Rhanna
Children of Rhanna
Rhanna at War

CHRISTINE MARION FRASER

Rhanna
Children of Rhanna
Rhanna at War

BCA

LONDON   NEW YORK   SYDNEY   TORONTO

This omnibus edition published 2000
by BCA
by arrangement with Hodder and Stoughton
a division of Hodder Headline

CN 7272

Typeset in Garamond by
Phoenix Typesetting, Ilkley, West Yorkshire

Printed and bound in Great Britain by
Mackays of Chatham plc, Chatham, Kent

CONTENTS

Rhanna

To Ken, Who Gave Rhanna Its Name

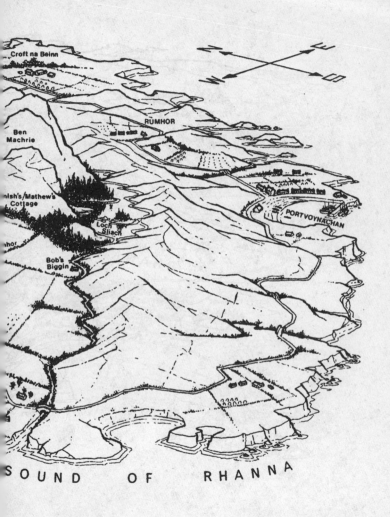

Croft na Beinn

RUMHOR

Ben
Machrie

nish's/Mathew's
Cottage

hor

Loch
Sliach

Bob's
Biggin

PORTVOYNACHAN

S O U N D   O F   R H A N N A

Part One

January 1923

Chapter One

The peat fire flickered in the hearth and the pale halo of light from the oil lamp cast long shadows on the camped ceiling of the room. A young woman lay in the big brass bed. Her face was pale, with beads of perspiration glistening on her forehead. Outside the warm shell of the big farmhouse a low moaning wind found its echo inside the cosy room as a soft groan broke from the lips of the young woman.

'Ach, there now, mo ghaoil,' soothed Biddy McMillan, bathing the fevered brow for the umpteenth time, and smoothing damp strands of red-gold hair from the pointed little face.

Wiry greying hair escaped Biddy's ancient felt hat. She felt tired and old, and her thirty years as midwife on Rhanna had stamped on her countenance the tenderness and toughness that went hand in hand with her calling. She sighed and turned to the young doctor at the foot of the bed.

'What do you think, Lachlan? There's no more strength in the lass. She was never fit to carry a bairn, never mind give birth!'

Dr Lachlan McLachlan shook his head, a dark curl falling over a forehead that was also soaked in sweat. He sighed wearily. 'I don't know, Biddy. She's not got the strength to push the bairn into the world. It looks like a forceps delivery. I didn't want it that way but if the infant isn't out soon it won't survive – the foetal heart is getting fainter by the minute. Go and fetch Mirabelle, we'll need all the help we can. Tell her to bring more hot water and some sheets. There's going to be much bleeding.'

Mirabelle, plump and homely, was in the kitchen. In anticipation of the doctor's needs she was boiling gallons of water on the range and clouds of steam rose from kettles and pans. She turned when Biddy came in and her round pink face was anxious.

'Well, how is the lass?' she asked curtly. 'I hope it won't be much longer for all our sakes. Fergus has been like a demon, with ants in his breeks since the start o' the pains. He won't keep from under my feet, asking endless questions about the time a bairn takes to be born. I could skelp his lugs so I could!'

Biddy ignored the sharp tones, knowing they were born of worry. Mirabelle had kept house at Laigmhor for twenty-six years but the title of housekeeper was a mere formality. She was the heart of the big rambling farmhouse. Without her, Fergus McKenzie and his younger brother Alick would have known a very different life. Since the premature death of their mother, Mirabelle had mothered them and cared for them. Hers was an ample heart out of which love flowed like a stream. It had flowed out to Helen, the girl who now lay upstairs in childbirth. Helen had come to Laigmhor three years before, a surprise to everyone. Fergus McKenzie had gone north on farming business and when he returned he brought Helen whom he had met and married in the short space of two months. Rhanna was amazed that strong-willed Fergus, who never did anything on impulse, should have behaved so untypically, and Malcolm McKenzie, Fergus's father, was angry and disappointed because he'd had hopes of a sturdy local lass becoming the mistress of Laigmhor.

Helen was eighteen years old, so small and slim that it seemed impossible that she could make a farmer's wife. But time proved everyone wrong. Her exuberance for life, coupled with her strength of character, oiled the cogs of Laigmhor so that life there ran more smoothly than ever before. She brought sunshine into the old house and even Malcolm, who had retained an air of dour, hurt silence for a time, eventually blossomed under her warm influence. She made him feel important and wanted, his cantankerous moods gave way to a new zest for life, and if the house was without her cheerful presence for any length of time he complained restlessly till she returned.

Laigmhor had been without a mistress for so many years that Mirabelle had come to accept the role as her own and she was wary about Helen. But though the girl was sweet and charming she was also discerning and wily. She discussed all household affairs with the old lady, and appeared to need advice about even the most trivial matter so that Mirabelle, flattered and secure of her position, remained sweetly oblivious to the fact that the girl got her own way without seeming to do so at all.

For Alick, Helen was a welcome addition to the household. He amused himself by flirting with her slyly and earned only gay peals of laughter from the girl who adored his brother with all her heart and took no bother to hide the fact.

Alick was the complete reverse of his strong, dominant brother. The farm and its running held no interest for him. He was flighty and perpetually in search of pleasures outside the demanding tasks of the farm. He was shy, yet glib, his greatest gift lying in the quick words of flattery he gave to the plainest of females. As a result, he was never short of women and at fifteen years of age had disgraced the family by making a local girl pregnant. His father, never very interested in his younger son's welfare because he regarded him as a weakling not fit to be a farmer's son, washed his hands of the matter and it was left to Fergus, barely eighteen, to sort out the affair as best he could. In the end the girl had miscarried and Alick had been sent to a school on the mainland. Well educated he returned to Rhanna with no real ambition for his life. He drifted around the farm, escaping as many of the manual tasks as he could and getting in the way of everyone. Finally he had left the island to seek his fortunes in Edinburgh. With the luck of his kind, he found a good job, married a girl as flighty as himself, and had only come back to Rhanna once in two years for the funeral of his father who had collapsed and died while helping with the harvest one ripe September morning.

Fergus now ran the farm, handling its affairs with the confidence of the born farmer. Those who had known him all his days said they didn't know him at all and were never likely to, for he was a man of few words and undemonstrative to boot, though this was not an uncommon trait in the dour demeanour of the Rhanna folk. But there was also a softness lurking beneath the surface of the main mass of the population and it was thought lacking in Fergus. He was labelled as hard and unyielding and had few close friends, but the more discerning of these knew that under the steel buffer beat a heart that was steadfast and fair despite his bouts of unreasoning temper.

Helen was his life now. The sight of her smiling could change anger to laughter. If, on rare occasions, she was displeased with him, he was like a little boy who had been naughty and wanted to make up. With every touch and glance she melted his façade and kindled in him fires of deep desire.

Now she was upstairs, struggling to bring his child into the world, her cries of agony searing into him till he could almost feel her pain himself. He had gone upstairs several times and she clung to him with hands that were cold and damp despite her fever. At times her body shook with uncontrollable tremors and she retched weakly, while he held a basin to her mouth.

'I'm sorry, Fergus,' she whispered as if the pain and sickness were her fault. 'I – I didn't think it would be so bad.'

You're sorry! You're sorry! his heart cried out and he thought, it was my doing! It's my fault you're going through this hell! But if desire was a fault, then they were equally guilty. Passion had engulfed them both with its eager searching for fulfilment, the warm lust they felt for each other coupling them in the dark intimacy of their bedroom as they lay together in the soft feather bed, the very bed she now occupied in her agony.

He sat by the peat fire in the parlour, the flickering flames outlining the bulk of his powerful body, his shock of black hair matching the coals in the hob, and his dark eyes bright with the unshed tears of anxiety. The springs of the old wooden rocking chair creaked protestingly as back and forth he rocked unable to still himself, the turmoil of his thoughts thrashing unceasingly till he felt he would go mad. He knew things were not going well upstairs. He had heard Mirabelle go into the kitchen and rattle pots and pans, filling them with yet more water that must be heated. Good God! What did they do with all that hot water? Biddy's voice floated through the door, requesting Mirabelle to go upstairs.

He bit into the stem of his unlit pipe then banged it back on the mantelpiece, finding no comfort in the familiar things of his life. He rose, and strode up and down like a caged wild thing, his stockinged feet making a soft padding sound on the hearth rug. All night long he had paced thus, hearing the low moan of the wind outside, feeling the chill of the fiendish snowstorm in the very marrow of his being. The blizzard was over now but the wind had gone raging on, piling the soft snow into every conceivable corner, humping it over windowledges and doorsteps. Several times he had left the warmth of the parlour to shovel snow from doorways, leaving paths clear for the morning when work must start no matter the weather. It was now 4.30 and another two hours would see the start of the farm tasks. Hamish Cameron, his grieve, had promised to come down for the milking. He would bring young Mathew, a local boy who had recently started work at Laigmhor. He, too, was a born farmer and tackled lowly jobs like byre-mucking and teat-washing with an enthusiasm that earned Fergus's approval. He took the milk cart on the morning rounds, filling milk cans from the big churns.

Fergus went to a frost-rimed window and peered out. The morning was eerily bright, the sky glittering with the farflung sparks of millions of stars. The snow reflected itself in strange haloes of light and it was quite possible to see the stretching white nothingness of the Muir of Rhanna and the sea a thread of silver in the distance.

Another cry came from upstairs and he stiffened. In a torment he cried aloud. 'Let the damned child be born soon. She can't stand any more, not my little Helen!'

He stared back into the cosy room and it looked so normal that for a moment he felt he was living alone in a world of unreality. Everything else was the same, but not he. He tried to think about the day before but could remember very little. Snatches came to him – small things, like taking Helen a cup of tea before he started his day. She had thrown her arms round his neck, laughing because the roundness of her body had prevented him getting too near.

'Can you believe you'll be a father soon?' she teased. 'I can't imagine it at all. The bairn will deeve you with its greetin' and you'll mump like an old man. Will you skelp your son's wee bum when you're in one of your moods?'

He had laughed with her. 'I'll leather yours now if you don't hold your tongue!'

He had pulled the sheet back to gaze at her, at her soft burnished hair spread over the pillows, and her blue eyes regarding him with the veiled fire of her vital attraction. It was a look he knew well and usually preluded sexual play. She knew she was desirable but she never used it as a weapon of control over him, rather she used it to make their love-making into something that took them both into a world of deepest intimacy and incredible sensual pleasure.

His hands had travelled over her rounded breasts to the hard swelling of her belly, feeling the warmth of her flesh through the soft flannel of her nightdress, and the contact started the familiar ache of longing in his groin. Sweat broke on his brow and he was ashamed of his hardness when she was lying there with his child almost ready to be born. It had been a long time since his cravings for her body had been satisfied. Really it had only been a few weeks but to him, lying beside her every night, with the perfume of her skin and hair in his nostrils, it had seemed an eternity.

Confused, he turned from her, but she had pulled him round and her hands caressed the hardness in his middle. Even through the thick material of his rough tweed trousers he felt the touch as though he were standing before her naked.

'My poor Fergus,' she said softly, 'you've been very patient but it won't be long now. Don't be ashamed of your feelings. You're a bull of a man but I'm not one to be complaining for I love every movement you make inside me. My belly won't always be this size, it's like a funny wee mountain and I'll be glad to be rid of it.'

He grinned, glad of the change of mood that allowed the heat to gradually go from his loins. 'I love your wee mountain because it has our child inside it. I hope it's a girl with your eyes and teeny button of a nose. But I hope she won't chase me round the kitchen table and clout me with the dishcloth the way you do when roused!'

She giggled. 'I want a boy, strong and dark like you and with eyes like coals burning in the grate. But he mustn't have your temper for I couldn't bear two going into tantrums.' She laughed in her abandoned way. 'I'll have to give you a few lessons on nappy-changing and the best way to break the winds, as Shelagh would say.'

An hour later, when the weak fingers of dawn were spreading out over the cold January sky, Mirabelle came panting up the slopes of the hill pastures to tell him that Helen's pains had started.

'I'll fetch Biddy at once!' he cried and ran to the byre where the horses were stabled. Mathew was hitching Mac the pony to the milk cart but Fergus stayed him with a quick order.

'The rounds can wait till later! I need Mac now!'

Mirabelle wheezed into the stables. 'There's no need to go right this meenit, Fergus! It will be a long whily before the bairn comes.'

'I'll go now,' he said and without another word led Mac outside.

Mirabelle shook her head in disgust and mumbled

under her breath, 'A real nipscart that one. As pig-headed as a mule!' She giggled, better humoured at having allowed herself the luxury of a quiet swear. It was a safety valve she used frequently, especially when she found herself harassed in the kitchen, often about Fergus because of his difficult ways, but mostly at the hens who clucked and strutted into the kitchen leaving droppings on her clean floor and poking into her pantry in a never-ending quest for food.

Fergus set out, excitement struggling with anxiety on the mile-long journey through Glen Fallan to the midwife's cottage.

At the sound of his imperative knock an upstairs window opened and Biddy looked out, her hair dishevelled and her face lined and yellow in the unkind light of winter. 'Ach! It's you!' she said indignantly. 'I thought it was thunder! What's wi' you? I've just had my breakfast and I'm not yet dressed so I can't come down.' She drew the folds of a thick wool dressing-gown round her neck and her eyes, small and tired without the aid of her glasses, peered at him in annoyance.

'We need you at Laigmhor,' he shouted, his breath condensing in the cold air from the moor. 'Helen's started!'

'How long since? Have her contractions been going on for a time?'

'Long enough!' came the short reply.

'Ach, away you go, Fergus! She'll keep for a few hours yet I'm thinkin'.'

'How do you know! She could be quick and no one there.'

'Not wi' a first! Never wi' a first!'

She fell to grumbling until Fergus exploded. 'Dammit, woman! Are you coming or not?'

'Och, haud your tongue, man, I'm comin'! Just give me time to put on my breeks if that's no' too much to ask!'

The window banged shut and Fergus was left to stamp his feet and swing his arms until the door opened and Biddy came out, calling a fond farewell to a big black cat which sat at the foot of the stairs mewing loudly.

'Bide a wee, my lamb. I'll try not to be too long. I've a nice bitty fish for your dinner!'

Fergus snorted and Biddy gave him a cold look before flouncing over to the trap. She grumbled at everything on the journey to Laigmhor. She told him he shouldn't have come for her so early. Babies didn't just pop out the minute a pain started. There would be a long wait ahead and she had heartburn from rushing about so soon after her breakfast. He remained silent throughout the tirade. He knew her so well; her bark was only a front. When she was with her patients her gentleness and patience were matchless. She had assisted most of the younger population of Rhanna into the world, and their own offspring. Everyone dreaded the day when age or death robbed them of the kenspeckle old figure who had devoted her life to her work. She was Rhanna-born as were her parents and grandparents, and had only left the island to take her training, returning to assist the existing midwife, then carrying on alone when 'Auld Murn' collapsed and died at the age of eighty.

Mirabelle had everything ready and Helen was curled in the chair by the bedroom fire looking very young in a blue nightdress. She giggled a little nervously when Fergus loomed big and speechless at her side. 'Don't look like that,' she chided. 'You'll make me more scary than I am already.'

'Pain bad?' he grunted gruffly.

'Getting worse now but I can thole it . . . och, c'mon now! We'll laugh at this later.'

Biddy intervened. 'Out, my lad.' She pushed him towards the door. 'Men are so feckless at times like these it just gets me angry!'

He tried to fill the gaps in his memory but it was useless. The day had passed in a blur with Mirabelle stolidly plodding up and down stairs, taking Biddy endless cups of tea and muttering under her breath.

Nancy McKinnon, the young daily help from Portcull, darted about from kitchen to yard to hang out wet dishtowels and feed the hens. she slopped soup into bowls and made thick sandwiches filled with dry mutton and told herself Fergus was lucky to get anything at all. He filled the weary hours with essential farm duties, his voice clipped and cold when he gave orders to the men. By the end of the day they were glad to be out of his sight.

Murdy McKinnon, a distant cousin of Nancy's mother, kicked dung from his wellingtons and chewed viciously at a plug of tobacco.

'He's a bugger o' a man is McKenzie,' he complained to Jock Simpson, the amiable ploughman, who was employed in no one place but gave his services to the widely scattered farms on Rhanna. 'My Cailleach just dropped our three lads like a ewe scatters its sharn.' He blew his nose on to the hard rutted road and rubbed the gob of mucus into the ground with his stoutly booted foot. 'McKenzie seems to think no one never had a bairn but his wife!'

Jock nodded placidly and was glad of the fact that he had never had the worry of a wife let alone a child. 'Ach, you canny compare Laighmhor to yoursel', Murdy. Yon wife o' yours is a real blossom o' a lass. Plenty o' meat to her bones you might say. The wee lass McKenzie wed's a nippet cratur – bonny, mind, but no' made for rearin' bairns.'

Murdy sniffed and plodded on, his mind on his cosy cottage by the Fallan river. A hot meal would be waiting and his three sturdy sons would clamour for his attention. Later, his wife would regale him with all the local gossip while he smoked his pipe with his feet on top of the warm oven in the range. The scent of snow was heavy in the freezing air and the men hurried on, the dim lights of Laigmhor already well behind them.

Teatime came and went, and Biddy decided it was time to call the doctor. She was getting anxious about Helen whose pains were violent but who was nowhere near giving birth.

Fergus, thankful for something to do, strode out of the warm kitchen and met the first flakes of snow from a leaden sky. Lachlan's house was but a short walk from the farm and later he remembered nothing of it. His memory was only of Phebie McLachlan, outlined in the dim light from the hall, her two-year-old son Niall clutched in her arms.

'Can Lachlan come?'

It wasn't so much a question as a demand, and Phebie's welcoming smile faded a little. She and her husband were incomers in Rhanna. Their four years there were a mere breath in time as far as the islanders were concerned and every move they made was watched warily by the natives. Lachlan was a Stornoway man and because he 'had the Gaelic' was more at an advantage than Phebie who hailed from Glasgow. They had met while he was at Glasgow University studying medicine, had literally 'fallen' for each other when he, late for a class, had bumped into her in the middle of Argyle Street and they had both landed in the gutter, he with a fractured wrist and she with bruises and a 'jelly nose'.

A year later they were married and moved to England where he had managed to get his first post as a doctor. But he pined for the Hebrides and when the post of Medical Officer became vacant on Rhanna he applied for the job and got it.

But being a doctor was one thing; earning the confidence of the canny crofters was another. They compared him continually with 'Auld McLure' who'd been Rhanna-born and bred and who knew every one of his patients and their ways. He had not been very well up on 'fancy modern cures' but that had not greatly mattered: he had healed with the wisdom of familiarity and age-old cures. Simply by spending an hour or so 'cracking' with a patient and having a dram or two had done more good than any medicine found in a bottle. 'Except for the stuff the tint o' an amber river,' the islanders joked with a glint in their eyes.

But Lachlan was making progress. His fluent Gaelic overcame a great many hurdles because the Rhanna folk were lazy, with the unhurried calmness of purpose passed down through generations, and they did not care to translate every thought or expression into English. Many of the older folk knew no other tongue than Gaelic. The young people had the English – they had to learn it before going to school or they didn't go at all – but even they found it more natural to use their native tongue and poor Phebie had been at a loss until she built up a reasonable Gaelic vocabulary.

'Auld McLure', now buried beside his wife and daughter in the Hillock Kirkyard, was still well remembered by his old cronies but his name was now less on their lips. Young McLachlan 'was a bright one and no mistake'. Lachlan, looking at bunions that ought never to have been, and administering to bronchial chests that could have been prevented with a little care, cursed 'Auld McLure' under his breath and set about righting the ails of the islanders. After four years of hard work they held him in respect and marvelled at his 'fancy ways' that really worked. His tall young figure and boyish smile, his kind yet firm way of dealing with even the most difficult of patients, had earned him a firm place in the hearts of the Rhanna folk. With patience and a good deal of understanding Phebie, too, had won her way into the affections of the islanders. Even so she'd been glad of the advent of Helen who was a 'foreigner' like herself but who didn't mind the tag in the least. With her vivacity and joy of living she drew people like a magnet and they came to her, the wary Rhannaites, because they could not help themselves. They spoke about her 'scrawny wee figure' and told each other she would 'never make a farmer's wife' but not a day passed without one of them seated cosily in the kitchen taking a Strupak and listening to her gay chatter, some of which they couldn't understand but which made them smile anyway it sounded so cheery. Ceilidhs were part and parcel of island life but the McKenzies had been a family who had kept themselves to themselves and Laigmhor had always been a quiet, dreaming place.

Now, with Helen it rang with gossip and song. Ceilidhs there were now a regular occurrence and Phebie was glad of Helen because she made life so precious a thing to be lived and passed the exuberance she felt to everyone she met.

The friendship between Fergus and Lachlan had developed with painstaking slowness. Fergus was a son of Rhanna, and caution and dourness had been his heritage. In his heart he admired the young doctor but it was not his way to let such feelings show. Enough it was that he could pass the time of day with Lachlan without feeling the impatience that others roused in him. With the exception of Hamish Cameron he had very little in common with his own kind. With them he experienced an anger because they squabbled like children over matters of little importance. With Lachlan he felt no need to indulge in silly superfluous chatter. Peaceable silences could fall between them and he didn't feel he had to search his mind for something to say to fill the time. He was at ease in Lachlan's company and Lachlan knew he was

honoured by the friendship – the islanders were quick
to tell him so.

'A real dour one that,' sniffed Behag Beag, the postmistress, when Lachlan went into her shop one day
to buy stamps. 'Aye was – even as a bairn. Used to
keek at me wi' thon queer brooding eyes o' his! Black
as his moods they are. Alick was a different laddie
altogether. A weak sort right enough but kindly in his
ways. Fergus did all the fightin' for him at school for
he couldny stick up for himself but he wasny to blame,
he never got the chance to prove himself – it's no
wonder he was aye in trouble when he grew older.
That poor lass . . .' She shook her head sadly and let
the words hang in the air before continuing. 'Fergus
had to stick his nose into that affair as well. Always
leadin' Alick's life for him – aye – you'll regret makin'
friends wi' that man! Not a word o' cheer you'll get
from him and that's a fact!'

Lachlan smiled to himself as Behag's mournful tones
fell on his ears. She was the soul of doom with her
down-turned mouth and jowls that hung from a
wizened face. Thin wisps of hair escaped a threadbare
headscarf and her whole demeanour reminded him of
a doleful bloodhound. She complained incessantly
about her rheumatism, her customers and her lot in
general and if Lachlan had cause to cross her path he
took care to always appear to be rushing off on some
emergency.

James Balfour, the laird, and his sickly little wife
were quite upset that Lachlan had made friends with
one of their tenant farmers. They lived in Burnbreddie
– a large gloomy house which stood on a rocky

outcrop on the western side of Rhanna. The estate reached back for three miles and more and Robbie Beag, Behag's brother, was the ghillie. Away from his sister's watchful eye he spent his days browsing through the estate, swigging whisky from a hip flask and shooting hares and rabbits which he gave to his friends. He also landed fresh trout and salmon from the two rivers and these also found their way to the tables of the crofters. Behag, unaware of her brother's generosity, gave lavish Strupaks, sublimely believing that she and she alone was the sole benefactor of Burnbreddie spoils, and her neighbours came and partook of her fare with a great show of surprise at the treats offered and all the while they shared with round-faced, blue-eyed Robbie, the greatest secret on the island.

The laird, big and blustering with a red face and a bulbous nose that told of too much rich feeding and an unrestrained tippling from the fine brands of whisky in his cellar, came from a long line of Gaels and had earned his father's disapproval when he'd come home from college in England and announced his intention of marrying an Englishwoman. All manner of threats had no effect and he'd married the woman of his choice in the end. Despite his English education he spoke a strange mixture of Gaelic and English so that words burbled from him in waves of almost unintelligible sound, his voice thickly slurred by a lifetime of drinking. Madam Balfour was much more articulate and honeyed tones dripped from a small prim mouth. She had been pretty at one time and had small delicate features, but time had twisted them, time and the bitterness she'd harboured for years at being brought to live on a remote island among 'peasants and barbarians who knew nothing of civilization.'

The young James Balfour had seemed a good catch. But when he came into Burnbreddie and its estate and decided to live there, his wife was furious at first, then resigned, but her feelings manifested themselves in an open ear for malicious gossip and a barely concealed superiority towards the crofting community of Rhanna. She was slightly more tolerant of the people who had tenanted their farms for generations, but when she spoke of Fergus the honey in her voice was tinged with bitterness and her beady, pale grey eyes glinted with malice.

'I really don't know what you see in that man,' she sniffed to Lachlan. 'A good farmer, I grant you, but not the type one would have for dinner, if you see what I mean. He barely speaks to me – I don't know why because I was brought up to be civil to everyone – but these farming people have a rough streak, would you not say? Mind you, his mother was a fine woman, more genteel, but then of course she didn't really belong here. She was from the north, farming people but better quality than the McKenzies. Alick was like her, a bit more manners than his brother. What a pity he was such a weakling in other ways, but then his father's blood is in him. Fergus is like his father all over, no control of his emotions at all! Have you ever experienced his temper? Dear me, it's frightening! I wonder he ever found himself a wife and such a flighty little thing too. Pretty as a bluebell in her way but she'll never make a farmer's wife. I . . .'

She had stopped in mid-sentence as the doctor lanced the boil that had ripened on her neck. He dressed it but his touch was less gentle than usual and she looked at him in pained surprise, wondering if she'd said anything to upset him. He had found himself wishing that he could have stitched her tight little mouth so that she could never speak again. He found her a hypochondriac nuisance with too many airs and graces. He disliked her all the more for miscalling Fergus to whom he had grown very close. In the beginning he'd found it difficult to get underneath the man's steel exterior but patience had won and he admired Fergus for being his own man.

He was glad too that Phebie had found a friend in Helen. When Niall was born, Helen was at hand like a gay sunbeam, helping in every way she could. Now it was her turn to bring a child into the world and Phebie was worried because her friend looked too frail for such an ordeal.

'Don't worry,' Lachlan said one night when Helen had had a Strupak with them before departing for home. 'The skinny wee ones are sometimes the best in childbirth. It's the ones with too much meat to them we've to watch!'

'Lachy! You're getting at me, you – you whittrick that you are! I'll – I'll . . .'

His brown eyes had twinkled and he shouted with laughter, throwing his arms round her warm plump waist. 'I love you the way you are – like a bonny pink rose just waiting to be plucked!' He nuzzled her neck and caught the roundness of her breasts with eager hands.

'Lachy!' she had cried, but softly, her voice enticing and her fair hair falling over her face. 'Lachy! Niall's crying, I must go up to him.'

'Later,' he said, his tanned skin flushed. 'A bit of crying won't do him any harm but waiting won't be good for me at all. Just feel and see what you've done to me. Now, Phebie – here – by the fire!'

But things like these were far from Phebie's mind when she opened the door of Slochmhor and saw Fergus standing against the black background of moor. Snowflakes were whirling around his muscular coatless figure and a keening wind whipped the black hair from his brow, tossing it over eyes that were darkly intent with the urgency of his quest.

She heard his clipped question and her heart leaped strangely in her breast. Niall stirred in her arms and gurgled happily. 'Where Elly? Elly comin' soon?'

'Weesht,' said Phebie, shivering in the bite of the wind. 'Come in, Fergus, you must be frozen. Elspeth will make you a Strupak.'

'I'm not here for tea! I'm here for Lachlan! Dammit woman, are you deaf? Helen needs Lachlan!'

'B-but – he's not here,' faltered Phebie. 'He was called out to Glan Fallan. One of the Taylor bairns at Croft na Beinn has pneumonia. He left three hours ago and I'm getting worried. If this weather keeps up there'll be drifts. Oh, Fergus, what if he can't get back over the Glen? It gets blocked so quickly at Downie's Pass!'

Fergus exploded. 'What about Helen? He must come!'

Phebie shivered again. 'There's no need to shout, Fergus McKenzie! Lachlan can't be in two places at once – and on a night like this I fear for his safety too.'

Elspeth Morrison, Phebie's housekeeper, came bustling into the shaft of light. She was thin and angular, her bony features always strangely immobile no matter her mood. When she saw Fergus she gave a horselike snort.

'Humph! I might have known who was shoutin' like the de'il! Can you no' come into the house like other folk? The heat is just fleein' out the door.'

'Hold your tongue, you old yowe!' roared Fergus with a glare that would have quelled the bravest heart. 'If you were in my house you'd know your place all right!'

Elspeth stuck her sharp nose in the air. She was inclined to be annoyed with Laigmhor in general because the previous week she'd fallen out with Mirabelle over a recipe for tablet.

'Your house!' She sniffed. 'I wouldny be seen dead in it! As for anybody you can get to work for you – they must be gey weak in the head if you ask me!'

'That's enough, Elspeth!' ordered Phebie sharply. From the corner of her eye she had seen Fergus's fists bunching with rage and she couldn't blame him. Elspeth's tongue was sharp and bold. Many blamed her bitterness on her husband Hector who was a fisherman. When he was away her whole demeanour softened. When he came home and drank the cold of the sea from his bones till he was a sodden lump of cursing humanity, his wife bore the brunt of his fists and foul language and she in turn spat cynical words at her fellow creatures and was not popular even among the fisherwives on the harbour. She vowed a hatred for all men and prayed that her husband would be lost to sea. It was quite common knowledge that she went about saying, 'The sea's the best place for his carcase. He'd make a nice feast for the gulls but the craturs would likely die of alcoholic poisonin'.'

After such terrible utterances she would sit in her cottage with her bible on her lap and folk looking in could not tell if she was using the good book to strengthen her evil wishes or if she was in fear of her salvation because of them and was relying on the bible to resolve her difficulties.

She came out to the door and glared at Fergus before stretching out her arms for Niall. 'I'll take the bairn inside – poor wee mite's blue with cold. I'll be off in ten minutes so I'll just finish in the kitchen.' She glowered malevolently at the snow. 'What a night! There'll be a blizzard come midnight. I'd better hurry. *He'll* be home waitin' for his supper! Drifts a dozen feet high there could be but *he'd* sit with his feet up waitin' for me to fetch and carry for him!'

She went off muttering, bearing Niall into the warmth of the kitchen.

Phebie turned again to Fergus who was stamping with impatience. 'I'll send Lachy the minute he comes home, there's nothing else I can do . . . except . . . could I perhaps come over and help out? I'd love to be with Helen, she was so good to me.'

Her eyes were appealing but Fergus turned on his heel.

'There's nothing you can do! I've enough women

cluttering my house! I'll be waiting for Lachlan. If anything happens to Helen and he's not there, he'll surely be to blame!'

The wind carried away his muttered words so that Phebie did not hear them. She watched his hulking figure till it was lost in the whirling snowflakes, then she turned gladly into the warmth of the house, her thoughts centred on Helen and on her husband out in lonely Glen Fallan.

She shut the door and stood leaning against it.

'Oh God,' she whispered. 'Please bring Lachy safely through the storm – and – Helen . . . give her the strength for what's ahead. Please God!'

Chapter Two

By nine o'clock the wind had risen to a howling shriek and drifts were piling everywhere. Mirabelle and Biddy huddled over the fire and gave voice to their worries.

'Ach, poor lass,' sympathized Mirabelle glancing at the small figure in the bed. 'She's havin' a struggle and no mistake! I wonder will the doctor manage. What if he doesny, Biddy?'

'Ach well, I'm no' a midwife for nothing, Belle. It's the girl's first born. The wee buggers have had a cosy nine months o' it and are in no hurry to come out. As for Lachlan, he's as much chance as a fart in a constipated cow gettin' through the Glen in a night like this. I'm sure the de'il himself bides yonder at Downie's Pass.'

Mirabelle's frown deepened. 'Pray God he'll make it! Fergus is rampin' like a bairn wi' the skitters! Everything will have to be done proper for Helen or we'll never hear the end of it! I'm afeard for Lachlan roamin' aboot in weather like this. Hamish was down at Portcull and he came by to tell me the waves are washin' over the harbour wall. Some of Ranald's boats have been smashed to smithereens and them lyin' on the scaup too!'

Biddy took off her glasses and wiped her weary

eyes. 'Ach well, we can only wait. I'm thankful the lass has fallen asleep. Restless it may be but it will give her strength for the rest of the battle.' She sighed and spread her legs wide to the heat. 'My, it's been a long day so it has. I'd love a wee nap and I've got heartburn again . . . no fault of your lovely broth, Belle, but my belly hasny given me peace since all the rushin' this mornin'. I'm all blown up like there was a wheen o' wind caught in my bowel. You wouldny have a wee touch o' bakin' soda, Belle?'

Mirabelle sighed too. All day long she had been on her feet tending to the needs of the household. She longed to put her feet up and sleep for hours. She'd missed her usual nap that evening. The kitchen was her kingdom at the day's end. With a long day behind her she could nap in the peaceful warmth with Lass the old sheepdog on her ample knee and Ben the spaniel making cosy little grunts of contentment on the rug. Three cats usually occupied the warm depths of the inglenook and Mirabelle drifted dreamily, enjoying the drone of talk and laughter from the parlour where Helen and Fergus sat together before a glowing peat fire.

But tonight was not like any other night and wearily she rose to fetch Biddy's soda.

Fergus, unable to settle himself in the house, was in the byre with Hamish who had come over from his little cottage to see if there was anything he could do. He knew only too well the havoc created by gale-force winds. Laigmhor, though well protected by trees, was nonetheless vulnerable. The winter before, a gust of wind had brought down one of the trees, crashing straight through the byre roof, killing three cows and injuring one of the horses so badly he had to be shot. A new roof had been built but door and windows could be blown in by the terrible winter storms that swept Rhanna, so Hamish was busy piling bales of hay against the windows and Fergus was nailing planks of wood over the doors in the milking shed.

The two worked well together for Hamish was as silent and purposeful as his young employer. He had been grieve at Laigmhor when Fergus and Alick were infants and knew every trick there was to know about farming on an island lashed by Atlantic gales. He was a big man with powerful shoulders. A shock of red hair matched a bushy beard and fair eyebrows beetled thickly over pale blue eyes. Dressed in a hairy tweed jacket and plus fours he was a fine figure of a man. Clad in a glengarry, lovat tweed jacket and the Cameron kilt he was not to be missed in a crowd. In his younger days he had carried off numerous honours at Highland gatherings all over Scotland and for years had tossed the caber as if it were a piece of driftwood. Women gazed at his tall sturdy figure and wondered why he never married, and his attentions were still sought by eager young maidens who could well picture themselves in his cosy cottage by the tumbling burn that flowed from Ben Machrie. It was a comfortable homely place with an ever open door, but Hamish seemed quite content to retain the freedom of his bachelorhood. Animals seemed to bring him more satisfaction than humans and he shared his home with two sheepdogs, three cats and several wild rabbits he had rescued from predators.

He worked quickly and efficiently at the windows and talked in soothing tones to the beasts who moved uneasily in their stalls as the sough of the wind whined round corners and rattled at doors. He finished tying ropes and went through to the stable to caress and calm Heather and Thistle, the two huge Clydesdales used for the plough. Mac snorted and Hamish pushed a piece of carrot into his mouth and whispered into ears that were twitching nervously.

Fergus came in, stamping snow from his wellingtons. Hamish saw that he was in a sorry state. Worry, impatience and nerves had made his face drawn and grey and it came as no surprise when he said thickly, 'We've done all we can here, Hamish. You get along home before the drifts get worse. I'm going up the Glen for the doctor!'

Hamish stared at him. 'I'm not one for interfering, man, but you'd be a fool to venture out tonight. Mac would never make the drifts at Downie's Pass!'

A small muscle in Fergus's jaw worked furiously. 'I'm walking!' he stated shortly.

Hamish bit back an angry retort – he knew his argument would be lost. Both men moved into the bitter night. Footsteps crunched somewhere in the dark and Hamish held up the lamp. Lachlan came into view, his greatcoat plastered in snow and his steps dragging.

'Lachlan!' The cry broke from Fergus in a great wave of sound that defied the wind. 'Thank God, man!'

'I just got back from Croft na Beinn,' said Lachlan through frozen lips. 'Phebie gave me the message and I came straight over.'

'Good God, man!' bellowed Hamish. 'How did ye get through the Glen? No pony and trap could have managed the Pass on such a night!'

'I left Benjie at Croynachan and came the rest of the way on foot. The Taylors wanted me to stop with them but I didn't want Phebie and the bairn to be alone and I knew Phebie would worry if I didn't come home.'

Lachlan's voice was breathless with exhaustion and his shoulders sagged. The struggle over the Glen had been a nightmare of whirling white spicules that stung his face till it felt raw. He had got stuck several times and bitter air froze in his lungs and numbed his hands and feet. He had cursed himself for not taking the Taylors' offer but he hadn't realised the severity of the weather. His administrations to little Fiona Taylor had made him oblivious to all else. The struggle to break the child's fever had been a hard one but he had won the battle, and, triumph making him jubilant, he had taken no need of Donald Taylor's pleas to wait till morning. It was only when he was going through the Glen with the great masses of Sgurr na Gill and Ben Machrie looming on either side did he realise how stupid he'd been. The mountains channelled the howling winds till it seemed all the forces of the terrible night were against him, and the blizzard hurled curtains of snow with such an intensity that Benjie reared and whinnied with fear.

Croynachan loomed out of the darkness and Tom Johnston, astonished at the sight of Lachlan, ushered him into the wonderful warmth of his kitchen and led Benjie to the stable where he had a meal of hay and a brisk rub-down. Mamie Johnston had wanted him to stay, her round kindly face dismayed at the idea of him going out again but Slochmhor was but a mile from Downie's Pass and stopping only for a cup of tea he'd ventured out again, little dreaming that the last part of the journey would be the worst of all, with drifts ten feet high at the Pass. Frozen to the marrow and at the end of his strength he'd decided to stop and rest awhile at Biddy's cottage but her house was in darkness and he'd battled on, his mouth covered by his scarf in an effort to keep out the icy snow-filled winds. After what seemed an eternity Slochmhor appeared like a beacon, a little haven sitting in the middle of a smothering world. Thoughts of a hot meal and bed hurried his steps and he almost fell into Phebie's arms at the door. She cried with thankfulness into his snow-caked collar and rumpled his wet hair with hands that trembled.

'Lachy! Oh, my Lachy! I'm so glad! I was nearly coming out to look for you but then I thought you might spend the night at Croft na Beinn! One half of me hoped you would and the other half wanted you home so badly. Come inside quickly. There's a pot of broth, salt mutton and boiled potatoes and . . .' she giggled with relief '. . . if you're good I'll make you a hot toddy to warm you while I get the meal.'

He collapsed into a chair by the fire and stretched every aching limb. 'Ach, it's good to be at my ain fireside,' he said shutting his eyes. 'I feel I've been away for years. Any calls while I was gone?'

'Y-es – but you must rest and eat first.'

'Are they that important?'

She knew it was wrong but she was reluctant to tell

him about Helen. Her love for him was strong and she knew his body was crying out for rest but the doctor in him would not let him do so if a patient needed him.

'Helen's been in labour since morning, but Biddy's with her, Lachy! You must stop in for a while! Please, Lachy! You're exhausted!'

But he was already in the hall struggling back into his wet coat. 'I must go to her, Phebie, I'll get a bite to eat there. Don't wait up for me, it might be a long night.' He gave a wry smile. 'To think I battled through the Pass so that I could be here with you and you will be on your own after all.'

'Och Lachy,' she whispered tenderly, 'I'll be fine but you – how weary you must be, my darling.'

He took her face in his hands and kissed her mouth gently, then turned into the bite of the storm once more.

Mirabelle gave a cry of consternation when he was ushered through the kitchen door. She stood with Biddy's soda in her plump hand but laid it on the table to rush over to help him out of his sopping coat.

She looked at his thin tired face and her kind heart turned over. 'My poor laddie! You're frozen and done in by the look o' you! Will you take a sup of hot broth? It won't take a minute.'

'Later!' interrupted Fergus. He looked at his friend with something near to pleading. '*Please*, Lachlan,' he added with unusual humility.

Lachlan put his hand on Fergus's shoulder. 'I'll go up at once. Don't worry, man, she'll be fine.'

33

Biddy jumped up at sight of him. 'Gracious laddie! You're like a spook but thank heaven you're here. I've just had a wee look and think the waters haven't broken just right.'

Lachlan strode quickly to the bed and touched Helen's hot brow. She looked at him with a smile lighting her tired eyes.

'Lachlan, how tired you look. I'm sorry I couldn't wait for better weather. I can hear the storm, whining and wailing like myself.' A flash of humour touched her mouth but another pain made her bite her lip and she reached for her husband's hand. 'Fergus, how are you managing . . . and poor Mirabelle? She must be scunnered running after us all.'

'Nonsense, lass,' said Mirabelle and turned away to hide a glimmer of tears. Helen looked so young in the big bed and delicate with the pallor of her skin showing the blue veins at her temples.

Fergus crushed her hand and she winced at the strength of him. It was as if he was trying to convey some of his power to her by his very touch.

'Sorry, my lamb,' he apologized. It was his pet name for her but he never used it unless they were alone. Now he was uncaring of the others in the room. 'You're going to be safe now, Lachlan will see to it.'

Lachlan looked up and a strange look of uncertainty shadowed his brown eyes. Fergus was laying so much store on him that the burden of his responsibility felt like a weight on his back.

'I'll do everything I can, but go now. I want to examine Helen.'

Without a backward glance Fergus left the room and

the doctor washed his hands and rolled up his sleeves. He checked his patient quickly, then went to Biddy and said, 'You were right, Biddy, the membranes haven't ruptured properly. Bring a bowl over, we can speed things up a little.'

At a little past six Hamish arrived with young Mathew. Fergus could hear them in the byre but he sat on in the rocking chair by the dying fire in the parlour. An immobility had gripped him so that his muscles, tense and stiff, were unable to obey the commands of his brain. The cold of the bitter morning stole through the cracks in doors and windows, seeping into his bones. Sounds came to him as from a great distance. The soft lowing of the cows, a gentle snicker from a horse, the clucking of hens, Peg and Molly barking happily at Hamish, the desolated bleat of sheep in the fields. Later he would have to go with his men and dig out the ewes on the high ground. In such conditions they could be lost in snow-filled corries and trapped in drifts. The bleak baa'ing came to him again and he thought how much it sounded like a baby's cry. A baby's cry! He leapt to his feet. A thin threading wail came from upstairs and his heart pounded into his throat.

'Helen!'

His body surged with life and he bounded upstairs, exploding into the room. In a split moment he saw Lachlan holding a red scrawny infant. It was fresh from the womb, its body glistening, a shock of jet hair plastered thickly over a tiny head. It was upside down, and Lachlan was slapping it, forcing it to cry that it might gulp the air of life into its lungs. Mirabelle was bustling with a tray containing cotton wool and olive oil. Biddy was bending over the bed working with Helen. In the dim light from the lamp Fergus saw her removing sheets that were red with blood, so much blood that Fergus felt his own draining from his face.

'Helen!'

He strode over to her but her eyes were closed, her head turned sideways on the pillow with her lovely red-gold hair spread out like a fiery halo round her white face.

'Helen.' His voice was a dull whisper. 'Helen, my lamb.'

Her eyes opened slowly and even in the dim light were a deep gentian blue. A smile of quiet radiance lit her pointed face. 'Fergus, we have a baby . . . is it a boy?'

Fergus looked at Lachlan who was washing his hands in a bowl, the baby now transferred to Mirabelle.

'A girl,' said Lachlan briefly.

Fergus took Helen's hands and gathered them to his lips. 'We have a daughter, Helen. A wee lass who's going to look like you.'

She smiled. 'A girl, och I'm so happy. A wee girl can be dressed in such bonny clothes . . .' Her voice trailed away and lids of softest purple closed over her eyes.

A hand fell on Fergus's shoulder. 'Leave us now, Fergus,' said Lachlan. 'There's a lot yet to be done. Helen's bleeding badly, complications with the placenta. We'll call you the minute we can.'

Fergus began to protest, but Lachlan and Biddy

were already busy and he went from the room, his feelings of joy already fading, leaving a new dread in his heart.

He paced the hall, the tick of the grandmother clock keeping time with his footsteps.

Hamish came stamping in. 'We're off now, Fergus. I don't know how far we'll get but we'll do our best. I thought it best I should go with Mathew. Murdy and Johnnie are away with Bob to the sheep. You take it easy, man . . . any news yet? Has the babe arrived safely?'

Fergus swallowed hard. 'It's here – a girl.'

'Och, man, that's grand! A wee lass, eh? We'll have a dram later to celebrate. How's the new mother? Proud as a piebroch I'll ken.'

Fergus merely nodded and went into the kitchen on some pretext. Hamish shook his head sadly. He knew that something was far wrong. A man newly made a father didn't behave the way Fergus was doing. Above him a door opened and Mirabelle stood looking down. Her plump face looked thin and old and her voice, low and shaky, barely reached down to Hamish.

'Bring Fergus,' she said dully, 'the lass has but a few minutes.'

Hamish took a deep breath. 'No! It can't be!'

'Hurry!' urged Mirabelle and turned away.

Hamish found himself bursting towards the kitchen where Fergus was gazing from the window. Hamish felt his throat go dry, making the utterance of his message harsh. 'Go quickly upstairs, man . . . Helen – she's – she needs you!'

When Fergus reached the bedroom it was empty but for Lachlan. He was by the fire and flickering flames found every hollow in his tired face. 'I'm sorry, Fergus,' he said tonelessly. 'We did all we could. It's a miracle we saved the baby but Helen . . .' He spread his hands in despair. 'It was too much for her, we couldn't stop the bleeding.'

He left the room quickly and Fergus turned to look at his dying wife. The bed was clean now, the whiteness of the sheets matching the small face on the pillow, a face from which life's blood was flowing quickly. The shadows round her eyes had deepened to blue and her lips were as pale as her face, emphasizing the vivid burnished gleam of her hair which surrounded her face like a delicate painting.

'Oh God, no!' The words were torn from him in an agony of grief.

Her eyes opened and the blueness of them pierced the depths of his crying soul. Her lips moved and he gathered her into his arms.

'The baby,' she whispered, 'call her Shona – it's a gentle name, don't you think, Fergie? And . . .' Her chest heaved as she gathered breath from her failing lungs. 'I love you, my darling – I wish I could have had more of you – I've been so happy. Don't be too hard on the little one – you haven't a lot of patience, Fergus. If she's like you she'll need . . . a lot of handling.'

He gathered her closer and the familiar warm smell of her filled his nostrils so that he felt he must cry out, scream his feelings to the world. Instead he murmured, 'We'll all manage between us. Mirabelle will help you to keep us in hand.'

But she seemed not to hear him. She had turned her head towards the window. 'Och, look, Fergus, it's a bonny morning. What a lovely day for our wee girl's birthday.' He had to strain to hear the whispered words. 'So clean,' she continued, 'with the sky all wet like a mountain burn. It's funny . . . the way it's always so calm after a storm . . .'

Her hands came up and stroked the dark tumbled curls on his head, then a long sigh came from her and her hands fell back to her sides.

'Helen, don't leave me,' he whimpered. Then he screamed aloud in his grief and crushed her body, his whole being burning with pain, an ache inside him so raw and deep it cried for some salve to ease it but the tears of release would not come. 'Oh God, why, why?' he said bitterly and rocked the slender body back and forth, feeling he could never let go of the lovely creature who owned his very being. A memory came unbidden to his mind, one he had thought forgotten.

He remembered himself, a small boy gazing at the dead face of his mother. He had loved his mother with a passion unusual in a child so young. But he hadn't thought it strange, the strange thing was that his mother didn't return his demonstrations of love. But she loved Alick for sure, she was always kissing him, making all his little ills better with a kiss, giving him her attention all the time. Alick was the one who got everyone's attention because he had a gay friendly smile and perfect manners, yet he could change so quickly to a little devil, mocking the people who made so much of him. Fergus didn't mind the other people, all he had wanted was the love of his mother. She treated him differently from Alick, almost as if he were grown up. He'd had to take the responsibility of the elder brother all his childhood. He protected Alick from bullies and fought battles for him because he knew it was expected of him and would earn words of praise from his mother. Sometimes he'd felt the burden of Alick too heavy a load to bear but in his child's way he knew his mother relied on him to keep Alick in order because their father had no time to spare for his younger son.

Yet, despite everything, Fergus had gone on loving his mother though he had learned to hide it behind a façade of indifference. But he never forgot her whispered words to him on the day she died.

She had clasped his small hand and he'd gazed at her dying face with eyes that ached with unshed tears and a heart full to bursting.

'Fergus, my lovely strong laddie,' she said clasping his hand till it hurt, 'you're the child of my heart. Poor Alick, he's not strong like you and his father can't understand him. You've been a wee man these years and I'm sorry but Alick needed you Fergus. Try to see it that way, my dear proud laddie.'

Fergus's heart had known no real feelings of love after his mother's death, not until Helen came into his life. Everything in him that had lain dormant for years had burst forth in a tide of love. She had captured his very spirit and had roused him to feelings that he hadn't known himself capable of.

He had had flirtations with girls since his school-days, fine buxom girls with big breasts and berry-brown skin. He had lain with them on the warm summer moors, ran with them over sun-kissed fields till laughter and the pretence of play had ended with rough kisses and caresses. Hidden by swaying stalks of golden corn he had enjoyed the feel of soft naked breasts, and love-play had satisfied his physical desires without actually possessing any of the girls, sometimes to their annoyance that the bounties of their bodies could not entice him further.

Helen had been his first complete union. Her delicate, enticing beauty had made him burn with a longing never before experienced because, mixed with his need for her body, was the deep and lasting emotion of his love for her.

Now she was gone from him. For the second time in his life he had lost someone who had captured his heart.

He sat holding her in his arms till a footstep behind made him turn. It was Lachlan, his eyes dark with sympathy.

'C'mon, Fergus,' he said softly. 'Come downstairs and have a drop of whisky. It will do you good. Try to think that Helen is at peace now.'

Fergus stood up, his face chalky white in the dawn light filtering through the window. He looked at the doctor and a new feeling took the place of grief in his heart. A cold anger slowly boiled in him. He could feel it churning in his belly and knew he was going to say things he might later regret. He'd had the feeling before but never so intense, so pressing as now. He fought to keep the words from coming and pressed a bunched fist to his mouth, all the time staring at Lachlan with an intensity that was almost tangible. But the bubbling rage kept on inside and finally exploded to the surface.

'You!' he whispered in a tight tense voice more commanding than the loudest cry. 'You let my Helen die! You ought to have known there would be complications but you did nothing till it was too late! She bled to death because you are incompetent! Why did it have to be her? Why not the bairn? Why save it and not Helen?'

Lachlan felt his heart beat strangely. He was exhausted, so tired that his legs felt weak beneath him. He hadn't slept or eaten properly in twenty-four hours. The day-long battle to save little Fiona Taylor had been bad enough, the struggle through the storm a waking nightmare, but worst of all had been the fight to save Helen and her child. Fatigue had lain like an old man on his shoulders yet he had given of himself all there was to give. He had felt a triumph in bringing the child live into the world. Complications that no one could have foreseen had taken Helen, and his heart was heavy. It was always bad to lose a patient and when that patient was also a personal friend, the loss, the feeling of failure at being powerless to save a life, was even harder to bear.

But despite his fatigue his voice was strong when he spoke. 'You don't know what you're saying, man! I tried everything to save Helen and it wasn't a choice between her and the bairn! I nearly lost the two of them! Dammit, Fergus! Can't you see you're lucky the little one survived? My heart's sore about Helen. I'm more sorry than I can say but at least be glad you've got one of them!'

He spread his hands in appeal but Fergus took no notice.

'Get out!' he said, his voice rising menacingly. 'Get out, McLachlan! I never want to see you in this house again!'

Mirabelle appeared at the door with the baby in her arms. Her face grew scarlet at Fergus's words and she looked at him in disbelief. 'You canny be serious, Fergus! I was here most of the night, remember! I saw the way this laddie worked and he so weary too! He fought like a Trojan to save poor Helen. If she could hear your bitter words, how do you think she would feel? We're all in the presence of her dear soul this meenit, let it rest in peace and be thankful you have her bairn – a bairn ye havny even set eyes on yet. Look at her! She's the bonniest wee thing. Look at her, Fergus and thank Lachlan for her life!'

But he turned away, everything in him so spent that his strong shoulders were stooped and his head sunk on to his chest. 'Get out,' he murmured dully, 'get out and leave me in peace.'

Lachlan was already running downstairs and Mirabelle went out leaving him alone in the room. He went over to the bed and touched his wife's smooth brow. It was already growing cold and he covered his face with his hands. A ray of winter sun stole into the room and turned the small figure in the bed into a pale golden statue. He looked towards the window, out to fields and hills unbelievably beautiful in a mantle of purest white, but his eyes saw none of the beauty. An abyss loomed ahead of him, one filled with incredible loneliness where he felt the sunlight would never penetrate again. Above the bed a calendar told him that it was the twenty-ninth of January, 1923. He shuddered and tried not to let his thoughts crystallize but it was no use. It was a day never to be forgotten because it was the day his dearly loved wife had left him behind and the day his daughter had taken her first breath of life. A life for a life that had no meaning for him. He shuddered again and banged his head with his fists in an effort to stop such thoughts, but they were etching themselves into his brain. He would have given anything, everything, to have his wife back and if he could have had one wish it would have been for the baby to be taken and Helen brought back in its place.

He could hear the child crying in the next room, the room he and Helen had prepared with such joyful anticipation. She had made the curtains, golden yellow like the sun, he had distempered the walls a fresh white and revarnished the old family cradle till it gleamed, waiting for the day it would be filled with the child of their love. Now it didn't matter any more. The child of their love had become the child of his sorrow and he put his hands over his ears to shut out the thin wailing of the newborn infant.

Rhanna was a jewel of beauty on the day of the funeral. The tattered peaks of Sgurr na Gill gleamed in a brilliance of white against a cornflower sky. The snow had melted from the lower slopes and churning burns frothed down from the mountains. The Sound of Rhanna was a rippling mass of liquid silver that hurt the eyes so that it was easier to look at the shoreline where soft little wavelets kissed the white sands that encircled the bay. The long finger of Port Rum Point enticed the water round its rocky length and there the sea spumed in frothing sprays.

The Hillock Kirkyard sprawled untidily on top of a wooded slope. Ancient stones, that looked as if they had been thrown by some giant hand to land where they would, surrounded the church which stood outlined against the sky, its fine old stone battered by the wind but withstanding the wiles of the weather like a sturdy old sailor.

Fergus looked down into the yawning black hole that awaited Helen's coffin and he felt sick. The mourners stood round the grave with bowed heads, waiting for the minister to speak. He was a tall, grey-haired man with piercing eyes and a compelling voice. He had come from Dundee seven years before and was an incomer who had never been quite accepted because he gave all his sermons in English and showed no intention of trying to learn even the odd Gaelic word. Because of this he always remained on the fringe, never quite understanding and never being fully understood. Nevertheless his congregation listened, or appeared to listen, when his powerful voice reverberated through the church.

The Reverend John Grey could see the blue smoke from the manse chimneys climbing into the sky and he followed the spiral upwards and looked for a long moment heavenwards before he started to speak. His mouth felt dry and he licked his thin lips nervously. He hated the island funerals because he never knew quite what to say. Confidence oozed from him on the

Sabbath when he had prepared his sermons so carefully and when he spoke from the pulpit he could be quite impersonal towards the parishioners. But a funeral involved so many personal feelings of grief and loss and he found it difficult to commune wholeheartedly with the tight-knit community of Gaels who made it so plain he would never be one of them. Help me, God, to say the right things, he thought wistfully and began his opening words, his voice drifting sonorously in the frozen air of morning.

Helen's two brothers moved restlessly, their feet crunching the blades of frosty grass and her father took out a large white handkerchief and blew his nose loudly, drowning the end of the minister's sentence.

He began the Lord's Prayer and the men joined in, their voices a drab monotone, blowing steam with the utterance of each word. A bird chirped sweetly from a nearby tree and the bleating of sheep came from the slopes. Alick gave a loud sniff and Fergus heard it like an explosion. He glowered at his brother's bowed head, momentarily hating him because of his display of tears. He could not show his emotions to the world. He watched Helen's coffin being lowered into the dark cold cavern of her last resting place and he wanted to reach out and enclose with his arms the hard wooden box that encased the body so dear to him. Instead he closed his eyes so that he wouldn't see the first scatterings of earth thrown over the coffin.

Numbly he sensed that the mourners were moving slowly away. An arm was thrown round his shoulders and Alick's voice murmured futile words of sympathy into his ears.

Fergus opened his eyes and looked into his brother's face. He saw the blue-grey eyes, red-rimmed but eager for an acknowledgement that his presence was of some use. He noted the handsome features, finely drawn, but the drooping lips too thin under the dark wiry moustache, and the prominent bulge of the Adam's apple working desperately to swallow his tears.

Automatically Fergus assumed the role that had been expected of him for as long as he could remember. He put a strong arm round his brother and led him out of the kirkyard back to Laigmhor where the parlour was crowded with black-clad women and sombre sniffing relatives. This was the time Fergus dreaded most of all. The condolences, the weeping, all the formalities he had to go through before his house was his own again.

He could hardly bear to look at Helen's mother. He'd never liked her but had put up with her for Helen's sake. She was a small fussy woman. She'd fussed because he'd wanted Helen buried on Rhanna and she'd fussed about every little detail since her arrival on the island till he'd felt like hitting her. Three years before she'd been delighted because her daughter was making a 'good marriage' to a fairly prosperous young man, but now she realised it had all been a mistake and Helen should never have married a farmer because she had been too unsuited for such a 'rough' life.

She sat in a corner dabbing her eyes with a lace handkerchief while her husband, a short balding little man, red-faced and uncomfortable in the hot stuffy room, patted her ineffectually on the shoulder. Alick's wife, Mary, a slim blonde, frivolously pretty even in her dark clothing, sat by the window primly enjoying the attention of several menfolk. Alick appeared not to mind in the least and after a time he followed his wife's example and began flirting with Tom Johnston's eldest daughter.

Hamish sat apart from everyone, quietly sipping at a glass of whisky and Fergus went to sit by him, appreciating the strong unassuming companionship that could be felt without words.

'Fergus!' Mary's high light voice floated clearly above the general murmur of voices. 'Aren't the doctor and his wife coming? I understood they were good friends of yours!'

It was difficult to know if her question was entirely innocent. She and Alick had arrived only that morning but gossip ran quickly on Rhanna. Fergus glowered at her and she giggled but turned red. The room had grown quiet and everyone was looking at Fergus. He grew warm with embarrassment and thought, Not a questioning! Not now when everything in me longs to have Helen at my side instead of in a cold grave on the Muir of Rhanna. A sick icy feeling gripped him and he longed to run from the room like a small inarticulate boy.

But before he could say anything Helen's mother fired another question at him.

'What's to happen to the bairn? Have you considered it at all? The wee mite will need a woman's care. Donald and I have talked about it and think it only right we should bring up the child. The Lord knows it won't be easy. You know yourself, Fergus, I don't keep good health but I think my grandchild deserves a good upbringing. We owe it to our own lass too. We have our boys but they have their lives to lead. The wee girl will make up for . . .'

She began to sob quietly into her handkerchief and Mr McDonald grew redder and patted her awkwardly.

The room was agog for Fergus's answer. He could feel the hush of the curious who had been wondering about his daughter and who would take care of her.

But now Alick broke the silence. He turned away from Tammy Johnston whose face fell because she'd been enjoying the surreptitious pleasures of having Alick's hand halfway up her skirt. He'd forgotten her now, his handsome face animated as he spoke.

'Mary and I have talked too. We're young and no doubt will have bairns of our own but we'd still like Shona to come and live with us. Isn't that right, Mary?'

She nodded with a distinct lack of enthusiasm. She didn't like the idea one bit. She and Alick hadn't talked about taking the baby, they'd argued. She didn't particularly care for children – if one of their own came along it would be different, but someone else's child, especially one that belonged to a man she had never understood, didn't appeal to her at all. She prided herself on her looks and these would soon go with the strain of continual washing, sleepless nights and all the other attentions a child demanded.

Fergus looked at her and saw her vanity. He looked at Mrs McDonald, fragile like Helen, but with none of her daughter's vivacity or zest for life. She was prim and prudish, with a hypocrisy that belied her religious beliefs. He couldn't imagine her bringing up a child, its spirit would be stifled from the beginning. He couldn't even begin to consider Mary. He could find no desirable quality in her that would render her fit to bring up Helen's child.

His thoughts were a surprise to him because he hadn't till then cared very much about his daughter's future. He had barely looked at her since her birth but he hadn't been able to avoid thinking about one picture that repeated itself continually in his mind. It was of Mirabelle feeding the child from a bottle that looked enormous beside a tiny elfin face. Wide blue eyes were open, gazing unseeingly at the ceiling, yet they held a world of wisdom as yet out of reach, un-developed beneath the smooth bloom of the high forehead, waiting for time to ripen each impression till the miracle of memory and learning blossomed from each living cell. And there was something else, some-thing so poignant that a needle of pain pierced the shell round his heart and hurt deeply. Helen stared out of those eyes. A glimmer of life-loving mischief lurked in the periwinkle depths and the mouth was Helen's, full and soft with upturned corners giving the impression of a permanent smile.

His voice lanced the expectant silence in the room. 'I think the child will stay at Laigmhor, it's her home after all. It's good of you to offer, Alick, I know you really mean what you say but Mary doesn't . . . do you, Mary?'

He looked her full in the eyes and she turned away guiltily. Then he swivelled to face Mrs McDonald. 'I thank you too – for wanting to do your duty by Helen but as you say yourself you're not really able to care for a young child. She will be far happier on Rhanna where she belongs.'

'How dare you!' She trembled and the hanky was in evidence once more.

'I dare because the child is mine.'

'But a child needs a woman to care for it! How can you, a man . . .'

She was interrupted by Mirabelle who appeared from the kitchen, the baby snugly asleep in her arms. Mirabelle was feeling harassed. The house had been in a turmoil all day and even with Nancy's help she was hot and tired. They had cleaned from top to bottom and aired and fired the spare rooms because several people were staying till the return of the ferry. It all meant a lot of extra work for her and some of the guests she didn't care for, in particular Mrs McDonald who had complained too much. On top of everything she had the baby to see to, but already she loved the tiny mite with all her kindly heart and enjoyed the wonderful trusting feel of the downy head against her bosom. She'd been having a rest in the kitchen when the heated voices drifted through from the parlour. She knew it wasn't her place to interfere but she hadn't been able to stop herself and she stood in the doorway and stuck out her chin proudly.

'And am I not a woman? I'll look after the little one and see she gets all the love that is her due. So long as there is life in me she'll get all the care it is possible for a bairn to get!'

Mrs McDonald blew her nose indignantly. 'Even the servants don't know their place in *this* house, it would seem. I can see I don't have a say about my grand-child at all. I'll be glad to get away from this place I can tell you!'

'Serves you right, you auld Cailleach,' said Jock under his breath and Fergus looked at Mirabelle with gratitude.

'Thank you, Belle,' he said quietly. 'The matter's settled.'

When dinner was over he made an excuse and went outside. Lass and Ben padded at his heels, sniffing the frosty air with silent joy.

Fergus found his steps taking him away from the farm over the road in the direction of the Kirkyard. He climbed the frost-rimed Hillock and saw a figure coming out of the rustic wooden gate, a plump familiar figure wrapped up tightly against the cold. It stopped and looked towards him and he saw clearly Phebie's bonny face, her skin whipped to a deep rose by the frost. For a long moment she looked at him then turned away, wrapping her shawl closer round her shoulders before hurrying down the hill.

Something tightened round his heart and he sighed, a sigh that told of all the sorrow in his heart and the regret he felt at having lost the friendship of two of the finest people on Rhanna. He knew that he was too proud to go cap in hand and admit his sorrow for his hasty words on the morning of Helen's death. He also knew that he would want to apologize a thousand times in the months to come but that he wouldn't do so because of his pride, the terrible pride that bound him in a lonely prison of body and soul.

Slowly he went to Helen's grave and saw on the

fresh earth a bunch of snowdrops, the petals tightly shut, lying on the hard ground like drops of exquisite purity.

'Phebie!' he murmured. The wrong that he had done tore afresh the caverns of his mind. He had denied the McLachlans the right to see Helen laid to her rest and the enormity of his feelings forced him to his knees. The setting sun had turned the Sound of Rhanna into a sheet of flame and Portcull thrust its peacefully smoking chimneys into the fiery sky. Sheep bleated mournfully on the moor and the shouts of children from the village were borne over the Glen to be lost in the corries of Sgurr na Gill.

Lass made little whining noises and buried her nose in his arm. He caressed her ears gently.

'You feel it too don't you, lass?' he whispered. 'The loneliness. It's all so lost . . . or is it just me?'

He shut his eyes and Helen came to him, laughing, her mane of hair blowing in the wind, her blue eyes crinkled with the joy of living and of gazing into a thousand suns of happiness. They had known it together, that happiness, but each memory was a locked door in his mind. Later – later, he would remember the happy times but just now he was too numb, too tired to think very much about anything.

'Goodnight, Helen, my lamb,' he whispered, so low it was like a sigh of the wind.

Part Two

1928

Chapter Three

Shona opened her eyes and lay very still under the warm blankets. The curtains of sleep still lay heavy over her eyes and she blinked long lashes in an effort to get them to stay open.

She liked to lie still when she woke, letting her eyes travel over her neat little room with its sloping ceiling. Her bed was in an alcove and there she felt safe. Sometimes she imagined it was a cosy cave, or that her bed was a boat tied in a hollow on the shore. The rag doll made by Mirabelle lay beside her. The floor was polished and shiny with a mat near her bed. A family of dolls and woolly dogs flopped lazily on a shelf and on the dressing-table was the china bowl in which she washed each morning.

The light of the January morning filtered through the gold curtains and she wondered what sort of day it was. There was something special about today but she couldn't quite remember what it was. Then it came to her – it was her birthday. Today she was five years old and grown up because being five meant that she would soon be going to school and would enter a new phase of her life.

Excitement churned in her at the prospect. Birthdays were exciting things altogether but today's birthday would have a special flavour because she

57

was going to feel grown up and very proud. But somewhere at the back of her mind a cloud hovered. It had something to do with her father because while all the people she loved celebrated their birthdays he withdrew into himself and became very strange and short-tempered.

She sighed at the thought of her father. He was so big and strong and she loved him with all her heart even though he was often brusque and impatient with her. Every day she longed to throw her arms round his neck and smother him with her love. Sometimes he let her kiss him and call him pet names. Sometimes he even swept her up in his big arms and crushed her till it hurt but she didn't mind because the feel of his strength made the hurt worth it because it meant that deep inside he loved her too.

She pursed her small mouth and said out loud, 'Today I am five! I am five years old today!'

The feeling of wanting to snuggle in bed left her and she padded over the cold floor to open the curtains. The wind whistled in from the sea making the rusty grasses cringe against the earth. The ocean was grey in the distance and white horses leapt and pranced to the shore. It was the kind of day she loved because inside everything was warm and cosy but outdoors the breeze would ruffle her hair and make her face tingle. On the breath of the wind would be all the smells she loved, the tang of the sea and peat smoke, the clean smell of tossing heather and the rich warm odour of the dung midden mixed with the scent of hay from the two big sheds.

She heard Mirabelle plodding upstairs with the jug

of hot water for her face and hands and she raced back to her bed and pulled the blankets over her head pretending to be asleep. Her heart beat faster and she waited, smothering her giggles. The door opened and the hot water gurgled into the basin.

'Ach mo ghaoil,' said Mirabelle slightly breathless. 'I know you're pretendin'. It's up wi' you this meenit. Your father will be in from the fields and wantin' his breakfast and you keepin' us all back wi' your mischief.'

Shona slowly peeped from the blankets and Mirabelle looked at her with an exaggerated frown on her round face. She had changed little in five years. The hair that escaped her mutch was a shade whiter and her shoulders stooped slightly, but otherwise she was the same Mirabelle who had undertaken the upbringing of Fergus's child. It had not been easy. Shona had been a lively, demanding infant, crawling at seven months, walking at a year and speaking fluently at two. Mirabelle often felt more tired than she would ever admit but the little girl's affection and love made up for everything, even the determination of will that had earned her many a spanking on her plump little bottom. But she never sulked and took the spankings and scoldings in her stride knowing she had earned them.

'Mirabelle?'

'Yes, my wee lamb?'

'You've forgotten what day it is so you have!'

'Indeed you might be right. I am always so busy I never know if it's Monday or Friday.'

'Mirabelle! You really have forgotten.'

A glimmer of tears shone in the big blue eyes and laughing, Mirabelle rushed forward to fold the child to her bosom.

'Ach, you're too quick by far to take offence. You're like your father in that queer wee way of yours. Happy birthday, my lamb. You're a big girl today and you must learn to behave like one. Now get your face washed, take your goonie off and put on your blue dress. We'll go down to Portcull after breakfast.'

'Truly, Mirabelle? Can we go to Merry Mary's and buy sweeties? I have a penny that Hamish gave me.'

'We'll see, but weesht now. Stop your blethers and get dressed.'

Shona hurried through her toilet and flew downstairs to the kitchen. Fergus was already at the table supping his porridge.

'Good morning, Father. Good morning, Ben.' She stooped to hug the old spaniel which rose stiffly from the hearth to greet her. Lass was gone now – she had died in her basket one night at the ripe age of fourteen. Mirabelle had cried for days and vowed no other would take her place but sheepdogs were a necessity on the farm. There was too much work for Peg and Molly who were now growing past their best so Kerrie came, a fine young dog who had learned fast but was a man's dog and preferred to stay with Bob the shepherd in his steading half a mile up Ben Machrie.

'Good morning, Father.' Shona repeated her greeting quietly but with a hint of stubbornness in her voice.

Fergus looked up slowly, reluctant to speak on a day that held so much joy for his daughter but none at all for him. He seldom looked properly at his little girl because the sight of her turned his heart to jelly. When he looked at her he saw Helen in every smile and glance, the way she turned her head, the glimmer of mischief always bubbling just under the surface.

But now he did look and saw his growing child, the blue dress matching her eyes, the deep auburn hair tied with a big blue ribbon to keep it from tumbling over the small pointed face. Something caught at his throat and he tried to turn away but her glance, powerful and compelling in such a small being, held his and unable to stop himself he rose and swept her into his arms.

Shona held her breath in delight, the hurt of his crushing arms only serving to heighten her happiness and she buried her face deep in his hair.

'Happy birthday, my wee chookie!' he breathed. 'Oh, God help me! You're so like her!'

Her happiness suddenly fled. The pain was there again in his voice and she didn't understand it. It puzzled her and frightened her. There was so much depth in his voice, such a force of longing that she felt him tremble. Something caught in his throat that sounded like a tear but which couldn't possibly be because he was so big and strong and never cried. For a moment she didn't want to be five. She wanted to be a baby again and to cry on his shoulder because she felt so sad. But he was putting her down and her sadness turned to hurt when he ordered her curtly to eat her breakfast.

She went to her place despondently but smiled when she saw the small pile of parcels by her plate.

'Oh Father, look! Please can I open them before I eat my porridge? I don't care if it gets cold. And please, Father, will you read the writing for me so's I'll know who they're from!'

He smiled despite himself and helped her open her gifts, losing himself for precious moments in her child's world.

'Look, father – a whirligiggy . . . from Mirabelle! Och, look at this bonny wee purse . . . . with a whole shilling inside! Who is it from?'

'It's from me,' said Fergus gruffly.

'Och Father!' She flew round the table and kissed him on the end of his nose. Another parcel was opened and proved to be a roughly sewn pink apron from Nancy. The last parcel was a puzzle. It was large and soft and she enjoyed guessing what it was before opening it. Out fell a long black pair of woollen stockings and a pair of navy blue knickers. She held up the stockings, her face a study.

'Father! who are they from?'

'Mirabelle!' he supplied.

'Och Father, look at them! They're like long tubes of liquorice. You don't think she expects me to *wear* them do you?'

She stared at him in consternation and he burst out laughing.

Mirabelle stood amazed at the kitchen door. 'What's a' the skirlin' for? Mercy child, have ye not started breakfast yet? And what's so funny I'd like fine to know? Fergus! Have ye taken leave o' yer senses?'

Shona held up the stockings. 'It's these, Mirabelle! They're so funny!'

'Funny!' exploded Mirabelle. 'I'll have ye know I near blinded myself knittin' the damt things. My een havny been the same since! They're for school, madam, that's what and I'll have none o' yer cheek. Would ye rather have frostbite than wear these lovely warm stockings I've sweated over for weeks?'

'Yes, Mirabelle, I would rather have frostbite,' giggled Shona, her heart aglow with joy because she had made her father laugh.

Hamish put his head round the door. 'Can I come in and wish my wee lass a happy birthday?'

Shona clapped with happiness. She adored the big red-bearded man. He was always spoiling her with sweets and pennies but more than these she loved his hearty laugh and unstinted affection, and a visit to his cottage was a highlight of her life.

'I've a wee surprise,' he said, his eyes twinkling. 'Shut yer eyes a minute.'

She screwed her eyes up tightly. There was a murmur and a scuffle then something soft and warm was placed on her lap.

'Och, it's a wee puppy,' she said softly, tears springing quickly at sight of a tiny golden spaniel. She lifted the furry bundle to her face and a pink tongue licked her nose and snuffled into her ears. Animals were the delight of her life. The big ones held no fear for her and she sat on Heather or Thistle while they stood quietly in the stable. She was already an expert at driving the cows and it was a laughable sight to see her small figure wielding a stick at a large stubborn bull.

She ran to Hamish and hugged him. 'Och Hamish,

I'll love you all my life so I will. What a dear wee puppy!'

'See you look after her well,' he ordered, his voice muffled in her hair. 'You've to walk her and train her. Remember she's just a wee baby and needs a lot o' care.'

'I'll do everything for her, I love her so much already. I think you're the most wonderful man on earth.'

Fergus watched the scene and a strange feeling came over him. He didn't recognize it at once, then he knew it was jealousy. He was jealous that another man had given his daughter a present that pleased her enough to single him out as her most favoured person. The violence of his feelings swamped him and he couldn't think clearly. He'd had the feeling before but it had been vague and he hadn't been able to place it. He'd kept thinking of her as a baby, an infant who toddled about asking tiresome questions. At times he had felt like striking her, so much did she disturb him with thoughts of what might have been if she had never been born. Lately she disturbed him even more because a real person was emerging, one who could form her own ideas and opinions with a determination that he knew she'd inherited from him. Also there were these other feelings, the ones he experienced on holding her close, when love for her swamped him so that he had to push her away, drive the love back into his heart because it claimed too much of him and he never wanted to belong to anyone again.

Now this other feeling annoyed him so much that he stood up and spoke sharply to Hamish. 'C'mon, man, there's work to do. We've got to drive the bull over to Croynachan. Johnston has some cows coming on!'

Hamish raised a bushy eyebrow but said nothing. Shona was too busy playing with her new puppy to notice her father's displeasure. She screamed with laughter when Ben rose with a grunt and waddled over to examine the newcomer. They snuffled for a while then the pup made a lunge and caught one of Ben's long ears, holding on with sharp little teeth till the old dog groaned protestingly.

Shona bent and smacked the newcomer hard on the bottom and the golden bundle looked up at her with surprise in its blue-brown eyes.

'Naughty!' reprimanded the little girl severely. 'You mustn't plague Ben, he's an old Bodach and you treat him with respect. Now – I wonder what I'll call you. Tot would be a good name, you're such a teeny wee thing!'

Mirabelle grunted. 'Aye, and ye'd better fetch a cloot for that lochy on the floor. She's your doggy and that means you must train her. I'm too auld for such capers!'

An hour later Shona was skipping beside Mirabelle on the narrow track to Portcull.

'A whole shilling,' she sang. 'Can I spend sixpence, Mirabelle, and buy lots of sweeties? I'll get you some Granny sookers if you like. Och, isn't it a lovely day? I feel so clean in the wind!'

But Mirabelle didn't agree and pulled her coat closer to keep out the biting wind.

Merry Mary's shop was a place beloved by all the island children. It smelled of apples and boot polish and everything from bootlaces to bobbins of thread could be had there. But it was the jars and jars of colourful sweets that interested Shona and she spent a lovely time pondering over her purchases while Merry Mary and Mirabelle gossiped. The shopkeeper's real name was Mary Merry but the islanders had repeatedly got it back to front and she eventually stopped correcting them knowing it to be a fruitless task. She was an Englishwoman; but she had spent thirty of her sixty years on Rhanna and instead of being a 'new incomer' she was now honoured as an 'old incomer' and, because she spoke Gaelic like a native, the younger generation could hardly believe she was an Englishwoman and loved her dearly because her nature suited her name. She was a quaint little creature with limp ginger hair, a big happy smile and a large wart on the end of her nose. The children were fascinated by the wart. Its hold seemed so precarious on the large square nose it had become a challenge as to who would be the first to see it fall off. The child to witness its demise would receive a half-penny from every child on the island, so Merry Mary's shop was very popular indeed. Though she sometimes wondered why her door would open to admit a solemn-eyed youngster who merely stared at her briefly before turning out of her shop without a purchase.

'Did you hear about Dodie?' she asked Mirabelle eagerly. 'He's gone and got himself a cow so he has.'

'Ach, away wi' you! Dodie will never manage a cow. He canny look after himself!'

'Well, he's got one right enough! It's a queer looking beast and its udder so big it near has to leap over the damt thing! But Dodie says it will give him plenty milk. He's that sick of trekking to the bottom of the hill where Mathew leaves his can and sometimes it's been knocked over by a damt yowe and nothing in it but grass and sharn!'

'And where did he get the cow is what I'm thinking? Poor Dodie hasny twa farthings to rub together and these beasts cost money so they do.'

'The laird gave it to him for doing wee jobs about the estate. Aye, and it was a dear cow sure enough for the laird doesn't give anything for nothing and Dodie has worked most of the winter to get the damt cow.'

'Aye, well he'll be lucky if he doesny have to go further than the end of the track to work the udder. These hill beasts just roam where the will takes them.'

'Ach well, he has a wee hut to keep the beast in but he'll have to comb the hill every evening to get her in for the night so that he'll get his morning milk.'

The two shook their heads sadly and murmured 'Aye' by way of sympathy for Dodie, the island's eccentric. He was what was quaintly referred to as 'a wee ways wrong in the mind' yet everyone knew by experience he was by no means lacking in intelligence and was not to be cheated out of a farthing. He lived alone in a tiny remote cottage in a treacherous hill track between Glen Fallan and Nigg, the minute Clachan perched on the cliffs near Burnbreddie. His real name was Joseph, conjured from the bible by his mother who had borne him out of wedlock and who had died when he was thirteen leaving him to fend for himself. He had never been able to pronounce the name and his childish pronunciation was so familiar to everyone his real name had been forgotten with the passing of time.

'Ach well,' sighed Merry Mary, 'it's good luck to him for he'll have a job getting milk from the damt thing at all with thon great hands of his. Ten thumbs he was born with and no mistake!'

Shona had made her choice and proudly brought out her new purse.

'My, what a fine purse,' commented Merry Mary. 'And a whole shilling to spend too. Have you been saving your pennies then?'

'It's my birthday and Father gave me the purse and the shilling.'

Merry Mary had argued with Fergus the day before over the price of tobacco and she wasn't feeling kindly disposed to him. Her lips pursed till they were almost touching her wart.

'Things are looking up indeed! He must have been in a good mood right enough for he'd fight over a half-penny like a bull over a cow when he has a mind!'

'Aye, we'll get going now,' said Mirabelle and hastily bustled her charge away.

Behag Beag looked up when the bell over her door jangled to admit Mirabelle and Shona, and a gleam of blatant interest showed in her beady eyes. Phebie and Niall were in the shop too and it was always vaguely exciting when Laigmhor and Slochmhor met.

'Ach, it's yoursel', Phebie!' Mirabelle's greeting was cheery for she was extremely fond of the doctor's wife. 'And Niall! What a big loon! Dodging school, is it?'

Phebie smiled. 'He's got a bit of a cold but feeling better today and driving me crazy so I thought to come out for a message or two. Hello, Shona.' She stooped and looked into the little girl's blue eyes. 'What a bright bonny lass you are this morning.'

'It's my birthday,' explained Shona.

'Y-es . . . I know.' Phebie stood up and Behag stopped rustling papers to listen better. A silence fell over the shop and Mirabelle glared at the postmistress.

'I'll have some stamps please, Behag . . . and you'd best pay attention to what you're doing! The last time I got stamps from you they were covered in blotches from your inky fingers!'

Behag stuck her nose in the air and went to get the stamps.

Shona and Niall stood beside the high wooden counter and regarded each other shyly. Niall, now a sturdy seven-year-old, was tall for his age with a mop of corn-coloured curls and his father's deep brown eyes and quick smile. Shona had seen him often, kicking stones on the road on his way to and from school, a whistle never far from his lips. It was his gay whistling that alerted her to the fact that he was passing Laigmhor and she would leave whatever she was doing to race to the gate and watch him in the distance. Sometimes he saw her and waved and she waved back wistfully, longing for the day when she too would be going to school. Now that day was drawing near.

'I'm going to school soon,' she volunteered.

'You'll be in the infants' section,' said Niall in slightly superior tones. 'In amongst the rest of the babies!'

Shona's eyes blazed. 'I'm *not* a baby! I'm five and you're cheeky for saying such things! Anyway, Mirabelle's been teaching me things. I can count to twenty and I can do the alphabet and – and I'm sure I can do a lot more than you!'

Niall's young face darkened. 'And you're nothing but a right wee crabbit baby and spoiled too! Why don't you ever come out to play instead of keekin' at folk on the road?'

Shona stamped her foot and tears of anger gleamed in her eyes. 'Because I was too little before! But I'm big now and I will be out to play! And I've got a new puppy who'll come with me everywhere but you won't because you're a nasty cheeky boy and I don't like you!'

'Wee baby!' he taunted but his eyes showed a regret at the turn of things because he had noticed Shona McKenzie often and in his toddler days had longed to play with her, but, for some reason, he wasn't allowed to visit Laigmhor and it had puzzled him because on Rhanna people Ceilidhed all the time. Eventually he had come to the conclusion that the McKenzies thought themselves above other people, so aloof that their little girl wasn't allowed to play with a doctor's son. Yet he admired the strapping figure of Fergus McKenzie and always shouted a cheery greeting when they passed, even though the big man's reply was hardly more than a grunt.

Phebie and Mirabelle had been having a quiet chat

at the other end of the counter but turned at the sound of shrill childish voices.

'Bairns!' cried Mirabelle. 'What on earth are you mumpin' about?'

Phebie came over to her son, 'Niall, I heard you call Shona a baby! Say you're sorry at once!'

Behag lurked in the little cubbyhole she proudly called her 'back shop' and listened gleefully. It seemed that even the children of Laigmhor and Slochmhor couldn't agree.

Niall shuffled his feet. His head dropped on to his chest and his words were low. 'I won't! She called me cheeky and I'm not! I'm not!'

Phebie grasped his hand and pulled him out of the post office, rushing him angrily away. Mirabelle grabbed Shona by the back of her collar and bull-dozed her outside away from Behag's long ears. It was seldom that Mirabelle got really annoyed but now her eyes shone with rage. She hurled Shona round a corner and whirled her round.

'You wee bitch that you are! Causin' a rumpus in that Cailleach's shop! It's a good skelpin' you're gettin' this very meenit, birthday or no'.'

And there, in the middle of Portcull, Shona found her knickers at her ankles and her bottom soundly spanked. The sharp sting of Mirabelle's heavy hand made her want to cry, but humiliation and determination would not allow a single protest to escape. Two Portcull children passed and shouted, 'Baldy bum!' and her face grew red with shame.

Mirabelle hastily pulled up the knickers and yanked her charge away. The two walked home in dejected silence but at the bottom of the track to Laigmhor Shona looked up at Mirabelle with a gleam of mischief in her eyes.

'Och, I'm sorry, Mirabelle! Don't look so angry, because your face was made for smiling and you look awful funny with your mouth all twisted like Behag's. I'm not sorry about that Niall though. He *is* cheeky and I'm *not* a baby!'

Mirabelle took a large hanky out of the folds of her voluminous attire and blew her nose soundly. She looked down at the child's upturned face. 'Ach well, I'm sorry too for skelpin' you on your birthday. We'll not mention a word to a soul for I shouldny have bared your wee bum and you shouldny have been so cheeky. It would be nice if you made friends wi' Niall so mind your manners in future.'

Nancy turned a rosy face from the stove at their entrance and the puppy pranced to meet them, leaving a pool in its wake.

'That doggy!' exclaimed Nancy in exasperation. 'I've had my feet chewed all mornin' and slipped on a great platter o' shit! I dropped all the spoons and they got covered in skitter. Poor auld Ben stood in it and I had to wash his feets, clean the pup and wash my stockin's for they were reekin' and me meetin' Archie tonight for the Ceilidh at Croft na Beinn.'

Nancy was very down to earth and never used dainty words no matter who she was addressing. Her entire family had the same indelicate use of language but were not less liked for it.

It had been rather difficult for Mirabelle when Shona first started to speak because Nancy's colourful expressions were the ones the toddler could pronounce perfectly. For a time the housekeeper had dreaded when someone dropped in for a Strupak and the day Madam Balfour came to discuss some business had been the worst of all.

Mirabelle had completed the delicate intricate embroidery of the chairback covers that had been given to her from Burnbreddie and the laird's wife had called to collect them. In raptures over the faultless work, with Mirabelle intent on explaining how a certain stitch was executed, neither noticed the small figure stagger unsteadily into the parlour till gleeful ecstatic baby tones announced, 'Vat bloody dog's farted! Vat bloody dog's farted. Fink he's shit the floor!'

Madam Balfour's mouth had dropped open and Mirabelle had scooped Shona under an arm and borne her hastily away.

Now Shona knew better than to repeat Nancy's words though she still giggled on hearing them. The young woman's language was more earthy than ever of late and there was a sparkle in her. She was 'walking out' with young Archie Taylor, eldest son of Croft na Beinn and a summer wedding was in the offing.

'I'm sorry about the mess,' apologized Shona, grinning. 'I'll train her as quick as I can, Nancy. And thank you for the apron. Now I can help Mirabelle make scones without getting in a mess.'

Mirabelle groaned at the thought of her charge making merry with flour and currants and Nancy sniggered wickedly. Fergus came in and they all sat down to stovies with cold meat followed by apple tart and fresh cream. Later, when Nancy was clattering busily with the dishes, Shona went with Mirabelle to scatter meal for the hens.

'Greedy creatures!' said Mirabelle mildly, watching while the hens squabbled and pecked.

But Shona's thoughts were far away. 'I'm a big girl now!' she said almost to herself.

'Aye, you are that,' agreed Mirabelle.

'And I'll have a lot more freedom now, won't I?'

'That's up to your father, mo ghaoil.'

'Och, but he's away with Hamish to Rhumhor to buy some piglets and I want to do something very badly.'

'Well, you know where to go. Is it a wee pup you are that knows not how to control itself?'

'Mirabelle! You're laughing at me! I want to go away up on the moor with Tot. All by myself . . . without you, Mirabelle.'

The old lady looked thoughtful. She was thinking of the scene in the post office and knew the time had come for the child to learn some independence. In a few weeks she would be off to school which was a very competitive world full of little humans who could be cruel to sheltered and inexperienced children. She patted Shona's head.

'Aye, my wee lamb, away you go.'

The reply was so unexpected that for a moment Shona was nonplussed, for she had expected an argument. She had been allowed to certain places on her own, like Hamish's cottage, and she had often gone on an errand to Portcull, but the wide open spaces of the island had demanded an adult escort because there were many hazards inland that were a challenge even to the experienced.

'I won't go far,' she promised breathlessly and ran indoors for Tot, then raced down the track and on to the road. She was like a wild thing that had been caged up for too long. She sped on to the moor and kept on running. The sound of a burbling burn was music in her ears, the cold sharp air streamed into her lungs and wakened every cell to pulsing life. Her hair streamed in the wind and the ribbon came undone to fall unnoticed in the rusty bracken. Eventually she rolled over in the heather, panting and laughing. The pup rolled too, barking and biting, and the child giggled, spreading her arms wide and looking at the racing grey clouds above, feeling herself riding with them in a great surge of freedom. Heather tangled in her hair and she buried her face in the sweet smell of the straggling shoots. Raising herself on one elbow she looked at the scenery spread below. Laigmhor sprawled untidily, tiny from this distance. She strained her eyes for a sign of life and saw Mirabelle, a tiny doll figure hanging out clothes. Suddenly she felt queer and sad. She loved Mirabelle, she loved her father, she loved Laigmhor, but she knew now that it wasn't enough. Now there had to be more loves, more people and places in her life and she felt a traitor to the people who had surrounded her for as long as she could remember. There were so many new feelings inside herself she didn't understand and she felt she wasn't ready for them because there was a lot of old feelings she didn't understand either. One of them was about her mother. She knew she ought to have a mother because Mirabelle read her stories and they always had mothers in them. She had asked Mirabelle where her own mother was and had been told she was in heaven. That was another mystery because no one seemed to know where heaven was though it was mentioned all the time in the bible and when Reverend John Grey came to visit her father she had heard him talking about this place called heaven but it hadn't made any sense because he'd used so many big words.

She knew her mother was buried in the kirkyard so she really couldn't see how she could be in heaven and in the kirkyard at the same time. How could something that grown-ups called a soul be with God, when the body belonging to that soul was deep under the ground?

Tears sprang to her eyes at the idea of her mother being in a wooden box buried in the earth. It must be terrible because beetles and worms and all sorts of creepies were in the soil.

She knew her mother had been beautiful because there was a photo of her in the parlour but she seldom saw it because the parlour was hardly used now. But Mirabelle had shown her another one that she kept in a little cardboard box in her room. It was a nicer one than the parlour photo because it was more natural and the delicate cameo face was smiling, the eyes alight with some secret joke. But to her it was only a photograph and she felt nothing except a great pride that her mother had been so beautiful.

It was very strange that her father never spoke of her mother because Mirabelle had said he loved her very much. How could you love someone and not speak of them even if they were dead?

Mirabelle spoke of her own mother and two sisters who were dead yet could be recalled by just talking about them.

It was all very mysterious and sad and difficult to understand.

She sighed and wrapped her arms round Tot who was sound asleep on her chest. It was lovely to feel the warm trusting bundle against her and she wished she had been able to let Niall see her puppy. She was sorry she had argued with him. It was the last thing she had wanted to do but her quick temper had let her down again and she vowed to try and keep it in better control. She chuckled. A temper was a funny thing because you could lose it yet still have it. Other things were easy to lose but difficult to find. She hoped he would never get to hear about her being spanked outside Behag Beag's shop. Just thinking about it made her face grow red.

Something flapped on the road far below and she looked down to see Niall's mother hurrying along in the direction of the woods near the Hillock. Shona wondered where she was going and wished she had been near the woods to talk to Phebie whom she liked very much. Next to Mirabelle, Phebie was her favourite woman person. Next to her father and Hamish, she loved Lachlan. He was like a big boy, he was so eager about everything. Once he had given Shona and Mirabelle a lift to Burnbreddie in his trap. Mirabelle had been going to see the laird's wife about cushion covers she had been asked to do for the sitting-room. Mirabelle hadn't been keen on the task because she had so little time, but she was an expert needle-woman and Madam Balfour insisted she was the only person fit for the job. There was going to be another house party soon with London people coming and new chair covers were a must.

Dr McLachlan had joked all the way to Burnbreddie and it had been a lovely ride over the high cliff road. When they arrived at the house he had gone to seek out the laird who was having trouble with something Mirabelle called 'piles'.

Going home Shona had sat silent thinking about the laird's piles till she could contain herself no longer and had asked the doctor to explain. Mirabelle's face had reddened but Lachlan roared with laughter and for the rest of the journey explained with great delicacy about haemorrhoids. Shona was delighted that another discovery was adding to her growing list and announced her intention of telling her father but Lachlan's face had clouded.

'Better not mention it, lass. In fact don't mention me at all.'

He had gone off quickly and Shona turned to Mirabelle. 'Why can't I talk to Father about the doctor? He's so kind and nice. I'm scunnered with all these secrets you big folk have!'

'Ach, don't worry your wee head,' Mirabelle counselled. 'You know your father's a bit ramstam and he and the doctor don't see eye to eye. Anyway – what a nice secret we have! We've had a ride in the doctor's trap and not a soul knows but us.'

Shona felt like a conspirator and her eyes gleamed.

'Ach, you're right, Mirabelle, we won't tell a soul. The doctor's our cronie even if he and Father don't get along. But Father will find out anyway because that Madam Balfour will tell him. I don't like her, do you, Mirabelle? She's got wee beady eyes that take off your skin and tries to look into your mind and her mouth goes all tight and thin like a wee red dash made by a crayon. I don't know why she bothers with lipstick because she has no mouth to put it on!'

'Weesht wi' you!' said Mirabelle sternly but hid a smile because she shared the child's sentiments. Sitting in the big formal parlour at Burnbreddie it had taken all her willpower to hold her tongue when told: 'Make a good job of the covers, Mirabelle. My friends from England must see that we're not all uncivilized on the Islands. I'll pay you well for your trouble, of course. If you were my housekeeper you would get a handsome salary. At Laigmhor you are . . . let me see . . . cook, housekeeper and nurse and no doubt only get paid for housekeeping. Yes, my dear, you're wasted and no mistake.'

Mirabelle straightened, stuck out her bosom majestically and said in her dourest tones, 'Money is not everything, my leddy, for there are those who are none too happy with the aid of it. I'll bid you good day and see you get your covers in good time for your English friends to rest their backsides on. We must let the gentry see that we aren't *all* peasants . . . eh, my leddy? There's some can put to use the hands that God gave them.'

Out she had flounced pulling Shona with her and an indignant 'Well!' had floated into the empty room.

79

In due course Fergus heard about his housekeeper's 'impertinence' and he had looked at the laird's wife with contempt when she also mentioned that the doctor had brought Shona and Mirabelle in his trap. He had put his face very close to hers, and his black eyes were like steel.

'And what is wrong with that? It's a fair trek from Laigmhor. The doctor must have saved my housekeeper a hard walk over the hill for no doubt you would not have thought to send your groom to collect her.' He had turned to go and, whitefaced, she had scurried off to her husband to inform him that 'something must be done about Fergus McKenzie'. But the laird had looked at her with bleary eyes and told her, 'McKenzie's a damned good farmer and you talk too much.'

Shona knew about this because she'd heard Annie McKinnon who 'worked to Burnbreddie', telling Mirabelle and she hugged herself with glee at the thought of her father scaring the wits out of Madam Balfour.

Her thoughts were interrupted by a scrunch of heather and Dodie loomed big and dark on the skyline. He was well over six feet, though a pronounced stoop belied the fact. Everyone said the stoop had something to do with the years he had walked Rhanna with his quick loping gait, his eyes glued to the ground and his neck thrust forward as if he expected to encounter some rare find at any moment. His skin was nutbrown, weatherbeaten by years of wind and sun. His grey-green eyes had an odd dreaming expression and his large mournful mouth rarely smiled. Brown broken teeth were stained forever by the juice of the tobacco he chewed continually. His most startling feature was his nose or rather the huge carbuncle that sprouted from its side. It was almost like a second nose, but nobbly, and shook with the movements of his head. Long arms hung down at his sides, useless-looking with short stubby fingers calloused from years of hard work, for he excelled in manual tasks and had worked on every croft and farm on Rhanna. Nobody knew if he had hair because his head was perpetually covered by a green frayed cap and his long lean body was draped in a threadbare raincoat that looked an impossibly inadequate garment to combat rain and wind, yet he refused kind offers of warmer outerwear. Enormous feet were encased in stout wellingtons worn winter and summer and the smell that emanated from them had incurred many a comment.

'He breeah!' Dodie greeted Shona mournfully but his eyes were alight with pleasure at seeing her. No matter the weather his greeting was always the same and even if it was pouring from the heavens people returned the greeting in kind because he was hurt as easily as a small boy and so inoffensive, but for his peculiar smell, that everyone liked him.

'He breeah!' said Shona. 'Look at my new puppy, Dodie. Do you like her?'

'Ach, but she is lovely just!' He gathered the puppy tenderly in his big awkward hands and it sniffed eagerly, obviously enjoying the smells so offensive to humans. His love for animals had endeared him to Shona and when he worked at Laigmhor she followed him about asking questions that he answered with unending patience. The pup nibbled at one of his long ears and his eyes gleamed delightedly when a wet nose was poked into his neck. Shona smiled when she saw that the portion of skin that had been licked was decidedly paler than before.

'I'm going home now, Dodie,' she said, taking Tot before she disappeared inside the greasy raincoat.

'I'll just walk with you. I was coming over to ask your father if he was needin' odd jobs done for I'm wantin' to bring Ealasaid when she comes to season.'

His candid way of speaking was no surprise to Shona. No matter the age of his listener he spoke freely about the facts of life with beguiling innocence. But Shona knew all about animals and their 'seasons'. Most of the children on Rhanna did – one could not live on croft or farm without witnessing animals mating and giving birth.

'Who's Ealasaid?' giggled Shona. 'Are you courting then, Dodie?'

Dodie's face reddened, for while he could talk freely about the habits of animals with complete candour, he grew embarrassed if anyone hinted that he had an interest in the human female. As a result he was always being teased.

'Ach Shona, my lassie,' he chided gently. 'Ealasaid is my cow. Did you not know I had a cow? A right bonny beast too.'

'Yes, Dodie, I heard you had a cow and what a fine name I'm thinking. The fanciest I've heard for a cow.'

'Well she's a real fancy cow but a bugger for all that. I've to trek miles with her hay and there I sits in the middle of the damt moor milkin' her and sometimes she kicks the pail away till there's nothing in it and her udder dried out. So I've to bring her home and wait till she's full again before I can get anything, but my . . . it's worth it! Damt fine milk it is, the cream to it inches thick and lovely spread over my tatties for dinner.'

'Och Dodie! You don't spread cream over tatties, it's for porridge.'

'Well mine's for tatties! Nothing finer wi' plenty salt and bread.'

'Och well, we'd best hurry now. Mirabelle might give you a Strupak. She was baking cake and scones this afternoon because it's my birthday.'

Mirabelle greeted Dodie with some reserve. She'd had a busy day and wasn't in the mood for a crack but, with her usual hospitality, she ushered him to a seat near the door in the hope that the draughts might carry some of his odours away. He munched scones and drank tea with relish, while Tot and Ben watched with dribbling muzzles. Fergus came in and was treated to a long list of reasons why Dodie wanted his Ealasaid to be mated with Fergus's bull, the main one being that it was a prize bull and in return for its services Dodie would do all the spare jobs till his debt was paid.

'It's to keep the cow in milk you see, Mr McKenzie,' he explained earnestly. 'She's a fine cow and if she and your bull came together they would produce a fine calf. Ach! It would be a fine day for us both, would it not?'

Fergus had to smile. He had seen Dodie earlier that

day, milk pail in one hand and a bundle of hay in the other, standing on the moor talking lovingly into the ear of a rather dejected looking cow. The beast was past its best and Fergus felt sorry that guileless Dodie had been cheated by the laird. He knew he should have refused the services of his bull because the cow looked unfit to bear a calf but he couldn't resist the appeal in Dodie's eyes. He had a soft spot for the old eccentric and admired the way he worked so willingly to provide the bare necessities for his simple life. Dodie had received less rebukes than any man to cross Fergus's path and the islanders told each other that McKenzie had a heart after all. Dodie was always quick to defend him.

'Aye, and a big heart just! He is a fine man, the best there is. A lot better than some o' you lazy lot!'

'Ach, maybe it's because you're a cheap way o' labour,' they'd counter.

'Mr McKenzie never gives me more than I'm paid for. It's that sly Bodach at Burnbreddie who would work your fingers to the bone and hardly a reek o' his dung in return.'

Fergus considered Dodie's proposal for a long moment. He opened his mouth to refuse but the pleading in Dodie's eyes made him say instead, 'Very well, Dodie, when your cow is ready, drive her over to Croynachan and put her in with the rest of the kie. My bull will be there for a while yet.'

'Ach you're a good man just! She should be comin' on soon for she was jumpin' on some o' the beasts up on the hill.'

The matter was settled and Dodie took himself off

well pleased. Mirabelle quickly cut an onion and tied it to the chair on which he had been sitting.

'That will clear the reek in no time,' she told Nancy. 'Now, mo ghaoil, I know you're champin' to be off. You've worked well today so away you go and have a nice time at the Ceilidh.'

Nancy's dark eyes lit up. 'Ach, you're good so you are, Belle. It will give me a chance to get home and put some scent on these stockings for they still reek a bit and I wouldny like Archie to think I had a natural smell o' shit off me. It might put him off the weddin'.'

Shona was out of earshot and Mirabelle chuckled. 'Aye, but keep a finger on your halfpenny just the same. If you had a bairn out of wedlock he still might not wed you. Men can be gey queer that way!'

'Och Belle! As if I would!' Nancy's smile was innocent but her memory delighted in recalling her last outing when Archie had walked her home to Portcull. He had pulled her into a boatshed and kisses had led to his hand creeping into her blouse while his whispers tickled her ear.

'You have the finest breasts on Rhanna,' he mumbled. 'I like them big with fine nipples like cherries that a man can get his lips over. Let me play with them, Nan!'

He had played and worked himself to a nice frenzy but even though her body wanted more, her quick mind warned her against it.

'Och, please, Nan!' he pleaded. 'We're as good as wed! I'll be careful, I promise.'

But Nancy had seen too many of her mother's pregnancies and knew how easy it was to get that way and she wasn't going to the altar looking like a Christmas pudding.

'No, Archie,' she told him firmly. 'Bide your time, it will come soon enough and think how nice it will be to have your first night with a real virgin!'

Further begging had got him nowhere and he had crossed his legs in agony and smoked two cigarettes while she tidied her clothes before going home. On the way they had passed her sister Annie who was also having a tussle with a young fisherman in old Shelagh's peat shed.

Nancy hurried off and Mirabelle went upstairs to tuck Shona into bed. The little girl lay with her rag doll in one arm and Tot in the other.

'And what way is that pup doin' here?' asked Mirabelle sternly. 'She'll have pools all over the floor come mornin' and I'm not going to clean them up.'

'Och Mirabelle, she's such a wee thing and would cry all night and Ben might clout her 'cos he's too old to bother with noise. Let me have her beside me, Mirabelle. I get lonely sometimes.'

Mirabelle's softening glance told her she had won and she reached up to pull the old lady close.

'I love you, Mirabelle! You'll never be a Cailleach with that nice face you have!'

'Is it trying to get round me you are?'

'Maybe just a wee bit. Has it not been a lovely day . . . except for that Niall McLachlan! It was grand on the moor all by myself. Father was nice today as well, he hugged me close and laughed. Do you think he loves me a wee bit?'

'Of course he does, my wee lamb. It's just he canny show his feelings easy.'

Mirabelle's voice was gruff because of the tears in her throat. She always felt unhappy when the child asked her such questions. Things would have been so different if Helen had lived. Oh, how happy a place Laigmhor then, and Fergus a completely contented being.

While they talked he was at that moment out on the dark windy moors, his steps taking him on a pilgrimage he made often but especially on this day of all days. The bare trees crackled in the Kirkyard and he could barely make out the dim lines of Helen's stone. Even dimmer was the mossy ground beneath but he knew without seeing them that the snowdrops would be there. He felt for them and picked them up, crushing the cool pale drops to his chest.

'Helen, my dearest lamb,' he murmured. 'I loved you – I love you with all my heart but she – Phebie – loved you too and I'm too proud to tell her I'm sorry.'

Chapter Four

The shrill cries of newborn lambs echoed over the fields. March was moving into April but to the uninitiated there seemed no sign of spring in the bare trees. But the expert eye saw the tiny swollen buds on the stark branches and the sharp new green of tender heather shoots through the tangle of rusty bracken and bramble on the moor. The air was still raw but there was a softness hidden in the rough caress, a hint of the glorious summers that could bathe the Hebrides in long days of golden sunlight.

Shona skipped through the lambing fields but stopped to watch twins running to their mother, tails wagging as they nudged her belly with no regard for her swollen milk glands.

Bob and her father were moving amongst the flock with Kerrie dancing in their wake. A trio of carrion crows rose from a hedge, their shrieks telling of their rage at being disturbed from a feast of a dead lamb dropped from the talons of a golden eagle.

'I'll shoot that damt bird yet!' said Bob, wiping his nose with the back of a brown hand on which a pattern of knotted veins told of a lifetime of hard work. 'The brute has its eyrie on Ben Machrie for I've seen it fleein' abouts there.'

A ewe, heavy and awkward, was in the last stages

of labour and the men went to help her.

'This one's in trouble,' said Bob, examining the swollen vagina with expert hands. Several moments later an unformed embryo was expelled on to the grass.

Shona watched with quiet interest. She had seen it all before but each lambing season brought renewed excitement. It was so lovely to see the newborn lambs taking their first wobbling steps, the legs shaking but miraculously supporting a perfect little body. Each year brought its casualties like the lamb now feeding the carrion and there were always orphan lambs needing care. Shona delighted in feeding the motherless babies and now that she was five her father had allowed her to go to the fields with him though he had forbidden her to bring Tot and she sulked because the pup went everywhere with her. But she soon got over her mood and watched fascinated while Bob worked with the ewe who was lying on her side with her eyes closed.

'There's a live one in there yet,' he said. 'The contractions are weak but wi' luck we'll have a lamb, though there's no' much chance for the poor auld yowe.'

The ewe was dying even as a tiny head appeared under her tail. For a minute the head hung helplessly for there was no more help to be had from its mother who had taken her last shuddering breath. Bob's hand disappeared into the birth canal and grasping the lamb gently but firmly delivered it from its mother's body. Shona's eyes filled with tears for the dead sheep but she gazed at the new lamb with tenderness. Bob had removed the delicate skin bag which encased the lamb and skinny ribs heaved to draw in life-giving oxygen.

Fergus turned to Shona urgently. 'Can you be trusted to run to Mirabelle with this wee lamb? It's a weak one and needs heat. I can't come but she'll know what to do, she's done it often enough.'

Shona gazed at her father in disbelief. The enormity of the trust he was placing on her took her breath away and her heart raced with pride.

Bob placed the fragile warm body in her arms and she turned to go.

'I'll take care, Father,' she promised. 'The wee lamb will be safe for I'll keep her warm with my jacket.'

Her feet barely touched the turf. She had two fields to cross going the shortest way but it meant crossing the burn and climbing over a stile.

The stepping stones were slippery and she held her breath when her boots slithered on slimy moss. The stile was more difficult because she couldn't use her hands to cling to the fence. Her heart jumped when she almost fell from her precarious perch but she steadied herself with an elbow and flew over the last field. The lamb bleated weakly from her jacket. The sound made her afraid, it was so faint, and her whole being urged her legs to go faster. If the lamb died, she would blame herself and her father would never ask her to do anything important again. The cobbles in the yard threatened to trip her tiring feet but in seconds she was in the kitchen, her heart light with the knowledge that the burden of saving the lamb would now rest with someone else.

She stood in the warmth looking expectantly round the room but it was empty but for a wildly ecstatic Tot, and Ben in his usual place by the range.

'Mirabelle!' The cry was torn from her in a torment of anxiety. She ran to the parlour, then to the hall where the ticking of the grandfather clock echoed in her ears. She had often noticed that the tick of a clock was so much louder in an empty house and it was then she remembered that Mirabelle had mentioned going to Portcull to visit Morag the spinner and wouldn't be back till teatime.

Shona's mind raced. Nancy! She would get Nancy to help! She was an expert at dealing with the new-born, both animal and human. But it was Nancy's day off and she and her mother were going to start work on the wedding dress, a grand ensemble which Mirabelle had promised to finish with embroidered white flowers on the bodice.

Shona suddenly felt small and very young, not at all like the big girl she had felt on her birthday. The lamb bleated again and the sound stung her into frantic action. The lamb was very weak and its small body, still wet with amniotic fluid, was cold and trembling. She ran to the linen cupboard and found a blanket and a rough towel then holding the lamb on her knee she rubbed briskly with the towel till the soft wool curled and the small body grew warm. She wrapped it in the blanket and laid it on the rug beside Ben who began licking the small white face with his warm tongue.

Food was the next thing and Shona rummaged in the pantry till she found the feeding bottle kept specially for weak lambs. She mixed cream with water and poured it into the bottle.

'But it's got to be warm!' she said in despair because all Mirabelle's pans were on a shelf out of her reach. But she spotted Tot's tin ashet in a corner and hurriedly washed it and poured the mixture into it and with the aid of the clothes tongs held it over the glow of the range. Panic made her try to pour it directly from ashet to bottle but it spilled and she uttered a frustrated curse and rushed once more for the jug.

A moment later the lamb was on her knee sucking slowly but firmly from the bottle. She held her breath in delight and felt like a mother with a new little baby. Milk dribbled from the small inexperienced mouth and she wiped it gently with the towel, helped by Tot who was entranced by the whole proceeding.

When Mirabelle came home she found Shona fast asleep in the cosy inglenook, the lamb clasped firmly in her arms, contented burping pops coming from its milky lips.

'Well! I'm blessed!' Mirabelle folded her arms over her stomach and chuckled. 'Two wee lambs snoring like thunder!'

Shona opened her eyes and her smile was triumphant. 'I saved the wee cratur, Mirabelle, all by myself. Look, it's warm and fed.'

Mirabelle removed her voluminous coat and bent to take both lamb and child into her arms. 'I'm proud o' you, so I am, and your father will be too. So proud he'll feel like burstin' the way I am!'

At teatime Fergus was greeted by his excited daughter.

'Look at the wee lamb, Father! Mirabelle wasn't here but I warmed and fed it. It's going to live!'

He looked at the fluffy lamb, now on wobbly legs, its tail wagging with pleasure as Ben licked it and Tot jumped around with the unrestrained antics of the very young, and a feeling of pride glowed in him.

'You're a daughter of the farm right enough,' he said briefly but it was enough for Shona.

'It's what I want to be, Father. I'm glad I can help you now. It's a lovely feeling to save a wee thing's life. It was a shame about its mother but at least her baby is alive.'

He looked at her, a long considering look, the strangeness back in him again.

Tears sprang to her eyes. 'Och Father, what is it that bothers you so? Did I say something wrong?'

'Shona!' He knelt beside her and looked into her blue eyes. 'You haven't said anything wrong. You just have a queer wee way of hitting at the truth. And I do like . . . love you but don't expect me to fuss about it. There's so much you don't know and so much I can't talk about.'

She folded her arms around his neck and nuzzled his rugged weatherbeaten skin. 'My poor father! Talk to me about the things that bother you. I'll understand.'

He unclasped her arms and stood up, a look of weariness in his eyes.

'Go and wash your hands, tea will be ready in a while.'

She turned dejectedly but his voice stayed her. 'You're a clever wee lass – I'm – proud of you.'

She didn't look at him but ran to her room, her heart singing. Living with her father was like sailing the sea forever. One minute it was calm and the next so stormy that each of her senses reeled till she didn't know where she was. But the squalls made the times of calm like lovely bounties of treasure, precious jewels that she could hoard in the caskets of her memory.

Saturday came and Mirabelle bustled about in Shona's room, laying out her best clothes because the next day she was going to church for the first time. She had mixed feelings about it. She had heard so much about the Reverend John Grey's sermons. Nancy had told her that he could see into a person's soul and Shona wasn't sure she would enjoy that. This soul that people spoke about must be a very important part of a person and she felt that it ought to be a strictly private piece of property.

'There we are!' Mirabelle laid the black knitted stockings over the back of a chair.

The child stared aghast. 'Och no, Mirabelle! I can't go to kirk in these!'

'These you are wearin' and no' another word. There's a bite in the wind still!'

'But . . .' Shona searched desperately for an excuse. 'What if I rip them and won't have them for school next week?'

'Rip them and your bum will be warmer than a hot toddy. What's the matter wi' them anyway? Are they not fine enough for madam?'

Shona didn't reply. She had put the 'liquorice tubes' to the very back of her drawer hoping that Mirabelle would forget about them till she had outgrown them. The thought of everyone looking at her 'liquorice' legs filled her with horror and when she got into bed she racked her brains for a way to escape wearing them but could think of none.

The Sabbath was a very pious day on Rhanna. Saturday evening was spent in preparation. Zinc tubs were brought to the fire and filled with hot water for the weekly bath. The less fussy 'steeped' their feet in a basin. All over the island people bathed and steeped. The latter was favoured by solitary old men who, safe from watchful eyes, kept their socks on and thus accomplished two tasks at one time all the while alleviating any twinges of guilt with the thought that economy was a saving grace and they were saving both soap and water. Old Bob, safe in his lonely biggin on Ben Machrie, simply bared his feet to Kerrie who, with ecstatic expertise, slapped his tongue in and around toes while his master lay back blissfully by his cosy peat fire. The women busied themselves preparing meals so that there was nothing to do but heat them and lay them on the Sunday table. Clothes must never be seen hanging to dry on the Sabbath though many of the womenfolk cursed the fact and surreptitiously hung sheets in the big airy hay sheds consoling themselves that 'cleanliness was next to godliness'.

The bell was pealing its rather mournful notes when Mirabelle patted her best hat and took Shona firmly by the hand. The little girl wriggled.

'Mirabelle, these stockings itch something terrible. I'll scratch all the time in kirk. Can't I wear my brown ones?'

'I'll skelp your lugs if you don't be quiet. Now – have you got your collection?'

'Yes, Father gave me threepence.'

'Come on then. Carry your bible like a real wee lady and put this nice clean hanky in your pouch. Remember, you mustny cough too loudly in kirk and don't keep squirming like an eel or folks will think you've worms.'

They met Hamish on the road, his beard smooth and tidy and his kilt flying proudly in the breeze. No one mentioned Fergus. He hadn't attended church since Helen's death though the Reverend Grey visited him regularly and never gave up trying to persuade the young farmer that his soul would find no rest till he came back to the Lord's house. But Fergus was not easily dissuaded and told the minister, 'God and myself understand each other all right. I'll be no better going to kirk just to listen to old wifies sucking mints and criticizing each other's hats.'

The trio wandered past the cold green waters of Loch Tenee but known better to everyone as Loch Wee. Scurrying figures were coming from all directions, something in their bearing suggesting the discomfiture they felt being rigged in stiff Sunday best.

Shona skipped between Hamish and Mirabelle till she earned a sharp rebuke from the latter. 'Bide still ye wee weasel! You're like a hen on a hot girdle!'

Hamish grinned indulgently. 'Ach the bairn's excited. It's no' every day we get goin' to kirk . . . thanks be to the Lord!'

Mirabelle pursed her lips. 'The de'il will get you, Hamish Cameron! You're a blasphemer and should know better than to say such things in front o' the bairn!'

Voices hailed them and they were joined by the McLachlans and Biddy, her best hat slightly askew.

'It's a queer way the Lord has o' givin' us a day o' rest,' she said with slight regret. 'Every other day I'm called to a confinement but no one seems to have bairns on Sundays. The very day I could put my feet up I've to drag myself to kirk!'

'You don't *have* to go, Biddy!' twinkled Phebie.

'What! And have that blessed meenister comin' to my door threatenin' my soul wi' a' sorts o' things! No thanks! I'd rather hae a snooze in kirk than risk that!'

Lachlan smiled at Shona. 'Our little lass is looking very smart today. Going to meet the minister in all her Sunday best, is it?'

Shona wriggled and tried to hide behind Mirabelle, her whole being concentrating on hiding the awful black stockings from Niall who was eyeing her with covert amusement.

A black speck was coming towards them from the hill track to Nigg. In front of the speck was a larger one with four legs that turned out to be Ealasaid mooing protestingly with every step because Dodie was driving her at a pace which didn't suit her in the least.

'Bless me!' exclaimed Mirabelle. 'It's Dodie wi' thon queer cow!'

'He's no' bringin' it to kirk, surely!'

Dodie came nearer and his mouth cracked into a mournful grimace which was the nearest he ever got to a smile.

'He breeah!' he cried with something akin to elation in his tone. 'I'm just drivin' Ealasaid over to Croynachan!'

'Bless me, what for?' asked Mirabelle, eyeing the cow who had seized the chance to nibble heather shoots at the roadside.

'She has just come on real strong and I'm wantin' to get her to the bull while she's in the mood.'

He nodded his head enthusiastically causing his carbuncle to wobble alarmingly.

Mirabelle was shocked. 'Not on the Sabbath, Dodie! She can't go to the bull on the Sabbath. Anyways, the Johnstons passed in the trap a whily back. They'll be in kirk now. You'll get no help wi' the beast!'

'Ach, Angus will be there. If Ealasaid's ready we'll get the bull on her between us.'

'I'm sure the Lord won't mind this once,' twinkled Lachlan.

Dodie nodded earnestly. 'Aye, you're right, doctor. I had a wee word wi' Him last night and I got the feelin' He was not annoyed at all.'

Biddy smiled dourly. 'I'm sure there's not just the beasts that go matin' on a Sunday. I've a funny wee feelin' half the bairns on Rhanna are started on the Lord's day.' Her smile changed to one of mischief. 'Folks have got to pass the time some way and there's not a lot to keep the hands occupied on the Sabbath, is there now?'

Mirabelle gave her friend a prim glance and pulled Shona hastily up the Hillock to kirk leaving Dodie to shout abuse at the cow who had wandered to a small green patch and now stubbornly refused to move.

Inside the kirk it was dim and musty. Light filtered through the ruby glass of the window above the pulpit and the colour splashed on to the floor. Shona stared at the rows of bowed heads all round her and was amazed that they were the same warm-hearted lively creatures who peopled the crofts and cottages in Portcull. Elspeth was near the front, almost unrecognizable in a black coat and bowler type hat, her sharp nose sticking out resolutely in the direction of the pulpit as if she expected to see her salvation at any moment. Hector was by her side, his hair plastered down with oil, his red nose tamed to a duller hue in the dim mists of the kirk.

Near them was old Joe who had spent all his life at sea, retired now and beloved by the village children whom he entertained with amazing stories hoarded from his many voyages. His white hair curled over his dark collar and his sea-green eyes were closed in prayer. Shona wondered if he was really praying because a smile hovered at the corners of his large mouth and she wondered if he was reliving his past adventures. Idly she asked herself if some of his stories were really true. That one about the mermaid sitting on the rocks near Mingulay was lovely. He had described her as having long golden tresses, a fish tail and 'never a stitch to cover her birthday suit'.

The Taylors of Croft na Beinn sat in a neat row. Little Fiona, small for ten, thirteen-year-old Donald awkwardly trying to arrange his gangling form on the hard pew, and strong thick-set Archie meekly staring at his shoes but every so often sneaking a glance at Nancy who sat with her family in an opposite pew.

Behag Beag sat with her brother, her headscarf exchanged for a blue felt hat with a discreet feather sticking out at one side. It looked like a grouse feather and Shona grinned to herself.

Merry Mary was staring trance-like at the window, her wart outlined in the ruby glow. Beside her sat deaf old Shelagh McKinnon, Mr McKinnon's aunt and old Joe's cousin. She too wore a long black coat and a round black hat trimmed with faded green felt daisies. Old Joe had described the hat as looking like 'an upturned chanty wi' the bile' but Shelagh, deafly oblivious, was very proud of her hat. She was a quaint figure altogether with a small inquisitive face, sloping shoulders and broad hips giving her the appearance of a walking pear. At seventy-two she was surprisingly agile yet it was a practice of hers to haunt Dr McLachlan in a never ending quest for a magical cure for 'the winds that make my belly rumble and causes me to fart all the time'. She sucked Pan Drops continually, her deafness making her sweetly oblivious to the loud satisfying belches she emitted at regular intervals. At the age of sixty-five she had acquired a set of false teeth, and had, for the first time in her life, taken a trip to the mainland to have them fitted, but after months of half-hearted effort she gave up trying to eat with them saying, 'They're nothin' but a damt nuisance and I'm chewin' the buggers wi' my dinner half the time!' Nevertheless the teeth were carefully wrapped and placed in a drawer to be brought out and worn on the Sabbath so that she could sing to the Lord with proper 'prenounshun.'

She was humming untunefully, singularly content

and oblivious to the frowns thrown at her by red-haired Morag Ruadh, the nimble-fingered spinner who was very proud that she was also the church organist. It took a lot of patient persuasion to get any sort of tune from the ancient harmonium and she had to pedal furiously to get the bellows inflated before the instrument wheezed into life. Prior to the minister's appearance she liked to play quietly to get the congregation in a properly sober mood and Shelagh, humming an entirely different tune to the one being played, was an annoying diversion.

The McLachlans sat in the pew opposite Mirabelle and Shona. Niall's golden head was bowed in his clasped hands but one eye was open and he was grinning over to Shona. Hastily she tucked her legs under the hard seat and peeped at him over the generous swell of Mirabelle's bosom. She smiled back and brown eyes met blue in a shared moment of suppressed mischief.

A door opened and the minister came in. Morag pedalled harder and managed to coax some enthusiasm from the harmonium. The coughing and rustling died down and the Reverend John Grey climbed to the pulpit, pausing for a moment to bow his head in prayer.

He raised his hand and everyone rose to sing *Rock of Ages* while Shelagh remained seated and sang one of her favourite Gaelic hymns. A small girl from Nigg shuffled to the front and read a passage from the bible and the old Gaels, not understanding a word, rustled in their pockets for a mint or a handkerchief, and wished it was dinner-time. But when the minister started his sermon, everyone paid attention, whether they understood or not. The church reverberated with his booming voice and Shona sat with her mouth agape, her expression of wonder a copy of every other child there.

Shelagh, conditioned to years of church-going, kept dropping off to sleep, only to be brought back by a sharp nudge from Merry Mary. Each time she woke she muttered, 'Eh? Ach leave me be! I canny understand a word he's sayin' anyways!'

Psalms were sung and another passage from the bible read by Lachlan. He returned to his seat and the minister held up his hand again. It was his habit to divide his sermon so that he could begin by gaining the attention of his parishioners and end by giving them something that would keep them going for the rest of the week. Today he excelled himself and extolled about the virtues of clean and sinless living.

'The day will come,' he boomed, 'when we must all come to the threshold of our existence. We must prepare ourselves for that day for when it comes, according to the way we have lived our earthly lives, so will we live our eternal lives. If we have tried to be truly good, chaste of mind and body, the angels of heaven will be there to meet us. Trumpets will sound! The gift of everlasting life will take us to the gardens of heaven where the gentle winds of purity will bear the scents of sweetness that we may breathe the clean good air we have earned. Will you feel those winds, dear friends . . . will you?'

He paused and looked round his congregation. It was a habit of his to stop at a vital question and fix his flock with his piercing eyes so that the full effect of his words would have time to sink into their minds.

Shelagh stirred and grunted, smacking her lips on the sliver of mint that had stuck to her top plate. She had been enjoying a nap but the minister's deep boom had penetrated both sleep and deafness. She was confused for a moment and was quite unable to stop the great surge of wind that burst from beneath her in a triumph of sound. One after the other the farts tripped merrily like a roll of drums, the hard wood of the pew only serving to heighten the boisterous echoes. Shelagh sat quite still and upright, her look of supreme innocence confusing everyone for a moment. The acoustics in the kirk made sounds difficult to pinpoint and those in the back pews looked at each other accusingly. But there was no confusing those who sat at the front. Merry Mary made a surreptitious but noticeable movement away from Shelagh while everyone choked to keep back their laughter.

Morag Ruadh's face, red from her fight with the harmonium, grew redder still and her fingers fluttered over the keyboard as if she were debating whether or not to take the huge responsibility of playing the congregation out of the kirk before the end of the sermon.

'God help us all,' muttered Maggie Taylor and dug her youngest son in the ribs before he burst out laughing.

Elspeth's face remained like a poker and she glued her eyes to the pulpit, ignoring Hector's hissed remark about Shelagh being even ruder than she was.

Shona sat rigid in her seat and fought to keep back

the bubbles of mirth but a glance at Niall, whose face was crimson with suppressed merriment, caused one of the bubbles to escape in a strangled snort. Mirabelle was very aloof and upright but Shona glanced at her and knew that if she were to allow one muscle to move she would shame herself for the rest of her life because the laughter was sparking out of her eyes. Old Joe had turned a strange shade of blue and Lachlan had his head in both hands while his shoulders shook like a jelly. He had heard Shelagh's 'winds' many times but today she had surpassed herself. The minister coughed discreetly then, with admirable calm, went on with his sermon. When it was over, the congregation poured hurriedly from the kirk. Shelagh bid everyone a reserved 'good day' and went calmly down the slope emitting a small belch in her wake.

'Ach, but that was the best laugh I've had in weeks!' said Tom Johnston. 'My God it was the trumpet voluntary right enough!'

Old Joe nodded. 'Ach! It's shamed I am just that she is a relative of mine but it was the best turn I've heard yet in kirk! It was heaven "scent" right enough!'

Merry Mary sniffed disdainfully. 'It's all very well to laugh but I was the one sitting next the old scunner. The minister gave me a gey suspicious look. As if *I'd* do a thing like that! The smell near killed me!'

Lachlan threw back his head and roared. 'Ach, don't worry, Mary,' he consoled, 'just think we'd *all* be dead if we couldn't do what old Shelagh did, only we might not make ours so public.'

'*Really*, doctor!' said a shocked Merry Mary and walked stiffly away.

Tom Johnston turned to Biddy who having laughed herself to exhaustion was sitting on a stone fanning herself with her hat. 'Can I give you a lift home, Biddy? The bairns can sit on each other's knees and leave a wee space for you.'

Biddy's face lit up, but Mirabelle, who was very fond of the midwife and liked her company, said quickly, 'Och, but I was going to ask you over for a bite of dinner. There's more than enough.'

'Och, that would be nice now,' acquiesced Biddy. 'I was only having cold mutton so it will keep till tomorrow.'

'I'll away then,' said Tom and went over to his trap where his family were waiting impatiently.

Shona and Niall followed in the wake of the grown-ups.

'Did you like the kirk?' asked Niall gruffly.

Shona, clasping her bible and walking like 'a real little lady', tried to sound polite. 'It was very nice. I liked your father reading, he has a nice voice so he has. But . . .' Her dimples deepened. 'Shelagh was the best of all.'

'I heard a cow do that once!' exploded Niall. 'But not so loud as Shelagh!'

They were still giggling when they came upon Dodie at the roadside at the same spot they had left him more than an hour before. Ealasaid, imperious to all his coaxings, was standing, sublimely chewing a mouthful of cud.

'God, man!' cried Hamish. 'Have you not got her over to Croynachan yet or are you on the way back?'

Dodie looked like a soulful bloodhound. 'She won't

come, no matter how much I calls her. I've tried pushing and pulling but the damt beast is like a consumed bowel! She just won't move!'

Phebie looked thoughtful. 'Dodie, it's maybe because she doesn't recognize your new name for her. What was she called before?'

'Buttercup,' he said disdainfully. 'I wanted her to be fancy-like and thought Ealasaid would be lovely just!'

'Why not call her by the name she's used to . . . just this once!' Phebie hastened to add as Dodie's eyes brimmed with tears.

'Ach, c'mon, man,' coaxed Hamish. 'Phebie's right. You can call her anything you like when you've got her safely to Croynachan.'

'Just this once,' agreed Dodie with a watery sniff.

'Buttercup! Buttercup!' they all shouted together but the cow lifted a bleary eyelid, bellowed disdainfully and remained where she was. A flock of gulls rose from a nearby field and flew to the sea that shimmered in a blink of sun peeping unwillingly from behind deep grey clouds.

'We'll *all* push her!' decided Hamish and strode purposefully forward. The others joined him, their shoulders against the massive hairy backside. Biddy pulled off her best hat and set it carefully on the heather before going into the fray.

'Damt cow!' she puffed. 'I'm too old for this! Get going, you auld Cailleach!'

But instead of going forward the cow took several paces backwards pushing everyone aside. Her tail flicked then curved into an arch and manure poured from her like thick porridge. There seemed no end to it and all the while the cow stood with a look of pure relief on her face.

'My hat!' screamed Biddy but it had disappeared under the deluge.

'My God!' Dodie's tobacco-stained teeth showed for a moment. 'It's maybe she was consumed after all!'

Without further coaxing the cow turned and lumbered gently in the direction of Glen Fallan and Dodie loped hastily after her.

Biddy stared aghast at the sea of dung that covered her hat. 'Damt cow! The dirty bugger has ruined my best hat! I'll never be able to wear it again!'

'Tut, tut!' admonished Hamish with a twinkle. 'Swearin' on a Sunday, is it?'

'Away wi' Sunday!' cried Biddy, outraged, and flounced away home despite Mirabelle's reminder that she was invited to dinner.

'And how did you enjoy your first kirk service?' Fergus asked Shona when they were seated at the table.

She looked up, a piece of chicken halfway to her mouth.

'Oh, Father! It was the best laugh I've had for a long time!'

He raised his brows and Mirabelle threw Shona a warning look but it was too late, she was already relating all that had happened and great gusts of laughter roared from her father.

Mirabelle's frown disappeared. Fergus was laughing more often of late and it was his daughter who could draw the laughter from him in such abandon. He wiped his eyes, eyes that were still alight with fun.

'And did you learn anything at all about God?'

'Oh yes,' Shona assured him, 'but mostly I learned about Shelagh's winds and Dodie's consumed cow! Ach, poor Biddy! She was very upset about her hat. Maybe God will see to it she gets another because the minister says He works to give us what we want and I think Biddy wants a new hat most of all.'

That evening Shona was so excited she could barely sit still while Mirabelle read from the bible. She was starting school the following day and it seemed a whole new world was opening up for her.

'You'd best behave yourself tomorrow,' Mirabelle warned. 'I hear there's a fine new teacher come from Oban. Old Roddy has retired and gone to live with his sister in Mull. He was aye too soft wi' the bairns but this one's a real tartar from all I hear and stands no nonsense.'

'Can I wear my brown stockings now that it's spring? My legs were terribly itchy and warm with these wool ones you made me.'

'The black ones it is, madam! It's still gey bleak and cold. Now into bed, say your prayers, and don't ask God for anything for yourself.'

Shona snuggled under the blankets and asked God to bless all the people on Rhanna especially her father and Mirabelle.

'And God,' she whispered. 'Mirabelle says not to ask anything for myself but there are one or two wee things that bother me. I want my father to love me all the time, not just sometimes, and I'd like Biddy to get a new hat because she's old and doesn't have a lot of money, so maybe you could arrange a miracle. Also

Mirabelle's the best there is but she's making me wear those black stockings tomorrow and I'll have to do it, but please God don't let any of the children notice them. They're cosy and warm but they're *black* and make my legs look like spurtles so be a good boy, God and I'll try always to be a good girl, Amen.'

She turned on her back and gazed at the ceiling. There was a little damp patch shaped like a man's head. A nice kind head and she knew it was Jesus's head because it had a little beard exactly like the picture on her bible marker.

'Goodnight, Jesus,' she said, and, hugging her rag doll, she cuddled into Tot who was snoring.

Next morning she choked over her porridge, left her boiled egg and got so excited that Mirabelle became exasperated and her father impatient and finally bad-tempered. She was ready long before Mirabelle who, because it was her first day, was seeing her into school.

Niall whistled past them on the road and children were streaming from all directions, some still with their breakfast 'pieces' in their hands. The school faced the sea. Waves thundered to the shore and the tang of salt was thick in the air. There were three new children to be enrolled and Mirabelle waited till it was Shona's turn before she turned away, her shoulders humped and a suspicion of tears in her eyes. Up till then Shona had felt very happy but when she watched Mirabelle walk away a lump came to her throat and she suddenly felt very small and deserted.

'Shona McKenzie?'

'Y-yes.'

'Come along with me, Shona. I'm new too so I think we're both feeling a wee bit strange, is that right?'

The new teacher was tall and slim with fair hair and blue eyes. Shona thought she was utterly beautiful and didn't know why Mirabelle had called her a 'tartar'.

The classroom was big and smelled of chalk and musty books. A sea of faces turned to look at Shona and the other new children. Fresh from the Easter holidays, and not liking being back at school one bit, the older children were ready to seize at any distraction and tittered when the newcomers were placed in a little section on their own. Shona went hot and cold and thought everyone was looking at her stockings. She tucked her legs under her seat till they hurt and concentrated her attention on a pale shaft of sunlight that danced through the window.

It was soon evident that the new teacher was a disciplinarian. The children, used to 'Old Roddy', sprawled untidily over their desks till a sharp reprimand brought them upright.

'Straighter! Straighter!' commanded Miss Fraser. 'Pretend you have each got a ruler up your jumper.'

The dumbfounded class sat like pokers and clasped their hands sedately on their desks. One boy sniffed loudly and drew his sleeve across his nose.

'What's your name?' asked Miss Fraser, fixing him with her clear blue eyes.

'Er – Wullie McKinnon, miss. It's the cold I've got so I have! The snotters are just trippin' me so they are.'

He was Nancy's youngest brother, the one she had delivered into the world, and his language was even more indelicate than the rest of his family. The class tittered but one look from Miss Fraser quelled them.

'Bring a handkerchief tomorrow, William,' she said and turned towards the blackboard.

Wullie gulped and wondered if the tail from one of his father's old shirts would pass muster as a hanky. He was bothered continually with a runny nose and his mother 'skelped' him regularly on the ear and said she could go for a slide on his sleeves. He was plied with bits of old sheets and bits of old shirts but more often than not used them to clean excessive mud from his shoes in case his father skelped his ear too.

The class was given a number of sums and a dejected silence fell while Miss Fraser turned her attention to the newcomers. She was delighted to discover that Shona could do the alphabet and asked her if she could write the letters down and show them to the other two little ones. Shona glowed with pride and spent a happy hour printing big coloured letters. But at playtime she was surrounded by a jeering group and she stopped gnawing at the big rosy apple Mirabelle had given her and stared at the chanting children.

'Teacher's pet, awful wet! Liquorice legs like wee black pegs!'

'Och, away you go,' she cried, angry tears filling her eyes.

'Will you give us a bite of your apple?' asked a freckle-faced boy whose hair stuck up in red spikes.

Niall suddenly burst into the group, his fists bunched. 'Leave her alone! he cried menacingly, 'or

I'll punch you all on the nose. You're just jealous because she's cleverer than you!'

'Stickin' up for a lassie!' yelled Wullie disgustedly. 'What's wi' you, Niall? She's a wee baby!'

Like a flash Shona darted forward and grabbed Wullie by the hair. His nose frothed and tears poured down his face but the hold on his hair grew stronger.

'Take that back,' warned Shona, 'or – or I'll pull all your hair out and leave you like a baldy old man!'

The other children screamed in delight and Wullie screamed in agony. 'I'm sorry! I'll no' say you're a baby again!' he promised in terror.

Miss Fraser came running. 'What on earth is happening?' she demanded. 'I thought someone was being killed!'

The children shuffled sheepishly and Wullie drew his sleeve across his streaming nose. 'We were just playin', miss.'

'Well, play quieter in future . . . and for goodness' sake bring a hanky tomorrow, William. You should be ashamed – a big boy like you.'

The children filtered slowly away and Shona was left to look triumphantly at Niall.

'Can you skim stones?' he asked gruffly.

'Not yet.'

'Well, I'll show you – at dinner-time.'

Shona smiled. She knew she would never be called a baby again.

Chapter Five

The summer of Shona's sixth year was spent roaming the glens and moors of Rhanna. She and Niall were inseparable. Sometimes they were accompanied by other children; more often they were alone, finding in each other an appreciation for the wide open spaces and the small creatures of nature. They were both sensitive and intelligent and felt a certain impatience with others of their own age whose boisterous presence chased away the wild life they so eagerly looked for. Birds' nests abounded on the long stretches of open moor. Trout flashed in the clear brown rivers and they spent hours lying on dappled banks, silently intent on a pastime enjoyed by many of the island children, that of guddling. Niall was well practised in the art and could easily bring an arching silver fish from the water, much to Shona's frustration because to her the whole thing seemed an impossible difficulty she would never learn.

On really hot days, when the world outside beckoned and the classroom was a hot stuffy prison, Miss Fraser took the school swimming. The shallow waters at the edge of Loch Tenee were ideal for beginners. Nothing was more delicious than easing hot feet into the cool water and the first breathtaking sensations were hailed with screams of ecstatic agony.

Miss Fraser's 'modern ways' and extreme good looks had already caused her to be the subject of much speculation. Local crofters and fishermen suddenly had very pressing tasks that took them suspiciously close to Loch Tenee where, through the cover of summer green, they could furtively inspect Miss Fraser's lithesome body in a swimsuit, comparing her mournfully to their 'Cailleachs'.

Some children had no bathing suits but splashed happily in underpants and knickers. Mirabelle had hastily sewn a piece of material into something resembling a costume and Shona proudly splashed in her bright red attire.

Dogs came and joined in the fun. Tot had grown into the habit of going off to school each afternoon to await her young mistress and naturally, if swimming was to be in the curriculum, it meant a welcome break from long afternoons waiting for school to finish.

Each day dawned blue and cloudless. Bees droned lazily in the heather. Dunlins called out with their peculiar buzzing whistle on the marshes and oyster-catchers probed unhurriedly with their long red bills for molluscs. The haze of heat caused strange effects and from a distance the white shimmering sands looked like burning snow. Old men sat on harbour walls smoking their pipes and dreaming of younger days when more than the mind could wander at will.

Yet though the island droned with the lazy sounds of summer the people themselves bustled about with great purpose. Summer was a time of preparation. Peats were lifted and turned, fields planted and the damage wrought by winter gales put to rights. But

Rhanna folk never hurried. A simple job like repairing a lobster pot could take a long time amidst agreeable companionship. Tar and salt titillated the sense of smell. The screaming of gulls, the wavelets slapping green barnacled stilts, made time a thing to hold on to rather than pass.

On such a day Fergus strode out to the fields to meet Bob and young Mathew. He braced his strong shoulders and took a deep breath of air heavy with fragrant scents. It was one of his good days. Everything had gone well and the sight of his corn fields already knee-high added to his sense of well-being. Memories of Helen still tormented him but time was gradually taking away the bitterness he had felt on losing her. At first he felt he hated God, hated the circumstances that had taken her young life. Utter loneliness engulfed him and his very soul pined for her. His dreams were filled with visions of her and he would reach out to take her in his arms only to wake up and find the reality of the empty room. He knew he called her name in his sleep because several times Shona appeared at his door, her eyes round and frightened.

'Father you were calling *her* again!' she said once, a sob catching her throat. The small white figure looked so forlorn and afraid he wanted to take her in his arms and snuggle her down in bed beside him but something held him back. He no longer thought of his little girl as the usurper who lived in place of his wife because when he looked at her he knew that Helen had been reborn in every glance, every dimpled grin. But he was afraid to love again. He knew his attitude was cowardly but the black shadow of death had already robbed him of his two loves and he couldn't risk giving of a heart that was already badly scarred by grief.

He looked at the field of corn and remembered the day he had coaxed Helen into the field on some pretext and then made love to her on the bed of sweet grasses. Passion had engulfed him and his senses reeled. Green corn and blue sky had merged into one. But she had escaped him and ran laughing, tantalizing him, her auburn hair glinting like fire in the sun and her breath coming fast when he had caught her and tussled with her, the struggle making the final conquering of her lithe body all the more satisfying. Perhaps that day of hot sun and warm bodies joining, had been the day their child was conceived.

Bob's harsh shout broke in on his thoughts. 'Have you seen Kerrie?'

'No, he's usually with you, man!'

Bob's walnut brown face showed impatience. 'Ach, the damt bugger has likely got wind of McDonald's bitch. I was needin' him to help old Peg to bring down the lambs and yowes from the top field.'

'I saw him at Loch Wee,' volunteered Mathew, now a strapping youth of nineteen. 'A lot of the dogs were in the water wi' the bairns and that new teacher.' His eyes gleamed. 'She's a bonny woman so she is, nice shaped without bein' skinny. I could see her bosoms peepin' out from the top o' her suit. It brought me out in a sweat just to look at her.'

'Damned woman and her swimming!' Fergus exploded. He had heard all about Miss Fraser – Shona was full of her, the men made eager remarks about her looks and the women also made remarks but none of them favourable. He turned on his heel. 'I'll go down to the loch! There's too much nonsense in that young teacher's mind. If Kerrie's there I'll get him back but not before I've given Miss Fraser a piece of my mind. Distracting everything from what I hear!' He strode away and Bob spat in disgust.

'See what you've done, you young upstart!' he told a shamefaced Mathew. 'From all I hear the lass is a real lady but a wee firework for a' that. If she and McKenzie has words the woods will be afire wi' a' the sparks fleein' abouts!'

Fergus reached the road and crossed over to take a short cut through the woods. Shafts of sun dappled the covering of pine needles at his feet and a squirrel scolded him angrily from a high, hidden place. The woods were cool and peaceful and his burst of temper was evaporating as quickly as it had come. A little burn tumbled nearby, the water sliding smoothly over green stones. He stopped to splash his face in the bracing mountain water and lifted his head to see a rabbit washing its whiskers in a patch of sunlight. He held his breath, keeping still till the little creature completed its toilet and ambled slowly away. The sight of the wild rabbit brought a strange thought to him. He was always so purposefully busy he seldom had time for any of the things that had once been so precious to him and he walked on slowly, thinking deeply. Shouts of laughter came to him from Loch Tenee and he pictured Shona, bronzed by the sun, splashing and screeching with joy. He knew her companion would be Niall McLachlan and he wondered if it would be through the innocence of the children that he could make his peace with Lachlan. The thought of a reconciliation had occupied a good deal of his mind of late for he knew the black cloud of guilt and shame would remain in him till he had made his peace. But he didn't know how to go about it. Mirabelle always took Shona to be treated for childhood complaints. When she'd had measles and Lachlan had had to come to the house to treat her he had been at a cattle sale in Oban and by the time he got home Shona was up and about. He himself had never had the need of a doctor since his boyhood so there was no excuse for their paths to cross. He had often passed Phebie or Lachlan but they were either accompanied by friends or Lachlan was trotting by in his trap and he had never been able to pluck up enough courage to shout a greeting, not after so many years of silence. He knew Shona was often at Slochmhor and he had pondered about going on some pretext to fetch her but somehow he was either too busy or she was home before he'd made up his mind.

He approached the thickly wooded slopes above the loch and paused to relight his pipe. It was very quiet except for the scurrying of small creatures among the ferns and he heard the audible gasp of dismay as clearly as if the sound was at his elbow. Less than four yards away stood Miss Fraser. He had seen her quite often at a distance, her tall slim figure not to be mistaken for any other. He couldn't mistake it now although she stood before him quite naked, her blue eyes round with shock and a red flush spreading over her neck and face. She had come into the woods to dry herself and dress, never suspecting that she would encounter anyone in the quiet sleeping glade among the trees. The swim had been good and her body glowed with the exhilaration of the freezing water. The children were getting dressed behind various bushes skirting the loch and she had come to her usual place, well away from prying eyes. Her costume lay at her feet where she had just dropped it and she was reaching for a towel when the twig had snapped nearby.

For a brief moment man and woman regarded each other, neither of them having the will to move. It was a fleeting tableau when all time seemed to stand still. The forest rustled with small sounds but the warm wind that had caressed the treetops seconds before now held its breath. A gull screeched overhead and a tiny vole scampered for cover in the moss but all else waited.

Fergus stared at the utter beauty of her slim body fresh from the water. He was unable to stop his eyes from travelling over every part of her. Her lithesome brown legs were long and shapely. Belly and hips curved to a narrow waist and her breasts were small but perfect, standing up young and firm, heaving because she was breathing rapidly. Her neck was slender and the bones of her face fine and sensitive. Her hair glinted like corn in the sun with crisp small tendrils drying round ears that were pink with embarrassment. His heart pounded into his throat and a sound like the sea on a stormy day rushed through his

121

ears. Passions that he hadn't felt for years gripped his body and his loins churned. Every fibre in him cried out and he felt the blood pulsing till every cell seemed to rush downwards and he felt a hardness rising up against his belly. He knew that she could see what was happening but he was powerless to stop it. He wanted to rush forward and crush her lovely body in his arms. He wanted to feel her naked breasts in his hands, to throw her down on the moss and take her there in the middle of the silent wood, and he wanted to hear her cry out in pain and ecstasy because he knew he would be brutal and rough in his over-whelming desire. Sweat broke from him and his legs felt weak so that he had to lean against the bole of a tree to steady himself. His heart raced while he fought to gain control over the pulsing heat at the pit of his stomach and his mouth felt dry.

She stared at his tall lean figure and her first impulse was to run. She had heard all about Fergus McKenzie. The Rhanna folk were wily with newcomers. They dropped hints and innuendoes and pretended that they didn't want to gossip but all the time the gossip went on and she had gradually learned that Fergus had lost his beloved wife in childbirth and had blamed Dr McLachlan for what had happened. It was the story of a bitter lonely man and Kirsteen Fraser had watched him from a distance and felt sorry for him. She also felt sorry for little Shona McKenzie, who was spirited and brave, clever and quick yet somehow forlorn and lost.

But the man that she had heard about was not the same one she was facing now, his deep dark eyes looking at her with an intensity that shook her. She looked at his bronzed arms and strong hands, clenched till the veins had knotted and she thought he would break the bowl of his pipe. His tightly muscled body strained against his thin shirt. The collar lay open and she saw quite plainly the pulse beating swiftly in his neck. His face was handsome with rugged strong features and his hair was so black it glinted blue in the light. She saw with a sudden catch of tenderness the damp tendrils clinging to the sweat on his brow. She no longer wanted to run but felt she could stay in that wood forever just looking at him. She let her eyes traverse every bit of his body and saw that her nakedness had roused desires in the strong rugged creature who was supposed to be without feeling and who was said to be ill-tempered and unapproachable.

She forgot her embarrassment and became aware of a strange feeling in the pit of her stomach. A pulse beat rapidly in her groin and her body became warm with an excitement she hadn't known since Donald. Donald! How sweet the name was to her. He had died of a cerebral haemorrhage only a month after they were engaged to be married. She hadn't wanted to live without him and after a time knew she had to make a complete break away from her home and her family, especially her mother who wouldn't let her try to forget Donald for a moment. She had mourned and cried over the loss, not letting go of the past, and constantly grieving about the future that her daughter would never have with a young man who had met with her approval in almost every respect.

In Rhanna Kirsteen was slowly picking up the pieces of her life and already she loved the green island. She had discovered that Rhanna people were furtive and secretive about many aspects of life yet the intricacies of human relationships were so intriguing to them they were always ready with a hinted account of unsavoury gossip, some of them so outlandish she had found them hard to believe.

People like Behag Beag and Morag the spinner were certainly too good to be true both in manner and prim speech, others like the McKinnons open and frank to the point of embarrassment, yet so likeable it was easy to feel natural in their company. She would always remember her first visit to the McKinnon home. She had wanted to have a word with Mrs McKinnon about Wullie's continual sniffing and had been ushered in by Nancy who immediately made her a Strupak and settled down eagerly for a talk. Nancy's wedding was imminent and she regaled Kirsteen for a full hour with tales of Archie whose strong desires for her body had made 'the buttons o' his fly fairly go poppin' every time they were alone together'.

'Ach, but I'm lookin' forward to my wedding so I am,' she had continued. 'It's taken me all my time to wait, so it has, for all my family are that way inclined. My two big brothers are wed now but they had poor old Roddy near off his head in school for they used to be puttin' their hands up the lassies' skirts in the classroom and Wullie's only going on ten and already he lets the girls see his rooster!'

Kirsteen cleared her throat. 'It's your little brother I

came about, Nancy. When will your mother be back? I can't wait too long.'

'Ach, she'll be awhily. She's taken my dress up to Laigmhor and will crack wi' Mirabelle for ages. Mirabelle's doing wee flowers all over the top of my dress. Och, I'll be just lovely in it so I will and because I've kept myself a virgin, though God knows how, I'll not be like some o' they hypocrites who go to the altar in white and are droppin' bairns like elephants seven months later and sayin' they've come afore time.'

'Nancy, I'll have to go but I wonder – I know you'll be leaving home soon but meantime, could you try and teach your little brother not to swear quite so much and could you ask your mother to take him to Dr McLachlan. He's got a continual runny nose and, as well as being annoying, there must be a reason for it.'

Nancy had stared at the earnest face of the pretty young teacher and burst out laughing.

'Ach Miss Fraser, it's funny you are. We could all swear before we could talk properly! You mustny mind it for we canna help it. I'll have a word wi' Mither about taking Wullie to the doctor but I'm sure that it won't do a bit of good. Wullie was born wi' a dreep at his nose! I should know that for I delivered him and he snottered from the start. But it's kind you are to think of him and I'll tell the wee bugger to watch his tongue in future!'

Kirsteen escaped the warm dim kitchen and hurried round a corner where she burst out laughing, then, composing herself, she went up a grassy lane to the Morrisons' cottage because she had wanted Elspeth to take a message to Phebie with whom she was very friendly.

Hector came home and Kirsteen heard the raised voices even before she reached the open door. Elspeth was baking and in her floury hand she held a rolling pin which she was brandishing at Hector who was steeping his feet in a basin by the fire into which he stared with glazed eyes. Neither of them noticed Kirsteen and she tiptoed hastily away from the scene, not knowing that Elspeth would not have been offended because her argument with Hector had been overheard. Hers was an open hostility and she didn't care who knew it and Hector, conditioned to years of nagging, was hardly aware that any other way of life existed.

But swearing or nagging, gossiping and laughing, the islanders were refreshingly different from any other people Kirsteen had met and she was growing to love their way of life. The gentry at Burnbreddie were a different story. Kirsteen had been invited to Burnbreddie for tea. It was Madam Balfour's habit to invite all newcomers to her home so that she could look them over. Kirsteen had hated every minute of it and had sat on the edge of a huge chintz sofa and been cross-examined to the point of rudeness, all the while aware that Madam Balfour's beady little eyes were taking in every detail of her. Afterwards the laird had taken her to his study to show her his collection of butterflies. He had pressed himself hard against her on various pretences and leered into her face with watery lustful eyes. When one big hairy paw came out and openly fondled her breasts she had slapped him hard on the face and asked to be taken home immediately. 'Pretty young woman,' Madam Balfour commented, watching the carriage drive away. 'Nicely mannered but nothing much of interest in the way of family. I wonder why she left so quickly. It was very rude, yet she *seemed* to have been well brought up.'

'Spirited little lass,' mumbled the laird, his bloodshot eyes gleaming at the memory of Miss Fraser's firm young breasts in his hands.

Kirsteen had settled well to her new way of life. The schoolhouse was cosy with its big fireplaces and exciting little neuks and crannies. Slowly her heart was healing and she felt a peace stealing into her. Now here she was, in the heart of a pine wood, her whole being tingling with the feelings Fergus McKenzie roused in her. Somehow she knew that even after the moment was over she would never again know peace of mind, not so long as the strong vital force of the man was in her thoughts.

He was breathing easier now though he still surged with a passion he thought had died with Helen. But anger slowly took the place of longing and he was unable to find a reason for it. Perhaps it was guilt, or shame that he could experience such a tide of excitement for a woman who wasn't Helen, he didn't know, but he was in control of himself again and with a slight nod of his head dismissed the incident as if it had been of no import whatsoever.

'Miss Fraser.' His voice was clipped and cold. 'Begging your pardon I will bid you good day!'

She watched him disappear into the greenery and her face flushed with shame and embarrassment. In a few words he had humiliated her, made her feel cheap and degraded. The power of the man, his virility, had touched cords she had never felt before, not even with Donald. She knew he had desired her but the tone of his voice, the elusive quality of his departing figure, made her wonder if she had only imagined his attraction to her. The fact that she was naked had played a big part she knew but there was something else, something that had burst out from each of them to meet in burning streaks of electric magnetism, a silent force that each of them had been aware of. She couldn't have mistaken it and it would be a long time before she forgot the dark passion glazing his eyes and his almost tangible depth of longing. She dressed slowly allowing her hot cheeks to cool and her hands to stop trembling.

The children were growing impatient but knew better than to wander. Shona plopped stones into the water and Niall sat on a mossy boulder, his hands clasping his knees and his brown eyes contemplative.

'Shona!'

She turned to look at him. His brown skin was glowing and his tumbled corn curls ruffling in a faint breeze. She was only five and he seven yet already she thought him the finest boy in the class. He was protective towards her and though they often had rough games and angry words he always knew when she had had enough.

'Yes, Niall?'

'Why does your father hate mine?'

She stared. 'He doesn't, does he?'

'I heard Father and Mother talking. It was at night

and I couldn't sleep I was so hot. Their room is next to mine and I heard my mother asking Father why they couldn't have another baby and he said no, not after what happened to Helen.'

Shona examined a piece of heather. 'That's a strange thing. My father cries out in his sleep for a lady called Helen!'

Niall frowned, his child's mind trying to grasp a mystery. 'But Helen was your mother's name. Didn't you *know* that?'

'N-no, I always just call her mother. It's a strange thing about her because I don't know very much at all. I ask Mirabelle and she tells me quite a lot but she's so busy she often tells me to be quiet. My father tells me nothing at all – well almost nothing. Hamish says she was a lovely lady with hair and eyes like mine.'

Niall glanced at Shona's deep blue eyes and auburn locks but he was not yet of an age to appreciate feminine beauty.

'Anyway,' he continued, 'my mother said, "Damn Fergus McKenzie! He knows he's been wrong all these years but not man enough to apologize."'

Shona's eyes flashed. 'My father's a fine big man! Say you're sorry, Niall McLachlan!'

He remained calm and plopped a stone into the glassy surface of Loch Tenee.

'Wasn't me that said it so I can't say I'm sorry. Anyway, it's true, your father never talks to mine and it's nasty of him because my father's the best in the world.'

Shona's eyes filled with angry tears. 'He's not – mine is! He is – he is – and he loves me the most in the world!'

Niall looked at her fierce, sad, little face and knew he had gone too far. He jumped from the boulder and put an arm round her with an unconscious gesture of affection.

'Look, Shona – over there by the bushes! Wullie McKinnon's showing off again! He's letting the lassies see how high he can pee!'

She wiped her eyes and saw Wullie, his body arched forward, and a thin spurting stream rising into the air. Several girls watched avidly from behind coyly raised hands and, thus encouraged, other boys joined Wullie till a row of fountains arched at varying heights.

Niall squeezed Shona's hand and they collapsed in a giggling heap till Miss Fraser appeared and gathered her little flock together.

Summer passed. The days were long and golden interspersed by fierce electric storms that threw rain on to the parched earth with such force that the grasses cringed under the onslaught.

But the crofters and farmers welcomed the rain and it was a good harvest with everyone reaping till last light. Carts were piled high with sweet hay and children and adults rode home in the gloaming, the lilting sound of Gaelic tunes filling the evening till melody and summer, birdsong and laughter, all mingled and became one.

It was the habit at harvest time for one farm or croft to help the other. Croynachan had been gathered and now it was Laigmhor. Heather and Thistle plodded up and down with the reapers and the air was thick with the warm fragrant smell of freshly cut corn.

Shona loved this time of year and had looked forward to Laigmhor's harvest. She raced home from school each day with Tot scampering at her heels and had a slice of freshly baked bread thick with jam and a drink of creamy milk before she went off to the fields. She knew her father would be there, big and strong, stripped to the waist while he worked. She loved to be near him, to watch his rippling muscles under his bronzed skin, and to smell him, the warm afternoon smell of him. His smells varied according to different times of day. There was his morning smell of shaving soap and freshness, his afternoon smell of earth and horses, hay and honest sweat, and his night smell of carbolic soap and wet hair, fresh breath and tingling skin. She wondered if he attached different smells to her and hoped they were mostly nice. She tried to stay clean but it was difficult. She loved to roll in the hayshed and get cobwebs and dust in her hair that made Mirabelle snort with disgust and bring out the bath tub.

It was nice to be working beside the men and she was quite useful with the rake. She looked at Hamish on top of the cart, his red beard glowing in the sun. Mathew raked with Bob and Murdy, and Dodie, who enjoyed harvest time because he was never out of work, was turning and lifting. There was a quiet elation about him these days. The dearest thing to his heart was Ealasaid and she was at last expecting a calf. She had not been ready for the bull when Dodie thought she was and he had walked her back and forth through the Glen till both man and beast were footsore and disgusted. The laird of Burnbreddie heard of Dodie's efforts to mate his broken-down cow with McKenzie's bull and he sent word that Ealasaid had always calved in spring and June was her month for mating. Dodie had fumed and waited till the great day finally came and the bull had joined with Ealasaid.

Dodie was now at the zenith of an excitement he had never known before. He owned a cow who was going to have a calf and for the first time in his life he really felt somebody. He was also in love with Ealasaid and spoke into her flicking ears in a mournful whisper which she seemed to understand because she bellowed in response. Certain other little riches had come his way. His greasy raincoat had been replaced by a smart navy macintosh and he had been able to solve a certain matter that had been on his conscience for some time.

Biddy was touched and pleased when he appeared in Glen Fallan one peaceful summer morning and presented her with a surprisingly attractive hat. She had watched him coming up the Glen and wondered where he was going at such an early hour though it wasn't unusual to see him at any time of day or night because he seemed to roam perpetually. The linnets were soaring and the wrens singing loudly and Biddy was enjoying her porridge when she saw the figure on the road. When it stopped at her gate and looked soulfully up at the stream tumbling down from Ben Madoch she knew the visitor was for her. Dodie never went straight to anyone's door but hung about dolefully at gate or doorway till he was asked in. The islanders knew his ways and never offended him by letting him stand about too long.

Biddy gave him the remainder of the porridge from the pan on the fire and he had supped, drank tea, and lingered till Biddy grew exasperated. She had been called to the other side of the island and was less able to hurry now. Sometimes a cart was sent for her or she met a trap going in her direction but on occasion she had to walk all the way and her varicose veins were getting no better.

Dodie was acting suspiciously, clutching at something under his coat, opening his mouth to speak then shutting it again without saying a word.

'What's wi' you, man?' burst out Biddy finally. 'Are you knowin' someone with child and wantin' my advice?'

He blushed to the peak of his cap and his brown teeth showed nervously. Suddenly he pulled a bundle from inside his coat and pushed it at Biddy, overturning his cup with excitement.

'It's a wee thing for you,' he gulped, his words almost unintelligible. 'To make up for the one Ealasaid shat on! She couldny help it bein' consumed but I was ay thinkin' how she ruined your hat. It will be fine on you, sit nice it will! I know leddies like hats to sit nice. Not like the other in colour but nice, nice it is, ay nice just!'

Biddy didn't hear the rather confused explanation. She was already trying on the hat, preening in front of the mirror on a shelf. It was a fine velvet hat with a nice trimming and she was so pleased she stooped and kissed Dodie on the cheek. He blushed again and rising quickly, almost knocked over the table. He opened the door and loped hastily over the winding road till he was lost to view. Never, never in all the years he could remember had anyone kissed him and he put up his large fingers to touch the favoured spot on his cheek, his mouth opening wide with pleasure. Biddy hadn't asked where he got the hat and he wasn't going to tell her or anyone else. There had been so many hats in the attics at Burnbreddie. Trunks of them and clothes too. He shouldn't have looked really because he had been sent up to clear out accumulated rubbish. But he had peeped and there were so many clothes – enough to keep the folk on Rhanna warm for years – the temptation had proved too much. The laird didn't pay him well for all the work he did, so the hat and the navy macintosh were a sort of bonus. He had worn the coat with a certain trepidation, savouring the warmth of it compared to his old one, yet dreading that it would be recognized by the laird and his leddy. But they hadn't given him a second glance and he knew Biddy's hat would go unrecognized too.

So he worked and dreamed of Ealasaid and her calf, his dreams taking him into realms of fantasy where Ealasaid would provide him with enough offspring to have a herd of his own, one that would be the talk of Rhanna so grand it would be.

Shona grew tired of raking after a time and Murdy helped her scramble on to the cart beside Hamish. She sank into the warm sweet hay and shaded her eyes to look at Slochmhor nestling in the hollow. She had wanted Niall to come to her father's harvest but he had refused. He could be stubborn when he liked and had set his chin, adamant about the matter. He dearly loved his father and couldn't understand anyone who didn't. Shona too had her own brand of determination and she too adored her father though she was hurt and puzzled that he couldn't show his affection the way Lachlan did to his child.

'I go to your house but you never come to mine,' she accused, trying to swing the argument in her favour.

'Your father must say he's sorry first!'

'But what for? Och, I'm fed up so I am! Do *you* know what he should be sorry about?'

'No and I can't ask Mother because I wasn't supposed to hear. Anyway, it's a grown-up thing and they can be gey queer if you ask questions.'

'Oh Niall, come to our harvest! We've been to all the rest together and I saw you working with my father quite contented. Mirabelle makes a grand harvest supper, she bakes piles of bannocks and fancy wee cakes and we have chicken and ham on new-baked bread. You'd fairly love Mirabelle. She's big and cosy with a nice smell of baking off her and though she cuddles a lot she doesn't do it *too* much!'

'I do like Mirabelle. She's grand! I wish we had her instead of Elspeth but I'm still not coming to your harvest!'

'Don't you like my father even a wee bit?'

'I've hardly spoken to him and when I did he sounded girny. He's fine and strong and I like the way he strides like a giant but he's still girny!'

Shona's face grew red because she couldn't deny this and she knew she had lost the argument as she always seemed to when she was discussing her father with Niall. Harvesting wasn't the same without Niall's presence. Other boys and girls laughed and tumbled but they weren't the same and she looked down at Slochmhor wistfully. Clothes were flapping lazily on the line and the tiny dot that was Niall ran in the garden. Two bigger dots were Phebie and Miss Fraser who was a regular visitor to the doctor's house. Shona sighed. She wished Miss Fraser would visit Laigmhor. The only people who ever came were for Mirabelle; no one seemed to visit her father. She looked at him, unaware that she wasn't the only one to sigh for things out of reach. Fergus worked purposefully but one eye looked towards Lachlan's house and Miss Fraser. She had occupied his mind many times during the long weeks of summer. In bed at night his thoughts whirled till sometimes he felt like one demented. There was so much he wanted to do. One of them was to apologize to Lachlan. He needed the friendship of the man he had wronged so badly. He knew he was a man apart from others but he had been in tune with Lachlan the way he was with Hamish. They both enjoyed the same things and they could be happily silent in each other's company. Yet Lachlan was so different in many respects. He was outgoing and friendly, everyone liked and respected him. Fergus was treated with respect by most people but only a handful liked him and he was a lonely man. He was glad of Hamish and often sought solace in the cosy friendly cottage. There was an atmosphere of peace there. He could enjoy a dram and relax like the animals lying everywhere. Farm affairs could be discussed with unhurried demeanour and he could forget his loneliness. But Hamish had been rather preoccupied of late. It was rumoured he was 'courtin' steady' but like most rumours on the island it had been lacking in concrete evidence. Word was passed from croft to clachan till original beginnings were lost in a sea of speculation and exaggeration. But this time fantasy turned to fact when Hamish was seen several times arm in arm with a lady, mature of years but attractive nonetheless. She was a widow who had come to Rhanna two years before for reasons of health. The hopefuls who had eyed Hamish for years fumed inwardly but smiled at Maggie McBain with admirable composure and hoped the affair wouldn't last long. When it was rumoured that Hamish was making marriage plans, Mairi McDonald, the blacksmith's daughter, cried for a week. She had adored Hamish for years and when he had reason to visit her father she stared at his red beard and fine figure with open longing in her rather vacant eyes. She was a plain young woman with none of the buxom quality the Rhanna men liked in their women but she had never cared for any other man but Hamish. She paid regular visits to his cottage when she knew he would be out and cleaned and tidied much to his annoyance because after one of her visits he could never find anything in its proper place. But more than Mairi were disappointed when it became known that Hamish had every intention of abandoning his long years of bachelorhood for Maggie McBain and those females who saw their years on the shelf becoming a near certainty sniffed and remarked disdainfully, 'And she an incomer too. Why could he not have chosen a nice local girl?'

Fergus was pleased for Hamish but while the big

red-bearded man pursued his courtship, he had nowhere to go in the evenings and he had a lot of time for contemplation. He longed for a change in his way of life. He wanted to open his heart to his little girl who gave so much love which he found hard to return because the years of locking his love away made it difficult to turn the key of release. And he wanted Kirsteen Fraser so badly that at times it took all of his willpower not to go blundering down to the schoolhouse and take her in his arms. His evening strolls took him to Portcull, there to walk along the lonely stretches of shore past her house in the hope he might get a glimpse of her. He saw her several times but she was always with someone else, though she had glanced at him and smiled – a quick, shy smile that belied her racing pulses.

He did not know of the nights she lay dreaming of him, her body tortured by longing and her mind throbbing with the remembrance of the meeting in the woods so many weeks ago. She visited Phebie more often than was necessary knowing she would have to pass Laigmhor and he might be about. Just to see him fed the love in her heart for one brief moment but knowing she had to pass him by made her ache for days. She went back to Loch Tenee where first they had met and relived each second of their few minutes there. The memory of his strong tawny limbs went with her everywhere but most of all the intense burning passion in his black eyes haunted her every hour of the day and night.

Part Three

1929

Chapter Six

The wind battered against Rhanna. Frothing white spume hurled on to the shore and the schoolhouse garden was awash with salt water and rain.

Kirsteen looked in dismay at her daffodils and wondered how long they could survive the gale. She sat at her window eating a boiled egg laid by one of the hens she had been coaxed to keep by various islanders.

'Nothing finer than an egg fresh frae the erse o' one o' your own hens,' nodded old Shelagh wisely. 'They give myself the winds but good they are for young folks ay just! I'm readin' in one o' they wimmen's papers Mistress Behag orders from the mainland that eggs are a fine source o' nourishment. If that's the case then I should be well nourished just for my mither gave me eggs till they were droppin' out my ears and I'm blamin' too much o' them in my young days for the farts I have now!'

'I didn't know you could read English, Shelagh,' said Kirsteen, smiling at the wily old lady.

'Ach well, just a wee bit. I picked it up when I worked to Burnbreddie though they never knew. It's handy when folks are gabblin' away and thinkin' that you only have the Gaelic. You can find out a lot. After I could speak it I learned to read it. But you won't tell

141

a soul, I'm sure. You have the two tongues yourself and you and I could have a lot o' fine wee secrets, eh?'

She nudged Kirsteen and twisted her wizened little face into a conspiratorial grimace.

'The magazines are rubbish mostly,' she continued with asperity. 'I would never buy them but Mistress Behag gives them to me thinking I'll like the pictures. I *know* what she reads in them . . .' She lowered her voice a note below its usually boisterous bellow. 'Prim is Behag on the surface but underneath she'll be sensual they calls it and there's a lot o' that in they magazines but then . . . there's some will read anything in place o' a man!'

Kirsteen had no time to answer because Shelagh confounded her still further in the next few minutes. She came closer and spoke in a confiding bass whisper.

'There was a wee bit once on the doctor's page. Someone wrote in about having a lot of winds and he gave a recipe for relief. I tried it and was worse than ever . . . skitters for a week and farts for a month. You've never heard the likes! I was never away from Auld McLure till he came back to my house and asked me to show him the recipe. Do you know what he discovered, Miss Fraser?'

Kirsteen struggled to keep back her laughter and looked suitably interested.

'I had put in liquorice powder instead o' bakin' soda and I was more generous than the recipe said. It said a teaspoonful and I just put in a tablespoonful for good measure. I just ignore the doctor's page now and tear it up for the wee hoosie. It's fine if you're in a long time and nothing to hold your interest, you can read wee bits so you can, while you're waitin' for a miracle.'

Kirsteen knew by now that the 'wee hoosie' was the name the islanders gave to the dry lavatories situated discreetly at the backs of houses amongst the bushes. Running water and indoor plumbing were unheard of on Rhanna. Except for Burnbreddie and the bigger farms with hand-cranked generators, it was a case of carrying water and suffering the 'wee hoosies'.

Kirsteen, after a year of sharing her own 'wee hoosie' with midges and horseflies, had become quite accustomed to it and she didn't mind bathing in a zinc tub before the fire.

She had bought a clutch of chickens and they were now fine big birds thanks to the 'hen's pot' that Phebie had shown her how to make. She was grateful for the huge eggs with which the hens rewarded her. She liked to hear the hens clucking about and it was not unusual for them to come strutting into the classroom if the door lay open.

Spring had started early and she was looking forward to it. Now, in the second day of April, winter seemed to have come back, with the storm rattling doors and windows. She glanced towards the road and saw the first of the children battling their way to school. Little Shona McKenzie was with Niall as usual. His curls danced in the wind and Shona's auburn tresses escaped her woollen hat. Kirsteen wondered if Shona resembled her mother. If so, Helen must have been beautiful because her daughter was like a glowing cameo with her peach skin and pointed face, her huge blue eyes and that hair tumbling down her back in thick fiery waves and curls.

Kirsteen had asked Phebie about Helen but had been careful to make the question sound like an afterthought. Phebie had spoken with tenderness, a little smile of wistfulness lurking at the corners of her mouth, but she had seemed reluctant to discuss her personal feelings and Kirsteen understood that the matter was a sore point at Slochmhor and didn't pursue the subject further.

She sighed and rose to make her way to the schoolroom. If Helen had been beautiful like her daughter, if, as Phebie said, Helen had been vivacious and gay, charming and loving, then Fergus must have loved her deeply, so deeply and devotedly that no one could possibly take her place.

Fergus was alarmed by the force of the wind and hurried through his breakfast. Shona came into the kitchen dressed for school and she came round the table to give her father the usual peck on his cheek. She was growing more restrained in her displays of affection and with a start he tried to remember when last she had thrown her arms round his neck and called him 'my big boy'.

She was only six, yet in many ways grown up for her years. She was still puckish and gay, moody and bad tempered on occasion, but there was a growing dignity in her, and looking at her pointed little face and deep eyes that withheld her innermost thoughts he suddenly wished she would hurl herself at him and cover him with kisses the way she used to. He studied her for a long moment and tried to fathom the look in her periwinkle gaze. There was a sadness there. He caught a fleeting glimpse of it as she matched his stare with hers and something tore at his heartstrings. It was the way Helen had looked when she was forlorn but with Helen he had been able to discuss the reasons for her sadness and between them they had been able to dispel it.

He knew he couldn't communicate with his own child. When had he ever spoken to her about her hopes and dreams? Had he ever asked her about her childish pastimes? He couldn't even remember when, if ever, he had taken her on his knee to cuddle her and let her know she was loved and wanted. He hadn't loved or wanted her at the beginning. Now that he did he was unable to know how to go about letting her know. How many of her lovely child's years had he missed because he was so wrapped up in himself? Six! Already six! He had missed all her baby years, they were gone from him and he would never know what they had been like because he had been blind to all but his own sorrow. She had sat on Hamish's knee hundreds of times and tugged at his red beard because he always hid a penny there for her to find. She had laughed with Hamish, a happy child's laugh, when he grasped her in his arms and gave her bear hugs, all the things her own father should have done.

Impulsively he put out his arms to hug her to him but she was turning away, kissing Tot goodbye and throwing her arms round Mirabelle before opening the door.

He went to the window and watched her battling against the wind to meet Niall who was waiting impatiently at the gate. He cursed under his breath at the sight of the two of them bending their young bodies into the gale. They were animated. Shona's laughter was tossed back by the wind, making Fergus scowl harder. That boy, with his sturdy good looks, his strong handsome little face, his openly resentful gaze when he met Fergus, he could make Shona laugh. He could talk to her and play with her and do all the things that her own father couldn't. They were an intimate pair in their child's way and Fergus felt shut out and very alone seeing Niall take his daughter's hand in an effort to hold her upright on windswept Rhanna.

Mirabelle was clattering the things off the breakfast table and he took his resentment out on her.

'Oh, woman! Stop your rattling!' His dark eyes snapped with temper and he nodded towards the window. 'That two! What's with you that they're always together? Can't you speak to Shona and tell her to find another bairn to play with? A wee lass would be better!'

Mirabelle stood with her hands full of dishes.

'Fergus! Fergus!' Her voice was weary. 'If you weren't so proud you'd make your peace wi' Lachlan! He's a fine lad and his son's a fine bairn. He knows there's something wrong between you and his own father and he knows it's you that should put it right. I've heard things, Fergus . . . about Lachlan and Phebie . . . things are no' right wi' them and I've heard tell it's because you accused poor Lachlan about Helen!' She shook her grey head wearily and sighed deeply.

He was about to hurl abuse at her but something in the stoop of her shoulders stayed him. He realised that Mirabelle had grown into an old woman under his very eyes and he hadn't noticed. She had always been in his life. Hers were the arms he had tumbled to for comfort in his troubled boyhood. She had scolded and loved, cared for and comforted people all her life. She was part of Laigmhor, she held it together in a hundred ways that had nothing to do with bricks and mortar. Hers was a life of utter self-denial. Half of it was spent in the kitchen, the other half devoted to bringing up his daughter. In a way Mirabelle *was* Laigmhor because she had been there even before he was born. The thought was strangely disquieting. She had come to Laigmhor in 1897, two years before he was born. She must have come in young womanhood, now she was old, the hair that escaped her mutch was white, her plump face was still smooth but her kindly eyes were tired. But it was her hands he noticed most of all. Years of washing, cooking, scrubbing had left their mark. The veins were knotted, the skin crêped and dry, the fingers slightly disfigured by rheumatism.

She stood at the table and saw the anger go out of him. Suddenly he crumpled and looked like the lost lonely little boy who had come to her with his troubles long years ago.

'Belle!' he whispered. 'I'm sorry . . . if it wasn't for you, my dear old friend, none of us would be here. What am I to do, tell me? For God's sake I don't even know my own bairn. Och! If only Helen had lived! I loved her, Belle. The very marrow went out of me when she died but I've fed on memories too long now and there's so much I have to put right!'

It was a cry from the heart and tears sprang to Mirabelle's eyes. She went quickly to take the dark head to her bosom, a thing she hadn't done for many a year. 'Fergus! My laddie! I know how you've suffered! Bless me, I know only too well!' She rocked his head gently. 'There, there, my poor laddie, auld Mirabelle's here. I know your hert is sair but Helen wouldny want you to grieve so. You've held on to memories too long now. You don't know your own wee bairn because you tried to shut her out. You've kept poor Helen a prisoner o' your hert for too long. Tell the bairn about her lovely mother, you'll both be the better for it, believe me.'

Fergus felt the gentle old hands stroking his hair and a strange peace stole over him. A feeling of release came to his whole being as the lilting Highland voice soothed him.

'Make your peace wi' Lachy,' she crooned softly. 'Rid your hert o' its burden o' guilt . . . och yes, you know it's true. You'll not be a happy man till you do as I tell you.'

He raised his head and looked deep into her wise old eyes. 'Aye, you are right, Belle . . . about everything. I'll do as you say, I must or I feel I'll go mad. I've to see to the yowes, I told Bob I'd be up at the field early, but when I'm done I'll go straight to Slochmhor and hope they'll want my apology after all this time.'

'Ach they will, they will,' beamed Mirabelle. 'Och, I'm so pleased and this will be a happier place I'm sure.'

A flapping movement in the garden caught her eye and she saw Dodie loping along, his navy raincoat ballooning in the wind. This time he didn't wait to be invited but came straight to the door and rapped imperiously.

'I'll be blessed!' exclaimed Mirabelle. 'There must be an emergency or Dodie wouldny be chappin' the door!'

Dodie opened the door with a quick gesture and the frenzied wind ushered him through without ceremony so that his ungainly wellingtons caught on the doormat and down he went.

'Ach it's glad I am just to have caught you, Mr McKenzie!' he panted, struggling to regain his feet. 'It's Ealasaid calving and me not knowing right what I'm doin'. She's a wheen overdue but she's been labouring all night and me up with her holding her and rubbing her belly! Now she's just lyin' down and bellowin' and I think she's dyin'. Och, Mr McKenzie! Will you come and help? I'm feart o' losin' my Ealasaid and you're the only man I'd trust with her!'

Fergus thought about all the work waiting for him but, as always, the simple faith of hardworking guileless Dodie touched his heart. Tears of weariness and anxiety had stained his coarse brown cheeks and his usually faraway dreaming eyes held a frightened urgency. The thought that he might lose his beloved cow had brought him out of the simple innocent world in which he lived and tossed him into one of harsh reality.

Fergus placed a firm hand on his bent shoulder. 'Don't worry, man, I'll come with you! Come with me to the byre, we'll need one or two things. Belle!' He raised his voice. 'I'm away with Dodie to help with the calf! I don't know when I'll be back!'

'Right, laddie!' Mirabelle's voice was jubilant. Things were going to be happier soon at Laigmhor. Fergus would apologize to Lachlan and there would be an easier atmosphere all round. Singing an old Highland love lilt she went as usual to halve an onion in the kitchen to dispel the smell of Dodie.

Ealasaid lay in a bed of fresh hay in the little shed behind Dodie's cottage. Fergus saw immediately that she was in difficulties. Her breathing was rapid, her bloodshot eyes half-shut with pain and weakness.

He examined her quickly. 'It's just as I thought, Dodie, it's going to be a breech and the cow hasn't the strength for it. Go and get the ropes. When the back legs come out we'll have a pull between us. The old beast won't be able to give much help.'

Half-sobbing, Dodie galloped away for the ropes. The morning passed slowly. Ealasaid was unable to stand. Dodie sat sprawled in the hay beside her and held her huge head tenderly in his lap. He stroked her and whispered in her ears and every so often sobbed out, 'Ach, my Ealasaid! I shouldny have let this happen. It's my fault! Dodie's to blame!'

At one o'clock Fergus was outside smoking his pipe when he saw a distant speck toiling up the track. It came nearer and proved to be Mirabelle wrapped in a thick tweed cloak, a basket over her arm. Her face was red with exertion and she was unable to speak for a few moments. Fergus made her sit down on a rickety wooden bench and scolded her thoroughly for coming so far.

'Ach weesht, laddie,' she gasped. 'I know you wouldny get anything to sup here so I brought a bite for the pair o' you. There's cold chicken and ham and a loaf fresh from the oven.'

She nodded towards the shed. 'What's doin'? Has the beast calved yet?'

'No, she's not got the strength for it and it's going to be a breech into the bargain.'

She shook her grey head sadly. 'Ach, poor Dodie. She's all he has and not for long I'm thinkin'. That old goat Burnbreddie needs his lugs skelped . . . givin' a poor simple man a cow like that!'

A sudden flash of lightning lit the lowering purple-grey sky followed by a rumbling growl of thunder. Mirabelle rose. 'I'm away before that blessed sky opens again! What weather – in spring too!'

Fergus watched her flapping tent-like shape till it was out of sight. He felt his hands trembling. He was in the role of the deliverer and the thought made him feel sick because he knew Ealasaid would not survive.

Dodie, tearstained and exhausted, refused to eat and went back to the shed to be with his cow leaving Fergus to peck half-heartedly at the piece of chicken.

'Mr McKenzie, she's pushin'! She's started to push!'

The wind hurled Dodie's urgent cries to Fergus and he ran to the shed. The cow was straining, using every last ounce of her strength. Fergus knelt and massaged her massive belly. He had delivered many calves in his day and was used to seeing the agony that went with birth but somehow, watching the dying old cow using all the life that remained in her to bring forth her calf, he was filled with admiration.

An hour passed. The world outside the little shed became a raging, wind-battered torrent. Ealasaid had been moaning softly but now her eyes opened wide and she began to struggle to her feet. The men helped to pull her up and she sagged against them as the hind quarters of her calf were expelled.

'Hold her till I tie the ropes!' ordered Fergus.

He secured the ropes to the calf and began pulling with all his might. Ealasaid cried softly and Dodie wept into her neck.

'Help me, man!' panted Fergus. 'Grab that other rope!'

Ealasaid sank to her knees and the men pulled and sweated. The calf came surging out in a sudden burst and both men fell on their backs.

Fergus quickly cut the birth cord. It was a lovely black and white calf, amazingly sturdy, and he carried it to where its mother had once again sunk into the hay. She licked the warm wet little face and her long-lashed eyes regarded it lovingly. Her breath was coming very fast and she was moaning quietly at the back of her throat.

'Will she live, Mr McKenzie!' asked Dodie, dropping on his knees. He was staring at Fergus, willing with all the might of his simple brain that the man he held in such faith would give him the answer he so desperately wanted.

Fergus stopped in the act of wrapping the calf in a blanket.

'No, Dodie, she'll die.' Pity and a feeling of inadequacy made the words sound blunt and callous. 'She's nigh on death now but you have a fine calf in her place.'

Dodie sank his head on to Ealasaid's heaving flank and broke into a torrent of sobbing.

'I dinna want the calf! I want my Ealasaid! Ach my poor beastie, I've done for you so I have! You canny die, you canny!'

But Ealasaid had drawn her last shuddering breath and Dodie rocked on his knees, his calloused big fingers scrubbing his eyes.

'Come on, man,' Fergus said gruffly. 'Look at the wee calf. She's a bonny beast – and remember she's part of Ealasaid. It will be like having the old beast made new again.'

Slowly Dodie raised his tearstained face and a look of childlike wonder gradually diffused his sorrowful countenance.

'Aye,' he whispered, 'like Ealasaid reborn.' His voice grew eager. 'A new wee Ealasaid! I'll call her that! Mr McKenzie . . . it's yoursel' I've to thank. Without your help both would have died just.'

Fergus felt uncomfortable. 'Let's go now, man,' he said awkwardly. 'We'll take the calf down to Laigmhor till she's weaned. I'll get some of my men to come up and shift the old cow.'

Fergus hustled Dodie down the track, making him carry the new calf which he had already fallen in love with, whispering into its silky ears the way he had done to its mother. Fergus strode quickly in front. He was tired and hungry but there was something he had to do before he could rest or eat. Years of fretting, of

living with his guilt, had finally culminated in an over-
whelming desire to make his peace with Lachlan and
simple, trusting Dodie had set the final seal in his
mind.

School was allowed out early that afternoon because
Kirsteen Fraser worried about the children living in
farflung corners of the island and she didn't want them
caught in the thunderstorm that was brewing. So it
was that Niall and Shona were making their way home
an hour earlier than usual.

'Come home with me for a wee while,' suggested
Niall. 'Mother will maybe give us a scone in jam.'

But Shona was in a strange mood. Thunder never
frightened, but excited her. She lifted her face sky-
wards and Niall could see the tumbling grey clouds
mirrored in her sparkling eyes. She laughed in abandonment showing a gap where one baby tooth had
come out and been magically taken away in the night
by a Fairy Moruach who had left a silver threepenny
in its place.

'Och, it's lovely so it is!' she cried spreading her arms
as if trying to capture the elusive force.

'I don't want to be shut up in a house,' she said
breathlessly. 'Let's go somewhere. We've an hour to
spare.'

'Where? To the caves at Sgor Creags? I love watching
the waves crashing into the caves and it's grand the
way the froth skirls round the Creags!'

Shona shook her bright head. 'That would take
too long. We'll go to the Kirkyard. It's creepy there in
a storm. I love listening to the elms creaking and

154

groaning. They talk to each other and the wee flurries sough through the bell tower and the bell rings – like a wee fairy bell.'

Niall snorted scornfully. 'There's no fairies.'

But the idea of the talking trees appealed to him and he took Shona's hand and they scampered through the trees to climb the steep brae to the Kirkyard. They opened the rustic wooden gate and made their way through the long grass. The tall elms bowed to them, their branches creaked and groaned, swayed and tossed, in the wind that was much stronger here atop the Hillock.

'Listen!' commanded Shona breathlessly. 'They're moaning like old Bodachs with the reaumys!'

She stood with her head thrown back looking at the tormented branches that laced overhead, shutting out any light there was to be had from the dark sky.

Niall looked about him and shivered. Some of the tombstones were very old and lay flat on the ground, the writing on them illegible, almost hidden by damp moss and twining ivy creepers. And Shona had been right about the bell, it was tinkling very softly in the bell tower.

'Old Joe told me a story about the bell,' said Shona in a hissed whisper. 'He said it's rung by a Moruach who got stranded and died on the shore and she rings the bell to let all the Moruachs and Caonteachs know what will happen to them if they stray too far from the water!'

Niall didn't dispute the story.

'It's skearie here, and these old trees are like ghosties moaning and wailing. Maybe they're the ghosts grown out of the bodies of all the dead folk, their spirits all mixing together and trying to speak!'

They stared at each other wondering if such a thing were possible, both of them feeling afraid but trying not to show it.

'I wonder what spirits are like,' whispered Shona.

'Todd the Shod says they give him a rare feeling,' grinned Niall deliberately misunderstanding.

'My mother's a spirit!' said Shona solemnly. 'She's here watching us.'

Niall shifted uneasily. 'Let's go home! There's still time for a scone in jam.'

But Shona was darting away to the newer part of the Kirkyard. 'I want to look at my mother's grave!' she called and Niall followed reluctantly.

They stood before Helen's grave with its white headstone. An old McKenzie vault lay in the older part of the Kirkyard but old Malcolm had been the last to be buried there.

Shona folded her hands behind her back and stared. She had been at the grave before with Mirabelle who occasionally brought a bunch of roses from the farmhouse garden. But it had been a year almost since her last visit because though she went to kirk on Sundays they always had to hurry home to get Sunday dinner laid. A year ago she hadn't been able to read but she could now, very slowly. Carefully she began to read out the words on the stone. Niall wasn't greatly interested and scrambled up the stone wall to sit astride and view the tossing Sound of Rhanna in the distance.

'Here lies Helen McDonald, beloved wife of Fergus McKenzie, Laigmhor. Born 14th June 1901, died 29th

January 1923. Wait for me beloved, on that distant
shore, when my life has fled and the storms of life are
o'er.'

Shona's eyes filled with tears. Wait for me beloved!
How well her father had loved her mother. She wished
she had known her, it would be lovely to have a
mother. Niall was lucky. Phebie nagged him sometimes and he got an occasional skelping but more
often she was loving, her round sweet face made
beautiful with her love for her child.

Shona thought of Mirabelle. She was soft and round
and her arms were loving. She scolded and skelped
too but mostly she loved. Yes, Mirabelle was really
like her mother though she was an old woman.

Something nagged at Shona's mind. It was to do
with the writing on the stone. She read it again, slowly
and laboriously while the wind wailed louder,
shrieking and darting round the headstones. She
halted suddenly. Something familiar nagged at the
back of her memory. 29th January 1923. Why, that was
her birthday! Why was her birthday on a stone that
read death and not life! She had been born on that day
and . . . She held her breath and for a second the storm
paused. All afternoon, streaks of lightning and claps
of thunder had played threateningly amongst the
mountains. Now Glen Fallan was lit by a blinding glare
and thunder reverberated in deafening roars directly
above. Shona's scream was almost lost in the volley
but Niall heard and came running, his face white.

'Shona!' He stared at her aghast. Her baby face was
distorted with the agony of grief her discovery had
brought her. Tears poured down her smooth round

cheeks and her small slim body trembled with her sobbing. She couldn't speak, but just stood there, her eyes blinded by tears and her mouth twisted with shock. It was difficult to believe that a six-year-old girl could be capable of such emotions and Niall felt strangely frightened.

'Shona, what is it?' he asked softly, placing an arm round her shoulders.

'I know now why my father has never liked me – not really!' Her voice vibrated with intensity. 'It's because my mother died when I was born – like the sheep that died when its wee lamb came! He blames me for being born, that's why he can never love me! He'd rather I was dead and my mother alive. Och Niall.' She looked at him from swollen lids. 'I wish I never had been born!'

'Ach, don't say such daft things,' he comforted awkwardly. 'I'm glad you're born. So's Mirabelle and Mother and Father and lots more folk.'

'But Father isn't.' Her voice was dull and the life had gone from her. 'Every time he looks at me he'll be wishing I was dead and Mother here!'

The heavens opened then and they were soaked before they were halfway home. Shona ran to Laigmhor and Mirabelle into whose arms she tumbled with her heartbreak, and Niall, his fair curls plastered to his head, raced for Slochmhor. The kitchen was warm and no one was about so, while he dried his thick curls, he helped himself to a scone from a plate on the range.

At first he thought the house was empty. His mother wouldn't expect him for another half-hour and might be shopping at Portcull. Confidently he helped himself to another scone and munched contentedly, though he couldn't stop thinking of Shona. The clock ticked in the hall and the house was very quiet. Then he heard voices from his parents' bedroom. He went to the foot of the stairs to announce his arrival home but the rising note of bitterness in his mother's voice stayed him.

'Please, Lachy!' she cried. 'Don't let McKenzie run our lives any more. Let me have another bairn! Please!'

Lachlan was tired. All day long he had battled against the storm, from clachan to croft, tending his patients. Home was still the haven he so badly needed. He and Phebie had their rows like anyone else but he dearly loved the sight of her bonny face and her warm rounded body still moved him to passion. But now he kept a check on his desires and when they made love it was he who was the careful one when he reached climax and as a result their love-making lacked the spontaneity that was once plentiful.

Helen's death by childbirth and Fergus's accusations had affected him deeper than anyone realised. He loved Phebie dearly and wasn't going to lose her in the same way that Fergus had lost his wife. Phebie couldn't understand him. She longed to have another child but over and over he refused her. At first it hadn't mattered greatly and she had been confident that Lachlan would get over the matter. But time was passing, he had grown even more adamant, and lately their quarrels were heated and bitter.

Today was no exception. He had gone to lie down for an hour. He had wakened to find Phebie beside him, naked and desirable. Sleep went from him. She was tantalizing, touching him till he quivered, her silky body pressed against him, urging him to a frenzy and her hands did things to him till he cried out and reached for her roughly. But she kept eluding him till at the peak of his desire she whispered, 'Let yourself go today, Lachy! Don't hold back!'

But he had pushed her away and the flush of anger took the place of passion.

'You don't want me to love you!' he cried. 'You want to use me like a rutting stag! I'll not have it, Phebie! God, woman! Don't you know I do it for you . . . to keep you safe!'

That was when Niall heard Phebie's impassioned plea. He stopped, one foot on the stairs then turned and crept softly back to the kitchen. A few minutes later he saw Fergus McKenzie striding along purposefully. Niall held his breath. Fergus stopped and clicked open the side gate, pausing for a moment to look uncertainly at the house. At the same time Phebie came flying downstairs in a headlong flight away from Lachlan, the house, and her misery. She had dressed hurriedly and her hair and eyes were wild. She didn't even notice Niall but ran past him out of the door and came face to face with Fergus. He was taken aback at the sight of her. He was soaked, his clothes plastered to his body, rain running in rivulets from his hair and down over his face. In seconds she too was drenched but she appeared not to notice. The fierce storm that raged over Rhanna was nothing to the look in her eyes at sight of him. Her breath came quickly and her voice was high and unreal. 'Get away from here, Fergus

McKenzie!' she screamed above the peals of thunder. 'Get away and don't come back! I curse you for the selfish devil of a man you are!'

She ran from him and sped like a mad thing towards Glen Fallan. The next moment Lachlan shot out of the house. He stopped in his tracks at the sight of Fergus and his face turned white. For a long moment in storm-racked Glen Fallan the two men stared at each other then, with a look of contempt, Lachlan raced past to catch up with Phebie.

Fergus felt unreal. For years he had nursed his grievances, never stopping to think that they might affect the lives of others. He had felt himself to be the master of his own fate but had come at last to the stage when he wanted to bury the past. He had made the great decision and, having made it, nothing would appease him till he made amends. He had been sure of the forgiveness of easy-going Lachlan, and Phebie with her good nature presented no obstacle to the reconciliation.

He felt he had dreamed the scene but Lachlan, pleading and coaxing with Phebie while the rain poured in torrents round them was no dream, nor was Niall's face, white and frightened, at the window.

He stumbled away towards Laigmhor. There at least he was sure of a warm welcome. But another storm awaited him the moment he staggered thankfully into the warm kitchen. Shona jumped from the rocking chair. She had cried her heart out against Mirabelle's bosom. The old woman had petted and stroked and whispered endearing words, and her tears had dried leaving her heart heavy.

Afterwards she sat in the bath by the fire while Mirabelle bathed her. Mirabelle sighed and wished the unhappy little being would have a tantrum or utter words of anger but wrapped in her blue dressing-gown with her fiery hair tied back from her pale little face she was like a lifeless wax doll. But now the big wonderful man that she had loved devotedly was striding into the room and she felt at that moment she could never love him again. She faced him and her voice was strong and even.

'I know now why you don't love me, Father. It's because God took Mother and let me live. It was all on *her* gravestone!' Her voice rose and Mirabelle wrung her hands in dismay.

'If only you had told me, Father . . . about *her*! We could have loved her together but you wouldn't let me and I hate you for it – I hate you, Father!'

She fell to a storm of weeping and Fergus put his hand to his head and swayed dizzily. He had been without food since morning. The long struggle with Dodie's cow had left him exhausted, Phebie's words had shocked him but the worst nightmare of all was the sight of his little girl, an infant still but the words pouring from her baby mouth were those of someone whose emotions were developed beyond her years, who loved and hated with an intensity that matched his own. All the thwarted longings of her short life had given strength to her torrent of words. She had wondered at his rejection of her. Through the misty learning years of her infancy she had sensed the barriers between them; now she had discovered the reasons for them in a way that should never have been.

But he could give her no comfort – it was too late for that. He knew she would have rejected him and he also knew, with a choking sob rising in his throat, that it would be a long time before those slender little arms would entwine themselves round his neck.

Mirabelle looked at his chalky face and dazed eyes and felt alarmed. He's a man demented, she thought. Her kindly heart turned over and she cried, 'Fergus, come in and sup!' But he was turning into the fury of the storm once more. It seemed as if all the forces of nature had saved themselves for this day. The heart of the storm lay directly overhead . . . the wind tore at fences and trees and shrieked with an angry voice on the open moors.

Fergus bent into the wind, his mind churning like the sea. He was drenched to the skin but was aware of nothing but his tormented thoughts. He wandered without direction or sense of time but his subconscious guided him till finally he stood, a lonely figure battered by the elements, on the seething shore by the school-house. The lowering sky had brought early darkness and a warm light shone from a downstairs window.

He stared at the light, trying to keep his eyes open in the sting of salt spray. The light signified warmth and he became aware of his numb extremities. He put his clenched fists to his frozen lips and murmured 'Helen'. But it wasn't Helen he saw in his mind. It was Kirsteen, warm, living, beautiful Kirsteen.

'Forgive me, Helen!' he cried into the wind and stumbled towards the schoolhouse door, the rain mingling with the salt tears that poured unheeded down his cheeks.

Kirsteen had bathed in her zinc tub before a roaring fire; now, in a faded pink dressing-gown, with her supper on a plate on her knee and a book in one hand, she was warm and comfortable. Rowan, her orange kitten, purred before the fire and the house was a cosy protective shell. Windows rattled, doors strained at their bolts, but the anger of the storm only served to heighten the peace and warmth of the room. Engrossed in her book it was some time before she became aware of the erratic tapping from the hallway. Vaguely she reminded herself it was time she got someone to prune the trees. They were always tapping the windows in a high wind. But the tapping became intensified and with a start she realised it was someone at the door. Annoyed at the intrusion she went to open it and drew an involuntary gasp of surprise. Fergus! The man she dreamed of had come to her at last but never had she imagined it would be like this. His face was grey and his black eyes sunken and full of a desperate despair. Rain fell in sheets around him and the bullying wind tore at his bedraggled clothes.

'Kirsteen.' His voice was soft with exhaustion. 'Help me! For God's sake help me!'

The plea was utterly heartrending and filled her with such compassion she wanted to take him into her arms, to love him with all the love she felt for him. But she stayed her wildly beating heart and drew him out of the storm into the warm shelter of her little home. She sat him before the fire and like a small boy he allowed her to dry his hair and help him struggle out of his wet clothes. It was like a dream; yet in all her wildest dreams she had never felt such tenderness for the vital young man who had come to her out of the storm and let her help and comfort him without protest. She dried him and wrapped him in a wool dressing-gown left behind by old Roddy. Leaving him by the fire she went to heat some broth which he took obediently and gratefully. His dark hair had dried and small tendrils curled round his ears. A feeling of such poignancy tore at her heart that she couldn't help reaching out and stroking his head. She had asked no questions since his arrival and he had uttered no words save those spoken with such pleading at the door.

He turned and looked straight into her eyes. Some of the pain had gone from his, replaced by a look of unbelievable longing.

'Kirsteen,' he whispered huskily and it seemed the most natural thing in the world that she should be in his arms, his hands gently stroking her hair, his fingers tracing the fine bones of her face. Her heart raced into her throat. She tilted her head and he kissed her eyes and nose. The warm smell of his drying hair filled her nostrils and the dear sweet nearness of him made her cry out.

'Kirsteen,' he said again and now his lips were hard against her own. The dressing-gown fell from her shoulders and the flames from the grate outlined her breasts and slim waist. He caught his breath and crushed her to him, his breath quick and harsh.

'Beautiful Kirsteen!' he cried pushing her to the floor. His pent-up emotions of many years were being released at last. She felt his gentleness turn into a passion that could only come from a man such as he. His mouth touched every part of her body till she trembled in ecstasy. She was as passionate as he, her feelings for him had smouldered for almost a year, now they kindled and caught fire till every fibre in her burned for him.

He was wild, almost rough in his eagerness but her frenzy matched his, their cries mingling with the shrieking moan of the wind that darted and howled outside.

Part Four

1933

Chapter Seven

They found the cave high on the Muir of Rhanna near the site of the old Abbey ruins. It was a hot glorious day in July. Bees droned lazily in the scrubs of heather. It was the school holidays and the days of every Hebridean child were filled with play. Groups of them were always to be found scrambling around the caves at Port Rum Point. At low tide it was possible to go into the caves to sit on rocky perches and watch the Sound breaking against the Sgor Creags. Wind and time had sculptured each crag to a sharp point to make pinnacles of treachery for the unwary boatsman. Rumour had it that long ago a stranger to Rhanna had been swept in his boat against the Sgor Creags one stormy night. His body had been harpooned on one of the Creags and because of the treacherous tides no one had been able to reach the body and it remained there till the gulls picked it clean and the skeleton was eventually washed away to sea.

It was one of the many legends that abounded on Rhanna. The old folk clung to the stories told by their ancestors and the children liked to believe all they heard. The story of the harpooned stranger was one of the most popular and Shona and Niall sat on the ledges to stare with morbid interest at the Sgor Creags, picturing the man's body slowly rotting away.

'It must have been terrible for the poor man,' Shona would comment, though her eyes shone.

'Ach, he'd be dead and never know,' Niall scoffed unfailingly.

'But he wouldn't be dead at first,' answered Shona trying to imagine such a plight.

It was also rumoured that the plentiful ledges high up in the caves had been used by smugglers to store their bounty. The caves filled at high tide but never quite reached the ledges so would have been perfect for the smugglers so familiar with the tides and the banks of slimy rock.

Shona and Niall, like many children before them, searched for signs of bounty but found nothing. Hopefully they also searched for parts of the legendary skeleton, one day unearthing an old bone which they excitedly took to Old Joe who was the leading authority on matters marine. He immediately identified it as a cow's 'knuckle' probably buried and forgotten by a dog.

As well as the excitement of the Creags there was swimming in Loch Tenee or in the calm little bay in which the harbour nestled. The latter was the best fun because the harbour was the heart of Portcull. Boats big and small plied in and out, and the fishermen let the children clamber aboard their boats to play among tarry ropes and lobster pots. Gulls screamed and old women leaned from rose-framed windows to chat with everyone who passed. Winter was the time for Ceilidhs but in summer, dances were held in hay-filled barns. The men got slowly but pleasantly inebriated while the young couples crept to haylofts to kiss and cuddle. Shona and Niall, with groups of other children, lingered at rickety doors and dared each other to rush in and grab handfuls of bannocks and fruit cake.

It was strange to see Wullie McKinnon, now a lanky youth of fifteen, march into a barn with a girl on his arm. His hair was neatly plastered, his shoes polished but he still sniffed continually and had long ago got used to his nickname of 'Dreep'. He had none of his sister Nancy's roguish good looks but like her he was extremely fond of amorous pursuits. It was a favourite game with the youngsters to climb into a hayloft before the start of a dance, to hide and await the appearance of the courting couples. 'Dreep' was the favourite. The watching children choked back their laughter while he panted and sniffed between kisses. He was awkward with his girls but usually managed to undo a blouse, and grab a breast to which he clung like a tenacious lobster till he was slapped on the face.

'Will *we* ever do things like that?' Shona wondered. 'It all seems a bit daft.'

Niall, tall and handsome at twelve years, scoffed at the idea but grew red in the face and changed the subject.

Shona was at the lanky stage, legs long and body shapeless though her plump cheeks were thinning, emphasising the cameo features of her infancy. She was inclined to untidiness and preferred her long hair to fly loose but Mirabelle made her tie it back with ribbons which she detested because of their femininity. She was a tomboy, perhaps through long association with Niall or perhaps in an unconscious effort to be like a boy in his eyes. There were times when he had gone off with boys to fish in the abundant rivers or to sneak into Burnbreddie to poach a grouse or pheasant just for the devil of it.

The first time he had deserted her she had sulked when next he sought her company. But Niall was not a boy to be trifled with and her mood had only served to drive him away for a much longer period and now she knew better than to have her girlishly subtle displays of disapproval, accepting him back from his manly sojourns as if they had never been apart.

But now he had changed again and they had spent that whole summer together, if anything closer than they had ever been before. Sometimes he put an arm round her and gave her an oddly affectionate hug which made her feel queer and protected, the look on his tanned boyish face near her own making the feeling of love she felt for her father steal into her heart, only with Niall there was something different and she didn't know why.

She loved her father with a love that was deep, her heated words of four years ago forgotten, but it was a love without the displays of affection she had shown so freely in early childhood. Now she felt even closer to him.

There were times when his strong arms reached for her, an indefinable longing in his dark eyes but something deep inside made her resist him, a pride, a stubbornness, she knew not what, but she recognised vaguely that it had all stemmed from the day she read her mother's headstone and discovered the secret that had shrouded her simple child's life for six years. She was happy but sometimes wondered what her life would have been like without Niall.

They had married each other when seven and nine respectively, a simple ceremony with Agnes as chief bridesmaid and Stuart Simpson as the minister. It had been a hasty affair, the 'marriage feast' that awaited them on a ledge of the cave which was serving as 'kirk', a much more attractive proposition.

Now they had found this other cave, stumbled into it really while playing amongst the Abbey ruins. The ruins dated back into the mists of time, nestling in a hollow and skirted by a rocky heather-covered hillock known as Dunuaigh which meant Hill of the Tomb. Because of the many ghostly legends attached to Dunuaigh the islanders usually gave it a wide berth but Niall and Shona found it an exciting place to play and defied the legends. They were children of whispering quiet places and anything with a legend to it enthralled rather than frightened. Niall had tripped and fallen on a tangle of gorse and bramble, then disappeared from view. Shona poised listening in the shadow of a crumbling wall, unable to pinpoint the direction of his calls. She went forward, tearing herself on the snagging bramble, then jumped when Niall's head suddenly appeared from a gorse bush.

'It's a cave!' he told her excitedly. 'All big and airy with recesses like beds.'

She crawled in beside him with difficulty. The cave's entrance was thick with overgrowth and the only reason that Niall had stumbled upon it was because a big slab of rock had fallen inwards. It was dry and very quiet without even the buzz of a fly to interrupt the silence. Niall pulled back a clump of gorse and secured it to a crack in the rock. Sunlight filtered into the cave which went backwards into the hillside for twenty feet. Several rough recesses had been hewn into the shelves of rock and two large stones in the middle of the floor resembled a rough fireplace.

'It's grand,' breathed Shona. 'So warm and dry . . . not like the smelly caves at Port Rum Point. But . . . you don't think it's a tomb of some sort? It *is* in Dunuaigh!'

'N-no, I think it's been a hidey-hole carved out by the monks *centuries* ago. Long ago the Norsemen came in great Viking ships and raided the islands. The ships were like dragons and the Norsemen plundered and stole things. I think the monks who lived here made this cave to hide their food. When the Norsemen came the monks likely came into the cave to hide – maybe for days, and they would sleep in these recesses till it was safe to come out again.' His eyes sparkled at the thought of the monks cowering in hiding while the mighty bands of Norsemen ravaged the island.

Shona drew in her breath. 'No one knows of it but us. It will be our wee house. We can come here to play, if it rains we have a shelter and if we want to hide from anybody we can come here.' Her enthusiasm grew. 'We can bring things to make it cosy. Mirabelle keeps a lot of old pans and dishes she's forgotten about. You can maybe bring things too. We can light a fire and cook things on it!'

Niall caught her mood. 'That would be grand. We'd be like explorers and Mother's always so busy with the baby she'd never notice if I took some bits and pieces.'

He referred to his little sister of four months who, with her constant baby demands, had caused quite an upheaval at Slochmhor. But it was a happy upheaval and Niall knew the atmosphere had changed since that long holiday last summer when he had gone with his parents to Stornoway. Lachlan, worn out after a bout of pleurisy, and Phebie, an unhappy shadow of her former self, felt they had to get away from Rhanna for a time. Leaving a locum to the tender mercies of Elspeth they went to Lachlan's brother in Stornoway.

Two months later they were back on Rhanna, the old boyish bounce returned to Lachlan, and Phebie sparkling in a way she hadn't done for a long time. In Stornoway, away from all the reminders of old quarrels, they had recaptured all the love and freedom of their early married life. Lachlan's hurt heart healed and Phebie forgot her grievances. Slowly they picked up the threads of their troubled marriage and twined them together again. Lachlan regained his confidence in his powers of healing, of delivering life and letting it go when nothing further could be done to preserve it.

Niall spent much of his time with his cousins, two boys near his own age, and Phebie and Lachlan walked hand in hand through summer days, discussing their lives in the frank manner of their youth. And the nights – Phebie never forgot the long golden nights with the scented air of summer drifting through the window. Those nights of love without fear were not to be forgotten and the result was little Fiona, pushing and bawling into the world after a short though violent labour, delivered by her own father who held her tiny form as if it were the most precious thing in the world. Phebie sang about the house again and Lachlan's manner was sure and firm.

Niall was fascinated by his tiny sister. He played with her and even changed her nappy when the need arose. He kissed and cuddled her, feeling proud that she was his little sister, but when she cried her loud lusty cry he was glad to let his mother cope.

Shona jumped into one of the recesses. 'Sit here till we eat our pieces, I'm hungry!'

She delved into the package Mirabelle had prepared that morning. Thick crusty bread with butter, apple pie, oatcakes and scones, nestled temptingly in their wrappings.

'Mirabelle's a great cook!' praised Niall, abandoning his own lunch to savour a piece of pie.

'I know and she's learning me. I can bake scones and make bread but it always turns out a wee bit wizened.' She sighed. 'Mirabelle's getting awful old – you know she was seventy-three the other day. I worry some-times in case she dies because I love her so. I heard her telling Biddy she gets sick betimes and Biddy said it was like her heartburn and caused by old age. Biddy's old too, she's sixty-six and says she'll go on delivering babies till she dies. She's delivered nearly all the folk on this island except old ones like herself. She even helped give birth to my father.'

'How could she give birth? She's not your father's mother!' Niall's tone was scornful through a mouthful of scone.

'Och, you know what I mean. It must be funny to see babies you've delivered grow into people.'

'Babies are people too, only little ones!' snorted Niall in superior tones. His two years' seniority put him on his mettle with her and just lately he had felt an impatience because she prattled on so childishly while his thoughts and feelings were becoming more adult. Sometimes he felt protective and strongly affectionate towards her, at other times she annoyed him but he couldn't think of a life without her. Yet soon he must because his parents were sending him to a school on the mainland.

His love of animals had helped him to decide his career. He wanted to be a veterinary surgeon. He would be a doctor like his father but instead of helping humans he would help animals. Phebie had shared her home with many strange, wounded or orphaned animals through the years. One of these had been a seal pup, fortunately weaned but hurt and unable to search for food. Niall, with a dozen of his contemporaries, had carried the seal from Portvoynachan, four miles over rough moor, to dump it in Phebie's vegetable garden. It was a favourite trip for the Portcull boys, to hitch a lift aboard a fishing vessel from Portcull to Portvoynachan then to walk back to Portcull overland.

For two months Phebie tholed the seal slithering in the kitchen door whenever it could. She didn't even mind when the seal lay in pot-bellied splendour in the zinc tub out in the sun with Niall labouring back and forth from the burn to throw buckets of water over it. She even grew very fond of the young seal, indulgently christening it Salach because it smelled so strongly of fish. But when she found it snoring contentedly into Niall's back one night, with its silky head planted firmly on a pillow, she insisted it be returned immediately to the deep. Salach was thus returned to her natural habitat, fully healed but her mind imprinted with all the little homely comforts she had experienced in the land of humans. Niall had moped for a week till it was reported a young seal was haunting the harbour at Portcull and for a whole lovely summer he, with crowds of other youngsters, swam with Salach till the autumn came and she deserted Portcull to seek a life with her own kind.

Animals were Niall's vocation and his father had encouraged him to become an animal doctor; but he knew that his education would have to be furthered for such a specialised career so in autumn he was leaving Rhanna, his parents, and Shona who had been such a part of his growing years. The thought softened him and suddenly he put an arm round her. Fondly.

'You're a funny wee thing!'

'I'm not wee and I'm not funny!' she said hotly. 'And I'm going home because Uncle Alick's coming today. I promised Mirabelle I'd help her get tea ready. I like when Uncle Alick comes! He lifts me up and gives me hugs. I wonder why his wife never comes with him?'

'Because she doesn't like getting her feet covered in dung,' said Niall who had watched Mary on one of her rare visits picking her way daintily through a field.

'Manure!' corrected Shona primly.

'Dung!' spat Niall viciously. He was a bit wary of Alick. He hated the way he fawned over Shona and he didn't like the way Alick laughed. It wasn't real somehow. If anything he disliked Alick more than Fergus. At least Fergus was manly-looking and didn't prattle like an old woman. Alick was good-looking and women liked him but he was too smoothly handsome for rugged Niall.

'You're a vulgar boy sometimes.'

'I can be rude *all* the time if I want. Come on then, don't keep Uncle Alick waiting!'

They plodded through the heather and by the time they got to the hill track near Dodie's cottage they were tired and stopped to rest. Niall sprawled untidily in the grass and Shona sat hugging her knees.

'We'll get ticks,' said Niall uncaringly. 'You'll get them mostly in your bum!'

'Bottom,' she said evenly knowing he was egging her into a temper because he was still dwelling on Alick.

'Bum!' repeated Niall. 'Bum! bum! bum!' and feeling the laughter rising in his throat dispelling his mood, shouted daringly, '*arse!*'

'Arse!' echoed Shona and collapsed beside him on the grass where they both screamed in delight.

'He breath!' Dodie's doleful greeting made them sit up.

'He breeah!' they said together and Niall added, 'Are you looking for your cow, Dodie?'

'Aye and not findin' her. She'll be hidin' from me. I have her potash ready and I'm wantin' some milk for my breakfast!'

'We'll help you,' said Shona promptly and ran off with Niall in search of Ealasaid.

Dodie followed with his long loping gait. He had changed little over the years and no one knew quite what his age was, but the years he had spent on earth were the least of his interests. His first and foremost was Ealasaid whom he cursed constantly but loved with the same slavish devotion he had lavished on her mother. She was a cow with the wanderlust and all year round he tramped miles to feed her and milk her. He'd been unwilling to let her have a calf after what happened to her mother but Fergus had persuaded him that she was fit for such an event so he had succumbed, and Wee Ealasaid had arrived safely. But after a while Fergus had bought the calf from Dodie who couldn't cope with a wanderlust cow and a stubborn young bullock.

Dodie's second interest was his tiny garden out of which he coaxed amazing vegetables. He sold the surplus to make a few pence and altogether lived in a self-sufficient little world. Ealasaid was forever bringing her four-legged friends from the hill in an effort to trample down the fence that surrounded the little garden. Once they had succeeded, making a tasty meal before departing, leaving the patch a trampled mess of cabbage leaves and manure.

But Dodie wasn't easily dissuaded and now the garden was like a fortress into which he alone could penetrate through a massive gate made of a tangle of wood, wire, and flotsam, all bound together with heather. The fence was high with a disconcerting array of wire round the top over which not even the deer could jump.

'Only the sun gets in,' said Dodie happily.

Niall found Ealasaid in her shed behind the cottage happily munching a bundle of old hay.

'Ach the bugger!' cried Dodie. 'Me trampin' miles and her doublin' back on me! Ach well, I'll milk her now. If you go into the house I'll bring you a stick of rhubarb to chew when I'm finished.'

Niall and Shona were the only children that Dodie had ever honoured in this way. The island folk had seldom seen the inside of his cottage and few wanted to. Knowing his untidy ways they were sure his house must reek like himself.

The first time the children entered the dim interior they held their breaths. But the tiny room was amazingly neat. The two upright wooden chairs were rickety and an old dresser was almost in pieces, but treasures, reaped from shore and woods, decorated every available space. A lump of driftwood shaped like a seal was nailed to the wall above the fireplace, sea urchins scraped clean were strewn among the pine cones on the dresser. A pot of wild honeysuckle stood in the deep recess of the tiny window. True, the curtains were like cobwebs, ashes spilled from the grate but there was no 'Dodie' smell in the room. A string of onions hung from the ceiling and Shona decided they were the magic remedy for all unwanted odours.

'Sit you down now,' instructed Dodie coming back from Ealasaid. 'I'll make the wee polkys then I'll go and get the rhubarb.'

He was a most mannerly host. Nothing would do till the children took the two chairs leaving him drooping in the middle of the room so that his head would not touch the low ceiling. He went to fetch the rhubarb and the children sat obediently. They longed to wander round the room and look closely at the ornaments but were afraid they would break Dodie's trust and not be allowed back.

Two paper 'polkys' were filled with sugar and handed to the children with plump sticks of rhubarb.

'This is the best rhubarb I've ever tasted,' appreciated Shona, licking sugar from her lips.

Niall nodded in agreement. 'It is the best, Dodie. My mother has a good patch, so she has, all the best manure goes on it but never is it anything like this.'

'Not the best,' mumbled Dodie blushing with pleasure.

'I beg your pardon?' said Niall politely.

Dodie showed his stained teeth. 'Not the best manure!'

'Oh yes, the best,' stated Niall positively.

'Mine's the best,' argued Dodie.

'From Ealasaid,' said Shona, so taken up with the treat she hadn't wanted to stop and discuss the merits of manure.

'*Not* from Ealasaid,' grunted Dodie. There was a cryptic pause in which the youngsters waited patiently.

Dodie opened his mouth, hesitated, shut it again, and time ticked on. He seemed to be coming to some great decision and finally blurted out, 'If I tell you a secret promise you'll not utter it to a livin' soul.'

The children, their interest fully roused, agreed solemnly to keep the secret. Dodie's face was as animated as they had ever seen it.

'It's mine!' His head shook at the enormity of his confession and his carbuncle wobbled.

Niall looked puzzled. 'Your what?'

'*My* manure!'

'From Ealasaid,' said Shona again.

Dodie was growing frustrated at their lack of understanding and burst out, 'From *me*! I empty my po on the rhubarb patch every day!'

'Your *what?*' cried the children in horrified unison.

'*My chanty!*' babbled Dodie excitedly. 'The best I told you!'

Niall stared at his stick of rhubarb with new eyes and Shona looked at the remainder of hers with fascinated interest. She sniffed. It *smelled* like rhubarb, there was nothing unpleasant about its looks yet . . .

'The best?' urged Dodie with childlike enthusiasm.

'Did you wash it, Dodie?' asked Niall suspiciously.

'In the wee burn, always in the wee burn!'

'Och well,' grinned Shona and finished her rhubarb.

Niall giggled and ate his also and Dodie was delighted. He trundled to a pot on the fire and poked its contents with a bent fork. In the pot was a piece of venison. Every year the laird gave out venison and every year the islanders grumbled because the portions got smaller. 'Mean auld Bodach!' was the usual comment. 'He keeps the best for himself to feed the faces o' thon fancy folk from England!'

Dodie prodded his venison and commented mournfully, 'The joints I've seen at Burnbreddie. Great muckle lumps o' meat! Ach! It would make you sick so it would. And *he's* at it again! The things I'm seein' up there!'

Dodie had a knack of making cryptic comments which never failed to rouse the interest of his listeners.

'What things?' asked Niall.

Dodie shook his head slowly. 'Worse since my leddy lies up most of the time. I'm not sure what they cry her ailment.'

'Hypochondria!' proclaimed Niall, triumphantly repeating the word his father used when referring to Madam Balfour of Burnbreddie.

'A queer trouble just,' mourned Dodie. 'And *his* is no better.'

'What *is* his trouble, Dodie? persisted Niall.

Dodie blushed primly. 'I shouldny say.'

'We won't tell anyone,' coaxed Shona.

The old eccentric hesitated, not because his knowledge wasn't for children, but what he had to tell involved human relationships which were always such an embarrassment to him.

'I couldny help seein',' he said apologetically. 'I was workin' in the big hayloft and *they* came in . . . the laird and one of his fine lady guests with . . .' He cupped his hands in front of his chest. 'Big udders!'

Shona giggled explosively but Niall nudged her. 'And?' he encouraged curiously.

'They shut the door but I could see, plenty light in a hayshed. He was kissin' her and gruntin' like a pig and the next thing . . .'

'Yes?' urged Niall.

'He pulled out her udders – big they were – very big.' He paused and his vacant eyes were lit with an expression that could be described as humorous. 'I never knew a lady's udders could be like Ealasaid's!'

He stopped and a terrible screech escaped him and his big hands clutched his stomach. It took a couple of alarming minutes before the children realised he was not in pain but laughing, Dodie the doleful who had never been known to laugh, making a noise like a rusty hacksaw, his mouth stretched wide with enjoyment.

'Did he do anything else?' asked Shona.

Dodie nodded, his carbuncle wobbling wildly.

'Lots more! She was laughin' all the time but she stopped when he threw her on the hay and went at her like a ruttin' stag and she was bleatin' all the time like an old yowe. It was terrible just! Not natural at all, not like the beasts, no, oh no!'

Niall's eyes gleamed. When he was striding home down the winding hill track he turned to Shona. 'Let's get Agnes and Stuart and go up to Burnbreddie after tea! We'll get into that hayshed and wait for the laird. He just might bring a lady in there tonight.'

'But we promised Dodie we wouldn't tell anyone.'

'Agnes and Stuart aren't anyone, they won't tell. They kept all our other secrets – our marriage and everything,' he finished significantly. Shona hopped joyfully. Her hair had long ago escaped the ribbon and tumbled over her shoulders in silken strands. Her face and arms were a golden brown and Niall noticed these things that hadn't been important enough before for a second glance.

'Your hair's nice,' he said and touched it briefly.

She looked at him quickly wondering if he was teasing because sometimes he called her Caillich Ruadh which meant Red Witch. The name infuriated her and if he touched her hair it was only to pull it. But there was a new look in his brown eyes and for a moment they stopped and stared at each other. Then she pointed down to Laigmhor.

'Uncle Alick's here! I'll see you after tea!'

She was off, a rushing bundle of windblown hair and long legs. He watched her and kicked a stone vigorously.

'Bugger Uncle Alick!' he muttered and felt better. He raced home to help his mother lay the table, thinking about the adventure to come.

'Mother.'

Phebie looked at her sturdy son expectantly.

'I know that oldish folk like you and Father make love to make babies . . . that was why you had me and Fiona.'

Phebie hid a smile at being described 'oldish' at thirty-three but waited with suitable composure for the rest of the question.

'If you can do it and *really* old people can do it . . . well, you must like it a lot.'

Phebie looked slightly startled. She and Lachlan had always been frank with their son and knew that now he was at the stage of puberty his questions would become intricate but Phebie wasn't always prepared for the turn they would take.

'Y-yes I suppose so,' she faltered wishing Lachlan was home.

'Why is it then that big girls like Fiona Taylor and Annie McKinnon let boys kiss and cuddle them and enjoy it fine but if the boys put their hands on the girls' udd – breasts they get their faces slapped?'

Phebie searched for the right answer. 'Well – I suppose the girls do enjoy cuddling, it's only normal, but it's the girls who have the babies and no girl wants a baby out of wedlock.'

'Some do.'

'It can't be helped sometimes but it's best to wait for marriage.'

'It seems silly but I suppose you must be right,' said Niall and Phebie went thankfully to tend Fiona.

Shona flew to the farmyard and straight into Alick's arms. He lifted her high.

'My, but you've grown into a bonny big girl,' he laughed, holding her against the backcloth of sky till his arms ached. His handsome face was alight because he was truly fond of his niece and often regretted that she hadn't come to them as a baby. Mary hadn't given him children. She told him she was too delicate but she was strong enough to go gallivanting to the French Riviera. She was there now with a 'friend'. Alick didn't know if it was male or female and cared less. He had his own way of making his life bearable. He had a good job and Mary had been left a legacy by a great-aunt so they both had the means to indulge their whims. But he wanted a child and sometimes he thought the only reason he came back to Rhanna was to see Shona. He knew Fergus wasn't particular about his visits but they tolerated each other well enough.

He put Shona down.

'I've brought you a present.'

'Where? Och, where is it?'

'Hidden in your room. You'll have to search for it –

after tea. Mirabelle will spank me if I dare to hold up tea.'

'You're too big to be spanked!'

'Not by Mirabelle! She might even do it with my pants down.'

They roared in delight but Alick broke off suddenly, his gaze lingering on the slim young woman who had just come through the gate. Her short crisp hair gleamed gold in the sun and her breasts were firm under her thin summer dress.

She waved to Shona. 'I'm just handing in some things Mirabelle asked me to get at Portcull. I'll see you later.'

'Who was *that*?' asked Alick in admiration.

'Father's friend and *my* teacher,' said Shona proudly.

He whistled softly. 'I think I'm going to enjoy my holiday, Shona. Now, will you allow me the honour of taking my arm? We shall go in to tea in style.'

From the kitchen window Mirabelle saw the look Alick threw at Kirsteen. The old lady liked Alick. He was dashing and gay, bringing a lot of laughter into Laigmhor. He hugged her and made her laugh girlishly with his nonsense. But somehow she knew that this visit was going to be different. He had never met Kirsteen before because she usually went home to her parents in Oban for the summer. But this year she had decided to have a summer on Rhanna simply because she could hardly bear parting from Fergus. She was his 'bit mistress' in Rhanna language but she had borne the label well. At the beginning the gossips tore her to pieces but she had held her head high though she knew that if she hadn't loved Fergus so deeply she would have fled the island's malicious tongues and endless speculation.

How could anyone know of the heartache her love had brought? They couldn't know of the nights when her empty arms ached for him. These nights outweighed the ones he came to her in the schoolhouse and they shared an intimacy that fulfilled her but couldn't compensate her aching heart. But they were the wonderful times when they shut out the world. Locked in his arms she was safe and wanted but the time always came for him to go back to his other world. In the four years of their relationship he had told her that she was beautiful, that he wanted and needed her but never once had he told her he loved her and she wondered if he ever would.

They had discussed Helen. She had persuaded him to talk of her and in time he poured out his heart till it really seemed he had brought the years of suppressed grief out of his heart forever. But Kirsteen asked herself if he clung to memories because they were safer than real life. You could think about them, laugh or cry then shut them away till something recalled them to mind again. She wasn't sure that Fergus really wanted to love again and sometimes she wondered how long she could go on with the affair. In her mind she left Rhanna many times but then he came to her and swept away all reason with his lovemaking. She was glad she had decided against going home to Oban for the holidays because that green and blue summer on the island was the most wonderful she had ever known. Fergus, once too busy to take time off, now left the running of the farm in Hamish's capable hands and spent every day with her. He cared nothing for the gossips and walked with his arm round her waist making her feel guarded against the covert looks that followed them. They walked for miles and picnicked in places as far away as Croy where tiny sheltered bays abounded. They swam in the warm waters from the Gulf Stream and made love on the hot white sands with only screaming gulls for company.

Once she cried against his broad chest and he was bewildered.

'What is it, my Kirsteen?' he whispered into her golden hair.

She looked away from him, far away over the blue-green waters of the Atlantic.

'I wish we could sail away over the sea, you – might forget then.'

He knew what she meant. 'I'll never forget, as long as I live, Kirsteen. It would be impossible to forget someone you were so happy with. Have you forgotten Donald?'

'No, but I wouldn't let his memories stand in the way of my happiness. He wouldn't want that.'

'Nor would Helen!' he cried, his black eyes clouding. 'She isn't standing in the way. She was a gay wee thing herself and liked others to be the same. Aren't you happy, Kirsteen?'

A look of incredible sadness came into her blue eyes and she turned away again but he cupped her chin in his hand and made her face him. 'My Kirsteen,' he said huskily. 'You're a daft wee thing sometimes. Don't be sad. When I say I can never forget Helen I mean it, but she is part of my past life. You are *now*. I'm not a fancy man with words but I could never picture my life without you now.'

He kissed away her tears and his strong arms held her close but she longed to cry out that she wanted to be his wife, to have him declare his love for her by marrying her, but instead she lay silently against him, content for the moment to be in the safe circle of his arms.

But Mirabelle did not mince words on the matter.

'When are you going to marry the lass?' she demanded regularly. 'The poor wee soul has waited well for you and had to thole a lot o' auld gossips into the bargain. How she's stood it I'll never know. She's a fine lass – too good for her name to be thrown about like a bit cow dung.'

'In my own time, Belle,' he told her unfailingly.

'Just like a man to think you can ay ca' the tune! A bonny lass like that could have any man o' her choosin'.'

Another time she told him, 'It's high time the bairn had a mother! Are you too selfish to see that?'

'She's done fine with you all these years!' he snapped.

'I'll not always be here!' she had said strangely.

'Are you ill?' he asked in some alarm.

'I'm old,' she said briefly and he couldn't argue with that.

Fergus couldn't really explain his reasons for hesitating. Kirsteen was sweet-natured and sensitive. He was happy when he was with her, she made him laugh. Her physical make-up was exquisite and his desire for her a constant torment when they were apart. She was an endearing, wonderful young woman and he knew he would never find another like her, but, he asked himself a thousand times, did he love her enough to let her take Helen's place in his home? Helen had loved him enough to tolerate his strange moody tempers but could Kirsteen? Did she love him deeply enough? Did he really love her or did she merely satisfy his physical appetites? He tortured himself with indecision. At times he cursed that storm-swept night when utter despair of mind and body had driven him to the refuge of her arms, yet common sense told him that fate would have found some other way of bringing them together in the end. She had haunted him since their first meeting in the wood and the night of the storm, when everything seemed against him, had merely provided him with the chance he had waited for. Sometimes the fear of losing her to someone else brought him out in a sweat. Mirabelle was right about Kirsteen. She was attractive and the openly admiring glances she drew from other men couldn't be denied.

The day Alick arrived his fears became stronger than ever. He came in to wash before tea and saw them together at the table, her golden head next to Alick's dark one. She was emptying her basket and Alick was making silly remarks that made her giggle. She turned when she heard Fergus and her face lit up but no one had time to speak because Shona came bursting into the kitchen holding an elegant and expensive doll. She didn't play much with dolls except in the long winter nights when her family were brought down to the kitchen to play at 'wee hoosies'. More often her doll's pram contained Tot who was very partial to being tucked up cosily with a frilly bonnet tied over her silky ears. But Tot had no time for such frivolities of late for she was the proud mother of five tiny pups. Their arrival had caused quite a sensation because they were purebred spaniels whose father could only be Hamish's gun dog. It was Tot's first litter. She had spurned every dog who had dared to attempt to court her but had obviously fallen for the charms of Whisky and was now too busy with her babies to share her time with such mundane things as dolls. But the dolls were neglected in summer anyway and sat droopily on the shelves in Shona's room, each one a reminder of every Christmas of her life, stitched patiently by Mirabelle so that a new doll would be hanging from the top of her stocking to greet her on Christmas morning. She loved her rag dolls but each one was really just a replica of the last so the extravagantly dressed 'town' doll took her breath away.

'I couldn't wait, Uncle Alick!' she cried happily. 'She's the most beautiful doll in the world!' She ran to hug Alick who lifted her to the dizzy heights of the ceiling.

Mirabelle, tired and hot at the stove, was hurt. She knew that the bought doll outrivalled all those she had ever made but love had gone into every stitch executed by the light of a paraffin lamp, causing her tired old eyes to smart with the strain. A lump came to her throat. She knew she was being childish but she couldn't help it. Lately her aching tiredness had caused her to be more than usually sensitive and the crushing pains in her chest made her come out in weak sweats. Lachlan had been blunt when she had asked him to tell her the truth and had told her she must ease up or he wouldn't answer for the consequences. But she had been as blunt as he.

'I'd rather go quickly, Lachlan my laddie. I've not been idle in my life and I'm not going to start now. You won't tell a soul, mo ghaoil?' she went on pleadingly. 'I'd not want anyone pampering me and looking at me like I was a frail wee chick just hatched.'

Lachlan looked at her ample figure and smiled, though his heart was heavy. Mirabelle's heart condition had shocked him deeply. She was the type of woman who gave everyone the impression she would go on forever; she was the tower of strength that people leaned on without thinking that she might possess the same human frailties as themselves. Her very appearance belied any hint of illness: she had been, and still was, a jolly rotund figure, ample of bosom and bottom. Her round face was cheery and her sympathy for others showed in the compassionate warmth of her grey eyes. Her skin was pink and white and she looked the picture of health except for a tiredness deep in her eyes.

Lachlan had been angry when he discovered she had felt ill for a long time and hadn't come to see him before.

'Ach, I was ay too busy,' she answered placidly. 'Besides I had too much to keep me occupied to have time to be ill. There's the bairn, a handful at times but a bonny bright wee thing. I love her with all my hert, Lachlan and . . .' She gave him a covert look. 'There's Fergus. If ever a lad was eaten up with loneliness it's him. If only he'd marry Kirsteen I'd die happy so I would. Shona would have a mother. I've done my best but I'm too auld to be much use. Ach, what will happen to my poor wee lass when I'm gone?' She gave a deep sigh. 'As for Fergus, he's my bairn too. I brought him up. Och, Lachlan! I wish you and he would make your peace. He's sorry for everything, I know. He tried to tell you a long time ago but it turned sour on him. I only know he's like a lost soul sometimes and my auld hert aches for him!'

Lachlan put his hands firmly over her bent fingers.

'Belle, Fergus nearly cost me my marriage. I think you can guess what I mean. That old windbag Elspeth must have overheard some tasty tit-bits and no doubt passed them on. But that's all in the past now. I'd shake hands with the man tomorrow but he won't give me the chance again. His pride has already been bruised and he won't risk it again and I'm damned if I'll go to him. But forget about Fergus for the moment! You must stop worrying that old head of yours! Time will tell all. You must rest more. I'll give you something to take for the pains and I'll come and see you from time to time.'

But she rose in alarm. 'Och no – no laddie! They'd find out then! I'll come and see *you*.' She winked. 'Who knows, the gossips might put us together and hint we've a wee thing goin' for us.' She giggled girlishly but he wasn't deceived by her jauntiness. He watched from the window and saw her heavy drooping figure go down the path, all attempt at gaiety gone now that she thought she was unobserved.

Lachlan sighed and tapped a pencil on his desk. He

had known great satisfaction in his life. He had plunged to the depths of despair and risen to pinnacles of glory and the joy of being able to save a fellow human was his euphoria. But when he had to tell people he knew and loved that their days on earth were numbered his heart plummeted to his boots. He had often been told that people who tended the sick became hardened to death but he had never found it so, he had simply learned to disguise his feelings in an effort to convey a strength he sometimes didn't feel to the people who relied so much upon his opinion.

'We'll sneak in at the back of the estate,' Niall instructed his three followers who were trudging through the heather at his rear. 'Near the old iron gate that's all overgrown. There's a wee bit we can get through – eh, Stuart?'

Stuart winked, the entrance being well known to most of the boys on their poaching expeditions.

Shona felt she should have been in on this secret long ago and she threw Niall a reproachful glance but he was looking ahead, his corn curls dancing in the scented wind blowing in from the sea.

'We could have climbed the stile and gone through the woods,' suggested Agnes who, hitherto a tomboy, was now becoming more careful of her appearance and didn't want her dress snagged. She was twelve, with black waving hair and brown eyes, and proud of her developing figure. She was beginning to giggle coyly at boys and Shona wasn't so keen on her company now that she was growing from a sensible child into a 'cackling yowe'.

Stuart was a tall lanky boy of thirteen with a keen sense of adventure. He was the best guddler in the school and could swim faster and further than most of his age. He was not in the least impressed by Agnes's efforts to gain his attention and at her suggestion he snorted: 'We'd get caught going over the stile so don't be daft. Do as *we* tell you or you'll never come with us again.'

They climbed to the top of a steep rise and could see for miles on either side. The sea sparkled in the distance, the deep blue contrasting breathtakingly with white sands and the green of hayfields. They were in Glenriach, behind them the steep crags of Glen Fallan misty blue against the heat hazed sky.

'It's bonny!' cried Shona spreading her arms and breathing clover and bracken, heather and thyme. But the boys were anxious to get into Burnbreddie and marched down to an ancient gate set in a tangle of fir and ferns. Niall pulled aside some branches to reveal a hole large enough for them to crawl through. Shona and Stuart did so quickly but Agnes grumbled when a branch pulled at her skirt and when another tore a gash in her frilly knickers she wailed aloud, 'I should never have come! Och, look at me! Mother will skelp me on the lugs! I think I'll go back. What way should I watch auld Burnbreddie kissin' and cuddlin' anyway?'

'Get going!' growled Niall, wishing he hadn't brought the vastly changed Agnes. He hoped Shona would never become all giggly and fuss about her clothes.

The boys led the way through a dense thicket then

skirted the cool waters of an amber river. To get to the courtyard and the haysheds they had to cross an open pasture and they were barely halfway over when they saw two riders: the laird was astride a gleaming chestnut mare and a glossy black pony carried the woman who fitted Dodie's description because her bosom was bursting out of her costume and her high giggle carried across the field.

Burnbreddie had visitors in all but the worst months of winter. Several island girls were employed by the laird and reported 'terrible goings on just' to the rest of the island. The honest people of Rhanna turned up their noses but listened avidly to the gossip. '*These* kind of folk make their own rules just,' was the general verdict. 'They're a gey mixed bag so they are indeed. A lot to answer for they have, not decent in the eyes o' God, oh no!' But the pious words belied the veiled curiosity over Burnbreddie affairs. Annie McKinnon was a reliable source of information. She was as fun-loving as her elder sister Nancy and though she could speak English perfectly, constantly annoyed the laird's wife by always conversing in Gaelic. One day she was busy with her duties when Mrs Balfour of Burnbreddie said tentatively, 'Annie?'

Annie turned, showing her white teeth mischievously. 'Mo Bantigherna?'

'Why is it you have never learned to speak English?'

'Och, Mo Bantigherna why does it ail you so?' grinned Annie. 'English is a foreign language to me, remember. Indeed I could ask you why 'tis yourself has never learned the Gaelic. It is a far more civilized language than your own, begging your pardon. Funny it is the way the English always expect others to know their tongue but are too put upon to learn another. If you'll be excusing me now, Mo Bantigherna . . . or would you prefer "my leddy" instead?'

She danced from the room and it took the laird's wife several astonished moments to realise that Annie had just spoken in the lovely lilting English the island folk used.

Stuart watched the riders from the cover of a bush. 'We might just go home or . . .' He brightened. 'We could guddle some trout while we're here.'

Niall was shading his eyes. 'They're not going, they're coming back. They'll go to the stables with the horses so we've time to race to the big hayshed.'

'How do you know they'll go there?' asked Agnes. 'And why the big hayshed? They might go to a wee one. There's a few up by the yard.'

'The big one has the only doors that shut properly, I was told by a reliable source. Come on!'

They scuttled along to the hayshed, arriving breathless and hot. It was a huge barn with sunlight slanting from the skylight to dance on dusty cobwebs that hung from the cross-beams. A mouse scurried and Agnes protested daintily.

'You played with them last year!' hissed Shona.

'Not this year,' returned Agnes primly.

They followed the boys into the hayloft which was warm and sweet smelling.

'This hay's awful jaggy,' complained Agnes who had been one of the happiest children on harvest hayrides.

'Och, you're a girny bugger!' scolded Shona.

'You *swore*!' said a shocked Agnes.

Niall grinned. 'You are a girnin' bugger! Shut up!'

Stuart lay on his back and watched the sunbeams. 'It would have been a grand night for guddlin',' he mourned.

Agnes wriggled up to him. 'Stuart,' she said in wheedling tones, 'do you like the way I do my hair?'

'It's not bad,' he said grudgingly.

'Do you notice girls at all? Their bodies and everything?' she asked gently, pushing out her growing bosom.

Stuart was now less interested in the roof. 'They're shaped nice,' he admitted placidly. 'But they're a bother mostly. My sister scunners me the way she giggles all the time. *You're* like her! She's older with bigger bosoms but you laugh the same.'

Agnes smiled secretively. '*My* bosoms will get bigger, Stuart. Will you like me then?'

Stuart wriggled uncomfortably and wished he was fishing. He yawned and folding his arms under head closed his eyes.

Fifteen minutes passed and they were all growing bored. Then a giggle came from below and two shadows darkened the doorway. It creaked shut and a bolt shot home, the bolt that the laird had had specially fitted on the inside doors. He liked to bring his ladies to the hayshed. There was something primitive about making love in the hay that appealed to him. He wasted no time in preliminary small talk.

'Come here, my bonny plump rose,' he grunted, pulling the lady to him. He had changed from his riding habit into a hairy tweed jacket, kilt, and lovat green hose. His legs were fat and very hairy and Agnes gave an explosive snort.

'Quiet!' hissed Stuart but the laird was making so many of his own he was oblivious to any other. Before long he was red and sweating. The children stared in amazement when, with a speed astounding in one so lumbering, he had exposed the lady's generous breasts.

Stuart gulped and Agnes whispered, 'I don't want mine to grow *just* so big! They'd be awful heavy.'

Stuart grinned. 'They'd make your back all hunch up and you'd be like an auld Cailleach. You might grow a big nose to match and you'd have a hump on your head because your nose would be such a weight.' He snorted into the hay in an ecstasy of silent laughter.

The laird was beginning to babble as his hands wandered. 'My kilt! Wore it specially – nothing underneath,' he groaned in Gaelic. The children understood but the English lady didn't. She was making sounds that fitted Dodie's description of 'an auld yowe bleatin'!' and soon discovered for herself the laird's urgent message. She threw back her head and giggled hysterically. Her mouth was large, painted liberally, and the children could plainly see her Adam's apple wobbling above her voluptuous breasts.

Dodie had likened the laird to a 'ruttin' stag' and he had never been more apt.

Niall blushed and wished he hadn't come. It was all very well listening to the description of something but the reality was embarrassing and somewhat crude.

There was no dignity about the old couple below and Niall, at a rather romantic and impressionable age, felt that love should have dignity. Even the young courting couples at the barnyard Ceilidhs had a certain respect in their attitudes towards each other. Niall felt he had cheapened himself and opened Shona's innocent mind to the wrong ideas about sex. His twelve-year-old mind groped for an idea of what love should really be like. It couldn't, just couldn't, be like that lustful scene below. He stole a glance at Shona and saw with surprise she was enjoying the whole thing.

'Look at his *bum*!' she hissed gleefully. 'It's pink and hairy and jumpin' the way the old boar does when he goes to the sow!'

Niall breathed a sigh of relief. She saw the scene with the eyes of the innocent. She had witnessed the mating of animals all her young life and to her the laird and his friend were two human animals doing the natural thing. Her ten-year-old mind lumped all living things together and nothing was more normal than the mating of two living creatures.

But Stuart and Agnes were different. They were older and more open to suggestive happenings. Stuart had forgotten about fishing and was fumbling play-fully with Agnes, kissing her in an awkwardly eager boyish fashion and she was egging him on by twisting herself into all sorts of inviting poses. Niall watched them and wondered. Was Agnes an indication of all girls of her age, tormenting boys, teasing them, little witches who used their bodies like a commodity to entice, then to reject like the girls did at the dances?

Would Shona change so drastically? Would she flirt and tease and boldly flaunt her body? He knew her so well but he was going away and each time he came home he would see the changes in her such as he wouldn't if he stayed on Rhanna.

She was too engrossed to notice his stare, her twinkling blue eyes showing her obvious amusement. He was free to study the long sweep of her lashes. Mirabelle had tied back her auburn hair; it was swept up from her face but tumbled down her back in a cascade of thick rich waves. A dancing sunbeam lingered on the tresses and turned them the colour of autumn leaves. Her ears were like small pink shells. Niall noticed them for the first time. They were exquisitely shaped, so delicate in the sun they were almost transparent. She was thin to the point of being skinny but he knew that one day her whole shape would change. It had happened to all the bigger girls in school and it was bound to happen to Shona. Would she be like Agnes? Would she taunt the Rhanna boys with him away and not able to do a thing about it? For years he had calmed her stormy tempers, soothed her troubled heart and scolded if she sulked. They had spent their childhood together but when he was away she was bound to turn to others for company. Would it be another boy? He couldn't see the tomboy Shona playing dull games with other girls and the older she grew the more natural it would be for her to want a boy. Something churned in his heart but he was too young to recognize the bitter taste of jealousy.

He couldn't believe she would turn out like Agnes, he didn't want to believe it. He knew she had a strength in her, a pride and a sensitivity that went very deep and somehow he knew she wasn't going to be like other girls. She had confided so much to him but there had been times when the depth of her emotions shook him. She was usually so happy but sometimes he sensed a sadness in her that he was too inexperienced to reach. He knew the cause, of course, but who was he to turn the tide of time and make possible a more satisfying relationship between father and daughter. It was all too complicated for him. He had lost his dislike for Fergus McKenzie long ago – he admired his strength of character. It showed in every aspect of his bearing. He held his head high and ignored the gossips, his pride visible for all to see.

'Och, Niall, that was the best laugh ever!' Shona's voice startled him out of his reverie. She leaned over and whispered in his ear, 'Will yours be like that?'

'My what?' he said, puzzled.

'Like *his*! The laird's!'

'They've gone,' said Niall amazed.

'Och, you're silly *and* deaf, like Shelagh! They banged the door quite loud and you haven't answered me. Will you have a big rooster like his?'

Niall reddened. 'Will you have big bosoms like hers?' he countered.

'Ach, I don't think so, I'm too skinny. You're all red in the face, Niall. You never used to blush when you went behind a bush to pee. You never really bothered to hide, and I saw your rooster. It was a skittery wee thing – not like *his*! I hope you don't grow like that! You'd have to wear your kilt *all* the time because you wouldn't have room in your trousers!'

'*Shut up!*' he snapped and she fell back in the hay in a fit of laughter.

Stuart had become disenchanted with Agnes who knocked his hand away every time he became too personal.

'Let's go and guddle,' he grunted, pulling hay from his hair. 'If Robbie catches us we'll tell him we'll tell the laird we'll tell his wife he's a dirty auld man!'

Niall gladly accepted the garbled suggestion and all four trooped rather thankfully into a perfect summer evening.

Chapter Eight

A week later Mirabelle went up to her room to rest before tea. It was breathlessly hot. Not a leaf or heather bell moved and the sun shone faintly through a thick haze of heat. There was thunder in the air and Mirabelle felt tired and headachy. She sat on her rocking chair by the wide open window fanning her flushed face with a corner of her apron. Shona was in the garden. Mirabelle saw her pluck a red rose, sniff its glorious perfume absently before sitting down on the grass to hug her knees, her eyes gazing unseeingly ahead.

'Poor wee bairn,' sighed Mirabelle. 'She'll miss that laddie sorely when he's gone.'

Niall had told Shona because he couldn't bear to keep the secret any longer. He had told her in 'their' cave, now made homely with various items they had smuggled from their respective homes. At first Shona thought him to be teasing but the look in his brown eyes quelled her laughter.

'I want to be a vet,' he explained, his hand in her small grubby one. 'After school it will be a college like my father went to but there will be holidays, Shona. We'll still see each other.'

There was a long silence in which she sat like a stone, not even an eyelid flickering.

'I'll miss you like anything,' he hurried on, his sorrow at having to impart the news making him babble slightly. 'I'll miss lots of folk. My parents and wee Fiona. Tot too, she was so much with us. I'll miss Dodie and old Joe and even old Shelagh farting in kirk on the Sabbath. I'll be staying with a lot of other boys but it won't be like here on Rhanna. I'll miss our caves and the sea and the fishing boats and those lovely scones Mirabelle makes. I wish I could have known her better because it seems *awful* to miss her scones more than her. It'll be really terrible to wake up every morning and not look to the sea, because though it's a country place it's not near the water. There's a wee town not far away so I can send you a postcard sometimes. Would you like that, Shona?'

She was strangely, awesomely quiet. She saw the future stretching without Niall and the whole world was bleak. All along she had known that he would leave the island one day but one day was always in the future in her child's mind. Now that day was drawing nigh. A lot of Rhanna boys left school early to learn fishing and crofting, the two mainstays of the island. Some went away to the big cities like Glasgow and London, some to places like Canada and Australia, names that were other worlds to her, places on the big map in the classroom that she liked to hear about but they were foreign to her. Rhanna, the little green jewel in the Atlantic Ocean, was her birthplace and she loved it with every breath of her being. She would stay. Girls stayed on Rhanna – some went to take up nursing on the mainland but mostly they stayed. But she had known Niall would go. He hadn't been full

of fancy ambitions for his future but had always clung
to one, to be an animal doctor.

'I like them better than humans,' he once told her.
'They don't moan but suffer in silence mostly. They're
nice to work with.'

Shona felt herself grow cold though the sun was
streaming through the cave. She shivered suddenly
and turned slowly to look at his boyish anxious face.
His hand tightened over hers.

'I'll be back,' he said urgently, trying to dispel the
dull look that had crept into her eyes. 'It'll be even
better than when I'm here *all* the time because we'll
have so much to tell each other. Och Shona, don't
look so sad! 'Tis sad I am to leave. Think of the holidays! Every time I come home we'll run to this cave
and talk till we're blue in the face. This cave will be
our wee den! We'll always come here!'

He was so eager to please her he gripped her hand
till it hurt, his tanned skin flushing with his need to
make her understand how earnest he was. She put up
a small brown hand and touched his golden hair
briefly. 'We will, Niall,' she whispered in a small tight
voice. She knew that if she gave way to her feelings
she would explode. She would cry and shout and do
all the things she tried never to do because they
stamped her with the mark of her femininity and she
wasn't going to give in now, not after all the years of
reining her emotions. She drew her hand away and
he was surprised and a little hurt that she hadn't
shown more feeling. A lump came to his throat and
he said defiantly, 'Mother and Father will miss me
anyway.'

209

'Yes,' said Shona and turned away to hide a glimmer of tears. Angry at herself she stamped out of the cave.

'Are you in a bad mood?' he called.

'Yes,' she said again, keeping a wobble from her voice.

'Well you can just grow out of it!' Hurt made his tone snappy. 'You're a wee baby and I'm fed up trailing you about 'cos you're a girl! I'm *sick* of girls!'

He stamped after her. She stared at his tall sturdy figure. The wind whipped his hair and his cheeks were red. He stood astride a moss-grown rock, glaring at her, his brown legs apart and his arms folded. Her pent-up emotions came out in a flood of temper.

'Ach, away you go! You're a stupid daft boy and I wonder I've tholed you so long! I'm sick of you telling me what to do! You're glaikit, that's what you are, Niall McLachlan, and I'm that scunnered I'm glad you're going so I am! I hope . . . I hope a seagull shits on your head every time you travel on that boat – you deserve a whole flock of gulls shitting on your head for the rest of your days so you do!'

She scampered wildly over the heather. Her hair streamed like the tail of a wild pony and her blurring eyes saw not where she was going but she plunged on recklessly, the deep heart-rending sobs rising in her throat at last.

Niall was left to stare after her. Now he knew how desperately she had fought to conceal her tears from him. The wild burst of words, the tempestuous flight all proved it. His lips quivered slightly as her terrible wishes touched the humorous side of his nature but he sobered on a more serious reflection of the scene.

He realized it was the first time in years she had allowed her deeper feelings to come uppermost. She had tempers, yes; but nothing like the tremulous storm he had just witnessed. He cast his mind back, trying to remember that last time. It had been more terrible then because she had been very young and unable to restrain herself at all. When and where had it been? He searched his memory and it all came back: the Kirkyard, her mother's inscription, the deep terrible sorrow that her discovery had caused her.

Young boy that he was he felt sobered and very touched because she hadn't cried like that till today – and this time the tears were for him.

Two days had passed since then. He couldn't go to Laigmhor. He had never gone there and he couldn't very well start now. She wouldn't go to him because she was so ashamed of her outburst. Also there was the matter of her pride: it was difficult for her to apologize even when she knew she was wrong. So she mooned around and got under everyone's feet. Normally she was a good help to Mirabelle. She could do a lot of household chores and it had become her job to make the hens' pot. She also milked the cows sometimes and every morning she cranked the handle to start the generator that pumped water into the farm. But now she snapped at Mirabelle and not even Alick's cheerful chatter could dispel her gloom. A visit to Hamish's cottage lifted her spirits a little. Maggie was a cheery woman and stepped over dogs and cats to fetch creamy milk and biscuits for her little guest. Hamish showed her a baby rabbit he had rescued from one of the cats. It was in a little hutch especially kept for injured creatures and was happily munching lettuce leaves. Hamish made her laugh and she tripped home gaily but her mood returned when she saw Niall with a crowd of boys coming back from the harbour. It seemed he wasn't missing her at all, and she scowled. She didn't even have Tot for company and felt no one really cared for her.

Her father was surprisingly sympathetic. He knew what loneliness was like and could feel something of her sadness at having to part with the friend of her childhood. He saw how empty her life would be without the boy who had shared her innermost thoughts for so many years. She had made his mistake, that of attaching herself too devotedly to one human being. When that person went away the void that was left could only be filled by dreams and these were not things that made for a happy life. So he was gentle with her and for one lovely fleeting moment she allowed him to hold her close, his compassion over-ruling his fear of rebuff. He felt the warm smooth bloom of her cheeks against his and the sweet delicacy of her slim little body filled him with such over-whelming love that tears sprang to his eyes. She felt his dear rough face against hers. The smell of him was the night smell. His breath was fresh and his damp hair tickled her nose. He was stripped to trousers and vest and she could see where the brown weather-beaten skin on his neck merged with the paler skin of his chest. His arms were warm and very strong and she held her breath with the ecstasy of his nearness. But the feel of his arms was so unreal to her she began to feel uncomfortable and she wondered how she could break away. She wanted the lovely moment to last forever but moments never did. She knew he had hugged her on an overpowering impulse but it was over now and he too would be feeling uneasy. She broke away and immediately felt she had stepped back into a world of lonely uncertainty. His eyes were hurt and she knew she had done the wrong thing but she couldn't go back to him now. The beauty of the moment was over and they both knew it.

The next day she was irritable and snapped at her father during breakfast. He had spent a sleepless night wondering what to do about Kirsteen and snapped back. Alick ate his boiled egg and searched for something to say to ease the tense atmosphere.

'You two having love problems?' he said cheerily and immediately knew he had said the wrong thing. Shona got up and with great dignity marched from the room.

'Come back here and excuse yourself from table!' yelled Fergus, but she pretended not to hear.

'A good skelping she needs,' muttered Fergus and he too left the table. Mirabelle sighed. 'I wanted the bairn to help me this morning. I'm tired wi' her tantrums so I am. It's yourself to blame, Alick. Never could hold your tongue!'

He put his arms round her plump waist.

'Don't fret so, my lady. Alick will be a good boy and help with all the kitchen chores this morning. They take too much for granted, Belle. How have you put up with us all these years? Haven't you ever wanted a family of your own? You must have been a bonny lass in your day.'

213

She giggled and pulled a lock of his brown hair.

'Ach, away wi' you. You're a flatterer and a flirt into the bargain. You're such a different laddie from Fergus.'

'Aye, he was the big brother I worshipped and wanted to be like. But it didn't turn out that way, thanks to Mother. She strengthened my weakness by pampering me and setting Fergus up as my guardian. Oh aye, I've thought about it a lot, Belle.' His voice held an unusual note of bitterness. 'I should have fought my own battles but Mother wouldn't have it. Fergus was the strong one but just as much a pawn as myself. I think it was all wrong, Belle.'

'Ach, your poor mother did what she thought best for you both, but it's all in the past now, laddie.'

His smile was rueful. 'Aye, but it's our past that shapes our future, dear Belle. I was made to lean on Fergus even though he didn't want such a burden. All my boyhood days I needed that prop. Now, here I am, with a wife as flightly as myself. I'm just floating around like a cork in water. No bottle for me to fit into. I've lost my prop, Belle.'

'Ach, you're full of fancies, laddie,' she said lightly; but she wondered if anyone had ever credited him with the deep sensitivity he covered so well with frivolous words.

His mention about a family of her own had touched a chord deep in her heart. All day thoughts of the past came crowding in on her till she knew she had to be alone to think. Hers were very special memories but hers had been a very special family. She had a spare hour before tea so she folded her hands over her stomach and rocked herself by her window. A smile hovered at the corners of her mouth and a reminiscent dreaminess crept into her eyes. No one knew the secret she had kept in her heart for . . . how many years? She puckered her forehead. Fifty-four! It couldn't be but yes, it was, she was seventy-three now and had been barely nineteen when her husband and little son were taken from her in that terrible tragedy of 1879. She could see the face of her husband John so clearly. In her mind's eye she saw him smile, that jaunty gay smile of his, his boyish face alight with his love of life. And little Donald, just three months, beginning to smile his lovely toothless baby smile. She tried to remember his tiny face but couldn't. Panic seized her and she rose hurriedly to rummage in a drawer. The box was there beside all her bits and pieces. It was full of old photos, of her parents and sisters. The familiar crushing pain in her chest took her breath away and she sat down heavily, the box in her lap.

After a short rest she searched through the box, desperately eager to find that baby face that eluded her memory. There were several sepia photos of the child but she found her favourite, the one with John holding his tiny son. She looked gently at the young face of her husband and could see that he was bursting with pride, the sparkle of his eye and the upturned corners of his mouth gave him away but he had remained suitably composed till the photographer was finished. Now she could recall that day so clearly. When they got out of the studio he had burst out laughing, the sobriety of the occasion too much for his sense of fun.

She studied the face of her little son. His eyes were roundly agape at some object placed so that he would face the camera. He had kept sticking his fist in his mouth and John had to constantly take it out. It was a sweet innocent little face with big eyes looking into a future that was never to be.

Mirabelle sat back in her rocking chair and was transported back in time, far from Laigmhor and Rhanna. She remembered again that Christmas of 1879. It was a happy gay Christmas spent with her mother who dearly loved all her children and grand-children. She was widowed, and Christmas was a time full of poignant memories for her, so Mirabelle had gone with John and little Donald to spend the festive season with her. She knew John would have preferred to stay in their own cosy little home for Donald's first Christmas but his kind heart was easily swayed and the journey had been worth the happiness it brought. Three days after Christmas they departed for home but at the station it was discovered they had left a case behind containing a lot of things essential to the baby's wellbeing. He was cutting a first tooth and wailing fretfully so it was decided that Mirabelle would go back for the case while John went on with the baby.

But there was no next train over the Tay that Sunday night or for many nights to come. The high girders on the wind-lashed bridge had collapsed and both engine and train had plummeted into the foaming waters beneath. Not a single survivor came out of the disaster and Mirabelle collapsed. For many months she lived like a shadow, unable to cope with reality, and her mother had nursed her through days of unending darkness. A year later her mother, too, was taken from her and she felt she had lost everything that made life worth living. Oh yes, she knew how dear proud Fergus had felt when he had lost Helen. The marrow had gone out of him, he had told her, and described exactly the way she had felt all those years ago. But at least he had the gift of his daughter, although unable to appreciate the fact. She had saved nothing from the wreckage of her young days.

Tears were coursing down her cheeks now but she wasn't aware of them. She was seeing the young Mirabelle, drifting, unable to settle into any kind of niche. She had lived with a married sister for a time but her natural sense of independence made her go out and find a job and she had become housekeeper to a demanding crotchety old lady who never seemed pleased with anything but who must have appreciated Mirabelle because she had left her several hundred pounds when she died. After that, each post was worse than the last and every ounce of her strength was drained by large demanding families or old demanding ladies and she had come to believe her life would contain nothing but meaningless service to others. Then came Laigmhor and the lovely healing peace of Rhanna. She had been thirty-seven then but had felt she was starting life afresh. She had become so used to keeping her private thoughts to herself she hadn't been able to change, not even on Rhanna. No one expected a housekeeper of many years' standing ever to have a life of her own. She was expected to immerse herself in the running of other people's lives and that had been easy enough at Laigmhor with two young children to love. But she had always felt herself to be part of the family, not just an outsider to be used as a convenience and she gave of herself every ounce of her loving heart. She had lost her own little son but the boys, then Shona, had fulfilled her motherly instincts. Two generations of children! She had been their mother really. When hurt or unhappy it was to her arms they tumbled. She thought of them as her own. She wiped away her tears and smiled, an inward happy smile of thankfulness for such a rich life.

Shona rocked listlessly on her heels. It was hot and she got up to seek some shade under the apple tree. She glanced at the house and saw Mirabelle at the window. She put up her hand to wave but there was no response and she guessed Mirabelle was asleep.

Miss Fraser was coming up the hot dusty road and she came through the gate and over to Shona. 'Hello,' she said warmly. 'Is your father about?'

She too had spent a sleepless night thinking about Fergus. She knew she couldn't go on in the present position much longer. Two nights ago she had lain in his arms but last night she was alone again and she was now convinced he only came to her to appease his physical appetites.

Shona nodded. 'He's in the big barn with Alick, stacking hay.'

'Thank you, Shona. I'll see you later.'

Shona watched her teacher walk away. She liked the way she held herself. She was quite tall and very graceful and there was that dignified tilt of the chin that had earned her the label of 'madam' by some narrow-minded locals. Shona liked the proud chin and the way the golden head was held high. She liked Miss Fraser altogether and wished she and her father would marry – that might put an end to some of the spiteful jibes she endured at school.

Kirsteen went into the barn. It was deliciously fragrant. Hens clucked lazily and poked for insects on the straw-littered floor. It was warm and quiet, and for a moment she thought it was empty.

'Fergus!' she called. There was a soft chuckle from behind a hay bale. She stepped inside and found Alick sitting beside a fat contented hen.

'Will I do instead?' grinned Alick. 'Fergus was called away to look at a cow who has hurt her foot. He and Hamish will be gone for ages. You know what they're like when they get talking about the beasts. I'm just resting from my labours. Brother is a hard taskmaster. He's making sure I earn my daily bread.'

'Oh . . .' she hesitated, 'well, I'll see him another time. Don't – don't mention I called will you?'

He looked at her standing poised for flight. She was wearing a very flimsy blue dress and her long legs were bare. He didn't answer but patted the hay at his side.

'Sit down and talk to me for a wee whiley. Och no, don't go! They're all in the doldrums here just now and I could be doing with a lovely lady to cheer me up!'

He was being very charming and she knew his eyes were taking in every bit of her body. She had always managed to avoid him on her visits to the farm because she knew he was a lady's man. Nevertheless she liked him and felt his cheery frivolities were just the tonic she needed to make her forget for a while all the problems her life held.

'Just for a wee while,' she acceded and sat, not in the spot indicated but on the other side of the hen. Before long she was laughing merrily. He had a way of making the most ordinary happenings sound funny. His dark eyes were sparkling. He knew his talent for making laughter had always been his greatest asset next to flattering women.

Kirsteen was enjoying herself so much it was a moment or two before she realised his flow of wit had stopped and he was looking at her with open desire.

'You're beautiful, Kirsteen,' he said in a low voice.

'No – Alick – no!' she cried and tried to scramble up. But it was too late. The fat hen ran squawking at Alick's lunge forward. He was quick, so quick that Kirsteen was pinned helplessly to the warm hay while he kissed her, small swift kisses on her face and neck.

'Let me go, Alick,' she panted. *'Please* let me go!'

'You're too good for him,' he mumbled. 'He doesn't deserve you. You're the kind of woman who could have any man.'

His mouth came down hard on hers and she fought for the breath to scream. His hands were caressing her body with such fierceness her flesh tingled with pain. Panic seized her. She couldn't breathe. The more she struggled the more he seemed to enjoy it.

'Will you give yourself or can I have the pleasure of taking you?' he whispered. 'Please let me, Kirsteen. I've dreamed of you every night since I saw you.

Touch me, dear sweet Kirsteen. I'm on fire for you!'

She screamed then, a half-sobbing sound that tore from her in a desperate succession of sound. The tall figure of Fergus darkened the doorway and he was tearing Alick from her while the cries were still choking from her throat.

Alick hardly knew what hit him. Fergus's sledge-hammer fists were raining down on him without pause. He put up his hands to defend his face but he was useless against the fury of his brother's onslaught. Kirsteen, wild-eyed and sobbing, could only watch while he was reduced to a bleeding mess.

'Stop, Fergus!' she cried. 'You'll kill him!'

Alick lay for several minutes. Blood streamed from his nose and frothy saliva mingled with the blood of a split lip. His face was a mass of bruises and one eye was already beginning to swell.

Fergus, his chest heaving, looked down at his brother with contempt. 'Get up,' he said softly, 'and walk out of here like a man. You'll get the next boat from Rhanna!'

Alick stumbled to his feet. He drew the back of his hand across his mouth and looked at the blood on it.

'A man!' He spat thickly. 'Oh yes, I'm that, despite the fact that you and Mother tried to turn me into a mouse! Not a man like you, Fergus, all fire and fury on the outside but soft like dung inside! People know what kind of man I am! Can you say the same, man? I show it when I feel afraid but you're too bloody proud even to be human!' He staggered outside and away over the breathless fields, swaying like a man drunk.

Kirsteen's eyes were full of tears. 'Och Fergus, you were too hard on him! He's not strong like you! He wasn't able to fight back!'

He looked at her, it was a strange look which she couldn't fathom. She couldn't know that he was seeing Helen again but this time as a lovely memory of the past. He would always see her because he knew he could never forget her. But the guilt he had felt, the uncertainty of being able to give his heart fully to another woman was gone and a burden lifted from him. He was certain now of his deep love for Kirsteen, the sight of her in his brother's arms had proved it and he felt light-headed with the knowledge. He held out his hands.

'Kirsteen, will you marry me? Will you share my life and make me a happy man? I love you, Kirsteen.'

The words were simple enough but they were the most beautiful she had ever heard. She ran to him and the whole world was at their feet in that magical eternal minute.

'Fergus, my dear Fergus,' she breathed. 'I've waited so long to hear you say that.'

He closed his eyes and held her close. Briefly he thought of his brother and felt both pity and gratitude. Pity because Alick was the unhappy, pleasure-seeking product of a pampered childhood, and gratitude because Alick had unwittingly brought him to a decision over which he had hesitated for so long. Later he would find Alick and make his peace with him, but not now when Kirsteen overwhelmed him with her dear sweet nearness.

*

Shona heard the rumpus coming from the hayshed. At first she paid no heed till she heard her father's angry voice followed by Alick's high-pitched tones, then she ran quickly and was in time to see Alick reeling over the fields. She stood by the big doors and heard the murmur of voices from within. Her father was asking Kirsteen to marry him and they were so wrapped up in each other they didn't notice her. She tiptoed quickly round a corner and leaned against the warm wood of the big shed. Hugging herself with joy she lifted her face to the sky. It was hot and hazy-looking with purple clouds piling on top of Sgurr nan Ruadh, the red mountain of the Fallan range. It was beautiful, everything was beautiful, Loch Tenee sparkling, the misty bronzed moors, the rough grass at her feet, even the midgie that landed on her hand, all were beautiful. But the midgie had a sting and had to be killed and her world of beauty was soon to turn to a devilish nightmare. But not now! Certainly not now when everything floated in such a happy haze. A bubble of joy rose into her throat and she knew she couldn't stand for long. She skipped away, over the cobbled yard and into the house to find Mirabelle. It was teatime, yet strangely there were no lovely savoury smells in the kitchen. It was empty except for Tot and her pups. She bent and stroked the bitch's silky ears. 'I'll tell you a secret, Tot,' she whispered. 'Father's going to marry Miss Fraser and we're all going to be happy. I'll have to find Mirabelle, she'll be pleased because she's getting too tired to be my mother and needs a wee help with things. After that I'll go and tell Niall, even though he's a boy. 'Tis he can keep secrets better than anyone I know.'

She looked into the parlour but Mirabelle wasn't there. She wasn't in the green taking in the washing that hung limply in the stillness nor was she searching the hen houses for eggs. Shona went back into the house. The grandmother clock ticked in the hall and the house had that strange empty feel when Mirabelle was out.

'Mirabelle!'

Her voice intruded into the peaceful house. Then she remembered – Mirabelle was in her room. She had been in her favourite rocking chair by the window and would be sound asleep forgetting all about tea.

'Lazy Cailleach,' chuckled Shona bounding up the stairs. Mirabelle's room was at the end of the landing. It was light and airy with its chintz curtains and gay patchwork cushions and covers. Shona knew it well. Mirabelle had often rocked her in the chair and crooned old Scottish lullabys. The room was full of knick-knacks but the reason she liked to go there was because it had a 'mother' air about it. Everything was homely and friendly, even the smell of the room. It had Mirabelle's smell of lavender and mothballs.

Shona giggled when she saw she had been right. Mirabelle was fast asleep, her chin sunk in her chest. She held something tightly and a box had fallen from her lap to scatter its contents on the floor.

Shona tiptoed forward. 'Mirabelle, wake up! I have something lovely to tell you. You're not going to be so weary now for Father and Miss Fraser are to be wed!' She shook the old lady gently by the shoulder. How fast asleep she was. Her head lolled strangely and there was something unusual about her face. It was all tinged with blue, nose, lips and cheeks, even her wrinkled eyelids, but her mouth was smiling and Shona sighed. 'Dreaming again! Och, wake up, Mirabelle till you hear my news!'

Mirabelle suddenly slid sideways against the arm of the chair. She looked like one of the limp rag dolls she stitched so often and the little girl's hand flew to her mouth. She backed away, frightened now of the stout old figure that had always spelled security.

'Mirabelle,' she whispered then turned and fled from the room, downstairs and into the kitchen. Sobbing she ran outside. A cool breeze had sprung from the sea and she shivered. Her head was spinning and the cold hand of fear gripped her heart with icy fingers. The farmyard was empty. Where *was* everyone? Normally Murdy or Mathew were about and Bob always came in for a cup of tea about now. She raced to the hayshed where she had last seen her father but he was gone. She was crying, a small whimpering sound that could have come from a lost puppy. Everything was blurred in tears, and fields and sky wobbled together. Then she spotted several figures on the road to Portcull. They were specks in the distance but she knew her father was there.

'Father! Father!' she screamed, knowing it was useless. The wind was strengthening and threw particles of dust into her brimming eyes. The masses of cloud over the mountains had changed to a muddy grey with wraiths of white mist sliding down over corries and scree. The sky was a slate-blue with curling smoky clouds creeping over the landscape.

She felt small, helpless and very lonely and ran forward to look for some familiar figure but she was all alone. The sweep of her glance took in the farmhouse and there was the open window with Mirabelle slumped in such a way that her white mutch was like a beacon in the dark window recess.

'No! No! No!' The scream tore from the child's throat in a series of anguished protests. She began to run swiftly like a terrified animal. She tripped half a dozen times but each time she got up and ran on, heedless that her arms and legs were grazed and bleeding. She had no notion of direction but her subconscious mind guided her tired legs to the haven of Slochmhor. She burst straight into Lachlan's surgery hour. Her auburn hair was windswept, her eyes wild like a young animal caught in a trap. Familiar faces swam in her vision. She opened her mouth but the wild hammering of her heart robbed her of breath to speak so she just stood there whimpering.

'Mercy!' exclaimed Kirsty McKinnon. 'The bairn hasny the wind to speak!'

Old Shelagh nodded knowingly and emitted a small belch. 'Ach the wind, a terrible thing just!'

Nancy Taylor, heavy and awkward in her eighth month of pregnancy, heaved herself up and put her arms round Shona's shaking shoulders. 'There, there, my wee chookie,' she soothed, 'come and sit down beside Archie and me and tell us what ails you!'

But the little girl shook her head violently. 'No – no. Get . . . doctor – I think Mirabelle's dead!'

There was a stunned silence.

'Ach no, she canny be.' Nancy spoke as if she was

convincing herself because she had a great affection for Mirabelle.

'God rest her soul,' said Kirsty piously and looked heavenward.

Elspeth's sharp nose hove into view in the dark passageway. The gathering clouds had brought early darkness and the small hall window gave little light. The people gathered for evening surgery looked like shadows and Shona's news had turned several faces pale.

'My, it's like a funeral to be sure!' barked Elspeth. 'And who's soul's needin' rested?'

'The bairn thinks Mirabelle's dead,' quavered Nancy. 'Could you fetch the doctor quickly?'

Elspeth turned pale. Mirabelle was her friend, the best she had because there were few who could stand her sharp tongue. Kindly Mirabelle could always be relied on for a sympathetic ear.

'Dead!' Horror made her tone sharper than ever. 'Are you sure, child? Did your faither send you for the doctor?'

Shona shook her head. She felt like screaming. All those questions and Mirabelle lying dead! Niall hovered in the dark hall. The commotion had brought him downstairs.

'Niall!' Shona's voice trembled with relief at seeing him. 'Please fetch your father! Mirabelle's dead!'

But Lachlan, ushering a patient from his room, heard. He reached immediately for his bag.

'You'll have to wait a while,' he told his patients. 'Niall, take Shona to your mother. I've no doubt the lass needs a bit comfort.'

But Shona broke from Nancy's arms. 'No, no, let me come! She might not be dead – she just looked it! Och, please let me see her! She's my Mirabelle!'

Lachlan rested his hand briefly on her head. 'All right, mo ghaoil. You're nearest her heart.'

He took her small hand firmly and hurried away.

'Ach, I'm goin' too,' said Elspeth whose features had softened with grief. 'Belle's my friend and if she's dyin' I have the right to say goodbye.' She peeled off her apron, threw it on a chair and grabbed her hat from the stand.

Nancy's eyes were brimming with tears. 'My, poor dear Belle! When I worked to McKenzie she was like an auld mither to me. Are you comin' up wi' me, Archie?'

In minutes the hallway was empty except for old Shelagh who hadn't the least idea what was happening. She shook her head and sucked noisily at her mint. The hall was warm and she folded her hands and dozed. Time meant nothing to her. She was quite content to wait in the doctor's house. It was a friendly house and Phebie would give her a cup of tea if the doctor was too long.

Mirabelle wasn't dead. Lachlan could see she had suffered a massive coronary and was deeply un-conscious. Shona looked at the dear old face and her heart was heavy with love for the woman who had tended them all so devotedly. Now she was so help-less, unable even to move one finger, but she was alive! At least she was alive!

Lachlan had pulled the rocking chair over to the bed and was trying to lift the old woman.

'Fetch your father!' he panted. 'Quickly, lass, I canna manage myself.'

'He's not here, nobody's here! They all went away and I don't know why!'

There was a scuffle at the door and Archie fell into the room. A tight knot of Rhanna people were outside the bedroom all eager to help.

'I'll lift her wi' you, doctor,' offered Archie. Getting Mirabelle's ample proportions into bed was no easy matter but after much heaving the task was completed.

'Ach, my dear auld friend,' said Elspeth gruffly, 'can I help get her into a goonie, doctor?'

But he shook his head. 'She's almost gone. Her heart has been weary for long but she wouldn't rest.'

Elspeth stared. 'You mean she knew her heart was that bad and she never told a soul? Och, doctor, and her listenin' to all my troubles and never a murmur about her own!'

She sat on the bed and began to cry. No one had seen Elspeth cry before and they looked at each other uncomfortably. The realisation that she had such human emotions was quite a revelation and Kirsty patted her awkwardly on the back.

Mirabelle stirred and opened her eyes. She looked as if she had come back from a great distance. Everyone looked at her and Shona snuggled against the bosom that had always spelled security.

'What way is everyone here?' she whispered stiffly. 'Why are you here, Lachlan?'

Lachlan ushered everyone from the room. He knew that the old lady didn't have long. Her breath was coming in quick gasps making each word an effort.

'Weesht,' he soothed, taking her knotted hand in his. 'Don't talk, lass. It's come as I told you it would if you didn't rest.'

Shona didn't know what he meant but his voice was so gentle, his face so beautiful in its compassion that she could feel the deep pain he was feeling. She knew the laughing boyish Lachlan who was Niall's father. Now she was seeing the Doctor McLaehlan whose love for his patients was so strong that the power of his love could reach out and comfort those in their last moments. Sometimes it was difficult for her to understand the world of grown-ups, the things they said were never easy to decipher, but at that moment, in the small dark room with Mirabelle dying, she understood one thing clearly. Niall's father could ease the fears of a mind that knew it was going to an unknown world. He had the gift of healing the body and an even more wonderful gift of bringing peace to a body he could no longer heal.

Shona could feel the peace in the room. Mirabelle's face was grey and old, but peace had replaced the weary look in her eyes. Lachlan held on to her hand, his brown eyes steady and reassuring as he spoke.

'There now, Belle, don't be frightened. You wanted it this way. No pampering an auld chookie – remember?'

She smiled. 'Aye, lad, a gey auld chookie.' She turned her head and looked deep into Shona's eyes. 'My ain wee bairn. Did I do right to bring you up and me too auld to see it through? I wish you could have had your own mother but it wasny to be.'

Shona felt the taste of salt from the tears pouring down her face. 'Och, Mirabelle you *are* my mother! The best in the world. Don't die, Mirabelle. Father's to wed Miss Fraser and we'll all look after you. I'll be a better help in the house and I won't get into tempers the way I do!'

A light came into Mirabelle's fading eyes.

'Fergus – to wed! Where is he? And Alick? My, these two laddies were a pair to rear. Alick was ay sae canty and Fergus – Fergus so proud but wi' a heart as big as a horse. Och, I'm glad he's to wed that bonny lass, but where is he? I'd like fine to see him before – before . . .'

Lachlan squeezed her hand. 'Don't worry, he'll be here in a whiley.'

She closed her eyes. 'If only you and he could let go of the past. He admires you, son, but he was ay too stubborn for his own good. Ach, the bothers we make in this life! It might be quite a wee change to get out o' it for a whiley.' She smiled but her eyes remained closed. 'Now, my wee lass.' She took the small hand in hers. 'I've a bit money put by and I've left it to you for when you wed. My lawyer will see to it for you.' She nodded smilingly. 'Oh aye, it sounds grand . . . auld Mirabelle wi' a lawyer, but even auld housekeepers can have their wee secrets. I never had need of money – not without John and wee Donald. It's a strange thought to think I'll see them in a whiley, John and my own bairn.'

Shona looked at Lachlan in puzzlement but he had Mirabelle's wrist between his fingers. She was breathing strangely. Shona could see the pulse beating under the thin skin of her neck but it was a funny beat, very jumpy and irregular.

Suddenly she gripped Lachlan's hand.

'Hold on to me, laddie. Shona, my wee chookie . . . coorie doon beside me – like you always did – when – your wee heart – was troubled . . .'

She drew a shuddering breath and the pulse in her neck stopped beating.

'Mirabelle!' screamed Shona. 'Please don't leave me!' She threw herself against the still figure in an abandonment of grief. There was the sound of sobbing outside the room and footsteps shuffling sadly away.

Lachlan lifted up the child. 'She's gone, Shona,' he said gently, 'we must cover her. Put her arms under the quilt.'

'She's holding something. It's like – like a piece of paper.'

Lachlan took the crumpled photograph from Mirabelle's clenched fist. He looked at a smiling young man and the tiny baby he held.

'Who are they?' whispered Shona.

'Who knows, except Mirabelle herself. People from long ago, no doubt, who meant a lot to her. Perhaps the John and Donald she spoke of a while back.'

Shona touched the white hair on the pillow. 'I'd like a wee bit,' she said softly, 'to keep in the locket she gave me for my birthday.' She began to cry again. 'Oh, I wish I had asked her to forgive me!'

'Whatever for, lass?'

'For sulking because Niall's going away. She must have been so tired and I've girned at her so. I was sulking today in the garden and saw her at her window. I should have been with her but I didn't even know she was ill. Och doctor, I loved her so!'

He sat down and gently pulled the forlorn little figure on to his knee.

'Weesht now, you mustn't blame yourself, she didn't want anyone to know she was ill. She loved you all and liked doing things for you. You were her life and she was happy. I know, she told me, you were like her own flesh and blood. Now, you are coming home with me. Phebie will see to you till your father comes home.'

Despite his gentle comfort she felt desolated. Mirabelle was dead and her father didn't know. His were the arms she needed more than she ever had done before. She felt cheated, deserted, and afraid. How could she live without Mirabelle? Who could she run to when she wanted to be the little girl she was and not the defensive dignified child her father thought her to be. How could she do without the homely routine created by Mirabelle? She had grumbled when told to do things that the old housekeeper had thought vital to her comfort but at the same time she had felt cherished and important. How often had she protested while Mirabelle brushed her hair till it shone? How many Gaelic lullabys had lulled her to sleep, how many fairy tales had been read to her while she sat in the inglenook hugging her knees? It must have been hundreds, perhaps thousands of times. Now these things would be no more. The homely 'mother' feel would be gone because no one, not even Miss Fraser, could fill the gap left by Mirabelle.

She sobbed quietly and allowed Lachlan to carry her

out of the room. She looked back but couldn't see for tears. 'Father,' she cried silently, 'Mirabelle's dead and you weren't here when we needed you!' She didn't know that only part of the nightmare was over or that her father needed help more in that moment than he had ever done in his life.

Lachlan carried her outside. The wind from the sea blew against them with deceptive calm and rain stung their eyes. She looked at Laigmhor through the mist of rain. It looked gaunt and empty against the grey sky. There were no flickers of lamplight to shine in the windows and they looked like empty dead eyes. She shivered. Mirabelle was in there. If she'd been alive the house would be warmly welcoming but she was dead and the house looked dead too and Shona knew it would be a long time before Laigmhor became alive again.

'We've left Tot in there,' she cried, making the house sound like an enemy.

'She'll be fine,' said Lachlan. 'I've got to go back with Biddy and I'll give Tot some warm milk and tuck her up for the night.'

She knew what he meant. Mirabelle had to be 'laid out' for her funeral. Biddy usually attended to such matters and was as used to dealing with the dead as with the living. But she and Mirabelle had been close friends and Shona thought how terrible it would be for Biddy to have to deal with such a matter.

Slochmhor was warm and friendly. Niall took Shona to the kitchen where Phebie made her drink hot milk and eat a biscuit. Little Fiona screamed delightedly at the cat who had recently adopted the house, and the belated surgery resumed. Shelagh wakened from a very satisfying nap and gave vent to her pent up 'winds'. 'Terrible just,' she consoled herself and rumbled into Lachlan's room leaving behind such a repelling odour that one or two people went home and the rest held their noses in disgust.

Chapter Nine

Fergus and Kirsteen were sitting in the hay making their plans for the future when Kirsteen looked up and saw the small knot of men coming towards the barn. They were very excited and shouted to each other in Gaelic.

'Come quickly, McKenzie!' panted Ranald McTavish. ''Tis your brother! Goin' to kill himself he is!'

'Aye, rantin' he was,' supplemented Todd the Shod. 'Says his life's not worth a bugger and he'd be better off wi' the de'il!'

'Says he'll prove he's man enough to kill himself!' said Canty Tam, named so because he was slightly simple and smiled at everything. He was smiling now despite the horror of his words.

Fergus's face had paled under his tan. 'What are you all rabblin' about?' he demanded, his fists bunching in a characteristic gesture.

Hamish placed a firm hand on his shoulder. 'Steady lad, 'tis true enough. Ranald was painting a boat when Alick came storming down saying he wanted to take a boat out . . .'

'It's true,' said Ranald who made his living hiring out small boats. 'Bad in a rage he was and I'm thinkin' it was odd because he's not like yoursel', Mr McKenzie – beggin' your pardon like. He pushed some money into my hand and I couldny believe my eyes, near on a pound he gave me. He was ay a kind-hearted chiel but a pound just . . .'

'For God's sake get to the point, man!' said Fergus grimly.

'Well, I gave him a boat – one of my very best and Canty Tam and myself helped him to push off. When he got out a wee bit he started to scream all the things we've been tellin' you. He was like a man demented, his eyes starin' out his head. It was a bit skearie, wasn't it, lads?'

Those that had witnessed the event murmured in agreement.

'It was to the Sgor Creags he said he was goin',' added Todd. 'Awful it was just. A man sair trauchled wi' life so he was!' Todd's eyes were round and the other men looked overawed.

Fergus stared. 'Did you say – the Sgor Creags?'

'Yes, terrible it was. He shouted he'd become like the chiel in the story my mother told me – the one who was caught on the Creags!'

'Aye.' Canty Tam nodded eagerly. 'He said the gulls would eat his flesh but his bones would stay there forever and we'd all have to remember him!' Canty Tam smiled in satisfaction at the thought.

'The tide, Ranald – what like was the tide?'

'Comin' in, sir – slow and peaceful like but – comin' in.'

Fergus strode away and the men followed, an assorted crowd but all curious, and eager to help. Hamish, kilt swinging and red beard jutting, walked beside Fergus.

'Don't worry, lad,' he said quietly, 'we'll get him safely aground.'

'Go home, Hamish,' ordered Fergus curtly but he was immediately sorry and put his hand on the arm of the man who had always befriended him. 'Don't worry about the McKenzies any longer. Maggie will have your tea ready and she'll wonder if you don't come home.'

'Ach, she's used to me bein' late but I'll ask young Mathew to run over and tell her I'll be a wee while.'

Mathew grumbled but went off over the hill. He was in a hurry to get the task over with and popped his head hastily through Maggie's door. Whisky rose quickly thinking his beloved master had come home but seeing it was just another human flopped back down, his nose in his paws.

Maggie raised her hand in greeting. 'Sit you down, laddie, and have a cuppy,' she invited. 'Hamish should be in soon and the kettle's on the boil.'

Mathew declined hurriedly. 'He'll be late home and thank you, Maggie, but I have no time to wait.'

He rushed off and Maggie took a pot of steaming broth from the fire. She looked at the table to make sure it was set properly and, content that all was ready for Hamish's return, made room between two cats and went for forty winks.

Mathew sped quickly over the fields to the village. He topped a rise and saw the unmistakable figure of Shona fleeing over Laigmhor fields below. He shouted and waved but she was beyond hearing range. He shrugged. She had Mirabelle and it might be better if she didn't know about Alick till his fate had been decided.

A skittish wind had turned the Sound into translucent green swells that broke in creamy foam on the boulder-strewn sands of Portcull. When Mathew arrived, the men were dragging a sturdy boat into the brown shallows. Fergus jumped aboard and many hands pushed him into deeper waters. Before the greedy sea took the boat out too far Hamish treaded water to his waist and jumped in beside Fergus.

'Get out, Hamish!' panted Fergus wildly.

'No.' Hamish's voice was calm but firm. His kilt plastered round his legs in wet folds and his fiery beard was bedraggled yet he still managed to retain the air of splendid dignity that was always his. 'You'll need help in yon sea,' he continued. 'It's rough out there by the Creags and if there's any swimming to be done better me than you. It was never one of your best assets.'

Fergus knew the truth of this. He feared the sea, its intensity and power. It could look calm and inviting but undercurrents were always a danger. He had swam a lot as a boy but never without fear. His head could be above the surface looking at the calm but underneath he could feel the water surging and swaying, restlessly roaming, tugging at the puny thing that was his body. In a way the sea reminded him of the unfathomed emotions of the human mind, the depths of which could be frighteningly strong yet appear so calm on the surface.

Alick knew that he feared the sea, but it was his unspoken triumph over the brother who was so good at everything else. During the days of their boyhood Alick had gloated quietly when Fergus floundered and had to be helped from some difficulty that was to Alick a simple matter of skill. Fergus now wondered if his brother was testing his boyhood fears. Was he throwing out a challenge that Fergus as his brother couldn't possibly ignore because if he did he would show the world there was something that could terrify him? Fergus was afraid. He felt it in every bone of his body. The sea was bucking at the boat and the Sound was growing rougher by the minute.

'Are you sure, Hamish?' he asked quietly.

'Will you try and stop me then?' grinned Hamish, looking with affection at the white-faced young man he had known since a baby. He saw Kirsteen on the shore. She stood to one side of the knot of islanders who had gathered like nosy gulls. He thought what a lovely lass she was with her slim body and fine sensitive face. Her eyes had shown her reluctance to let Fergus take the boat out but she had uttered no protest and now stood, quietly dignified, with her hands at her sides. Hamish wished that just one of the islanders would go up and offer her some crumb of comfort but the women were in clannish groups and the men too interested in the proceedings to bother with one unhappy young woman.

Fergus seemed to read his thoughts. As he pulled at the oars, he said in a quietly jubilant voice, 'We're to be wed, Hamish. I'll stop the gossiping old Cailleachs. She's a fine lass is Kirsteen and I've been a fool of a man not to have wed her sooner.'

Hamish smiled happily. 'That's what I've been waitin' to hear, lad. When is it to be?'

'Not soon enough, Hamish. It's strange, but I feel a

different man altogether, not like myself at all. I was so tightly bottled up this morning I felt I could burst, now I feel I could shout to the world how happy I am. I haven't felt like that in years and it's all because of Kirsteen.'

Hamish felt honoured by the confidence and touched by the eager happiness of a man usually so withdrawn. Hamish was a happy man himself. All his life he had been contented but it wasn't until he married Maggie he felt really fulfilled. Maggie had brought him an ever greater contentment. With her he had found the richness of companionship coupled with a steadfast love and he thanked God every day for having allowed their paths to cross.

'I'm happy for you, Fergus,' he said simply. 'You've been a lonely man these years.'

Fergus drew a deep breath. 'If only Alick . . .'

'Don't worry about him,' said Hamish who silently cursed Alick his childishness. 'He won't spoil things for you, son! We'll find him out there and a damt warmed arse he needs for doin' such a thing!'

They were well away from the shore now.

'Mind my boat, Mr McKenzie!' yelled Ranald anxiously. 'She's a good one so she is!'

Canty Tam smiled secretively at the green swelling waves on the Sound.

'The Green Caillichs will get them,' he said softly, but with devilish assurance. 'They're out there waitin', their auld hag faces smilin' because today they'll have a Rhanna man!'

'You're daft, man,' said old Bob but he turned his eyes quickly from the boat. Many of the islanders

believed the legend of the Green Uisga Caillichs of
Rhanna Sound. They were the spirits of witches of
bygone days who had been cast from the island for
various evil practices. Now their ghosts roamed the
Sound and anyone venturing too far in a small boat
were likely victims. The Caillichs took many forms but
the most famous was a beautiful mermaid who turned
into a green, one-eyed monster when the victim was
lured far enough from the shore. Some claimed they
had seen the mermaids sitting on the rocks near the
treacherous Creags. The oldest man on Rhanna, ninety-
seven-year-old Tam the Plough, claimed he had
actually seen a mermaid turn into a green monster
and had managed to escape. 'Just by the skin of my
trousers' – because he had held a Celtic cross before
him and shouted for St Michael to smite the hag.
His simple faith had saved the day and earned him a
reputation for bravery. No Ceilidh was complete
unless Tam was there to repeat the tale which he
lavishly embroidered with each telling. He and Bob
had a friendly rivalry as to which was the best
Seanachaidh but both were equally popular with their
unending tales of water beasts, fairies, and witches.
They spoke with reverence about St Michael who
stemmed from the dim past of pagan rituals and who
was the patron saint of all who were in danger at land
or sea.

'St Michael will guard them,' muttered old Bob, but
Canty Tam shook his head.

'Not, it won't be so. The Uisga hags are gaining
strength. Look at them over yonder. I can hear their
skirls of laughter from here. It's the kind of sea they

like, all soft and swelling on the surface but below . . . boiling like a cauldron.'

Bob looked and saw the green swelling on the Sound and heard the thin threading moan of the wind rushing low over the water.

'You're daft, man,' he repeated but his voice was uneasy just the same.

Kirsteen stood nearby and listened. She knew all about the legends of Rhanna and she knew that the inhabitants held firm to their beliefs. Though they wouldn't always admit to it, they took precautions against those evil spirits that were said to abound in and around the island. Most of them wore Celtic crosses round their necks. Some of them were roughly carved from wood, but no matter how crude, they were a protection from a host of evils. Kirsteen had thought the ancient beliefs quite enchanting. She had been to several Ceilidhs in the homely crofts around Portcull. Curled warmly at blazing peat fires she had listened entranced as Gaelic songs filled the air or the plaintive notes of the fiddle brought the sigh of the sea and the rush of wind into the rooms. The highlight of the evening came when everyone settled to listen to the Seanachaidh, children and adults silently attentive while a lilting old voice told the tales that had passed through generations. Folklore, myths, and legends became frighteningly real in the warm, smoky rooms and, long after the stories were finished, the magic transmitted by the storyteller lingered on so that people scurried homewards clutching their crosses and children kept looking behind to make sure that no Caonteachs had deserted their water haunts in favour in haunting humans.

Since her affair with Fergus, Kirsteen had found her invitations to Ceilidhs growing less though she was still invited to partake of the odd Strupak. Suspecting that these gestures were merely a ruse to spier her into confiding her private affairs she had now started to refuse 'a crack and a cuppy' and by doing so incurred the islanders' hostility. Apparently nothing offended more than the refusal of a neighbourly gesture and she began to feel more and more outcast.

The charm of the islanders lay in their simple faith and barely concealed curiosity. Now that the curiosity was directed at her she was somewhat disenchanted and the islanders sensed her defensive attitude. Though she still received the customary exchanges she felt herself excluded from the vital centre of things though she knew a lot of it was her own fault. The folk-lore she had found so charming was crude and rather frightening when applied to everyday life and she shivered at Canty Tam's words of doom and moved away.

The boat was lost to sight now. Portcull lay in a bay, sheltered by rocky outcrops on the southern side, and by the steep cliffs that rose from Port Rum Point, a finger of land half a mile out to sea on the western side. It was on the other side of this finger that the Sgor Creags lay and the opening of the caverns known as Claigionn an Garadh which meant Caves of the Skulls.

Kirsteen made her way past the schoolhouse and began to climb the rough track to the high grassy base of the Point. She was aware that several islanders were dispersing to their cottages along the track and she quickened her pace to get away from their following eyes. A drizzling rain was beginning to fall and the mist was coming down quickly. She glanced inland and saw that the mountains were blotted out and thin curls of vapour floated in patches over the moors.

A group of sturdy mountain sheep were grazing contentedly on the short turf atop the cliffs but when she approached they bleated plaintively as if complaining about the weather. Kirsteen gazed at the greeny-grey waters far below and her heart leapt when she saw the boat heading round the Point. It looked tiny, the two men in it almost invisible. One of those men, a tiny dot barely discernible, was the man she loved more than her own life, the other a dear friend whom she knew had been a trusted member of the Laigmhor household for many years. Of Alick's boat there was no sign. She thought about him with pity and anger. She liked him and was sorry that his life was so shallow and empty but she was angry because he had ruined some of the most beautiful moments of her life. She cast her mind back to Fergus's marriage proposal, his words of love, the safe comfort of his arms, and his lips on hers, firmly sealing their love. Then those plans, so full of happiness. He had sworn his life to her and she had promised she would give him five sons, one of whom would surely carry on tilling Laigmhor soil. He had laughed then, a loud happy laugh, and swept her up in his arms as if she were swansdown.

It seemed impossible that a mere thirty minutes later she would be standing alone on top of a cliff with the gulls crying and the rain clinging to her eyelashes till she felt she was looking through a gossamer curtain. It was a fine rain but damp and cloying. Her dress was cold against her skin and she shivered again and wished she had stopped off at the schoolhouse for a cardigan. The mist was closing in fast and she could barely make out the sea below. A finger of icy terror curled round her heart. Abruptly she fell to her knees and put her wet hands to her face.

'Oh God,' she sobbed, 'keep them safe! And . . .' She stopped and looked far beyond the cliffs to the Sound of Rhanna. 'Please, St Michael,' she whispered, 'bring my Fergus back to me.'

Somehow just saying the words comforted her. She had dismissed all the tales she heard as folklore but she believed they had a grain of truth at their core and realised that below her so-called civilised veneer she was perhaps just as superstitious as the islanders themselves. She felt sick and dizzy and didn't hear the footsteps behind. Old Bob was there, his gnarled hands helping her to her feet, his voice rough but soothing.

'There now, lass, dinna greet so! My, you're cauld as ice. Here, take my jacket. Och yes now, I'm warm from the climb up!'

He tucked the hairy tweed round her cold body and put an awkward arm round her slim shoulders.

'Come away down now, you'll not do any good up here. The gods are wi' your man and as soon as the tide turns we'll all be out on that old finger down yonder, so dinna fear, lass. I came up to tell you we are all having a Strupak down at Todd's house. His wife says to tell you she'll keep you some hot broth. Come on now, there's a lass.'

Kirsteen leaned against him and cried. He was old and tough and it felt good to let herself be led by him. He murmured soothing words of comfort all the way to Todd's cottage where a small group of villagers had gathered. Without knowing how it happened she was sitting by a cosy fire with a mug of broth in her hands. Words of reassurance drifted to her ears and she looked up to see well-known faces whose concern for her showed in kindly glances. Somehow she knew she was in the bosom of the island once more and even more a part of it than she had ever been.

She listened to the men laying plans to man one of the bigger boats when the mist cleared a little and her heavy heart lightened with hope.

Alick wasn't out to sea ten minutes before he was regretting his hasty flight. It had been warm five minutes before but now a nasty wind knifed through his thin shirt. Boy of the seas of Rhanna many years ago, he was still master of the waves but years of soft living had weakened his fibres and he began to shake with a mixture of cold and the subsiding of an anger that had tensed his whole being. It had been a rare spurt of temper but extremely violent. In a welter of feelings he had stormed over the fields, hating Fergus for his strength. His face throbbed where his brother's iron fists had struck and the warm taste of blood filled his mouth. He spat out two teeth, dismayed to discover that one was from the front. His looks were his passport. His charming tongue and quick warm smile had won him endless nights of intimacy with endless women. He was a womaniser and knew it, yet there was never any fulfilment. Once he had won them over, his appetites satisfied, he soon tired of them and went on restlessly, hopelessly, plunging deeper into loneliness.

Kirsteen had been an exciting challenge. He had spent his nights at Laigmhor thinking about ways to win her over. She was even more of a challenge because she belonged to Fergus and because there was a dignity about her, a quiet, sweet burning of her inner strength that set her apart from all the women he had ever possessed. Today that slim body of hers had almost belonged to him. He wanted her more than any woman he had yet known and would have taken her against her will if there had been no other way. What a triumph then over Fergus, to have been inside the body of the girl that Fergus thought was his alone. The nearness of her had driven him crazy and all the time he was talking and laughing the heat inside him had risen to an unbearable pitch. Then the feel of her, the cool flesh under that thin dress, her breasts heaving with her struggles.

Then those awful pounding fists crashing into him, hurting every bone of his body. He was defenceless against the bullying power of his brother. He felt deflated and unmanly, humiliated beyond measure in the eyes of Kirsteen, the woman who moments before he had rendered helpless under his own lustful strength. What kind of man did he look now? She would pity him and wonder what he was made of. Only able to prove himself in the bedroom, a coward at all other times.

Well, he would show everyone what he was made of. He meant the words he hurled at the men on the shore. He wasn't afraid of the sea but Fergus was. They would go off and tell him and he could hardly refuse to come looking for his own brother. Let Fergus show them what he was made of . . . if he dared.

The boat rocked and Alick cried like a little boy. The tears mingled with the blood frothing from his nose. 'It hurts! It hurts!' he sobbed like the small boy who had ran to his mother with every little wound.

'Oh Mother! Fergus is a bugger for hitting me! I hate him so I do!'

He shipped his oars and buried his face in his hands. He had rounded Port Rum Point and was out of sight of Portcull. His little boat bobbed in the green swell coming in from the Sound and he sobbed, great heartrending sobs that were snatched greedily by the threading wind and tossed over the sea. For quite some time he cried out his heart and gradually felt better. Mirabelle was always saying, 'A good greet cures a host o' ails', and she was right. A man couldn't sit down and weep when he felt like it but he was alone now. Bobbing in his little boat out on the Sound he felt completely alone and very peaceful. The sea had always soothed him and he felt a regret that he hadn't stayed on Rhanna and become a fisherman. The water had peace and power; wind and tide decreed its moods and it was a force to be respected. But it could be kind to the unafraid. If a man could float and hold on to his courage the sea would carry him without the shell of a boat under him.

Alick stopped crying and looked about. The sea was strengthening. He had left the shelter of Portcull Harbour and was facing a glassy heaving swell at the tip of the Point. The tide was coming in quite fast but there was still a narrow strip of shore all round the high finger of land. He looked at the Sgor Creags standing out of the sea, stark and grey. The water seethed at their base and the glassy troughs of sea slid towards them to break in waves several feet high, washing the pinnacles in creamy spray. It was a wild sight. Alick was well aware of the presence of countless smaller rocks that surrounded Sgor Creags that were covered at high tide and a death trap to the unwary because they could trap a small boat and finally lure it against the Creags.

He stared up at the wind-battered cliffs that ran the length of the Point, getting steeper as they went inland. At their base they were barnacled and green, slimy with rotting seaweed, but above the tide line they rose dark and forbidding, hewn into fantastic patterns by wind and time.

The cold whipped through Alick's clothes and goose-pimples rose on his flesh. He was in a dilemma of his own making. The heat of his anger was burned out and he had no intention now of letting himself be battered to death on the Sgor Creags. But how could he go back with his tail between his legs? He would be the laughing stock of Rhanna. He couldn't stay out on the Sound too long either. He was hungry and cold and his whole face throbbed like a giant toothache.

For a time he rowed aimlessly, his dark head sunk on his chest, his shoulders hunched miserably. He was drifting nearer the Creags and he started when his keel crunched ominously against a hidden rock. He pulled away and came to a swift decision. He would hole up in one of the tunnels. He shuddered as he looked at the black holes in the cliff face but at least they would afford some protection from the elements. He knew the caves would fill with water but he would scramble to one of the tunnels higher up. He gave little or no thought to the men who would doubtlessly come looking for him. At the moment all his planning and motivation were for the comfort and preservation of Alick McKenzie, and time was running out because barely a foot of sand remained uncovered at the caves.

He pulled steadily and the keel grounded. Swiftly he jumped from the boat and, pulling it to one of the higher caves he knew never completely filled at high tide, tied it firmly to a rocky spur. He began clambering up the slippery rock but it was no easy matter: he slipped several times, tearing his clothes, cutting hands and knees on jagged holds. Eventually he slithered into a tunnel and lay panting. It was dark and smelled of rotting seaweed but at least it afforded shelter. He propped himself against the rough wall. He was trembling and sore all over and he sucked peevishly at his bloody hands. Edinburgh, with its clean streets and buildings, seemed a million miles away. He thought of a lot of things but most of all about his own plight. Something scuttled in the dark depths behind him and he stiffened when he heard the unmistakable high whistling of rats.

'Oh, God help me!' he sniffed. A thought came unbidden to his frightened mind. Those nights of the Ceilidhs of his youth and the old men with their stories of sea hags. What did they call them? Green water Caillichs? He looked down at the sea. It was green, a deep sea-green. He had laughed at the old men behind their backs and scoffed at the old legends but now – in this horrible dank tunnel with the waiting sea churning below – he could begin to believe anything. He would wait till dark then he would go back to Laigmhor, collect his clothes, and leave Rhanna in the morning. He was thankful that tomorrow was the day the ferry came: how awful if he'd had to wait a few days and everyone laughing behind his back.

The plan was simple and seemed quite feasible. Despite his state of discomfort a smile curved his cracked lips. He felt in his pocket, found his cigarettes, lit one, and leaned back against the damp wall to wait for the tide to turn.

Fergus and Hamish came round Port Rum Point and met the strong green swell from the Sound. They were surrounded by rolling mist and could just discern the looming cliffs.

'We'll use them to guide us,' said Hamish. 'But we can't go too far along or the damt Creags will tangle wi' us.' He laughed cheerily and Fergus, looking at his solid kilted figure, was glad of his reassuring company. It was eerie there in the mist with everything familiar blotted out. The slap of the waves against the boat seemed strangely loud but he knew it was because the thick blanket of har had deadened other sound.

'We'd better shout,' he said and proceeded to bawl Alick's name. Alick, dozing in his tunnel, heard the sound faintly. He recognized his brother's voice and for a reason unknown to himself his heart pounded with relief. He was feeling ill and miserable and didn't care now if he went back to Rhanna in disgrace. He had been a fool to behave the way he had and had deserved the beating he got. He crawled to the edge of the tunnel and cocked his head to fathom the direction of sound. There were two voices frantically calling his name and he cupped his hands to his mouth but only a croak came out. He swallowed hard and grimaced in pain. His throat was swollen and sore. He had slept with his mouth open because his swollen nose had made breathing difficult. Dried blood had gathered at the back of his throat and he swallowed again and again in an effort to relieve the dryness.

The voices were growing fainter. He cupped his hands once more and managed to shout, 'Here, I'm here!' but there was no answer. 'I'm here!' he cried again in despair. He sank to the floor and hugged his trembling body tightly. Fear made him feel sick and he vomited, retching agonizingly till he emptied his stomach.

Fergus had shipped the oars while he shouted. So eagerly did he listen for an answering cry that several vital minutes passed before Hamish noticed that the cliffs were no longer visible. Both men looked at each other in dread. Curls of mist drifted wraith-like over the water and the steady leaden rain soaked them to the skin. It was frightening not knowing which way to go. Too near the Sgor Creags and their boat would be smashed to driftwood, too far and they could drift into the open sea. Sweat broke on Fergus's brow and his eyes searched desperately for the cliffs but the mist had swallowed them up. The boat rocked alarmingly and his stomach churned in fear. It wasn't a particularly rough sea but there was a calm menace in the green swell that was far more forbidding than a superficial show of strength and Fergus knew that deep undercurrents were meeting and boiling.

Hamish wasn't afraid of the water, it was the mist that worried him. The sea was charitable enough as long as they could see where they were going but they couldn't and were in an extremely precarious position. He would have felt happier if they had been further out on the Sound away from the Creags and the numerous rocks surrounding them. The rain had drenched him. His red hair was plastered against his head and his kilt clung in miserable folds round his legs. He thought of Maggie and the warm meal she would have waiting. He thought of the warm happy feeling the sight of her always brought and just thinking about it brought a small measure of that feeling now. Life was so good; he loved his work but now he looked forward to the evenings, Maggie with her knitting, he with his pipe, Whisky and numerous cats draped over the furniture. They could be silent, so peacefully silent with Maggie's needles clicking, Whisky snoring, and the clock ticking sonorously. Or they could talk for hours about all sorts of things. Maggie wasn't just a woman who kept the house, she was extremely well versed in many subjects for she had travelled a good deal and could tell him about places he had never been to. He smiled when he thought about the intimate little habits they had adopted. Before bed they each had their own tasks, his to secure the hen runs and rabbit hutches, hers to wind clocks and settle the fire. Before he got back to the house she would hide from him then pounce from some dark recess and loudly cry, 'Keek a boo!' It was a kind of hide and seek they had played when first married and somehow the habit continued. It was 'their game'. They chuckled about it, wondering what the more sedate islanders would say if they knew. In kirk he only had to whisper 'Keek a boo' to make Maggie hide her laughter in a hanky.

He was still thinking of Maggie when an enormous silky swell hurled the boat on to a hidden spur of rock. For a moment he was aware of everything, the seething foam choking and blinding him as the boat tilted him into the sea, the wild crashing roar of water meeting rock, the white face of Fergus bobbing nearby, the cold ruthless water pulling relentlessly. He raised both arms and grabbed at the boat but even as he did so he knew he should never have pulled at the bow. It catapulted towards him. He heard the thud and knew it was deep inside his own head. He saw the blood foaming in the waves. Before the world and all his senses left him he heard Fergus screaming his name, over and over in nameless horror. His lips moved forming the name 'Maggie' before all that he had known and loved in life went blank and empty and the sea threw his body scornfully against the waiting Sgor Creags.

Fergus saw all that happened through a curtain of water. He heard a hysterical voice calling over and over for Hamish and hardly recognized it as his own. All the self-control that he had built round himself gave way and he began to scream in panic. He watched Hamish's helpless body being smashed over and over against the rocks till it was broken and bleeding. A giant wave lifted it and for a moment it was suspended before it was thrown high to wedge between two of the smaller pinnacles. Fergus looked at the once proud body, at the shining red hair, and the sightless staring eyes and he knew he was crying like a child. He thrashed wildly, trying to free himself from the horror of the Sgor Creags and their victim, but found that only one of his arms would work. The other hung in the water and now he felt the excruciating pain. His whole being had been so tortured at the sight of Hamish he had given no thought to himself. He tried again to lift his arm and cried aloud in agony. The sea was lifting him, taking him to the Creags, and he threshed wildly with his legs and one arm. He looked for the boat and saw that it had completely capsized and was being smashed to driftwood. With an awkward sideways scuttle he fought the tide and gradually took himself away from the rocks. His heart was pounding and he felt giddy. For a moment he stopped to rest and wondered why the water round him was tinged with pink. He looked up and noticed that the mist had cleared enough for the cliffs to be visible and thought bitterly that if it had lifted a few minutes before Hamish would still be alive.

He had managed to get well away from the Creags. They loomed like grey ghosts through the thinning mist. He shivered and his throat constricted when he thought of his friend dead because he had again wanted to help the McKenzies. His head was spinning alarmingly and he knew he could swim no further. Why had he come out here anyway? Alick! To find Alick! He tried to shout but couldn't. He blamed himself for everything. There had been no need for him to have beaten Alick the way he did. It was an unfair fight. Alick had never been good with his fists but it had been the sight of him with Kirsteen . . . Kirsteen, dear lovely Kirsteen, she was like Helen sometimes the way she laughed. Helen and Kirsteen, Shona and Helen, they all looked the same because their faces were blurring in his mind.

Mirabelle came to him suddenly – she darted into his mind and wouldn't leave it. She seemed very near and he held out his arm to cling to her motherly bosom. It was growing dim, and briefly he wondered if it was getting dark. His senses reeled; he was floating in the sky and looking up at wavering water and the sky he was floating in reminded him of a sunset because of the pink patches all round him.

Alick looked out of the tunnel and saw that the mist was clearing. He trembled with relief. It was horrible in the tunnel: rats scampered in the dark and insects crawled everywhere. He wondered where Hamish and Fergus were; it was a good half-hour since they had called. He hoped they hadn't gone out too far but knew that once the mist cleared they would be safe because a fishing boat would pick them up. Alick was worrying more about himself. The claustrophobic panic he had experienced in the dank misty tunnel had made him resolve to get out as soon as possible. It would be easy enough to scramble down the cliff for a few feet then jump into the water where he could swim to the cave where he had left the boat. The thought of the cold water didn't appeal to him but it was better than waiting in the rancid tunnel till the tide turned.

He stripped to his underpants and shivered. It wasn't cold but damp and cloying and he wasn't used to such discomfort. He peered out again and saw that the mist was clearing. At first it had hovered several feet above the water but a warm wind was dispersing it. He smiled to himself. No one would give him much sympathy when he got back, except perhaps Mirabelle. She would fuss discreetly and make him drink hot broth and a toddy or two. Yes, good old Mirabelle would salve the wounds of mind and body. He gathered his clothes into a bundle and tied them together to throw them into the water. He would have to change into the sodden garments because he couldn't very well prance through the village wearing nothing but underpants. He smirked. That would give the old gossips something to get their tongues round. He glanced at the dark object floating about a hundred yards from the caves and thought nothing of it. There was always flotsam coming in with the tide. But something oddly familiar about the object made him look again and he saw his brother's dark head sticking out of his brown working jacket.

'Fergus!' he cried and without hesitation dived straight into the water. He reached his brother with a few swift strokes. At first he thought the helpless figure was without life. The face was deathly pale and there was no sign of breathing, but a pulse beat faintly at the temple and Alick let out a sigh of thankfulness.

'Fergus!' he shouted again but there was no response and he realised his brother was deeply unconscious. He wondered what had kept him afloat then saw the piece of driftwood Fergus had clung to before his senses left him. It had wedged into his shirt causing a thick weal on his chest but at least it had saved his life – what was left of that life.

Alick worked swiftly. He pulled Fergus to him and removed the piece of wood, then he put him on his back, holding his chin above water. He had decided to swim to the cave where he would try and haul Fergus into the boat and get rid of some of the sea from his lungs. It was then that Alick saw something that made him feel faint with shock. His brother's left arm was a mangled bloody mess. Skin and flesh mingled together and the bone of the upper arm had splintered and projected several inches from torn flaps of skin. Alick looked away in horror. He retched but nothing would come from his empty belly. In that moment he felt a sorrow and a love for his brother that he hadn't experienced since those far-off days of hero-worship. He felt it was all his fault and he gathered Fergus to him and wept into his wet black hair.

'Forgive me, Fergie,' he whispered brokenly but he knew that his brother had a long battle for life ahead of him and the thought spurred him into action. He swam to the cave with his burden. The boat had risen with the tide till it almost touched the roof but he struggled gamely to get the helpless body aboard. It was an impossible task. Fergus was slim but muscular and heavier built than Alick, and after several exhausting minutes Alick gave up trying. He leaned against the boat wearily.

'It's up to God now, Fergus,' he panted, 'if He can give me the strength to keep us both afloat till help comes.'

He didn't know how long he floated. It could have been minutes or hours. Dazed with weariness he kept drifting into sleep only to jump into wakefulness at the feel of Fergus slipping from his grasp.

He had no idea of time, but in fact only thirty minutes had passed. Voices floated over the water.

'Here! Over here!' he croaked joyfully. He summoned his remaining strength and floundered out of the cave. The men saw him and two jumped into the water to help.

'Mind his arm,' warned Alick as his brother was taken from him and dragged into the boat. The men stared.

'Good God, what a bloody mess!' whispered old Joe. 'It's the doctor for him or he'll die if he's not gone already!'

Alick slithered into the boat. There was no willing hands to help him.

'What's become o' Hamish?' asked old Bob grimly.

Alick shook his head. 'Don't – know, Fergus was alone – no one else.'

'And where is my boat?' asked Ranald, but no one was listening.

The mist had cleared considerably and the sun was breaking through. It gleamed on the Sgor Creags and the men saw the small splash of colour that was Hamish's kilt. They looked harder and saw that the Sgor Creags had claimed one of the finest men of Rhanna. They hung their heads and in silence took the boat round Port Rum Point to Portcull.

Kirsteen was waiting with a knot of others. She saw Alick stagger from the boat. In different circumstances he would have been an object for laughter in his drooping sodden underpants but no one gave him a second glance. They were watching the helpless figure of Fergus being carried ashore. In a dream of horror she watched the men carrying him up the shingle and for several moments she remained in a trance-like state. Her hands had turned icy cold and she felt numb. She so desperately wanted to run to that beloved figure, to find out if he was still of this life, but she was paralysed with the enormity of fear that he had been taken from her. Then her feet took wings and she fled over the shore.

'He's in a bad way, lass,' said Bob before she could speak. He raised his voice. 'Will someone ride over for the doctor? Tell him to come quick!'

'To the schoolhouse!' cried Kirsteen.

Todd the Shod scurried off and the men carried Fergus gently away.

'Where's Hamish?' asked Mathew anxiously. 'I told Maggie he'd be late but I didny think this late. She'll be keepin' his supper warm. Is he comin' in another boat?'

'He'll never sup again,' said old Bob grimly.

Canty Tam smiled with satisfaction. 'I knew the Uisga hags would have a Rhanna man . . .' He glanced towards the group of men carrying Fergus. 'And maybe another before the night's over!'

Bob was old but his fists were iron hard and Canty Tam never quite knew how he landed with such force on the rough shingle because by the time his head stopped spinning old Bob had joined the rest of the men toiling towards the schoolhouse.

Chapter Ten

Fergus floated in a nightmare world of fever and pain. He knew not where he was. At times he felt himself bobbing in an inky black sea. The water roared in his ears and his bursting lungs fought for air. From afar he heard terrible groans that he knew came from himself yet they were part of another self over which he had no control. He was drenched in moisture and someone with gentle hands kept wiping his brow but how could they be so foolish as to think they could wipe away the sea that kept engulfing him. Hamish bobbed beside him but always just out of reach. It was awful the way Hamish stared at him, a blank stare from eyes of death, but how could anyone be dead who had been so vibrantly alive moments before? That sea near Hamish was spuming with red, bloody foaming sea, washing in and out of the battered gaping hole in Hamish's skull. That other self with so little control over its emotions let out a hellish scream and Fergus laughed and cried with pity.

Sometimes the black curtains that veiled his mind were pulled aside and he saw white muslin curtains blowing in the breeze and white wallpaper sprinkled with blue flowers.

Voices came to him and his senses struggled to place them in the faces that floated before him. A little girl with bright hair and blue eyes, a lovely little lass, but sad and lost looking.

And a young woman, with hair that gleamed like corn, and a delicate sensitive face. Her mouth was firm but soft and the very grace of her features made her beautiful. It wasn't Helen; no, she was of another life, one which he felt himself to be on the brink of. It was there, barely out of reach, stretching into the caverns of velvet infinity. It would be so nice, so peaceful, to let himself drift through those caverns, to reach Helen who floated like a dazzling star at the furthermost depths. He called her name and the sound of it reverberated back, back, into the black tunnels, vibrating till he felt he must scream. He was afraid now of those depths and he struggled; great weights pulled at him dragging him down, down, but he gritted his teeth and pulled against them. He tried to cry out but now no sound would come. He knew he was opening his mouth but his throat was paralysed with fear of the dark depths surrounding him. Over and over he tried to call out and the wet tears of weakness and frustration mingled with the salt sea dripping from his forehead.

Kirsteen watched his struggles and her heart lay like a stone in her breast. Once more she wiped away beads of sweat from his face with a hand that trembled. She was so tired but would let no one else nurse him till she knew he was going to get better.

The folk of Portcull were kind. Fresh bread, bannocks, and bowls of broth were brought every day. Kirsteen was touched by these gestures yet she was too tired and worried to listen to the solicitous condolences offered by all and sundry. No matter how Rhanna folk felt about each other personally, when sickness came to one of them it was a matter of duty to call in and offer sympathy and help. A steady stream came and went from the sick room. It was Kirsteen's own bedroom; she had moved into a smaller room and Shona slept with her, snuggled in close like a lost little kitten.

All day feet clumped up and down stairs.

'Terrible, terrible just!' Behag Beag said the same thing each day. 'Ach, the poor laddie! A dreadful thing to be sure.'

Kirsteen knew the postmistress disliked Fergus and each day she tried to tell her not to utter her hypo-critical condolences but somehow she couldn't get the words out.

Shelagh wheezed in and did nothing but cry at sight of the deathly pale face on the pillow. 'Ach, my poor lad, he's like death warmed up and him not knowin' about poor Mirabelle and poor Hamish. It's terrible just! I don't think I'll ever complain aboot my winds again and all these good folk dead and dyin'.'

Her words weren't designed to cheer a flagging spirit and Kirsteen breathed sighs of relief when the old woman left.

Dodie was the most constant and surprisingly the most comforting of visitors.

'He breeah,' he unfailingly greeted, stooping low to allow his tall gaunt figure through the low door. Because of the camped ceilings he always stood in the middle of the room and from this vantage point offered all sorts of hopeful predictions about Fergus's future. He was gruff and shy but in his guileless way he gave Kirsteen hope. Each day he brought a small gift; perhaps a sea urchin dried and cleaned, an unusually shaped pebble, carefully chosen shells, or simply an early autumn leaf glowing with red and gold. 'To press into one o' these books you read, miss,' he explained shyly, anxious that so humble a gift would be acceptable to a fine lady.

Kirsteen was deeply touched by the gifts. Dodie's simple mind saw beauty in the treasures of nature. He looked at the sunset and saw its glorious colours where a man of keener mind might look and see nothing but the sun going down.

He clearly worshipped Fergus and stared at him for minutes at a time. Love looked out of the normally dreamy eyes. Each time he went away he left behind his peculiar odour but he also left a feeling of hope and Kirsteen was grateful for even a grain of that.

The forty-eight hours since Fergus had been carried to the schoolhouse were like a nightmare. Fergus, unconscious on the couch in her little sitting-room, and the blood, so much blood from that poor mangled arm; she sitting beside him; thoughts, reality, all mixing together while she bathed the deep gash on his forehead. Alick hovering, making demented half-statements, blaming himself, crying like a baby, looking to her for a comfort she could not give.

Lachlan had seemed a long time in coming but it was only because each tick of the clock was another moment lost in the fight to save Fergus.

Then Lachlan, white-faced from a day already filled with painful feelings. His examination was quick and he wasted no time making a decision.

'Get ready the kitchen table, Kirsteen. The arm will have to be amputated or poison will set in.'

Kirsteen felt faint but went to the kitchen. Water was already boiling on the fire. Kate McKinnon and Merry Mary had kept a big pot ready for the purpose of making tea. Bob and several of the men had stayed, suspecting their help was going to be needed. They were drinking mugs of tea and smoking their pipes with the slow deliberate enjoyment of their generation. Word had got round about Mirabelle and there was a lot for them to talk about.

Kirsteen hadn't known about Mirabelle and she leaned against the doorpost.

'No,' she whispered. 'Oh God no! Mirabelle – Hamish . . . the bairn, where is she?' Her voice rose. 'Poor little Shona, she'll be so lost already and she doesn't even know about her father yet! He's to lose his arm! I've to prepare the table, Lachlan is operating here!' Her voice broke with utter despair. Kate McKinnon put a heavy arm round her shoulders.

'There, lass, greet now for it will do you good. Don't worry about the bairn, she's wi' Phebie.' She led Kirsteen to a chair. 'Sit you down – we'll get ready the table. It's no' the first time an operation's been done o' the spot. Auld McLure had to tak' off a pluchie's foot that got mangled wi' a heuck. Right out in the middle o' a field it was. Poor Sandy, he died – pneumonia set in but it was himself to blame. He swung that damty heuck like it was a wee pocket-knife. And there's myself,' she puffed out her bosom proudly, 'all but brought our Wullie into the world without help. Nancy was there right enough but she was only a bairn and couldny do very much! Aye, there's many a thing has to be done in a hurry, lass!'

But Kirsteen was listening with only half an ear. She was watching the sturdy wooden table being scrubbed with soap and boiling water and she shuddered at the thought of Fergus lying on it, not knowing he was losing his arm. She dreaded to think of the time of his knowing. Another man might at first be shocked but would learn to accept what had happened, but would Fergus? Could he, with his stubborn, independent pride, be happy to live without every one of his faculties in perfect order? Would he in time thank God it had been his left arm or would he blame God for what had happened both to himself and Hamish?

She wondered if he knew about Hamish. He certainly didn't know about Mirabelle. She prayed for his recovery yet dreaded his awakening to a world from which he had lost so much. But he still had his little girl and he still had her. Would he weigh those things against his losses? Did he love them both enough? Tears coursed down her cheeks and she shivered though the fire had brought a flush to her face. Merry Mary handed her a cup of tea. It was laced with brandy and made her throat burn but the heat glowed through her and when the men came in carrying Fergus she was able to help lower him gently on to the table.

Biddy had arrived. She looked old and very tired and Kirsteen realised she had just come from Mirabelle's deathbed. Her eyes were red and Kirsteen shook herself from her stupor and went to the hall where Biddy was removing her coat. The two women looked at each other. Biddy's chin trembled and Kirsteen gathered her into her arms. Neither said a word but the unspoken bond of their heartache was enough. Biddy gave a watery sniff and blew her nose. 'I'm fine now, lass, just an old fool I am but she was – ach she was my good friend – none better – there's gey few o' them left I can tell you! But it's sair your ain hert must be, my poor lass.' She laid her hand on Kirsteen's arm and a smile lit her weary eyes. 'Come on now, into battle. We must patch together that young upstart in there.'

'Biddy!' Lachlan's voice was threaded with impatience and unease. It was a disquieting sensation to see powerful, self-willed Fergus McKenzie lying so helpless, so completely reliant on the help of others. Lachlan's profession made him only too aware of human frailties but he had learned to accept its demands. How to tell loving parents their child was doomed, how to impart the news of the passing of a loved one, how to speak of a wasting disease? Time had given him the answers but it did not lessen the pain or joy of each experience. He had learned much about people and, early in his career, found that the humblest of humans had their dignity.

Fergus had dignity – that was a good point in anyone – but he also had a fierce pride.

Lachlan looked at the waxen features of the man who had ignored him for ten years. God, was it really that long? Yes, it did seem a long time, yet, was it not just yesterday that Fergus had accused him of Helen's death? Fergus had killed everything with those accusations of long ago. For a long time he had wondered about his abilities. Could he have saved Helen? He had fought so hard for her life but the battle had been in vain. Doubts had crept into his mind like thick black poisonous threads. No one but Phebie had known about them but even her staunch love had weakened at his continuing refusal to let her have another child. In the end, love had won but it had been touch and go, just another example of how susceptible human beings were in the face of adversity, yet love itself was strength and its power couldn't be denied.

Love and hate. Which was the stronger emotion? Fergus had loved with an intensity that made love itself a frightening emotion. He had hated too. Lachlan still remembered the dour black hate in Fergus's voice but it had been a hate born of grief and Lachlan had known that Fergus would one day regret his bitter words. He had regretted them and tried to make amends but by then it was too late.

Lachlan felt the sweat break on his brow. Everyone was looking at him strangely. He was delaying too long, they knew it as he did. In that moment all his old doubts came back, but he knew now that ten years was too long for two men to hate each other. But he didn't hate Fergus, on the contrary he liked the man in a strange sort of way. In the old days Fergus had brought an excitement to him, not the thrill a woman brings, but the excitement of shared male pursuits. There had been an affinity between them, a feeling of respect for the other's mood, when they spoke it meant something, when they were silent it was a shared contentment.

Carbolic fumes and tobacco smoke filled the stuffy atmosphere and Lachlan's head reeled. He knew why he was delaying. Fergus had accused him once before of letting go of something he should have saved; when he woke, and found his arm gone, would he accuse Lachlan of removing something he could have saved? Lachlan knew he couldn't bear such an accusation again. From someone else yes, from Fergus no, because after all these years he wanted to know McKenzie again, he couldn't waive the chance of a reconciliation by removing that arm.

Biddy had sterilized the instruments and laid them on a small table by his side. Everyone was motionless, the silence only broken by old Bob wiping his nose on his sleeve. He was at the head of the table ready to hold Fergus still if he should move during the operation.

Kate McKinnon was presiding over pots of water, keeping them at boiling point. Kirsteen had come forward, ready to help if needed, though she looked so pale Biddy ordered her to sit down.

'No, Biddy,' she said with quiet determination, 'I must help.'

They all turned as Alick came through the door. He had gone back to Laigmhor to change from the baggy trousers loaned by Tam McKinnon. The memory of the quiet house, with Mirabelle dead in her room, was with him still and his face was gaunt and grey. He was exhausted but unable to rest.

'Is . . . it done?' he croaked painfully.

Lachlan shook his head. 'No . . . no I can't! It's a job for a hospital.'

A general murmur or horror filled the air and Biddy looked at him sharply. 'Havers, laddie! There's no way of gettin' him to a hospital in time!'

'I can't save that arm,' groaned Lachlan. 'Bone, flesh, nerves, they're all mangled together! It's not humanly possible!'

'We know that, lad!' cried Bob gruffly. 'Just tak' the bloody thing off! If you leave it it will just poison the rest o' him! McKenzie's not a god, man! He's flesh and blood like the rest o' us and can die the same!'

Sweat ran into Lachlan's eyes making them smart. His hands trembled. 'He'll never know how bad the arm was! He'll say I could have saved it! He'll blame me if I cut it off, damn him!'

It was a cry from the soul and Kirsteen knew what his thoughts were.

'Lachlan, listen to me,' she said quietly. He looked at her and she saw the naked doubts in his brown eyes. 'Bob's right – Fergus is no different from any of us. You're a fine doctor, everyone on Rhanna trusts you.' There was a murmur of assent. 'Take off the arm, he'll die if you don't. Fergus will thank you, not blame you. I love him, Lachlan! Och, please give him a chance to live! Take off the arm!'

Another murmur of agreement rippled gently but still Lachlan hesitated. Alick whispered to Kirsteen, then went to a cupboard and uncorked a bottle of whisky. He took it to Lachlan and held it to his lips.

'It will steady you, doctor,' he assured gently. 'Take

a good swig, we all know what it's like to have a bit of the shakes!'

Lachlan drank. The bottle was passed from man to man and Kate McKinnon took a generous mouthful.

'I'll have a sip,' said Biddy with dignity and gulped so much old Joe had to thump her on the back. The incident relaxed the tenseness of the atmosphere and Lachlan scrubbed his hands once more. 'Ready, Biddy!' he said evenly.

'Ready, lad,' she said and passed him the scalpel.

Kirsteen never knew how she managed to stay on her feet but every pair of hands was needed. Blood ran under the knife and she swabbed it away. In a sick dream she heard the saw rasping on bone. Her legs wobbled but she mopped the life blood of Fergus with one hand and wiped sweat from Lachlan's brow with the other. Biddy was busy with instruments and Bob, stolid and calm, held Fergus's dark head in his gnarled brown hands.

Fergus groaned but Bob cradled him as if he were a baby and spoke in his lilting voice though he knew Fergus couldn't hear a word.

The operation was finished by the dubious light of paraffin lamps and it was Alick who carried away the bucket containing the grisly remains of his brother's arm. He stumbled to the shore, barely able to see for the tears coursing down his face. It was a night of fresh salt wind and racing green waves. He waded into the sea and disturbed a flock of gulls resting on a sand bank. They rose and screamed at him. He swung the bucket, throwing the contents far into the water, the gulls wheeled and cried, then descended in a cloud of flapping wings and tearing beaks.

'Eat it, you filthy scavengers!' cried Alick, his voice choking with sobs. 'It's no use to him now! Eat it, damn the lot of you!'

Fergus was in bed when he got back, the thickly wrapped stump of his arm resting on pillows to stop the blood flow.

'He's needing blood badly,' said Lachlan. 'I must take samples from everyone to find his group. Will you go and ask Biddy to round up as many volunteers as she can, Alick? I've still a lot to do here.'

In the end it was Alick who was the donor. He watched his blood being drawn and felt strangely satisfied. The act was a salve for his conscience and he even managed to pull Biddy's leg, telling her she was the most glamorous vampire he had ever met.

Elspeth came in to relieve Kate McKinnon from tea-making and she reported that Shona was in bed and had cried herself to sleep.

Alick started up. 'That poor wee bairn! I'd nearly forgotten her and her heart bursting with grief. The devil take this hellish day! None of it will ever be the same again!' He took a few steps forward and collapsed in a dead faint.

Elspeth looked at him with contempt and her sharp nose went up in the air.

'A weakling if ever I saw one.' She inclined her head upwards. 'And the other, too proud for his own good. It's no wonder poor Mirabelle has gone to the grave. The McKenzies spell nothing but trouble. The Lord knows how the wee one will turn out! A wildcat like her father, I havny a doubt!'

Kirsteen went forward and deliberately slapped Elspeth on both cheeks. 'One for Alick and one for Fergus,' she said with a venom she hadn't known she possessed. 'Pity you only have one face, Elspeth, because I should have liked to have slapped you for Mirabelle who loved her family, and for Shona who's a lovely sweet child! Now please get out from under my roof! I'll make the tea.'

Elspeth held her red cheeks and backed away.

'You deserve Fergus McKenzie, you wee spitfire,' she spat. 'He might make an honest woman o' you yet!'

She flounced out and Lachlan put his hand over Kirsteen's.

'We'll have nothing but outrageous tempers and tight lips for a week now. Phebie will have a hell of a time and I'll be regaled with it all when I come in weary from my rounds.'

Kirsteen's chin trembled. 'Och, I'm sorry, Lachlan but I couldn't help myself.'

He grinned. 'Don't be sorry, she had it coming. Now, young lady, it's bed and rest for you. We'll dump Alick on the couch and let him sleep it off. He's just exhausted like the rest of us.'

The whole of Rhanna seemed to be gathered in the yard at Laigmhor for the double funeral. The two coffins lay side by side, set on chairs brought from the kitchen.

Hamish's body had been recovered the day after he had been smashed to death on the Sgor Creags. The men had found him washed up on the white sands of

Port Rum Point. He looked crumpled and small in death, so unlike the splendid figure that had graced Rhanna for nearly sixty years. His red beard was tangled with seaweed and his clothes were in tatters. The tide had tossed him uncaringly so that he lay face downwards, exposing the terrible gaping hole in his skull. Brain and tissue were gone, picked by sea birds, and the remaining shell had been cleaned out by the sea.

The men were sick at the sight. They were tough men, hardened by years of reaping the harvests of sea and land. They were used to grim sights and were not easily sickened but it was hard for them to look upon the pathetic sea-sodden man who had been beloved by all who knew him. One or two of his closer friends turned away quickly and young Matthew cried openly.

They wrapped him hastily and took him to shore. Maggie was there, old-looking, a black shawl thrown over her shoulders as she waited for the men to bring Hamish. They hadn't been sure of finding him. If the Sgor Creags held on to him no one would get near enough to bring in his body; if they released him the tides and cross currents of the Sound could take his body far away.

She gave a little cry when the shapeless bundle was lifted from the boat. She ran to it but the men wouldn't let her look. 'Remember him as last you seen him, Maggie,' said old Joe kindly. 'He was a fine proud big chiel and these must be your memories.'

She stood now at the front of the huge crowd that filled the cobbled yard. It was a warm blue day, bees droned, and the scent of roses from Mirabelle's garden hung heavy in the air.

Two minutes before, the crowd had been astonished at the arrival of Mr and Madam Balfour of Burnbreddie. The carriage turned into the yard and the islanders parted to make way. They looked suspiciously at Mrs Balfour. Was she simply being nosy? She had never come to an island funeral before. It wasn't unknown for the laird to make an appearance when the older inhabitants of Rhanna departed life. He had played with many of them in his boyhood and got quite sentimental over their respective deaths, but his wife attend an island funeral . . . never.

She stepped down from the carriage and her diminutive figure crossed the yard. The laird followed, splendid figure in lovat tweed jacket and swinging kilt. At his side walked Scott Balfour younger of Burnbreddie, not so spotty as in adolescence, but still weak of chin and pinched at the nose, his full, drooping mouth almost hidden by a large drooping moustache. His mother laid a posy of red roses on Mirabelle's coffin. For a long moment she stood looking down at the coffin lid. Wullie the carpenter had done a fine job. The wood of each coffin was as smooth as silk and a small metal plaque was affixed to each. Not all the islanders could afford such grand caskets – some were buried in no more than plywood boxes – but no matter the style the departed were always given a good send-off.

The laird's wife suddenly burst into tears and went quickly back to the carriage. She had genuinely liked Mirabelle. There had been a quality about her, a devotion to those she loved that went far beyond the call of duty. She also had dignity and a spirited defence for anything she thought unfair. She had given 'my leddy' the rough side of her tongue once or twice but that hadn't detracted from her character; in a way it enhanced it and all she stood for. Oh yes, she liked Mirabelle and she would miss – oh how she would miss the exquisite needlework that had enhanced Burnbreddie over the years. She would never get anyone else to do such lovely work. Madam Balfour of Burnbreddie sniffed into a lace handkerchief.

The laird stood, with his son, beside the coffins. The laird thought of Hamish. They'd had many a dram together, and sometimes a game of cards in the long winter evenings. Often they'd gone shooting on the moors and fished the rivers. He'd regaled Hamish with stories of his female conquests and the big man had laughed, his deep, full-chested laugh, that red hair and beard of his matching the fire of autumn's splendour. The laird did not know that Hamish laughed because the pictures presented in his mind were hilarious. The laird thought the laughter was sheer admiration for his wiles with women and he had puffed with pride. He hadn't seen so much of Hamish since his marriage to that Edinburgh woman. The laird glanced quickly at the unhappy widow and his watery eyes gleamed. He would have to see what he could do to take her mind off things.

Young Burnbreddie stared at the coffins with no feeling but resentment that his mother had coaxed him to come. He felt foolish and knew that many eyes were on him. One day he would be laird. He didn't fancy the idea much, but at least he could do a better job than the old idiot who was his father. He had caught the old boy too many times fooling around, his hands up the skirts of those giggling middle-aged frumps who were never away from Burnbreddie.

He knew Hamish of course, but Mirabelle – she was that old woman who, according to his mother, had licked the boots of McKenzies most of her life. Mirabelle . . . a thought came to mind . . . a sunny day on Rhanna, himself a small boy tripping and falling into bramble thorns his screams bringing a nice motherly-looking woman from a nearby farm. She had taken him in, bathed his wounds, then plied him with freshly baked scones and strawberry jam. He had gone back several times and played with Fergus and Alick, who was about his age. But he had been sent to boarding school and had learned social refinements that had taken away his natural ability to make friends from all walks of life. School taught him to speak in a rather nasal way, certain things just weren't done, but it was considered smart to laugh at nothing and to browbeat those weaker than oneself.

A pang went through young Balfour's heart. He looked again at Mirabelle's coffin. The sun was hot and the scent of roses strong. The impulse that took him to the rose garden was entirely unpremeditated. He took a penknife from his pocket and cut a single pure white rose which he took back to place on the old housekeeper's coffin. 'Goodbye, Mirabelle,' he said softly and went quickly back to the carriage.

A few of the men were drowning their sorrows. One of them held up the bottle and shouted, 'Will you drink to our departed friends, laddie?' It was a jeer more than an invitation because few liked the 'college cissy' who would one day be laird.

Young Balfour hesitated, then he turned into the crowd and took a hearty swig from the bottle. His back was slapped by several crofters. 'Guid on you, lad,' said one. 'Share our bottle and our spit. You're no' so proud after all.'

A smile touched Scott's lips. 'I'd sup whisky from a chanty,' he commented cheekily and the crofters smiled dourly, recognizing a wit to match their own.

It was time for the coffins to be taken to the Kirkyard. The pony and cart were brought into the yard. Maggie watched dry-eyed. She hadn't cried yet, her grief was too deep for tears. Whisky was whimpering at her feet, a small puppy-like sound of utter misery.

Shona watched Mirabelle's coffin laid next to that of Hamish and she clutched Phebie's hand tightly. She had lived at Slochmhor for the past three days, though she slept at the schoolhouse. Occasionally she was allowed to see her father but the sight of him made her want to cry. She could hardly believe he had lost one of those lovely strong brown arms. She wanted to hold his dark head in her own arms, to touch him and tell him she loved him but he didn't know her, he didn't know anyone and tossed in his own world of dark fantasies. It was awful to hear him cry out. She wanted to comfort him yet she herself so badly needed comfort. At night there was Kirsteen's warm arms and soothing words but during the day Kirsteen was so busy nursing her father and had little time for much else. Slochmhor became a haven with its smells of baking and medicines, baby powder and wet washing. She played with little Fiona but for some reason couldn't talk to Niall. He comforted her in his awkward boyish way and she wanted to feel safe in his arms but he wasn't mature enough and she was too young to put her feelings into words. She mourned for Mirabelle yet didn't really believe she was dead. Tomorrow or the next day she would go back to Laigmhor and the familiar smells of baking and lavender would greet her.

She felt the same about Hamish. It was all a bad dream. He was still in his homely cottage with Maggie fussing and the animals weaving in and out of his legs. Soon things would be back to normal and Mirabelle and Hamish would be back where they belonged. Her father would get well – he had to get well. Nothing could take away the tower of physical strength that was her father. So she set up the pathetic barriers of self-deception.

The cart trundled on to the road with the line of mourners, stretching behind like a curving caterpillar. Hamish had relatives from as far as England, but Mirabelle had no blood relations to weep for her. Her sisters were long dead, nieces and nephews scattered afar. Nevertheless there was many a wet eye as she was laid to rest.

Elspeth stood apart and tears cascaded down her thin cheeks. She felt she had lost her last friend. Mirabelle had been the only one who had been kind enough to give her comfort or advice. Now she was gone and she felt very alone. She didn't even have the stimulation of an argument with Hector to sharpen her life. He had died the year before. The manner of his death had surprised everyone and dumbfounded Elspeth. He had gone to bed one night, very intoxicated, and was found dead the next morning choked by his own vomit. Elspeth couldn't believe that, after all the years of wishing a dreadful fate on him, he should die so suddenly and uneventfully in his own bed.

In a strange way she missed him. Life had held a certain uncertainty when he was alive. She had something to anticipate even if it were only a verbal battle during which they poured out venomous words and malicious jibes. He taunted her for not being woman enough to bear children and she goaded him to fury by pointing out that their childless marriage was caused by his impotency through drink. 'Your very seeds are burnt dry, you drunken pig!' she would rage and in a blind anger he would throw her on the bed and forcibly take possession of her angular body. Secretly she had loved those times, the feel of him ripping into her rousing her in a way that none of his ordinary attempts at love-making had ever done. The brute force of him inside her, his animal cries of satisfaction, thrilled her every fibre and she had pressed her hands to her mouth to stop from crying out in pleasure. Guilt at such heathen feelings took her hastily to kirk on the Sabbath where she prayed half-heartedly for a deliverance from her barbaric desires.

Without Hector she was lost, without Mirabelle she was alone, and she cried sorely as the minister's sombre words boomed into the hush of the Kirkyard. Biddy bustled over. 'Here,' she hissed, passing Elspeth a small hip flask. 'Take a droppy, it will do you good.'

Elspeth quickly composed herself and looked disdainfully down her nose. 'I don't drink – thankin' you just the same!'

Biddy straightened her hat. 'Och well, if you feel like that . . .'

Elspeth looked at the old nurse's moist sad eyes. 'Och well, a wee drop then . . . to bid Mirabelle a guid journey.'

Biddy guided Elspeth round the bole of a large tree. 'To Mirabelle,' she whispered hoarsely.

'And Hamish,' said Elspeth taking a large gulp without a sign of distaste.

'You've tippled before?' said Biddy, whose eyes were rather dazed.

'Betimes,' agreed Elspeth and gulped greedily.

Far below, a little girl with sun-bright hair walked to the schoolhouse clinging to Alick's hand.

'Father might be awake,' she said, trying not to sound too eager because she knew that Hamish's death and her father's illness were all somehow linked to Uncle Alick.

'He might,' said Alick too brightly. He lifted his face to the breeze from the sea and prayed to God for strength. He thought briefly of Mary and his life in Edinburgh but it was unreal. Rhanna, the dear green island of his boyhood was, for the moment, his reality and he would not leave it till he had made peace with his brother.

Fergus wakened peacefully. He saw the shaft of sunlight dancing on the blue counterpane and wondered what time it was. It must be afternoon because the sun didn't come round to his bedroom till then. But what was he doing in bed in the afternoon? And it wasn't his bed or his room. There was a huge bowl of roses on the window ledge and the breeze from the open window wafted their scent to him. There was another smell, a smell of medication, the way Shona smelled when Mirabelle dressed the many wounds of childhood. Fergus hated the smell, it made him feel sick it was so strong. His mouth was dry and he felt himself floating strangely. He sat up quickly and his head swam. The room wavered and he blinked to clear his vision. It was a glorious day. The fields were green and a bee buzzed frenziedly in the bowl of roses: a summer sound. He had always liked to hear the bees droning and he smiled with pleasure. He could see the Kirk Brae from the window and a long procession winding slowly to the Kirkyard. It was very bright and he raised his hand to shield his eyes but something was wrong! His hand wouldn't come up: he looked and saw the bandaged stump at his left shoulder. For a long moment he stared, frowning in puzzlement, then the shrouds unfolded from his mind and he remembered. It all came back slowly but the weight of each memory pushed him back on the pillows where he lay staring unseeingly at the ceiling, his thoughts turned inward, raking up each hellish memory that had been the nightmare fantasies of his unconscious brain. The search for Alick, the mist that had caused the boat to drift on to those terrible Sgor Creags that had killed Hamish. But no! It wasn't the Creags, it wasn't the Creags, it was the boat! Hamish had grabbed the boat and the bow had smashed his head to pulp. Fergus felt his heart twisting in pain. The memories were growing clearer by the second. He remembered knowing that something had happened to his arm but he hadn't felt anything, just the blood flowing round him in that awful sea of death. And Alick! They hadn't found Alick! Was he dead too? He looked again at the window. The funeral procession, could it be his brother? But how could it be? They wouldn't bury him so quickly. Everything had happened so short a time ago. He gave a short cry of terror and sat up to look at the procession again. He saw the cart turning and twisting up the brae and on it were two coffins. Alick and Hamish! His heart pumped wildly and he dragged himself from his bed to stare from the window but his legs wouldn't hold him and he fell in a crumpled heap on to the window seat.

Kirsteen rushed into the room. 'Fergus! My darling, come back to bed!'

She gathered him to her and led him back to bed and she sat beside him and smoothed his dark hair. His forehead was hot and he was coughing, a harsh dry cough. She looked at the pallor of his cheeks and his black eyes staring at her intensely. She took his hand gently.

'How are you feeling, my Fergus?'

He ignored her question. 'Kirsteen, you're ill,' he cried with concern. 'You're so – so white and there's black circles under your eyes.'

'Don't worry about me, Fergus. I'm just a wee bit tired.'

He closed his eyes and his breath was laboured. 'Everything . . . so strange,' he whispered. 'I'm in your bed . . . that's right, isn't it, Kirsteen? We've loved in this bed, haven't we?'

'Yes, Fergus,' she answered huskily.

'My arm . . . it's gone . . . I knew it – out there in the sea – I knew I'd never use it again.'

She breathed a sigh of relief. The moments of truth were coming but the one she had dreaded most wasn't so bad as she had expected. He was struggling to ask more questions, feebly astonished that he had been unconscious so long.

'That's why – the funerals . . . I knew about Hamish! God, will I ever forget the sight of him . . . but the other – Kirsteen . . . ?'

Footsteps came quietly upstairs and Alick entered the room with Shona. Fergus struggled up, his eyes burning into Alick's.

'Alick . . . y-you're not dead?'

Alick's chin trembled. He wanted to cry, he wanted to run to his brother and beg his forgiveness. Instead he said, 'No, Fergus, 'tis me still here – though I deserve to die for all the ill I've caused.'

Fergus shook his head. 'Havers, man! Everyone here knows I'm at fault, I shouldny have been so hard on you. I wanted to . . . say I'm sorry before but I'm saying it now . . . maybe too late for a lot of folk.'

Alick opened his mouth but could think of nothing to say. A breeze blew the muslin curtains, tossing the scents and sounds of summer into the room. The words of a well-known hymn were born faintly.

Fergus licked his dry lips. '*Abide With Me* – 'tis my favourite.'

Suddenly he noticed his daughter standing quietly by the window. He held out his hand. 'Shona, my wee lass, her hair all bonny with a blue ribbon.'

She ran to him and buried her face in his neck. He took some of her hair and fondled the silken strands. Suddenly he remembered something. 'The other coffin – was it old McTavish? I know he's been ill.'

'Oh Father,' Shona began to sob. 'It's Mirabelle! She's dead, Father! She died three days ago, she was ill and didn't tell anyone!'

'Oh dear God, no!' He turned his head on the pillows but too late to hide the glimmer of tears. Kirsteen went to him quickly. 'It was very quick, Fergus. She wanted it that way.'

He didn't answer but went on stroking his daughter's silken hair.

Alick shuffled uneasily. 'Don't worry about the farm, Fergus. I'll see to everything till you're well.'

Fergus remained silent. He was staring at the window but he wasn't seeing cotton wool puffs in a blue sky. His thoughts were bleak and he saw no glimpse of blue in the black of the sky. He felt drained. All his old power of mind and body were gone. Mirabelle floated into his mind but he pushed her quickly away. Hamish, tall and laughing, strode past the eyes of his mind but he blotted him out. He didn't want to think. His arm throbbed and pains shot through his chest. He turned to look at Kirsteen and the love in her eyes made him shut his own tightly. He didn't want to see that shining selfless love because he knew he couldn't marry her now. How could he ask a lovely girl like Kirsteen to tie herself to a one-armed cripple? His thoughts were wandering: he was going up and down; one minute it was light, the next dark.

'Lachlan – want to see him,' he mumbled. 'Must see Lachlan.'

But Kirsteen had already sent Alick to fetch Lachlan. She knew that Fergus's racing pulse and burning fever weren't normal.

Lachlan pronounced the diagnosis that Kirsteen had dreaded.

'Pneumonia! I was afraid of it, but luckily only one lung is affected! Even then it'll be a fight, his body hasn't got over the shock of losing that arm.'

Fergus slowly came out of the stupor into which he had sunk. 'Lachlan,' he rasped hoarsely. 'I'm – sorry . . . friends again?'

He lifted his hand from the coverlet and Lachlan took it almost roughly. 'Friends!' he said, swallowing the lump that had risen in his throat.

That night Shona slept at Slochmhor. She tossed and turned but sleep refused to come. The barriers she had erected in her mind were falling fast. She could no longer deceive herself into believing that Mirabelle and Hamish were going to come back. Her father would never be the same again. His arm was gone for good and he was ill, so ill that Kirsteen had made up a bed in his room to be near him all night. Biddy had been with him all evening and all visitors had been turned away. Not even Dodie, with his unquestioning faithful love for Fergus, had been allowed into the sickroom. Shona remembered the quick childlike glimmer of tears in his eyes when he heard that Fergus was worse.

He had stood in the schoolhouse kitchen, awkward and gangling, his huge wellingtons making scuffling sounds on the linoleum. To many he would have appeared a comic figure with his wobbling carbuncle and strange, inward, dreaming eyes. To Kirsteen and Shona he was a figure of tragedy. The tears had spilled and sobs choked him for a moment. Then he fumbled in his ragged pocket and laid something on the table.

'He'll get better,' he whispered huskily, convincing himself. 'This will make him better, och yes, it will just!'

It was as if he were trying to summon all the powers of healing to hasten Fergus's recovery. 'He'll get better,' he repeated and stumbled out of the kitchen to make his way back over the hills to his lonely little cottage.

Shona picked up the horseshoe he had laid on the table. It was an old one but it had been polished over and over till it shone. She could picture the old eccentric spending hours of love and devotion on the horseshoe. His initial was scratched on it, sprawling and untidy, but another mark of his faith.

Kirsteen took the horseshoe gently. 'We'll hang it beside your father's bed, it *will* help him to get better.'

Shona turned her face into the pillow and the hot tears spilled over. She heard Fiona crying and Phebie coming up to her. It was a nice house, homely and comfortable. She was in the little guest room and the sheets smelled of lavender. Lavender! Mirabelle!

Mirabelle and lavender! Laigmhor and Mirabelle! Laigmhor and her father! All the years of their life together. Lovely moments like today when he had caressed her hair and called her his bonny lass. His neck had been so hot and she could hear his heart thumping loudly in her ear. She loved his heart, it was a strong wilful heart but it could be so loving, so dearly loving.

In the still darkness of the little room she thought she could hear his heart beating-beat-beating, then she realised the beat came from within herself. She had never paid much attention to hearts before, they were just another part of the body to be taken for granted, now she knew when they stopped everything that had been a person stopped too. What if her father's stopped! He would be gone forever, all that lovely big man person would go away from her life! She couldn't take any more of her thoughts. Terror made her sob loudly and she could do nothing to stop herself.

The door opened softly and Niall padded in, holding aloft a flickering candle that threw leaping shadows all over the room. 'I heard you,' he whispered. 'My bed's right next to yours through the wall.'

'Is it?' She felt oddly comforted.

'Yes, we can tap out wee messages to each other.'

She felt the bed sagging as he sat on it. The tears were still catching her throat. He laid the candle on her dresser and his hand caught hers.

'I know how you feel,' he whispered sympathetically.

'Do you? Do you really and truly, Niall?'

'Yes – well, about Mirabelle anyway.'

'Do you know how I feel about my father? Is your heart all funny with wee shivers all through you?'

'N-no, but I'm trying to think what I'd feel if my own father was very ill.'

'It's terrible, Niall, so terrible you wish you were dead yourself.'

'Don't say that,' he scolded. 'Your father will get better, my father will make him, he's a good doctor. He's going to be friends with your father after this, I heard him telling my mother so. Grown-ups are awful daft, they wait till they're dying before they start speaking and then it's too late 'cos they might not live to speak to each other.'

She sucked in her breath and immediately he knew he had said the wrong thing. She was crying again, great sobs that shook the bed. Frightened, he tried to make his unthinking words sound reassuring, but it was no use. In despair he lay down beside her and stroked her warm brow in a shy attempt to soothe her. 'Och weesht now,' he whispered, 'we'll say our prayers and God might help your father. Don't greet so.'

His curls tickled her nose and she felt better.

'Stay beside me, Niall.'

'Very well then, give me a bit blanket and the coorie in. I hope you don't snore.'

She giggled, suddenly warm and secure in the embrace of his thin arms. 'Kirsteen said I talked a wee bit.'

'I don't think I'll hear you,' he mumbled into her hair and in minutes they were both sound asleep.

At the schoolhouse, Fergus was delirious and Kirsteen sat at his bedside bathing his forehead. Oh, how tired she was; every bone in her body ached for rest. Her eyelids were like lead weights and several times she almost dropped off. Lachlan had said he would come back after he'd snatched a few hours' rest. He'd wanted to let someone else sit with Fergus but she wouldn't hear of it.

It was a warm night. The window was ajar and soft moorland scents wafted in, a mixture of peat, bell heather and thyme. A dog barked from a distant farm and a sea bird 'cra-aked' close by. Kirsteen lowered her head on to the counterpane and slept.

She woke with a start and looked at the clock – 1.30 – she had been asleep for an hour. Fergus was moaning, repeating something over and over.

'Can't marry you, Kirsteen – not now – not now, Kirsteen. It's a better man deserves you. One arm – only one arm – can't marry you, Kirsteen . . .'

Her heart was like a cold heavy stone. She had been stupid enough to think he had taken the loss of his arm lightly, how wrong she was. He was too proud, his pride was like a disease, there was no fighting it, no curing it, she was a fool to think he'd come out of the accident unscathed in his mind. She covered her eyes with her clenched fists. She couldn't cry, all her weeping had been for Fergus and his battle for life. For herself she could only feel the exquisite agony of a mourning soul. She had lost Fergus as surely as if he had died. Her love for him was a growth, swelling in her heart till she felt it must burst, yet she must relinquish him if she were to keep her sanity. She would nurse his dear beloved body back to health then she would leave Rhanna while she could still go with some dignity. The decision left her drained. Lachlan found her sitting by the bed, her golden head resting on Fergus's hand, her blue eyes empty, gazing at nothing. She didn't even stir at the opening of the door.

'Kirsteen, are you all right?' asked Lachlan sharply.

'Yes, Lachlan, I'm fine.'

Her voice was hollow. Fergus stirred, coughed feebly, and once more began his fevered ramblings.

Lachlan took Kirsteen's hand. 'He doesn't know what he's saying, the man's delirious!'

She withdrew her hand gently. 'But he knows what he means, Lachy, the thoughts are there.' She shook her head and he saw that she had turned very pale.

'Are you ill, Kirsteen? You're tired, I know – exhausted, God knows – but is there something else troubling you?'

'No, Lachlan – nothing . . .' But she gripped his arm looking deep into his eyes. 'You're such a good man, Lachlan, you understand things – maybe . . .'

'Yes, Kirsteen?'

But she shook her head again. 'Don't worry.' She inclined her head towards the bed. 'Whatever way it goes – and God knows I pray he gets better – I'll be leaving Rhanna. I couldn't stay here now.'

'But your job! Dammit girl, you can't just give it all up!'

She smiled wearily. 'I'll write to the Education Authorities pleading illness. Don't worry, they'll send another teacher!'

'I'm not thinking about your job!' He was angry now. 'I'm thinking of you . . . and him, you can't leave him now, not when he needs you most!'

'Oh dear heaven, don't you think I need him! I need him so much I don't know how I'll live without him but I can't take any more, Lachlan. You've heard the gossips. I thought that was all going to be finished with but it seems not and I'd rather go before he tells me to! At least I owe myself some self-respect!'

His brown eyes were sad. 'There's nothing I can say?'

She shook her head vehemently but couldn't stop the brimming tears. 'Nothing, but thank you for caring enough to want to help. Now I must go and make us both some tea.'

For four days Fergus hovered on the brink that separates life from death. At times he was quite rational and recognized everyone who came and went. Alick was constantly at his bedside and the brothers rediscovered the kindred spirit of their youth. When Kirsteen was resting it was Alick who spooned broth into his brother's mouth. Fergus was inclined to refuse the nourishment but Alick was firm in a way he had never been before. It wasn't because Fergus was too physically weak to protest, for even in his fight for life he wasn't to be taken advantage of. The assertion that Alick had lacked all his life was at last coming to the fore. The last week had brought out a strength in him he hadn't known he possessed, but it was a strength of mind, a power born of a realisation that the thing his life lacked was the opportunity to make decisions for himself. During his brother's illness he had been responsible for the farm. There was no Hamish to turn to and he'd had to make many decisions. The men came to him and asked him things he knew little about, but his quick brain had helped him work out the best methods for coping.

Such a lot of tragedy had happened that summer on Rhanna yet he felt happy. Oh, he would go back to Edinburgh but Mary might not get so much of her own way in future. He wanted children and she was going to provide them. Perhaps a firm hand was what she needed. He had also decided to pull himself out of the rut of his easy job and look for something where he would have a say in decisions of importance.

His new mood must have showed. Fergus saw something in his brother that hadn't been there before. 'You're doing grand,' he would assure Fergus when his breathing was at its most difficult and he hadn't the strength to clear his lungs. Alick made him sit up and his back was pummelled till he cried aloud in pain but there was no mercy till he coughed up the thick red sputum.

Shona flitted from house to house like a pale little ghost, feeling she didn't belong anywhere. Phebie was gay and warmhearted but her life was a busy one. Alick was occupied with the farm. Kirsteen was loving and sweet as always but Shona sensed a withdrawal of the spontaneous affection she had displayed so readily in the past. Shona wondered why and shed lonely tears. She so badly needed to love and be loved. It was a time of great adjustment in her life and she needed to turn to someone. She couldn't know that Kirsteen, knowing she must soon leave all that she loved, was unconsciously steeling herself for the parting. She loved Shona whose every glance was her father's. His blood flowed in her veins, his defiance and pride were hers, and Kirsteen wanted to hold on to any spark that reminded her of the man she loved. Instead, she turned away and fought to hide her feelings from Fergus's child. Shona was hurt, but the pride that had been born in her wouldn't let her show it.

She went every day to the schoolhouse. She bathed her father's head and held the cup to his lips when he was thirsty. He smiled at her, a funny wistful smile and held her hand tightly. Often he fell asleep holding her hand and she liked to sit there just looking at him. He had always been so active and elusive she hadn't often had the chance to study him closely. How beautifully sensitive his mouth was; his jaw was strong with a tiny dimple in the middle of his chin; the tip of her pinky fitted in perfectly. It was strange to watch the pulse beating in his neck, it made her afraid, yet it fascinated her. Often she counted it beating to a hundred and more. It was a funny sad feeling to see him lying in bed. She hadn't often seen him in bed till this awful illness. His lashes were long and dark, curling a little at their tips. His hair was so black; she had always loved the way it clung round his head in crisp waving curls. Sweat plastered tiny baby curls at his ears. It was during one of her 'private looking times' that she noticed one or two small white hairs in his sideburns, they were very wiry and stood out from the black. The sight of them made her want to cry. She had always thought of her father as a big boy but those little white hairs belonged to a man not a boy. Each day after the discovery she studied his black curls and was thankful she could find no more of the wiry white ones. Eventually she grew to love the tiny white hairs; they were part of him and she loved all of him. She even knew how many there were, seven at the right side and three funny jaggy ones on the left. She hugged herself because they were her secret. Probably not even Kirsteen knew *exactly* how many of the little white hairs he had.

She could never look at him as long as she would have liked because either Biddy or Lachlan hustled her away. She didn't have Niall to talk to. He had gone to an aunt in Dumfries for a few days, to be fitted for his school uniform. He had grumbled about going.

'I canna stand the way Aunt Elly fusses,' he confided. 'She hops about like an old chookie and makes me eat salads all the time. I don't think she's *heard* of mealy herring or chapped turnip and Uncle George does awful things like picking his teeth at the table.'

Nevertheless his eyes gleamed. He liked the shops in Dumfries. His father had given him a whole pound to spend and he liked Aunt Elly's two boys who were very worldly without being superior.

Shona longed to see Niall's sturdy boyish figure. She wondered what it would be like when he was away all the time. There were only three weeks left but she pushed the thought far away and took Tot over the moors to the cave. Together they snuggled on a mattress of moss and heather. She was as lonely as Tot whose babies had been taken from her. Each afternoon they slept together on the bed, snug in the cave.

*

The days dragged on, each one feeling like a year to Kirsteen who spent most of her waking hours by Fergus's side. When he was asleep she just sat looking at him, engraving a picture in her mind that she might carry it with her forever. One day Biddy caught her staring trance-like at the strong handsome face.

'Aye, he's a bonny man, my lassie,' said Biddy with assurance. 'But time he had a woman to look to him.'

Kirsteen looked at the old nurse. 'What was he like, Biddy . . . when he was a wee boy?'

'A fine laddie but a strange one. Always quiet – not in a shy way but a quiet kind of strength – funny in a wee laddie but then his mother put too much upon his young shoulders. It wasn't right to make him feel he should never give in. But it was her way. She loved her bairns but ended up making one too reliant and the other . . . ach, poor Fergus – to him it's a sin to show weakness. It's hard to shake off the habit of years but I see a change in him, he's learnin' we're all weak in one way or another.'

Kirsteen looked over her shoulder at Fergus and a wry smile twisted her mouth.

'His pride is his weakness, Biddy.'

Biddy frowned in puzzlement. 'He's proud I'll grant you, too damty so for his own good, but what way is it a weakness, mo ghaoil?'

'Because he is not its master, it rules his head and his heart. His pride is the master . . . and oh God! how I wish he'd get the better of it! It has touched too many lives with its greedy need for power. A little pride is a good thing, Biddy, we all need it, but too much is a curse!'

Biddy looked mildly astonished. She didn't understand Kirsteen's logic but sensed that the words were a cry from the heart. 'There, my lassie,' she soothed kindly. 'You have a queer way of putting things but I think I understand a wee bit. Now, let's get his bed changed, you'd think a herd o' cows had trampled it for weeks!'

Kirsteen had already informed the Education Authorities she was leaving her post for health reasons and had asked that a replacement teacher be sent for the start of the autumn term. It was short notice but she didn't care, she was beyond caring about her responsibilities, she only knew she had to leave Rhanna. Every moment spent near Fergus weakened her resolution to leave him. Every sense in her was dulled except those that reeled with the engulfing love she felt for him. All else was unimportant and she knew she had to get away so that she could get a truer perspective of her feelings.

She tried not to think of a life without him, she only knew she wasn't going to wait for the moment when he must tell her he couldn't marry her. She couldn't bear that, she couldn't bear to go on as before, so she had to break away while there was still time.

The day dawned when Lachlan examined Fergus and pronounced him well.

'You've a heart like an ox or you'd never have come through. We'll fish the Fallan yet! It's been a while since I had a nice fresh trout for supper.'

301

Fergus glowered at the stump of his arm. 'Fish? With this? Don't haver, man!'

'The Fergus I once knew would let nothing stop him. Is it letting a little thing like losing an arm stand in the way then?'

Fergus struggled up. 'Dammit!' he exploded. 'It's fine for you to stand there and . . .' The rueful twinkle in the doctor's brown eyes compelled him to smile. 'Aye,' he said slowly, 'we will fish the Fallan and a damt red face you'll have when we weigh in our catch!'

With returning health came a growing awareness of all that had passed since the scented summer evening of his marriage proposal. He had lost so much, yet, when he thought of Alick and Shona, he felt he had gained a lot too. He felt closer to them than he had ever been. Alick was no longer a boy, the days of crisis had turned him into a man; Shona was a loving little girl again, throwing her arms around him with a zeal that sent him flying backwards on the pillows. His journeys near the deep valleys of death and his eventual escape from them made him vividly aware of the dear things of life. It was so good to feel those child's arms, the sweet, near, earthly touch making him respond with equal warmth.

In the lonely hours he journeyed back in time, reliving the years with Mirabelle. She had always been in his life and her going left a gap that he had only begun to appreciate. He still expected her ample motherly figure to come bustling through the door, scolding or fussing in the way they had all taken for granted, and tragically had never realised how much it meant till her motherly arms were no more. He couldn't bear yet to think of Hamish. The loyalty of the big Highlander was too near, too poignant to remember. Instead he forced his mind into the present and Kirsteen. In his darkest hours she had always been there. Even when his strength had reached its lowest ebb and his mind sank into one timeless abyss after another he had been aware of her presence, the power of her love reaching down, down into those dark depths, willing him to struggle out of them and upwards to meet her love with his. Because of her he had wanted to make that awful endless struggle to live and because of her he had won.

Propped up on pillows he watched her. He noticed that she was very pale with dark smudges under her eyes. His heart turned over with love. Her nights of nursing him had drained her, yet she uttered no word of complaint. She was quietly jubilant that he was getting better, yet he sensed a change in her. It was indefinable, but he knew that in some way she was different. He was suddenly afraid. He couldn't bear it if she loved him less than before the accident. He looked down at the useless stump of his arm. Was that it? Did his appearance repel her to some extent? But not Kirsteen! They had loved too deeply, he knew her better than that. Yet he needed reassuring, he had to know.

'Kirsteen.' He reached out for her, his voice husky. 'My dear little Kirsteen . . . do you still love me? I watch you and thank God for you! Are you still just a wee bit glad we met that day in the woods by Loch Tenee?'

She was taken unawares. She had steeled herself for such a moment but when it came she wasn't ready. She looked at him, at his hand reaching out for her, the naked doubts of her love for him in his burning dark eyes.

A sob caught in her throat and she was beside him, holding his head against her breasts. She ran her fingers through his thick hair and kissed the nape of his neck.

'I wish – oh how I wish we could have that day again,' she whispered brokenly. 'I loved you the moment I saw you. I wish we could have a thousand moments like that again, my Fergus!'

He wiped her tears away with a gentle finger. 'We'll have a million moments like that, Kirsteen.' He kissed her tenderly on the lips.

Three days later Kirsteen watched Rhanna fade into the blue of the sky. It was a hot day and there was no horizon. Sky and sea were one and the green island with its blue mountains was ethereal in the distance.

A group of sheep huddled on the boat, their plaintive cries rivalling the lost threading mews of the circling gulls. To Kirsteen the whole scene had a dreamlike quality. She felt she must soon waken to see Fergus smiling at her. She hadn't said goodbye to anyone, not even Phebie or Lachlan, because she knew they were hurt at her going and would try to talk her into staying.

The cross currents in the Sound swayed the boat, making her feel sick and giddy. Deep in her womb something quivered and stirred and she knew that she was leaving Rhanna with a child growing in her, its tiny foetal heart already pumping the blood of Fergus McKenzie through its living tissues.

Part Five

Spring 1934

Chapter Eleven

It had been a winter of severe winds tempered by mild damp spells. A short, cold snap in February brought the deer down from the hills and it was quite usual to see them sharing a potash from the same pail as an unruffled cow.

Dodie kept a special little supply of hay for the deer. Strewn a few yards from his cottage it attracted a number of the gentle-eyed, gracious creatures which he loved to watch.

Dodie was very contented with his lot these days. He had acquired several hens who supplied him with his breakfast eggs; as well as Ealasaid, he had a ewe in lamb. Fergus had given him the sheep in return for the horseshoe which he said had helped him to get well.

When March came the ewe gave birth to twin lambs and all three were housed cosily with Ealasaid because Dodie couldn't bear the idea of the baby sheep weathering the high winds. The ewe and her family trotted after him like devoted dogs and he shouted at them or waved his arms but to no avail. Inwardly his heart brimmed over with love for his animals and he strode over hill and moor in his flapping raincoat and flopping wellingtons with the sheep plodding faithfully behind.

He was helping with the lambing at Laigmhor and three figures in the field watched his coming.

'Dodie had a little lamb . . .' chanted Shona, giggling.

Mathew shook his head. 'Ach, he'll never sell the damty things. He'll make pets o' them and keep them forever! It's wondering I am you gave him the yowe, McKenzie.'

Fergus looked at the stooping tattered figure whose mouth was forming the familiar 'He breeah!'

'He has more in him than meets the eye,' said Fergus quietly. 'Dodie is smelly, dirty, and eccentric, but his heart's as big as his head! When he came to see me . . . the time of the accident, he left behind his stink but he also left behind his faith and I needed all I could get then. He's a cratur nearer to God than any of those kirk-going hypocrites who talk behind each other's backs. Aye, Dodie's a good man.'

Mathew said nothing. It was hard-going, working side by side with Fergus. Mathew was grieve now and honoured, yet awed, that he had been given such a responsible position. He was eager to please, yet in his own reserved way tried to appear nonchalant before Fergus. He was also embarrassed at having to give orders to men twice his age yet they had been pleased that he had been given the job. He was the likeliest choice. The other men had their specific skills whereas he knew a little about everything. It was what he didn't know that frightened him. He was marrying in the summer, the little cottage that had been Hamish's awaiting him and his bride. Fergus had given Maggie the option of staying on but she was unable to bear Rhanna without Hamish and had moved back to Edinburgh to live with a sister.

The prospects of the job excited Mathew. He liked and respected Fergus but he wished a thousand times that he had some of Hamish's strength of character and maturity.

'Bide your time, lad,' advised Bob. 'McKenzie didny pick you for your looks! Just ca' canny and don't put these muckle great feet o' yours in the shit afore it sets. McKenzie canny eat you, damn it! He's a thrawn bugger and respects a body wi' a bit gumption but see you don't tell him his business. Mind you . . .' Bob stroked his grizzled chin reflectively. 'He's no' so girny since his accident. I'd say he's learnt a bit about patience.'

Mathew took Bob's advice. He didn't indulge in superfluous chatter; he respected Fergus's supremacy yet, if he felt he was right and Fergus wrong, he clung to his opinions and was surprised to find that the older man acceded quite agreeably.

Shona ran to meet Dodie at the gate. He handed her a little bunch of snowdrops he had found growing in a sunless corner of his garden. It was March, late for snowdrops, so they were therefore all the more precious.

'Thank you, Dodie,' she breathed and held the frail white drops against her cheek. Snowdrops made her think of her mother because two months before, on her eleventh birthday, she had gone with Phebie to the Kirkyard and on her mother's grave had placed a huge bunch of snowdrops. Phebie had helped her to understand so much about her mother that she had missed because all the jealously guarded memories had been hoarded from her. Shona thought the story of her mother and father was a lovely one and she cried in bed when she thought about it; but for her it was really just a story – when she looked at her father she saw him not with her mother but with Kirsteen whom he had been going to marry but didn't. She wondered why. She had thought about it over and over and could find no answer. She didn't know why Kirsteen had left so suddenly and her father didn't seem to know either. No one seemed to know, not even Phebie who had been Kirsteen's close friend, but Shona suspected that all the evasive answers she received were the usual grown-up solutions for things they didn't want to discuss.

She would have found out from Mirabelle. Mirabelle had been evasive in her own fashion but in her guileless way she would let little things slip. She had solved many a mystery through the old lady's unguarded remarks.

Thinking of Mirabelle still brought a lump to her throat. A lot of the cosiness had gone from her life. Laigmhor had lost a lot of its homeliness since Mirabelle's going but the old housekeeper had taught her well. She was now adept at baking and could prepare reasonable meals. Kate McKinnon, all her family married except William, came in three times a week to clean the house and wash clothes. With her earthy tongue she was a colourful intrusion into the drowsing quiet of the farmhouse. Sloshing clothes about in a big tub, with soap suds piling over on to the floor, she regaled Shona with accounts of her family's latest exploits.

Shona knew that Nancy liked the physical aspect of marriage, everyone on Rhanna knew, but Kate had the privilege of knowing more than most.

'Aye, in heat is our Nancy,' she informed Shona as she lustily swished clothes on the scrubbing board. 'She tells me she makes poor Archie so tired of a night he can't get up in the morn to milk the cows. His father's sick o' it I tell you . . . mind you, he was a bit of a lad himself in his younger days! Aye, fine I know it too! We came home from a Ceilidh one night and he got me into a shed. Before you could blink, there they were! All hangin' out! Balls on him like a prize bull! His hand was up my skirt in no time and I had to slap his face for him. 'Tis a pity we have to pretend not to like the things we like but a lass had to hold on to her self-respect in those days.'

Despite Kate McKinnon the winter had been quiet. Niall's going caused a huge gap in Shona's life. She had plenty of friends. She played with them and Ceilidhed in their houses but there was no real intimacy, none of the real talks or lovely easy silences she had known with Niall. Always there was the feeling she was suspended in a world of expectancy, waiting for the holidays that brought Niall. When he was home she dropped into place again, and Rhanna, the lovely green island of wheeling gulls, windblown heather, ice-cold burns, and fragrant peat fires, was the same dear place of her yesteryears.

Christmas had been the loveliest she remembered at Laigmhor. For a week the weather was like spring with warm winds blowing in from the sea. It had been a Christmas of Ceilidhs, each one going into the small hours of morning. Tables groaned with turkey and mince pies, mealy black puddings, and potted herring. The fiddlers played and the Seanachaidhs told their well-worn tales. It was Shona's first experience of such traditional revelry, for her father had lately become less reserved than she ever remembered. Whether it was due to the influence of the McLachlans she never knew but he had changed.

While Ceilidhing, he sat quietly in a corner, but his feet tapped to the gay tunes of the fiddle. Sometimes he caught her eye and winked and a happy glow warmed her heart yet, though he appeared happier, sometimes there was such a look of sadness in his eyes that her breath caught and she wished there was some way she could dispel the look.

But that week of Christmas was no time to be sad. It was enough that for the first time in many years her father was mixing more with the folk of Rhanna and they admiring and respecting him for it. Many had thought that after his accident he would become even more of a recluse but he had gritted his teeth and faced the world, doing things with his one arm that astounded the observer.

Shona had completely accepted his disablement. It was no surprise to her that he could hoist her up in his one arm and carry her home from Ceilidhs. In the safe circle of that strong right arm she felt herself being jogged home through a world of night breezes and twinkling stars then being helped into pyjamas and tucked into bed, the last thing remembered the warm, fleeting touch of his lips on her cheek.

The Hogmanay Ceilidh at Laigmhor was the

loveliest of all. The whole of Rhanna seemed to be packed into a parlour that normally knew only the ticking of clocks; now it rocked with merriment. Biddy, praying that no Hogmanay babies would decide to arrive, got slowly and deliciously inebriated on the rather uncomfortable perch of the coal box.

'The wee buggers will keep till the morn,' she told a large glass of whisky and lapsed into a garbled Gaelic lullaby.

Elspeth had swallowed her indignation at the way Fergus had treated her in the past and condescended to help in the kitchen. She had smuggled a bottle under her apron and took frequent sips in the privacy of the pantry. Within half an hour she was humming untunefully while she buttered hot scones. Each utensil she used brought quick tears to her eyes.

'Ach, they were used by you once, Belle,' she sighed, gazing dazedly at a bread knife. 'It's honoured I am to be in your kitchen.'

Lachlan and Phebie came crowding in. Niall immediately armed himself with a handful of scones and deftly escaped Elspeth's scathing tongue. That night he tasted his first glass of wine and got up quite unbidden to sing one of the loveliest Hebridean boat songs. The lilting tune filled the air and everyone hummed quietly, swaying dreamily on the crest of each note.

Shona watched Niall. The room was lit only by one lamp and his tall kilted figure was outlined in firelight that made his fair hair gleam. It was then she noticed the change in him. His face was still soft but hovered on the brink of young manhood. His skin was smoothly tanned as always but on his upper lip was the faintest shadow, a mere breath of downy hair. His voice was different too, still sweetly falsetto, but occasionally an unaccustomed gruffness crept into the child's tones. She clasped her knees and swayed with the others but she thought about the changes in Niall. Barely five months had elapsed since he had left Rhanna but already she was seeing things in him she might never have noticed if he hadn't gone away. She wondered if she had changed and looked furtively down at her long legs and skinny arms. No, she decided quickly, she was still the same, perhaps a bit taller, thinner too. How awful! She was so shapeless and lanky. She wondered if she would ever get fatter. Mirabelle would have fussed and given her cod liver oil. Mirabelle! How she would have loved this night; a banquet would have groaned on the kitchen table. She would have grumbled a bit and been very hot with her mutch slightly askew and her long white apron floury from a day spent baking.

Shona dashed away a tear. This was no night to be sad, not with Todd holding the floor with his melodian and Shelagh 'hooching' loudly, her skirts held aloft to allow her black-clad legs better freedom. Her 'winds' forgotten for the moment, she gave a delightfully wrong interpretation of an eightsome reel, till finally she collapsed on top of an unwary Bob who was unfortunate enough to be lighting his pipe at the moment of impact. The pipe broke, Bob cursed, and Shelagh staggered to a seat leaving behind a loud 'Trumpet Voluntary' as an encore.

'Dirty auld bugger!' fumed Bob but Shelagh, sweetly oblivious, was sipping rum by the fire.

It was some time before Dodie was discovered waiting at the gate. Fergus had gone outside for a breath of air and saw the familiar, stooping figure, embarrassed, wiping his nose on his sleeve, and muttering profuse apologies because he hadn't known 'Laigmhor was Ceilidhing'.

Fergus had to hide a smile. The Laigmhor Ceilidh had been the talk of Portcull for days, everyone knew about it. 'Go away in, man,' he invited gruffly. 'It's daft you are hanging about here! They're having a good time in there.'

Dodie protested feebly. He had never been known to Ceilidh, a Strupak yes, a Ceilidh never.

'Come on, I'll go in with you,' offered Fergus. Dodie showed his teeth in a nervous grimace but allowed Fergus to push him gently in the direction of the door. Fergus got the impression that Dodie looked different somehow but for a moment he couldn't think why. Then he realised. Dodie had left off his greasy cap to reveal a head covered with fine dark hair. It had been combed into a middle parting, but though tamed by water, still sprouted upwards in jagged clumps. It was like a field of new grass and Fergus could not help staring; everybody stared when Dodie tripped on the rug and catapulted into the room. There was a sudden silence and Dodie patted his head self-consciously while his face grew bright red. Instinct had made the folk near the door move away, thus leaving Dodie all alone in a little clearing. But there was no need. Dodie had made history appearing at a Ceilidh hatless; he had broken all records by also having a bath. Carbolic fumes wafted from him and were even more powerful than his usual peculiar odour.

A loud bellow from the window broke the silence. Lachlan pulled back the curtains to reveal Ealasaid blowing steam against the glass.

Bob roared with laughter. 'The damty cow has followed you, Dodie! She wants to Ceilidh too!'

Everyone joined in the laughter and Tam McKinnon slapped Dodie's back. 'You'll be havin' a dram, Dodie! A large one. This is an occasion we must celebrate!'

Dodie grinned with relief and raised the glass. 'He breeah!' he said dismally and downed the drink in one gulp.

Shona smiled whenever she thought of that night. Dodie had become completely intoxicated and had been carried home by four equally merry crofters. Ealasaid had trotted behind the unsteady revellers, her bellows breaking uncaringly into the velvet blackness of the wee sma' hours.

The rest of the winter passed uneventfully except for the weather. Gales churned the Sound of Rhanna into fury and strong gusts forced the lobster boats to stay in harbour. Trees were uplifted by the roots and one had fallen over the schoolhouse, badly damaging the roof. The children were given an unexpected holiday while Mr Murdoch, the balding new teacher, tried to hustle the placid Rhanna builders into unaccustomed speed.

The winds screamed round Laigmhor making the inside feel all the cosier. Shona liked the evenings when it was just herself and her father. She read or knitted while Tot snored and Fergus smoked his pipe, his slippered feet up on the range. The clocks ticked and the firelight flickered and at bedtime she made hot milky cocoa. Sometimes the McLachlans left ten-month-old Fiona with Elspeth, and came over to spend an evening with Fergus. They brought a warm, happy feeling with them and when Shona went up to bed Phebie tucked her in and read to her. Afterwards she liked to listen to the murmur of voices from downstairs and it was so good to hear her father's deep laugh ring out.

It was good to fall asleep listening to the wind and the sound of laughter.

Now it was spring, with daffodils poking green buds to the sky, and the lambs arriving in ever-increasing numbers. She watched Dodie and Mathew go off to the lambing fields, then she ran into the kitchen to put her snowdrops in water.

Lachlan was coming along the road on the bicycle he used for his local calls and Fergus went to the gate to have a chat. He took out his pipe.

'Like to see my new trick?' he said, with his rueful grin. He'd had trouble lighting the pipe with only one hand. Now he placed the pipe in his mouth, held the box of matches under the oxter of his stump, and, with his right hand struck the match against the firmly held box.

'How's that?' he asked after the triumphant demonstration.

Lachlan smiled. 'You're nearly there, man, just as good as new.'

Fergus frowned suddenly. 'Do you think I'm as good as any man?'

'Better than some.'

'Then why . . . dammit why did she leave me, Lachlan? I've overcome most things. Did she think I'd be less of a man than I was? Why did she go away?'

Lachlan sighed. Fergus had confided in him over Kirsteen and he had been asked the same question several times. There were times when the trust Fergus placed on him felt like too big a burden, yet he was honoured that Fergus had trusted him with his innermost thoughts. 'You know why, man,' he answered firmly. 'She had some dignity left and she went before it was all taken from her.'

'But we were to wed! I told her that before the accident!'

Lachlan nodded and asked gently, 'Would you have wed her after the accident? Would that damt pride of yours let you?'

'In time yes . . . oh God yes, Lachy! I've been lonely too long!'

'But she didn't know that, she was at the end of her patience. She knew you weren't going to marry her and she had no guarantee you would do so.'

'Dammit, man I was raving! She believed things I said when I wasny my own master! She could have waited!'

'For what? You were rantin', man – aye, I'll grant you that! But these were the wanderings of what was in your mind. Admit it, Fergus! When you knew I'd amputated your arm you had already decided not to marry Kirsteen.'

Stark misery looked out of Fergus's black eyes. 'Aye

– you're right. But that was then. Now I'd marry her a thousand times over!'

'Then go to her – tell her! Don't let that proud heart of yours rule you any longer!'

'But she left me! And I've written! A dozen times . . . aye, and more, yet never a word back.'

Lachlan placed his hand firmly on the other man's shoulder. 'Go to her Fergus. For once in your life think more of her happiness than your own. She left Rhanna with a broken heart. You could heal it – and your own.'

'I'll think about it,' said Fergus gruffly, embarrassed that he had bared so much of his thoughts to another human. He returned to everyday talk with character-istic brusqueness. 'Have you a busy morning ahead?'

'No more than usual. I've to lance a boil, change a few dressings, Shelagh insists she needs an enema . . .'

He waved cheerily and pedalled away. Fergus walked slowly to the fields, his head bent, his thoughts going back to the time he realised that Kirsteen was no longer on Rhanna. He'd sunk into an abyss of lonely despair. Over and over he asked the same question. Why had she left him? They'd loved together – oh God, how they had loved. She'd given herself to him completely. He'd done things with her he hadn't even done with Helen, things that only a man of ex-perience and maturity could know of. The exquisite beauty he'd known in her love for him couldn't be denied and he'd loved her with a depth he didn't think possible after Helen.

He had admired her sweetness of character and her quietly happy personality; there was so much about her he had loved and he had thought that she returned that love, that life would be an impossibility for her without him just as it was such an impossibility for him to exist without her. The realization that she had shown she could live without him had hurt him deeply.

After the misery and aching longing, came anger. How dare she leave him? He could well live without her, there were other things in his life! She could go to hell for all he cared. He went through a spell of being angry at everything. The curious, guarded looks of his neighbours goaded him to fury. They were waiting – waiting to see what course his life would take, now that he had a disability to contend with, now that Kirsteen had fled from him, leaving him to look a fool in the eyes of everyone. His temper had acted as a good barb for his pride; it was temper that first took him among the people he had known all his life, inwardly he fumed but outwardly he showed the world he wasn't a maimed object of pity.

Maintaining a deliberate calm he threw himself into the work of the farm. The men watched him, hearts in mouths, while he attempted impossibly difficult tasks, but he conquered each one and the men nodded their heads and told each other, 'Nothing will beat McKenzie!'

It was defiance that took him to the first Ceilidh but a joy in renewed acquaintances that took him to the rest.

Anger wore off and gradually the old feeling of hurt took over. He thought about Kirsteen continually; sometimes he could spend a whole evening staring into the fire, reliving some experience they had shared in the past. He grieved for her and his grief was all the keener because it was for a beloved person who was still of the earth. Often he would stop and wonder, What is Kirsteen doing at this precise moment? Was she thinking of him? Did she think of him with the deep ache he felt for her? Was she well? Was she – happy? But how could she be? Was not every one of her waking and dreaming hours tortured by memories in the same way that his were?

He wrote letters and tore them up again. Why should he write? She left him! But there came a day when he could no longer bear the burden of his thoughts. He poured out his heart and sealed and posted the letter before he could change his mind.

For three weeks he waited and hoped. The sight of Erchy whistling cheerily along made his heart lurch. It became an obsession to look out for Erchy's stubby; weatherbeaten figure. Mail came, but not a word from Kirsteen. In desperation he wrote one letter after the other but to no avail. There was nothing, not even a polite note to tell him not to hope any more. He'd written the first letter in January, now it was March and he felt empty. Was there really so much in his life? He had recaptured the love of his little daughter and in return he treasured her for the precious gift she was. There were Lachlan and Phebie, warm and trustworthy, so much more than mere friends. The rift between them was healed, and he valued them perhaps even more than if they had never known those years of misunderstanding.

Alick! Yes, there was Alick too, so close to him since

his accident and turning into a real man at last. He and Mary had paid a short visit just recently and everyone was astonished at the change in Mary. She was helpful and kind and so amusing with her dry sense of humour that everyone held her with a new regard. She was even persuaded to don wellington boots and explore the farm. Murdy's son, Hugh, was mucking the byre at the time, and the aroma of disturbed dung was somewhat overpowering, but she had held her breath and doggedly plodded into the milking shed.

She no longer spoke to Alick with contempt. Instead they wandered off for walks and laughed a lot. Inevitably they argued but Alick no longer gave her her own way and Mary looked at him with a new respect. He had left his office job and had found a less comfortable post in an Edinburgh store. He was assistant supervisor, his pay was less but the job was so much more rewarding.

Yes, Alick was a brother worth having, no other child was as endearing as Shona, no friends finer than the McLachlans; yet, despite them all, he was empty, feeling the hunger pains for a love which had no fulfilment.

He thought about Lachlan's words. 'Go to her, go to her, man!'

He'd reached the lambing field. Bob was whistling orders to Kerrie and the sounds of new life filled the air. New lambs wobbled on unsteady legs, tails bobbing frantically as they darted under their mother's belly for sustenance.

Dodie was skinning a dead lamb and putting its fleece round an orphan in the hope that a bereaved ewe would accept it as her own. Tears were coursing down Dodie's face because the task was distasteful to him but if such ruses helped orphans to a new mother then the job was worthwhile.

It was a mild, fresh day, and the scent of new heather blew down from the mountains. Fergus lifted his dark handsome face. He had always loved the rugged changing hills on Rhanna. They were like himself. Sometimes stormy and moody, at others peacefully calm. Today they were clear, slate blue scree showing through the bronze of last year's heather on the deep corries of the higher masses, new grass and bracken furring the lower slopes.

Fergus took a deep breath and made up his mind. At Easter he would go to Oban. If Kirsteen was teaching again she would be on holiday then. Shona would have Niall for company. Mathew was a good efficient lad, well able to run the farm for a spell. There was nothing, nothing at all to stop him going to Oban, to see Kirsteen again, to talk to her, be near her. His breath caught and suddenly he was like a small boy, wishing the hours away till the Easter holidays.

Fergus felt very strange leaving Rhanna. It had been a long time since he'd left the island. There had been cattle sales in Oban but that had been some years ago; he had been inclined to leave such things to Hamish who had enjoyed the buzz of the sales and who had needed little help when it came to choosing good dairy cattle.

The day was cold with a fresh wind blowing from the east. Fergus shivered slightly with a mixture of cold and nerves. A tight knot of apprehension coiled deep in his belly and he wanted to shout to the boat's captain to turn round, to head back for Rhanna and security; instead he picked up his small suitcase and went below to the saloon.

The picture of Shona and Niall waving him off from the harbour was still with him. Shona's chin had trembled slightly but Niall had placed a firm arm round her shoulders and she was soon smiling. He had watched them till they were tiny specks against the white blur of Portcull. Alick and Mary were staying at Laigmhor for Easter, and Kate McKinnon was coming in to help with the meals. Alick had been aglow at the thought of helping Mathew to run the farm and Fergus had felt strangely superfluous.

He was awkward and uncomfortable in his suit and he was also very conscious of the loosely pinned left sleeve. In his working clothes it didn't matter but in the suit he felt conspicuous and very aware of his disability. He lit his pipe awkwardly in a little corner and settled down to the long journey. Only Lachlan and Phebie knew where he was going, everyone else thought it was a holiday, a break after all his sad experiences.

He thought of Kirsteen. The idea of seeing her again made his heart beat strangely. A quiet elation gripped him but it was tempered with doubts and the terrible fear she would reject him. He didn't want to think beyond that, he couldn't think of a life that held no hope of reconciliation with the woman he loved.

Oban seemed big and busy after Rhanna. How different the busy harbour was from Portcull. Men shouted and groups of noisy children helped the crew with the ropes, hoping their labours might earn a penny or two.

The town had changed little since Fergus had last visited, there were more shops but the happy bustling atmosphere was still the same. He booked into a small hotel. It was homely and its unpretentious character suited Fergus. After a wash he felt better and, it being teatime, he went rather nervously into the dining-room. It was almost empty. The season was quiet because of the cold weather and the hotel was peaceful and uncluttered. Nevertheless he was careful not to dunk bread in his soup. Mirabelle had snorted disapprovingly at the habit but in his own kitchen he hadn't cared; now he was in unfamiliar ground and felt hot and uncomfortable. Though there were only two other people in the room he was aware of every move he made. The stump of his arm grew in propor-tion till he felt it filled the room and when his pudding came he pushed it away untouched and rose hastily.

He strode into the cold air and took a deep breath. He looked down at the piece of paper that carried Kirsteen's address and his hand trembled. A passing fisherman gave him directions and he climbed to the top of a steep hill with legs that felt like jelly. He looked at the house. It was clean and whitewashed with tiny attic windows. It was perched on top of a hillocky garden filled with crocuses and budding daffodils. A light shone in a downstairs window. It looked warm and inviting yet he felt a stranger, an intruder into a scene that held no invitation to him. It was an oddly sad experience. On Rhanna he had been so sure of Kirsteen's welcome – he had expected it – now he felt he had no right to expect anything.

He looked again at the house she had grown up in. How often her light, eager step must have trod that path – this road. He pictured her toiling up the hill, the long climb behind her, her face flushed and her breath coming quickly. He wished she were coming up the hill now, it would make his task so much easier. The light of welcome would surely come into her eyes. They would look at each other, not speaking for a moment, then they would laugh, take hands, and he would know that she loved him still.

For several minutes he waited, his eyes straining downhill. The lights of the town twinkled, a boat tooted, and a crowd of young men laughed in the street far below. His ears listened for the sound of those well-known footsteps uphill but he knew he was waiting in vain.

Again he looked at the house. The wind whistled up from the sea and, pulling his collar closer, he went slowly towards the little green gate set in the wall. For a long moment he hesitated at the door then he knocked demandingly before his courage left him. Seconds of eternity passed then quick, light steps could be heard within.

His heart pounded into his throat. Kirsteen! At last, Kirsteen!

But it wasn't Kirsteen who answered the door, though for a moment the dim glow of a paraffin lamp gave the illusion that the woman who stood there was the one he had come to find. The likeness was so marked he nearly cried out but in time he saw a woman much older than Kirsteen and her hair was brown instead of fair.

'Yes?' The voice was softly Highland but it held a note of impatience.

'Can I . . . is Kirsteen here?'

She held the lamp higher and stared at him. 'And who might you be?'

'Fergus – Fergus McKenzie. I knew Kirsteen on Rhanna and I was in Oban for a few days . . . and – I thought I'd look her up . . .'

The hissing sound of her indrawn breath made him falter like a small boy.

'So,' she breathed, 'you've come at last, McKenzie! Just a wee bit late, I'm thinkin'.'

'You – know of me then?'

'Know of you! My poor lass nigh broke her hert – aye – and her health too because of you!'

'But I wrote – my letters – she never answered!'

She inclined her head backwards. 'I never thought I'd be askin' you over my doorstep but you'd best come inside, for it's cold standin' there.'

The house was warm, with a cosy lived-in atmosphere, but Fergus was barely inside when he sensed that the homeliness was an echo of the past. The shabby furniture had known a lot of use, the polished floors and squares of carpet were well trampled and on the piano top the faces that smiled from photographs were of happy years the house had known. The firelight danced over the shadowy figures. There was Kirsteen, a tiny girl on her father's knee; Kirsteen, her arm thrown round the shoulder of a friend, happy tomboys with bare feet sinking in the sand; and

Kirsteen, lovely in young womanhood, her eyes solemn but a smile curving the corners of her mouth. And pride of place, Kirsteen on her graduation, the sombre gown and cap serving only to heighten the sweet youth of the girl who wore them.

Fergus felt an indescribable sadness creep over him for he knew, as surely as if he had been told, that photographs and memories were the only things of Kirsteen left in the house. There was no feel of her tangible presence and he wished that he had never made the journey to Oban.

'Sit down, McKenzie! Let me see the man that tore all our lives apart. I'd like to look at you properly!'

Mrs Fraser's tone was imperative and Fergus felt angry at being addressed in such a derogatory fashion. She was a match for him, he had sensed the ruthless strength of her instantly, and he resented her for it.

But he sat down on the edge of a chair. 'Where's Kirsteen?' he asked flatly.

'You may well ask.' Her tone was so bitter that he looked up quickly. 'Gone she is, my own daughter. She wouldn't bide wi' me and all I wanted was to take care of her, even after all the shame she brought on us! It's no wonder her poor father died! A broken hert it was. Och, he doted on that girl so he did!'

'Her father . . . dead?'

'Aye, just six months ago. She wouldn't do as we asked! We wanted her to go away and have the bairn adopted when it came! But no! She got heavier and the whole of Oban seeing it – and her – like a hussy she was! Holding her head high, saying she was *proud* to be with child!'

Fergus turned white and stood up to face her. 'Did you say . . . Kirsteen is having a child?'

'*Had* a child, McKenzie! Your child, two months ago! A wee mite of a thing he was and her so ill she nearly died. But she came through, she and the wee laddie! Och, a bonny wee thing – dark, like you, McKenzie. We can only beseech the Lord he doesn't grow up to have your selfish streak in him!'

Fergus sat down heavily. He stared at Kirsteen's mother. 'Oh, God no,' he breathed, 'why didn't she tell me? I loved her! I wanted to marry her. I didn't know about the baby. I swear I didn't know!'

'Hmph! And the pair o' you livin' in sin! *She* said you didn't know but how could we believe her after all the lies she told us about her nice, clean-livin' life on Rhanna! We brought up that girl to tell the truth and she was a good God-fearin' child till you warped her, McKenzie. *Proud* of her pregnancy she was! She wanted the child to remind her of you! When I think of her poor father! Och, he was a good man, and he'd already forgiven her when he died. It was too much for him . . . the shame, the disgrace of it all! He sacrificed so much for that girl and that was how she repaid us.'

'Where is she?' Fergus's voice was tight.

'God knows, I wish I did but I wouldn't tell you! She walked out taking that poor wee mite with her!'

Fergus gritted his teeth and stood up again. 'WHERE IS SHE?'

Her hands clenched together till the knuckles showed white.

'I tell you I don't know and it's the truth. She said

she was going to one of the big towns to find work. I begged her to stay but madam was too proud. Didn't want to be beholden to her own mother. Despite all, I was willing to keep her in my house. I knew all the neighbours were whisperin' behind my back but she was my lass and I stuck by her and that was my thanks. Gone three weeks now and not a stroke of a pen. I could be dead for all she cares!'

In a flash Fergus saw it all. The long weary months of pregnancy, Kirsteen, that lovely head of hers held as high as it had been on Rhanna; her father's death; the recriminations, the hints that it had been all her fault. Her mother's continued air of martyrdom; the birth of the child. Kirsteen's lonely soul tortured in a world where it must have seemed everyone had turned against her. He could almost feel her ceaseless torment till finally she had fled from all that was familiar in her life to an uncertain existence in some noisy, frightening city.

He put his hand to his forehead in an agony of remorse. But something nagged at him, his letters! He had poured out the love in his heart, his pen had written things that he hadn't felt himself capable of expressing. Surely Kirsteen must have known that he had mourned for her.

He looked directly into Mrs Fraser's eyes. 'Did she not get my letters? I asked her over and over to come back to Rhanna to be my wife.'

Mrs Fraser could not hold his look. She fidgeted but when she spoke, her voice was coldly defiant. 'The first came when she was in hospital too ill to be bothered with anything. The others came when she was home but I made sure she never got them! I didn't want her to go to you! Not after you treating her like a hussy! I wanted her to stay here – with me – her and the wee one, but she went – just like a stranger she walked away from her own mother . . .'

His hand dug deep into her shoulder and she cowered under the strength of his blazing fury. 'She never got my letters! You call yourself her mother yet you wanted to rob her of any chance of happiness! I love her! Do you hear me, woman? Now, because of you she's in some God-forsaken place and we might never find her!'

She struggled to free herself. 'Let me be,' she demanded furiously. 'Yes! I'm at fault, McKenzie, and I'm sick with the knowing of it, but who put her with child then said he couldn't wed her! You, McKenzie, live with that on your conscience if you will!'

All at once he was deflated. 'We're all to blame,' he said softly, 'but you're right, I am most of all. I want now to find Kirsteen and I want you to tell me of anyone who might know where she is.'

Her own fit of indignation had subsided and he got a glimpse of a lonely woman.

'Do you not think I've asked? Her friends, everyone she knew – aye, and they were many for she was a popular lass, but not a soul knows of her whereabouts after me burying my pride to ask. Fancy, her own mother not knowing, eh? Aye, the tongues have been wagging here for sure!'

'If you hear, will you let me know?' he asked abruptly.

She smiled coldly. 'If I hear.'

'And the letters, can I have them back? If I find her I'd like to show her those letters.'

'I'll not be having them any more.'

'You destroyed them?'

She didn't answer but was already at the door to usher him out.

'I'll be bidding you goodnight then, Mrs Fraser.'

'Aye, goodnight.' Her voice was so distant he got the impression that she had already dismissed him from her thoughts. He took a last look round the room. Kirsteen smiled at him from the piano. A photograph . . . if he could even have a photograph.

But she had read his mind. 'I'm sorry but I have none to spare.'

The door closed behind him. A cold wind whipped round his legs and he felt that what had passed had been a dream. He had imagined it all and in a minute he would knock on Kirsteen's door and she would answer it. But already he was in the busy part of the town, that little house in the dark hilly street far behind him. His mind was numb. All that he could think of was that, somewhere unknown to him, Kirsteen struggled to keep herself and their little son. Their son! He caught his breath and was only then aware that he was crying, there in the street, where people could see him. The salt breeze whipped him and his legs carried him aimlessly. Light streamed on to the pavement in front of him. He looked up and through a glimmer of tears saw a public house. He didn't remember opening the door but suddenly he was surrounded by talk and laughter, warm smoke, and the fumes of beer and whisky.

Two hours later he staggered once more into the cold night air. He was drunk, so drunk that he had to lean against a wall for several minutes. Shadows passed and the disapproving ghost glances of strangers made him laugh, a slurred lunatic laugh, induced by the disposal of nearly a full bottle of whisky. Fergus was used to a good dram. He had always been able to hold his drink but now he careered along the streets in the weaving motion of the drunk. He fumbled and found a cigarette. Standing still to light it was an even greater problem than walking. Over and over the wind blew out the matches.

'Bastard!' he shouted stupidly. 'Daft bloody bastard!'

He staggered on, gulping in smoke and coughing, the inside of his head feeling as if it were stuffed with cotton wool.

'Kirsteen!' he shouted into the wind. A light rain began to fall but he was unaware of it. Tears of self-pity poured down his face; his nose was running and tears and mucus mingled together. He bounced against a wall and hung there, his shoulders hunched and his eyes staring wildly.

'I've a son!' he told several passersby. They gave him a wide berth and he bawled out his lunatic laugh, over and over, till his ears rang. He was so drunk he felt neither grief nor pain. His cigarette burned into his fingers and he giggled; he unpinned his sleeve and let it flap in the wind from the sea, and all the time his numbed thoughts for Kirsteen and the son he hadn't known existed were expressed in the hopeless tears that kept trickling from eyes that were swollen and red.

He lurched and mumbled through the quietening streets. He began to feel sick and the lights in the streets were wobbling alarmingly. He was sweating and shivering and had to urinate. Drunk though he was, he looked round desperately for a toilet. There was none. Deep in the recesses of his mind his human dignity struggled to assert itself. He tried to make for a doorway but had no time. A young couple were courting in a dark little wynd. They were kissing and giggling and the girl was making little noises of protest. They saw Fergus at the exact moment he saw them. He felt the hot liquid coming from his bladder and he was horrified even in his stupor. Quickly he undid his buttons and the stream flowed from him, weaving down through the cobbles in little steaming rivulets.

The girl stared and giggled. The boy grabbed her hand and tore her away. 'Dirty drunken pig!' he hissed at Fergus. 'You should be locked up, so you should!'

Even then Fergus was unable to stop. He stood where he was till his bladder emptied itself then he leaned against a wall and was sick. Afterwards he felt better but still dizzy and drunk. He stood in the rain till his head cleared, then he made his way back to his hotel, thankful that it was quiet and he was able to creep up to his room unseen.

He fell on to the bed, dimly aware that he smelt of alcohol and vomit. His sleep was deep but unsatisfying and he woke early, shuddering when he saw the state of his clothes. He coughed and knew that sleeping in wet clothes had brought on a bout of bronchitis. Lachlan had warned him to guard against damp because his pneumonia had left him with a weak lung.

He lay back and looked at the ceiling. His head ached and he felt fevered but over-riding all were the hopeless thoughts that crowded into his mind. Dimly he remembered his drunken wanderings of the previous night and bitter shame made him cry out. He felt he had sunk to the very depths of degradation by allowing himself to get into such a condition. He was Fergus McKenzie, strong of mind and body; he wasn't some poor helpless animal who cared nothing for dignity. He was a man, a *man*!

He put his hand over his eyes and tried to will his aching body to move from the bed. He craved for a drink of water but his body wouldn't obey his mind and he fell back exhausted on the pillows and sank again into the abyss of sleep.

From a long way off a voice called him. He forced his eyes to open and the plump, good-natured face of his landlady wavered above him.

'Are you ill, Mr McKenzie?'

'A drink . . . just want a drink . . . water . . . that's all.'

She touched his brow. 'Why, it's fevered you are, sir, and you're coughing real bad, heard you on the stairs I did! It's the doctor I'm fetching. Now, now, lie back, I'll get Maisie to bring you a nice cup of tea and a bit toast. But first we'll get you into pyjamas . . . in your case are they?'

He struggled to sit up. 'Mrs Travers, I'll be managing these myself!'

'Ach – a thrawn one I see! You can put them on

while I phone the doctor. You're in a terrible mess so you are! I didn't think a gentleman like yourself would get into such a state.'

'Nor did I, Mrs Travers,' he said ruefully. 'Just a wee thing I had to sort out for myself.'

'Aye.' She folded her hands over her stomach and looked at him. She was a cheery little woman with pink skin and greying hair. Her experience of human nature had made her a good judge of character and she could tell that the crumpled big Gael was no habitual drunk. 'Aye,' she repeated softly, 'you'll sort it out in this bed for that's where you'll be bidin' for the next few days I'm thinkin'.'

She was right. Dr Mason was slow and lumbering but he discovered Fergus's weak lung immediately.

'Bed,' he said briefly, folding his stethoscope and stuffing it into a large pocket. 'For at least four days. I'll give you some pills to clear the inflammation and a bottle to ease your tubes.'

Mrs Travers had come into the room to hear the verdict. 'I'll see he takes them, doctor . . . and don't worry, the laddie will get the best of attention here.'

The doctor winked at Fergus. 'A real tartar but a heart of gold for all that. You stopped at the right hotel, lad – Maggie Travers is the best unqualified nurse in Oban.'

Fergus was strangely content to stay in bed in the bright cheerful room; it was a little haven; he felt shut off from the world and for the moment he didn't want the world so he was as happy as it was possible to be. He knew he was living in a fool's paradise but he didn't want to think of the future. One half of him wanted to go back to Rhanna but the other half rebelled against it. For the past seven months he had fully believed that the day would come when he must meet Kirsteen again, it had been there, always at the back of his mind, that lovely romantic illusion of their reunion. Now it had all been taken away and he was numb. He didn't want to think of a life without Kirsteen, he didn't want to face the thought of the empty years ahead, so for the moment, he pushed Rhanna, with its familiar things and people, far into the recesses of his mind. It was enough just to lie and listen to the outside world, the sounds of the waterfront, people laughing and shouting, just as long as he didn't have to take his place in that demanding world outside his room he was content.

Mrs Travers coddled him and reminded him so much of Mirabelle he put his hand out once and squeezed hers gently.

'You're good to me so you are. Why are you so?'

'Och, because I always wanted a laddie like you, and because that old bone-shrinker's right – I enjoy nursin'. My poor old Murdy only has to sniff and he's in bed cuddlin' a hot bag . . . besides . . .' She patted his hand. 'I liked you, son. You have a troubled hert and though I might not mend it at least I can try and keep it cheery.'

Murdoch Travers blustered in to see Fergus. He brought beer and a pack of cards and amiably helped Fergus to forget himself. He spoke about shinty and fishing, sunsets and boats, showing a breezy enthusiasm for everyday topics till even mundane things like having a bath sounded like a crazy adventure.

Maisie Travers dimpled into the room with washing bowls and food trays. She was the Traverses' only child and at the age of twenty-five giggled coyly like a schoolgirl and blushed prettily. She flirted with Fergus, bending low over his bed so that he got an unparalleled view of her smooth firm breasts.

One day he ran his fingertips over the smooth skin of her face and the feel of it brought back memories of what it was like to love a woman.

'You're a nice girl, Maisie,' he said softly. 'Why have you never married?'

'I've never met the right man,' she answered. Her green eyes looking into his and her lips parted showing small white teeth. On an impulse he drew down her dark head and kissed her briefly on the mouth.

'You will, Maisie,' he said gently. 'You're a bonny lass.'

He was well enough now to go into that world which had seemed so hostile to him. He stepped into a world of spring. Daffodils were bursting everywhere and the birds were singing. He looked around. This was Oban, Kirsteen's home town, he had to know the places she had known. He walked to the school where she had been a teacher; like a small boy he peered through the railings and pictured her there, blowing her whistle, calling the children to order.

He went to the hospital where she had given birth to his son and tortured himself with mental pictures of her writhing in pain, the way Helen had writhed giving birth to Shona. He trod again up the hill to the cottage with its gay blooming garden and its air of waiting for people of the past to step into the present to bring it back to life. A curtain fluttered at a window and he knew he was being observed. In a way he felt sorry for Mrs Fraser. She was like him, lonely and waiting and knowing it was hopeless.

He was grey and tired when he got back to the hotel. Mrs Travers tutted disapprovingly and made him go back to bed.

'First day out your sick bed and you tramp the streets for hours. Are you demented, laddie?'

He pulled the sheets round him. 'Aye, you could say that.'

'I know fine. It's a lass, isn't it?'

'You know too much!' he said grimly.

She folded her hands over her stomach in characteristic fashion. 'No, laddie, not enough! You puzzle me, you puzzle us all.'

'You've been talking! I should have guessed.'

'Discussing more like. A fine young man like yourself shouldn't be alone! You are alone, aren't you? Why else would you be here breaking your hert?'

He sighed and put his hand over his eyes. 'I was married . . . a grand lass she was! We were happy, very happy, then came the bairn, my daughter Shona, and Helen died having her. I was a bitter man for a long time – dammit I even resented my own child! But the years healed and a time came when I met another lass, fine she was, too good for me but we were to be married, then . . .' He indicated his empty sleeve. 'This happened. I thought she wouldn't want me and she knew it, she'd waited too long already! So she went away and it's nigh on eight months since I last saw her.'

She nodded. 'So you came looking for her?'

'Aye, I'd written but her mother kept back the letters, now Kirsteen's gone and no one knows where, she never even told her mother. What chance have I of finding her . . . she could be anywhere in the world!'

Mrs Travers sat down slowly on the edge of the bed. 'Kirsteen . . . you wouldn't be talking of Kirsteen Fraser, would you?'

He looked at her wildly. 'You know her? You know Kirsteen?'

'Of course I do,' she said softly. 'Oban's quite a big place but we all know the other and Kirsteen being a schoolteacher was well known – aye, and well loved too. Poor child, her mother wanted her to be a saint and her father just fell in with everything Maudie Fraser wanted. He was a kindly wee man but henpecked if you know what I mean. He loved his daughter and was proud of her – they both were – maybe too proud. When she came home from that island where she went to teach she came home with child and they nearly died of the shame! Oh . . .'

She stared at him and he nodded. 'Aye, Mrs Travers, my son – and I swear I knew nothing about him till that first night I set foot in Oban. Mrs Fraser would barely let me over the door but she told me enough to make me wish I'd never been born.'

'Your son, Mr McKenzie?' She studied him. 'Aye, right enough, that dark hair, and the dimple, just plunk in the middle o' his wee chin. A bonny wee mite he was. Kirsteen brought him round here often before she went.'

'Kirsteen's been here?'

'Aye, she was never a stranger in this abode. Near demented she was with her mother accusin' her o' bein' a hussy and a shame to the family. Blamed she was for her father dyin' and he with a weak hert for years. The lass was so good to her parents too, she kept them in bread and butter ever since she graduated. Her father wasn't strong enough to work, you see, and it was Mrs Fraser going out on wee jobs that saw her girl through college. But Kirsteen paid them back in full . . . oh aye, she did! She even sent money from Rhanna. Mrs Fraser was always going on about her good lassie.' She nodded sadly. 'That was why she took it so bad – the bairn, I mean. She gave the girl no peace. Oh, she offered to give them a home but can you picture it? The accusations and the tears? She could turn them on like a tap could Maudie Fraser. Yes, Kirsteen came round here often, Mr McKenzie, I saw her getting near to breaking, then I heard she couldn't take any more and she just went away one day and never came back.'

He grabbed her arm eagerly. 'Do you know where, Mrs Travers? Oh please God that you do!'

'Ach laddie, I wish I did but somehow I'm thinkin' we'll not be seein' Kirsteen again.'

He lay back on the pillows and her kind heart turned over when she saw the long dark lashes glistening with tears. 'There, laddie,' she said huskily. 'I know fine you love that lass and she will be loving

341

you too. Ach, it's a funny old world so it is, but God will let you meet again.'

He opened his eyes and looked at her pleadingly. 'If you hear anything . . . any little thing that will help me find Kirsteen . . . will you let me know?'

She pulled a hanky from her apron and blew her nose loudly. 'You can count on me, son. I'd like nothing better than to bring the pair o' you together again.'

He looked at her seriously. 'I'm glad I met you, Mrs Travers, I don't take to a lot of folk and they don't take kindly to my dour tongue. Last year I lost two of the finest friends I had in the world and I've felt a gap at their going. You're a nice body and Murdy's a fine man, I'd like fine if you'd befriend a man like myself – maybe come to Rhanna for a holiday now and then. Laigmhor's a big place and there's only myself and Shona.'

Her face beamed with pleasure. 'Och, I'd like nothing better. We're quiet here out of season. I've never been to the Hebrides and Rhanna sounds a lovely island.'

Fergus looked out of the window at the grey clouds scudding across the sky. It was a windy, salt fresh day, the kind of day Shona loved. All at once he felt homesick.

'Rhanna is lovely,' he said quietly.

'And Maisie too?' Mrs Travers was saying.

He came back from his thoughts and smiled.

'Yes, Maisie too, though Rhanna might be a bit quiet for such a spirited lass.'

'Och, Mr McKenzie, Maisie's a shy girl, she's country

bred . . . and she's very fond of yourself too and I'm sure would love to stay at that bonny farm you talk about.'

But he wasn't listening, his mind was wandering over the sea to Rhanna, and he knew he was ready to go back. There was nothing now to keep him in Oban.

Part Six

Summer 1939

Chapter Twelve

Shona raced to the top of the hillock behind Laigmhor and shaded her eyes to look towards Portcull. She had heard the ferry tooting its funny little horn while it was still in the Sound of Rhanna.

It was a morning of pearly mist and though it was nearly the end of June the dew lay heavy in the fields. There was the promise of another long hot day and she was breathless when she reached the top of the rise. Her breasts rose and fell quickly and when she saw the ferry tying up in the harbour she fell to her knees on the wet grass and a soft little chuckle of pleasure escaped her slightly parted lips.

'Niall.'

She spoke the name gently, savouring the sound of it. The smell of peat smoke drifted lazily from Portcull and she breathed in the scent of it ecstatically. Everything was going to be wonderful that day. Niall was home. They had the long summer days ahead. He could forget about his studies at the vet-erinary college in Glasgow. Together they would roam Rhanna and while away the lazy hours of all the lovely lazy days. They always had so much to talk about yet just being quietly together was a queer intimate kind of happiness.

Tot came labouring up the hill. She was eleven now,

rheumaticky and slow, but still willing to leave her basket to follow her mistress.

Shona swept her up and kissed her silky ears. 'You're a lazy Cailleach,' she said lovingly, 'and I'm going to carry you the way I did when you were a silly wee pup. It seems a long time ago, I was just five and Hamish gave you to me for a birthday present.'

She stood with the old dog clasped to her and that day of her fifth birthday came back with blinding clarity. She remembered all the moments she thought were forgotten. Her father giving her the purse she still treasured; Mirabelle and the patiently knitted black stockings she had hated; Hamish with the wriggling bundle inside his coat. That had been the day she'd fought with Niall in the post office and Mirabelle had smacked her for her rudeness. She remembered it all as if it had only just happened but Mirabelle and Hamish were dead, her father was still as lonely as he had been on her fifth birthday. Tot was old and no longer romped.

Shona felt a little catch of sadness in her throat. For a long moment she stood, a slender graceful figure silhouetted against the sky, then her deep blue eyes looked again to the harbour and bubbling joy took the place of poignant memories.

She hoisted Tot against her shoulder and ran over the field path, taking the short cut to Portcull.

She saw him first and for a second she said nothing but stood among the trees watching. Every few months away from Rhanna brought changes in him. She had noted each different aspect of his growing years with surprise but with an acceptance that it must be so. Yet, though there were the inevitable changes, he had still remained boyishly handsome, his voice was gruff and a fine fair stubble grew on his tanned face if he forgot to shave, but the boy had been more predominant than the man.

Now she gave a little gasp of surprise at sight of him. She hadn't seen him since Christmas because he hadn't managed home at Easter. He had broadened and his chest was deep, his bare arms muscular and strong, and he was even taller than her father. But more than anything she noticed the fair little moustache. It changed his whole appearance and made the boy a man.

She shrank back among the trees, afraid that because he looked so different his whole character and personality would be different also. Then she heard the gay jaunty whistle and saw the corn curls bobbing in time to the tune.

A leaf tickled her nose and she sneezed. He looked up and she went flying out to him, a jumble of petticoats, sunburnished hair, and breathless giggles. He threw out his arms and she ran into them and he hugged her so tightly Tot wheezed in protest.

'Shona,' he breathed against her warm silken hair. He tore her away from him. 'Let me look at you – you skinny wee thing.'

'Och, Niall I'm not.' She laughed protestingly, wishing he hadn't pushed her out of his arms so quickly.

He saw the beauty of her slender, sixteen-year-old figure, and his heart beat swiftly. She was wearing a flimsy white dress and he could see the top of her breasts, the skin there was white and looked like satin and her neck was long and graceful. His eyes travelled to her face and he could see the tiny fair hairs on her smooth, peach-bloom cheeks. She was standing against the breaking sun and gossamer strands of hair gleamed like copper.

'You . . . look nice,' he said casually. 'You've filled out a wee bit since Christmas.'

'Is *that* all you can say?' she cried angrily. 'I don't like that silly wee bit hair on your face! You don't look like you at all!'

He threw back his head and roared with laughter. 'Well, *you* haven't changed! Still a damt wee spitfire! Caillich Ruadh!'

'I hate you, Niall McLachlan! Gordon McNab from Portvoynachan thinks I'm beautiful!'

Niall glowered at her. 'And who's he then?'

'Just – a man! I've Ceilidhed with him and I danced with him at Neil Munro's wedding. Four nights it went on – it was grand. I was drinking port and got quite merry and he kissed me twice.'

Niall grabbed her arm. 'You've never mentioned him before! Did he only kiss you?'

'I'm not telling! Anyway, it's none of your business. *You* never kiss me – well only like a brother – not that I'd be wanting it any other way,' she added hastily.

'I'm not letting you go till you tell me about Gordon McNab!'

His fingers were digging into her bare arm and she winced but he wouldn't give in.

'What about all the girls at the college?' she countered. 'Don't tell me you haven't kissed some of them!'

'And what if I have?'

Her nostrils flared. '*Oh*, so you have a fine carry on in Glasgow have you?'

'That I have, and a girl called Isabel is my special favourite. She lets me cuddle her a lot . . . nice wee arse she has too.'

Her cheeks were scarlet and tears of rage danced in her eyes. 'Och, you're a dirty bugger, Niall McLachlan – always did swear like a heathen!'

'You're swearing!'

'Who's Isabel?'

'Who's Gordon McNab?'

She looked at him and a twinkle shone through the tears. 'A lonely old man of sixty who's just come to Rhanna and does odd jobs at the farms.'

'And Isabel is the college cat who sleeps on my bed and has kittens twice a year.'

They burst out laughing and he threw his arm round her and hugged her close.

'Silly wee thing,' he said affectionately.

Dodie came loping behind them. 'He breeah!' he greeted mournfully. 'I have just come from Shelagh's house! She is asking for the doctor.'

'I'll tell him, Dodie,' said Niall.

Dodie paused to study Niall. 'My, but it's growing you are just. I thought you might have failed a bit in Glasgow. I hear tell it's a dirty smelly place with thon motor cars killing people all the time.'

Niall laughed. 'It's not like that really, Dodie. It is noisy and a bit smelly but it's interesting and I appreciate Rhanna all the more for being away.'

Dodie rubbed his grizzled chin thoughtfully but his

eyes were far away. 'Aye, there is that! I'll be goin' now, I'm needin' my dinner. Shelagh gave me a nice bit salt pork she couldny eat herself. Roarin' like a bull so bad in pain she is . . . terrible just so it is. He breeah!'

He galloped away over the hill track. The years had made little changes in him except that the stubble on his chin had changed from a dirty brown to a dirty grey.

Shona stopped at her gate and Niall squeezed her shoulder.

'The cave after dinner,' he whispered. 'I have something for you.'

The colour tinged her face. 'It's not my birthday.'

'It's a special thing, something I hope . . . och well you'll see for yourself. I'll be a bitty late for I have something to tell my folks.'

He strode off and she fancied his jauntiness was somewhat forced but she dismissed the idea as a mere whim of her imagination and flew up the path to burst into the kitchen.

Fergus turned from the sink where he was washing. 'Niall's home then?'

'Yes, did you see him?'

'No, but you're all pink and there's a sprite in your eye.'

'Father.' She smiled and reached up to kiss his sideburns. They were almost white, though the rest of his hair was still jet black. The touches of white only served to enhance his strong handsome features but it was one of Shona's favourite jokes to tease him about it. It was one of their 'alone together' intimacies, and he would laugh and retaliate by calling her his

'Sibhreach'. She had been thin and elfin-looking for years and the endearment had infuriated her at times. Now her mirror told her she was no longer an awkward bundle of arms and legs and she could laugh at the idea of being likened to a fairy spectre.

'I'll get dinner, Father,' she told him, putting an apron over her dress, and bustling about with a gay tune on her lips.

Fergus sat at the table and watched her. 'You're so happy when Niall's home,' he observed.

She set soup on the table and pulled in her chair. 'I'm happy all the time, Father – with you here – we're so warm and peaceful together. But – with Niall I feel a big bubble – just here,' she placed her hand over her heart, 'and I feel it growing to a million bubbles all bursting in funny little excited pops! Does that sound daft, Father, or have you ever felt like that?'

He stopped with his spoon in mid-air. 'Aye, I've felt like that, Shona, but it all seems so long ago I've almost forgotten what it feels like.'

She studied him and wanted to reach out and transfer some of her happiness to him.

'It'll happen again, Father, you'll meet her again. I know you loved her so much.'

For a moment he was startled and angry. He had guessed that his daughter knew far more about his thoughts than she ever revealed. She was quick and sensitive and a strange telepathy ran between them. He appreciated her deep intelligent mind, she knew how to be diplomatic, but at times she was too aware of his innermost mind and he resented it. A quick retort rose to his lips but her incredible deep blue gaze held his with unwavering love. 'I hope you'll never be hurt too much,' he found himself saying. 'A little hurt must be expected, we all know we can't go through life with our head in the clouds, but too much hurt can tear a heart to pieces and somehow the bits never fit into the right places again.'

It was the most he had ever divulged about himself. She felt honoured but tried not to show that the moment was so laden with intimacy.

'Och Father, be quiet and sup your soup,' she scolded. 'I've all those greedy hens to feed yet and I want to collect some eggs to take later to Shelagh. Poor old Cailleach, an egg is about the only thing she enjoys now.'

Soon she would be alone with Niall in the cave. The cave! Her eyes gleamed. It was their haven and as soon as she was free she ran over the heather with winged feet. The sun was shining in a blue sky and the world was a wonderful place.

The cave was cool and dark and she pulled bracken and heather back from the entrance so that sunlight found its way inside and dappled on the floor of mossy earth. She had come the day before to add new touches. The bed of stone was soft with sheepskins and cushions; the stone ledges were full of knick-knacks and some of Mirabelle's rag dolls sat next to cups and plates. Two old wickerwork chairs were positioned on either side of the fireplace on which stood a spirit stove and a paraffin lamp. It was like a real little home, each item lovingly gathered bearing a memory. She thought back to the day when the chairs had been smuggled from a shed at Laigmhor. She was twelve, Niall fourteen. They hadn't wanted the risk of anyone seeing them so had arranged to meet at dawn on a June morning. Five o'clock saw them struggling over the moors, each with a chair humped over their head. They had arrived exhausted at the cave and after fortifying themselves with liquorice sticks and chocolate fell asleep together on the sheepskins.

Shona fell on to the bed in a fit of laughter at the memory. A shadow darkened the doorway and Niall stood looking at her. He had changed into a kilt and old sweater, his favourite Rhanna clothes.

'Niall!' she said, the breathless laughter still in her voice.

'I thought I was hearing a demented spook of the Abbey laughing his lunatic dying laugh!' he chuckled, sitting down beside her. He looked round appreciatively. 'It's nice, mo ghaoil,' he said quietly. 'A real wee hoosie, is it not?'

'And would his lordship like a Strupak?' She giggled, placing an old kettle on the stove.

'And tea too? It's setting up house we should be.'

Her eyes were suddenly serious. 'And what could be nicer in the whole world than that? You and me in this cave and no one knowing where we were.'

'Ach, you'd tire of me and start throwing cups,' he laughed, but his tone was strange. She was kneeling, lighting the stove, and suddenly he bent and taking her face in his hands looked directly into her eyes. 'You're beautiful,' he said simply.

She felt hotly embarrassed and so acutely aware of his manly nearness that she rose quickly. 'I suppose you say that to all the girls.'

'Only the ones I like,' he teased.

She took down the cups and, keeping her face deliberately turned from him, asked, 'Niall, be serious and tell me – have you made love to a girl – really I mean?'

He clasped his hands round his knees and studied a patch of sun on the floor. 'We've known each other a long time, Shona, and we've always been honest. I'm a man now and I'm as human as the next lad. Yes, I did make love to a girl once but . . .'

She turned to face him and her eyes sparkled with unshed tears. 'Niall!' she cried.

'Let me finish, you wee spitfire. I did make love but I couldn't see it through because – because I kept thinking of you – dammit, I just couldn't do it!'

She turned once more into the shadows to hide her look of relief.

'Are you such a saint yourself?' he questioned roughly. 'I've been away a lot and – and I know for a fact there's a lot of lads daft on you! What about that then? Are you so prim as you make out?'

She met his blustering questions with a steady gaze. 'No, Niall, I'm not prim, I never was and you know it. I have been out with a few of the lads – I admit to it for you'll hear it anyway. Ti Johnston kissed me once and do you know what? I nearly spewed so I did. His mouth was wet and he smelled of potted herring!'

They looked at each other and laughed till the cave echoed.

'Och, Shona!' Niall wiped his eyes. 'You're a terrible girl but I'm glad Ti wasn't nice to kiss for you might have enjoyed it.' He grew suddenly serious. 'I've something to tell you, something you might not like, so promise you'll hear me out and not go running off in a temper.'

She glanced at him quickly, knowing now she hadn't been mistaken when she sensed the restraint in him. 'I half promise,' she said, forcing a smile. 'I can't help myself sometimes so it's no use making a real promise.'

He watched a spider making a web between some ornaments. 'I'm only going to be on Rhanna for a week then I'm going off to training camp. I volunteered for the Army and passed my medical and everything. There's a war coming, Shona and I don't feel right just sitting back and doing nothing. I want to fight for my country. I'm a man – and – and anyway, I'm going.'

There was a stunned silence. Shona couldn't believe her ears. The war and all it meant seemed very unreal to her. Rhanna was like another world. The islanders listened avidly to the progress and destruction of war but it was like an adventure story. Most of the men on the island couldn't possibly be spared because their existence, and that of their families, depended too much on the harvests of land and sea. A few of the young boys had spoken tentatively about joining up but families too often depended on young hands for the heavier crofting tasks and, as yet, it was all just a topic of conversation to most people.

Shona could feel nothing but an incredulity.

'Och, Niall, stop pretending! Your parents won't let you go. They've given you all those chances of a better education. You can't let them down.'

He took her hand gently. 'Shona, my parents know already. Och – of course they wereny pleased – not at first! I've just had an awful row with them! Father can understand but Mother is near demented.' He smiled indulgently. 'She has me dead already and me not even begun my training. She was begging Father to stop me but he's a sensible man my father. He's not pleased but he can see I must do what I feel is right. I'm young, Shona, I can go back to my studies later. Try to understand, mo ghaoil.'

Shona was barely listening. She was thinking how senseless it all was. She had read about the bloody massacre of the First World War. Between the wars there had just been enough time for boy babies to grow up and go marching into another bloodbath. They could all go if they wanted; if they had to prove they were men. Let them fight for medals that were often granted to them after they were dead – but not Niall, she was already proud of him, she knew the stuff he was made of, he didn't have to prove it.

She tore her hand away and raced outside to lean against the sunbathed rocks. It was very hot but she felt cold and trembled. She could do nothing to stop the tears coursing down her cheeks. The sunshine was blotted out and Niall appeared through a watery veil. 'Shona – my dear little Shona,' he breathed, 'do you cry with anger or with sorrow that I am going?'

She turned her face away but he took her pointed chin and gently made her face him. His head was very near; she saw the golden threads caught by the sun; his eyes were close and held her own with such a powerful intensity she couldn't turn away again. His skin was flushed and small beads of perspiration stood out on his forehead. He put out his hand and touched her hair and in a dream she felt his own hair running through her fingers. She hadn't even been aware of reaching out to him. Somewhere close at hand a bee buzzed but it was a sound outside of the world into which she had stepped with Niall. She heard her heart beating very fast then, in a rush of beauty and wonder, she was in his arms and he was kissing her. They had kissed before; short little pecks of affection, but now she was drowning in a tide of excitement. His lips were warm and firm and for a brief moment she could feel his tongue touching hers. But it was all so quick and changing. Their mouths were mobile instruments of pleasure. She heard a little cry at the back of his throat and felt his breath quickening. She sensed rather than felt his hands on her breasts, his touch was like a feather, yet it sent electric impulses deep down inside and awakened chords of desire she hadn't known existed. The feeling reached down even further till she was throbbing with a heat that had nothing to do with the sun. She too cried out and it was then he pushed her away almost roughly. She was still in the trance and he put her head on his shoulder and stroked her long burnished hair. 'Shona – I love you,' he said savagely. 'I've known now for a long time and – and there have been times in the last year when I didn't dare touch you or come too close in case – in case . . .'

She traced the curve of his ear and whispered, 'I've loved you since you were a wee boy and I was always so afraid you would meet someone each time you left

Rhanna. I love you, my Niall, and now you are going away.'

He didn't answer for a few moments but kept stroking her hair. The nearness of her, her sweet female scent, made him burn with desire. She had grown so beautiful; each time he came back to the island he saw some change in her. She wasn't very tall, her head came barely to his shoulder, she was fragile looking but so beautifully proportioned and so very feminine that, in the past, it had been difficult for him to be near her without wanting to take her in his arms. Now she was, and her lips, and that fleeting moment of touching the firm roundness of her breasts, had driven him so crazy with the need for her that he couldn't trust himself to keep her in his embrace.

He pushed her gently away and held her at arm's length.

'My little tomboy, when did you grow up to be so bonny? I've known you most of my life yet in a way I'm just getting to know you properly. You're new somehow, not like the old Shona at all!'

'That's how I feel about you,' she breathed. 'I feel we've played and talked all these years but we were just marking time – waiting for the moment when we would throw our old selves away and – and put on our grown-up selves. Does that sound daft?'

He smiled. 'It sounds like the old Shona, but I'll settle for a mixture of the old and the new. Now, would you close your eyes for a wee minute?'

She squeezed her eyes shut and felt him placing something round her neck. It was a gold locket, beautiful in its simplicity and when she opened it a tiny heart-shaped picture of Niall gazed out at her.

'Put one of yourself, next to it,' he said, 'and we'll be together even when I'm away.'

Tears of sadness and happiness made her voice funny. 'Niall – it's beautiful – I think I'll treasure it for the rest of my life.'

A return of boyish embarrassment made him redden slightly but again he clasped her hand in his.

'It's – it's a kind of engagement present really. I didn't want to get a ring in case you wouldn't accept it but – it's as good as a ring . . . isn't it, Shona?'

He looked at her anxiously and she leaned forward and kissed him tenderly. 'Better,' she murmured, 'much much better! You can't put photos into a ring.'

He pulled her close and whispered. 'You know it means I want to marry you . . . after the war.'

'I hate that man Hitler.' Shona's voice was vehement. 'With his silly wee moustache and cow's lick! Oh, I wish I wasn't a girl! I'd go to the war myself, so I would!'

'I'm glad you're a girl,' he cried with such passion that she held her breath. 'So very very glad! Sometimes you were a wee pest but that was a long time ago. I'm glad you're Shona McKenzie and I'm glad you belong to me.'

For the rest of the afternoon they walked hand in hand in the sunshine, not speaking much because the wonder of their love was too overpowering to be expressed verbally. Their eyes spoke volumes, they laughed at little things and squeezed hands, hearts pounding with the awareness of each other's nearness. Everything was doubly beautiful, a droning bee, the sea shimmering in the distance, the smell of earth from which sprouted the tough, swaying moorland grasses. Time flew on wings and Shona gasped when she looked at her watch. 'It's almost teatime, I'll have to run! Father will be in and not even the table laid!'

Niall clung to her hand at the gate. 'After tea?'

She nodded breathlessly. 'Yes, I promised Shelagh some eggs but later we could go down to the harbour. It's lovely there in the gloaming.'

Kate McKinnon had left scones and bannocks to keep warm on the range. Fergus had washed and was laying the table.

'Och, Father, I'm sorry!' gasped Shona.

He chucked her on the chin. 'When are you ever late, lass? I'm early. Mathew's a good lad, we got those bottom fields cut today. If the summer's a good one we'll have two crops this year. It's needing it we are. Last winter there was little feed for the beasts.'

She was dreamy and withdrawn all through tea. He watched her and knew that something big had happened in her life. He was afraid of change yet knew he couldn't hold it back. He had watched his daughter changing from a gawky child into a beautiful young woman. It was to him she had turned when, at the age of thirteen, her bodily changes had manifested themselves. Phebie had told her what to expect so she wasn't afraid but nevertheless needed reassuring. He remembered her pale child's face that day and thinking she was still too much of a little girl for such womanly things to be happening to her. She had looked too young with her long hair tumbling over her shoulders and her big blue eyes looking up at him as she sat in the inglenook hugging the hot bag he had given her to ease the cramp.

She hadn't been embarrassed, speaking to him with a natural ease about her changing body. Her simple trust in him had swept away any reserves he might have had and in the years that followed they discussed life and its facts with a freedom that made him proud of her faith in him. But he had known that one day she would have her secrets from him.

In the years since Kirsteen's going from his life he had desperately needed comfort and he had found it in the child he had once rejected. She, lonely without Mirabelle, and lost without Niall, sought to fill the needs of her warm and loving spirit and turned to the father she loved so unashamedly. All the love she had yearned for in her infancy was now hers a thousandfold; there was a kindred intimacy, so richly fulfilling, it was enough for her to be near him without the need for words. Her greatest wish was that one day he would find the happiness he had waited so many years to find. Even she had never been very successful at drawing him out but she loved him enough to let time work for them both. But that was when her own heart was happy and carefree. Now she struggled with a welter of powerful emotions, her mind whirled with thoughts of Niall and the implications of their love for each other.

Absently she fingered the locket at her neck and Fergus leaned over the table curiously.

'That's new,' he remarked. 'A present?'

'In a way, an engagement present from Niall, instead of a ring. Oh Father . . .' She sucked in her breath and her eyes swam with tears. 'Niall wants to marry me – after the war! We love each other! I suppose we've known for a long time but today it all just came out! I think it was when he said he was joining the Army. I'm happy . . . yet at the same time my heart is all funny and achey! I'm so much in love I could burst, yet I'm so frightened I could cry and cry! *You* know how I feel, don't you, Father?' The tears poured over and she ran to him.

'There now, my lassie,' he soothed, stroking her hair gently. 'Yes, I know how you feel – so well I know – only with you and Niall there's so much youth and hope. I'm losing my hope – and my youth!'

She tore herself away. 'No, no,' she cried fiercely. 'You're not getting old! You're so big and strong and I've always thought you were like a big boy! Even when I was a tiny wee girl you were just such a boy. You're not even forty yet!'

He laughed. 'Thirty-nine, mo ghaoil, but I've heard tell life begins at forty, so maybe there's hope for me yet. But you are just beginning and have all the strength of your convictions I once had. I'm glad about you and Niall. He's a fine lad and he'll come marching out of the war with his head held high. I'm not surprised he joined the Army, he's got Lachlan's spirit.'

She buried her face into the warm hairy flesh at the top of his neck. It was good just to feel his strength and listen to his soft lilting voice and by the time she had put eggs and cake into a basket and was walking to Shelagh's cottage she was feeling much better.

A gay whistle made her turn and Niall came up to

her. They said nothing but their finger entwined in an unconscious gesture of affection.

Shelagh wheezed and grumbled at them but they knew she was glad to see them. She was eighty-three. Her hair was snowy white and her skin unblemished and smoothly pink though in the last six months she had failed rapidly, her once pear-shaped bulk thin and frail. She was dying of cancer. Lachlan had discovered it long ago and had wanted her to go to a mainland hospital for treatment but she was adamant that her pains were merely caused by her 'winds' and no force on earth would make her leave Rhanna.

'I won't be having a strange doctor prodding at my belly,' she scolded Lachlan. 'And I won't be lying in some foreign mortuary like a lump o' frozen meat and maybe gettin' cut up like a yowe on a slab and me never there to do anything about it. No, no, laddie, it's the Kirkyard for me beside the friends I've known all my days.'

Niall seated himself on a raffia stool beside the old lady's chair.

'And how's my lass these days? Still driving all the men crazy, are we?'

'Ach, dinna be daft,' she answered with asperity. 'The only way I ever drove anybody daft was wi' my farts! Mind you . . .' Her old blue eyes twinkled. 'There was a time when I had the lads at my skirts but the dirty buggers were all after the one thing!' She chuckled wickedly. 'I watched you two holdin' hands outside. Is it in love you are?'

'Yes, Shelagh,' said Shona simply.

'Ach well, keep a grip o' your dock, mo ghaoil. This one looks a real buck.'

'You know then, Shelagh?' grinned Niall cheekily.

Shelagh was enjoying herself enormously. 'Aye, we all have our moments, and of course there's the things I was after seein' when I worked to the gentry. I could write a book but it would never be published for it would indeed shock the Sunday people!' She giggled.

'I brought you some eggs and a cake, Shelagh.' Shona wanted to divert the conversation. It was strange. She had always enjoyed the earthy humour of the islanders but now she didn't want to hear it in front of Niall. She felt embarrassed and a little angry that he obviously had no such reserve. His corn curls were almost touching Shelagh's snowy locks as they laughed heartily together. The old lady's high-pitched cackle filled the little cottage. A late sunbeam streamed through the open door and shone on the two heads, turning one to gold, and the other to silver. The anger left Shona and in its place came sadness. Shelagh had so little time, yet she showed no sign of fear and could still laugh merrily though she suffered constant pain. Shona's anger was turned against herself for grudging the old woman a little pleasure. 'I hope you like the cake, you daft Cailleach,' she smiled. 'I made it myself with a wee spot rum to warm you up.'

Shelagh smiled coyly. 'Oh did you now? And what would I be wantin' wi' rum in a cake? It's a good measure in a glass I'm needin' but I'll eat a wee bit o' your cake though it will likely give me a bad dose o' the winds.'

A spasm of pain twisted her mouth and Shona saw that she was very weary.

'We'll be going, Shelagh,' she said gently. 'Let you get on with that awful shocking book you're going to write.'

Shelagh gripped her hand. 'I doubt if I've enough time to write a letter, my wee lass. Away you go now, it must be good to be young and to know that death is far away. I'm glad the pair o' you have discovered each other. All those years . . . I've watched you both growin' . . . never one without the other . . . it's right you should fall in love. And thank you for the eggs, they're grand so they are. I miss a fresh egg since I had to give up my own hens.'

Old Joe came in, his cheeks as smooth and round as ever, and his sea green eyes twinkling but not quite so brightly when he looked at Shelagh.

'How's the whining old bugger?' he greeted his cousin with brusque affection. 'Still weathering the storm, is it?'

'She'll see the snows of many a winter yet,' said Niall too brightly.

Shelagh nodded her head calmly. 'The autumn will see me out. I'll go wi' the leaves o' summer.'

Niall bent and kissed her on the cheek.

'You young bull,' she cackled but she was thrilled.

'You're fond of old Shelagh,' observed Shona when they were strolling down to the harbour. 'It was nice – the way you kissed her.'

'I know she won't be here when next I come back to Rhanna,' he said quietly and when she glanced at him she saw the glaze of unshed tears in his brown eyes. She knew his heart cried for the dear, familiar people they had once thought immortal.

It was peaceful at the harbour. The smell of tar hung in the air and the gulls mewed placidly as they rummaged in the seaweed for small marine creatures. The sky was pure blue with a touch of gold on the horizon and darkness would never fall completely on such a June evening. Hand in hand they ran over the wooden planks of the pier and stopped to look breathlessly at the unbelievably brilliant royal blue of the Sound of Rhanna.

'Such a night,' whispered Shona. 'It's perfect.'

He drew her close and kissed her full on the lips. 'I'll never forget this day and I'll always remember how you look now – with your hair on fire against the set of the sun, and a smudge of peat soot on your nose. Hold still till I wipe it off.'

He took out a rather grubby handkerchief, wet it in a salty puddle, then scrubbed her nose till she giggled, 'Och Niall, they'll be peeking behind their curtains and thinking we're daft. You know what they're like.'

'I want them to know about us. The world can watch me kissing you and washing your face with water from the sea. I want to shout to everyone that I love you. I don't care what anyone thinks!'

He grabbed her hand again and they ran to the end of the pier. A number of fishing boats were bobbing gently, shadowed waves slapping against their hulls. A dog barked from one; an old fisherman, pipe hanging from his mouth, worked with lobster pots on another, but several craft were deserted.

'C'mon,' said Niall and they clambered aboard the

nearest to snuggle among tarpaulin and ropes. They lay in each other's arms and the sea rocked them.

'I love boats,' said Shona. 'They're lovely, smelly, exciting things.' She propped herself on an elbow. 'It's lovely to see Portcull in the gloaming. The men will be eating supper and the children maybe having a scrub in the zinc tub before bed. Look at the reek from the chimneys – spiralling into the sky without a breath to blow it away.'

He propped himself up to look at the picture she described but her nearness disturbed any attempt at concentration. He slid his arm round her waist to pull her closer. For a moment she was dimly aware of the cloudless sky above before his head blotted every-thing out and she was once again oblivious to all but his lips doing things with hers that made her feel she was drowning in a world of ecstasy. She knew she was responding to him with the desires of a full grown woman. That morning she had still been a child; tonight she was a woman and she knew her life would never be the same again. She would think of Niall but her thoughts would hold all these lovely inti-mate secrets that were happening now. For a moment she was afraid of the strength of his passion. Fleetingly she tried to remember what he had been like on his last visit home but strangely she was unable to visual-ize the boyish, mischievous Niall of yesteryears; not now, when he was groaning deep in his throat and she could feel the hardness of his young body pressed to her own. He was murmuring her name over and over and his brown eyes held a look she had never seen before. She ran her fingers through his hair, feeling the warm dampness at the nape of his neck. Again his hands caressed her breasts and she closed her eyes, wanting the night of warm desire and clinging bodies to last forever, but a screaming gull, and voices on the shore called her to reality. 'Niall,' she whispered urgently, 'stop now please.'

He fell back on the deck his breath coming quickly. After a while he caught her hand and kissed it. 'I'm sorry, mo ghaoil. You make me forget everything when I'm near you. It's as well you stopped me.'

She kissed his warm forehead. 'I heard people but – I think I would have stopped anyway. We – we don't know each other well enough yet.'

He saw that she was serious but he couldn't suppress a yell of mirth. 'You dear funny wee thing!' He leaned on an elbow. 'Look, the water's lovely. Let's go for a paddle, I need something to cool me down.'

They were carefree again, divesting themselves of shoes and stockings to splash in the clear brown shallows. A few Portcull children watched longingly till, unable to resist, they too were dancing in the water, risking a scolding from parents for coming home with damp hems and wet knickers.

Morag Ruadh came along, combing the beach for driftwood. 'A fine night,' she observed, looking disapprovingly at Shona's skirt tucked into her knickers, 'but 'tis chilled you'll get with the sea splashin' up your backsides.'

'Och, it's lovely, Morag,' laughed Niall. 'It's up with your skirt, off with your shoes, and in you should be yourself!'

'Havers,' sniffed Morag, 'it's stiff feets I would be

getting and not able to get a note of sense out of the
harmonium on the Sabbath, forbye the fact that I
would not be able to spin my cloth and there's some
of us must work for a living.' She glanced proudly at
her long nimble fingers. 'Without me our house would
go to ruin. I tell you. My mother has hands like cow's
feets and my father just spends his days damping the
peat with his spit. But the day will come . . .' She was
already drifting away . . . 'when I'll be after marrying
and where will we all be then?'

Shona giggled. 'Poor Morag Ruadh, she's waited for
a man for years and thinks that the world will fall to
pieces if she ever gets wed. I know for a fact Totie
Little has waited years to get a chance to play the
organ and poor old Mr and Mrs McDonald love it
when Morag's out the house so that they can get a rest
from her tongue.'

Niall grinned. 'It's her red hair that makes her tongue
go – just like yours. All you Caillich Ruadhs have bad
tempers!'

She bent to pick up a shoe to throw at him but he
was already halfway up the beach, leaving a trail of
footprints in the sand. She ran after him and they
walked hand in hand through Portcull carrying their
shoes. They took the path through the fields and
the delicious fragrance of new-cut grass filled their
nostrils. At the top of the field they stood for a moment,
looking down at the roofs and chimneys of Laigmhor.

'Father will be making cocoa,' she said softly. 'I'd
better put on my shoes and stockings or he will
wonder what I've been doing.'

She squatted down on the grass and Niall sat beside

her. He caught her hand and kissed her briefly. 'We won't give him any reason to worry,' he said seriously. 'We won't give ourselves the opportunity for being alone very often. I love you too much to want to do anything to harm you so I think it would be a good idea to take Fiona with us. I promised her a picnic and a day in one of Ranald's boats. She's a wee pest I know but she'll keep me in order. Do you mind?'

'No, I don't mind, Niall, it would be for the best and I don't think Fiona's a nuisance at all. She asks a lot of questions but so did I at seven.'

He grinned. 'You still do, and daft ones at that, but I can thole them now – because I love you.'

She held his hand briefly, then she was flying downhill, her hair a mane of red in the setting sun.

Fergus had the milk ready for the bedtime cocoa. He studied her flushed face as she buttered scones at the table.

'You're late in,' he said lightly, trying not to sound as if he were interfering with her life.

She giggled. 'Do you know what I've been doing, Father? Paddling with Niall down at the harbour! It was lovely – the water so cool!'

'Paddling?' He laughed. 'And not a finer night for it. I wouldn't mind myself but could you imagine what Portcull would have to say about that?'

She gave Tot milk, then sat opposite Fergus to sip her cocoa.

He looked again at her face, which was partially curtained by her long hair and knew that the time had come for her heart to hold its secrets. 'Take care,' he said softly, 'now that you're a woman.'

She looked up quickly but knew instantly what he meant. 'Yes, Father, I'll try.' She shrugged her shoulders, looking at him pleadingly. 'There's so much that's new – feelings I never knew existed. I know I still look the same – but – inside I've changed. I think I grew up today, it's a wee bit frightening.'

His strong, dark face relaxed a little. 'You're still such a little lass really. Mirabelle would have you in black stockings and blue ribbons.'

'Do you remember these things, Father?'

'You'd be surprised at what I remember. I see everything, though you might not always think it. I'm not old and feeble yet, you know.'

She looked at his slim, powerful body, and burst out laughing. 'Och Father! Do you think I see you as a withered old Bodach? You're so good-looking I'd marry you myself if I could. Oh – if only Kirsteen could come back – we could all be happy.'

He stopped laughing and the shadows of his loneliness veiled his dark eyes.

'You know too much,' he said angrily. 'I can't remember discussing my private life with you!'

'Father, don't shout so,' she chided angrily. 'Perhaps if you did talk to me of such things it would help. I'm old enough to understand now.'

'I never could talk about myself,' he growled, his voice tightly controlled, 'and I don't know what makes you think you'll have a privilege no one else ever had.'

She got up and touched his shoulder lightly. 'It might be because I'm your daughter,' she murmured and bent to kiss his bowed head before she turned and went upstairs to bed.

*

The week flew past. Shona and Niall were seldom alone and never even managed a return visit to the cave. Niall's original idea to take Fiona on an occasional outing turned sour on him because Phebie took a bout of summer 'flu and had to take to bed. Elspeth was kept so busy managing the house and the surgery she had no time for anything else.

Niall was assigned the task of shopping and each morning left the house with Elspeth's shrill orders ringing in his ears. He refused to carry a shopping basket. The first morning they set out Fiona skipped at his side, swinging the basket high in the air, and imploring him to give her some pennies for sweets.

'Oh shut up, you wee nuisance!' he rapped. He was in one of his rare tempers. Elspeth had nagged him since breakfast which he'd had to get for himself because he'd lain longer than normal and arose after everyone else had breakfasted.

Tears sprang into Fiona's eyes at her adored big brother's sharp words. She was a tiny sprite of a child with straight brown hair cut in a heavy fringe and button bright eyes alive with mischief. She was the opposite of her brother, both in looks and temperament. He had always been easy-going but she was stubborn and had tantrums that were the despair of Mr Murdoch at school and a puzzle to her good-natured, placid parents. But despite her moods she could be angelic and loving when she wanted and Niall could always get the best from her with his easy calm manner and quiet affection.

Now they were both out of spirits and trudged

sullenly along the road. A twite uttered a note of alarm from its nest in the heather and a group of scaup crooned contentedly on the calm green waters of Loch Tenee. A frog hopped unhurriedly into the moss at the road's edge and overhead, soaring in the wide blue of the sky, a skylark trilled notes of pure merriment. Normally, one of these things would have brought Niall at least from his mood, but not this morning, and the very fact that Fiona ignored the frog showed that her stubborn little heart was badly hurt.

They trudged into the post office in disgruntled silence and while Niall purchased groceries Fiona made a face at Behag behind his back. Behag sucked in her thin lips and banged a packet of tea viciously on the counter. 'Cheeky wee upstart,' she sniffed. 'Got your mither's sense o' humour, I see.'

Niall looked up quickly. 'What's that about my mother?'

Behag sniffed disdainfully. 'I was just sayin', your mither has a funny wee way o' sayin' things – sarcastic if you know what I mean – and the wee lass has the same quirk, only she's not so open natured – oh no, makes faces at folk only she's to hide behind her brither's back to do so.'

Niall's jaw tightened as he paid for the messages. When he was lifting his change he looked steadily at Behag and said, 'My mother was never one to make sarcastic remarks but it might be there's a wee quirk in your own nature that brings out the worst in people. Good day to you, Mistress Behag.'

He left the postmistress with her mouth agape and pulled Fiona outside. Without a word he lifted her frilled petticoats and smacked her hard on the bottom. For a moment nothing happened, then she dropped the bag of sugar she had been carrying and simply bawled with hurt pride.

The sugar had burst all over the road and Niall's face was red with temper and embarrassment.

Shona had come out of Merry Mary's at that moment and she ran over to survey the scene with amazement. Suddenly she burst out laughing and had to steady herself against the wall of Morag Ruadh's cottage. Her peals of mirth made several people turn and smile but Niall's face was a study of indignation. He glowered at her. With the sun in her hair, laughter creasing her face, and a pale green dress setting off her glowing tan, she was the picture of summer freshness but he was angry that she was enjoying his obvious plight.

'Girls!' he snapped. 'Nothing but pests!'

'Niall,' she gasped, 'it's just so funny – you slapping poor wee Fiona – funny strange I mean – history repeating itself in a way! Don't you remember? That time we met in the post office? You called me a baby and I said you were glaikit and we bawled at each other till your mother pulled you away and Mirabelle took me outside and skelped me on my *bare* bottom! I was so mortified I couldn't even cry!'

Fiona wiped her tears and giggled at the idea of lovely, graceful Shona being spanked for being naughty. Niall relaxed and chuckled, his eyes dreamy as he travelled back over the years. 'Yes, I do remember that day now,' he said, 'but I never knew Mirabelle gave it to you.'

'Right here – outside the post office – she was so

ashamed because I'd thrown a tantrum in front of your mother and nosy old Behag in there.'

Niall handed Shona the basket and put his arm round her, then he put out his other hand and grasped that of his small sister. 'Do you know what, bairns?' he grinned. 'I'm going to treat you to a bar of chocolate and we'll get down to the harbour to eat it. The old bitch Elspeth can wait for her messages! It was through her Fiona and I were grumpin' at each other in the first place.'

After that, the morning trip to Portcull became a treat instead of the drudge Niall thought it would be. With Shona everything was different. Whenever she could she went to Slochmhor and helped Elspeth with the chores, and prepared pretty trays for Phebie. As a result Elspeth was less put upon and her tongue lost its edge.

In the little spare time left, Shona and Niall took Fiona for picnics and in the process taught her to swim. They also spent lazy hours fishing offshore in one of Ranald's boats. Fiona was a lively interested child, always engrossed in whatever she was doing. Niall and Shona could steal the odd kiss and hold hands occasionally.

'Go ahead,' Fiona told them once. 'I know big boys and girls enjoy these things. Kiss all you want – I'd rather kiss a cat myself.'

Shona had smiled. 'I used to feel like that too, Fiona.'

The little girl screwed up her face. 'I'll *never* change. I don't like boys at all. They're dirty and cheeky and try to lift your dress so they can see your knickers, *and* they do awful things like picking their noses behind their reading books!'

The day before Niall's departure Shona went over to Slochmhor to prepare lunch for Phebie who was up but still feeling shaky. She was a young thirty-nine, plump and pink-skinned.

'My doctor is allowing me to Ceilidh tonight,' she smiled as she sprinkled salt over cold lamb, 'so I was wondering if you and your father would come over. We could have a nice crack.' She placed her hand over Shona's. 'It's sore your heart is that Niall's going.'

It was more a statement than a question. Shona nodded. Her heart was brimful of suppressed emotions. It had been a week of restraint both for her and for Niall. There had been so much they had wanted to say but no opportunity except for brief assurances of their love for each other. She couldn't trust herself to say too much to Phebie because she knew she might break down so she merely nodded at Phebie's words.

Phebie sighed. 'Och my lass, I wish he wasn't going. I know the war's not right begun yet and if we're lucky it might not get off the ground at all but I can't help fretting for my laddie.'

Shona bit her lip. 'Please don't talk about it,' she whispered.

Phebie saw the blue eyes brimming and she put out her arms and Shona went into them and cried quietly.

'There, there,' soothed Phebie, 'have a good greet. Niall's going from us and we would all like to grab him and hold on but Lachlan and I have talked it over. It won't be easy for any of us but he has to do this thing, Shona. He'd grow discontent and sour if we held him back. But yet our hearts will be heavy. It's the ones who are left behind who should be given the medals right enough.' She held Shona at arm's length and chuckled suddenly. 'Why do women always cry for men? Do they cry for us I wonder?'

Shona gave a watery sniff. 'In a different way I suppose.' She put her hands over her breasts. 'They cry more in here – in their hearts. Father's been doing it for years and it hurts him so. First it was for my mother, now it's for Kirsteen. I watch him and I want to take away the ache but there's nothing I can do.'

Phebie looked into the girl's incredible eyes. 'You've been doing something all your life,' she said softly. 'You've loved him and without you he'd be a sorry man today.'

'Do you really think so, Phebie?'

'I know so, mo ghaoil, and Fergus knows it too. If Kirsteen Fraser came back tomorrow she could turn round and thank you for holding together the body and soul of her man.'

'I wish she would come back to Rhanna. I'd love to see Father really happy. D'you know, Phebie, I don't believe I ever really have – not really.'

Phebie looked thoughtful. 'No, I don't suppose you have. It must be terrible – to be so deeply unhappy. Thank God he and Lachy made up their differences or he could have been even worse.'

Shona nodded. 'I know, thank God for that at least.'

Phebie's little crack snowballed into a gay Ceilidh that went on till the small hours of morning.

'Och, Mother, you shouldn't have bothered,' said

Niall, looking at the laden table in the kitchen.

Phebie placed her hand briefly on his fair head and said softly, 'It's not every day my son gets himself engaged, so be quiet and put those pancakes down. Engaged or no' I'll skelp your lugs for stealing. Your eyes were ay bigger than your belly!'

The house was filling. Todd the Shod came in bearing his bagpipes and old Bob was settling down to play the fiddle. Todd's daughter, Mairi, now Mrs William McKinnon, came into the kitchen to see if her help was needed.

'Ach, it's all ready you are, Mrs McLachlan,' she said with her simple but radiant smile. 'I've brought some wee buns so I'll just leave them on the range. They're nice warmed a bitty. If you'll be excusin' me I'll just go and see will William dance with me. My mither's mindin' wee Andrew so I can have a good time.'

Faithful, doting Mairi spent a restless night looking for Wullie while the pipes skirled and the fiddles haunted the soul. Toasts were drunk to the newly engaged couple till everyone was crapulous and merry. Doors and windows were flung wide to let smoke and whisky fumes escape.

Niall and Shona held hands and tapped their feet to the pipes and each wished they were alone with the other.

Lachlan danced with Phebie and kissed her warm brow gently. 'Are you happy, my bonnie, plump peach?' he whispered.

She looked at her son with his bright hair and eager young face. 'Yes, happy that our son is going to marry Helen's bairn. It's strange the way of things, eh Lachy?'

He knew what she meant and his brown eyes were thoughtful. 'Aye, strange, if I'd saved Helen and lost the bairn or lost them both . . .'

She put her fingers over his mouth. 'Hush, no more of that, things are as they were meant. I wish Kirsteen had never left Fergus though – look at him – Shona's right – I doubt if we've ever seen him really happy for years.'

Fergus was sitting in a corner getting quietly drunk. His thoughts were crowding him that night and he couldn't sort one from another. He wanted his daughter's happiness yet he knew that her marriage to Niall would mean more emptiness for him. It would be a while yet but it was there, looming on his bleak horizon.

He looked at the revellers and noticed that nearly everyone had a companion of some sort. Even empty-headed Mairi, dithering about in her search for Wullie, had someone to look forward to. When Shona went he would have no one, what then would he do with his life?

Fiona Taylor, flushed and breathless from a gay highland fling, threw herself down on the seat near him. She was the child Lachlan had saved on the night of the awful storm of Helen's death. She was now in her early twenties, dark and vivacious with a firm bosom and a neat waist. Fergus looked at her and felt an open desire for her warm, young body. It had been so long since he'd held a woman close to his heart. He had lived with thoughts and hopes too long now and he was hungry for love. Kirsteen had taken all that was left in his heart; she had robbed him so that he knew he could never love another woman mentally. But the physical need in him for the contact of a female body couldn't be denied. He worked hard on the farm so that most nights he fell into bed exhausted but there were those other nights when sleep wouldn't come and he throbbed with heat.

These were the nights he conjured up the memories of Kirsteen till she beckoned in the dim mists of his mind. Sometimes it was difficult to get a clear image of her lovely face but he could imagine loving each part of her body that his memory could provoke till he could almost feel her beside him in the warm bed. His mind could make his body love, but when it was over there was no real, living body to snuggle into with contentment, only the big double bed with himself, humiliated and unhappy beyond measure.

He could smell Fiona's perfume and the smile she threw him raised a response in him. He leaned forward to ask her to dance but she was already jumping to her feet. 'Och, that Jimmy,' she laughed, her eyes sending messages to the young man who was beckoning her from the other side of the room 'he won't sit still for a minute – loves dancing he does and just because we are to be married at Christmas he thinks he owns me.'

She was off, her petticoats whirling and a wild skirl breaking from her. Fergus put his head in his hand, letting his veneer fall away for a moment of longing. A light touch on his shoulder made him look up. 'Would you dance with an auld wife like me?' asked Phebie quietly.

'I prefer to dance with the bonniest lass in the

room,' he answered lightly and whirled her away.

While the Ceilidh was still at its height Niall and Shona stole away unnoticed into the summer night. Biddy was ensconced in Fiona's swing, her hip flask clasped to her bosom while she rocked herself gently back and forth to the lilt of a Gaelic boat song she was humming untunefully. She didn't notice the two shadows stealing past. Shona stifled a giggle and Niall took her hand and they ran beyond the halo of light from the house.

It was a soft velvet night of country scents. The sea sighed in the distance and a dog barked from a distant croft. They walked to the small wood at the top of the field above Slochmhor, stopping to listen to the laughter that drifted from the open windows. Laigmhor was a dark shadow and Portcull a blur of whitewashed cottages against the subdued shimmer of the Sound of Rhanna.

Niall pulled Shona close. 'It's been a grand night, mo ghaoil. But it's glad I am to have you to myself for a wee while.'

She turned to him with a sudden movement and buried her face into his neck. 'Och Niall, I love you so much. I've got so much I want to say yet I don't know where to start.'

'That's how I feel,' he whispered into her hair. 'I've wanted to be alone with you all week; now all the words have gone I wanted to say. Now, tomorrow, I must leave you and I am wishing tonight would last forever. Promise me you'll write. I'll be lost for a time and looking for your letters.'

'Niall, of course I'll write,' she chided gently. 'But

will you answer I wonder? You never wrote much before.'

'This is different,' he assured her. 'Before we were just bairns playing ourselves – now one day you'll be my wife.' His voice was full of awe at the over-whelming implications of his words. He held her hand tightly. 'I'll miss you,' he said huskily. 'Will you think at all of me?'

'Maybe sometimes,' she answered as lightly as her heavy heart would allow.

He smiled in the darkness. 'It's a skelped bum you're needing, my girl.' He reached for her but she eluded him and like children they played hide and seek in the rustling wood. When he caught her he kissed her over and over and whispered, 'No more kissing Ti Johnston or flirting with Gordon McNab or I'll spank you when I get home!'

'And when will that be, my canty lad?' She tried to keep her voice steady but in the darkness tears were on her cheeks.

'I'll not be knowing for a while but I'll be home whenever I can.'

'I'll try and be here. Who knows where I might wander? I might even join the ATS and be away when you get back.'

'Don't dare!' he said fiercely. 'You're mine and a man has a right to claim what's his! When I come back to Rhanna I want my Shona here to welcome me . . . Now, turn round till I pee.'

She giggled loudly at the sudden change of mood. 'Och, you're rude, so you are, Niall McLachlan. It's so unromantic to say such things.'

384

'I can't help it, I'm burstin' with all that beer big Tam McKinnon kept giving me. I think he makes it himself for I'm sure I've smelt it coming from that wee washhouse near the cowshed. He must drink gallons of the stuff too for every time I've been with Tam he's always burstin' to pee and when he does it's like the wee waterfall up by Brodie's burn – never-ending. I remember one time –' he chuckled at the recollection – 'Tam was burstin' and a crowd o' lassies coming along. He couldn't wait so he popped the milk can he was carrying inside his breeks, did up his buttons, and was peeing merrily into the can as the girls were passing. It made quite a noise and between that and the bulge in his trousers the lassies' eyes were goggling. He looked like a prize bull with breeks on!'

Shona shrieked with mirth and she and Niall returned to the Ceilidh in a light-hearted mood.

Next morning she overslept and was kept so busy there was no time to see Niall off from the harbour. In a way she was glad because she knew she would have cried at the parting.

She was in one of the top fields, driving two straying cows, when she saw him on the road far below. He looked up and waved, shouting something she couldn't hear, then he was off, his beloved, familiar figure a dark little blob on the road to Portcull. She stood silhouetted against the sky. She knew he turned again and again because she could see the tiny stick that was his arm raised in farewell. She sank into the lush grass, the cows forgotten. She watched the boat leaving the harbour and kept on watching till it was just a speck in the misty distance.

'Ca' canny, my Niall,' she whispered and a cold little wind dried the tears on her cheeks.

That summer Alick and Mary came with their four-year-old twin sons. The farmhouse rang with wild yells and screams of joy. Shona was an adored cousin and she took the boys for picnics to the sheltered little bays at Nigg. She taught them to ride Thistle, the tiny Shetland pony she had long outgrown, and they clattered along with her to feed the hens or help with the milking.

She was laughing and gay, yet Fergus looked at her and could feel her loneliness.

The twins departed and Laigmhor reverted to its drowsing norm. Erchy the postman paid more than his usual number of visits and he lumbered slowly through a Strupak while Shona fingered Niall's letters nestling in her apron pockets and wished she was alone.

'Love letters, is it?' twinkled Erchy unfailingly. 'That young buck must have it bad, I'm thinkin'. His poor mither only gets half of what you do.'

Niall's letters were colourful and his descriptions of life in the training camp so full of wit that Shona often laughed aloud, but there was also a yearning for her in every line he wrote and she hugged each little intimacy to her heart.

The summer days grew shorter and autumn came with a sharp tang. The rowans winked fiery eyes and woodsmoke hung in the misty air. The bronze of beeches and the twinkling golds of silver birches turned Rhanna into a patchwork quilt of colour.

Bracken rustled on the mountains and towards the end of September the deer rut came and the strange, plaintive roar of the stags echoed in the glens.

Biddy was seldom away from old Shelagh's cottage and one morning the old lady said to her, 'See that I have my teeths in when you lay me out, mo ghaoil. The damt things were never much good to me when I was alive but they'll help me to look better when all my friends come to see me in my box. And . . .' She laid a frail hand on Biddy's arm. 'Will you be saying a wee prayer for me in the Gaelic when they put me into the Kirkyard? I know God has all the tongues but thon minister is not even speaking English right and I'd like fine for God to know I'm coming so that all my friends up yonder will know to greet me.'

Biddy brushed away a tear and said gruffly, 'Ach of course I will, you old blether, but it's a bit early to be talking of such things.'

But Shelagh, a small wizened figure in a bed full of patchwork quilts, shook her head. 'You should know better than to try and fool me. I've lived too long to be taken in by kind words. Just say that wee prayer for me, Biddy, and don't worry. If I have any trouble getting into Heaven I'll just blow my way through the gates, my winds will see to that.'

Three days later, on a morning of gentle sun and mellow amber tints, she passed peacefully away. Everyone who had loved the kenspeckle old sprite who had spent her entire eighty-three years on the Hebridean island, toiled up the leaf-strewn path to the old kirk.

Old Joe watched his cousin laid to rest. 'Gone with

the winds right enough,' he chuckled but there was a mist of tears in his green eyes and he blew his nose loudly on a spotted red handkerchief.

Dodie, resplendent in a black coat and grey soft hat no one had seen before, wept quietly into his big tobacco-stained hands. 'He breeah!' he said in a funny choked voice. He was conscious of the strange hat on his head but proud that he had managed to dress decently to see his old friend off. He had 'borrowed' the clothes from Burnbreddie many years before and was pleased of the chance to wear them, even if it was for such an unhappy occasion.

He looked at Biddy, who was standing by the open grave saying a beautiful Gaelic prayer that brought the tears to the eyes of all the Gaels present, and his broken teeth showed for a moment. It was nice to see her wearing the gift he had given her a number of years ago. She too was wearing her very best in honour of old Shelagh.

Chapter Thirteen

Shona rubbed at a pair of thick woolly socks with an energy that had nothing to do with enthusiasm. Mrs McKinnon had been unable to come to Laigmhor because of a bout of sciatica and Shona had had to contend with all the chores both in and out the farmhouse for nearly a fortnight. She had been so busy she had deliberately ignored the pile of washing, but when Fergus came down to breakfast that morning, with no socks to wear under his wellingtons, she was so ashamed she set about the tasteless task after lunch was over. Soapsuds spilled out of the tub to the floor and Tot, who had skated the length of the kitchen twice, was now taking refuge under the table.

The kitchen was warm and the door was thrown wide to let in the few stray breezes from the Indian summer day outside. Sunlight streamed over the flagstones and Shona sighed, raising her head for a moment to look at the russet gold shoulder of Sgurr na Gill outlined against the deep blue sky. She longed to be outside to feel the sun on her skin. The outdoor sounds were enticing, a Hebridean song-thrush 'tchuck-tchucked' from the apple tree, cows lowed gently from the fields, and the hens clucked peacefully and every so often wandered into the kitchen, combs waggling and beady eyes bright. Shona rushed at them with a besom and they flew clumsily outside, shrieking indignantly amidst feathers and droppings.

'Silly fools!' Shona spoke vehemently to the empty kitchen, and the ticking of the grandmother clock from the hall, and Tot's snorting, only served to heighten the silence.

She sighed again and rubbed her nose with a soapy hand before going back to the sink. Clothes slopped once more and she looked absently at the calendar. October was halfway through and it was three and a half months since Niall had left Rhanna. She had been parted from him for longer spells but it was different now; now that their love was no longer the secret of the other, the months apart were like years.

Her hair fell over her face and she was so engrossed in her thoughts that she didn't notice the shadow that loomed on the sunlit flagstones.

'Is this the wee hoosie where the washwife lives?' Niall's voice was full of suppressed joy. She looked up, her expression one of startled disbelief. His strong young figure filled the doorway, a handsome stranger in his Army uniform. With a few quick strides he crossed the room and lifted her high; then the warm firm mouth she had dreamed of was on her own and she gasped for breath.

'You smell and taste of soap,' he grinned, holding her away to look at her. She wiped her hands on her apron and backed away from him, trying to take in the fact that the suntanned young man in the neat uniform, his hair severely cropped under his cap, was really the same person who had left her months before.

'Hey!' he laughed, 'it's me – Niall! Remember – the glaikit wee laddie you played with!'

'You look so different, it's difficult to believe you're Niall McLachlan!'

'I'm just the same, it's the uniform that's different – aye, and the Indian crop! C'mon! Are you not pleased I'm here?'

She went into his arms then. 'I've missed you so,' she whispered into his ear, 'and I imagined when you came home I would be beautiful and perfect and instead you've caught me with my peenie on.'

'You *are* beautiful and I've longed for this moment so much I wouldn't care if you'd nothing on.'

They burst out laughing then she grew serious. 'How long, Niall?'

'Seven days but I'll miss two of them because of travelling so it leaves only five. I'm being posted to France.' She turned pale and went quickly back to the sink but he was at her back, turning her face gently towards his. 'We must make the most of the time, mo gaolach, so it's off with your peenie and out with me. I've been home and sent my folks crazy with delight at sight of my bonny face. Mother has made me a big parcel of sandwiches so we can go off for the whole afternoon.'

'I can't,' she wailed. 'I look like a spey wife and I'm in such a guddle with the washing! Father hasn't a single pair of socks to wear!'

He slapped her gently on the bottom. 'Give me your apron and you get along and clean yourself up.'

She left him wrapping the apron round his uniform and she could hear him singing while she washed and tidied herself in her room. She surveyed herself in the mirror and sparkling eyes and rosy cheeks looked back at her. She put on a blue dress and brushed her hair till it shone. For a moment she stood still and thought, 'Five days, five precious days with Niall. I'll hold on to every minute and turn them into hours.' She put down her brush and flew downstairs, chuckling when she looked outside and saw Niall hanging out the washing, his singing somewhat distorted by the rows of pegs sticking from his mouth. She didn't dare inspect the newly washed clothes too closely. They were hanging in comically unusual positions but looked clean enough in the searching rays of the sun.

Niall came back to the kitchen and threw his apron on to a chair. 'All set?' he said, crooking his arm in a dashing manner.

She nodded breathlessly, 'I've left a note for Father in case he comes in and wonders where I am. I just said you were home.'

They went outside. 'Where will we go?' she wondered though she knew what he would say.

'Where else but our own wee hideaway?'

It was a day borrowed from summer and Niall took off his jacket and threw it over his shoulder. He put his arm round Shona and they walked with their heads together, their feet light and swift on the dry moor grasses.

They hadn't been to the cave since June and it was full of cobwebs. Shona dusted them away and made tea on the spirit stove while Niall washed the cups in the nearby burn. It was too warm to stay in the cave so they spread a rug outside and sat on it to drink tea and eat chicken sandwiches. The ruins of the Abbey made a perfect sun trap. Through the crumbling walls held together in places by an overgrowth of tree roots and fern, they could see the moor stretched for miles, a sheet of golden ochre merging with the blue-green mists of the sea.

Shona looked far into the distance and felt frightened, knowing that Niall was soon going to a place where the serenity of Rhanna would be very far away. She shivered and snuggled against him.

'Hey, why all the shivers?' he asked gently. 'The sun's warm enough for July.'

'I'm afraid, Niall. You are too – I can feel it. It's happened – I've tried not to think about it but now the time has come – you're going off to fight and you might get hurt.'

'I am a wee bit scarey, Shona,' he admitted. 'I think most of the lads are, but we're not going out there with the idea we're going to get hurt. We're going to fight and probably not even right away. I'll maybe get a chance to come home if things aren't too bad.'

She pulled herself away from him angrily. 'When are you going to give me peace of mind? When will you stop leaving me? I can't deny it any longer, Niall! I've always hated you leaving but I didn't want to behave like a silly wee girl so I pretended not to care every time you went. It's different now! I love you! And you're supposed to love me but how can you when you worry me so with all your stupid ideas about adventure? War's not an adventure. You might get killed, Niall and have you thought – you'll have to kill other people if you want to stay alive!'

She burst into a torrent of tears. Niall's face had turned white with anger. 'I know it's not an adventure, Shona,' he said harshly. 'I've lain nights in the billet sweating when I think about it. I don't want to kill anyone but you're right – if I don't, they'll kill me, even though they might not want it either. It's the whole conception of war that's rotten and evil but if I don't fight, and thousands like me, there would be no freedom for anyone! Everything would be swallowed up by all the greedy little Hitlers of the world! Do you want that to happen, Shona? Would you like to see Scotland taken over by the Nazis?'

She had never seen him so angry. She hadn't realised his convictions were so strong and she wanted to run to him and hold him but her stubborn nature wouldn't allow it. The sun was still shining, but the beauty of the day was ruined for both of them. She began to gather up her things while he watched miserably.

'Will I see you tomorrow?' he asked.

She flounced about, her chin set in the determined lines he knew so well.

'I really don't know,' she answered, coldly polite. 'I have so much to do with Mrs McKinnon not well. You'll be about no doubt and know where to find me if you need me!'

She hardly dared look at him because she knew if she did she would melt. From experience she knew how he was looking. From the side of her eye she saw him sitting dejectedly, his hands hanging over his drawn-up knees. What she couldn't see, but could guess, were deep brown eyes, dark with growing misery, and tanned skin flushed with fading anger. A lump came to her throat but she forced herself to walk away, her head high and her step nonchalant. He didn't come after her and her face was pale with hurt when she arrived home. Tot wheezed to greet her but it was still too early for anyone else to be about.

She held the old dog close and went to the cobbled yard then through the little gate to the drying green. Niall's washing, a gay jumble on the line, made her cry out with remorse and shame. She wanted to run back over the moor to tell him how sorry she was but instead put potatoes and turnip to cook on the range and laid the table with a precision calculated to pass time quickly.

Fergus came in smelling of dung and he stripped to the waist and ran water into the sink. 'I hear Niall's home,' he called through a lather of soap. 'Well, you can go off and enjoy yourselves while he's here. Mrs McKinnon sent a message that she'll be here in the morning.'

He reached for a towel and wiped the water from his eyes, expecting to see his daughter's radiant face. Instead she was at the stove, her back to him while she furiously mashed turnip and potatoes.

'Clapshot tonight, is it?' he asked, wary of her mood.

'With salt beef,' she snapped.

'I'll mask the tea then.' He poured boiling water into the teapot and set it on the range. He sat down, still wearing only his trousers, and drew his plate towards him. 'I hear tell Dodie's ram's been going at the yowes up on the hill,' he said conversationally. 'The crofters from Nigg will be moaning about it though they know fine none of their rams can compare with Dodie's. He should be charging a fee, so he should.'

'He should have sold that ram,' said Shona sullenly. 'And you should never have given him that old yowe in the first place. One of her lambs just had to be a ram and one of these day's there's going to be a fine stramash over the whole thing – that's if the old ram doesn't drop dead first from all its matings!'

'There's already been a stramash, I think. The sun's gone out of your eyes, my lass.'

She lifted her head, an angry retort on her lips, but the look of caring in his black eyes made her instead jump to her feet and go to him. His body was warm and still damp from his wash, and she bent over to put her arms round his neck.

'Oh Father, I'm a bad-tempered bitch and deserve a skelping! Niall's going off to France and all I could do was shout at him that he thought it was all just an adventure. I'm afraid for him and when I'm frightened I get crabbit.'

He smiled strangely. 'An inheritance from me! It's a devil of a thing to control and even worse if there's a bit of thrawn pride alongside it. You're the one who should apologize but I know how hard that can be.'

'You understand so much, Father.'

'I've been through it all, that's why. When I was your age I could never bring myself to admit being wrong. Now I see all the time I wasted with my pride and it's too late to be sorry. Don't make my mistakes, Shona, or you'll live to regret it. How long has Niall got?'

'Five days – and one of them nearly gone.'

'Precious hours,' he said briefly and turned back to his meal.

That evening she wanted to run over to Slochmhor but she didn't. Her father was going up the hill to old Bob's biggin for a night of chess and when he had gone she curled herself on the inglenook and gazed into the leaping flames in the hearth. Minutes passed, then a tap at the door made her leap up, her heart racing. Niall had come to her! But it was Nancy on her way to Portcull to visit her mother.

'I'm just dropping in for a crack,' she dimpled, her merry dark eyes full of life. 'Archie brought me over in the trap and now he's away to Ranald's for a dram and a game o' cards. Och – but you and that bonny Niall will make a fine pair. If you just let me put Jeemie down and give me a cup o' tea I'll give you a few hints for your weddin' night.'

Shona listened to the busy tongue and felt that Nancy's vivacity could be somewhat overpowering at times.

Half an hour later she left in a whirl of laughter and Shona sat down thankfully, feeling tired and unhappy. At nine o'clock she took her cocoa, her hot water bottle and Tot up to bed and lay gazing at the small damp patch on her ceiling. She had loved the patch from childhood because it was shaped the way she imagined Jesus's head would be. The slates of the roof had been fixed and her ceiling repapered but still the little patch came through till the paper was stained in the gentle profile that always brought her a certain measure of comfort. She turned and snuggled into Tot who groaned in ecstasy. It was the time the old dog loved best; the dregs of cocoa from the saucer, the cosy bed, and the warm loving arms of her mistress hugging her close.

Shona pictured Niall sitting in the homely parlour at Slochmhor. Fiona would be in bed and he would be talking with his parents in that intimate close way they had with each other.

A tear slid on to Tot's ear and Shona whispered, 'Oh dear God, let Niall know it's because I love him I'm angry he's going away and – and I'm so frightened.'

Tot snored and Shona heard her father come in. It was comforting to hear him moving about. The light from his lamp illuminated the crack under her door. She knew he had stopped and she could picture him, a tall lone figure surrounded by the darkness of the house, listening for a sign from her that all was well. He wouldn't say anything for fear she was asleep, and he would go to his empty room, with its masculine traces of untidiness, without the comforting sound of a human voice bidding him a good night.

'Goodnight, Father,' she said gently.

His soft lilting voice floated back. 'Goodnight, Ni-Cridhe.'

'Ni-Cridhe'. My dear lassie! The unaccustomed endearment made her heart swell with love for him and feeling oddly comforted she buried her face into Tot's silky ears and slept.

The next morning was one of calm mists and damp dewy grass. Mrs McKinnon came and talked incessantly while she made bread and prepared vegetables. It was good to hear her earthy tongue and Shona laughed despite her restless mood.

'Are you not going out?' asked Mrs McKinnon, looking from the window to fields and moors now bathed in mellow sunshine. 'I hear tell Niall's home for a wee while before going off to fight. You should be making the most of your time together. When I was your age the blood was leapin' in my veins – rearin' to be off I was.' She chuckled. 'Aye, and look where it got me – a man that could still teach a young buck a thing or two about ruttin' and a gift for breakin' everything he touches. Still, I'm happy with my Tam, no brains he has but he's done not bad without them. Yon Niall's got brains – and a fine handsome laddie into the bargain. He'll go far, will young McLachlan.'

'If he stays alive,' said Shona, unable to keep the bitterness from her voice.

'Och havers! You mustny think so! Bide a wee – he'll have the Germans runnin' like gowks and thon wee man Hitler will be frothin' like a bull without its balls, mark my words. Now, away ben and get me some dripping from the larder.'

The morning passed quickly, thanks to Mrs McKinnon, but when she departed after lunch and the house was quiet again Shona still had not thought of a way to make amends with Niall. She didn't want to go to his house because that would make her appear too anxious. He hadn't come to her so she knew he was still hurt and angry and was making it clear that the first move must come from her. But it was so hard to apologize when stubborn pride seethed within. Unable to bear the house any longer she threw a cardigan over her shoulders and went outside.

It was another day stolen from summer and the heat

from the sun made her shed the cardigan quickly. Tot had opted to come out too and the golden dog and her slim, golden-skinned mistress walked together over the shaggy amber moors. Without conscious intention Shona was breasting the Hillock of Dunuaigh and looking down at the ruins of the Abbey nestling in the hollow. There was still a good half mile to go and Tot, pink tongue lolling, was tired and lagging behind. Shona picked her up and went on down the hill. The ruins of the Abbey loomed against the blue sky and she paused for breath, hoisting the sleeping old dog higher against her shoulder. Through one of the crumbling windows of the Chapel she suddenly saw Niall. He was sitting in the same place she had left him the day before and she might have thought he had spent the night there but for the fact he had changed from his uniform into his old kilt and jersey. Her heart pounded and she felt faint with her love for him. How dearly familiar he looked in his Rhanna clothes. He was disconsolate and sullen-looking and idly threw pebbles into the foaming little burn that wound its way from the mountains.

Tot had wakened and was struggling to get down. The lovely scent of rabbit was in the air and she still enjoyed a mild chase. She whimpered with excitement and stood for a moment, torn between going to greet Niall or going to sniff out rabbit.

Niall looked up, a pebble poised in his fingers. He stood up and, though he was more than a hundred yards from her, Shona sensed the tension in him. He began to run towards her and her own feet took wings, his name a soft breath on her lips. For a moment it seemed eternity divided them, then she was throwing herself into his outstretched arms, her mouth meeting his in a kiss she knew would hold in her heart forever.

'Don't ever walk away from me again,' he gasped, holding her face and covering it with kisses.

'I'm sorry, my Niall. I didn't mean half of the things I said – please forgive me.'

They walked to the cave, arms entwined. Shona fell on to the sheepskin rugs, her legs weary from the long walk. Niall sat beside her and stroked her hair. 'I couldn't sleep last night,' he whispered, 'and all because of you, you wee wittrock.'

'Love me, Niall,' she breathed her blue eyes serious and her lips, warm and inviting, parted to show her even white teeth.

'I do love you.'

'Love me with your body, Niall. I thought about it last night. Father was out and all I could think about was you. I love you so much I want to give you all of me – my heart and my soul – and – and my body. Please, Niall, give me something to remember when you're gone. I want to be able to think of us belonging to each other. Our memories are the only things we're going to have for a long time.'

He had turned away from her and didn't speak for a few moments. Outside Tot barked and a light wind rustled the ferns. 'I want you, Shona,' he said at last. 'God knows I've wanted you for a long time now. You're beautiful – so beautiful that I can hardly bear to be alone with you without wanting you. I've watched you growing lovelier each time I came back, but because I love you I can't do anything that might hurt you. When we're wed your body will belong to me but, till then . . .' He spread his hands helplessly, unable to express himself further.

'We are wed,' she laughed softly. 'We've been wed for years. Don't you remember our marriage in the cave at the Point?'

'Och, Shona, it's teasing you are. Get up from there and we'll go for a walk . . . or something.'

But she lay where she was, strangely inert, and tears fell helplessly on to the sheepskin. 'I'm afraid, Niall, I'm frightened you'll be killed and I won't ever know what the completion of our love would have been like. I won't be able to remember because you won't give me now what would be my memories later.'

He looked at her intently. 'You really mean it, mo ghaoil?'

'You know I do. It's not the sort of thing to speak of lightly.'

She was exquisite, with her burnished hair spread over the white sheepskin and he felt his heart beating up into his throat. 'We'd better go outside,' he mumbled before his resolution left him. 'I won't be tempted to do something we might both regret later. Please Shona – don't look at me like that – those eyes of yours all soft and with a look I've never seen . . .'

His words were lost because she had reached up a slender arm and pulled his head down to her breasts. He heard the throb of her heart and felt the softness of her. His body wouldn't obey his mind. He was beside her, their mouths meeting and parting over and over, their bodies pressed together till he could think of nothing but her. Briefly her hands touched his hardness and for a moment he was embarrassed because he was still in possession of his sensibilities and he thought she might be shocked that the playmate of her childhood could have changed to a virile young man, capable of doing all the things they had once thought so foolish. But her touch had been no accident, and she caressed him again till he felt himself to be on fire and the hard swelling of his passion became a thing apart, something that seemed to move and press without any conscious direction from him. His pelvic muscles seemed to be made of fluid, so easily did they allow him to move up and down, and her body was a supple thing of wonder, moving with his in such perfect unison they might have been of the same flesh. But not yet; he wanted to keep the ultimate moment at bay, to enjoy her lips and the feel of her breasts for as long as he could. The cave was warm and quiet, an intimate little world into which no one could intrude. Slowly he undressed her till she lay naked on the sheepskin. For a moment her blue eyes looked at him, an awareness in them of everything that was happening. 'Shona,' he whispered, 'are you sure?'

But she closed her eyes without answering and he looked at the sweep of her long lashes and the pulse beating in her slender neck. His eyes slowly travelled to her body, seeing how white was the skin of her torso compared to her arms and legs. He reached out and his hands cupped her small high breasts, then he bent and kissed her hard pink nipples, over and over again till she was making soft little moaning sounds.

She put out her hands and again caressed those intimate parts of him till there was no turning back. Trembling, he undressed. For a moment she opened her eyes to look at him. Her gaze travelled over his penis. She looked at it wonderingly and touched it again, like a little girl who had unlocked a secret door and discovered adulthood. Their childhood was far behind them now – those long days of innocence, of exploration of the things of nature, now turned in on themselves and the joy of finding such ecstasy in each other.

But the real ecstasy was still to come. Niall quivered at her touch and could wait no longer. He gathered her to him in a frenzy of excitement and went into her with the drive of an animal. She hadn't expected the pain and bit her lip to stop from crying out. He had forgotten everything but the intense pleasure he was getting from her body. His brown eyes were glazed and each thrust he made inside her brought a strange low moan from his throat. She endured the pain, it was the ultimate proof of her love for him, and she stroked his neck and shoulders till he finally let out a cry that echoed through the cave. Still he kept moving, releasing every bit of fire that burned in him till finally he fell against her exhausted.

'Shona, my lovely Shona,' he whispered and tears glistened in his eyes while he kissed her with such tenderness that she cried soundlessly. They were still joined together but he made no attempt to withdraw, falling asleep with his young, boyish face so close to hers she was able to study every little detail. His skin was smooth, the little fuzz of his moustache a shade deeper than his fair head. She put up her hand and touched his firm, sensitive mouth and he awoke with a start, withdrawing from her almost guiltily. 'Shona, I'm sorry.' He was full of remorse. 'I shouldn't have done it – oh God – after all the times I kept from touching you!'

'Please don't be sorry, Niall. I wanted you to love me, I'm not sorry and . . .' she giggled unexpectedly. 'Shelagh was right, you are a young bull. Now I know something else about you I didn't before.' She leaned on her elbow and touched him. 'Look at it now, it's a wizened wee Bodach, yet before it was so – big. Does it go like that often?'

'Sometimes,' he said evasively.

'When you think about girls?'

'When I think about you – and if you don't stop poking at it you'll make it happen again.' He reached for his clothes and noticed a stain on the sheepskin. 'Shona, I've hurt you, you're bleeding!' he cried in alarm.

'Only a little,' she confessed. 'But don't worry, my Niall. I loved the pleasure I could give you. The bleeding only means I'm no longer the virgin I was.'

He fell on his knees and cradled her head. 'I'm sorry I hurt you so. I should have been gentle but you drove me crazy. It was wonderful but it can't have been very good for you.'

'It will be – the next time.'

'The next time?'

'We only have five days together, Niall, and I want to belong to you every minute you're here.'

'Let me bathe you,' he requested, still ashamed that

he had hurt her. 'I'll get some water from the burn while you dress.'

He made tea and while it was masking he cleansed her with warmed water. She had protested but his argument stilled her.

'Please let me, I drew the virgin blood from you and it is my right to clean it away.'

'Are you not shocked?' she asked when it was finished.

'No, I love every bit of you and besides, I know what girls are like. I've bathed Fiona manys the time; you're much the same, though bigger with fluffy red hairs. It's funny, I often wondered if they'd be red.'

She gasped. 'You've thought of me in that way then?'

'Of course – a long time ago in fact. I used to try and see but you always had knickers on.'

'NIALL MCLACHLAN!' She threw a cushion at him and he lay back on the bed and roared with laughter.

It was growing dark and the air was damp and frosty when they arrived at her gate. He took her hand. 'I loved you so much this morning I didn't think it was possible to love you more – now I know I was wrong.'

'Do you, Niall – really? I wanted to prove to you how much I care. I don't want you to think I'm just a cheap . . .'

He put a finger over her lips. 'Hush, don't dare think the thing. Now I must go. Will you be over tonight? My mother will be expecting you – and your father if he's not busy.'

'I'll come even if he doesn't.'

She was halfway up the track when she stopped,

wondering suddenly how she would face her father. He had an uncanny knack of reading her mind and always knew what her mood was even if she tried to conceal it. Tonight she felt jubilant and very womanly. She didn't feel ashamed or guilty. Her father had warned her indirectly about the trappings of emotion and she had promised him to be careful. Today she had thrown caution to the wind and she was afraid now that he would guess at her indiscretions.

But the warm kitchen was quiet and empty. She lit a lamp and saw a note propped against her place at the table. Her father had been asked over to Burnbreddie to dine and discuss farming business with Scott Balfour, laird of Burnbreddie for two years now since his father had died.

The new laird of Burnbreddie had made slow progress with the wary Rhanna crofters. They didn't trust a 'college cissy' to handle their affairs but gradually they realised they were getting a fairer deal from him than they'd ever had from the whisky-loving womaniser who had been his father. He was generous with the harvests of his land and distributed game and venison equally to all and even those who had criticised him with the sharpest tongues had to grudgingly admit he had some gumption after all.

His wife was no society girl either but a sensible young countrywoman of Scottish landed stock, and she endeared herself to the islanders by taking an active and genuine interest in their lives. Little boys of two and four livened the former gloom of the big mansion house wherein old Madam Balfour, under the firm hand of her daughter-in-law, simpered and ailed less, complained still, but less vehemently, and even enjoyed her two little grandsons.

Shona took her dinner on a tray by the fire. Tot lolled on one side of her and two cats sat grimly to attention on the other. Three pairs of eyes watched her emptying plate intently and Tot's mouth watered profusely. Normally, such blatant bad manners would have earned a rebuke, but Shona was barely conscious of her surroundings and sat for a long time gazing dreamily into the fire. Eventually Tot's snuffling and wheezing brought her to her senses. Shona patted the silky ears and went to the larder and soon the cats were lapping milk and Tot eating her fish and oatmeal.

Shona went outside to shut the hen-houses and check the cowsheds. Her breath clouded in the air and she looked up to see a million stars. Mirabelle had taught her the various constellations and she stared at the panorama of the heavens, her arms folded over her breasts in delight.

'Oh great God up there,' she breathed, 'I thank you for this lovely day with Niall and for all the things I have that are so good. Mirabelle – if you're listening don't think bad of me. What I did today was for love, I don't feel it was wrong though I know you won't think it was right. Tell Hamish and my mother I send my love – and old Shelagh too.'

She always prayed in the fashion of her childhood, simple words that gave her great satisfaction and, since the old housekeeper's death, she had passed messages through her to others who had gone from her life.

She went indoors and damped the fire. She had

already laid the table for breakfast and the big kettle was filled for bedtime cocoa and hot bags. She stepped once more into the frosty night air and met Dodie hovering at the gate.

'He breeah!' he moaned unhappily.

'He breeah! Is something not right, Dodie?'

'I'm lookin' for my damty ram so I am. He's having a fine time with the yowes on the hill and I hear tell the lads from the sheiling of Nigg are girnin' about it. It's just talk with them for Dan Russell was blawin' last spring about his fine lambs and knowin' fine my Murn was the father.'

Shona had to hide a smile. After his experience with Ealasaid's offspring he had decided that the females of the domestic animal kingdom were easier to manage and had hopefully bestowed feminine names on the lambs at birth. When the mistake became apparent the names had stayed because the young ram would only answer to Murn.

'We ought to call him,' suggested Shona. 'Was he seen hereabouts recently?'

'Not long since.'

After a few minutes of calling Shona paused for breath. 'You know, Dodie, you ought to sell Murn. He's just causing trouble and with Ealasaid to look after you have enough of a handful. I've seen you tramping miles with her potash.'

'Ach, she's worth it – and I'm not selling Murn. He would miss me too much.'

'Och, c'mon now, Dodie, it's not right that a fine ram like Murn should be mixing with all those common yowes on the hill. Murn should have hand-picked yowes and you'll never manage that letting him roam freely.'

Shona could be very devious when she liked and Dodie stroked his grizzled chin thoughtfully. 'I never thought on it that way just. Murn is a fine ram, I'd like to see him get goin' with good yowes. That lot on the hill are a scruffy lot.'

'Well, just you have a good think about it. I'm having to go now.'

'Is your father at home? I'd like fine to ask his advice about Murn.'

'He's out tonight, Dodie.'

'Ach, what a pity just.'

She expected him to lope away but he trailed behind her and it was obvious he was in the mood for company. She paused at Niall's gate. 'Are you coming in to Strupak?' she asked kindly.

'Ach, the doctor will be busy.'

'I'm sure he'll be delighted,' she said uncertainly.

'Ach well, maybe for a wee while. I'd like fine to ask somebody about Murn. I'll hold the gate while you go through.'

Phebie was less than delighted to see Dodie. She had scrubbed the house till it smelled of soap and disinfectant and she knew that a few minutes of Dodie in any enclosed space would allow his odour to linger for hours but she concealed her feelings admirably and ushered both callers into the parlour.

Lachlan was dozing by the fire. Dodie immediately settled himself in the opposite chair and very soon the heat from the hearth was coaxing all the trapped smells from his boots.

Niall came pounding downstairs and burst into the room, his eyes meeting Shona's in a brief moment of unspoken love.

'Hello, Dodie,' he acknowledged cheerily, holding his breath as the smell hit him. 'It's yourself then?'

'Just for a whiley. I'd like fine to ask the doctor here what he thinks I should do about Murn.'

'I saw him chasing some of Croynachan's sheep,' volunteered Niall. 'Just round about teatime.'

'Aye well, that's the trouble, chasing too many damty yowes and myself gettin' into trouble because of it. Wee Shona here thinks Murn's just wastin' himself on thon scruff on the hill. She thinks I should sell him and see he gets a chance with some better yowes.'

Lachlan's eyes twinkled but when he spoke he sounded so seriously concerned about Murn's welfare that Dodie listened intently.

'Shona's right, Dodie. I've watched that ram and thought what a fine beast he is. I know old Jock from Nigg is looking for a good ram.'

'Is he that now?'

'Aye, I heard him telling Johnston just the other day.'

'Well now, that would be fine. Murn would be happy with Jock for he's a kindly wee man and loves his beasts the way I love mine. But I wouldn't know what price to be askin'. Murn might be a fine ram but he's been usin' himself up you might say. Not that he'll run dry on Jock – oh no, never that, but it's a wee rest he's needin'.'

Phebie, coming in with a laden tray, could hardly keep a straight face and Fiona, a sparkling nymph in a white nightgown, came in for a scone and looked sympathetic at Dodie's words. 'Ach poor Murn,' she consoled. 'I think he plays too much with the sheep. I saw him jumpin' on a scraggy old yowe yesterday and her wool must have tickled his belly for his eyes were rollin'.'

It was the cue everyone needed to release their laughter. Phebie lifted her little daughter high and kissed her. 'On up to bed, ye wee wittrock. Remember to say your prayers.'

Shona helped Phebie to hand round the Strupak but when she made to put milk in Dodie's tea he stayed her with a big hand. 'Not in my tea, lass, over my bread in a saucer.'

'But Dodie, there's jam on the bread.'

'Aye, lovely just. I like a bit jammy bread with milk over it. Merry Mary makes me jam from my own rhubarb and quite often she gives me bits of her new baked bread. I spread on the jam and pour over Ealasaid's best cream and have it for my dinner. It's a fine meal, you all should try it.'

He scooped the soggy bread from the saucer and smacked his lips to catch the dribbles on his chin. 'Lovely,' he approved. 'You make fine bread, Mistress McLachlan. I'm thinkin' now you'll be tryin' my recipe on the family.'

'Aye maybe,' said Phebie while Shona smiled as mention of Dodie's rhubarb brought a memory of two suntanned children listening round-eyed while the secret of the thick, juicy sticks was divulged.

Dodie was sublimely happy eating his Strupak and chatting in his native Gaelic. Most of the islanders, except the very old, had a good English vocabulary and the youngsters could speak both languages equally well but Dodie, with his speech difficulties, was sadly lost trying to pronounce the 'foreign' words. Rumour had it that an English visitor, lost in the hills, had come upon Dodie and had asked the way back to Portcull. Dodie, arms waving and carbuncle wobbling, had tried to give directions but the Englishman was unable to understand. Eventually Dodie had summoned Ealasaid and tied a rope round her hairy neck. The stunned visitor was bidden to climb aboard and, with a proud Dodie coaxing and pulling, Ealasaid lumbered into Portcull to safely deliver her ashen-faced passenger.

He dusted the crumbs from his knees and got up reluctantly.

'I'll have to be going now.' He patted one of his voluminous pockets. 'I have a neep here for Murn and I'd like fine to see he gets it for supper.'

Phebie sighed. 'Och Dodie, no wonder there's a smell,' she scolded. 'The neep's near roasted with the heat from the fire! I've been trying to fathom the reek.'

'Ach well, that's what it was,' said Dodie who was sublimely unaware of his own strange scent no matter how many innuendoes were cast at him.

'I'm going over to Nigg in the morning,' said Lachlan kindly. 'If you want to see Jock about the ram I'll pick you up around ten. I'd like fine to see you get a fair price for Jock's gey canny with the shillings.'

'Och, it's kind you are.' Dodie's broken teeth showed for a moment. 'I'll be off now, bidding you thanks for the Strupak. He breeah.'

He backed to the door and Phebie held her breath as his ungainly figure narrowly missed tables and other obstacles. Lachlan went to the door and watched till the untidy flapping figure was lost in the dark though the moaning cry of 'Murn! Murn!' could be heard for a long time in the calm frosty air.

When Lachlan got back to the parlour he chuckled to see everyone fanning the air with newspapers.

'I'm sorry about bringing him,' grinned Shona, 'but he was so forlorn out there I couldn't leave him. Poor Dodie, he must get lonely sometimes.'

She was on the sofa beside Niall and he squeezed her hand. 'Will you think of me, a poor lonely soul, out there in muddy, smelly trenches with bullets whingin' round me?'

It was meant to be a light-hearted comment but everyone in the room tensed.

'We'll think of you, lad,' said Lachlan quietly. 'Every day we'll spare our thoughts for you.'

Shona's eyes glinted in the firelight. 'Will it really – be like that?'

Niall made his answer sound uncaring. 'I canny really imagine what it will be like. It might be a bit like going into a dark room and not knowing if there's ghosties there or not.'

Shona shivered despite the warm room. 'I can't imagine you in a strange country,' she whispered.

'Ach, I'm used to being away from home.'

Phebie was clearing the tea things but she stopped to look at her son and when she spoke her voice was sharp. 'Are you used to fighting? And what about killing. You that never hurt a living cratur no matter

414

how wee. What about a man, Niall? How will it be killing a man?'

She didn't wait for an answer but rushed from the room, her face crimson.

Lachlan sighed and studied his slippered feet intently. 'Take no heed of your mother, Niall,' he said gently. 'She's having a hard time trying to cope with her feelings. She canny believe you're going off to war. We're all feeling a bit strained at the moment.'

Shona got up silently and went to the kitchen to help Phebie.

Lachlan tapped his pipe on the grate. 'How's she taking it?'

Niall played with his thumbs. 'Bad at first. She ran from me yesterday when we spoke of it.'

'I thought you were out of temper last night but you're sweethearts again I see.'

Niall flushed and his bowed head glinted in the firelight.

Lachlan looked at his son and felt such a rush of love that he wanted to cradle the young head in his lap. Ah, it seemed but yesterday that a merry little boy laughed and played at his feet. Was it not a short time ago that the harvest carts trundled homewards in the gloaming and his sleeping son lay heavy in his arms? How could he ever forget the family outings with Niall, the only child in their lives then, leaving a trail of tiny footprints on silver sand? Those had been the days of picnics in sheltered coves, the thundering foam of the Atlantic spuming high in the air while Niall, a suntanned sprite, embraced the world with his outstretched arms, screaming with joy as the frothing spray bathed his sunkissed body.

How golden had been those far-off days and how easy it had been to laugh. Lachlan didn't feel like laughing now, knowing that each interlude with his son would become a precious memory later – later when all he might have would be memories.

Niall stirred restlessly and Lachlan sensed his impatience.

'I'll see Dodie gets a good price for his ram tomorrow,' said Lachlan trying to take the strain from his son by keeping matters on an everyday level.

Niall looked into his father's brown eyes and felt the love and understanding reaching out to him.

'I'd like fine to come over to Nigg with you. I want to see Tammy and one or two others. Could Shona come too, do you think?'

'Well, it's only a wee trap but Shona's just a wee lass so I think we'll manage, but don't blame me if you're all squeezed up against Dodie.'

Niall put his hand on his father's shoulder and his usually laughing eyes were serious. 'I know there's a lot you'd like to say, Father, but thanks for not saying it. I always knew I chose a sensible father.'

Lachlan's fixed smile did not betray his inner emotions. 'And I always knew I picked a lad with a lot of gumption. Now see me over those tuffers before the fire goes down and I get a warmed lug from your mother.'

It was a mild misty day when Niall left Rhanna. He felt himself doing things as in a dream yet he was so aware of individual sensations he felt he could reach out and

416

put each one in his pocket. Shona's head nestled on his shoulder as they walked away from Slochmhor. The smell of her was of roses and shining hair, mingling with all the scents of Rhanna the breeze brought to him. The healthy smell of dung and hay came from Laigmhor. A herd of cows, scratching hairy necks on the fence, blew clouds of steam and chlorophyll into the air. Smoke, fragrant with peat, floated lazily from chimneys and over-riding all was the faint, ever-present tang of salt sea.

The memory of saying goodbye to his father was keen on his mind. It hadn't been a spectacular farewell, just a few murmured words, and a pair of strong hands gripping him on the shoulder. He was glad his father had turned away quickly because he felt the hot tears blurring his eyes, his throat constricting as he watched the tall, familiar figure striding away, clutching the black bag that marked him as a healer of men. How often he had watched that beloved man going off on his rounds. When he was a little boy he'd sometimes gone with his father, thinking it a treat to visit croft and farm, biggin and cottage, where constant Strupaks were offered and dogs and cats would submit to being his very own 'pretend' patients, obediently sitting with patient resignation while he prodded the old stethoscope his father had given him into furry bellies and examined tongues. In the dogs' cases that had never been difficult as a pink tongue was usually lolling anyway, but cats were never quite so forthcoming and he often ended with a scratch or two which the real doctor had to see to.

He had waited that morning for the final wave from the striding figure and when it didn't come he had felt like the little boy of long ago, cheated out of something he felt was his right. Then he saw his father's hand go up to his eyes and he knew, with a poignant tearing of his senses, that his father wept too.

The time for leaving came quickly. Shona came breathlessly from Laigmhor and his mother, wiping floury hands on her apron, kissed him briefly and promised she would come to the harbour to see him off. She was aloof and too bright and he was grateful to her for giving him the obvious opportunity to spend those precious last minutes with Shona.

She was very quiet on the walk to Portcull and he wondered if she was in the same wakeful dream as himself. Tot trotted beside them and her squatting on every patch of grass that appealed to her brought a sense of normality to the morning.

The gulls were whooping and screaming in the harbour. He could see them in the distance, looking like torn fragments of paper blowing in the sky.

He kissed the delicate shell of Shona's ear and felt that even if he were to die in the war his last days on Rhanna had brought a fulfilment to his short life that could never be surpassed. He had loved Shona with his body and his soul. She had given herself to him with such unquestioning love that he had cried in the act of joining with her and she too had wept so that their tears mingled as their bodies became one.

Suddenly she twisted her head to look up at him, her incredible eyes dark with emotion.

'Oh Niall' she murmured, 'I feel so unhappy – yet

in the last week my life has been so full I think I could live for ever and never know such happiness again.'

He put both arms round her and held her close. 'You even steal my thoughts, Caillich Ruadh. Is it not enough you already have my heart? Five days ago I came home my heart afire with love for you, now I leave, knowing that what burned before was only a candle to what I feel now. Oh God, I love you, mo gaolach! These days together will be my crutch when I'm low in spirits and I ask you to spare your thoughts for me whenever you can.'

'It's going to be a long winter, Niall, there will be time to think and wonder – what you are doing, when you'll be home.'

'I might get a bit of leave if things are quiet.'

'Not enough to allow you to travel to Rhanna. It would be fine if you could walk over the sea because those daft ferries of ours only come twice a week *if* the weather's good.' She fingered the gold locket at her neck. 'I have something for you. Niall – nothing as grand as this locket but it's a wee keepsake to remind you of home. I made it when I was nine and think well of it, Niall McLachlan, for each letter was sewn in tears and blood. I hate sewing but Mirabelle made me unpick it and do it over and over till it was as perfect as I could get it.'

It was a sampler of rough linen, beautifully embroidered in different coloured silks. Tears shone in his brown eyes as he whispered the words of a Hebridean poem: 'From the lone sheiling of the misty island, mountains divide us and the waste of seas; But our hearts are true and our hearts are Highland, and we in dreams – behold the Hebrides.' He gathered her to him again. 'I'll treasure it, mo gaolach, but I won't need reminding of home. I can assure you of that.'

The harbour was strangely quiet. Usually, when the boat was due there was a subdued excitement in the knots of people waiting about. Today there was hardly a soul to be seen. A few cows, waiting to be shipped to the mainland, lowed dismally in a nearby pen, but otherwise Portcull was deserted.

The boat appeared like a ghost ship on the horizon. 'I thought Mother would have come,' said Niall looking towards Glen Fallan. He felt strangely deflated. He was leaving the island of his birth to fight for its people and not one familiar figure was there to wish him luck. His thoughts were self-righteous and with them came an unaccustomed pang of self-pity.

Shona squeezed his hand. 'Your mother will come, Niall. She'll leave it to the last because she won't want time to cry.'

The boat came closer and they watched in silence, suddenly finding nothing to say to each other while the boat loomed, filling the span of their vision. Ropes were thrown, men shouted and the ever-present gulls glided in the warm air from the ship's funnels.

The boat was unloaded. Chickens clucked in subdued tones from several crates and a young bull swung gently in the cradle of the sling attached to the derrick. Old Joe sauntered from nowhere and lit his pipe, keeping a nonchalant eye on the sling. His appearance was like some kind of trigger. All at once the harbour swarmed with all the warm-hearted, familiar faces that Niall had known all his life. They gathered round him showering him with gifts.

Morag Ruadh pressed a small parcel into his hand. 'A wee bit tablet, just the way you like it. Mither moaned at me for using up the sugar and Father just missed the pan I was making the tablet in with his spit.'

Niall wasn't sure if she meant the tablet had been made with a recipe using some of old McDonald's spit but he took the package gratefully and kissed Morag Ruadh on the cheek. She looked astonished for a moment then she smiled slowly, a rueful gentle smile that softened her ruddy, weatherbeaten features.

Ranald beamed into the scene, pushing a bundle of rather tattered magazines into Niall's hands, and Todd the Shod gave him a tiny horseshoe. 'Just for luck,' he said in his apologetic fashion, though the keepsake had been cast with exquisite attention to detail.

Canty Tam smiled in his vacant fashion, murmuring something about no horseshoe on earth being a match against the evils of 'furrin parts' but his mother, a widow woman of mighty girth, prodded him sharply in the stomach, leaving him without further breath for his prophecies of doom.

Merry Mary, who had simply shut up shop for a few minutes, handed Niall a parcel, her usually radiant smile somewhat forced on this occasion. 'Just a wee bit sweets,' she whispered sadly. 'Not so good for the teeth but fine for the nerves – the wee kind in your belly that can make you feel sick.'

Righ nan Dul came limping along from his cottage perched close to the lighthouse at Port Rum Point. He had inherited the name from his father who had manned the lighthouse before him. It meant governor of the elements and Righ thoroughly deserved his title. His limp he owed to a fall on the twisting stairs inside the lighthouse but, despite it, he still kept his lonely night vigil, year after year. His weatherbeaten face creased into a grin at the sight of Niall and he shouted, 'I'll keep my torch burnin' for you, laddie, and may the Lord guide you home safe.'

'Thank you, Righ,' said Niall, feeling a lump rising in his throat as Righ's horny hand took his in a firm grasp.

Old Bob had stolen away from the fields to see Niall off. He was extremely fond of the doctor's son but his words were gruff as he hastily slipped a small heavy package into Niall's pocket. 'For fear you get drouthy, lad,' he mumbled and seized Niall's hand in his large calloused one. Niall couldn't speak. He knew if he did he would make a fool of himself. His dreamworld was growing in proportion yet still he felt and saw everything with an intense clarity.

Dodie galloped into the crowd. 'He breeah!' he sighed dismally, 'I thought I would miss the boat for I couldn't find Murn and old Jock comin' for him early. He's away now so he is and I just hurried down to give you this wee present.'

He was embarrassed and unsure of himself. Tears had sprung to his odd, pale eyes and Niall wasn't sure if they were for him or the going of his beloved Murn, but when he looked down at the exquisitely polished conch shell, with a shaky 'N' laboriously scratched on its surface, he knew that eccentric old Dodie wept for him.

'It's a bonny present, Dodie,' he said brightly.

'Ach well, you were a fine brave laddie,' came the reply and Niall knew that he was already as good as dead in Dodie's simple mind.

'Niall, Niall!' Fiona's small figure hurled itself at him. 'Old Murdoch let me away to say goodbye!'

He swung her into his arms. 'We said it this morning, you wee wittrock.'

She giggled, her dark eyes snapping with mischief. 'Old Murdoch doesny know that for I said you were in bed when I left for school.'

He nuzzled her warm neck and put out his free arm to his mother.

'I'm late,' she apologized, her concealed emotions putting a sharp edge to her voice. 'Mathew tore his knee on barbed wire and I had to bind it for him.'

Shona stood to the side. She felt shut off from Niall's world but she knew she was being foolish. She wondered if love was always such a strong influence on a person's normally sensible reasonings. Portcull was alive with people all claiming Niall's attention. A short time ago it had just been the two of them and selfishly she wanted it to stay like that, to have all his thoughts directed at her. She wanted to be the last person in his vision of Rhanna, instead it seemed the whole of Portcull would predominate over his final impressions.

She folded her arms behind her back and let the sounds wash over her. The cry of the gulls seared into her brain, the babble of voices made her want to scream.

A terrified bellow came from above and she looked

up to see a shaggy cream-coloured cow rigid with fright on the sling. It was perfectly safe in the strong canvas sling and the men winching her aboard were experts but the poor cow could know none of these things. Her eyes rolled and the rigid limbs thrashed the air. Shona felt sorry for the frightened animal. It was terrified of the unknown and, like herself, didn't know what the future held.

At the moment her own future looked bleak and she felt sick and empty. But a warm arm came round her neck to hug her close and Niall whispered, 'Don't desert a sinking ship! All these folk seeing me off as if I were some sort of hero and now all I want is you, mo gaolach.'

She was secure again but in minutes he was gone from her, striding up the gangplank to the deck to become again a dear, familiar, but unattainable figure.

Phebie gripped her arm. 'Hold on, mo ghaoil,' she urged. 'I know well how you feel but don't let go now.'

A sob rose in Shona's throat but she choked it back, looking up to smile and wave at Niall.

Fergus burst into the scene, tall and wonderfully calm. He slipped his arm round his daughter and drew her close. 'Thought you might like a shoulder,' he murmured. 'They come in handy betimes.'

She leaned against him and he felt hard and strong. The boat was casting off. Niall leaned on the rail shouting something she couldn't hear for the bellowing cows and the ship's loud, mournful horn. The crowd cheered and Niall raised his hand, a handsome slim figure in his Army uniform. For a moment

Shona swayed against her father. Her times of loving Niall were already folded into the caverns of her mind, the memories that would sustain her in the long days ahead. Already quarter of a mile of swirling green water was between her and the young man she loved. He was just a dark speck, indistinguishable from the other little specks that merged around him.

She was inclined to linger but her father pulled her away.

'I'm going back to make a Strupak,' said Phebie lightly. 'Anyone care to join me?'

'Just what we all need I'm thinking,' said Fergus leading his daughter firmly in the direction of Glen Fallan.

Barely a week later Shona was restless and unsettled. She had looked forward to the annual visit of the Travers family but a letter came from Oban containing the news that Murdy had fallen and broken a leg so their holiday would have to be cancelled.

'Maisie would have come alone,' wrote Mrs Travers, 'but she is going steady with a nice boy and doesn't want to leave him alone.'

'Frightened he would get away,' said Fergus with a grin.

Shona tossed her mane of bright hair impatiently. 'Och Father, you've never been very kind to poor Maisie.'

'Ach, it's just my way and if you must know the truth I was always frightened she would get me in a dark corner.'

Shona giggled absently and fingered the letter. 'I like

old Murdy, and Mrs Travers is such a cheery wee body. I could fair have been doing with them for a whiley. Alick and Mary won't be till Christmas and that's a long time away.'

Fergus tapped out his pipe on the edge of the grate. He looked at his daughter's brooding young face. 'Why don't you go to the Traverses'? The break will do you good, stop you thinking too much.'

She turned to him in surprise. 'But I'd have to leave you and you'd never manage on your own. Who would get your meals and darn your socks and feed the hens and – and . . .'

'I don't put a hole in my sock every few minutes,' he smiled, 'and I'm not a baby to be coddled by a daughter who's fast becoming a Cailleach before her time.'

The tears, never far away lately, sprang to her eyes. 'Och Father! How could you?'

'Because it's true. I know you love Rhanna but I think the time's ripe for you to get away. We all need fresh stamping ground at some time in our lives. Your time has come.'

She hesitated, her elbows on the table, the letter clutched in her hand. She knew her father was right. The things that had charmed her from babyhood now seemed to have no meaning. Her lonely walks could only take her to the places she and Niall had haunted. The white beaches and long stretches of moor now seemed bare and lonely and she returned from her lone wanderings disconsolate and uneasy. She tossed in bed unable to sleep and as a result she felt weary and disinterested. She reached across the scrubbed table top and caught her father's hand.

'Will – you write and ask, Father?'

'Get my pen and paper and I'll do it now. If we hurry we'll catch the boat before she leaves. Erchy says she had to bide in harbour for a minor repair but she'll be leaving soon.'

Mrs Travers's reply came the following week. She wrote saying she would love to have Shona, they were all looking forward to it, especially Murdy who was wearying and needing a 'cheery wee soul like Shona to cheer him up'.

'I don't feel very cheery.' Shona stared from the window at the blue-green Sound of Rhanna in the distance. It was a windy fresh day, the sort she had always loved. Behag Beag, her black coat flapping, was making her determined way to Lachlan's in time for morning surgery and Bob, his pipe hanging precariously from his lower lip, had hold of a ram by the horns and was dragging it to a small field of noisy sheep. The scene looked so familiar and dear that she suddenly felt she must sit down and write to let Mrs Travers know she couldn't manage after all.

Fergus was reading over the letter. 'They're expecting you by the next boat – the mail boat to Oban . . .' He paused as a memory came back to him. 'So you'd better iron your petticoats, mo ghaoil.'

'I wonder if Kirsteen ever goes back to Oban.' She said it absently, still staring from the window, but he looked at her quickly.

'Why do you say that?'

'You went there to find her, didn't you? I was only eleven, I think, but I remember you coming back. You had changed in a funny kind of way. You were so gay but your eyes – all empty and sad. I think I loved you more then than I ever did. It was after that I became your wife – yes, in a way, Father. I've looked after you and worried about you the way a wife would. Now I feel like you must have then – lonely and terribly empty.'

He put his arm round her. 'You'd better start packing. I know women take long over such things.'

'I think I'll only stay for a week, Father, so I won't need much. Now, you'd better get over and help Bob with that ram. I've never seen one so unwilling before.'

Her week dragged into a month and Fergus had never been so keenly aware of his own loneliness. The nights were long. Clocks ticked, Tot and the cats snored peacefully while he gazed into the fire and thought his lonely thoughts. He made work for himself, gathering in peat till the shed was piled high, scrubbing the milking shed till the cows looked uneasy at such cleanliness, and redecorated Shona's room for her return. Before bedtime each night he took to going to the byre to smoke his pipe in the company of the cows. They were such peaceful animals with their calm, long-lashed eyes, and they transferred some of their serenity to him. The cobbled byre was a place of warm breath, rich smells, and solid hairy backs to lean on and St Kilda, who had lorded the byre for years, would bellow at him till he was obliged to put a few strands of hay into the racks.

Letters came from France and he readdressed them to Oban knowing how eagerly his daughter waited them. She returned to Rhanna three weeks before

Christmas and he was quietly pleased to see the change in her. Her eyes sparkled with life, her cheeks were pink, her slim body had filled out slightly. She flung herself on him and he felt his heart bursting with the joy of having her back.

'Oh Father, I've missed you so but I've enjoyed myself with the Traverses. I've got all my Christmas presents – the shops in Oban are bonny. Murdy's a terrible man, he taught me all the card games there are, so you and the McLachlans had best be careful if I'm playing with you.' She paused to look at the fields and the blue-grey shoulder of Sgurr na Gill. 'Och, isn't Rhanna beautiful?' She turned back to him, her blue eyes quizzical. 'It's strange, Father – I had to get away from Rhanna and I love you for making me go but I *knew* when I was ready to come back. I was pining for you and for my island. I suppose Phebie's told you Niall's well? He doesn't really describe what it's like out there but he never did explain things – even when he was away at school.'

She danced into the kitchen and Tot grunted delightedly to meet her. 'Oh, it's lovely to be back.' She was ecstatic. 'Dear old Tot and everything just the same. I hope it's always like this!'

'Things change,' he said lightly.

'Not Laigmhor, not you, Father. Now, I must unpack and hide my presents! I don't want you poking about . . . oh, Mrs Travers gave you this, she said she was going to send it but I was coming home so she gave it to me.'

She tossed a package on to the rocking chair and raced upstairs.

Fergus heard her exclaiming over her room as he picked up the parcel. It was wrapped in brown paper and tied tightly with string and he put it on the mantelshelf to open later.

He served out dinner and Shona felt like a queen being made to sit down while he ladled steaming soup.

'Just today,' he smiled ruefully. 'Tomorrow it's back to normal. I've a pile of socks to be darned and all my shirts need buttons.'

'I knew you needed me, Father,' she said triumphantly.

She was exhausted that evening and went to bed early. He sat for a time beside the fire, drinking his cocoa and sucking his unlit pipe. He reached to the mantelshelf for a taper and his hand brushed the-parcel. Suddenly he felt quite excited about it and opened it quickly. He recognized the contents at once and his heart lurched into his throat. They were his letters to Kirsteen, each one opened but still in their envelopes. It had been so long since he'd written them yet it seemed only yesterday he'd painstakingly scrawled each loving word. But why were they sent to haunt him after all this time? There was a note from Mrs Travers and he read it, his hand trembling:

'Dear Fergus,

I should have written before but with Shona here the time has flown by so quickly. Mrs Fraser died two weeks ago and I went to clear out her bits and pieces for, though she was a selfish wee body in many ways, she grew to trust me over the years and would let no one else do things for her.

As you know I tidied for her now and then so it was natural enough for me to clear the things out. She has a sister somewhere and one or two nephews and the lawyer tried to trace them without success.

I found some letters from Kirsteen to her mother. She had been writing after all but Maggie Fraser never once hinted this to me and myself her good friend the besom. However I'm not one to speak ill of the dead. It was obvious Kirsteen had been sending money to her mother but there was no address on the letters and never a hint where she was staying so it was easy to see she never wanted her mother to know of her whereabouts.

The old lady has eaten her heart out these years since Kirsteen left. I used to see a tear in her eye on the few occasions she spoke of her lass. I know she was sorry for driving her away but she was a stubborn old lady and would never admit to being wrong. There's a hint she's left her house to some charity. She hadn't much else but her house and her memories. The lawyer will likely put something into the leading papers in an attempt to let Kirsteen know that her mother has passed on and if I hear anything I'll let you know.

The letters are your property, I think, and I feel it's your right to get them back. I didn't look at them, well, maybe just a wee keek and they were that lovely I had a quiet wee greet to myself.

Murdy and Maisie send their regards. I think the

break here has done Shona some good. She's a bonny bright lass and we'll all miss her. Take good care of yourself, my lad.

Your friend
Maggie Travers.'

Fergus picked up the sheaf of letters and crushed them to his breast. 'Kirsteen, Kirsteen,' he murmured brokenly, 'it seems everyone has read my letters but you.' He cradled his head in his hand, the firelight giving the dark curls on his brow the sheen of a raven's wing.

He remained where he was for some time, a strong motionless figure in his thick tweeds and Fair Isle pullover, lovingly knitted by Shona. The room was dark behind him and a faint wind rattled the window. A daring mouse nibbled crumbs by the dresser and Snap's ginger fur bristled but he was too lazily comfortable on the hearth to bother further.

The fire's glow found every hollow in Fergus's handsome face and iridescent colours broke on a tear poised on his lower lashes. His knuckles tightened on the letters and the sudden movement of his arm, drawn back to hurl them into the fire, made Snap sit upright, nostrils aflare with fright.

The bundle landed on a piece of unlit turf and remained unharmed but for the wraiths of smoke already blackening the edges. Fergus watched, his chest heaving. A flame curled greedily and with a small strangled cry he snatched the bundle back from the fire. Something that was beyond his understanding made him want to keep this reminder of the past. The letters were a link with Kirsteen, the girl who lived somewhere in the world and who cared for the son he had never seen. If he ever found them, the letters were proof of a heart that had never stopped mourning for a love he couldn't let go of.

Part Seven

Christmas 1939

Chapter Fourteen

The smell of snow was in Shona's room when she woke three days before Christmas. She was aware of it, even as she was aware of the feeling of nausea that was becoming a familiar sensation of her first waking hour. She lay snugly under the patchwork quilt she had started with Mirabelle's help when she was nine years old. She loved the quilt, it was a dear familiar thing in her life because each triangle and square was a memory. There were several patches from Mirabelle's thick tweedy coats and from old jackets of her father's. Many bits were from her own childhood clothes and two very precious patches had been begged from Niall to mend a torn square. He'd been fifteen when he'd given her the fragment of tartan from one of his discarded kilts. She ran her fingers over the rough homespun and thought about him. He wouldn't manage home for Christmas or New Year. He had leave but not enough to allow for all the travelling time necessary to get to Rhanna. She searched under her pillow and found his letter from the week before. One passage tormented her with its unconscious pathos:

'The thought of you is the one thing that keeps me going out here, mo gaolach. It's a cold place, a different cold from Rhanna, and it curls inside till it reaches every bone. I make myself remember each moment we shared then I get warm again. It's not that I find it hard to think of you but a man gets gey tired playing at soldiers and weariness does odd things to the memory.

'It will be strange not being home this Christmas. I've always had Christmas on Rhanna with my ain folk but I'll imagine you all, the peat fires, the plum puddings, and Bob playing his fiddle. Give your father my regards. Funny, I used to be a wee bit skearie of him, now I'm glad that one day I'll be his son-in-law.

'I look at the sampler you gave me often and, in my thoughts, I can see those misty islands.

'I love you, mo gaolach . . .'

She folded the letter and slid it back under the pillow, her arm frozen though it had only been exposed a few minutes. She covered herself again, reluctant to leave the warm bed. She heard her father in the kitchen and felt guilty. He was always up and about by six and in again for breakfast at half-past eight. Usually she had the fire going and his breakfast ready. Lately she'd felt too sick to move from her bed and the cold searching light of a winter dawn was something she hadn't seen for almost a week now. She'd felt the same nausea when she'd been staying with the Traverses but it had passed quickly and hadn't detracted from her enjoyment of the holiday. Oban seemed far away now and her visit belonged to another time.

Cups clattered in the kitchen and with quick decision she got out of bed, making Tot groan at the intrusion into her slumbers.

Shona was aware of the heavy dull soreness of her breasts as she swiftly pulled on clothes. She'd been aware of the feeling for some time but her mind was always so active with other things that she hadn't bothered very much about it, she always got it before a period only this time the heaviness was more acute. She pulled on a cardigan and her eyes fell on the calendar above her bed. She stared at it, her eyes growing big, while her hand went slowly to her mouth. She hadn't stopped to think before, to count the weeks, or to analyse the reason for the lack of menstruation. She sat back heavily on the bed and her hands went automatically to her stomach. She was going to have a child, Niall's child, it was growing inside her now and she hadn't been aware of it! The surprise of the discovery made her feel faint. She tried to think, to count the weeks of her pregnancy, but she couldn't. Pregnancy applied to people like Nancy and Mairi, to animals like sheep and cows, dogs and cats, not to beings like herself, in love but unmarried, and barely seventeen. Her time of loving Niall had been a time of joy, of innocent wonder of the untamed passion they had shared. It was their secret, a thing of beauty to be held in the heart and unlocked from the mind in the dark hours when others slept. She was shocked by her discovery but she wasn't afraid, there was going to be time enough for all those emotions later. The only real emotion she felt at that moment, other than surprise, was a growing certainty that she'd known all along that this was the thing that had motivated her to give herself so freely to Niall. She was afraid he wouldn't return to her and she'd wanted him to leave a part of himself, his seed was growing inside her, into a baby that would be like him.

In a daze she got up and splashed her face with cold water from the basin but the freezing water did nothing to rouse her from her trance. Her father shouted from below, 'Are you up yet, lass? The porridge is bubbling!'

'I'm coming, Father!' she cried and went downstairs with Tot at her heels. Warming flames leapt in the grate and the porridge made soft plopping sounds in the pan. Fergus was pouring water into the teapot but he turned to look at her.

'It will snow before the morn's out,' he forecast. 'I'll have to go out with Bob and Jock and put out neeps for the hill sheep and you'll have to look for Thistle again – he got out from the field, the rascal. Most of the beasts will need extra hay so it will be all hands to the plough.' He looked at her keenly. 'You look wabbit, Shona. Are you sleeping bad of late?'

She forced a laugh. 'Och no, Father, it's just lazy I am and afeard of the cold outside the bedclothes. I'm sorry you had to get breakfast and you out so early. It won't happen again.'

But he wasn't deceived. He ate his porridge thoughtfully and noticed she only toyed with hers. He'd noticed the change in her after her return from Oban. She was different in a subtle way. Her lovely elfin face was still rosy and her summer tan hadn't faded completely but there was a pinched look at her nostrils and her morning lethargy was very noticeable. She'd hardly missed a morning since Mirabelle's passing, therefore her behaviour was all the more noticeable.

There was something about her that stirred chords

somewhere in the recesses of his mind but he couldn't think what it was. He was used to Helen's fragile loveliness looking out from her face so it wasn't that which tormented him. He knew she missed Niall more than she would admit and he decided it was his absence so near Christmas that was causing her such distress. He remained silent till she was clearing the breakfast things then he said casually, 'I'll have an hour or two to spare this afternoon. Mathew has a few wee firs growing near his cottage and I thought we could cut one down and decorate it for Christmas. Alick and the bairns will be here next week and it would be nice to have a tree for them.'

Shona's eyes sparkled. 'That would be grand, Father. I'd like that fine, so will Alistair and Andrew. Oh, it will be nice to see them again. Mary's so different now. Do you know, she made better scones than me last year.'

The first flakes of snow began to fall while she was looking for Thistle. Somehow, the thing that she had discovered about herself that morning was so unreal that she pushed it to the back of her mind. Later she would think about it, later she would worry about telling her father, but not now, not with the calm cold air stinging her cheeks and the Sound of Rhanna glinting dull silver in the distance; not when snowflakes fell like silent fairies and were draping fields and dead bracken in white.

She found Thistle sharing a meal of sliced turnip with the shaggy sheep of the hill. He was unwilling to go with her because he was a creature of the wilds himself but she tied a rope round his neck and led him back to the pony shed where fresh oats soon settled him down.

By early afternoon the snow was two inches deep and Shona put on her wellingtons to cross the cobbled yard with her father so that they could check the out-buildings before setting off. The snow was powdery and crunched under their feet and she looked at her tall handsome father looming above her and felt a quick upsurge of happiness. He strode briskly, his pipe in his hand and the axe under the stump of his left arm.

Rhanna was like a Christmas card with the croft and byre huddled under a white blanket. Snow clung to bare trees and turned everyday objects into things of beauty. The crags of Glen Fallan blurred against the leaden sky and the tiny huddled houses of Portcull sent smoky banners into the snowflakes. It wasn't often snow came to Rhanna, it was therefore a novelty to the young but a hazard to the more mature who knew of the danger it could bring to livestock.

Shona lifted her face appreciatively. 'Oh, isn't it lovely, Father?'

'It's nice stuff to look at I'll grant you.'

'And to play in. I used to have such grand snow fights with Niall.'

Fergus had half-expected the snowball but hadn't bargained for such an exact aim at his neck. The snow melted and some slithered down the woollen neck of his jersey. Very deliberately he laid down his axe and pocketed his pipe. Shona yelled and looked for cover but there was none. His aim was even better than hers and the absence of an arm was no deterrent to him in the battle that ensued. Shona's cheeks glowed and even while she darted about she knew she was sharing with her father a precious moment. He loved her and trusted her and now she carried a secret, the disclosure of which could only be a matter of time. When he found out . . . She dared not think further and the tears of laughter in her eyes mingled with the tears of sorrow.

Lachlan joined them on the way. 'Tina's near her time,' he informed them, referring to Mathew's wife. 'Are you walking my way?'

'The very place,' said Fergus. 'We're cutting down a tree for Christmas. Mathew has some nice firs, some that Hamish planted a few years back. He never thought they would survive that wind that whistles up from the sea but they have, though they're a wee bit twisted.'

Lachlan looked at Shona. 'The fishing boat brought in some extra mail at dinner time. Erchy's just brought a letter from Niall so no doubt there will be one for you too. It's a shame he can't be home for Christmas but Phebie sent him a food parcel. She's certain he's starving to death out there. There's enough shortbread and tablet to go round the regiment.'

Shona drew in her breath and wanted to run home to Niall's letter but she marched steadily beside the men. 'I've sent a parcel too, not a foodie one, I knew Phebie would do that. I knitted him gloves and a scarf that just got longer and longer without my realising. Poor Niall, he'll be sharing it too with the regiment, I'm thinking!'

They scrunched up to Mathew's cottage. Three-year-old Donald drifted to meet them, a purring cat draped round his neck. The little boy followed Fergus and watched solemnly while the tree was being cut.

Shona went straight to the kitchen to make a Strupak while Lachlan examined his patient. Shona felt at home in the cottage. It was little changed from Hamish's day. Dogs and cats were heaped by the fire; the sofa was covered in hairs, and Tina always half-heartedly apologized to visitors, but she was a pleasant, easygoing, young woman who spent her life dressed in a smock and slippers. She muddled through each cluttered day and she and Mathew were extremely happy.

Fergus came in with the tree and Donald, still with the cat round his neck, went to sit on the rug to gaze dreamily into the fire and pick his nose. His mother, oblivious to his bad manners, sat on a chair beside him, her body arched forward so that she wouldn't squash a large ginger cat who had lost an ear in some nocturnal battle.

Shona plucked a hair from her tea and studied Tina quietly. Was it possible that one day she would look like that, her stomach an enormous protuberance and her breasts hanging heavy with milk? Tina looked like St Kilda, the old cow who lorded the byre, somehow always escaping the fate of most cows past their best; a trip to the slaughterhouse on the mainland. St Kilda's udder swayed with the slightest movement and almost touched the ground.

Tina bent to re-turf the fire and Shona could see right inside her loose garments. Her breasts flopped heavily, and there was darkness where the belly swelled relentlessly. There was no grace or dignity,

444

from the shamelessly splayed legs to the hair scraped back with kirbies. Shona shuddered. She couldn't get like that – she was too slim, her breasts were high and tight. Tina was normally a pretty girl but inclined to plumpness and there was simply no comparison. Nevertheless she was aware of Tina's every move, noting the awkward walking gait, with the belly thrown out and the feet spread to withstand the weight.

'When is the bairn due?' she heard herself asking.

'Och, it will come at any time now.' Tina patted her stomach affectionately. 'It's a wee bit skearie I am with Mathew out all day. I'm thinkin' the snow will last a while and me here all by myself. It's a quiet wee corner and sometimes it's only Erchy I'm seein' in the daytime. My sister from Croy said she would come and bide with me for a whiley but I hear tell she has a bad cold and in bed. I dareny think how auld Biddy will get up in time to deliver me. I was so quick with Donald! Just came out like a wee skinned rabbit he did after only four hours' labour. 'Tis afraid I am just.'

Lachlan patted her arm reassuringly. 'Don't worry, lass. When has Biddy ever let anyone down?'

'Och, I know she's a good sowel but she's a mite too auld to be gallopin' about in this weather!'

'I'll come.' Shona's impulsive offer surprised her own ears. 'I'll manage to sit with you in the afternoons till your time's past.'

'Ach, it's kind you are, Shona, mo ghaoil.' Tina beamed with gratitude and Fergus smiled quietly at his daughter's sudden look of apprehension.

445

They stood up to go and Tina ushered them to the door with Donald toddling at her back, wiping his sticky fingers on her apron.

'No skinned rabbits at Christmas,' ordered Lachlan jokingly. 'It's turkey for me that day and a dram, with my feet up at the fire.'

Snow was still falling heavily and it was good to get back to Laigmhor and the cosy kitchen. They seldom used the parlour now but after tea Fergus went through and lit the fire. Coal was piled on and the flames licked it greedily. The air of gloom, always present in a room that hadn't been fired for some time, dispersed quickly. He recalled the days when the parlour had been one of the most used rooms in the house and he remembered vividly the family Sundays with he and Alick sitting stiffly to attention while their father read from the enormous family bible. He had spent some of his happiest days in the parlour when Helen had been alive. The warm fragrant kitchen was Mirabelle's domain in those days but the parlour had been his and Helen's kingdom. In it they had made their most important decisions and, huddled cosily on the big settle, they had sometimes made love there.

He looked round at the dark walls where phantoms made by the fire cavorted and darted. The dresser held the best china and two large soulful-looking plaster dogs guarded the hearth. The mantelshelf was covered with photographs and from the top of an old wind organ that he and Alick had pumped to death as boys, the sepia-tinted features of his parents regarded him solemnly.

It was a room with a feel of the past and Fergus

shuddered. Shona called on him to help her with the tree, already potted in an old tub.

'I think I'll do up the parlour,' he told her. 'It has an odd feel about it now. It would be nice to brighten it up with some paint. It feels as if it's waiting for something to happen.'

She dusted her hands on her apron and looked at the dark walls. She seldom came into the parlour except to dust but now she took stock of it and knew what he meant. It was a 'dead' room, full of reminders of people long departed life.

'Yes, Father,' she said slowly, 'it's fusty and needs doing. Mirabelle used to say "Make the old thing new and meet again an old acquaintance".'

He didn't reply but heaved the tree up to the window and she decorated it while he sat on the settle and watched her. The decorations were mere paper chains and fir cones, baubles of silver paper and cotton wool, but they nestled against the dark green of the needles and looked lovely.

Shona stayed on in the room long after her father had gone up to bed. 'Don't be too late,' he warned before going upstairs. 'You know you can't get up come morn.'

She lay down on the settle, staring at the tree and wondering for the first time what Niall's reaction would be to a baby. Till now he was the one whose opinion she had feared the least but now her thoughts were crowding in on her and she was afraid. Niall might be horrified at the idea. He would come home from war, expecting the slim girl he'd left behind and instead he'd find a lumbering monster. Even though it was his baby he might not want it. They'd barely courted each other and suddenly he would be confronted with the enormous responsibility of fatherhood. Then there were his parents, how would they take it? How would her father react to a daughter who shamed him so? She felt she couldn't bear any of it and she felt sick and utterly lonely.

A star was twinkling in the window behind the tree. She was so dejected she was ready to grasp at any straw and she saw the star as a symbol, a sign that Niall would love her no matter what happened. She sat up and wiped away a tear with a slim delicate hand then rose and went to the window, rubbing away the steam to see a moon-bathed snowscape. The sky was ablaze with stars and the moon spun a pathway of silver on the sea. A movement at the wire fence surrounding the garden caught her eye and she laughed softly. The deer had come down from the hills and were eating some old kale stalks, past their best and higher than the fence. For a long time she watched the graceful creatures then she went to the kitchen, put on her shawl and her boots, and went out to the hayshed and scooped out forkfuls to spread behind the outhouses. The deer had magically disappeared but she knew they would be back. It was bitterly cold. She huddled into her shawl and looked at the sky and particularly at the brilliant star she had noticed before.

'Twinkle, twinkle little star . . .' she chanted childishly and scooped a handful of snow to throw in the air. It was strange to be out there on the sleeping island. Lights from fishing boats were visible though they were well out at sea and the world was hushed and very peaceful. Small sounds were to be heard, a rustling from the byre and a snort from the pony shed, but otherwise all was silent. Tot waddled into the path of light from the kitchen and sniffed the air. She shook a paw, disgusted by the snow, then squatted hastily before turning back to the warmth. At the door she stopped to look at her mistress, undoubtedly puzzled by the quirks of human nature.

'In a wee minute, Tot,' called Shona softly and reluctantly abandoned the world of white peace. The clock in the parlour was at half-past eleven and guiltily she remembered the promise she had made her father to be in bed early. She took the lamp and went upstairs. The halo of light revealed Fergus outside his door.

'Where have you been?' he demanded rather sharply. 'You should have been in bed long ago.'

'Yes, Father, I . . .' Impulsively she wanted to throw herself at him and unburden her heart. How interwoven the pattern of their lives had become when he was unable to sleep because she had broken their usual routine. His face was dark and angry and she could only say, 'I'm sorry, Father, the tree was so bonny and the deer were down from the hill. I gave them some hay.'

'Aye well, you won't get up in the morn.' His voice was softer now.

'I will, I promise you won't come in to a cold kitchen again.'

'It's not that, lass, it's . . . never mind now. Goodnight.'

'Goodnight, Father.'

449

*

Tina was pacing the floor when Shona arrived on the afternoon of Christmas Eve. Donald was playing with lumps of peat from the turf box, mixing small bits with saliva and spreading it carefully on a black and white collie who looked dejected but resigned to such happenings. Two hens squawked in the kitchen, cocking beady eyes at a black kitten who was stalking them under cover of dirty pans on the floor.

Shona grabbed a besom and chased the hens outside and Tina sighed gratefully. 'The buggers came in when I was fetching water and I was putting them out when the pains started bad.'

'Pains?' faltered Shona. 'You haven't started, Tina? Did you tell Mathew when he was in at dinner?'

'Och well, they weren't bad enough then. It's hard to tell because you get a lot o' funny wee pains in the last month. I didn't want to worry poor Mathew, he was going to thraw some turkeys this afternoon and he never did have a stomach for such things.'

Shona held her breath and wondered at girls like Tina. She was a grotesque figure with her belly lumped before her in menacing splendour. Her pleasant pink features were twisted in pain and all she could think of was Mathew. She was the most unromantic sight on earth yet she loved with utter self-denial.

'Are you sure . . . now?' asked Shona, hopeful of a negative reply.

'Aye, sure as daith! My waters came you see, near as much as came out o' Brodie's burn in a week . . . but och . . . I shouldny say such things to a wee lass like you.'

450

'I'm nearly seventeen,' asserted Shona faintly, 'and I'd better go for Lachlan and send a message to Biddy.'

'Ach, the puir auld Cailleach will never manage. She near died when Donald was coming. She was so wabbit from the walk I'd to give her brandy and me the patient!'

Shona darted to the door but Tina let out such a cry that she turned back and helped her to lie down on the sofa. Donald turned, and with an angelic smile, rubbed his lovely muddy mixture into the sole of his mother's slipper.

Tina grabbed Shona's arm and her usually calm brown eyes were gently worried. 'My – pans – the dishes – could you wash them, mo ghaoil? I know I'm not very tidy but the doctor will need hot water and he can't have it mixed with clapshot can he?'

'I'll do them later, Tina! I'd better go! Lachlan might be out on rounds and it will take Biddy a while to get down from the Glen. If I see Father, I'll ask him to fetch her in the trap – if he can get it through.'

Tina let out a cry and gritted her teeth. She was unable to speak for a moment, then her face relaxed and resumed its usual beatific expression. She lay amongst patchwork cushions covered with cat's hairs and suddenly looked so radiant it was difficult to believe she was in childbirth.

'It'll be a girl, I know it will be a girl! A bonny wee lass that I can cuddle and dress in fine frocks.'

Shona smiled with affection at the bulk on the sofa. 'I'm going now, Tina. I'll run if I can.'

'Och, mo ghaoil, wait a minute. Och I wish my sister was here – you can be more at home with your own.

I meant to have everything ready but I never seemed to have the time. Shona, would you get me a pair o' knickers? The others got all wet with . . . well you'll find them in the top drawer in the bedroom – the pink ones with the wee bits o' lace at the legs.'

Shona was exasperated. 'Tina! The doctor will just make you take them off again!'

'Och, I know, but a lass has to be respectable.'

Shona fetched the desired garment and left Tina pulling them on with Donald, an interested spectator, admiring the bits of lace.

Lachlan was out. The pony and trap were gone and with it seemingly the whole family. Shona rapped the door till her knuckles were sore but no Phebie or Fiona appeared to greet her. She looked round desperately. Sometimes her father was about but today the fields were deserted and she knew he had gone to the high ground with Bob and Mathew to bring the sheep to lower ground in case there was more snow. Her eyes searched in all directions for a sign of life. The children were on Christmas holidays and those who lived in the Glen were often to be seen making the journey to and from Portcull but today the road was empty. Panic gripped her. She had to get a message to Biddy. If she went herself it meant leaving Tina on her own for at least an hour, probably more because of the snow.

Something black and ragged flapped in the distance. She recognized Dodie coming from the hill track, obviously bent for the village. She almost screamed his name but for a moment he appeared not to hear, then she realised he'd slipped on the hill and couldn't stop for a time but his arm was raised and she heard his familiar, 'He breeah!' with something akin to hysterical laughter. He loped up, dusting snow from his coat, his stained teeth showing his pleasure at being hailed.

'He breeah!' she greeted him swiftly. 'Could you take a message to Biddy for me, Dodie?'

His face fell and his peculiar mourning eyes brimmed with tears. It was obvious he was disappointed and she suspected he'd been hoping to partake of a cosy Strupak at Slochmhor.

'It's a fair walk,' he pointed out sadly, 'and Merry Mary was keeping my baccy.'

'Father will give you some later and . . .' She gripped his arm impulsively. 'Come over tomorrow for a bite of Christmas dinner. I'm cooking it myself though Kate McKinnon made me the dumpling but – hurry now to Biddy and tell her Tina's baby is coming.'

His face lit with joy. Christmas dinner for Dodie was hardly different from any other day. People were kind and gave him tit-bits but other than that his festivities were sparse. He flapped away with his giant lolloping gait.

She scrunched back through the snow to the cottage. A squadron of hens raced helter-skelter to meet her and she realised they probably hadn't yet been fed.

'Where's the hens' pot, Tina?' she called.

'On the bunker,' answered Tina through clenched teeth.

Shona spent the next half-hour washing up and boiling pans of water. She was glad to be doing something because the moans coming from the sofa frightened her more than she could have believed. She piled peat on the fire and removed a skelf from Donald's finger.

'Muvver's greetin',' he observed in his childish lilting voice. 'Muvver's belly sore.' He drew his hand across his eyes and screwed his nose with the back of a dirty hand. The threatening tears spilled over to be scrubbed away on Dot the collie's floppy ears.

'Weesht,' soothed Shona. 'We'll get mother cooried in bed. Doctor will be here soon because there's going to be a new baby. Biddy will be here too.'

'Biddy,' beamed Donald who loved the green-cloaked, kenspeckle figure. A visit from her meant a boiling to suck and spectacles to play with and the most amazing teeth that simply lifted from her mouth in two whole pieces.

Tina didn't want to go to bed. 'A nice cup o' tea first, mo ghaoil. I've such a drouth on me.' She got up and began to pace again, her hands gripping her back, her legs splayed wider than ever.

Shona got the tea and wished someone would come. She looked from the window and saw a blanket of whirling snowflakes.

'Is anyone coming at all yet?' asked Tina who had collapsed again on the sofa, her face very pale and her eyes showing her pain.

Shona shook her head wordlessly.

'God, make them hurry,' prayed Tina aloud. 'The pains are coming so fast now, I don't think it will be long. 'Tis hell so it is, lass, just hell!'

She let out a sharp cry and both Donald and Shona stared wide-eyed.

'Muvver's dyin',' yelled Donald and his nose frothed profusely.

Shona ran to the door and looked out along the path. Nothing moved in the swirling snowstorm, only the trees stood like sentinels on the fringe of the fields. Another cry came from within and she hurried inside. Tina was writhing and the sweat stood on her brow. Shona felt sick and giddy but she took Tina's hand. 'They won't be long, Tina. It's just the snow's so heavy and walking will be difficult. I'll put on my boots and go up the track for a wee bit. I can give Biddy an arm though Lachlan will most likely be there . . . pray God!' she ended in a fervent whisper.

But Tina kept hold of her hand. 'Stay wi' me, Shona. Och please! The bairn's coming, I can feel it! It's been making me push for the last two pains. Could – could you have a wee look? Just a quick peep. Biddy could tell me the colour o' Donald's hair at this stage.'

Shona's heart was racing and she pushed copper strands from her eyes. 'I'll – I'll get a bowl of water first! I think I'll bathe your brow.'

Her hands trembled as she lifted a heavy black pot from the fire. The fact that she had to step over cats and dogs strewn uncaringly on the rug, made her task all the more difficult, but she held the steaming bowl aloft and went to Tina.

Donald sat solemnly amidst the animals, his thumb in his mouth, watching the bulk of belly, all that he could see of his mother, heaving on the sofa.

'You'll need some sheets and cotton wool,' whispered Tina, her eyes dark and pleading. 'It's all in a wee bag under the bed. The – baby's shawl is in there too.'

Shona's eyes were very blue in her white face. 'Tina – I – I – can't. I've brought forth a lamb before and helped my father pull the calves from the cows but never – never a *baby*!'

'It's the same thing,' urged Tina. 'Easier than a calf. I'll do most of it but you've got to help a wee bit. I'll tell you what to do. Och – mo ghaoil – one day you'll have a bairn of your own and you'll need all the help you can get.'

Shona looked down at the young woman and said gently, 'Tina, tell me what to do for I'm shaking like a newborn lamb.'

'Have – a wee look and tell me how much you can see o' the bairn's head.'

Donald sucked his thumb and rocked himself, looking calmly up the dark tunnel of his mother's legs ending in a pit of blackness where, from his position, nothing was visible. But Shona saw a crown of fine hair and the sight made her draw in her breath and feel unaccountably thrilled.

'Your baby's got fair hair, Tina.'

'Never! Och, it'll be a girl, I know – I wish I could see the other end.'

Shona tucked the sheets over the sofa then bathed Tina's face and gave her sips of cold water. She was panting and pushing and gripping Shona's arm till it was red and bruised.

Half an hour passed. Shona went to the door again

but the snow was heavier and she could see nothing. Mathew will be home soon, she thought. Father won't keep him in weather like this.

The cottage was unbearably warm and she wished she hadn't piled the fire so high.

'Shona!' Tina's cry pierced the air. 'The bairn's coming now!'

She was pushing, her face red and her lips clamped in a straight line. Her legs were spread, one braced against the back of the sofa, the other waving in mid-air. She grabbed the limb and held on to it, uncaringly displaying the huge pale dome of her belly with its untidy sprinkling of pubic hair. Donald looked up from the absorbing pleasure of licking butter from a scone.

Shona had no time to be afraid. She stared breathlessly at the gleaming circle of the baby's head. Tina's whole being was absorbed in getting the child out from her body. Her face was upturned, her eyes were closed, and elbows dug into the couch to further the terrible, supreme effort a woman has to make in childbirth.

The small circle grew bigger. Tina gave a mighty push, her voice catching in her throat in a half sob. Suddenly the small head was expelled and with it a rush of amniotic fluid. Instinctively Shona supported the warm slithery little head. She was still apprehensive but now a sense of wonder held her and she wanted to help the small thread of life all she could.

Tina lay back exhausted and the baby's head hung helplessly. Tina gathered her remaining strength and strained for a moment. The baby shot out in a rush of fluid to lie still and lifeless in the pool that had buffered it for the last nine months. The waxy white coils of the umbilical lifeline were yet attached to the placenta inside Tina and Shona stared helplessly at the awesome sight.

'The – the baby's a funny blue colour,' she whispered.

'So was Donald, it's natural, hold it up by the feet and smack its wee bum.'

But there was no need. The tiny form jerked and gasped, its mouth opened, and it cried loudly and clearly.

Donald toddled over and pointed. 'Doll's crying!' he reported happily and clapped his hands. Tina lifted her head to look and the tears of joy sprang to her eyes. 'It's a wee lass, och, wrap it in the shawl away from the mess. Everything else will keep for a whiley.'

Ironically, everyone arrived at once. Biddy, supported by Mathew, slithered in, her coat hem soaked and her spectacles askew. As always she was slightly indignant about everything. Dodie's rude awakening of her cosy afternoon nap had given her 'bellyache' and he'd been no help at all on the treacherous Glen road. She was soaked and frozen and needing a 'cuppy' but as always the sight of the newborn softened her kindly old face and brought forth as much excitement as the new mothers felt themselves. She stared at Tina's new baby and threw up her hands. 'Mercy! It's come! And the deliverer wee Shona McKenzie none other! Mathew, get the whisky. We'll all be needin' a dram, I'm thinkin'!'

She went to cut the birth cord and deliver Tina of the placenta. When Lachlan arrived he found a clean mother and baby and a slightly inebriated old midwife, minus teeth and spectacles, reclining beside two cats in the armchair. Donald peered from behind spectacles and grinned at him with a mouth grossly misshapen by its burden of extra teeth.

Mathew, overjoyed by his tiny daughter's arrival, was in danger of collapsing on Biddy's knee as he refilled her glass from the almost empty whisky bottle. 'It's a wee lass,' he greeted Lachlan, 'a bonny wee lass. I couldny have given Tina a nicer Christmas present if I'd tried – eh?' He grinned in a gluttony of self-satisfaction and knocked Biddy's hat off for the third time.

Lachlan had to smile. It was usual for new fathers to take most of the credit for their offspring till sleepless nights and cold meals, served late by a disgruntled wife, brought them quickly to their senses. Mathew was wallowing in his hour of glory and Tina, only slightly weary looking, was letting him have his way. She was quietly radiant and it wasn't easy to believe she had just endured an afternoon of agonising labour. Her daughter slept warmly and peacefully by her side and she stared at the tiny red face in wonder.

Lachlan went over to admire the newborn infant. 'A bonny wee lassie right enough and she arrived on the eve of Christmas. She'll be a blessed bairn.'

'Doctor, you have just given me her name, I'll call her Eve.' Tina's satisfaction was complete. 'It's a bonny name for a bonny wee lass.'

'And thank Biddy for getting here in time to deliver her,' said Lachlan. 'It's a treacherous road over the

Glen today and myself out with the family would never have got here in time.'

'Och but doctor, it was not Biddy either! Wee Shona McKenzie brought my bairn forth and the Lord be thanked for her. I don't know what I would have done without her. She fetched and carried and saw to Donald.'

Biddy staggered upright holding her glass aloft. 'Praise be to the Lord for Tina's safe delivery and thanks be to our Shona.'

Lachlan turned his dark head to look at Shona and saw that she was fast asleep on a small hard rocking chair. She looked very young with her smooth flushed skin and long tresses of silken hair hanging over her shoulders. Biddy's words brought back the long ago night at Laigmhor with the storm freezing his marrow and the terrible tragic aftermath of the weary struggle with the dark angel of death. The results of that night had been many but the most loving and lasting had been Shona. She and his son loved and because of them the lives of all of them were inextricably bound together. He knew she was missing Niall badly. Despite her vivacity and spirited nature there had always been an aura of contentment about her; now he sensed a restlessness and looking closer he thought there was a weariness in the youthful shadows of her face. She stirred and uttered a small cry but smiled when she realised where she was.

Lachlan took her hand. 'Doing me out of a job, I hear. It's proud I am of you, lassie, and thinking you deserve a cuppy. If our new father would care to stop patting himself on the back he might make us all one.

After all – though he did most of the work according to what I'm told – there were other parties who just *might* have helped a wee bitty.'

Mathew reddened and hastened to put on the kettle and Biddy, toothless and barely able to see, nodded with satisfaction. 'Just what we all need. The daft bugger might have given the bairn birth himself the way he's carryin' on. Ach well, I suppose it's only natural.' She fixed her dim eyes on Shona who was yawning and stretching. 'It'll be the same wi' you my wee lass when your time comes. Young Niall will take all the credit – it's the way o' things.'

For a moment Shona's arms remained in mid-air. She wondered wildly if the cunning old midwife could possibly have guessed her secret. But Biddy was toasting her feet and had apparently forgotten her surroundings. Her smile was very toothless and alcohol appeared to have taken her mind faraway.

Shona held her breath because she wanted to cry. She was beginning to misconstrue innocent remarks and knew she would go on doing so till the truth was out. She glanced at Lachlan and wondered sadly if she ought to unburden herself to him. He was always so fair about everything and wouldn't be likely to fly into a rage like her father. But telling Lachlan would be the easy way out and something in her make-up had always prevented her taking the easier course. She was proud and stubborn but above all else she was true to herself and that had always meant being true to those she loved most. No matter how nasty or unpleasant, her father was the person to know first. She fingered Niall's letter in her pocket. If only he were coming home that would solve a lot but his leaves were not long enough and the war was getting more serious which meant young men like Niall were desperately needed in the fight.

She sipped her tea and felt very scared because she alone carried the burden of her knowledge. The man she loved could do nothing to help her. She wasn't even going to tell him about the baby, not until it became more real to herself. At the moment it was all like a dream. She looked at Tina crooning over her baby but the sight did nothing to cheer her. Her baby wasn't real like Tina's and she couldn't imagine herself going through the ordeal she had witnessed that day.

Childlike, she turned her mind away from herself and thought about Christmas. The snow made it all very real and created just the right atmosphere for presents, turkey, and plum pudding, Christmas trees and carols. Alick and Mary were coming with the twins: the thought of their cheery, lively presence at Laigmhor made her smile.

She jumped up. She had a lot to do and she had to get home. Biddy groaned and began pulling on her boots. Everyone was making a move to go and she wasn't letting Lachlan away so easily when he might offer to take her home in the trap. She didn't relish the thought of plodding up the Glen in the snow. She sighed and wondered how long she could go on. She was seventy-three and beginning to feel it but she would be lost without her patients and her babies. She was greying and old-looking, with her grizzled thin hair escaping her hat and her cheeks wrinkled and sunken, but there was still a dignity about her bearing.

She gently prised her belongings from Donald and went through to the kitchen to rinse her teeth.

'Let's go, mo ghaoil,' she said to Shona, grinning resplendently. She took the girl's arm and wanted for a moment to hold her close and tell her not to worry. She wasn't going to find the months ahead easy and the old woman prayed that Niall would come out of the war alive so that Shona's child would have his name.

Her throat felt tight with sorrow for all the torrential emotions that girls like Shona must bear alone. She had given herself away so easily, the reddening of the face and the long silence at Biddy's words. Oh, they had been innocent enough until they were uttered, but the reaction to them had caused the seemingly unobservant old midwife to note all the usual signs, the thickening of a normally diminutive waist, the pinched face, the tired pallor, all so plain to an expert looking for them.

Biddy sighed again and hoped that Helen McKenzie's daughter would give birth easier than her mother had done all those years ago.

Part Eight

1940

Chapter Fifteen

The swelling sounds of spring filled the air, the most compelling being those of the newborn lambs. Shona, coming from Portcull with a laden basket, paused to catch her breath and gaze at the lambing fields. She saw her father with some of the men, dark specks in the distance, with two smaller dots that were sheep-dogs frisking busily.

Biddy was coming down the hill-track from Nigg, her green cape lifting in the gentle breeze from the sea. She was panting and slightly askew as usual. A smile lit her face when she saw the girl leaning by the dyke.

'It's yourself, lass? My, I'm damty tired so I am. Been sitting with Mamie McKinnon for three hours so I have and then the pains go – just like a puff o' wind. It happens sometimes. How is it with you, my wee one?'

Her scrutiny appeared careless yet she took in everything.

'I'm fine, Biddy,' answered Shona pulling herself up quickly. Her clothes were loose-fitting and she was neat to be in her sixth month of pregnancy but never-theless she knew she couldn't hide her condition much longer.

'Aye,' Biddy gazed into the distance, 'fine you look too, mo ghaoil – for a lass so far gone with child.' She heard the surprised intake of breath but stayed the stammered protestations with a gentle touch of her hand. 'Weesht, lassie,' she whispered kindly, 'I'm an auld hand at the game – remember? I was tendin' pregnant lasses afore you were born and I know the signs fine. I've known for a long time about you and I'm thinkin' it's high time you told your father. You haven't yet, eh?'

Shona shook her head miserably.

'Aye well, the time has come, mo ghaoil. You canny hide it any more. It's a wonder Lachlan hasny spotted it.'

'I – I haven't been over for a time.'

'Aye, he mentioned that you were keepin' away these days. I knew why of course. He's a doctor and a good one. Mind you, he wouldny be lookin' for such a thing and you're such a mite of a lass still. We're all inclined to think o' you as a bairn yet. Some are wed at your age, I know, but you have the look o' a wee lassie just out o' school . . .'

She was expecting the tears and her arms were ready. She hugged the sobbing girl to her scrawny bosom and uttered words of comfort, 'Weesht, my bonny one. Tell your father, you'll feel the better o' it. He's near at hand to give you comfort whilst Niall, the poor laddie, is too far away to help at all. He'd be pleased I'm sure if he knew someone here was helpin' you.'

'But he doesn't know either,' wailed Shona. 'I meant to tell him in every letter but somehow I'm afraid it will take away all the lovely things we shared!'

Biddy nodded significantly. 'And wasn't the making

o' the bairn a thing you both had a share in? Och, pull yourself together this meenit, girl! You must be near out your mind keepin' such a thing to yoursel' so long. Niall wouldny be pleased. Surely he's more o' a man than you're givin' him credit for. It's time for the truth, my lassie. Mirabelle taught you well, don't let her down any more than you have already!'

Shona made her way home, oddly comforted by the old midwife's blunt words. She made up her mind to tell her father that night.

But there was no need. He was kept late in the lambing field and when he arrived home she was asleep in the inglenook. He tiptoed to retrieve his dinner from the oven and sat to eat it quietly. He looked at his daughter and wondered at the little naps she seemed to find so necessary now. It was so unlike the vivacious, almost untamed vitality he was so used to, that he was beginning to wonder about her health and the very thought of anything wrong made him pause, the fork halfway to his mouth. He studied her intently, knowing there was something different yet unable to place it. Living with someone, seeing them every day, it was difficult to pinpoint changes, yet he knew there was change in her. She was lying awkwardly, her head pillowed on her arm in a familiar childlike pose. Her dress had caught under her and was pulled into the contours of her body. The thing he had imagined to be so subtle now glared at him and he drew in his breath sharply, his meal forgotten. He tried to tell himself it wasn't true, the distortion of the slim child's figure had something to do with the way she was lying, but how could anything lumped

into such an obvious place be a figment of his imagination? It all fitted, the sickness, the fatigue, the
gradual change from flimsy garments to the loose
smocks and dresses he'd thought to be a mere girlish
whim.

He got up and went to look down at her. He could
feel the muscle in his face working the way it always
did when traumatic feelings seethed in him. He knew
of course whose child it was but at the moment he
had no thoughts for the young man at war in France.
His fury was all for his daughter, the child he had
come to trust and love with an intensity that he was
afraid of at times. She was all he had, he knew his life
revolved round her too much but he couldn't help
himself. They needed each other, each a buffer for the
other's loneliness.

The strength of his presence reached into her sleeping brain. She stirred and her eyes opened, a smile of
pleasure lighting them. 'Father!' She struggled up. 'I
left your dinner in the oven. Did you get it?'

The black fury in his face deepened and when he
spoke his voice was hoarse with the depth of his
hurt. 'Tell me, girl, tell me about the thing that has
turned you from a bairn into a clumsy tired Cailleach!
You're with child, aren't you? Dammit, I should have
guessed but I thought you had more sense! You're
having Niall McLachlan's child after all my warnings
and all your ill-kept promises! You're no better than a
tramp!'

The whiplash of his words made her cringe back
against the cushions, afraid of the temper that was
boiling over in such frothing fury. She had seen his

rages before but never one so furious as now. Her heart pounded and the room spun round.

'Say it damn you,' he roared. 'Let me hear from your own lips you've lain with McLachlan and now carry his child!'

She felt faint and strangely breathless. 'I tried to tell you, Father, I wanted to but I was afraid! I was going to tell you tonight – Biddy knows and thought you should too! But you were late and I fell asleep . . .'

'So – the word is already getting round! Biddy knows – before your own father! Soon the whole of Rhanna will know that McKenzie's daughter's a slut!'

'I'm not ashamed, Father,' she sobbed. 'I love Niall and because of that I am proud to be carrying his child! It might be the only part of him I'll have left in the end. I am *not* ashamed, Father!'

His hand came down and crashed into her face with such force that she fell back against the cushions. Tot whimpered and struggled up to lick her mistress's bleeding lip.

The door slammed and the house was quiet but unnaturally so. Shona's tears were soundless though she wanted to scream and run to someone for comfort. She thought of Niall but even he was unreal in her mind. He was her life yet he could not help her. Somewhere he too fought a lonely battle in some stinking trench in faraway France. Seas and mountains divided them when they needed each other most. She couldn't know if there was any comfort in his life but she had people she could turn to, those who were the flesh of her beloved Niall. She rose from the couch and ran from Laigmhor to the warm beckoning glow of Slochmhor nestling in its shelter of Scotch pines.

Fergus walked as he had walked on that other night of tortured mind and spirit, blindly without thought of direction.

The infant Shona had pointed the screaming finger of accusation at him then, her child's mind infuriated because of the tight band of secrecy he had woven round the truth of her existence. Now he was the accuser and his hurt wouldn't let his seething mind see anything, other than the fact that the child he had come to worship had deceived him by her very silence.

The cool night wind lashed over him and he was aware of the sound of the sea. He walked on, stumbling over rocks on the shore, his head bent in misery. He came then to the place he had sought once before. From the lonely washed shore he looked towards the schoolhouse, its windows aglow from the soft lights within. It was the same place it had been on that other night, a dark mass of stone and chimneys outlined faintly against the endless moors. But within moved little Mr Murdoch and his family. There was no Kirsteen beckoning him wordlessly with the beauty of her body and soul. He could run to no one for the comfort he so desperately needed.

He sat on a barnacle-encrusted rock and cradled his dark head in his hand. The sound of the sea and the soft sigh of the wind gave peace to the night and gradually his reeling senses cleared. He began to collect each of his thoughts and sort them out.

An hour passed. The beautiful peace of the Rhanna night seeped into him and he raised his head to look at the soft glow of silver on the water. He reached for a pebble and threw it into the water and as it sank it seemed to carry all his furious feelings to the bottom of the sea.

Now his heart cried for the little girl who had wreaked so many emotions in him throughout her life. She had always been there, wanting only his love and gradually he had given her all the love that should have been hers in her infant years, yet, despite his love she had been afraid to tell him about herself because she feared he would love her less.

He hurried now, back to Laigmhor, his heart full of remorse, seeing in his mind's eye a pale little wraith without Niall, carrying on her duties at the farm, tending to his every need and all the time a child growing within the confines of that delicate body.

But the farm was quiet, with only the animals sleeping by the kitchen range. He ran upstairs to her room but it too was empty. He guessed though where she was, the people she was with, the folk who had been her comfort and stay from her early years.

It was Phebie who answered the door and she looked wordlessly at his wild dishevelled figure.

'Where is she?' he demanded urgently, looking past her into the dimly lit hall.

'Upstairs – in Niall's room! Lachy gave her a sedative, she was worn out but couldn't rest. I've never seen a lass so lost of heart.'

Phebie's voice was softly accusing but Fergus was only aware of his need to see his daughter. He pushed past and went upstairs to Niall's room. It was a real boy's room with all its boyish collections of model planes, pictures of animals, and fishing tackle propped in a corner. In the bed, with its gay patchwork quilt, was Shona, half asleep, her face warmly flushed, and her copper hair cascading over the pillow.

At sight of him she started up quickly, the sleep going from her eyes leaving them big and frightened. He stood for a moment looking down at her; noting the lovely elfin little face, eyelids puffy from heart-broken weeping, he saw the bruised cut lip caused by the brutal strength of his own hand and his heart twisted in a rush of remorse and terrible shame.

'Shona.' The whisper of her name was barely audible. He bent and took her to his heart, crushing her to him in a moment that gathered the years together and brought forth all the love he felt for her. Her silken hair was smooth against his lips and the warm heat of her body surged through his hand and at last the flesh of his flesh was openly acclaimed for its worth.

She lay against him and sobbed quietly, giving herself up to the exquisite moment. After a time he pushed her gently away and taking her hand looked deep into her eyes 'It – it's difficult for me, Shona – you know that. I never could show my feelings much.'

'I know, Father,' she said softly.

'This – thing that has happened – we'll see it through together. I'll take care of you till Niall comes home then we'll get the pair of you to the altar as it should be. Bugger the auld Cailleachs and their wagging tongues!'

'Aye, bugger them, Father,' she said softly. 'They will

talk and though I'm not shamed at having Niall's baby I'm sorry for the disgrace I'll bring on you.'

He was silent for a time and his dark eyes were faraway. His hand gripped hers tighter. 'My lass, I've never spoken to you much – of things. I loved your mother. God knows I loved her too much and when she died I didn't want to love another. I was afraid of love and I didn't even want to own you, my own bairn. But no man can be an island forever. I met Kirsteen, you were just a wee lass then. I loved her –' he lifted his face to the ceiling – 'I loved her in the way a man loves a woman but I couldn't bring myself to wed her. She was all any man could want, more, God knows, but I didn't want to commit myself – not after your mother. Then, something happened that made me ask Kirsteen to wed me but then . . .' He paused and she held his hand tightly, her love reaching out to him in the agony of his revelations. 'There was the accident. Kirsteen knew I was too proud to ask her again to be my wife – so she left Rhanna – carrying my child!'

Shona gasped aloud, her mind racing with the implications of his words.

'It's true, Shona,' he said softly. 'Somewhere I have a son I've never seen and . . .'

'I have a half brother,' she finished in dazed tones.

'Aye, it's true you have. The words you spoke tonight of being proud to carry your lad's bairn were spoken nigh on six years ago by Kirsteen herself. I found it all out that time I went to Oban. I was looking for Kirsteen but she had gone and me not knowing where to this day.'

'You'll find her again one day, Father.'

'Aye, maybe.' He touched the cut on her mouth gently. 'I'm sorry, mo ghaoil, I've hurt you but I couldn't believe the truth of my eyes. I'm a fine one to judge but at the time I saw black with rage. I had thought better of Niall yet I'm no better myself.'

She looked at him, a strange mixture of pride and pleading in her eyes. 'I wanted him to love me, Father, I asked him. I was afraid of the war, I had to know what love with him was like in case – in case . . .'

'Weesht now, he'll come back. It'll take more than a war to put down that young de'il.'

She lay back on the pillows, blue smudges of weariness under her eyes. 'Now I can tell him about the baby,' she whispered.

'He doesn't know?' His words held disbelief.

'No, somehow I couldn't tell him without you knowing first and I was afraid to tell you so I couldn't tell anyone.'

Something tightened in his throat at her confession and his voice was sad when he spoke. 'You've borne your burden alone, my lass, and I know what that feels like. Aye, you're a McKenzie right enough.'

Her eyes were closing despite herself. 'You'll let me bide in Niall's room tonight, Father? I'm so tired.'

Lachlan appeared at the door. the eyes of the two men met. 'Let her rest now,' said Lachlan quietly.

Fergus stood up. 'Aye,' was his brief answer before he went quickly from the room.

In the hallway Lachlan gripped his arm. 'My son's a young bull and deserves to be whipped for this. I'm sorry, McKenzie.'

Fergus drew a deep breath and looked straight into the deep compassionate eyes of Lachlan. 'I'm not – not now that the first shock is over. Those two were created for each other and the coming of a bairn is but a bit sooner than any of us expected.'

Lachlan's eyes crinkled with relief. 'Good God! Are you not a man of surprises? You're mellowing, Fergus, and it's as well. Will you come down now and have a dram to celebrate the fact that soon we'll both be grandparents?'

Fergus stared. 'I hadny thought of that! I'm not yet forty!'

'And I have just a year over you and poor Phebie only thirty-nine like yourself. It's a nasty shock for us all.'

Phebie appeared in the hall below. 'Are you not coming down? You'll waken Fiona with your blethering!'

'Coming, Grandma!' answered Lachlan and both men gave a bellow of mirth.

Fergus had been right about the gossips. Shona's condition provided ample fuel for the wagging tongues who openly declared their piety by regular church-going but who kept stout keys for the many skeletons rotting in the cupboards of their past. The more sensible islanders gossiped eagerly in the beginning but soon grew tired of the subject, even solicitously asking after Shona's health when she appeared in the shops at Portcull.

Behag Beag remained tight-lipped and distant whenever Shona's ungainly little figure appeared on her premises.

'Serves McKenzie right,' Behag told her cronies. 'His nose might come out of the air now his lass is known to have such lusts of the flesh.'

'You're a jealous auld Cailleach,' grinned Erchy. 'It's for want of a man up your own skirts you're such a greetin' baggage.'

Erchy had always enraged Behag by his teasing remarks which were too much near the truth for comfort and she flounced to kirk on Sundays to stare at the stained glass window and pray for the salvation of Erchy and sinners like him.

Tina gave Shona endless cups of tea and lots of advice and Mairi delighted in detailed accounts of each of her confinements always ending up with, 'Ach, poor Wullie was always afeard I wouldny come through and promised never to touch me again. But he's a man! He's a man so he is and likes fine his wee bit play.'

Nancy came more to the farm than ever with her four sticky children trailing at her heels. She beamed at Shona's hard lump of a belly and became motherly and comforting, all the while listing gory details 'Ach, but never mind, you'll be fine. Biddy might be an auld Cailleach but she'll see you come through. My, she must have seen more bums in her lifetime than she's had cups o' tea.'

Shona listened and waited and grew increasingly impatient with her clumsy stomach which was tight and neat to be harbouring an eight-month foetus but which nevertheless made her feel ugly and untidy.

The war was worsening and she fretted for news of Niall. His last letter had been angry that she hadn't told him about the baby sooner. 'It is the child of our love, mo gaolach, and it was my right to know about it. I dream of you and our times of love and I long to be back on dear clean Rhanna. The stink of war is growing worse by the minute. I smell of it, the mud and the filth and the first thing I'll do on Rhanna is sit naked in Brodie's burn and let the sweet cold water from the mountains wash the war out of me. I love you, mo gaolach, and I'm worried and unhappy that I can't be with you when you need me most.'

It was the beginning of June and the warm winds of the Gulf Stream fanned gently the sweet new heather on the moor. Cows and sheep grazed contentedly in the lush pastures and the island had the browsing lazy feel that summer brings to green places.

Shona felt hot and uncomfortable and spent a lot of time by the open window of the parlour, now fresh with new paint and white muslin curtains. Fergus had acquired a wireless set, powered by accumulators which had to be recharged occasionally by the generator on the young laird's estate. The islanders were dourly impressed by the strange piece of machinery that could make enough power for such a modern wonder as electricity to come on at the turn of a switch.

Todd the Shod already owned a small generator which proved its worth in the smiddy and he had felt himself to be a man of some importance since its acquisition. But he guarded it jealously and continually bemoaned the cost of its running, considering it unprofitable to use it for anything other than the blacksmith business. The arrival of the young laird's generator, and the fuss of its unloading on to the harbour, was a day to be remembered in Portcull. The huge piece of machinery swayed precariously on the end of the cattle pulley and Todd watched from his doorway and wished mildly that the whole contraption would go crashing on to the cobbled pier.

But stout ropes and many hands loaded it safely on to a strong cart and two wheezing Clydesdales trundled the burden away on the steep twisting road to Burnbreddie.

Few on the island owned wireless sets but those who did took their accumulators to the laird who proved most obliging and didn't charge a penny for the use of the ever-running generator.

'Noisy damty thing!' spat Todd, his self-esteem much lowered in his own eyes.

News of the war wasn't good but to most of the island it didn't mean much. There was the excitement of watching extra vessels sailing up the Sound and British reconnaissance planes roaring overhead but, other than that, the threat of war didn't touch the peace of Rhanna.

But Shona hung on every report that crackled from the wireless in the parlour. Niall had been very hopeful of a leave that would give him enough time to come home but now now, not when the Germans had invaded Holland, Belgium and France and were pushing the British Army on to the beaches at Dunkirk. The sombre voices of the newscaster intoned the bloody massacre the Germans were leaving on their trail and Shona shuddered and wondered about her dear Niall. He had only hinted at the horrors of war and it was difficult for her to think of him in any setting other than that of the island.

She forced her mind away from her imaginings of what the war must be like and looked towards the green fields where she had so often walked with him. Her memories carried her back to the times she had run nimbly over the fields and into the trees to await him coming off the boat. She sat by the open window, her face cupped in her hands, and dreamed of the past, till the familiar strong movements in her belly brought her to reality and she sighed with the knowledge that she could barely walk let alone run.

Her fears of becoming like Tina had been allayed. Her breasts were still firm and high and her loose garments gave no sign of the round little dome beneath.

'Are you *sure* there's a bairn in there?' laughed Lachlan, but his careless merriment was only for the benefit of her spirits. He was keeping a sharp eye on the small child-like form who carried his grandchild. He had examined her and found her perfectly healthy; nonetheless he was watchful and Phebie was aware and tense, spending more time at Laigmhor than before.

Fergus was snappy and irritable. Lachlan and Phebie knew that it was because his daughter's time was drawing near and he was recalling, with a painful reawakening of buried memories, that other time when the birth of a child had brought tragedy. Then he had lost a wife who meant his world, he had gained a baby whose tiny helpless life had meant nothing but which was now everything he couldn't bear to lose.

Shona sensed the mounting tension building round her. Coupled with her inner anxiety about Niall, she became withdrawn and no more did the rooms of Laigmhor echo with her singing and laughter. The one thing she feared no more was the actual birth of her child. During the earlier months she had come out in sweats of terror remembering Tina and the awful pain of her labour. Now she was strangely peaceful and thought no more of the pain her baby would bring in its struggle into the world. Instead she tried to imagine what it would be like and formed the picture of a tiny boy with Niall's corn curls and deep brown eyes. She knitted tiny garments and cleared a drawer to keep them in, hardly able to believe they were for a real baby and not one of Mirabelle's dolls that still smiled at her from the shelves in her room.

One hot night she undressed and stood naked before the wardrobe mirror. She was a small girl with tumbling copper hair and eyes big and tired in a pale face. Looking at her head and shoulders she still looked like the restless tomboy that Mirabelle had scolded to be still while a ribbon was tied to keep her shining mop of hair in order. But her eyes travelled her rounded breasts and the swelling that began just beneath them. Briefly she touched her breasts then her belly for a long breathless moment. She tried to remember what it was like to be flat but couldn't. The hard tight little mountain seemed to have been part of her for a long time now; she couldn't visualize herself without it yet how she longed to be rid of it.

A picture of Mirabelle smiled at her from the dresser. 'Oh Mirabelle,' she whispered and the tears spilled over. 'I wish you were here just for a wee whiley. I miss you, so I do. You would have grat at me in the beginning but then you'd have mothered and loved me and I could have talked to you. Father's worried in case I'll die like my mother, I can feel it. Lachlan and Phebie know about that time too and they think they're being kind not mentioning it at all. Niall's away so I've no one – not a soul to talk to – not *really* talk.'

She hugged the photo to her breast and fell on the bed to weep sadly but silently so that her father wouldn't hear.

He lay in the darkness of his room and tried to still the restless agonies of his mind. He was afraid for his daughter but, by very reason of his manhood, felt inadequate. He wanted to comfort and reassure her and tried his best to do so, knowing all the time it was the understanding of a woman she needed. He was grateful to Phebie but she couldn't spend all her time with his daughter and in the still emptiness of his room he listened to his own heart beating and wished that Kirsteen could fill his arms and his life once more.

June grew hotter and the island merged with the sea in a haze of heat. Shona sought the coolness beneath the spreading boughs of the gnarled apple tree but mostly she liked to sit in the cool parlour by the window.

One morning she stared towards the hazy blue sea and imagined Niall was coming home over the water from France. She watched the mail boat gliding through the smoky horizon towards the harbour and wasn't aware that her nails were digging into her face till she took her hands away and saw blood on her fingers. Fear and hope knotted tightly together in her belly. She had felt sick with fear since the sombre tones of the newscaster had intoned that the British army had withdrawn to the beaches at Dunkirk. It was a hellish nightmare of retreat against a spitting wall of enemy fire and the soldiers were being taken off the bloody beaches in an armada of pleasure craft.

At sight of the mail boat her heart beat swiftly. There might be a letter from Niall, a wonderful letter to tell her he was safe and coming home in time for the birth of their child. Men were arriving home, straight from the terror and stench of the trenches, still caked with the mud and blood of the lost battle. Niall might be one of them, he had to be.

She got up and was aware that her legs were trembling but she went into the kitchen and began to set the table for lunch. Her father wouldn't be home for another hour yet but she needed something to do to fill her time. She cut cold ham and thick slices of bread. The door was open, with Tot drowsing in the cool draught and the chickens clucking past her, cocking beady eyes to look for crumbs. Shona hadn't the will to chase them so they picked crumbs from the floor and squabbled with each other. A fly buzzed, caught in the muslin curtains, and a spider hung on the sash, busily wrapping a neat parcel of midgies in its web.

It was very peaceful but Shona felt tense and nervous. When Fergus came in she fidgeted and toyed with her food and his stomach tightened with worry which made him irritable.

'Eat your meat, lass! There's no room for waste in this house.'

But she wasn't listening. Erchy was coming up the road faster than was usual for him. He was mopping his brow, his usual jaunty whistle absent as he approached their gate.

Shona held her breath and Fergus too found himself waiting, the very action of chewing a mouthful of food stilled for a moment. But Erchy went on, past their gate and into the Glen. Shona let go her breath and lifted her cup to her lips with trembling hands. She felt the tears brimming in her eyes and desperately tried to stop them spilling over but Fergus saw the swelling gleam drowning the gentian blue eyes and he said quietly, 'No news is good news, mo ghaoil, remember that.' He stood up. 'I must be off! Old Thyme is calving up on the hill. It's a bad one. Bob and Mathew are with her now but,' he smiled ruefully, 'all hands are needed. It's a breach and I think we'll have to use ropes on the poor beast.'

Shona was dozing under the apple tree when the small, dancing presence of Fiona woke her up. The little girl was hopping with impatience. She was a sprite, never still for a minute, every thing about her a complete contrast to calm, unruffled, big brother Niall.

'Mither said can you come?' she imparted quickly, looking past Shona to the swing that hung on a stout branch of the tree. 'She wants to tell you somefing. I think she was greetin', and Elspeth too, the auld Cailleach. She's always that crabbit with me when she's out of temper. I hope St Michael sends her a plook on her bum so's she can't sit down for a week!'

Shona giggled despite herself. She loved Niall's little

imp of a sister with her quick smile and roguish tongue.

The child hesitated. 'Can I have a swing? I'm going up to play with wee Donald and I hear tell Eve is crawling now and goes into the hooses with the hens. I like it fine up there but I'd like a swing before I go.'

'Don't go too high,' Shona warned and went down the track and through the gate with Tot at her heels. Shona was feeling heavy after her nap and Fiona's message hadn't rung any warning bells in her mind. The little girl was inclined to exaggerate and was always wishing some mishap on the unlovable Elspeth.

Slochmhor looked very serene against the green pines and Elspeth, sitting in a chair in the sunshine busily crocheting, completed the picture, though, on closer inspection, the old woman's sharp discontented features detracted somewhat from the illusion.

'He breeah!' cried Shona pleasantly.

Elspeth looked up and there was an odd look in her red-rimmed eyes. 'What's good about it, lassie?' she said huskily. 'Away you go in. Mistress McLachlan's away to meet the doctor. She asked Erchy to send him down from Croynachan. Is your father to hand or is he busy as usual?'

'He's up on the hill with a cow in calf,' said Shona with a puzzled frown.

'Aye weel, he'll need to leave it to the others. He'll be needed down here for a whiley. I'm gey auld to be climbin' up hills though and you're no' much good in your condition. We'd best leave it till the rest get back. Do you think that would be best? Aye, it is, right enough.'

Shona felt a mounting impatience. Elspeth, with all her veiled hints and self-answered questions, could be very exasperating. 'Leave what, Elspeth? Why must my father be here?'

Elspeth gazed into the distance. 'There's that young upstart Angus McKinnon. I'll go and get him to fetch your father. Whereabouts on the hill is he?'

'Just up by Brodie's burn, near the Seanachaidh's Stone. But he's busy, Elspeth, and I wish you'd tell me what you want him for. Has somebody got a sick beast? Is that why you want my father and the doctor?'

There was no vet on Rhanna and Fergus, with his knowledge of the ails of farmyard beasts, was often called upon for his services. If the case was very bad Lachlan's advice was also sought and at the moment no other reason for them both being called upon entered Shona's mind.

'Mercy on us,' was Elspeth's reply, 'is that young Angus comin' or goin'? I canny see in this haze! There's a pot o' tea on the stove. You'd better have a cup for you'll need it.' She shook her wispy head and pursed her lips. 'The Lord has a way wi' Him. I'm no' one to judge but you've made your own bed and it's punished we all are so it is!'

She scurried away, her spindly legs carrying her with surprising rapidity.

Shona wandered into the kitchen but it was warm there and she didn't feel like tea so she drifted into the parlour which was in the shadow of the hill and cool in the late afternoon.

It was a pleasant room, chintzy and homely with pictures of Niall and Fiona smiling from the dresser.

She went to gaze at the boyish features of Niall at fourteen and her hand knocked some letters to the floor. With difficulty she stooped to retrieve them and froze suddenly. One of the envelopes was buff-coloured and would have escaped her attention but the letter inside had partly fallen out and words leapt at her like living things. It was a War Office communication and she snatched it from the floor to read it, her whole body trembling while her eyes devoured the terrible message.

She whispered aloud, 'It is my painful duty to inform you that a report has this day been received from the War Office that Number 206 Private Niall Iain McLachlan has been reported missing, believed to be dead . . .'

She could read no further. The letter fluttered back to the floor and she put her hands to her head, shaking it and groaning over and over, 'No, it's not true! Not Niall! Not Niall!'

She backed away from the piece of paper and knocked over a small table. Unheeding she tottered backwards to stand for a moment against the wall, staring with huge unbelieving eyes at the white scrap of paper on the floor. Then, with a sob, she turned and ran from the house and into the hot sunshine.

She looked round desperately but the only sign of life was Elspeth, a small speck in the distance. A great welling terror rose in her throat and she began to run, as if by the very act of flight she could leave behind the knowledge contained in the letter. The moor shimmered and danced in the haze of heat and it was to its lonely wild stretches her legs took her. Tot, lying in the shade of the porch, whimpered and sat up, looking intently at her mistress's fleeing figure. She got up and walked a few paces but thought better of it and flopped down again, her head in her paws, her brown eyes looking towards the moor.

Shona ran through heather and gorse. Brambles snatched at her, tearing her bare legs but she was unaware of physical pain. Mentally she was in agony and her pumping adrenalin would not let her stop in her flight. Her heart pounded and there was a sharp pain in her side but she went on till she tripped and fell, her face scratched and bleeding by the shaggy moorland heather. She was sobbing, harsh dry sobs, but her eyes were dry.

Sheep, grazing nearby, looked up momentarily at her intrusion into the hush of the day, but she was of no moment to them and they went back to cropping the sparse grass among the bracken.

She lay where she was, stunned by her fall, uncaring that her face rested on sheep's droppings and that her hair and clothes were matted and torn. The only sounds on the unending stretch of moor were her own harsh breathing, the biting of the nearby sheep and a greenshank, startled from its nest in the peat to utter its alarm of 'krji, krji'.

After a time she raised herself on an elbow and saw nestling in the distance the rotting crumbling stones of the old Abbey. She knew now where she was going, the only place in the world it seemed to her, in her numb deep sadness, where she could ever find any peace. Her aching stumbling limbs carried her on to her destination. Was it really possible that less than a year ago she had flown with Niall, on the swift, tireless limbs of youth, to the place where they had woven their child's fantasies; dreamed of magical impossible dreams of their young adulthood and finally, loved with the tender over-riding passion of a love that could never die because it was still at the stage of spring, yet to blossom forth into a summer never yet surpassed.

'He's not dead,' she whispered, stopping to lean against a slender rowan. 'HE'S NOT DEAD!' she shouted in a defiance of her mental torture but the words died quickly away and only the soft sigh of empty spaces answered her. Her ebbing strength forced her to rest again at the walls of the old chapel. Her eyes swept over the gorse-covered hillock where her final footsteps must take her but for a moment she could see no familiar sign to tell her where the cave was. It was so long since she had last been to the lonely windswept spot where it seemed the thin voices of spirits of the past were borne on the breezes of moor and sea. It was a wild forgotten place, inhabited only by sheep and wanderlust cows, but with Niall it had been a happy place and their voices had echoed in the Abbey ruins and their laughter rang in the ancient cloisters of the chapel.

But she wasn't afraid of lonely places, they had always been a balm to her spirits, yet panic now seized her because her wildly searching eyes couldn't find the little birch tree that marked the cave's entrance. Niall had planted the tree and it had grown into a sturdy sapling, twisted by the wild storms of winter, but flourishing despite the moods of the weather.

Then she saw it, almost hidden by the prickly gorse that abounded in the hollow. She walked unsteadily towards her goal till she stumbled through clumps of bracken and heather into the cave. It was cool and dark after the glare of the late afternoon sun. For a moment she could see nothing but blackness but gradually everything that was familiar came into focus. The shelves with Mirabelle's dolls, the kitchen utensils, the little spirit stove, all covered in cobwebs but there just the same, their lovingly gathered possessions.

She dragged herself on to one of the dusty wicker chairs and it was while she struggled to regain her breath that the first pain seized her, like a gripping vice in her belly. She gasped and held on to the arm of the chair and in a few moments the contraction subsided. She lay back, closing her eyes, so exhausted that she fell into a half sleep. But there was to be no rest for her. The second pain was longer and more intense, like something inside tearing her apart. She put her fist to her mouth and even as she endured the pain she knew she was going into the first stages of labour. Sweat broke on her brow, she felt sick with fear and her hands grew clammily cold. She fingered the locket at her neck and fumbled to take it off so that she could gaze at Niall's smiling face, to see the dark honest eyes she loved looking back at her.

'Oh Niall, Niall,' she murmured brokenly, 'if only you were here. Our child's going to be born soon and I need you so.'

She clutched the locket and looked slowly round the cave and all the memories it contained came crowding into her mind. More pains came and in between each one she remembered some incident in time she had shared with Niall. It was their place of dreams and of a love that had conceived the child she was going to have. Slowly, fear was replaced by a new feeling, one of confidence in herself. She knew how to deliver a child, she had all but delivered Tina's daughter, and it hadn't been so difficult. She knew what to do with the birth cord too, she had watched Biddy doing it. A smile slowly lit her small tired face. What more fitting than that her baby should be born in the small haven where it had been conceived?

'Our son will be born here, Niall,' she said gently. 'In time for you coming home.'

Her mind was blotting out the awful message contained in the letter from the War Office and now her whole being was diffused with excruciating pain yet through it all she trembled with joy at the thought of Niall's face when he saw their child for the first time.

She was physically exhausted and suffering from shock but she struggled up to make ready the bed. Everything she needed was in the cave; blankets, cushions, utensils. But something niggled at her. Water! There always had to be plenty of hot water at childbirth. She bent to shake the spirit stove and discovered that it still contained some fuel – but matches, there had to be matches! They had always kept a box on a shelf but they might be too damp to strike. She found the box hidden behind a cobwebby cup and her hand shook so much some spilled out.

She held her breath as she struck one, it flared but died immediately. Several crumbled on contact but another flared and stayed alight. She stared at the small bright flame with tears on her cheeks, realising she should have waited till later to try the matches. She had no water and she didn't want to light the stove too soon and the rest of the matches might not work. Another pain came relentlessly and a dry sob shook her. Then she saw the candle stuck in a cruisie beside one of Mirabelle's dolls. The match was almost spent and the pain in her belly made her want to double up but she reached up to the candle and held the flame to it. The wick smouldered and smoked.

'Oh, please God!' she cried. The match was burning her fingers but quite suddenly the wick robbed the charred remains of its flame and a white oval of light burned steadily.

'Thank you, God! Oh, thank you,' she whispered and sank to the chair to rest for a moment. But not for long. She had to get water from the little mountain stream nearby. She pulled bracken and heather away from the entrance, tied back the gorse bushes then she began the laborious task of going back and forward to the burn for water. She had no bucket; only pots and a kettle. The usually tinkling little outlet was almost dried up and water trickled into the utensils with unhurried tranquillity.

She had left her watch at Laigmhor but she had a vague idea of the time because the sun was setting in a sheet of flame over the Atlantic. The cool night air brought forth the scent of thyme and moss and the sheep cried plaintively over the moor. She was glad of the breeze because it kept away the midges that could hover in dense clouds of torment if the air was too still.

It was very peaceful and the June night would bring no real darkness to Rhanna. She sat by the burn and even in the agony of childbirth breathed in the sweet scents of the moorland with an appreciation of one who had always loved the earth.

Fergus paced the parlour at Slochmhor. 'Where in God's name is she?' he said for the umpteenth time in the long nightmare of a day.

Phebie sat very still and her face had the frozen immobility of one who was in a stupor of grief.

Lachlan cradled his dark head in his fine doctor's hands and Elspeth, her features sharper than ever in her anxiety, said again, 'I shouldny have left her but it was only for a wee whiley. I had to find someone to fetch McKenzie.' She rocked her gaunt frame and a thin wail, which was a mixture of grief and self-pity, escaped her.

Fergus turned on her. 'Will you be quiet, you old yowe! You should be away home for all the good you do here!'

Elspeth gripped her lips together. 'You're a hard man, McKenzie, but for all your fine airs you're no better than the rest o' us. If you'd given your lass more of your iron hert she might not have needed to look so hard elsewhere for a bit o' love!'

Fergus whitened and the muscle in his jaw worked furiously. 'You dried up old baggage! Who are you to . . .'

Lachlan sprang to his feet. His face was deathly white and his brown eyes were dull with the burden of his sadness. 'For pity's sake, the pair of you! Stop it! We'll do no good miscalling each other!' He faced Fergus.

'I'm thinking the time's come to go out and look for Shona. It looks as if she's not coming back tonight. God knows where she'll be nursing her grief. If we could have broken the news to her gently . . . but she saw the letter first and must be in a state of shock.'

Fergus nodded acquiescence. Lachlan turned to put his arm round his wife. 'You go up to bed, mo ghaoil. I'm going to give you something to make you sleep.'

But Phebie shook her head violently. 'No, I'm coming with you! I couldn't sleep – I must be doing something and Shona will be needing a woman to comfort her.'

Elspeth looked up dourly. 'Away you go, I'll bide with the bairn.'

There was a scuffling outside and a murmur of voices. Lachlan went to the door and saw a crowd of Rhanna men outlined against the clear sky in which a pale moon hung like a lantern. Bob and Ranald were at the front of the group, their rough, homely features touched with anxiety. Bob spoke first, his gnarled fingers working nervously on the bone handle of his shepherd's crook. 'We heard about the lass and thought you'd need help to find her. And – we're sorry to hear about young Niall.'

There was a subdued murmur from the men and Lachlan looked at them with swimming eyes. 'Thanks, lads – and you're right – we'll need all the help we can get. We have no idea where the lass might be but if we split into groups our task might be easier.'

Phebie, wrapped in a tartan plaid, joined them. She, together with Fergus, Lachlan, and Bob, were going to comb one section of the Muir of Rhanna, and

Robbie Beag with three others were going over the high rise that led to Nigg. Mathew and Neil Munro went to search the shore round the harbour while the fourth party went overland, south-east, where fields and moors separated them from Portvoynachan.

Bob was well acquainted with the moors; he had roamed them for miles with his sheepdogs, rounding the sheep at various times of the year. Dot, the younger of the sheepdogs, was with him now, keeping just ahead of her master, running in the silent gliding fashion of a good sheepdog.

Nobody noticed the golden, slightly tubby, form of the old spaniel till she pushed her wet nose into Phebie's hand and whined.

'Tot,' said Phebie gently. 'You can't come with us. You're too old to be roaming the moor.' But Tot had waited patiently all day outside Slochmhor. She ran ahead and stopped to look back, a low moan rising deep in her throat.

Bob spat impatiently. 'Ach, get away back girl. You're of no use to us.'

But Tot was a dog with a purpose. To Dot the whole thing was a game, an unexpected outing for a working dog, and she frisked and poked into heather tufts with delight. The old spaniel ran on again on rheumaticky legs and whimpered, her nose testing the wind, one paw raised in the pose typical of the gun dog.

Fergus looked at her and frowned. 'The old girl looks as if she knows what she's about. She seems to know where she's going.'

'Of course,' breathed Phebie. 'Who would know better? She's been all over Rhanna with Shona.'

Bob blew his nose disdainfully. He had time only for sheepdogs; game dogs were all right in their place but not much use on the farm. To his mind they were 'gentry beasts', good for all the useless sport indulged in by useless fowk with little else to occupy them but shooting and fishing.

Tot was well ahead and everyone was running to keep up with her. They covered a mile, then had to pause for breath. The air from the hill was clean and they gulped it in greedily. Tot, tired and panting, had collapsed in a heap and old Bob leaned against a boulder, shaking his head at what seemed an impossible task. They had shouted themselves hoarse and now that they were quiet, the silent, eerie loneliness of the moor enclosed them in a hushed blanket. The sky was clear and everything could be seen quite plainly, with the moor stretching on either side, flanked by the ridges of Sgurr nan Gabhar that separated them from Glen Fallan.

They were on the outskirts of the Burnbreddie estate and a dog howled mournfully. Tot was too tired to even prick her ears but Dot sat on her haunches and, lifting her nose to the June sky, wailed loudly.

'Be quiet, you stupid fool!' ordered Bob sharply. He knocked his pipe against the stone. 'I think we've seen enough o' this part – the lass would never have come so far in her condition. I'm for cutting over to Fallan. Maybe Croynachan or Croft na Beinn would know something of her whereabouts.'

'It might be best,' said Lachlan wearily, getting up stiffly from the heather.

All but Fergus changed direction. He was watching

Tot who, groaning, had roused herself and was heading once more on the course she had set. She disappeared in amongst gorse bushes and Fergus ran forward, his mind and body exhausted, but every fibre of his being urging him onwards.

It was some time before the others realized he wasn't with them. They were plodding over the rough peat bogs to Glen Fallan less than quarter of a mile on.

'He's chasin' that damty dog again,' cursed Bob.

Phebie began to cry, the slow silent tears of despair and grief. 'We'd best go back,' she said, clinging to the rough tweed of Lachlan's jacket.

Lachlan hesitated in an agony of indecision. He felt they were all on a wild goose-chase yet he trusted the strength of Fergus's decisive mind more than any other on the island.

'We'd best,' he said quietly.

'It's daft us all goin' back,' said Bob. 'I'll get along to Croynachan and get Johnston to help me look along the banks o' Loch Sliach. It was a place favoured by the lass and Niall. She might be there.'

He trudged away, his crook helping him over the peaty ground.

Lachlan put his arm round Phebie and they went back to the moor.

Fergus strode after Tot. His breath was harsh and sore in his throat but he was positive the old dog knew where she was going. Her nose was to the ground, her floppy ears hiding her whitening muzzle and intent brown eyes. She was wheezing, her tongue lolling and dry but she kept gamely on.

'Good lass, good lass,' encouraged Fergus at intervals and a memory came to him of a big laughing Highlander handing over the tiny golden pup to a little girl on her fifth birthday.

Dog and child had grown up together, played and romped through youthful years. Now Tot was old, with cysts on her ears and watery eyes; she slept most of the time and romped no more. Yet some force was driving her on over that shaggy unkind moorland, a deep spirit of loyalty for the child she had known all her life was urging her to the very last ounce of strength in her loving old heart.

They had come two and a half miles and now they were breasting a rise. Tot stood looking down, breath rasping and flanks heaving. Fergus looked down also, down into the hollow where the stones of the old Abbey lumped together like the grey stooping figures of old men. His heart sank. Shona would never have come to this eerie place. The islanders avoided it, believing it to be haunted by the 'ghaisties' of the monks that had been slain there hundreds of years before. Peat Hags were said to roam the ruins at night, howling and screeching in glee at the plight of the monks.

People like Fergus knew the screeching to be no more than the wind whistling in and out of cracks and empty windows. Nevertheless even sensible, level-headed people had the seeds of ancient superstitions buried deep, and he shivered at the sight of Dunuaigh and the ruins. But his need to find his daughter was stronger than all else and his deep voice boomed out, echoing over the moor reverberating in the hollow. Over and over he called out but only the plaintive cries of the sheep answered him.

'You were wrong lass! You were wrong!' he scolded the dog. He looked down and saw the old spaniel was lying on her side, her eyes closed. He dropped on his knees and laying his hand on the golden fur felt the flying pulse. Even as he knelt there the faithful old beast drew a shuddering breath and the heart beneath his hand stopped beating.

'Och no,' cried Fergus to the stars. 'Not this above all else!'

He remained where he was for several minutes, the burden of his grief and anxiety stooping his shoulders and bowing his head. His dark eyes stared dully at the lifeless little body lying on the ground, the curling red-gold fur a shade darker than the tough moorland grasses. A cold wind skittered from the sea and he shivered then rose, stiff and cold, with the limp little dog over his shoulder.

He stumbled back the way he had come and in the distance saw Lachlan and Phebie coming towards him. They came closer and Phebie put her hand to her mouth when she saw what he carried.

Like a man drunk he came towards them and wordlessly they all made their way back to Slochmhor little knowing that down in the hollow, among the Abbey ruins, the girl they sought lay drenched in sweat, her belly torn apart by the pains of childbirth. She had heard the faint echoes of her father's voice and had answered, but her voice was a mere whisper in the deep cloisters of the cave.

Dawn was breaking, a faint streak of gold and silver above the dark corries of Glen Fallan. Elspeth was asleep in the rocking chair by the dead embers of the fire. Her face was gaunt in the morning light and she got up slowly at the opening of the door. She looked at the grey hopeless faces before her and her usually edgy voice was soft with pity. 'The men found nothing, though they searched till nigh dawn. They've all gone home save Murdy. It wasny worth his while he says for he'll be out in the fields in an hour or two. He's sleepin' in the kitchen. I'll just go and put the kettle on.' She paused at the door where Fergus stood with Tot draped over his arm. 'Even the old dog,' she murmured quietly and the unfamiliar glimmer of tears shone in her eyes though they were quickly wiped away and she brushed roughly past Fergus.

They were all desperately tired yet unwilling to leave the comfort of each other's presence and the ever flowing cups of whisky-laced tea.

Bob arrived as the sea brightened to a deep gold and the morning chatter of birds drowned the air with song. He looked yellow and old and drew his hand across his nose irritably. 'Croynachan reports nothing unusual,' he said gruffly. 'He's seen nothing up the Glen or by Sliach but sheep and kie. But don't worry, McKenzie, we'll find her but we won't follow the old dog next time, I'm thinkin'. She led us a fine dance.'

'We won't follow her again – she's dead,' said Fergus briefly.

Bob's inscrutable old face softened. 'Ach, but that's a shame, a shame right enough. She took too much upon herself. It was strange, very strange.'

He accepted a glass of whisky then went off muttering, Dot tired and limp at his heels.

Fergus cradled his cup in his hand and stared into

the rekindled fire. 'What are we going to do?' he asked hopelessly.

Lachlan stood up. 'Get a bit of sleep and look again. You'll bide in – in Niall's room.'

'Dammit, man, I can't sleep!' exploded Fergus. 'She could have fallen somewhere, she might be hurt. I must go out again!'

Lachlan's hand came down firmly on Fergus's shoulder. 'Bide a wee, man! You'll do yourself and the lass a lot more good if you do. Heed what I say! Go out now and you'll fumble around and do no good at all.'

Fergus sank back into the chair. 'You're right, Lachlan, but I'll just rest in the chair.' He was asleep even before Lachlan closed the door. In the chair opposite, Elspeth snored softly, her jaw sagging and her lips making little popping noises.

A babble of voices below the window woke Lachlan first. Still dazed with sleep he struggled into his trousers and looked out. Biddy was there, her spectacles falling from the end of her nose as she shooed away the folk who were gathering for morning surgery.'

'Have you no respect?' she shouted severely. 'The doctor's had word his lad's missing and you all crowd round wi' your wee aches and pains like nothing's happened!'

'We didn't know,' said several voices, genuinely shocked and sorrowful. They turned and dispersed slowly, leaving Biddy with a wildly gesticulating, almost hysterical Dodie who was babbling over and over, 'It was ghaisties I'm tellin' you! Moanin' and screamin' like the dead!'

'The dead don't scream,' said Biddy firmly and cuffed him on the ear the way she did with the cheekier of the village children.

Lachlan looked at the clock and was shocked to see that it was nearly ten o'clock. Phebie was struggling to waken and Fiona was singing in her bedroom.

Downstairs Fergus was opening the door to Biddy and a flustered Elspeth was scuttling into the kitchen. It was obvious everyone had just wakened.

Dodie's voice was rising to a higher pitch, his mouth was frothing and he was obviously terrified.

'Johnston told me about poor wee Shona missing,' shouted Biddy above the din. 'I came over quick as I could to see could I help and met this demented cratur shouting about hearing screams over the muir.'

Dodie's nose was dripping on to his saliva-filled lips. 'It was Ealasaid, doctor! I was looking for her last night but she didn't come so I went out again this mornin' – a bit o' cream I wanted for my bread. I went away over the muir and had just got hold of her by the ghaisties' place when they started screamin' at me and Ealasaid run away so bad a fright she got!'

Biddy clucked impatiently but Fergus was looking intently at Dodie. 'Do you means the ruins of the Abbey, Dodie?'

'Aye, Mr McKenzie. Demented spirits screamin' and the Peat Hags moanin'. It was terrible just.'

'How long ago, Dodie?'

'Nigh on an hour! I ran, so I did, it was so skearie. Ealasaid will likely have died o' fright!'

Fergus turned to Lachlan. 'The old dog was right.' His voice was soft but hurried. 'Shona is out there somewhere in the ruins. It was she Dodie heard screaming. It may be the bairn is coming.'

Lachlan was already picking up his bag. 'Let's go,' he said briefly.

Biddy followed though the doctor protested. 'You canny stop me,' she said in a voice that brooked no interference. 'I've walked the island all my life and if I canny walk the moor to deliver the bairn o' the bairn I delivered years ahent then I'm no' worth my worth.'

They met Bob, shamefaced because he had over-slept. 'I'm comin' with you,' he said in tones that didn't invite refusal. 'Mathew and the rest can see to things. If the lass is where you say you might need help to bring her back.'

The hollow was a trap of warm sun and honey-laden bees. There was no sound but for those of nature and the men stopped to mop sweat from their faces while Biddy went to the trickling stream to wet her handkerchief so that she could wipe her red exerted old face.

And there in the stillness, they heard a voice singing a Gaelic lullaby, so faint that it could have been the sighing of the wind.

Old Bob, his grizzled head filled with folklore and tales of ancient myths of the Hebrides, looked round the grey silent ruins of the Abbey with fear in his watery blue eyes. He was one of the best Seanachaidhs on the island and proud of it but cosy hearths were very different from this eerie place where souls from the past wandered forever. He gripped his crook tighter and drew a brown hand over dry lips.

'Weesht,' warned Biddy. "Tis the fairy folk singin' to be sure.'

But Dot, whining and scratching at the gorse of the hill, suddenly disappeared and Fergus and Lachlan ran forward. 'There's nothing here.' Lachlan stared at the huge moss-covered boulder in front of them. 'I don't understand.'

Dot reappeared leaving tufts of hair on the snagging gorse and Fergus ran forward to pull the bushes back.

Shona showed no surprise to see them. She lay on sheepskin rugs and blankets which were saturated with the blood of childbirth. Her copper hair tumbled over her shoulders, framing a face that was pale and strained. But her blue eyes were brilliant and a soft little smile hovered round her lips. 'Hello, Father.' Her voice was low with pride. 'Look now at your grandson. Isn't he the bonniest baby in the world? I did it all by myself, just like I did for Tina. I'm calling him Niall Fergus – it's a grand name I think. I can hardly wait for Niall to see his son.'

She was holding a tiny bundle wrapped in a tartan plaid. Lachlan ran forward while Biddy made a quick examination of the girl. 'The lass is fine,' she murmured thankfully. 'Just a wee clean up and you'll feel lovely, my little one.'

Lachlan had taken the baby over to the light at the door. It was a perfect little boy with downy fair hair. The birth cord was tied as neatly as if Biddy herself had done it and the little waxen body had been wiped clean. Lachlan looked down at the tiny lifeless face and the slow tears burned his eyes. It was the final blow in two nightmare days. The son of his own dear son as dead and cold as a piece of marble.

Fergus was behind him, his tall strong body stooped like an old man. 'Was it – because we never got here in time?'

Lachlan shook his dark head. 'Stillborn – the mite was dead before it came into the world. We'll never know why. She's so young and there was the shock – of – of Niall. Also it was a premature birth – nearly four weeks.'

'But why – why in God's name!' The cry was torn from Fergus in an agony of torment. The cruel irony of the devious twists of life was too much for him and the tears of hurt grief, and pity for his daughter, coursed down his face. He went to her and took her into the fold of his strong right arm, his tears falling on to the bright copper hair under his chin.

She pulled away to look at him with eyes that were unnaturally veiled and dreamy. 'Och Father,' she chided gently, 'don't cry so. Are you not pleased with your grandson?'

'He's dead, Shona,' he sobbed. 'The baby never drew life.'

Lachlan came and pulled Fergus away, shaking his head warningly. 'Don't – she can't take it! Not now, man! She's suffering from shock already. The sooner we get her home and to bed the better.'

They wrapped her in blankets and between them carried her over the warm summer moors. Behind them trailed Bob, his tough weatherbeaten face gaunt and sad and beside him Biddy carried the pitiful little bundle of Niall's dead son.

Chapter Sixteen

When Shona finally accepted the fact that her baby son was dead she withdrew into a lonely shell which nothing seemed to penetrate. She moped around looking like a lost child and Fergus could find no way of reaching the sad, bruised caverns of her mind.

'She'll need time,' said a weary Lachlan, himself struggling to bear his own sorrow. 'She's lost so much – even the very dog she had most of her life. Give her time, Fergus.'

The days stretched into July and four weeks after the tragedy Erchy came whistling up the dusty road from Portcull. He saw Shona, listlessly sitting by an open window and waved cheerily, then went on to Slochmhor where he propped his bicycle at the gate. He clutched a letter in a hand that shook slightly. They had all speculated about the missive at the post office because it was a War Office communication. If he accepted a glass of Phebie's blackcurrant wine he might be able to hang around long enough to find out the contents of the letter.

'A letter, Mistress McLachlan,' he shouted to Phebie who was hanging washing in the sun-drenched garden.

'Leave it on the table, Erchy,' she answered through a mouthful of pegs.

Erchy's heart sank. 'It's a thirsty day,' he said chattily and made exaggerated puffing noises.

'Aye, it is that! Go away ben to the kitchen and take some wine from the larder. I'm too busy to come in now.'

Erchy pulled in his breath. 'It's from the War Office,' he said and exhaled quickly.

Phebie turned slowly and looked at him. Her round sweet face remained immobile but a strange mixture of hope and hopelessness shone in her eyes. She came over the fragrant grass slowly and took the letter with a show of calm. Methodically she opened it with a thumbnail. Erchy watched her, his breath held in his lungs. He saw the slow flush creeping over her face and the slight tremor of her head. She looked up and the glimmer of tears shone in her eyes. 'He's alive, Erchy,' she whispered disbelievingly. 'Niall's alive – wounded but alive.'

Erchy let go his breath once more and grabbing Phebie's plump waist whirled her round and round. The island had mourned with Lachlan and Phebie. The love and respect earned by Lachlan throughout the years went deep. Rhanna loved him and his family and they had wept, the hidden silent tears of the dour, loving Hebridean folk. Phebie was laughing and crying and Erchy whirled and kissed her in an abandonment of spirit.

'Niall's alive!' shouted Phebie and ran on to the road. Clutching the letter she sped with Erchy at her heels to Laigmhor. Shona was still at the window, seeing nothing of the lovely day outside, her thoughts turned inward, on Niall, on the little son who had never known the sweetness of breathing life. She didn't even have the comfort of Tot's head resting on her feet, giving the silent undemanding love she had grown to accept as part of her life. It seemed to Shona she had nothing very much to live for. Nothing was worthwhile any more and not even the strong quiet love of her father could reach into her hopeless world.

She didn't notice Phebie and Erchy wildly gesticulating at her from the garden. Not until they burst into the peaceful dreaming silence of the parlour was she aware of them. Phebie's breath was squeezing from her lungs in short little gasps and for a moment she couldn't speak. She collapsed into a chair and, unable to find the breath to explain, motioned Erchy to break the news.

He ran his hand through his thinning sandy hair and, bursting though he was with emotion, controlled himself enough to say calmly, 'Your lad's alive, my bonny lass. Niall's alive – it's all in the letter I brought to Mistress McLachlan!'

Shona slowly turned her head to look at Phebie. Her dull eyes showed no sign of having interpreted the message, but slowly, like a pale rose opening to the sun, her face diffused with a glow that lit the transparency of her skin.

Phebie nodded and spoke jerkily, the excitement of the past few minutes making her light-headed. 'It's true, mo ghaoil, our Niall's alive.'

Everything about that time had a dreamlike quality. Shona got up and glided over to Phebie. She stared trance-like at the letter, then she was on her knees, her head in Phebie's lap and she cried, all the lonely, tragic tears she had bottled up for so long. Phebie stroked the copper head and let the tears run their course, knowing they would help to wash away some of the agonies endured by such a young heart too many months.

When Shona finally looked up her eyes were red but they contained something that had been missed so much of late – hope and the small beginnings of the joy for living. 'Where is he?' she whispered, drying her eyes on the hem of her dress.

'In a military hospital in England. He was badly wounded in the neck and head and his identity disc got shot off. Just before he was wounded, he'd taken off his jacket to cover another laddie whose clothes had all but been blown off. He was still alive when Niall gave him his jacket with all his papers. But the boy died and they thought he was Niall and Niall couldn't tell anyone who he was because he's had concussion and loss of memory until recently.' Phebie shook her head as if to clear it. 'He's on the mend now and will be home soon, but he'll always be deaf on one side – his ear-drum was damaged very badly.'

Shona's face was wet and swollen but she was smiling the first smile for weeks. 'He's alive – and because of his deafness he won't have to go back to war. I'm so happy I could cry all day.'

'You're happy he's deaf?' asked Erchy.

'Och no, of course not! I'd wish that he was the same as he went away.' Then she paused and continued thoughtfully, 'No – you're right, Erchy, I am glad, if not he'd have been home for a wee while before he went back to war and he might never have come out

510

alive. He mightn't have been so lucky the second time. What's a deaf ear compared to a chance of life?'

Phebie shuddered but she knew Shona was right. To other people it might appear foolish and selfish but to her, at that hour of knowing her son was alive, she would have been lying to herself if she'd wanted him whole and well enough to go back to war, perhaps to get killed in the spring of his life. Far better a deaf ear and a live son than a dead son and memories.

Erchy rubbed his hands together and cocked an eye at Shona. 'I'm thinkin' the occasion calls for a wee dram, does it not?'

Shona nodded. 'You're right, Erchy – and I'm going to have one too. I'm needing it I feel so shaky. Then . . .' She looked at Phebie. 'We'll go and find Lachlan and Father and tell them the news.'

Fergus leaned against the dyke that ran parallel to the road and lit his pipe with the expertise of long practice. He had grown used to only one arm, doing so much with it that he often found himself looking in astonishment at people who could do less with two arms than he could with one.

It was a mild calm morning with a fine mist of rain from the hills and the smoke from the farmhouse chimneys curled lazily.

He puffed contentedly and watched Shona in the garden, gathering flowers and humming a gay little tune. She looked very slim and sweet in her youth with her hair gleaming brightly and it was difficult to believe that her childish form had, until recently, carried a child. He'd never given the child much thought until he'd seen the small features and perfect body of the tiny baby. When he'd realised it was the flesh of his flesh he had known the hopeless longing for the little life that might have been. But his compassion for his daughter had overridden all else and he had suffered with her in her darkest hours. Now Niall was alive and he rejoiced with her yet for reasons he could barely understand he felt that she no longer needed him as desperately as before. She was loving and mindful of his every need, yet he knew that the biggest part of her waited longingly for the time of Niall's return to Rhanna. He was jealous and hated himself for it but was unable to stop from thinking of a future when his house no longer breathed with the life his daughter gave it.

A chestnut mare came cantering along the road. Riding it was the young laird of Burnbreddie, a man now held with respect on the island.

He brought the mare to a stop when he saw Fergus.

'Good day to you, McKenzie,' he nodded. 'Things are a bit more settled now, I hear.' He had glanced towards Shona, and Fergus knew what he meant.

'Aye, the lass is to have her lad back soon.' Fergus didn't want to talk about any of the events that had happened in the last months and people were talking again, saying that he was, 'the dour bugger he was before'.

The young laird dismounted and the mare, her coat polished to the shade of a ripe chestnut, nuzzled delicately at the fragrant clover amongst the long roadside grasses. 'A fine beast,' commented Fergus wishing he'd been left in peace. He liked the laird well enough and could talk easily about the weather and the health of his beasts but it was to Lachlan alone he confided his real feelings.

The laird nodded and brushed a hair from his impeccable tweed jacket. 'I've just come back from the south. Rena was with me and we looked up one or two old friends. We had an invitation from the Campbell-Elliots, people I knew in London years ago. They had gone down to the country for a spell – to get away from all the bombs.'

Fergus shifted impatiently and the laird idly stripped the heads from the knee-high grasses and looked speculatively at the sky. 'Dashed strange coincidence,' he murmured casually. Fergus knocked his pipe on the wall and opened his mouth to make some excuse to escape. 'Couldn't believe my eyes when I saw her,' the laird was continuing absently. 'She's the Campbell-Elliot's governess now. Last time I saw her she was teaching here at Portcull.' He shook his head. 'Funny how things go. The Campbell-Elliots think the world of her. A fine young woman she is. Got a little boy, nice as kids go, not like her at all – black hair and eyes. I only saw her once or twice when I came to Rhanna but I remember thinking what a fine girl she was. I got talking to her, she went a queer colour when she found out who I was and where I came from – and . . .' He looked sideways at Fergus. 'She was asking about you, McKenzie.'

Fergus had frozen, the inside of his stomach felt weak and the laird's voice sounded far away. He stood there, glad of the support of the dyke, unable to speak, yet longing to ask a million questions. Finally he found his voice and looked straight into the laird's pale blue eyes. 'You – know, don't you?'

'Y-es, I knew you were to be married, then you had your accident and I don't know anything after that. Canny the Rhanna folk may be but they've never fathomed what happened between you.' He paused. 'The boy's yours, isn't he?'

'Yes, Goddammit man, he's mine and I've never seen him. Where is she, Balfour? When did you come back to Rhanna? When did you see her last?'

'Hey, hold on, old chap! She's not going to disappear! I saw her a fortnight ago – I got back to Rhanna yesterday. As a matter of fact I rode over specially to tell you. I thought you might be pleased.'

'PLEASED!' Fergus held out his hand and the young laird gripped it.

'Go to her, McKenzie. She still loves you – stupid thing love, isn't it? We botch it up all the time. Anyway – good luck old man. There's a mail boat out of Rhanna tomorrow.'

He mounted and rode away. Fergus felt his innards had turned to jelly. He couldn't believe it. After all the years of waiting and longing he had found Kirsteen at last. No wonder she hadn't seen the notices the lawyers had put into the London papers, she was deep in the English countryside and possibly didn't even know her mother was dead.

Joy washed over him in waves but after the first excitement came fear, fear that she would slip through his fingers again and he couldn't let that happen.

Sweat broke on his brow and his hand felt clammy. He wasn't aware of anything but the great urgency of finding Kirsteen and bringing her back to Rhanna. In his mind it would be as simple as that – it had to be. The laird had slipped a piece of paper into his hand with the address in England written in neat small letters. Fergus stared at the paper as if it were his most precious possession, then he ran to the kitchen where Shona was arranging roses in a bowl.

'Father,' she said on the alert immediately. 'What's wrong?'

He was panting and laughing. 'Everything's *right*, mo ghaoil! I have discovered where Kirsteen is – I'm away on the mail boat tomorrow!'

'Father!' She ran to him and held him close, feeling the trembling of his strong masculine body. 'Oh, my father, I'm so happy I could cry!' she buried her face into his warm neck, feeling his pulse beating swiftly. Her hands caressed the crisp curls at the nape of his neck. At last their world was falling into place. Her happiness was complete now – if she married and left Laigmhor, she wouldn't feel like a betrayer. Her father would have a love of his own and they could stop being so dependent on each other. She sighed deeply and pulled away to look into his deep dark eyes. 'Do you know what, Father?'

'Tell me.'

'I'm looking forward to meeting my wee brother.'

'So am I,' he said softly and climbed the stairs to his bedroom to pack.

He went early to bed, hoping to sleep the hours away. Instead he tossed and turned, sleeping fitfully, wakening just as daybreak crept through the curtains. He lay for a time thinking ahead, trying to visualize what the following days would bring. It was very early, too early to get up, in case he disturbed Shona. He slept again briefly then got up to wash his face and bathe his body with the cold water from the pewter basin on his dresser. He dressed and looked from the window. A white blanket of mist covered the fields and the scent of wet earth was nectar to his nostrils.

He stole down to the kitchen to put kindling on the fire and when Shona came downstairs the kettle was singing and eggs boiling in a big pan. Snap and Ginger had been fed on cream and were washing their faces by the fire.

'You didn't sleep well,' she stated simply when she saw his tired drawn face.

'Not very.'

'Don't worry, Father. Och, I know you must feel all queer and excited. I feel the same about Niall and he's only been gone ten months. You haven't seen Kirsteen in six years. The wee boy will be – what – about five?'

'Aye, he would have been that around January, funny, the same month as yourself, mo ghaoil.'

Her blue eyes were gentle. 'It will be funny having a wee brother here. I wonder what he's like . . . if he's like you at all, Father.'

'Balfour says he's dark so the colouring anyway he's inherited from me. I hope not the temper.'

She laughed. 'He wouldn't be a McKenzie without one. Sit down now and I'll get the eggs. You mustny be late for this boat. Oh, it will be lovely to see you happy, Father, you haven't been in years – not really.'

He squeezed her hand and sitting down forced

himself to eat an egg. His belly was tight with nerves and the food tasted repulsive. He was glad to see Lachlan striding past the window and into the kitchen. It was an excuse to leave the table.

'Good luck,' said Lachlan simply. 'I'm going to Croynachan but wanted to see you first.'

'Thanks,' said Fergus. 'You'll see this lass of mine gets up to no mischief while I'm gone.'

'Father!' chided Shona laughingly. 'How can I with all the work of a farmer's wife to be done. Anyway . . .' she coloured. 'I think I've learned my lesson about mischief-making.'

Lachlan held out his hand and Fergus gripped it briefly. 'Take a good dram before you set out,' recommended Lachlan. 'Doctor's orders.'

He went away quickly and Fergus busied himself with any task that would take his mind from himself. Mathew had been given his instructions but Bob came in with Murdy to go over a few details.

Shona didn't come down to the harbour. She was very emotional these days and didn't want to weep before her father. She hated his going and, though overwhelmed with happiness at the turn of events, felt naturally apprehensive about the great changes there would be at Laigmhor with another woman to run things and a small boy who was her half-brother and a total stranger. But she had always admired Kirsteen and felt excited at the thought of seeing her again, though she couldn't help but retain most of her excitement for Niall.

He had written a letter full of sadness and remorse for all that she had gone through, blaming himself bitterly for everything, even the loss of their son. She had written him letters of reassurance but couldn't wait to see him to prove that her love for him burned even more brightly. They had both known tragedy, each apart from the other, both had grown up and had still to see the changes in each other but she was confident that all they had survived would bring them even closer in the end. She had made up her mind that they wouldn't marry for a while. She would let Niall get over the shock of war and she herself now felt she needed time to let her own scars heal.

She watched the boat leaving the harbour and hoped fervently that her father's journey would be fruitful.

Fergus hadn't left the island in five years and the journey passed in a dream. Glasgow frightened him and he jostled with people in the streets, suddenly conscious that his best suit was drastically out of date. In Rhanna no one bothered about clothes. Suits hung in wardrobes for years, only brought out for funerals or weddings. They never went out of fashion because each man's garb was much the same as the other.

In the city it was different and Fergus felt himself sticking out like a sore thumb, easily picked out as a country farmer. His heart bumped with dismay as he wondered if Kirsteen would see him as such, perhaps be ashamed of him.

On impulse he went into a big store and stared at racks of clothes without seeing them. A sales assistant hovered and he sweated. She came over to offer her help but he muttered something about just looking and she took the dismissal with the smiling mask of a good public servant. He drifted aimlessly and she hovered again. 'Is it a suit or casual wear, sir?'

'Casual – I think.'

'Then might I suggest a nice tweed jacket, a green check would go nicely with your hair and eyes . . . and flannels in a natural shade, plain to offset the jacket.'

He acceded gruffly and was hustled into a cubicle to try the things for size. 'Just right for you, sir,' she enthused when after five minutes of indecisive sweating he finally stepped out of the cubicle. 'Do you want to change back or will you wear them now?'

'I'll keep them on.'

'Right, I'll just put your – er – old things in a bag and we'll go along to the desk.' She smiled and fluttered her eyes at his greatly changed appearance and made polite sounds of approval. 'Now you're more like the thing.' She nodded and he fumed, his black eyes snapping while he waited for change.

Fergus stood in Argyll Street and felt like a tailor's dummy, surely more conspicuous than ever. But no one gave him a second glance.

He ate in the station restaurant and was aware of the uniforms of the armed forces all round him. In Rhanna one was lulled into a sense that the same peace that existed there must surely be in the rest of the world but the cities were full of young uniformed men.

Fergus drifted in and out of slumber while the train rushed him through the night to London.

Before Euston, Fergus splashed his face with cold water but he still felt bleary-eyed and conscious of the dark shadow of stubble on his face. He breakfasted on a greasy egg roll and a watery cup of tea and felt sick on the train to the home counties.

But in a homely country inn at his destination he found solace at last. The innkeeper was unhurried and friendly and guided him to a room with oak beams and a sloping floor. The window looked on to rolling fields and for the first time since leaving Rhanna he felt some of the tension uncoil from his stomach.

'Bathroom's right along the passage,' said Mr Trout showing two aged front teeth. 'We're none fancy here you know, sir. No 'ot water except on Fridays and Mondays for baths but I'll get the missus to bring a pan of 'ot water for you to shave if you want. You look a bit of a gentleman to be stopping 'ere. We're for travellers mostly and locals.'

'I couldn't have wished for a better place,' said Fergus gratefully. 'It suits me fine.'

Mr Trout folded his arms. 'Ah! It's a nice tongue you 'ave there. Where in Scotland do you hail from, sir? Went for a holiday there once and it snowed in May! Would you believe it?'

Fergus smiled. 'It's colder in the north. I'm from the Hebrides, an island called Rhanna.'

'Is that so, is that so? The 'ebrides, eh? Sounds lovely – nice names they 'ave these islands but far, too far they be for the likes of myself. At first I thought you were one of these posh gentlemen from Edinburgh or the like – the clothes you know, I like to dress casual-like myself.'

He looked at his baggy trousers and voluminous cardigan and gave a small apologetic grin. 'Can't be bothered being stuffed up with a tie, the bloody things choke me. Now come down when you're ready, sir. The missus made some nice soup and there's a bit of roast beef if you've a mind. Apple pie for afters – can never resist it myself.'

He went out and Fergus fell on to the big feather bed and laughed with joy. He loved Mr Trout already – Trout, he'd thought that was merely the name of the inn.

Mrs Trout could have been her husband's twin so alike were they in shape and manner. She plied Fergus with platefuls of food and her round face grew quite sad when he refused a second helping of apple pie and cream.

'You're a fine big lad but you need feeding,' she scolded severely. 'Now Mr Trout will eat it and 'im with pounds of blubber already. Ah well, I like 'im that way – we're two of a kind Mr Trout and I.'

'I believe Teesdale House is quite near here?' said Fergus tentatively.

'Bless your 'eart, yes. 'Alf a mile back near Farradale Farm. You know the Campbell-Elliots then?' Her voice was slightly overawed.

'Just someone who is employed there.'

'Nice people they are for the gentry,' Mrs Trout murmured, her voice changed to an unnatural politeness at the very idea of her guest being even remotely connected with Teesdale House. 'Comes in 'ere sometimes, does Mr Leonard. Seems to enjoy an occasional beer with the locals. It's the way he talks, can never understand 'im myself but we're all alike in the eyes of God I say.'

It was a warm evening and the scent of honeysuckle filled the air. The rolling countryside stretched green for miles. It was so different from the wild beauty of Rhanna. There was a gentleness about the fields and the hedgerows and the peacefully grazing, orderly looking cows, so unlike the shaggy self-willed beasts that freely roamed the island. But Fergus felt he would fall off the world at any moment. He needed the strong shoulders of mountains to keep him in place, he was lost without the thunder of the sea and the wild cry of gulls. England was pretty but too fashioned by man, there was none of the sense of freedom of lonely open spaces where one could lose oneself and be alone to think.

He passed Farradale Farm and drew the familiar scent of dung into his lungs. A farmhand nodded at him. 'Nice evenin'. You goin' up to the big 'ouse?'

'How did you know?'

'Gentry clothes you're wearin'.'

Fergus realised how he must appear to a farm worker whose trousers were splattered with mud and whose shirt was patched in sweat. He shook his head, anxious to dispel the illusion his appearance created. 'Forget the clothes. I'm more used to wearing duddies like yourself. It would never do to work a farm wearing tweeds.'

'Wh-at? Duddies?' beamed the farmhand.

'Work clothes.'

'Ah! Isn't that quaint now? You a farmer dressed like a lord?'

'I am going to Teesdale though.'

'Well, just you come with me and I'll show you a

short cut. Not for the likes of everybody mind but seein' as you're a farmer an' all . . .'

He led Fergus through a cobbled yard and opened a gate into an overgrown path. 'Follow it till you come to a copse,' he instructed. 'The 'ouse is on the other side of the copse. Save you a half mile or more goin' this way. Biddin' you goodnight, then.'

The copse was cool with sunlight dappling the grass. Fergus heard the laughter before he saw anyone. His heart hammered into his throat. How many times that same laugh had rung out for him – it was unmistakable, melodious and high.

He stepped into a sunlit clearing and there was Kirsteen standing by a huge oak tree, her hair shining like pale gold in the sun. She didn't see him, she appeared to be hiding from someone and a small peal of laughter was smothered quickly.

He was able to drink in every detail of her, the slim figure in a dress that matched her hair and long brown legs with feet in open sandals. He could hardly believe it, the dream of Kirsteen was now a reality, her living flesh there before him and fate, the force that weaved lives into a pattern, had stepped in once more to fashion a strange twist to their meeting. With woods again as the setting he was about to surprise her as he had done in another time. His heart pumped madly but this time it wasn't desire that made his legs tremble; it was love, pure and naked, the emotions of years culminating in this final moment of nerve-shattering triumph.

A small boy burst into the clearing, a child with crisp dark curls and sturdy limbs. A shout of laughter died in his throat and he stared past Kirsteen to Fergus at the edge of the trees.

Kirsteen turned slowly to look at Fergus, their eyes meeting in a moment when the world held its breath. He saw that she had changed but only by reason that she was more beautiful than he ever remembered. The years had honed the girlish features of his memory to the delicately boned structure of mature young womanhood. Her eyes were very blue in her smooth tanned face and reminded him of the blue of the Atlantic on a summer day. He heard the quick intake of her breath and saw her hands clenching at her sides but her voice when she spoke was calm and held a trace of an English accent.

'I knew you'd come,' she said without emotion.

He stepped forward feeling that such a moment should have been without words. He wanted to gather her to him, declare his love, but their years apart had robbed them of youthful impulses and it was no longer his right to take her intimate responses for granted.

There was so much to say yet he could think of nothing, only the small talk that meant little. 'Balfour told me,' he said, his voice rough with longing.

'I knew he would.'

'And – you didn't run away?'

Her head went up defiantly. 'Why should I? I ran once, now I have no reason to.'

He couldn't believe that the cold toneless words were coming from her lips. Surely, if she'd loved him in the way he'd always believed, she must feel something. The years did not take away the kind of love they had known.

He spread his hand in a gesture of despair and she bit her lip to stop from crying out. The sight of him, bronzed and handsome in his new clothes, despite them, with every lilting word, so endearingly a son of the Hebrides, made her want to run to him, to tell him of the years of her lonely exile away from a love that would not let spirit rest.

Her heart fluttered so fast she was afraid she would faint. She'd counted the days since the laird's departure, waiting and praying for the moment that was now here. She had wondered how she would feel seeing him and had thought that perhaps her mind had magnified her loving memories out of all proportion to what was real in her heart. But it wasn't so; he was here, real and near, and she knew if she touched him that all the resolution and pride she had built round herself would vanish in a puff, leaving her with nothing, no will to deny him anything he asked of her.

'Mother, I found you!' The child's voice broke the silence. 'It's my turn to hide now.'

She looked at Fergus. 'We were playing – it's my day off. I don't get much time to spend with him.'

Fergus bent down to his son. 'What's your name?'

'Grant Fergus Fraser,' said the boy shyly but with pride. 'It's a real Scottish name because although I live in England I'm a Scot really. My father belongs there and he's been living on an island all his life but some day we'll go to Scotland and find him. Who are you, sir?'

Fergus dropped on one knee so that his face was level with that of the little boy. He saw dark, deep eyes with a touch of defiance in them, and a small tanned face with a dimple set in the chin and he felt he was looking at a picture of himself at five years old.

'My name is McKenzie,' he said quietly. 'I come from an island, an island called Rhanna in the Outer Hebrides.'

The boy gasped. 'My *father* lives there! Do you know him? He's big and strong. Mother told me, didn't you, Mother?'

Fergus looked towards Kirsteen. 'You told him the truth. Dear God! Thank you for that!'

Kirsteen struggled to maintain her calm. 'I told him the truth yes, to a certain extent. I saw no point in lying because these things have a habit of rebounding. Ever since he could start asking questions he asked about his father and I told him that you were alive but that was all. He makes things up, that he's going to live some day on Rhanna beside his father. I didn't put the idea in his mind.'

'You're my father!' the boy yelled and a flock of crows rose from the trees in alarm. He held on to Fergus's sleeve and his dark eyes were pleading. 'Have you come to take us back to Scotland? It's terrible not having a father. Other boys are always telling me things they do with their fathers and – and they call me funny names.'

'That's enough, Grant! Come over here!' Kirsteen held out her hand and the boy went reluctantly. 'You mustn't say a word to anyone,' she said severely. 'Promise you won't, please, sweetheart.'

The child scowled. 'Oh all right, but I think it's nasty of you. I've waited a long time for a father and now he's here you won't let me tell anyone!'

'He needs a father's hand,' said Fergus with a faint smile.

'He's needed it for years.'

'Kirsteen, och my Kirsteen, you left me, remember? Please let me talk to you. Could we go somewhere?'

'I'll ask Beatrice to put Grant to bed. She's the housemaid and has been very good to young Grant. Wait . . . here for me.'

Fergus was left in a haze of doubts about everything. His golden dream of carrying Kirsteen and his son back to Rhanna belonged to a fool's paradise. She hadn't even been friendly towards him. He watched her walk towards the big Tudor mansion set in velvet lawns. She had made a good life for herself, she might not want to live on a farm on a wild lonely island. They were worlds apart. She had changed, everything had changed, even his son had grown from a baby to a boy with a mind of his own. They were all strangers to each other and he'd been living in a world of dreams for so long he'd been unable to separate dreams from reality till he'd come face to face with reality and found that it didn't make any sense of his dreams at all.

He felt deflated and uneasy and wanted to walk away from the sun-drenched woods. Instead he sat down on a tree stump and was surprised to find the taste of salt on his lips. He was crying like a lost child, the tears of frustration and sadness, once begun, flowing down his face helplessly. He hid his face in his hand and the sound of his harsh dry sobs made him hate his weakness but he couldn't stop.

Kirsteen's heart was torn in two when she came

back and saw him there, strong, proud Fergus crying like a baby. A sob caught in her own throat and she knew she was going to run to him, to rock him in her arms and tell him how much she loved him. But he looked up and mistaking her look for pity he cried out in anger, 'That's right, look at me damn you! Look at me! It's not the first time, Kirsteen! I've cried for you for years. I cried when I knew you'd left me and I cried when I went to Oban and your mother told me you had gone.'

'She never told me. She wrote – I wrote her – but she never told me you had been to see her, Fergus!'

'Too damned well I know it! She wouldn't tell anyone where you were! Even when she died she had everyone in circles trying to locate you.'

He didn't mean to deliver the blow so hard but the words were out. Her face went pale but she showed no emotion. 'I – didn't know. I haven't written since we came down here last year but she knew this address. She didn't write much so I didn't suspect. I . . . this may sound hard but I can't feel anything very much, pity perhaps and regret that things went the way they did but . . . that's all.'

Fergus stood up and looked deep into her eyes. He made no attempt to touch her. 'Your mother was like me, Kirsteen – too much pride. It's a heavy burden and she died with pride choking her. I've had to swallow mine and the taste of it was bitter and sour. Now I fear I have none left and you've a mite too much. I was too proud at one time to ask a lovely woman like you to be my wife, I drove you away. Now I'd go on my knees to you if you asked me.'

She kept her eyes fixed on the grass at her feet because his nearness was turning her into an un-resisting being without control of heart or mind. 'It's not that easy, Fergus. It wasn't easy having a baby in London and finding a place where I could work and keep my son. He was the only thing that kept me sane. That first year away from you I had to fight not to go running back to Rhanna and you. I left the biggest part of myself on that island; the rest of me, the living shell that walked and talked, had to eat and sleep. I went from job to job and hated them all, then I found the Campbell-Elliots and for four years now they've treated me like one of the family. I work for them but they make it a pleasure and it's not many would bother with a single woman and a young child.' She inclined her head towards the house. 'I can't just go off and leave them after all they've done. Try to under-stand . . . my dear, dear Fergus.'

He looked at her quickly, trying to catch her eye as she whispered the endearments, but she eluded him.

He took a step backwards. 'I'm – glad I saw my son, he's a fine lad – Shona was looking forward to having a wee brother.'

She turned quickly. 'Oh, how is she? I've thought so much about her.'

'She's . . . been my life these years. She's had sad times but they're over now. Niall and she are to be together again when he comes home from military hospital. He was wounded at Dunkirk.'

'Oh, I'm sorry, but glad it's turning out for them. In my heart I always thought they'd end up together, they were so close as children.'

He was turning away from her and a beam of evening sun found the small white hairs among the jet black of his sideburns.

'Oh!' She strangled a cry and moved away. 'I'd better see if Beatrice is managing.'

He nodded, slowly and deliberately signalling his defeat. Then he remembered something and pulled a package from an inner pocket of his jacket. He held it out. 'It's a bit late but these were meant for you. I wrote them four months after you left Rhanna but your mother kept them back from you. I have to thank Mrs Travers for their return – she found them in a drawer after your mother died. They're of little use to me now.'

He pushed the letters into her hand and strode away seeing nothing before him.

She stood where she was, tears coursing down her cheeks, clutching the letters like a drowning person clutches at a straw.

Rhanna was determined to give Niall a hero's welcome. They were all there at the harbour, leaving work behind for the occasion. Todd, with two horses to shoe, had simply taken them to an absent neighbour's barn and let them have a feed of hay. Wullie the carpenter had left some newly cut wood to ripen nicely in the sun and Merry Mary, even Behag Beag, had closed their doors for a whiley.

Canty Tam, with his peculiar leaning stance, grinned aimlessly at the sky and Dodie was lolloping anxiously from Glen Fallan. Biddy, Robbie, Beag, old Joe, Bob and Murdy, all the dour, loving familiar faces were there in the crowd, waiting with a subdued excitement as the boat bringing Niall foamed into the harbour. Hardly a cottage had an empty window, faces peered and the fishermen's wives leaned ample arms on window sills and 'cracked' with each other to fill the time.

Elspeth stood proudly by Phebie and Lachlan, holding the hand of an excited Fiona, and Shona waited quietly with her father. A little behind them stood Alick and Mary with the twins, on Rhanna for their summer holidays.

Shona was wearing her blue dress, the one Niall liked her in best. Her copper hair, tied back with a blue ribbon, tumbled down her back, and her eyes sparkled blue in a face pale with excitement.

Fergus puffed his pipe and the smoke curled in the haze of the autumn day. Behind him the hills were bronzed with bracken and the moor stretched, a sea of purple heather.

The approaching boat brought a swelling tide of green which slopped and swirled against the piles of the pier.

Fergus could sense his daughter's tension and she caught his look and smiled, a quick nervous smile that wakened in him the usual responses of protective love.

'Not long now, mo ghaoil,' he whispered.

'I'm – afraid, Father.'

'I know exactly how you feel, I've been through it too but it's to be sure your meeting will be happier than mine.'

An involuntary little cry broke in her throat and she

gripped his hand tightly. 'I wish – oh how I wish . . .'

'Weesht now, lass, it's all meant for us. Things canny be changed.'

The boat sounded its horn and the pier swayed with the bump. Ropes were thrown and tied. There was quite a crowd of passengers, the last of the summer people visiting relatives. Among them bobbed two heads of bright hair. At first Shona couldn't distinguish Niall then an arm came above one of the heads and she knew it was him.

'Niall,' she whispered, then 'Niall!' in a shout of joy that echoed above the general hubbub.

In a minute he was down the gangplank and in her arms, wordlessly clinging as if he would never let go. A cheer went up and he stared in amazement.

'For you,' she murmured, looking at him, seeing a very pale thin face, so different from the boyish contours she remembered, but still Niall, his brown eyes aglow with joy. 'Why me, sweetheart?' he said. 'I'm no hero, just another soldier who got crocked up in the war.'

'You're a son of Rhanna and to them you're a hero.'

Phebie and Lachlan came over and Niall was smothered with the love of his family. Fiona clung to his neck and he was jostled and welcomed, the tongue of his native Gaelic sweet and dear to him.

Fergus knocked out his pipe and was making his way to the core of the crowd when he stopped frozen, his black eyes looking in disbelief at Kirsteen coming uncertainly towards him, her hand clutching that of their little son.

Fergus was immobile, unable to move while hope

and love churned in his heart. She too had stopped. Grant was looking about him in a wonder of delight. 'Mother, look at the caves!' he cried. 'Look at the mountains! Look at the seagulls!' He broke from his mother's grasp and ran, a sturdy little boy, filled with the magic of his new discoveries, ran to the screeching gulls perched along the harbour and chased them into the sky where they soared in silent majesty of flight.

His parents beheld each other in a daze of longing then the years were bridged in one short moment. She was beside him and he was holding her so tightly she gasped and laughed before their lips joined in a kiss that swept away all doubts in a tide of love.

'Was it the letters?' he whispered in her ear.

'Partly, but mostly because after you left I was so miserable and sad Mrs Campbell-Elliot asked me what was wrong. I told her I had seen you and she said I was to come to you at once. I waited till they had another governess – it was the least I could do. It seemed the longest month I've ever gone through in my life – except when I left Rhanna.' She looked towards the mountains and breathed deeply. 'It's so good to be home . . . do you think it will work for us?'

'My dearest Kirsteen,' he said huskily, 'how could it not? You'll be my wife, tomorrow if possible.'

She laughed. 'Rhanna will be shocked. Fergus McKenzie with a wife and ready-made son.'

'Let them,' he said and kissed her again, uncaring about anyone or what they thought. He caught Lachlan's eye and received a mischievous wink and he raised his hand to the doctor who had devoted himself to the people of Rhanna and who had honoured him with a friendship that was all the stronger the second time round.

Alick and Mary were bearing down on them.

'Welcome aboard,' grinned Alick holding out his hand to Kirsteen. 'Are you all coming along now? It's high time we had a bite to eat. Mary here will thraw a chicken for us.' He put an arm round his wife's waist and they laughed at the look of disgust on her face at the idea of killing a chicken singlehanded.

Shona had just spotted Kirsteen through the crowd and she gasped, 'I can't believe it!'

Niall nodded with quiet satisfaction. 'She came on the boat with me. I knew her but she didn't recognize me – I was only a glaikit wee boy when she went away!'

She smiled at the jibe but continued to look in her father's direction. 'That wee boy – the one with the black curls must be . . .'

'Your brother,' finished Niall before he was lifted to the shoulders of two brawny fishermen. The crowd sang a triumphant Gaelic air and Canty Tam shut his eyes and thanked the Uisga Hags for the return of a Rhanna man.

Phebie and Lachlan each took one of Shona's arms. 'He belongs to the people for a wee while,' said Phebie with a sigh of contentment.

'Then he's ours again,' said Shona.

Lachlan nodded towards Fergus and Kirsteen. 'There will be at least one wedding soon,' he prophesied. 'We'll Ceilidh for days.'

A small boy came running, his face red with exertion. 'Biddy – where's Biddy? Mrs McPherson's started!'

Biddy broke from the crowd. She had lost her hat and her hair straggled over spectacles that were characteristically lopsided. 'Will the folk on this damty island never stop havin' bairns?' she wailed indignantly but as she followed the small boy on legs that were spindly but strong from a lifetime of walking glens and moors, her face was serene and smiling. Nothing gave her more pleasure than seeing a tiny new life come bawling naked into the world.

Dodie, his thoughts already taking him over the moors in a search for Ealasaid and his morning milk, loped after the crowd going into Glen Fallan. 'He breeah!' he shouted dismally to Morag Ruadh who was searching the beach for driftwood, then he wailed to the disappearing crowd, 'Will you wait for me? I have a present for Niall so I have!'

The harbour was quiet once again but for the sound of waves and the cry of gulls. Triumphant in the distance Niall's head bobbed above the rest, a blob of gold against the wild yet dreaming hills of Rhanna.

Children of Rhanna

To Tracy, for her timely reminder about the
S.S. *Politician*

Part One

Winter 1941

Chapter One

Fergus paced the kitchen at Laigmhor, his footsteps eerily enhanced by the silence that enshrouded him. The black cavern of the window with its drab covering of blackout blinds, gaped at him like the blank eye of a dead fish and added to his sense of desolation. Going over, he pulled the blind back a fraction. The mist lay over the moors and he could see nothing but dismal swirling wraiths floating and billowing over the landscape. The night sounds of Portcull came to him as in a dream; the echoes of a dog's bark from Murdy's house by the bridge that spanned the Fallan; faint sounds of merriment from one of the village cottages; the hoot of the steamer's horn from Portcull harbour; a wail from the siren. Captain Mac was certainly making the most of his enforced stay at safe anchorage. He had told Fergus he would ceilidh the night away with the help of Tam McKinnon's home-brewed malt whisky. From the sound of it one half of the ceilidh was on board ship, the other half no doubt in Tam McKinnon's cottage. A light flashed out at sea, filtering uncertainly through the hazy curtains of haar that warped everything that was normal and real. It all added to Fergus's own sense of unreality and he hunched his broad shoulders wearily and dug his hand into his jacket pocket, reassured for a moment as his fingers curled round the familiar stem of his pipe.

His thoughts were sluggish, mixed, taking him back over the strange events of that long exhausting day. It seemed years since they had boarded the steamer at Portcull harbour: At 6 a.m. the village was hushed and peaceful, the sea dark and calm, the ship's crew subdued and heavy-eyed after a night of ceilidhing with relatives on the island. Kirsteen was pale and drawn, heavy and awkward in the advanced stages of her pregnancy. Lachlan McLachlan, the doctor who tended the population of Rhanna, had advised Fergus to take Kirsteen to a mainland hospital because she was expecting twins and it was safer for her to be under constant medical supervision. She hadn't wanted to go. 'I want to have my babies at Laigmhor,' she had told Fergus somewhat defiantly. 'It seems right that they should be born here. I'll hate it in hospital.'

But something deep inside Fergus had rebelled at the idea. A flash of cowardice perhaps, a knowledge that in a hospital he would be divorced somewhat from the stark drama of birth. He hadn't wanted to go through that again. Far better a hospital, away from Laigmhor, away from Rhanna.

In the cabin she snuggled into him, fragile despite the swollen bulk of her belly, resentment and rebellion making her silent and uncharacteristically sullen. Her hands were cold but her face was warm against his and she smelt of fresh air and freshly laundered underwear. The faint fragrance of lavender clung to her and the smell reminded him vividly of Mirabelle, so much a part of Laigmhor for so many years, so much a part of everyone she had tended in her selfless years as housekeeper. Though she was gone now, she still lived in his memory and he had found himself wishing at that moment that she was still there with them all, fussing, comforting, scolding, safe, so safe.

He nuzzled Kirsteen's wheat-coloured curls and in a rush of protectiveness crushed her to him in a fierce embrace.

'I love your strength, you great brute of a man.' She laughed and he thought, 'I'm not strong, not now, not strong enough – for this.'

She lay in his arms, quietly, no resistance left in her, hardly even a smile for Kate McKinnon who came breezing into the cabin, her strong homely face full of sympathy as she surveyed first Kirsteen's stomach then her face. 'Ach, my poor lassie, just about well done they are from the look of the oven – ready to pop out any time, I'd say from the look of you – are you feeling all right, mo ghaoil? You look a wee bit tired.'

'I'm fine, Kate, I never was a good sailor, that's all.'

'Well at the rate we're going, we might as well get out and walk,' Kate said vigorously. 'Would you listen to that damnty siren! It's worse than Tam's snoring when he's had a bellyful of whisky.'

It wasn't till then that Fergus became fully aware that the ship's siren was blaring out at regular intervals and he stared at Kate. 'What's wrong?' he demanded. 'Don't tell me the mist has come down?'

'Ay, as thick as my head feels this morning,' Kate imparted cheerily. 'It will be tonight before I get to Barra at the rate we're going now.'

'You're going over to Barra then?' Kirsteen smiled, already feeling better in Kate's boisterous company.

'I am right enough, I thought I might go and visit some of my relatives there – and o' course to see how is the *Politician* doing. These damt salvors have made a fine mess o' things.' Kate's cheery face became sad. 'Fancy the likes – blowin' up a boat and all that good whisky still in her hold – but ach we might get a bit o' peace then and have no more o' thon officials sniffin' about the islands to see if we have been hidin' whisky and foreign money.'

Kate had every reason to sound huffed. Up until recently she and her husband, Tam, had been making a tidy little profit from the produce of his illicit whisky still, which was safely tucked away in a 'secret room' in old Annack Gow's blackhouse. The whisky had been bottled in small brown medicine containers and, in the guise of cough mixture, had found its way all over the island and spilt over into neighbouring islands. Tam and Kate had kith and kin living the length and breadth of the Hebrides and his superb-tasting malt whisky had found a ready market. Annack and a few of Tam's contemporaries had shared some of the 'takings', but it was to the crafty Tam that most of the profit had gone.

In February of that year the S.S. *Politician*, en route

from Mersey to Jamaica and the United States of America, had run aground on the rocks in Eriskay Sound. A large part of her cargo had consisted of twenty thousand cases of Scotch whisky, which the salvors had been unable to reach. The Hebrideans had heard the news with delight and from all over the islands, boat parties set forth, braving the dangerous waters of the Sound of Eriskay and the Minch. Bottles had bobbed in on the tide, crates full of whisky had been thrown onto sandy beaches, the whim of the wind deciding which island would be next to benefit from the water of life. Money had come in too, Jamaican ten-shilling notes, floating tantalisingly on the silken waves before being tossed ashore. It had been as if an Aladdin's cave had erupted under the sea to spew out its treasures. No one had known what to expect next; the chief occupation of the day was beachcombing. Bicycles and thousands of shirts had come from the *Politician*'s generous holds. It had been carnival time in the Hebrides, a spree of endless ceilidhs and uninhibited revelry. Jamaican money had circulated through the islands, as far north as Benbecula, and the Customs and the police, in a furore over the whole affair, had begun searching, finding a lot of the whisky but missing the bulk, recovering and destroying large amounts of Jamaican notes, though vast amounts had been left unaccounted for. A sweating Tam had closed down business for an indefinite period, being careful however to hide away a few casks of his malt 'for emergencies'.

At sight of Kate's soulful expression, Kirsteen burst out laughing. 'You're the limit, Kate. See how the *Politician* is doing indeed! Away to see what you can find more like! And I know fine that Tam's whisky is still popular despite the glut and folks are still willing to buy it.'

Kate looked suitably downcast. 'Ach well, times are hard so they are and Tam hasny the brains to be doin' much else but the odd job and brew a drop or two o' whisky on the side.' She sniffed dismally. 'Things was goin' fine for us till that damt boat hit those rocks and now my poor Tam has had to suspend his business for a whily. We might as well make the most o' things till the Customs have satisfied themselves that we are no' doin' them out o' anything . . .' A wide grin split her face. 'Fly they may be but no' as fly as us when it comes to hidin' things. Now – I'm away to see Mollie. She is needin' a shirt or two for Todd and is goin' to see will her sister in Uist slip her a few.'

She breezed away and the cabin was quiet again. Kirsteen smiled at Fergus and they settled down to read the magazines they had bought.

They were barely twelve miles out to sea when the first pain seized Kirsteen, so violently it took her breath away and made her tremble. But then the mist had crept thickly and insidiously over the water and the ship's engines had slowed till it seemed they had all but stopped.

Kirsteen lay back on the narrow bunk bed and tried not to let Fergus see that she was in pain but there was no fooling him and he stared at her, his eyes black with apprehension.

She forced a smile. 'Fergus, I'll be all right. These aren't proper pains, false I think they call them. It's too early for the babies to be born yet.'

'Lachlan says twins can be premature,' Fergus said tersely. 'What if they are coming? We're stuck out here and the mist is getting thicker. Dammit! It will take years to get to Oban at this rate.'

'We have to make a stop at Barra and then the Uists – if the worst happens we'll get a doctor there.'

'It's hours to Uist, we're only a few miles out from Rhanna. I can't let anything happen to you. I'm going to ask the Captain to turn back!'

'No, Fergus!' she cried, her face so white he felt his heart racing with dread. 'Stop it! I know what's on your mind! For heaven's sake, it's only a few wee twinges. Oh please don't be so afraid for me, darling, I'm perfectly healthy, I've had Grant; now I'm having twins, it's natural for me to have some pains now and then. Don't worry so.'

'I'm not worried!' he shouted at her.

'Oh yes you are! I've felt your worry for more than eight months now! You're terrified of birth, Fergus. I don't blame you, it's only natural after what happened to Helen – what Shona went through.'

'I am not terrified,' he gritted. 'What do you take me for? Some kind of damned cissy?' His jaw was tense with rage because he knew that she was right. He was terrified; memories were starting to engulf him, forcing him back over the years to Helen, his first wife, upstairs in the bedroom at Laigmhor in the throes of childbirth; the cold sharp light of a January dawn; a child's thin wailing cry – and Helen, dying, her fiery hair framing the delicate cameo of her face. Later came his torture of mind and soul, a heartrending grief that had made him turn away from his infant daughter Shona, rejecting everything that reminded him of Helen's death. He had thought it all forgotten, buried in the ashes of his past, but now it was all coming back. A cold prickle of foreboding touched his spine and made him shiver.

'I'll get you a cup of tea.' Anxiety clipped his tones. She lay back with a sigh and he went to fetch the tea which she drank gratefully.

'There, I'm fine now.' She smiled, her eyes a startling blue in her pale face. Briefly he clasped her hand then he got up. 'I'm going on deck for a smoke. Try and rest.'

He stood on deck and looked down at the grey water below. It was glassy, deceptively calm, the same kind of sea that had robbed him of one of his finest friends, Hamish Cameron, the big laughing Highlander who had been grieve at Laigmhor when Fergus was still an infant. Hamish had died in the sea by the treacherous Sgor Creags, jagged masses of rock near Port Rum Point. Fergus, too, had nearly died but in the end he had been saved, though his left arm had been amputated by Lachlan because it had been so badly crushed by those pinnacles of rock it was beyond repair.

Fergus looked again at the glossy swells rising and

splashing against the hull and he shuddered. He feared and hated the water and here he was, with Kirsteen, gliding slowly along on the steamer, cradled by his enemy, yet relying on it to carry the boat safely to land. The mist enveloped him and he could almost hear Canty Tam's voice saying, 'The Uisga hags love the mist, they can make things happen to people that never happen on land. See, their auld hag faces are smilin' for they like nothin' better than the mist to cast their evil spells.'

'Silly fool,' Fergus thought, but nevertheless he moved away from the rails and went down below to the cabin. Kirsteen was moaning in pain and she gasped, 'I – I think it's the real thing, Fergus. It's too soon – but you mustn't go losing your head over it – I'll keep till we get to Barra.'

Without a word Fergus turned on his heel and went to seek out the Captain. 'How long till Barra?' he asked curtly.

Captain Mac was a Lewis man with a shock of white hair, a bulbous red nose, and calm brown eyes. He blinked at Fergus sleepily and said with a wry grin, 'About the time it might take us to get to the moon. We canny go like the clappers o' hell in mist like this. What ails you, McKenzie?'

'Not me, it's Kirsteen. I think she's started to go into labour.'

Captain Mac's eyes twinkled and he slapped his knee. 'Bugger me, would that not be a fine thing for you? The first twins ever to be born on board the old girl and myself acting as chief midwife. I tell you it would give me something to tell my grandchildren and the lads would make a fine tale of it at the ceilidhs . . .'

He was brought to an abrupt halt as Fergus gripped his arm painfully. 'Bugger your grandchildren and your ceilidhs! My wife isn't some sort of object in a circus. I want you to turn back – to Rhanna – now.'

'Ach, get a hold of yourself, man,' Captain Mac said somewhat peevishly. 'If you must know I was just about to give the orders to turn back for I am no' daft enough to think we'll ever make anything o' it in this kind o' weather.' He glanced at Fergus reproachfully. 'By God, you're a de'il o' a man when you're fighting for your own – but . . .' he was remembering how Fergus had lost his first wife. 'I admire you for saying outright just what's in that stubborn buggering mind o' yours.'

He glanced at his abused and battered clock on the shelf. 'I tell you what, son, that old witch Behag should just be opening the Post Office by now. How would it be if I get a message through to her on that wireless contraption thing o' hers? The old bugger will spread the news about before you can undo your fly, but at least she can alert Lachlan that we are coming back and that bonny wee Kirsteen will get attention the minute we get to shore.'

Fergus gripped his shoulder. 'Thanks, Mac, that's a grand idea, we'll share a bottle next time you're in port – celebrate in style.'

Captain Mac chuckled heartily. 'Ach, I won't be

waiting for the next time. I'm for a good celebration tonight. If the mist holds I'll get along to Tam's for a taste o' his cough mixture. My first grandson was born last week and I have wet his head so much I doubt I've maybe drowned the poor wee mannie.'

When Fergus arrived back at his cabin, it was to wonder what sort of telepathy existed among women for there was Kate and Millie filling the air with sanguine utterances while they took turns at rubbing Kirsteen's back. Kate's big capable hands squeezed and pummelled till Kirsteen protested but Kate would have none of it. 'Weesht you now,' she ordered authoritatively. 'I'm an expert on matters like these, for haven't I went through it often enough, and the last time on my own wi' never so much as a pat on my bum to help me on – ach, Nancy was there right enough but she was only a bairn herself and could do little more than gape at my sufferings – near died I did, but the Lord pulled me through – wi' a good bit o' co-operation from myself o' course. Did I tell you how?'

'Yes, Kate, you did,' Kirsteen broke in hastily. She had heard Kate's story many times before and was in no mood just then to listen to gory details about birth. She felt sick and afraid and when Fergus came in she stared at him wordlessly.

'We're turning back,' he told her, his dark eyes lingering on her lovely face with its finely honed features and beautifully shaped mouth. 'Don't worry, there's no fuss, Mac was about to go back anyway.' His voice was soft, intimate and Kate's eyes flashed.

'Would you listen to him – makin' love to her wi' his voice!' She grinned at Kirsteen. 'It's no wonder you're lyin' there wi' a belly like a Christmas puddin'! If Tam had used that voice on me all our married life I'd have spent my days on my back doin' all the things we aren't supposed to like and churnin' out bairns like sausages!'

Everyone laughed, even Fergus, because it was impossible not to like Kate with her blunt tongue and earthy humour. She was reliably strong in difficult situations, never panicking, enjoying any challenge that chanced her way.

'Look you here,' said Mollie, wife of Todd the Shod, the village blacksmith. 'You won't get to see your relatives in Barra for a whily yet, Kate. It wouldny go amiss if you was to share a droppy o' your cough mixture wi' us.'

'But you don't drink, you just turn up your nose and sip at a glass of good whisky like a hen wi' a sore throat,' Kate accused firmly. Mollie's face grew red, but she persisted. 'Ach, it's no' for myself, Fergus here could be doing wi' a dram, I'm sure. It's no' every day a man is about to become the father o' twins and it's no' every day that Kirsteen here gives birth to them. A droppy would do her good.'

'Ach, you're right enough.' Kate delved into her bag. 'Tam won't mind a wee bottle or two going to his friends.'

As if on cue Captain Mac appeared at the door, his words for Fergus but his gentle brown eyes surveying with languid joy the bottle that Kate was pulling from her bag. 'Just to tell you, McKenzie, I got the message through to Behag and she has promised to have Lachlan standing by at the harbour.' His eyes roved slowly from the whisky bottle to Kate's ruddy fresh face. 'My, would you look at what this bonny woman has smuggled into the innocent-looking shopping bag o' hers.' His eyes twinkled. 'Cross my palm wi' a full bottle and I won't be telling the Customs mannie.'

'You haverin' de'il, Isaac MacIntosh!' an outraged Kate yelled. 'You blasphemin', twisted old sea dog! How could you say a thing like that, after all my Tam's given you in the way o' free whisky?'

'Oh, he's a good man all right, my bonny Kate, but a crafty bugger for all that. Last night he made me stump up a shilling for a half-pint of the malt. I've never had a free drink from him yet.'

Kate's eyes bulged with chagrin. 'Never!' she breathed. 'Wait till I get my hands on that lazy lying cheat . . . Just for that . . . here.' She thrust a bottle at Captain Mac. 'Drink it all and there's more where that came from. Now –' she said, turning to Kirsteen, 'you take a good swallock o' this, mo ghaoil, and then me and Mollie here will give you an arm and help you walk about for a bit. It's the best way to keep your muscles goin'. When he's fu' enough, Captain Mac will give you a song, that's another thing that helps when you're in labour.'

'A song?' Kirsteen asked rather dazedly.

'Ay, if the wee buggers are at all musical they will be in quite a hurry to come out and see what it's all about. When I was having Angus, Tam was in the kitchen, stupid wi' the drink and singin' his head off, and there Angus popped out so quick even auld Biddy was taken aback.'

Fergus threw back his head and roared with laughter. Putting his arm round Kate's shoulder he whispered in her ear, 'You're a wild wild woman, Kate McKinnon, but thank the Lord for you right this minute – and I wouldn't mind a good dram from that shopping bag of yours.'

When they arrived at the harbour Lachlan was waiting with his motor car, which he had managed to get started after much pushing from one or two stalwarts making their leisurely way down Glen Fallan. Captain Mac's predictions about Behag's ever-busy tongue had proved true enough.

As Kirsteen was helped down the gangplank and into the car curtains twitched all along the length of the harbour and Lachlan's thin face broke into a smile. 'Just think of yourself as royalty,' he told Kirsteen. 'They were all agog when they heard you were going to have your twins on Rhanna after all. I might add that Biddy, too, is delighted. She was quite peeved at the idea of another midwife bringing Rhanna babies into the world.'

All that had been hours ago, or it might have been yesterday to Fergus's confused mind. It seemed as if daylight had hardly broken at all during that drab misty day, which had merged into evening without much noticeable difference. Lachlan had gone away to take evening surgery, and now he was back upstairs with Biddy and Babbie, the young nurse who had come to Rhanna earlier that year for a holiday and had stayed to become Biddy's assistant.

Fergus knew he would only be in the way if he stayed in the house, so he busied himself around the farm, glad of the company of old Bob the Shepherd, and Matthew the grieve of Laigmhor. But he couldn't escape Kirsteen's cries of distress when he came in with Bob at teatime. Seven-year-old Grant had been all for coming home after school, delighted to know that his mother hadn't gone to Oban after all, but Fergus had chased him up the road to Slochmhor where he was staying till everything was over.

'Rotten babies,' the little boy had sniffed, his black eyes flashing scornfully. 'We don't need them, Father, it was fine the way it was. I want to come home. Fiona bullies me all the time. This morning she skelped my ear just because I went to see old Joe's new boat and was a wee bit late for school.'

'You needed a skelping then,' Fergus had told his young son firmly. 'You play on Mr Murdoch's good nature. Off you go now to Phebie's. She'll have your tea ready.'

Phebie, the doctor's wife, had prepared a meal for Fergus and Bob, which they ate in an uneasy silence while round them bustled Biddy, scuttling on spindly legs from sink to fire with pans of water. She was seventy-two now, age was showing in her lined face and knotted fingers but she wouldn't hear of retiring. 'I'll work till I drop,' she sharply informed those who dared to suggest she was past it. 'Auld Murn went on till she was eighty. I'll push up the daisies when *I* decide the time is ripe and not before.'

Everyone who knew and loved the kenspeckle old nurse fully believed that she was capable of dying when it suited her. 'She's as tough as cow's hide,' said Kate. 'She's seen that much o' life and death in her time I fine believe she has learnt the secrets o' both. It wouldny surprise me if she does just what she says. The day she knows she can work no more is the day she'll die.'

Bob's grizzled old face was serious as he tackled his meal. Across from him, Fergus went rigid as yet another agonised sound rent the air. 'Kirsteen, Kirsteen,' his heart cried out helplessly. 'I love you, my darling, yet I can't share your suffering.'

Bob looked at his ashen face and muttered, 'She's a strong lassie. Dinna fash yourself, lad. By God, it's a terrible struggle for the women right enough. I thank the Lord I'm a man and will never know the pain o' givin' life. It's times like these I'm glad I never married, though betimes I think what a grand comfort a wife and bairns must be. I'm used to livin' alone but I often wonder what it would be like to have a daughter lookin' after me in my auld age. At sixty-eight I'm still a bit of a spring chicken . . .' He chuckled, not because he didn't believe that he was indeed still in the prime of life, but at the spark of amusement in the other man's eyes. 'Ay, smile, lad, for at forty you are still that, but I'm tellin' you, in another twenty years or so you'll take bad at the idea o' folks thinkin' you're gettin' on, for you will still think much the same things you're thinkin' now. Forbye that you're a lucky man, you'll never know an auld age without your bairns around you, for you have provided yourself wi' plenty and enough to guarantee that one at least will look to you when you're nothin' but a heap o' dry bones.'

He rasped the back of a gnarled hand over his stubbly chin and scraped back his chair. 'I'm away down to Todd's to see if Conker has been shod yet. I might stay and have a game o' cards wi' Todd but I'll look in on you later.'

'I doubt it.' Fergus smiled faintly. 'Captain Mac and his crew will be ashore and there will be ceilidhs all over the place, so you'd better take your fiddle along with you.'

'Ay, right enough then.' Bob sounded apologetic. Quickly he pushed his feet into his wellingtons, waved his crook at Dot, who sprang up obediently and glided to his side, waved his stick in farewell to Fergus and plodded away over the cobbles of the yard. After that it was so quiet in the kitchen Fergus felt he might have been alone in the house except for the tread of feet in the room above and Kirsteen's muffled cries.

The flames from the fire gave the room a mellow hue; shadows danced on the ceiling and distorted everyday objects into strange shapes. Light spilt golden over the hearthrug, falling on a quivering little bundle of curling amber fur. The three-month-old spaniel was a new arrival at Laigmhor, yet was so familiar a sight lying there in the pool of warmth that Fergus's heart turned over. It might have been old Tot breathing gently in contented slumber. Tot had been Shona's dog, given to her by Hamish when Shona had been just five years old. Tot was dead now, but this little dog was one of her offspring. His master had offered him to Fergus just recently.

'I'm going off to stay with my sister in Australia,' the old man said rather sadly. 'I'm getting too old now to enjoy living on my own.' He had glanced down at the pup. 'Thought you might like this wee devil. You mind auld Tot had pups? Well this one sprung from one o' them. The bairnies will like him. Children should never grow up without a dog they can call their own. Farm dogs is all right in their place but they know better how to work than play, this one will play wi' a body till they are just about dropping.'

When Grant first saw the pup he immediately christened him Squint. It was an appropriate name as one of the limpid brown eyes was badly crossed, yet rather than detract from the dog's appearance, it added to it and endowed him with an irresistible appeal. Fergus could hardly wait to see Shona's face. She would be home for Christmas.

The thought made his heart bound with joy. He hadn't seen her since her marriage to Niall, the doctor's son, nearly two months ago. God, how he missed the child of his first marriage. Her departure from the island had left a void in his heart. They had spent so many of her eighteen years together at Laigmhor, comforting each other in the days of their loneliness when his heart had pined for Kirsteen and when Shona had been plunged into an abyss of despair on learning that Niall was thought to have been killed at Dunkirk. She had been expecting his child at the time, and in a state of shock had given birth to a little stillborn son. Fergus could still see the child in his mind's eye, the neat perfection of it, the small head covered in downy fair hair, the flesh waxen and cold as marble. It had taken her a long time to get over the trauma, but it was all behind her now. Niall had come back from the dead and they had married and gone to live in Glasgow where Niall was training to be a vet, and Shona a nurse. Fergus breathed deeply. Often he was so busy in the bustle of farming and family life that he had no time to miss his firstborn child, but sometimes he fancied he heard her light step on the stairs or her singing in the kitchen and he never quite got over the feeling that she still occupied her bedroom upstairs. He missed going to her door, whispering goodnight to her and hearing her whisper softly back, 'Goodnight, Father.'

He stopped pacing and sat down in the inglenook. Squint opened one eye, got up, stretched lazily, then on big, gangling puppy paws padded over to Fergus and climbed calmly onto his lap. His body was warm and soft. Fergus caressed the golden ears and felt again he was back in the past feeling Tot's fur under his fingers.

A light tap came on the door and it opened quietly. Phebie stood there, her sweet face smooth and rosy, her expression slightly defensive. 'I hope you don't

561

mind, Fergus,' she said rather hesitantly. 'I have left Grant to Fiona's tender mercies.' She smiled. 'It's strange how these two snarl at each other so much. How unlike Shona and Niall at their age.'

'It would be asking too much for history to repeat itself,' Fergus said as he lifted Squint from his knee and got up. He looked at Phebie and the knot of tension in his belly uncoiled a little at the sight of her calm face. He knew of course the reason for her defensive attitude. Once, long ago, he had rejected Phebie's offer of help at a time such as this and he had lived to regret it sorely. He stretched out his arm to her. She was soft and warm, like a plump little rosebud that smelt of antiseptic, for she quite often helped Lachlan out in the surgery.

'I'm glad to see you, mo ghaoil,' he told her in his deep lilting voice. 'I've been sitting here feeling sorry for myself. I feel so strange, as if the clock was turned back and I'm re-living that hellish night of Shona's birth.'

'I know how you must feel.' She felt drawn to him in this moment. Often he was a dour, unapproachable creature, though she had learnt that underneath his hardness there lay a soft heart.

'I'm a coward, Phebie,' he continued, shamefaced. 'I wanted this to happen in hospital. To be near Kirsteen yet to be apart from her. I should go to her now but I can't. I don't want to see her pain because there's nothing I can do to help her.'

'Nonsense,' Phebie became brisk. 'Kirsteen knows you're down here and not miles away like some husbands are when their bairns come into the world. I'll make tea, a good strong brew; I could be doing with a cup myself.'

In minutes the kettle was singing on the hob. She poured two cups and handed him one and he was annoyed when his trembling hand slopped some of the liquid into the saucer. 'You are in a state,' she said. 'Sit down for heaven's sake before you fall down. I don't think I'm strong enough to catch hold of a man your size – not that it wouldn't be nice, but think of what Lachlan would say if he found us in each other's arms . . .'

He glowered and she giggled. 'Och c'mon now, let's see a smile. Would you like me to make you a sandwich? No doubt you haven't eaten very much of what I left earlier.'

'Ay, that would be fine.' His tones were brusque in the effort to conceal his emotions. Babbie danced into the kitchen, smiling smiles he felt she had no right to in such a situation. Her red hair gleamed in the lamplight, her green eyes sparkled.

'Relax, Mr McKenzie,' she said. 'Kirsteen is coping beautifully, but these things take time. Labour isn't known as such for nothing, you know – but of course –' her eyes crinkled again – 'what would a man know of that?'

There was no smile in response in the dark, ruggedly handsome face looming above hers. Instead, the well-shaped, sensual mouth tightened with annoyance.

Babbie went to the fire and lifted the teapot, her

face glowing in the fire's light. In her pocket was a letter from Anton Büttger, the young German Commander who had crash-landed his plane on Rhanna in March of that year and who had been badly wounded in the process. She had nursed him back to health and during that time they had fallen in love. He was now in a prison camp in England and she longed to see him again. His letters to her were the one thing that illuminated her life. The present one had come on yesterday's boat and she had read it so often she knew every word by heart. The war could end next week or next year, whatever way it went she would wait for him to come back to her. Dreamily Babbie poured tea into large cups. 'I've been sent to fetch a cup for Biddy – laced with a drop of brandy if you've got any. She's grumbling like mad up there, even though she's so thrilled you would think she was having twins herself.'

She went off with a laden tray and the kitchen was quiet again. Phebie was not a demanding companion and Fergus found himself thankful for her presence. Each little night sound made his ears crackle with awareness. A strange mewing cry filtered through the silence but it was a sound outwith the sturdy walls of Laigmhor, a seabird's cry, a haunting, lost sound that melted away into the night.

Fergus could sit still no longer. 'I have to go out to the cowshed,' he told Phebie, and lifting a lamp from the dresser, he made his way outside, not to the cowshed but to the little garden at the back of the house. Mirabelle had planted roses here. Despite storms and howling winter gales they somehow managed to survive and in the summer the air was filled with their fragrance. Carefully he set the lamp down on the mossy earth. Yesterday he had noticed a perfect red rosebud shining like a jewel amidst withering foliage. The light from the lamp picked it out, red as a ruby as it loomed out of the chilly mist. It was studded with droplets of moisture that lay on its satin-smooth petals like teardrops on a baby's cheek. He cut through the stem with his tobacco knife and the rosebud lay in his hand, marble-cold, an object of perfection. It was then he saw another bud on the same bush, a fragile-looking red blob, smaller than the first, drooping slightly on its stem as if cowering away from the threat of winter that ought to have killed it but hadn't. With a gentle finger Fergus touched it, a strange thought coming to him. It deserved to live; he couldn't leave it to die after such a game struggle for survival. It needed to be cherished, protected. Gently he plucked it and tucked it into his pocket along with the other.

Chapter Two

Just before midnight the first baby was born, and half an hour later came the second, a feeble little mite, with hardly a flicker of life in its tiny body.

'Get water,' Lachlan instructed Babbie. 'Two basins, one hot, the other cold.'

Babbie flew downstairs, brushing aside Fergus's questions, urging him instead to help her with the water, which he did silently, not daring to ask for further details from the young nurse who told him quickly what was happening. Biddy busied herself with Kirsteen, while Lachlan and Babbie between them worked with the baby, bathing it alternately in hot and cold water. For fifteen minutes it seemed as if there was no life in the infant. A pall of eerie quiet surrounded the doctor and the young nurse, broken only by whimpers from the first arrival, Biddy's voice soothing Kirsteen, the plop, plop of water, accompanied by splashes as the infant was plunged from basin to basin.

'Come on, come on,' Lachlan rasped. 'Cry, for God's sake, cry!' His face was shiny with sweat, his brown eyes alive with desperation.

'The skin is turning pink. Look, Lachlan,' Babbie's voice was jubilant. The baby jerked and trembled, the tiny fists clenched, the chest heaved and filled the lungs with air, the pink mouth opened wide to give vent to a life-saving cry that was music to the ears of everyone in the room.

'The Lord be thanked,' Biddy beamed as the baby was wrapped in blankets and brought to Kirsteen's side. She stroked the young woman's hair tenderly and whispered, 'There, there, lass, have a good greet, it's all right now. My, my, are they not lovely just?'

It was nearly two o'clock when Lachlan came downstairs and into the kitchen. He stood for a moment, shoulders drooping with weariness, unruly locks of dark hair falling over his brow. The lamplight found every hollow in his thin boyish face, sweat gleamed on his upper lip but his eyes were luminous, the slow breaking of his smile like a summer dawn pouring sunlight over the dark earth.

Fergus leapt up at his entry, his muscular body taut with suspense, his strong brown right hand bunched into a knuckle of steel. 'Well?' His voice was breathless, strange to his own ears.

Lachlan held out his hand. 'Congratulations, Fergus, you have sons, identical twins. Kirsteen is naturally very exhausted, but she's fine, just fine, man.'

'Thank God – oh thank God!' Fergus's voice was husky with relief. In a few quick strides he was across the room, grabbing Lachlan's hand, pumping it so vigorously the doctor gave a little laughing yelp. Phebie, too, was on her feet, laughing, kissing Fergus, kissing Lachlan, waltzing him round and round.

'Hey, go easy,' Lachlan protested. 'I'm feeling a wee bitty fragile right now. It's not every day I deliver twins.' Fergus was making for the door but Lachlan put out a hand to stop him. 'Not yet, Fergus, there's something you should know first.' He was silent for some time and it seemed as if the house held its breath in suspense of what must follow. 'You know of course we had quite a fight to save the life of your second son . . .' He spoke slowly, almost unwillingly. 'Both babies are premature, and therefore small, but the youngest is well below what I consider to be a healthy weight. He – well – the next few days will be critical for him. His breathing may fail, by rights he should be in an incubator in hospital, but it's impossible to move him, he would never survive a journey of any length. Also –' Lachlan took a deep breath – 'I think I can detect a heart condition. It's difficult to tell at this stage how serious it is, only time will tell us that. Otherwise he seems normal enough, but he is very frail and there's no knowing if he'll survive. Kirsteen doesn't know any of this and it's best not to worry her just now.'

Babbie appeared in time to hear his last words. 'I'll stay for as long as I'm needed,' she said quietly. 'The babies will need constant supervision, and if an emergency arises I'll be nearby to cope.'

'Ay.' Fergus nodded dejectedly. 'The bairns are to have Mirabelle's old room so you can sleep there; the bed's made up. I lit the fire earlier, so the room should be warm.' He looked from one to the other. 'Thank you both – for everything,' he said briefly but it was enough for Lachlan, who nodded.

'On you go up now,' he said. 'Don't let her see anything is wrong. We'll give you ten minutes and then we'll all have a dram together – I could be doing with it,' he finished with a weary sigh.

Fergus walked into the hall. All was hushed, even the ticking of the grandmother clock seemed more subdued than usual. It had ticked just as sweetly, just as steadily on that morning of Shona's birth more than eighteen years ago. No doubt it had been lazily swinging the time away when he and his younger brother, Alick, had been born, because he remembered as an infant gazing solemnly up at the round serene face of it. It had appeared a huge object to him then, and even now, when he loomed above it, it still seemed bigger than he, solid, reassuring.

The oak-panelled walls were rich yet mellow in lamplight, the pictures that hung on them were as familiar to him as his own name. He had known no other home, he had trodden these floors, these stairs, for more than forty years. He climbed up the wooden stairs as he had done countless times before. Routine was so much a part of life it often seemed to stagnate and it was easy to think that nothing could ever change. But changes, when they did come, were sometimes so dramatic they brought feelings of panic, a sensation of being unable to cope. Such things were happening to him now. He went on upwards but felt he was stepping back over years, living again things his mind had buried. Eighteen years had gone by, yet it was all so near, so real. The first stop in the mists of time came when he went into Mirabelle's old room to check the fire. This was to be the nursery. Everything that the babies needed was here. To one side of the fire stood the old family cradle, gleaming with a fresh coat of varnish. Beside it was an exact replica, beautifully fashioned by Wullie the Carpenter; the only things it lacked were the tiny cracks of age, the gnaw-marks made by babies cutting milk teeth. Fergus saw the cradles like someone looking at a scene from a dream, for more real to him was the feel of Mirabelle's presence in the room, the lingering perfume of lavender, the vision of her sitting on her rocking chair by the window, her snowy white mutch cap appearing like a beacon in the black oblong of the window when you looked up and saw her from the garden. So Shona had seen her the day she died, worn out from a lifetime of caring for others.

'Mirabelle, my dear old friend,' he whispered into the warm silence. 'Two bairnies are going to shatter your dreams with their cries, but you'll look to them like you looked to the rest of us.' An odd peace stole into his heart. Somehow he felt that the old lady was still here, watching over them all, all those she had called my bairnies.

He put more coal onto the fire then went out of the room and along the passage to the bedroom he shared with Kirsteen. When he opened the door he was transported back to a morning in January 1923. Peace lay over everything and everyone the room held; the shadows were full of secrets, kept yet shared; by the fire Biddy was sound asleep in a deep comfortable chair, skinny black-clad legs spread wide to the heat, hands folded over her stomach, her head falling forward onto her scraggy bosom, the big pin in her felt hat glittering in the soft light.

Kirsteen lay depleted against the pillows of the big double bed, her ruffled curls damp with perspiration, her eyes closed, her face beautiful as the sculpture of a young girl whose innocence hadn't yet been violated. For a brief moment Fergus saw again a pure white bed, a girl still with the face of a child, blue-lidded eyes closing as death beckoned her away from the life she had so loved, a girl who had laughed, who had cried, who had adored him with all the exuberant passion of youth – and who had died at the age of twenty-one. In a blinding flash, filled with clarity of each small detail, Fergus saw it all, then in a dizzy sensation of whirling forward through time, he was back in the present, seeing not a bed of death but one filled with life, three lives.

Kirsteen opened her eyes and saw him standing motionless in the doorway. She lifted her hand and held it out to him. 'Fergus, my darling, come and see what we have made together.' Her voice was low, laden with an intimacy that made his heart turn over. He tip-toed over to the bed, not knowing if he did so to allow Biddy to sleep on undisturbed or because to break the tranquillity in the room would have been a violation. He stood tall above her, drinking in the sight of her lying there with the children of their love at her side.

'Kirsteen, my dearest,' he whispered huskily. 'How do you feel?' Though weary beyond measure, her face was alive with joy, tears of thankfulness drowning her eyes, a smile curving her soft lips. 'I feel – happiness. It was a sore struggle but it's over now, it's over, Fergus.'

No, he thought, it's only just begun, the heartache of the unknown. Pain, sharp and overpowering, filled his heart. Surely having gone through so much, her sweet happiness couldn't be shattered by the death of one of their newborn sons. It would be too cruel to give life only to have it taken away. Tears choked him and to hide them he bent his dark head to kiss her warm lips. Even though her body was racked by fatigue she was overwhelmed as always by his nearness. She caressed the black curls at the nape of his neck and in the passion of love he put his arm under her head to pull her up close so that she was lying against his powerful chest, hearing the dull steady throb of his heart. 'I love you, my Kirsteen,' he murmured, 'and I thank God for keeping you safe.'

'I promised I would give you more sons,' she smiled. 'Don't you want to see them?'

He straightened and gazed at the two bundles cocooned in white blankets and saw two thatches of jet-black silken hair, the indentation of the fontanelle on each little head making them look fragile and vulnerable. She pulled the blankets away from the puckered faces, identical faces, though one was smaller than the other, the skin so transparent he could see the delicate fretwork of veins. This was the one who might not live, and it looked to him to be already on the brink, but he couldn't let her see that anything was wrong.

'They're very small.' It was all he could find to say and he wished immediately he could take it back.

A frown crossed her face. 'I know Lachlan says it's natural for twins to be smaller than single babies but I never realised – how tiny – especially –' her slender fingers stroked the cheek of her youngest son – 'this one. He was all but dead when he was born. Lachlan and Babbie between them saved his life. She's a fine nurse and Lachlan's a wonderful doctor – but will this baby survive, I wonder.'

'Of course he will; he's a McKenzie, remember,' Fergus said, changing the subject quickly. 'Wait till Alick and Mary hear about this; now we have two sets of twins in the family. Grant might feel better when he knows he's got brothers. He was dreading the idea of sisters. There's only one girl in his life at the moment and that's Shona. He worships her, though he tries hard to let on he doesn't.'

'I wonder how he's getting on at Slochmhor. I hope he isn't fretting.'

'Not him! He's filling his time nicely. He made himself late for school this morning by going to see old Joe's new boat. He loves that old man with his stories of the sea.'

Her hand tightened over his. 'He will never be a farmer. He's not yet eight and already the sea is in his blood. I wonder will one – or both of these babes

grow up to love the earth – to till Laigmhor soil . . .
If not I'll have to give you the rest of those five sons
I promised.'

'Hell no! Never again! I couldn't go through another
day like this and you're not going through more hell
just to please me. I don't care if all my sons grow up
and go to sea – or to the moon for that matter – you're
more precious to me than a few acres of soil.'

Footsteps sounded on the stairs and Lachlan came
into the room with Phebie and Babbie at his heels.
Biddy grunted and groped among the cushions for
her specs. 'Where are the damty things?' she
demanded irritably. 'If it's no' them losin' themselves
it's my teeths playin' hide-and-seek wi' me.'

'If it's your specs you're looking for, they're on the
end of your nose, Biddy,' Babbie giggled.

'Ach, it's a cailleach I am indeed.' The old nurse
smiled sourly and sniffed the air. 'Here, is that whisky
I'm smellin' and no one ever offerin' me a drop!'

Lachlan handed her a well-filled glass and Biddy,
snuggling back contentedly into the chair, gazed into
the fire and began to croon a lullaby. Phebie was
over by the bed, utterly enchanted at her first glimpse
of the twins. One of them stirred and gave a weak
cry and Babbie moved quickly to pick him up. 'I'm
taking them through now, Kirsteen. The cradles have
been nicely warmed with hot bags and there's a fire
in the room.'

Anxiety creased Kirsteen's smooth brow. 'But –
they'll be hungry,' she protested. 'And I wanted to
feed them myself.'

'You will,' Babbie promised kindly but firmly. 'Just now they only need some boiled sweetened water and you must have a good night's rest. Don't worry, they'll be fine with me. I'll attend to their every need.' With a small bundle on each arm, she went to the door where Lachlan had a few quick words with her before she went along to Mirabelle's old room.

Kirsteen lay back and Lachlan went to put his hand over hers. 'It's for the best, mo ghaoil. You get a good night's rest and I'll be back in the morning to check up on the bairns and to make sure you're behaving.' He put his arm across Phebie's shoulders and was about to offer Biddy a lift in his trap when he saw that she was asleep once more, the empty whisky glass clutched against her bosom.

'Leave her,' Kirsteen said softly. 'It's been a long day for her. She can go through to Shona's room later.'

'I had a mind to sleep in there tonight,' Fergus protested.

Phebie laughed. 'Well, just think how nice it will be for you if you waken in the night feeling lonely and there's auld Biddy snoring beside you.'

Kirsteen gave a small tired smile. 'Use Grant's room, darling. There's room in the house for every-body – you can all stay if you like.' Her eyes were closing despite herself. Lachlan led Phebie away and their footsteps receded downstairs. From the room at the end of the corridor a thin little wail pierced the night, then all was silent once more. Fergus felt uneasy. He stood for a long time looking down at

Kirsteen. The firelight brushed her pale face with gold, her hands were relaxed and still on the coverlet. He felt alone and more than a little afraid of the thing that he knew but she didn't. She stirred and gave a sigh. 'Fergus, you're there, aren't you?'

'Yes, darling, I'm here.'

'Go to bed,' she murmured. 'You must be tired.'

'I am . . .' His fingers curled over the two rosebuds in his pocket and he took them out and placed them on the white pillow by her head. They looked like two drops of blood that had been preserved for all time.

She opened her eyes and saw them. Slowly she picked them up and holding them to her lips she kissed them. 'They're beautiful, one for each of our sons – but where on earth did you find roses in December?'

'In the garden, growing on the same bush. I wish I could give you an armful – I will yet, I want to get you something special for Christmas. I've a mind to go to Oban next week and do a bit of shopping.'

'You could buy me the world but nothing will be as precious to me as these; I shall keep them always. You know that big family Bible that belonged to your grandparents? I'm going to press your rosebuds into that.'

Biddy was snoring gently, her lips making little plopping noises as she sucked in and expelled air.

'Dear old Biddy.' Kirsteen's eyes were like leaded weights and in seconds she was asleep again, the rosebuds clasped to her breasts. Fergus tucked the blankets round her, and brushed her hair with his lips, then he padded soundlessly away to Grant's untidy room.

Glass net floats hung over the bed like bunches of gaily coloured balloons, crayoned pictures of boats were pinned askance on the walls; opposite the bed hung a big gilt-framed painting of the sea, the first thing the little boy saw each morning when he woke. But child of the waves and wind though he was, a floppy teddy bear was tucked carefully under the quilt. Fergus picked it up and looked at it. Quite unthinkingly he put it back in its place, undressed and got into the small narrow bed. In the darkness the rough fur of the bear brushed his face. The bed was cold and he thought longingly of Kirsteen's warm body beside his. How had he borne all those years alone in an empty bed? He had almost forgotten what it was like. Curling up into a tight ball he fell into a restless sleep, unaware that in the night he hugged his son's teddy bear to his chest like the little boy of long ago who had cuddled a battered cloth bear made by Mirabelle. Three doors from where he slept Babbie kept a lonely vigil on a helpless baby who barely appeared to be breathing. In the dark hours before dawn Biddy came through to relieve the young nurse, and there, by the fire, in Mirabelle's big chintz armchair, she held the tiny infant to her old bosom, smelt the fragrance of silken hair against her face, said silent prayers for the preservation of the youngest McKenzie son, and, as always, she felt so much love for the newly born it might have been her own babe cradled so lovingly in her arms.

Several critical days passed, days in which the fragile baby held to life by a thread. Lachlan was hardly away from Laigmhor, Biddy was in constant attendance, while her young assistant made the strenuous rounds of croft and cottage. She was exhausted, but insisted on spending her nights at Laigmhor. 'Ach, what did I ever do without you, lass?' Biddy said with misty eyes, pulling the girl to her and fondling her fiery red hair before pushing her away in embarrassment and toddling off on spindly legs.

Kirsteen cried when she heard that her smallest son was fighting for his life, but with the determination that Fergus knew and admired so much, she spent little time indulging in useless tears and instead set about positive action. She breast fed the babies, cuddled them, whiled away the long hours in bed doing everything she possibly could to help in the battle, and everyone was overjoyed when Lachlan finally announced the crisis was over.

'The bairnie will live,' he said simply. 'God and McKenzie between them put a spirit into the wee lad that wouldn't be beaten. He'll need a lot of care, mind you. His heart isn't strong; he might never be as big or as strong as his brother; but the chances are the older he gets, the stronger he'll be.'

After an extended stay at Slochmhor, Grant came home, utterly disgusted at the first sight of his baby brothers. 'They're ugly,' he stated with a toss of his black curls. 'I hope I didn't look like that when I was a baby.'

'Ach, you'll have looked worse!' Fiona scolded, her bright eyes flashing under her dark fringe of hair. 'And you're no better now – at least they'll likely get better looking by the time they get to your age.'

The little boy's dimpled chin jutted out in indignation. With his snappish black eyes and rosy cheeks he was the ultimate in childish beauty, though when he scowled he looked very much like his father in a rage. 'At least I don't look like a Robin with beady eyes and a funny wee beak.' He glared into Fiona's laughing face. 'I'm going down to the harbour,' he went on peevishly. 'Ranald is building a big new boatshed and I'm helping him,' he finished off proudly.

After that a steady stream of visitors came to Laigmhor, all bearing small gifts for the twins, whose arrival had caused a great stir of interest. For the sake of convenience the cradles were brought down to the kitchen where the womenfolk gathered to stare and admire. Knitting needles had been busy for months and very soon heaps of tiny garments lay everywhere.

'My, my, is it no' just like the stable from Bethlehem itself?' Mairi McKinnon observed, her round-eyed, rather vacant gaze absorbing the scene with quiet bliss.

Fergus had cut and brought in a small spruce tree. Shiny with baubles and tinsel, it sat in a corner of the room; a few stray hens clucked in the pantry; the women stood, shawled heads bowed over the cradles, their faces bronzed in the warm flicker of firelight. Mairi, in her unsophisticated way, had described the scene perfectly.

But it was Dodie, the island eccentric who lived in solitary existence in his tiny cottage on the slopes of Sgurr nan Ruadh, whose gift touched Kirsteen the most. She was in the kitchen drinking a well-earned cup of tea when she saw him standing by the gate looking with soulful eyes at the languid activities of the sheep that dotted Ben Machrie. Unlike the rest of the islanders to whom the business of visiting was a normal habit at any time of the day, he never entered a house unless specifically invited to do so. Kirsteen felt only in the mood for solitude but no one ever hurt the old man's feelings by ignoring his presence.

'Come on in, Dodie,' she called from the doorway. 'I have just made a strupak.' He loped up the path with agility, his large wellingtons making slapping sounds with every long step.

'I was just passing on my way over to Croynachan,' he stuttered in mournful apology. Shy of women in general, he was only just growing used to Fergus's comparatively new wife, and he stopped short at the doorstep, his stooped gangling figure blotting out the light. He was dressed in a threadbare raincoat and hairy tweed trousers that were tucked carelessly into the wellingtons. A greasy cloth cap was jammed on his head so tightly his ears stuck out on either side, giving him the appearance of an oversized gnome.

From the end of his carbuncled nose a large drip dangled precariously; his strange, inward-dreaming eyes were full of water from the bite of the December air; his calloused, ungloved hands were mottled with purple. If he had taken the charity the islanders were only too willing to give, he would have been well-off indeed, but simple though he was, he maintained a fierce pride and accepted without complaint the harshness of his own existence.

Kirsteen's heart swelled with pity even though she was somewhat repulsed by the smell that emanated from him in waves. 'Sit down, Dodie,' she invited kindly. 'Elspeth sent some fresh scones over from Slochmhor. They're still hot and delicious with butter melting over them.'

'That cailleach,' he sniffed, momentarily causing the drip to ascend in his disapproval of Elspeth Morrison, the sharp-tongued housekeeper of Slochmhor. He had never forgiven her for chasing him up the village street brandishing a broom just because he had accidentally stumbled into her clean white washing and pulled it to the ground. Despite his grievances however, he tucked heartily into the scones, a finger placed strategically under his chin to catch the rivulets of melted butter, which he expertly scoped back up to his mouth.

'Are you no' sittin' down yourself to have your strupak?' he asked Kirsteen politely.

'Er – no, I prefer to stand at the moment,' she told him with a faint smile.

'Ay.' He nodded wisely and his carbuncle wobbled

slightly. 'Your backside will be sore for a whily after havin' two bairnies.'

Taken aback, she stared at him, and he himself, utterly dismayed at the audacity of his statement, blushed crimson and choked so violently on a crumb she had to rush forward and thump his bent back. Though prim to the point of being prudish, the old eccentric was astonishingly frank about the facts of life, even though normally he reserved his observations for the animal kingdom. Animal matings and animal births filled him with joy and in this case he had simply forgotten which category Kirsteen came into.

'I'm sorry, Mistress McKenzie!' he wailed, getting to his feet so hurriedly the table tilted and the cups slid gently to the edge. 'I'll be goin' now, thankin' you for the strupak.' He babbled on unintelligibly. 'I have a potach in my pocket for Ealasaid so I have, and if I could find the bugger I might get some milk too. I left my pail down by your gate.'

He lurched to the door but Kirsteen stayed him by saying kindly, 'Don't you want to see the babies? They're asleep just now and you'll see them at their best – not like poor Mrs Gray. They roared their heads off when she came and she couldn't get a word in.'

'Ay, indeed just,' he gabbled. 'I have a wee somethin' for them – somethin' really special seein' they are doubles.'

The 'wee somethin'' proved to be two beautiful silver teaspoons, which he withdrew from some hidden pocket inside his coat. With reverence he placed a spoon at the foot of each cradle then stood with his hands folded over his chest, the big thumbs pointing upwards.

'Dodie,' Kirsteen gasped, picking up one of the spoons. 'These are beautiful but . . .' She left the question hanging in mid-air for she knew he would be offended if asked outright how he had come by such items.

'I paid for these myself,' he volunteered with pride. 'I took them as wages for some wee jobs I did to Burnbreddie. Her leddyship said your bairnies would not be born wi' silver spoons so I decided it would be a fine thing for the auld bitch to be proved wrong and . . .' he paused, stretching his lips to show tobacco-stained teeth, the nearest he ever got to a smile, 'herself providing the very things she said they would never have.'

'They're lovely, Dodie,' Kirsteen said, deeply touched not only by the gifts but by the thoughtfulness that lay behind them. Once before Dodie had bestowed a simple treasure on Fergus when he had lain at death's door after his accident. It had been a discarded horseshoe, polished over and over till it gleamed. 'It will make him get better,' the old eccentric had whispered tearfully but with deep conviction. Fergus had always maintained that the charm had helped to speed his recovery and to this day it hung above the fireplace in the bedroom.

'I am after hearin' that one of the bairnies is no' very strong, so these will maybe bring him luck and, of course,' he said, his lips stretched again, 'they will come in handy when they are breakin' their milk teeths and are learnin' to sup food.'

A tiny fist boxed the air and Dodie stared in awe as Kirsteen pulled the blankets back. 'My, would you look at that!' Dodie was completely enchanted. 'By God, they are beautiful just – I had two just like them myself a good few years back – like two wee peas in a pod they were. Even the black socks on their feets were all alike.' Kirsteen was rather taken aback but she had no time to utter a word because Dodie was racing on. 'Ay, lovely they were just. I had a hand in bringin' them out o' the yowe for they were her first and she was that grateful neither she nor the lambs ever let me out of their sight after it. Ach, they were buggers betimes, but my – I was that proud inside myself I could have burst wi' happiness.' His odd dreamy eyes filled with tears and into them he scrubbed a horny knuckle. 'I'm sorry, Mistress McKenzie – it's just –' He swallowed hard. 'I never got over havin' to sell my lambs – they were causin' a nuisance, you see, them bein' like pet dogs and runnin' into folks' houses lookin' for biscuits. Old Behag says she came home one day and there was one o' my sheeps at her fire and sharn all over the floor. The old hag nearly killed my bonny bairn wi' that witch's broom she keeps at her fireplace – ach – they were the nicest lambs you ever saw and these is the same, two bonny wee lambs.'

Kirsteen thought it was a beautiful comparison and she was minded afresh that there was more to Dodie than met the eye. He had a compassionate love for all of God's creatures and would literally never harm even a fly. He was a figure that invoked pity, yet his artless beliefs and philosophies lifted him high above the more sophisticated and materially well off.

'I'll be goin', then.' He shuffled to the door, nervously playing with a loose button on his coat.

'Wait a minute and I'll sew that on,' Kirsteen offered and he submitted to her swift repair work with surprisingly little objection.

'I like it fine here,' he enthused, gazing fondly round the homely kitchen. 'I never feel like bein' myself in other folks' houses but here it's different. I mind Mirabelle aye made me welcome though I never right understood what way she needed to cut an onion and place it beside my chair for I was never one for the smell of them – they make my eyes cry.'

Kirsteen hid a smile. Fergus had told her of Mirabelle's method of drowning out Dodie's offensive smell, her belief being that to cut an onion was to kill unpleasant odours as well as all 'living germs'.

'There.' Kirsteen gave the button a pat. 'That should keep for a while.' She went to the larder where she stuffed scones and cake into a bag. 'Here, take these for your tea,' she said, pushing the bag at him. She reached up to the mantelshelf. 'This, too. Merry Mary didn't have Fergus's favourite brand and he put it up there and forgot about it.'

'But – it's – baccy,' Dodie protested even while his eyes shone, for he liked nothing better than a good chew at 'thick black off the roll'.

'It is that,' Kirsteen agreed. 'Put it in your pocket.'

'Ach, it's kind you are just.'

'No more than yourself. These bonny spoons will be treasured always. By the way, it's Christmas soon. If you stop by you will get some turkey and plum pudding and there might just be a wee gift on the tree with your name on it.' On impulse she reached up and kissed his nut-brown cheek, vowing to herself that warm woolly gloves and socks would be waiting for him on Christmas day. His face immediately blazed a brilliant red and he turned away so quickly he tripped over the doorstep. Picking himself up, he galloped away up the glen in a daze of breathless joy.

Chapter Three

A week later Fergus left for his trip to Oban. During that time he had collected all the clothing coupons he could find. His own supply was barely depleted because he seldom had reason to buy new clothes. Many of the older men were delighted to sell him their coupons including Dodie who was overjoyed and somewhat bemused that the scraps of paper he had always regarded as useless could actually fetch him money.

'Ach, McKenzie will have cheated that poor simple cratur',' Behag Beag, the fault-finding postmistress of Portcull, stated sourly. 'Fancy having the cheek to offer money for things as scarce as clothing coupons. It's like this black market I am hearing goes on over yonder on the mainland. It's only villains do things like these.'

'McKenzie of the Glen is not a man to cheat anybody!' Kate McKinnon stoutly rose to Fergus's defence. 'Especially would he never cheat Dodie out o' a farthin'! He's kind to old Dodie – no' like some I could mention.' Kate leaned across the counter and gave Behag a conspiratorial wink. 'Am I no' after hearin' that you sold your own coupons to my Nancy and the poor soul payin' more than they were worth

– and her wi' all these bairns to clothe – ay.' Kate shook her head sorrowfully while Behag's wizened jowls fell in dismayed layers over her neck for she had sworn Nancy to secrecy.

'There's some would do anythin' for sillar,' Kate went on, thoroughly revelling in Behag's discomfiture, 'but my, you had better no' be throwin' your coupons about too much, Behag, or you'll end up with no' even a decent pair o' breeks to cover the cheeks o' your bum – now o' course that might have been all right in your younger days when you were maybe tryin' to tempt a man up your skirts but the only thing you'll get up there now is a chill in the bladder that will keep you runnin' to your wee hoosie for weeks!'

Kate went off, skirling with laughter, leaving Behag to fume and vow that one day she would report the McKinnons to the Customs mannie and rid the island once and for all of a sinful and illegal product. But Behag knew that her vow was just a shallow one and she prayed to the Lord to forgive her for being too weak to face up to the certain wrath of the islanders if she dared to expose the McKinnons, for they were a family beloved by many. Forbye that, she was not averse to a drop of McKinnon's brew herself, entirely for medicinal purposes, of course. The preservation of a person's bodily functions could in no way be construed as a sin and after Kate's triumphant exit Behag flounced to the back shop where she took a good swallock of the malt to help her get rid of the lump of rage that had risen in her throat.

'I'll only be away for a night or two,' Fergus told Kirsteen. She was going through a spell of depression and was inclined to be unusually irritable. He nuzzled her ear, feeling the softness of her breasts against his hard chest. He had been gentle with her since the babies' birth, contenting himself with just kissing and holding her though his desire for her was so strong he wanted to crush her to him and take her without constraint.

'Why do you have to be away at all?' she whispered sulkily, drawing away from him and lowering her face so that it was veiled by the shadows of early morning.

'Because I want to buy you something special for Christmas – I've never given you a proper present, so just for once let me do this.'

'But you won't be able to get anything! It's wartime – remember?' she told him rather resentfully, thinking of months of watered-down tea, of scrimping to save a little out of each week's rations so that they could all enjoy a real feast at Christmas.

'I'll get something,' he said with a conviction he was far from feeling. 'Don't you worry about a thing. Shona and Niall will be here within the next day or two and Matthew will see to things around the farm.'

'Oh – to hell with the farm,' she cried, throwing her head back in a fit of pique, an action that curved her neck into a slender arch. Her blue eyes were rather dull and weary-looking, for her days were filled from morning to night with the constant demands of two infants and a lively son. Phebie was a wonderful source of help but there were the nights of broken sleep to contend with and Fergus felt a pang of guilt.

'We're going to get someone in to help you here,' he said firmly. 'When I get back I'll see to it, and I don't want any of your refusals. Nancy's eldest daughter, Janet, is a good sensible girl and she's grand with bairns.'

'Yes,' Kirsteen said dully.

Fergus's black eyes snapped. 'Och to hell! I won't go and leave you like this! Dammit! You know how I've always hated leaving home even for a few days. It was for you! Just for you! I only want to make you happy.'

'Oh, Fergus, I'm sorry,' she said with a rush of remorse. 'I'm being childish and bad-tempered. Lachlan says it can happen like this but I don't like myself very much at the moment. When you come back I'll be a ray of sunshine, I promise.'

She straightened his jacket and pushed him towards the door, which she opened decisively. The morning was dark with pearly mist hanging over the fields and clinging to the hills. The chill breath of winter rushed into the warm kitchen. Putting her arms up she drew his head down and kissed him so deeply his heart quickened.

'Little seductress,' he murmured. 'If you want to stop me going that's the surest way. Why couldn't you have done that last night?'

'Too soon, my darling, but you wait, I'll give you

a Christmas present that won't cost anything but that you will never forget.'

'Promises, promises,' he chuckled, his breath condensing in the frosty air. 'I'll keep you to them but right now I must go if I'm to catch that boat.'

'Fergus.' He was halfway down the path when her voice stayed him. 'We haven't given our sons names yet. I want them to be special and I want them to come from you.'

Many hours later Fergus arrived at Oban. The mist hung in a purple pall over the fishing port, huddling the town into a clammy blanket. Ghost shapes of trees probed the dour sky and spread winter tracery over the wet slates of rooftops. In the bay the needles of masts pierced into the haar; pinpricks of guide lights shivered over the grey water, ending the subdued dance on the glistening cobblestones by the harbour. The remoteness of the night made him hurry through the near-deserted streets towards the small homely hotel run by Maggie and Murdy Travers. They had befriended him when he had come to Oban seven years before in a fruitless search for Kirsteen.

Maggie welcomed him with delight and led him into the cosy parlour where Murdy was snoring in the depths of an armchair with his feet atop the range. At their entry he opened an enquiring eye then rose with agility to pump Fergus's hand heartily. After that, it was like old times, with Maggie plying him with platefuls of food while she reminisced about the time of his exhaustive search for Kirsteen and his eventual travels to England to find both her and his little son.

'Ay, and now you have two more,' Murdy said, gazing thoughtfully into his whisky glass and gave a dignified hiccup. 'I tell you this now, lad, never show you have a favourite. My mother favoured my elder brother more than me and never took pains to hide the fact. To this day I have never got over the hurt of that. Maggie and me only had our lassie, so we had no problems there. It's easy to spoil a lassie and you can get away with doin' it to that bonny wee girl of yours – but treat the lads the same, son, and remember – the heart that hurts most least often shows it.' It was an unusually serious speech for the jovial Murdy. He hiccuped again and grinned. 'By God, I'm on my soap box tonight, I must be soberin' up – where's that whisky? . . .' He struggled out of his chair and Maggie rushed to hold him upright. 'You auld bodach,' she giggled. 'Drunk as a lord and sayin' things you'll regret come mornin' – but mercy on us! It is mornin', nearly one o'clock. Up to bed wi' you this very minute and if you think I'm goin' to help you off wi' your clothes you've another think comin' for I doubt it will take me all my time to get myself under the covers.'

Though he was fatigued Fergus slept only fitfully and wakened as dawn was creeping coldly over the sky. It was the habit of years that made him get up and dress quickly. The room was chilly but he was used to that at Laigmhor. There was no sound of life in the house and he guessed the Travers must still be asleep. Noiselessly he crept downstairs and let himself outside. The wind had freshened during the night and swept the mist away, leaving the morning bright and bitterly cold. He turned his steps in the direction of McCaig's Folly, which reared up against a turquoise sky washed over with gold. As he climbed the steep deserted hill, the Folly became more than just a giant landmark: the great circle of weathered stone loomed above him, powerful in all its Colosseum-like splendour. The deepening gold of the dawn filtered through its double row of tall windows and he couldn't help thinking that the building was like some great Roman temple lit from within by thousands of candles. With the slow measured tread of the Hebridean he walked across the unroofed inner gallery. Scrambling up to one of the window apertures he perched himself on the grey stonework and gazed out over the shimmering landscape. Today the horizon was cloudless, the rich hues of sunrise diffusing into a brilliant blue that deepened to purple in the dome of the heavens where stars still sparkled faintly. His gaze travelled downwards to the dream-like splendour of the Mull hills whose corries were erased by distance, though a faint glimmer of snow was discernible on the high sullen peak of Ben More. For a long time he looked at the hazed island of Mull, thinking how much it resembled Rhanna, though on a much grander scale.

He felt contented and very peaceful and had to

force his mind back to the reason he had come to this high place of solitude. Kirsteen had told him to think of names for their sons – and he had never been over-imaginative about things like that. It was easy enough to make up names for horses and cows – but boys! He smiled at his thoughts and watched as the sun rose higher to inject the water with shades of blue and silver. The nearer islands lay in shadows of damson and jade, though the long tawny shape of Kerrera was touched by fingers of golden light, which were reflected in the deep dark water of the Firth of Lorn. Lorn. Lorn! Fergus sat up straighter. Blue and languorous. That was how the Firth of Lorn looked this morning. The twins had the bluest eyes he had ever seen. Kirsteen said their eyes would change, grow dark like his, but he was convinced they would stay like hers.

'Lorn.' He murmured the name softly. One of his sons would be Lorn – and the other – he suddenly thought of Lewis. Shona and Niall had spent their honeymoon in Stornoway on the island of Lewis. Lachlan had relatives there . . . 'Lorn and Lewis.' He spoke the names aloud and they echoed round the cloisters of the Folly like a melody. 'Lorn and Lewis!' he cried again and gave a deep chuckle of satisfied laughter. Wait till he told Kirsteen. He wanted to go home right away but there were other matters to settle first.

Maggie came with him to help him with his shopping. 'You have no need to be buying toys now,' she told him as she pulled on her gloves. 'I doubt you would get them anyway but I have been busy this whily. I've made things for you all and look – come over here,' she said, and opened a drawer in the sideboard and proudly withdrew an exquisitely carved model of a fishing boat. 'For that wee rascal Grant,' she said, beaming. 'My Murdy made it. He's no' as green as he's cabbage lookin'. Took him months to do, mind, but och, he knows fine the wee laddie is mad on boats and will take care of it.'

Maggie had been right about the shortage of goods in the shops and here he was looking for fur jackets for Kirsteen and Shona. 'Fur jackets!' Maggie shook her head doubtfully. 'You will be lucky if you manage to find a fur purse! But wait you, I know the very place! Not much to look at mind but the wee mannie there has stuff in that shop you would never credit.'

The shop was situated in a back street and its appearance was so dilapidated it was hard to imagine that it was occupied at all. But the 'wee mannie' was there all right, shuffling from the back shop in answer to the rusty tinkle of the bell above the door. The interior of the shop was dismal and matched well the proprietor's gloomy expression and his greeting of, 'A bitter day is it not? I canny get my blood goin' in the right direction in weather like this.'

Fergus swallowed and wondered why on earth Maggie had dragged him here but his heart lifted somewhat when, having voiced his request, the little man's eyes lit with interest, though he hummed and hawed so much Maggie burst out, 'Ach, stop fooling around, Mr McDuff, you know fine what the laddie means. Have you got what he is wanting or haven't you?'

'Fur jackets,' Mr McDuff said thoughtfully. 'These are no' easy to come by, no' easy at all. Times are hard, hard indeed . . .' He looked over his specs at Fergus. 'You will need plenty money and plenty coupons.'

'I've got enough of both.' Fergus placed the coupons on the counter and taking out his wallet he fingered the contents provocatively.

Mr McDuff tapped the side of his long nose and whispered, 'I might have the very thing, though I wouldny say that to just anybody. Seein' I know Maggie here . . .' He shuffled away into his back shop and several minutes later re-emerged with two beautiful jackets over his arm, one the colour of dark honey, the other a rich grey that glowed silver in the feeble light from the window. 'These are all I have,' Mr McDuff said, laying them on the counter. 'They are not what you would call new, mind, but near as good as. I forgot I had them. There's no' many folks rushin' to buy fur jackets the now.'

Fergus could hardly believe his luck. 'I'll take them,' he said rather breathlessly, seeing in his mind's eye the look on Kirsteen's face when she beheld his gift to her.

'Plenty money, mind,' the old man said, rubbing his hands together gently, a nervous twitch lifting one corner of his mouth as Fergus counted his notes one by one and placed them on the counter.

Mr McDuff's fingers scrunched over the money quickly before he scooped it up and placed it with a show of nonchalance into a drawer. 'I will wrap the jackets up –' He paused. 'I have a nice bitty paper I was savin' for my special customers and by God! You're the most special I've had this year and I'm thinkin' you've maybe made my Christmas too.' Methodically he wrapped and tied the boxes. 'It's no' everybody gets string to put round things these days but I'm thinkin' these jackets must be for two special ladies so I'm makin' an exception in your case.'

'Very special ladies,' Fergus agreed soberly, though the minute he was outside the shop he grabbed Maggie's waist and pulled her to him. 'You're a witch, Maggie Travers! The most magical witch I've ever known I tell you, you beat all of Canty Tam's water witches for tricks and spells. Come on, I've got a few coupons left, your wee mannie was so excited he didn't take them all, and I'm going to get you something really grand for Christmas.'

Maggie giggled and protested but Fergus swept her along. 'Really, laddie,' she told him with a twinkle, 'that old bodach is known as McDuff the Bluff in these parts. He was a furrier before the war and I know fine he still has plenty of furs in that back shop of his even though he told you you got the last two.'

'No matter. I never thought I'd get anything so grand, so you and Murdy are getting presents whether you like it or no.'

The next morning Fergus left for Rhanna on the

mid-morning boat. Murdy and Maggie saw him off, the latter in tears as she pushed parcels into his grasp. 'You come over and visit us whenever you can now,' Fergus told them firmly. 'Let us repay you for all you've done for us. The doors of Laigmhor are always open to you.'

'Ay, we will that,' Maggie sniffed. 'Away you go now and don't forget to give all our friends on Rhanna our love.'

It was very late when the craggy drift of the Rhanna hills at last reared up on the horizon. The sea was like a crumpled piece of ebony paper, a shade darker than the vast reaches of the star-studded sky. The boat pushed its way through the Sound of Rhanna, lifting the waves to foam, cutting steadily along. The water in the harbour was velvet-smooth, the village so silent that the noise of the boat's engines was like a profanity, tearing the peace apart. Ropes were tied, the throbbing of the engines lessened, then ceased. The crew languidly saw the few passengers off. Niall was at the harbour with the pony and trap.

'You shouldn't have bothered,' Fergus protested, though he had been wondering how he was going to carry everything up to Laigmhor.

'Orders,' Niall said grinning, throwing parcels into the back of the trap. 'Shona is at Laigmhor waiting.' He laughed. 'Ay, and a fine time I've had with her all day – like a wee lass she is waiting for Father Christmas to come down the lum. Come on, in you get.'

In the darkness Fergus smiled and listened with pleasure to the slap of the sea beating against the shore. The little white houses of Portcull sat solid and serene against the black slopes of the night hills; scents of salt and peat smoke filled the air. The pony plodded up Glen Fallan and now there were other smells. The men had been spreading dung on the fields. The rich reek of it mingled with the sharp tang of frost. The air was cold against his face. From the hills a stag roared once then was silent. The burns frothed down into the river, shimmering in a glint of moonlight. In the distance he saw Laigmhor, a dim white blob against the slopes of Ben Machrie. Chinks of light shone from the windows and his heart leapt. No matter how short was his separation from his beloved home, he never failed to feel excitement and joy on his return.

They clattered into the cobbled yard and he turned to Niall. 'I'll take my cases in but leave these other things by the back door till I get settled.'

'Right, I'll just get Dusk into the stable and I'll be right with you.'

Fergus stepped over the threshold to see a sparkling-clean kitchen. A peat fire sang in the grate, throwing showers of sparks up the chimney. On the hearthrug, three cats were piled on top of the obliging and good-natured Squint, who appeared to be sound asleep, but at Fergus's entry he got up hastily and a shower of indignant felines landed on the floor. The little dog hurled himself at the dark man standing smiling in the doorway and Fergus threw up his arm to catch the ecstatic, quivering bundle of golden fur. A delicious savoury aroma filled the room. Shona was by the range, lifting a crusty brown steak pie from the oven. Her glorious curtain of auburn hair hid her face but at the opening of the door she pushed it back impatiently from her flushed face. 'Damned hair! I'll get it cut, I swear I will no matter what Niall says —' She stopped short in her tirade and a smile lit her elfin face. 'Father,' she said softly, rather shyly, 'it's so good to see you.' She rushed at him and Squint groaned in protest as the air was squeezed from his tubby little body. One of his floppy ears fell into Fergus's mouth together with a lock of Shona's hair.

'Hey, give me air! he shouted laughingly. 'I'm smothering.'

'Och, be quiet, it's not every day I get to coorie into you,' she scolded, nuzzling her face into his neck.

She was radiant in her youth and beauty. Her hair was silk under his fingers, the vibrant love she had for him pulsed into him and a lump came into his throat. Gently he pushed her away and studied her sparkling face. 'Married life suits you, mo ghaoil, you're bonnier than I've ever seen you.' Over Shona's head his eyes met Kirsteen's. She looked different. The weariness had gone from her eyes; there was an aura of quiet elation about her. And when she caught the message in his glance she blushed and was once again the young girl he had chanced upon in the woods by Loch Tenee where she had been swimming. She had been drying herself when he had come upon her. Shock had turned her into an immobile golden statue with droplets of water gleaming on her smooth skin and wet little tendrils of blonde hair clinging round her pink ears. Vividly he recalled the scene and his legs felt unsteady beneath him.

'Hello, Fergus.' Her voice was soft, her smile secretive, filled with gladness to have him back. 'This child has been spoiling me. I've done nothing since she came. She's fussed over me and coddled me and looked after the twins.'

'Ach, I've enjoyed it,' Shona broke in. 'Though if I have some of my own I think I'll start off with just one. Now, we're all starving to death waiting for you, Father. I want everyone seated at the table in five minutes and that's an order! Wash yourself first, Father, there's hot water in the pan . . .' She giggled and looked from one to the other. 'It's so lovely to be home,' she said, her blue eyes shining with the brilliance of a summer sea. 'I love being married to Niall and I'm very happy – but this . . .' she said, glancing round the room, 'this is where I belong – at Laigmhor – on Rhanna. I miss it so much, but one day we'll come back – though of course we'll have to find another house. It's crowded here, I can hardly believe I've got more brothers, when will it ever stop?' Her eyes travelled to the little golden spaniel draped once more by the fire. 'Dear wee dog,' her voice had grown husky. 'When I first saw him the years just rolled away – I thought Tot had come back, then this wee devil opened his eyes and instead of crying I laughed instead. I love him, he's so silly and playful, the way Tot was when Hamish first gave her to me.'

'You can take him back with you, I took him knowing how much you missed Tot . . .'

She shook her head. 'No, Father, let the babies grow up with a dog of their own. My childhood would have been a less precious memory without dear old Tot – besides, Grant loves Squint already, he says he's going to take him to sea and he'll become an old sea dog.' She choked with laughter. 'Grant puts me in mind of myself when I was his age. Yesterday he dressed that poor wee pup in a scarf and bonnet exactly like old Joe's. When I came in and saw Squint lying at the fire I thought he was a hobgoblin. Then to make matters worse, Grant leapt out at me from the larder and near scared the wits out of me. We had a job getting him off to bed tonight. He was all for staying up till you came home.'

Niall came in, his tanned face glowing from the sting of the night air. He rubbed his hands together and sniffed the savoury fragrances mingling together. 'Mmm, my mouth is watering. I'm starving. Do you know, Fergus, this daft daughter of yours hasn't let me eat a thing since this afternoon. Favouritism that's what it is, pure neglect of her new husband in favour of her father.'

There would have been a time when he would never have uttered such things to dour, unapproachable Fergus, but things were different now. Fergus was different, though he was still, and probably always would be, a man of few words. He had a pride of bearing that many took for arrogance, but he was not nearly as formidable as of yore. He laughed more, and took things less seriously – though he protected those he loved with such fierce passion few dared to rile him openly. It was perhaps because of that, that 'McKenzie of the Glen' as he was now becoming known, was more talked about behind his back than anyone else on the island.

Shona giggled and clouted her husband playfully with the dish towel as he was drawing his chair into the table. After that everyone seemed to talk at once. Shona was immediately busy and so efficient that Fergus watched her in delight. She had always been a mercurial creature, a tomboy who rarely sat still, but now she glowed with an inner radiance, her movements swift and graceful. Marriage to Niall had certainly been her salvation, though Fergus knew that this daughter of his would never know complete contentment until circumstances allowed her to come back to live on the place she had loved since her first stirrings of awareness to the beauty and enchantment of her island home.

Proudly she set food on the table and smiled at Fergus. 'You see, Father, I've learned to cook now that I'm a sedate married woman.' She dimpled mischievously. 'No more awful dumplings or burnt porridge – well just sometimes. For did not Mirabelle say herself more than once that "no' a body in the whole wide world is perfect, even those that put themselves on a pedestal so that they can spit and

605

do other nasty things on the lowly and imperfect".'

Fergus's deep laugh boomed out. 'A sedate married woman uttering profanities that would make Mirabelle turn in her grave . . . If I mind right she was quite prim and proper in her way!'

'Ach, she was right enough, but if things riled her enough she could come out with some surprising observations. She used to mutter a lot under her breath when she was harassed, and once, when she thought I was too young to understand, I heard her saying, "Ach, that Behag, she has a face on her like a threepenny bit in a cow's backside waiting for change."'

Everyone shrieked with laughter and the meal was a merry one with Fergus and Kirsteen giving the two young folk all the latest gossip and news about the island. When the table was being cleared Fergus went to the door and brought in his parcels, though he was careful to leave the huge bouquet of red roses he had brought for Kirsteen by the lobby door.

'Peenies off,' he ordered. 'I've got something for everybody to be opened on Christmas morning, but these,' he said, indicating the biggest packages, 'are for now, for the two women in my life. I hope to God you like them. I'm not very good at choosing things for females, but Maggie helped me. Anyway, see what you think.'

Kirsteen and Shona were like children in their eagerness to discover what the parcels contained, though they were careful to preserve the precious pieces of paper and string. In awe they stared at the contents of the boxes.

'Well!' Fergus's voice was frayed with anxiety, his cheekbones tinged red with embarrassment.

Kirsteen lifted up the silver-grey fur and looked at it in disbelief. 'Fergus, oh my darling, it's beautiful, the most beautiful jacket I've ever seen. How on earth . . . ?'

'Ask no questions. Presents should be accepted without question . . .' His face relaxed into a smile. 'All I can tell you is that we owe a lot to Maggie Travers not forgetting McDuff the Bluff of Oban.'

'I'll never get a chance to wear it,' Kirsteen said, her voice was low, 'but I shall treasure it always. Thank you, oh thank you, my dearest.' She kissed him on the cheek. Her lips were warm and he could sense the depth of her emotions.

Shona had said nothing, she just stood staring at the gift, stroking the soft honey-coloured fur with trembling fingers, her blue eyes swimming with tears. 'I don't know what to say,' she whispered shakily. 'Oh, I do know!' Impatiently she brushed her eyes. 'But I can't get my tongue to make the words come out properly!'

Niall put his arm round her slim waist and pulled her against him. 'You'll look so grand in that you'll be ashamed to walk down Sauchiehall Street beside your poor tattered husband.' He grinned at Fergus. 'And I thought I was doing well getting a rabbit's paw to put in the nylon stockings I managed to get her. Ach well, she can always put it in the pocket of her jacket – it will bring her luck.'

Later, when Niall and Shona were busy at the sink washing up, Fergus went to get the roses, and then, taking Kirsteen by the hand, he led her into the parlour where he made her sit down. Tentatively he presented the bouquet to her. She saw the discomfiture in the big ruggedly handsome Gael and her eyes filled with merriment, which made his own flash in chagrin.

'Oh don't,' she laughed. 'You looked so handsome holding them. You suit red roses, my darling. You should carry them more often.'

'Even when I'm mucking out the byre?' he hissed, and they both burst out laughing, though his eyes devoured the sight of her so vibrantly lovely in a blue wool dress, her corn-coloured curls clinging round her head, fine little tendrils crisping round the delicate shells of her ears. Her smooth skin was flushed, her eyes were very blue and she looked ten years younger than her thirty-five. They were acutely aware of each other. She put out a slender hand to him and his big work-hardened one closed over hers so tightly she gasped. 'I've missed you so,' she told him rather breathlessly. 'And yet – I don't know what to say to you.'

He fell on his knees beside her and enclosed her in his embrace, his lips caressing her hair. 'Then don't say anything,' he breathed. 'Just listen to me. I can't remember when I've felt so happy. You have given me two fine new sons, but most of all you have given me your love and that means everything to me. It's going to be a wonderful Christmas. I'm going to hold you and kiss you and love you. I want you all the time and never more than at this minute. You look like a wee lassie sitting there, your skin all pink and your nose like a shiny button off a Sunday dress.'

She lowered her head quickly to hide the tears that had sprung to her eyes. His two nights away from her had seemed like years and her heart beat swiftly at his nearness. She took his face in her hands and gazed deep into his eyes. 'I am going to be very wanton and let you do anything you want with me – and I'm so much in love with you I almost forgot to ask – names – did you think of names for the twins?'

'Ay, I did that. I couldn't sleep my first night with the Travers and I got up at dawn to walk up to the Folly. The view gave me inspiration and I thought of Lorn and Lewis.'

She stared at him, and he reddened. 'You don't like them,' he accused.

With a gentle finger she traced the curve of his rebellious mouth. 'Fergus, my Fergus, they're beautiful – perfect. Lorn and Lewis, they're poetical. There's more to my strong farmer than meets the eye. You have a romantic centre under that tough shell you show the world.'

'Och, get along with you,' he said uncomfortably, and she smiled and took his hand.

'Come on, let's go up and christen the babies. The poor wee souls are just numbers at the moment.'

He looked into the kitchen to bid goodnight to Niall and Shona and was astounded to see that the room was filled with rainbow-coloured soap bubbles. Squint was sitting entranced, one eye roving towards the ceiling, the other fixed on a large bubble that had landed on the tip of his nose. He snapped and the bubble burst, the look of comical surprise on his face sending Niall and Shona into shrieks of laughter. Fergus, too, laughed – though he asked rather sourly, 'Am I to believe there is a sudden glut of soap? According to Merry Mary it's more scarce than gold at the moment.'

Shona wiped her eyes. 'Ach, don't worry, Father. I gathered all the bits and pieces I had and made them into liquid soap. I brought a few jars with me, so we're having a bubble party.'

'Well, see and don't flood the place,' he warned, eyeing Squint who was joyfully skating about on the wet floor. 'We're having an early night, so see you two behave yourselves.'

'We'll get along over to Slochmhor the minute we're finished here,' said a rather flushed Niall, and Fergus nodded and went on upstairs.

Kirsteen had gone on ahead. The nursery was hushed and peaceful. The babies had cried a good deal that day but now, though awake, they were quiet, their huge blue eyes gazing in wonder at the dancing shadows on the ceiling. Kirsteen buried her face in the roses Fergus had brought her. They were exquisite, but not nearly as precious to her as the two rosebuds he had given her on the morning of the

babies' birth. She went to the dresser and softly
pulled out the drawer where lay the family Bible. It
opened at the book of Job in the Old Testament
where the pressed rosebuds nuzzled the yellowed
pages. Reverently she touched the roses, which
though faded still retained a whisper of colour.

'Lorn and Lewis,' she murmured. She held the lamp
higher and a sentence on the page seemed to leap
out at her. 'Though thy beginning was small, yet thy
latter day should greatly increase.' She mouthed the
words to herself then said aloud to the silent room,
'And so be it.'

'Talking to yourself – or to them?' Fergus came in
and stood gazing down at the babies. 'They're
awake, yet they're not crying,' he said in wonder.
'Have you bewitched them, little witch?' He put his
arm out to her and drew her in close to him. 'Which
will be which?'

The youngest baby had a tiny dimple on his chin,
a replica of his father's. 'This shall be Lorn,' she said
softly. 'He will grow up to be strong like you, strong
and self-willed, stubborn and wonderful. Oh, I know
Lachlan is worried for him just now but it won't always
be so.' She picked the child up and propped his
downy head under her chin, very aware of his frailty.
His heart fluttered swiftly against the softness of her
breasts but she vowed silently never to let him be
aware that his was a lesser strength than his brother's.

Fergus scooped the other baby into the crook of
his strong right arm, and in a mood of abandonment,
danced with him round the room. 'Lewis!' he cried

joyfully. 'Lewis Fraser McKenzie! How's that for a grand title, eh, my bonny wee man?'

Kirsteen watched him and felt that all the joy on earth belonged to them in those wonderful moments. Fergus's shadow pranced on the ceiling and she felt such an unbearable love for him rising in her breast she wanted to sing aloud in her happiness, knowing she would remember him like that, dancing with his son in his embrace, for the rest of her life. 'And I have here his bonny lordship, Lorn Lachlan McKenzie!' she said, her breath catching with the pain and passion of her emotions. 'Lachlan has a few namesakes on the island but none will bring him greater credit than this precious infant.'

Fergus caught her by the waist and they danced together, their laughter ringing out, the babies in their arms gurgling in keeping with their parents' mood.

Downstairs Niall grinned. 'Would you listen to them up there? Like a herd of elephants. If that's what babies do to people we must have what these two have.'

'Not twins!' Shona said, shocked.

'No, babies will do,' he yelled gleefully, and, pulling her to him, he kissed her deeply. She lay against him, cherishing the warm nearness of him. 'Babies can bring pain too,' she said eventually, and rather sadly. 'I didn't bring Father much joy when I came into the world, but things came all right for us in the end because ours was a mental rather than a physical battle. It won't be so for Morag Ruadh. I feel sorry for her, but more for the bairnie – so bonny but for her poor wee leg. Other folk would just accept it as a natural thing, but Morag will see it as a damnation brought about by her throwing away all her saintly scruples and giving herself up to the lusts of the flesh. I know fine what I'm talking about, for the besom said the self-same things about me when I lost our wee boy and me with no wedding ring on my finger.'

Niall stroked her hair. 'Hush now, my babby, these things are in the past now but I can well believe that Caillich Ruadh made your life a hell at the time. I can't feel sorry for her, all my sympathies are with the bairnie and poor old Doug. Mark my words, she will become a religious fanatic after this, and she'll drag Doug down with her. His life will be hardly worth living, though the bairn might bring him some comfort – even though it might not be his.'

Even Niall couldn't know how apt his words were to be. At that very moment at Dunbeag House, Portvoynachan, Morag Ruadh held to her breast the little daughter to whom she had given birth a few days before. Moaning and crying in a paroxysm of remorse and shame, she rocked the baby back and forth, back and forth, then she laid it down and for the hundredth time since its birth, she clasped her long supple fingers to her lips as if in prayer. The child was beautiful, perfect, so perfect – except . . . Morag lifted up the skirt of the baby's flannelette gown, and through a watery blur she gazed in disbelief at the skinny little legs; one completely normal,

613

the other as twisted and shrivelled as a piece of unravelled yarn. Morag's thoughts travelled back to the night of the manse ceilidh held by the Rev. John Gray for the Germans who had arrived so unexpectedly on Rhanna. For the first time in her life, saintly Morag had thrown caution to the winds and had seduced two Commando guards in the minister's fuel shed. Later, Dugald had also succumbed to her wild abandonment, and when she had discovered she was pregnant he had married her without question. But Morag didn't know who the father of her child was; all she knew in those dreadful despair-filled hours after her daughter's birth, was remorse so deep and tortuous she fully believed the child's deformity was a punishment sent to torment her for the rest of her days.

She held the infant high above her head and cried aloud in her grief, 'I did this to you, my babby, but I will make it up to you. From this day forth you are a daughter of God! As long as there is breath in my body no man will tarnish your purity! As sure as God is my Judge!' The hair of the child was golden. Morag stroked it with reverent fingers, tears flowing from her eyes. 'My bonny one, so bonny. Your name shall be Ruth. When words come to your lips you will say unto me, "Whither thou goest, I will go and thy God will be my God and nothing but death will part thee and me". Don't cry, my little one, no evil will ever befall you as long as I'm here to look to you. You will be a servant of God and the angels and I was aye a body who kept my word.' She muffled her sobs into the soft folds of the baby's neck. Dugald came into the room with a tray. Already he adored his tiny daughter. To him she was perfect and to him that was all that mattered.

Morag looked at her husband. His mop of silvery hair shone, his honest grey eyes regarded her with steady affection. She didn't love him; she never had. Oh, he was a good man and she was fond of him, but she had only married him to give the child a name. She would be a good wife to him, she would cook, clean, sew – but never again would she share the marriage bed with him and in sacrificing her lustful and ungodly urges she would perhaps allay in some small measure the dreadful sins that lay in her mind like festering sores.

But it wasn't due to sin that out of four babies born on Rhanna in the December of 1941 three of them had congenital defects. Lachlan suspected something other than coincidence when three days before Christmas in a cottage at Portcull he delivered Kate McKinnon's daughter, Annie, of a healthy eight-pound baby girl who, though rosy and sound of wind and limb, made not the slightest whimper in her entry into the world. Annie was Kate's youngest daughter and there were some who had said she should never have married Dokie Joe, a cousin twice removed. The child was their firstborn and Annie was thrilled at first sight of the chubby pink bundle, but her joy turned to dismay when several hours elapsed and no sound escaped the baby's rosy lips. 'She doesny cry, Doctor,' Annie told Lachlan in a frightened voice. 'She is bewitched an' no mistake. There are some who would think it a mercy to have a bairnie who doesny greet, but I'm thinkin' it's no' natural – I'm thinkin' that my bonny wee Rachel has maybe been struck dumb. These folks were maybe right when they said that Dokie an' me shouldny have wed. Even Mither said that close blood doesny make for wise bairns.'

But Lachlan dismissed this. If Annie and Dokie had been first cousins, there might have been something in what she said, though Rhanna was full of close blood marriages and one had yet to produce a defective child.

'It's early yet, give her time,' he advised gently.

'But she's struck dumb, I'm tellin' you, Doctor.'

He uttered words of comfort, though in his heart he knew that Annie had stumbled onto the truth. Lachlan thought about little Lorn with his weak heart and frail body, he thought of baby Ruth, beautiful but for her pathetic twisted leg, and he looked now at Rachel and knew that it wasn't just chance that had brought about such tragic malfunctions. Desperately he sought the answers from his personal store of medical knowledge, from medical textbooks, but at that time there were none. He didn't know the reason, and the knowledge of that brought him sleepless nights and frustrating days, for he was a man dedicated to his profession. In time, the answers would come, but not then, in the winter of 1941, when two sons and two daughters of Rhanna emerged from their mothers' wombs to breathe the sweet air of hill and sea; suckled at their mothers' breasts, fought their separate battles for survival in those first tender stirrings of life, in their dreamings and their awakenings as yet unaware that the delicate threads of their lives were even then being woven into a pattern binding them together in a tapestry already planned by fate.

Part Two

Spring 1950

Chapter Four

The last nine years had brought some changes to Portcull, the greatest being the conversion of the largest house, which was next door to the Smiddy, into an hotel. This innovation pleased all the menfolk, delighted Todd, but disgusted Mollie, who claimed the establishment not only brought the Smiddy down, but encouraged drunkenness.

Bed and breakfast signs had sprung up outside croft houses all over the island, many of which greatly puzzled and misled the tourists. One at Nigg grandly proclaimed 'Bed and Breakfast with all conveniences', the conveniences being the dry lavatory situated in the bushes at the back of the house and the rickety bus that shook and rattled its way over cliff roads only suitable for horse-drawn traffic. Another sign at Portcull laboriously extolled 'Mrs McKinnon invites you to bed'. Here Tam had run out of space and in tiny letters at the bottom had added, 'and breakfast with home-made mealy pudding and home-cured bacon.' Outside old Joe's cottage a large white notice screamed in red letters: 'Fresh lobsters and crabs for sail. If owner out, take crabs from coal bucket – carefully, they nip – leave money in tin marked nails.' Elspeth Morrison, though turning up her sharp nose at what she called money grubbing, nevertheless placed a minute notice on her gate, which read 'Eggs laid while U wait – duck, hen, goose – take your pick – hard boiled for picnics in peat creel'.

At the bottom of the hill road to Nigg was the most mystifying and tantalising notice of all. At Ranald's urging, Dodie had finally capitulated to the 'towrist boom', and Tam, who spoke English but thought in Gaelic with its grammatical charm, painted a sign that even he could hardly understand when it was finished. 'Is a head two miles,' the sign read, 'German swastika genuine – old relic from world war two. A hundred thousand welcomes all.'

Tourists had been baffled to follow the trail only to find an embarrassed Dodie working in his fort-ressed garden. Tempers had flared at the idea of him being the ancient relic they had laboured over hilly moor to find, but when it was discovered that the roof of his wee hoosie was indeed formed from the tail-piece of the Heinkel bomber that had crash-landed on the island, dismay turned to amazement and cameras soon began clicking. News of Dodie's swastika soon spread, and regular visitors to the island brought friends to look. Over heather hillocks they scrambled to get a better view, and the tin that Dodie had hitherto placed too discreetly on a window sill was now painted pink with a bold sign on it saying, 'Donations here, no buttons thank you. He breeah.'

Ranald had suggested to Dodie that he open up

his wee hoosie and charge folk to have a look inside, for here the old eccentric had brought bits and pieces from the bomber and had arranged them till the inside of the dark little hut resembled the cockpit of a plane.

'It would be to their advantage,' Ranald earnestly told Dodie. 'These folks is sometimes burstin' for a pee, and them bein' townpeople they're no' likely to go behind a bush like us. Charge them for the use o' your wee hoosie, and while they're in there havin' a pee they could put a collection into a tin for bein' allowed the privilege o' playin' wi' that control column thing and lookin' at all these instruments on the back o' the door – I tell you if it was me I wouldny hesitate,' Ranald finished rather enviously.

But Dodie drew the line at this. For one thing he couldn't imagine the sophisticated tourists clapping their hands with glee at the idea of using his large chamber pot, the only 'convenience' he had in the wee hoosie. For another thing, he was a creature who liked his privacy and wasn't entirely happy at the invasion of that peaceful spot drowsing amidst the heather. The task of clearing up picnic litter fell to him, and though not fussy about personal hygiene, he couldn't bear to see his environment violated.

All over the island a variety of home-made jams and heather honey was temptingly displayed to catch the visitors' eyes, and always there was the battered old money tin which so endearingly betrayed the trusting Hebridean nature that only the guilt-ridden few did not leave their coppers.

Because it was the Easter holidays the children, barefoot and free from the rigours of the classroom, went about their various tasks and pleasures without hurry yet with an intentness that ensured they made the most of every precious minute. In the yard at Laigmhor Lewis took his brother's hand and they ran to the big barn, which was cool and dim, full of slanting sunbeams and ancient cobwebs. Here were the growing posts, two massive uprights, fashioned from tree trunks. A jumble of dates and niches had been etched into them, an untidy scrawl of red paint on each spelling out the names Lorn and Lewis. The growing posts had been Lewis's idea, conceived at the tender age of five when he had just learned to write. 'One day you'll be as big as me,' he had earnestly told his brother. 'Every month we'll measure ourselves just to see how fast we're growing.'

Lorn had eagerly accepted the idea. His greatest ambition in life was to be as tall as his brother because the first five years of his existence had thwarted all attempts of his to be 'normal'. Childhood ailments that only temporarily affected Lewis had left his brother ill for weeks. One crisis had followed another, and Lorn's infant years had been severely restricted. Wullie the Carpenter had fashioned a little cart for him and he rode about in this, pulled by a tiny Shetland pony, all over the island roads. Wherever Lewis went, his brother went alongside in his miniature trap. When Lewis followed his father out to the fields, Lorn went too, sitting astride Fergus's strong shoulders, loving the feel of the wind in his face, the smells of the earth, the reassuring hardness of his father's body. Grant, too, carried him about in this fashion, striding with him down to the harbour to watch the boats, holding him in the water to teach him to swim. Fergus didn't know about that, or he would most certainly have forbidden his eldest son ever to take Lorn out again. Lewis and Grant between them let their brother do a lot of things that might otherwise have been forbidden because they sensed that their father was afraid for his youngest son and this had perhaps made him over-protective, a point brought home to him one day by Lachlan.

'You must let him do more, Fergus,' the doctor had advised quietly. 'If you don't, he'll be an invalid for the rest of his days.'

'I think I know what's best for my son!' Fergus had snapped defensively.

'And I think I know better,' Lachlan had said gravely. 'Be careful with him, yes, but for God's sake, man, don't pamper him; he won't thank you in later years.'

Fergus had said nothing more, but, as always, he took Lachlan's advice, with the result that Lorn now ran free beside his brother, and though his heart was still weak and he wasn't physically robust, his fierce fighting spirit continually urged him on.

Lewis, tall and straight for nine years, grabbed his brother and pushed him against a growing post where after a few seconds of silent concentration he made a new notch on the hard wood. 'Half an inch taller than three months ago,' he reported earnestly.

The look on Lorn's face was worth the lie. 'I knew I was growing, I could *feel* myself getting bigger – now, it's your turn.'

Lewis stood to attention beside his post, his broad shoulders straight, and Lorn stood on tip-toe to make a mark above his brother's curly head. 'Half an inch – we've both grown the same amount – you're still three inches taller than me, but I'll catch up with you all right.'

''Course you will,' Lewis said off-handedly. 'Now stop blethering and let's go. Old Conker will be fed up waiting for us but I'm going to get us a scone an' jam first – I'm starving.'

He dashed over the yard to the kitchen, leaving Lorn standing stroking the silken nose of Conker, a magnificent Clydesdale with not a grain of temperament in his sweet and placid nature.

Children adored Conker, whose time was divided between working in the fields beside Maple, his stablemate, and acting as companion to all the children who came and went from Laigmhor. Fergus now had a tractor and several other pieces of farm equipment, which made the hard business of farming a whole lot easier, but many of the older farmhands scorned the new-fangled stuff and adhered to the old ways, particularly Jock and Murdy who claimed that nothing but a Clydesdale could plough a true furrow. Likewise, the twins cared nothing for machinery. They were as much at home on the backs of horses as they were on the ground. Under Jock's guidance, Lewis was able already to handle a plough. Lorn could only stand by and watch, but Lewis swore to him that as soon as he was old enough to handle a plough on his own he would teach Lorn everything he knew. With the clearsightedness of youth, Lewis knew of the unspoken dreams in his brother's heart, and though Fergus trusted him to look after Lorn, Lewis did so up to a point but was determined that he wouldn't turn him into a cissy. With this in mind, he let his brother fight his own battles at school, and even though Lorn invariably emerged from them pale, shaken, and breathless, he was able to hold up his head with pride and in time he had shaken off the nickname, Tumshy, that had been bestowed on him when he had started school as a skinny little six-year-old.

Biddy was coming along the glen road, riding a bicycle she had acquired from the SS *Politician* back in the fateful year of 1941. Her green cape flapped behind her in the wind; her skinny black-clad legs ground the pedals round with jubilant energy; the hair that escaped her felt hat was now snowy white; her lined old face was serene even though she had left her 'teeths' steeping in a glass by her bedside. She was still the same teasing, grumbling, fun-loving Biddy, but age had cloaked her with a look of venerable dignity and everyone honoured her convictions. The medical authorities had officially retired her but she would have none of that. 'Damt officials!' she had snorted indignantly. 'They think they can just sign a bitty paper and put folks out to grass – well they can just bugger themselves! No one but God will ever stop me workin' and only then when He has a mind to take me.' So she still carried on with the work that was her life and no one dared to sway her from her path. Indeed, they were delighted at her decision: to them she was 'auld Biddy', a part of Rhanna, as much a feature of any sickroom as the very walls themselves.

'Hello, Biddy,' Lorn called, knowing that her almost-blind old eyes would never see him. She raised a hand to wave and had such a frantic struggle to regain her balance she wobbled the rest of the way down the glen.

Fergus came striding down from the fields and Lorn ran to him. 'We're going to meet the boat, Father, we're going on Conker.'

Fergus smiled at his son. 'Ay, there will be quite a crowd coming off. We'll be having a few visitors ourselves over the next week or so, plenty of folks to keep us busy. It's well seeing Easter is here.' He took Lorn in his strong right arm and swung him onto conker's broad bare back. Lorn wriggled and protested, 'I can manage up myself, Father, I'm not a baby.'

Fergus laughed, his black eyes crinkling in his weatherbeaten face, 'Ay, and you're not a man either.'

'But you never help Lewis the way you help me,' the little boy persisted, his blue eyes darkening with chagrin even while he remembered those early days sitting on his father's shoulders, the good solid feel of power beneath him making him feel safe, safe and wanted. These were times to be cherished in his heart for ever, but now he was feeling more and more that he had to make a stand for himself, to prove to his father that one day he would be strong enough to make a farmer.

Fergus ruffled his son's earth-brown curls and without answering went over to meet Lewis, who was emerging from the kitchen.

'See and be back in time for dinner,' Kirsteen's voice floated from within.

'Ay, Mother, don't worry.'

'You watch your brother now,' Fergus warned. 'Don't let him do anything daft, and see and help him on and off Conker.'

Lewis smiled up at the big man looming above him. 'Ach, Father, of course I will.' He grasped the hard brown hand briefly then raced over the yard and took a flying leap onto Conker's back. The horse was used to such wild behaviour, and with a flick of his ears he began to amble out of the yard.

Lewis had a love of life that bubbled out of eyes vibrantly alive with excitement and laughter – except when he went into one of his rare tempers. Then they grew black and crackled like a thunderstorm in full fury over lowering hills. He sat on Conker and ran an impatient hand through his tangle of curls, which, like Lorn's, gleamed chestnut in the sun. 'Ach, c'mon with you, Conker, get along now,' he urged the horse. 'Auld Todd's new limousine is coming on the boat and everybody's going to see it. Move your backside or I'll give you a good hiding!'

It was an idle threat. Both boys adored the animals of the farm as much as the soil itself.

'Born farmers,' Kirsteen told them with pride, though her heart cried out for her youngest son with the love of the land ingrained in him and the wistful, stubborn tilt of his chin trying so hard to show everyone he didn't care that he couldn't do the things he longed to do. And all the time she knew how much his bruised young heart hurt him. He held onto his brother's waist, delighting in the feel of Conker's strength under him. He was a slightly built child, full of a temperament that could raise him to the heights or plunge him to the very depths of despair. Dour and sullen with all but those he loved, he was not as popular as Lewis whose buoyant charm won many hearts. Physically, Lewis was his father's image, but it was a skin-deep resemblance. Lorn was the one who had inherited Fergus's mental and emotional make-up, and because of it his path through life was as rough as his brother's was smooth.

'Fancy auld Todd winning a limousine,' Lorn said, his voice full of awe for the news that had taken everyone's breath away. Todd openly scorned the 'rubbishy wimmen's papers' that his wife avidly devoured, but in the blissful privacy of his wee hoosie he secretly enjoyed many of the juicier items and he had tried a very tempting competition, never dreaming that he of all people would win the first prize of a silver limousine. Of course, the news had had to come out along with the fact that he was, in the words of the villagers, 'an auld pretender and a hypocrite just'. But in the excitement of the moment all the talk had gone over Todd's head as he and Mollie impatiently awaited their big moment. Now it was here. An important personage escorted by reporters from various newspapers was arriving with the car to ceremoniously hand over the keys. The whole of Portcull, together with spectators from other villages, would be at the harbour, trying to appear very nonchalant and not in the least interested in one of the greatest events to come to the island for many a long day.

'What will he do with it?' Lorn wondered. 'He canny drive a car, only horses.'

Lewis brushed the flies off Conker's mane and laughed. 'Him and Mollie will treat it like a baby. They'll clean it and pamper it and likely sit outside the Smiddy all day just admiring it.'

In the distance the Sound of Rhanna shimmered like a blue satin ribbon. As they reached the bridge by Murdy's house they could see a black knot of people gathered at the harbour. The boat would take some time to unload passengers and small pieces of cargo before dealing with the more ungainly items, but even so Lewis wriggled with impatience and tapped his heels on Conker's sides.

In the grassy yard of Annie McKinnon's house, two little girls sat on the old swing, locked into a small world of their own. 'I have some grand news for you, Rachel,' Ruth Donaldson said rapturously. 'You know Merry Mary's retiring soon – well my father is going to take over the shop so we're moving here – to Portcull, to a house near my grandparents . . .' Ruth paused for a moment, remembering the look on the faces of Jim Jim and Isabel McDonald on hearing the news. They had been astonished and apprehensive, certainly anything but pleased when their daughter, Morag Ruadh, told them, 'You are both getting a mite too auld to be managin' on your own, so I will be on hand to look to you. The Lord knows it will no' be easy but I was never a one to shirk my duties and the more sacrifices we make in this life, the more we will be rewarded in the next.'

Jim Jim's pink pleasant face had taken on an agitated frown at her words, and in the trauma of the moment he had made a faultlessly aimed spit into the peats burning in the grate, much to Morag's disapproval. Isabel had said not a word. For almost ten years now, since Morag's marriage to Dugald, she and her husband had led a life of unparalleled peace; but now the bliss was about to be shattered, things would be worse than they had ever been because of their daughter's fanatical devotion to the church.

'I'll get back my old job as church organist,' Morag had told them with prim happiness, 'Totie was never much good at it and was more than pleased when I told her I was coming back. We are all going to be very happy together, wait you and see. Oh ay, family worship will just be like it was in the old days when I was here to keep an eye on you.'

Rachel absorbed her friend's news thoughtfully and showed her approval by making the swing go higher. The breeze ruffled her dark curls and she reached out a rapturous hand as if to touch the blue sky. The clip clop of hooves on the stony road made them both look up.

'Look, Rachel, there's Lorn and Lewis,' Ruth said, pointing excitedly, the violet of her eyes darkening and her solemn little face lighting up. 'They're going to Portcull. I'll have to go too. Mam will be out looking for me if I'm not down the road for dinner time.'

Rachel pushed her silken black hair back from her face and her brown eyes flashed. She was a stunningly beautiful child, tall and slim, brown as a gypsy, wild as the wind that blew down from the mountains, as mercurial as the sea that lapped the Rhanna shores. Strangers couldn't help staring at her nor could they resist speaking to her, but when she stared back wordlessly they took her silence for insolence, and told each other she was nothing but an impudent urchin.

Some of the older islanders said she was possessed of 'the power' and could take things away from folk just by willing it. She had taken Squint away from Lorn and Lewis. Some years ago he had simply deserted them in favour of her. All attempts to win him back had failed. He adored the little girl. Without uttering a single word she could make him do her will by a few simple gestures. He flopped beside her now with lolling tongue, his alert brown eyes gazing up at her, ready to obey the commands of her expressive hands.

Rachel knew that the only reason Ruth was allowed to play with her was because she could not communicate orally, and though she might hear evil she certainly could not speak it. Her assumption was unerringly correct. In committing herself to a sinless life, Morag Ruadh had sentenced her daughter to a rigorous existence bound by endless religious rules that, if broken, not only brought hell down on the head of the sinner, but misery to the entire household. 'You mustny mix with blasphemers,' she warned Ruth repeatedly. 'Folks these days is corrupt and take a delight in corrupting others. Oh ay, I know fine they talk abut me behind my back, but I am strong in the Lord, therefore I shall not falter.' Thus it was that when she came to visit her aged parents in Portcull she allowed Ruth to go and play with Rachel. 'But mind her now,' she never failed to warn. 'Thon wee lassie might be dumb but I am hearin' she has other powers that are no' natural. That can happen to folks wi' a faculty missing; another can take over and it might no' always be to the good.'

Rachel held Morag in contempt but suffered her because she loved little Ruth with her big languorous violet eyes and golden hair, glorious features in a child otherwise rather plain. Her callipered leg made her walk in an ungainly fashion and her mother dressed her in rough drab homespuns because vanity was sinful – all of which effectively hid the otherwise lithesome grace of the child's small-boned figure.

Ruth saw the expression in Rachel's eyes and she took her hand. 'Och, Rachel, c'mon now, you mustny be angry. Is it no' good news I am after tellin' you? When I come to live in Portcull we'll play together all the time and go to school together. But look you, come with me to the village now. The twins will give us a ride on Conker. We'll go and ask your mother. Quick now, I hear tell Todd the Shod is getting his new motor car today and if I give Mam the slip for a wee while I might see it arriving on the harbour.'

Annie nodded her acquiescence at the request. She was bathing the youngest of her three sons in the kitchen sink and was much too harassed to bother where Rachel went or what she did. She and Dokie Joe loved the little girl after a fashion, but had long ago given up trying to understand her, for she was clever to a degree that left them feeling bewildered and inadequate. Her gift for music made them proud, and they were able to boast that she had inherited it from her great-grandfather, whose violin, in its red velvet case, had been merely a toy for countless other McKinnon children. But to Rachel, finding it one day at the back of a cupboard, it was a dream come true. She had plucked fiddle strings since the age of four.

Old Andrew had recognized her talent and had taken her in hand, and now she could extract from her great-grandfather's scratched old fiddle tunes that amazed everyone who heard them. In music Rachel found expression for all her unspoken thoughts and fears, hopes and dreams.

635

Annie wiped her soapy hands on her apron and, reaching for the biscuit tin, gave each of the children a biscuit. Rachel held up two fingers and Annie said in exasperation, 'Two more! Is it made of money I am? Doesn't your poor father have to work his fingers to the bone out on that cold raw sea and sometimes no' enough fish to fill a sardine tin . . .' Through the window she saw Conker plodding up the road and her face broke into a smile. She pushed two more biscuits into Rachel's waiting hand. 'At least you're no' a selfish wee lassie. Away wi' you now before Dave catches his death in the sink. Mind now, Ruth, get along to your grandparents' double quick, for I won't be havin' that saintly mother of yours sayin' my lassie leads you astray.'

Rachel pushed half her biscuit into Squint's ready jaws and hurried with Ruth out onto the sunlit road. Boldly she stood in Conker's path and when the horse stopped she grabbed Squint, and without preliminary hoisted him up to Lorn, who took him without question. The boys had long ago forgiven him for his desertion. There was a wealth of animals at Laigmhor and they much preferred working dogs to any other.

'We're going to watch Todd's car coming off the boat,' volunteered Ruth while Rachel grabbed her to give her a leg up.

The boys regarded her steadily. She wasn't as well known to them as Rachel, but like everyone else they felt sympathy for her in the restricted life she led. Unlike Rachel, she was shy and awkward; she lisped and blushed easily and was self-conscious about her limp, she also wasn't easy to talk to. Lorn sensed in her the same feelings of inadequacy that were in him and he was, at nine years old, unable to help anyone else to cope with similar feelings. But Lewis had no such complications to hamper his spirit and he gave Ruth a friendly grin.

'Your mother will be keeping a lookout for you,' he predicted, 'so just you keep with us and she might not see you in the crowd.' She blushed crimson and stirred up in him a memory of Dugald standing red-faced and silent in the kitchen at Dunbeag while his wife lectured him for 'idling away the Lord's time in useless pursuits', these being an innocent visit to Portvoynachan harbour at sunrise to watch the fishing smacks coming in, and a quiet sojourn over the moors with jotters and pencils in the hope that the solitude would give him the inspiration he needed to write his beloved poetry.

Ruth didn't answer. She was having difficulty mounting Conker and Lewis was about to scramble down to help her when he spotted a figure proceeding up the glen. Though it was some distance away the children knew it was either a tinker or a tourist because of the forward-leaning gait, which suggested the burden of a rucksack or a poc, the name for a tinker's sack of wares.

'If it's Stink the Tink I mustny speak to him,' Ruth said nervously. 'Last time I did Mam made me stay in my room the whole of the Sabbath to learn by heart three of the Psalms.'

'Ach, it won't be a tink at all,' Lorn said. 'Most of them will be down at the harbour or up by Dunuaigh, and Stink was round the doors yesterday selling colanders so it won't be him back again.'

The figure came closer and proved to be a bearded young hiker dressed in shorts and thick wool stockings draped over stout walking boots. 'Good day to you,' he nodded pleasantly, his accent suggesting he was a foreigner who had picked up English well. Wriggling the pack from his back he laid it on the grassy bank and flopped down beside it.

'Good day, sir,' the children chorused in polite unison, though Lorn eyed the stranger with reserve, and Rachel, hands folded behind her back, stared at him openly. The young man stared back, unable for a moment to tear his gaze away from the untamed gypsy-like beauty of the golden-skinned child with her unruly black curls and unwavering brown eyes.

'I wonder if you could help me,' the young man said, drawing a map from his pocket and studying it intently. He was thin and boyish, his dark-rimmed glasses giving him a studious appearance. 'I am looking for a place called Croft na Ard. It isn't marked on this map and everyone at the harbour seemed so excited about something I couldn't quite understand the directions they gave.'

'Ach, they speak in Gaelic when they get het up,' Lewis said, grinning. 'Has the cargo been unloaded yet?' he added anxiously.

'No, there was bother with one of the Highland beasts, which caught its horns in the rails. There's quite a commotion down there at the moment and everything has been held up.'

'Good.' Lewis climbed down off Conker and went to look at the map, though there was no need as he knew fine where Croft na Ard was situated. But he loved people and enjoyed finding out about them. Lorn hid a smile as he watched his brother studying the map, tracing fields and roads with a grubby finger, which stopped suddenly. 'There it is, Anton Büttger's place. He came back here after the war and married Babbie, our district nurse. We have two nurses; the other is auld Biddy. She's past eighty but still sprachles about, delivering babies and drinking whisky.'

'Biddy.' The young man's eyes grew dreamy. He gazed round him, at the hills and the drowsing moors, and retreated into a trance. 'Ah, I remember Biddy all right and I'm so glad she's still alive. I've dreamed of this island for years and vowed I would come back one day. How is Mr and Mrs Gray and Tam McKinnon and that wonderful old man who played the fiddle like a dream – Andrcw, his name was Andrew?'

'Old Andrew's fine, although he's the oldest man here. Old Madam Balfour of Burnbreddie swears the island people live long because they are pickled in drink. Mr and Mrs McKinnon are just grand – especially Tam. This,' Lewis said indicating Rachel, 'is their granddaughter, Rachel. She canny speak but she can hear and is the cleverest girl in the school. She's as tough as any boy and can fight with her fists.

She had to learn to do that because the others used to call her names but don't dare do it now. She's so good at everything she even teaches auld Murdoch, our teacher, how to teach. You don't have to be afraid of her though because she only gives black eyes to people her own size.'

His laughter rang out and the other children relaxed and smiled too. Lewis did that to people; to him strangers were just potential friends and he had the knack of putting them at ease.

The young man smiled at Rachel. 'Tam McKinnon's granddaughter. Tell me, does he still make whisky that slides down the throat like nectar?'

Still wary, Rachel tossed her dark head and her eyes fell on the violin case slung over the stranger's shoulder. Her face immediately lit up, and laying her head to one side, she made an action as if playing the fiddle.

The young man nodded eagerly. 'Yes, it's a fiddle. I carry it with me wherever I go. Do you play?'

Rachel nodded vigorously and Ruth spoke for the first time. 'She could play almost before she could walk. Old Andrew taught her.' Ruth's heart raced at her audacity and trepidation rose in her breast as she wondered what her mother would say if she knew her daughter had been conversing with a strange man.

'Lewis and me play too,' Lorn said, his deep blue eyes holding the young man's gaze. 'We practise with Bob and old Andrew in Ranald's boatshed and sometimes we have our own wee concerts there.'

The stranger's eyes were sparkling behind his glasses. 'That sounds wonderful. Perhaps you will allow me to come and practise with you in Ranald's shed. I am here for two weeks' holiday and would love to get together with people who play the fiddle. After the war I became a music teacher, but always I wanted to come back to Scotland and now I have a post in the high school of Oban.'

Rachel was enraptured. The stranger watched her expressive hands trying to convey her joy and he said casually, 'You do not speak with the language of those who cannot speak? I can teach you if you will let me. When I was in prison camp, there was a boy there so badly injured in the head he was deaf and dumb. He learned the language and taught it to me. Look, Rachel, this means the sun is shining and the day is beautiful.'

He made a few swift gestures with his long nimble fingers and Rachel followed them intently, her fingers fluttering as she copied the signs.

'Good girl, you learn swiftly. You will soon be able to speak without words and you can teach your friends to speak your tongue.'

This delighted the little girl. For the first time she showed her pearly teeth in a radiant smile, and the young man felt sadness in him for the absence of laughter in her, for a joyous sound that would never peal out from her soft child's mouth.

Something that might have been a tear gleamed in Rachel's eyes but she brushed it away. Lewis put an arm round her and gave her an affectionate hug, but he didn't speak. The stranger seemed to have enchanted them all. Then, the hooting of horns from the harbour brought Lewis to his senses. He made to walk away over to Conker but the young man put a hand on his arm. 'Please, I can see you are twin brothers,' he said, looking from one to the other and smiling.

When the twins were apart they were identical to the inexperienced eye; it was only when they were close together that the difference in them became apparent. 'Yes, but I'm the eldest,' Lewis told everyone, not to boast, but in his child's way, trying to save his brother the embarrassment of having to explain why he was so thin and small.

'Where do you live? What are your names?'

Lorn didn't answer, the stranger was being too inquisitive. But Lewis couldn't help saying with pride, 'We are Lorn and Lewis McKenzie. Our father is McKenzie of the Glen.'

'Fergus McKenzie, ah yes, the big proud man with eyes of steel and a heart of gold – he was the one who found me – on the moors. I remember his voice, soft, full of light and shade, like music. I knew he felt he should hate me but couldn't . . .'

The eyes of the young man were far away. The children watched him rather apprehensively, fascinated by him, yet something telling them to tread carefully.

The stranger came back from the past and came forward to gallantly lift Ruth onto Conker's back.

'And you, little golden-haired princess, what is your name?'

'Ruth Donaldson,' murmured the little girl hesitantly. 'My father helps Totie Little in the Post Office at Portvoynachan and my mother is Morag Ruadh. She is a spinner and everyone wants the things she makes.'

'Of course, Morag Ruadh. Does she not also play the piano? I remember the Reverend Gray had a great regard for her music . . .'

'Please, sir,' Lorn broke in rather rudely, 'who are you?'

This was received with a delighted laugh. 'At last you ask! No one at the harbour recognized me – perhaps the beard – I am Jon Jodl. I was one of the Germans who crash-landed on Rhanna almost ten years ago . . .'

'A Jerry!' Lewis exclaimed and pulled Conker's head up so sharply that the horse snickered and drew back. The four children sat on his broad back and stared rudely at the bemused young man.

Lorn's face was white. 'Have you got German measles?' he asked rather breathlessly. 'Have you brought them with you?'

Jon Jodl spread his arms in appeal. 'German measles! No – I don't understand – did I say something wrong?'

Annie came out to her door with a basket of washing under her arm. 'Rachel, you get along,' she called. 'You mustny idle your time away with the towrists. Get along or you can just come right back and do the dishes!'

'He breeah!' A familiar cry rent the air and Dodie came galloping down the hill path from Nigg, temporarily stopping the children in their flight. Now in his late fifties, he had grown more bent with the passing years but otherwise he was the same Dodie, travelling the island in all weathers, accepting the changes that tourism was bringing to Rhanna with a reluctant elation because though suspicious of the foreign invasion, he was not averse to the opportunities it brought to his life. 'I am just going down to the harbour,' he mournfully told the children. 'Torquil Andrew of Ballymhor was after tellin' me that Todd the Shod has a fine new motor car comin' on the boat. He got it in a magazine for nothing.' He pulled up short at sight of Jon, his wellingtons scrunching on the stones.

'Dodie,' Jon said, beaming. In his mind he had pictured many times the folk of Rhanna, their charm and hospitality, the simplicity of their uncluttered lives. To come back and hear all the names he had cherished in his memory was a dream come true.

Dodie rubbed his grizzled chin. 'Ay, that's me right enough, I'm Dodie.'

'Ealasaid – do you still have your Ealasaid?'

Dodie's eyes immediately swam and he gulped. 'My bonny cow died a few years back but I have a calf of hers, her name is Ealasaid too, for they are all alike – all from my first Ealasaid.'

'Rachel!' Annie's voice came again. 'Come you

back this minute and get the dishes done!'

Rachel gave Jon a last lingering look then tapped her heels into Conker's flanks. The horse began to amble away and Dodie was left to gaze at Jon with real liking. Anyone who spoke to him about his cow was worth a few minutes of his time.

Lorn turned. 'Come on, Dodie! He's a Jerry! You'll get the measles!'

The old eccentric immediately took fright, but for different reasons than those of the children. 'A Jerry!' he threw back over his hunched shoulders. 'You've no' come to take the roof off my wee hoosie! You canny do that. The towrists pay to come and look at it!'

'No, Dodie, no!' Jon cried, and in an effort to convey his sincerity he shouted out the only Gaelic word he knew: 'Slainte! Slainte!'

His Gaelic 'health' echoed round the hill corries but except for Annie peeping curiously from her window it fell on deaf ears.

Chapter Five

By the time Conker had plodded on into the harbour, many of the visitors were making their way to the hotel, ably assisted by the children out to make an easy shilling by carrying luggage. The majority of people were watching the unloading of the boat's cargo. Up the shore came Grant, a brawny young man dressed in an old blue jersey. His arm was linked through that of his sister Shona and with them strode Niall holding two-year-old Helen in his arms. The twins scrambled off Conker, shouting for joy and raced forward. It was quite a reunion. Shona and Niall hadn't been expected for some days yet. Lorn buried his face into Shona's hair. She smelt of roses, and the little boy clung unashamedly to her for he loved his big sister with all his heart.

'You've grown, you wee wittrock,' she laughed, holding him at arm's length to look at him.

'Have I really, Shona? Lewis measured me on the growing post this morning and he says I've got half an inch taller than last time.'

Helen stirred in her father's arms and pointed a chubby finger at old Mo. 'Pwam!' she squealed in delight and they all went over to the crowd gathered by old Mo's pram. The ancient tinker was sitting up, a whisky bottle next to him, a bow in one hand, a beautiful violin in the other. From it he was extracting haunting melodies that soared above the general hubbub to merge with the soft wind hushing over hill and moor. Jon Jodl stopped on the road above to listen in wonder and Rachel saw him standing there looking rather lonely. On impulse she scrambled away from the crowd and raised her hand to him. He glanced down and saw her and waved back. 'I'll see you later, Rachel,' he called, though he knew she couldn't hear him. Shouldering his ruck-sack once more he plodded up the road to Croft na Ard, which lay south about a mile and a half from Portcull. Rachel went back to join the throng. The visitors were entranced by the old Irishman's playing, but none more than Rachel, who shut her eyes and concentrated on the ethereal strains. She loved and admired old Mo with all her heart and quite often she took her own old fiddle over to Dunuaigh to join the tinkers in their camp-fire gatherings.

'Delightful!' Rachel's reverie was broken by a high gushing voice. Coppers were raining into old Mo's pram as his long fingers, so out of keeping with the rest of his tough appearance, skilfully guided the bow over the strings, bringing to a finale the tear-jerking *Dark Lochnagar*.

'What's the old boy's name?' asked one man of a squinty-nosed youth.

'Mo.'

'Mo? – how strange. What does it mean?'

'Moses.'

'Moses? But surely not! How did he come by it?'

'Ah well, that is indeed a fine mystery, sir. We found him floating in the sea in a big wicker basket and we gave him the name of Moses. He knows not where he came from or where he's been, and might be a leprechaun for all we are knowing – but there you are, sir, strange things happen in Ireland that can't be explained away. We took old Mo into our family and will look after him till the angels think it's time he should be joining them.'

'But surely a leprechaun is a sort of Irish fairy?'

'Indeed that is right, me fine sir. You are lookin' at an old man who might have come from the land of the little folk itself.'

The glib-tongued young Irishman kept a straight face throughout this monologue. The tourist eyed him suspiciously then shifted his gaze to old Mo's battered countenance. 'Fairy indeed!' he said contemptuously and stalked away without putting a penny into the pram.

'Is he not a mean sod now, Grandfather?' The young man grinned at the leprechaun and began to count the takings.

Rachel clapped her hands in delight as old Mo took up his fiddle once more but his efforts were lost in the ripple of awed comments that heralded the appearance of Todd's car dangling from the wire hawsers of the ship's crane.

'Would you look at that now, Mollie,' whispered Todd in hushed tones, his mouth hanging open in his benign craggy face. 'Is she no' a beauty just? I never pictured the like.'

Mollie was momentarily speechless. It had never occurred to her that the motor car would be anything as grand as this. Rhanna boasted quite a few powered machines of one sort or another, but mostly they were dirty temperamental affairs that banged and rattled their way round the island roads. Everyone was speechless at sight of the sleek gleaming machine dangling against the blue sky.

Tam McKinnon was first to find his voice. 'By God, it's beautiful just! A body could live in a motor car like that. It's near as big as my house!'

'Ach, you'll be sellin' it,' the money-conscious Ranald told Todd. 'What good is a car like that to a cratur' who knows more about servicin' horses?'

'No, indeed I will never sell her,' Todd said with reverence. 'She is so beautiful she is like a – like a . . .' He fumbled for words to describe the car.

Old Joe, now ninety, his snow-white hair frisking out from his peaked cap, his sea-green eyes as serene as the sheltered waters of Loch Tenee, murmured gently, 'Like a mermaid, all shiny and silvery and as slender as a birch tree with a shape to her that makes you want to touch her.'

'You romantic old sea dog!' said Fiona McLachlan who was standing nearby. A slender, bright-eyed seventeen-year-old, her bobbed hair shining in the sun, she was now at university studying marine biology, but had arrived home for Easter two days before. She took the old man's arm and snuggled against him, remembering how as a child she had listened enthralled to his wondrous tales of the sea.

He squeezed her hand, smiling at sight of her fresh youthfulness. 'You're growing more bonny each time you come home, lassie. How many young men have you got dangling on the end of a fish hook?'

'None,' she stated emphatically. 'Well, none that matter anyway. I'm a career girl, Joe. Boys can be a nuisance and I'm not taking any of them seriously.'

The photographers and newspaper reporters were following the progress of the car from crane to terra firma. The hubbub rose to a crescendo mingling with the screams of the gulls and the strains of old Mo's fiddle. Fisherwives leaned ample arms from windows and watched the proceedings in comfort. Fishing boats began tooting their horns as two very distinguished-looking gentlemen joined the throng. It was difficult to make sense of the jumble of faces, but Grant had just spotted Fiona and he came pushing towards her.

At sixteen he had the face of a boy and the build of a twenty-year-old, with muscles that rippled from battling against the seas, for he had joined the fishing smacks at fourteen. His smooth skin was tanned by salt and wind; with his dimpled chin and black curls he was a young Fergus all over again. Often he was away from home for days at a time, and there was already about him a toughness that came from combat with the sea and from mixing with hardened sailors. A boy became a man quickly under those circumstances. He had just arrived home after a sojourn at sea and it was his first sight of Fiona for many months.

'Well, well, if it isn't cheeky wee Robin herself!' was his rather cutting greeting. 'Are you going to spend your holidays hunting for frogs and poking about in the water for things that normal folks canny see unless they are wearing microscopes instead of specs – or are you going to behave like a normal girl and be seen at a dance or two . . . wearing a dress?' he finished, eyeing the slacks that had sent shock waves of disapproval through the community of womenfolk when first they had sighted them as she came off the boat.

'Fiona McLachlan – wearing the trowser!' they had told one another in round-eyed dismay. 'Whatever next? That lassie! She was aye a wild one – peety her poor parents – they have a handful there.'

Fiona tossed her head and looked down her pert little nose. Every time she saw Grant McKenzie he seemed to grow bigger, broader, more handsome, more impertinent. From infancy they had bickered with each other, indulging in splendid verbal battles that made Phebie squirm and wonder if her daughter would ever become a lady – especially now she was 'wearing the trowser'.

'Ach, hold your tongue, lad!' spat old Joe. 'Is that any way to treat a lass with her feets no' long on the island!'

But Fiona was more than a match for Grant. He might tower above her but the look of dislike she threw him made him visibly shrink. 'As if you could tell a dress from a sack, Dimples McKenzie – or would know what to do with a girl if she was hanging naked in front of your nose! You should be in the pram with old Mo there! That's the right place for big babies who sook the bottle still – only now it's whisky instead of milk.'

Grant reddened, but hid his chagrin in a shout of derisive laughter. 'I wouldn't like you hanging naked in front of *my* nose! I doubt there would be anything to tell me you're a girl.'

'You McKenzies are all the same,' Fiona said, her voice cold, 'self-centred, hard, selfish – you should all go and live with Elspeth – you'd make a fine team.'

'Even Shona?' taunted Grant. 'You should go and tell her that – she's standing over there with Niall.'

Fiona walked away, very dignified, her eyes shiny. Disapproval flitted over old Joe's face as he looked at Grant. 'You shouldny be so hasty wi' that tongue o' yours, you young bugger. Fiona is too fine a young lady for you to be saying the things you do to her. The sea is making you hard already.'

'It never did you any harm,' answered Grant, sulky and abashed. 'And Fiona was never a young lady – she was always more like a boy than a girl.'

'Then you must be needin' specs! Stop gabblin' now and look at that old show-off Todd, gettin' his photos taken inside the motor car as if he was the lord o' the manor – ready to drive the damt thing away and him no' even knowin' where the petrol goes.'

Fiona ran towards Niall and Shona, the joy back in

653

her eyes. 'Niall! Shona!' she yelled, and threw herself at them in delight.

'I never thought I'd see the day you would look so elegant,' Shona said, smiling in welcome. 'And wearing trousers too. The cailleachs' tongues will have had a field day.'

'Red-hot!' giggled Fiona. 'You ought to wear them, give the old hags something to fuel their fires.'

'Where did you spring from?' laughed Niall. 'I didn't see a thing of you till this moment.'

'I was in the crowd. How did you come? I didn't see you getting off the boat.'

'We came with Grant in the *Magpie*. He was tied up at Campbeltown and the chance was too good to miss. It was a smelly journey but this wee devil loved it – the smellier the better,' Niall said, lifting his daughter up to the sky. She chuckled with glee, a rosy-cheeked bundle with deep brown eyes and fair hair touched with red.

Niall and Shona were now living in the Mull of Kintyre, a handy gateway for the islands. Until recently Niall had been assistant vet to his toothy senior, Mr Frank Finley, nicknamed 'Fang' by the mischievous Shona, but he had just been made a partner in the firm, and Fiona hugged him when she heard the news.

The ceremony of handing over the keys was over and Todd and Mollie now posed beside their bene-factors, both in and out of the car. Their daughter, Mairi, together with her husband, Wullie McKinnon, was being asked to pose too.

'Any more relatives?' asked a beaky-nosed photographer rather sarcastically, and was immediately swamped by a deluge of the McKinnon clan. Tam and Kate rushed forward pulling with them numerous grandchildren. Reporters were jotting furiously, losing track of all the McKinnons who swarmed round them.

'Get a hold of that little gypsy girl and stick her on the bonnet!' cried one ambitious photographer, but Rachel was having none of it. She backed away and at a safe distance stretched her lips into a hideous grimace.

'Little brat!' cursed the photographer while the delighted crowd clapped and cheered. The scene was becoming shambolic. The reporters had spotted old Mo and they surrounded him, cameras clicking, tongues wagging, as old Mo lay blissfully in his pram swigging at his whisky. One of the tinker women rattled her stack of colanders amidst the reigning chaos, and then Dodie came into the scene, his fascination of the flashing cameras getting the better of his shyness.

'What's these?' he asked. 'They're no' like the ones the towrists use to take pictures of my wee hoosie.'

'Get that old boy!' yelled an excited voice and a flashbulb popped in Dodie's amazed countenance. The tinker woman rattled her colanders again and Dodie leaned over old Mo's pram to touch the shiny objects with joy. 'These is lovely just,' his broken teeth flashed. 'What are they?'

'A new kind of po!' shrieked the incorrigible Kate

joyfully, but Dodie took her seriously.

'Ach, they'd be no use at all.' He shook his head and his carbuncle wobbled. 'Everything would go straight through.'

Kate was bent double in a spasm of mirth but she managed to gasp, 'Ay, you couldny trap even a fart in a colander, Dodie.'

'Priceless, priceless,' mouthed one reporter, scribbling furiously. Todd, feeling neglected and outdone, had climbed onto the bonnet of his new car, and with arms folded stiffly over his chest, one leg crossed over the other, he shouted, 'Right, lads, here is the man himself, the fastest driver on the island. I tell you, I was driving cars afore any o' you cut your milk teeths! Am I no' worth a pop o' these flashes in your wee boxes?'

'The lying old cheat!' Grant gasped, laughing so much Lorn almost fell off his shoulders. 'If you asked him where to put the key he would stick it in a horse's backside!'

Portcull had never seen the likes of such a day. The noisy squabbling of the gulls along the harbour walls was lost in the din; the children danced about, making faces at the cameras, their peals of mirth ringing out.

Ruth had laughed till she was sore. She had forgotten everything but the complete and glorious joy of the moment. To laugh like that, with such careless abandon, was a new and totally wonderful experience for her. It was good to laugh; it was life; joyous, bursting, bubbling life. She wanted to know more of it, to become familiar with it, to feel that laughter was right and good and not sinful.

Ever since she could remember Ruth had felt as if she had been in mourning over something she didn't understand. The only times she came near to feeling like today were when she was with her father on his tramps over moor and shore. She loved him, the feel of her hand in his, his arms lifting her over rough or difficult ground, the gentleness of his fine ascetic face, the goodness burning in his grey eyes like the steady flame of a candle. His poems were beautiful, his stories, when he took her on his knee by the fire, so filled with sensitivity that often she cried quietly, the tears marking a slow course down her cheeks. She sensed the sadness in him, the loneliness brought about by visions lost, hopes long faded of a man who had dreamed of becoming a writer but hadn't. She knew that he was unhappy but that in some way she brought him joy because his eyes glowed when she came home from school. He was the only reason she liked going home. It wasn't a happy place. Other houses rang with laughter, with nagging and bickerings. There were no rows in her house, it was too quiet, too clean, too orderly. The atmosphere was oppressive, as if all the life the house had ever known was held down by an invisible force that had robbed it of light, shade, tears, joy, all the things that went on in normal homes. Her red-haired, quick-tongued mother did all the talking, she nagged, scolded, but in a strange quiet flat voice, as if she was afraid that someone, other than the occupants of the house, was listening. Once Ruth saw her on her knees in the bedroom, praying passionately, calling on God to cleanse her soul, to forgive her sins, vowing over and over to recompense for all the evil things she had done. She did all the things that other mothers did, like cooking, cleaning, sewing and weaving, often well into the small hours of morning, but she did it all mechanically. She didn't gossip like other women, yet with a mere tightening of her lips and a toss of her red head, she could say more than all the gossipmongers put together. She tended her husband and daughter devotedly, saw to their every need, yet somehow she couldn't give them the thing they needed most – her love. Occasionally she took Ruth to her bosom and stroked her hair, her long nimble fingers playing with the silken curls while she said over and over, 'My babby, my babby,' but the gesture, the words, conveyed no love, only a fearful sort of apology to someone unseen and Ruth always felt uneasy and knew there was something strange about her mother.

But these things were far from her mind that day at Portcull harbour and Lorn, sitting on Grant's strong shoulders, felt an echo of her emotions touching a chord in his heart. Without knowing why, his eyes sought out Ruth, standing with her golden head thrown back, her usually solemn little face transformed into beauty by the light of sparkling happiness. She looked round and caught him watching her and the violet of her eyes darkened to purple, the dimpled smile remained fixed on her face for an eternal moment. Then the familiar flush spread over her cheeks and her features composed themselves into wistful solemnity.

Lorn wanted suddenly to go over to her and take her hand. She looked guilty, as if to laugh was wrong. He felt compassion turning to anger, at Ruth, at her mother, at the strangeness of life. He didn't know why, but he was overwhelmed by the feeling and his heart pounded, the way it always did when strong emotions swamped him. He wanted to touch Ruth with some of his own joy, share some of the love he knew in his own life. His mother was so different from Ruth's. She was beautiful, but not in an obvious way. Hers was a subtle beauty, natural and sweet: she loved without fussing, more with her deeds than with her hands. She conveyed her love through her eyes so that there was no embarrassment, just a warm glow brought about by knowing how much she cared. From his elevated position on top of Grant's shoulders Lorn spotted Morag Ruadh emerging from her parents' house and watched her walk swiftly along. Lorn opened his mouth to give Ruth a warning but Morag had easily spied her daughter's bright head.

'Ruth!' she called imperiously. 'Come you up here this minute.' Ruth limped away up the shore, feeling that every eye was on her, when in fact the engrossed crowd hardly took notice of her, only those up by the bridge hearing Morag's voice and seeing the anger burning her cheeks to red.

Rachel took Ruth's hand in passing and both

children gazed at each other in understanding before Morag's arm shot out to pull Ruth away from the harbour. At a safe distance she whirled the child round so abruptly she stumbled and almost fell. 'So – this is how you spend your time,' Morag gritted, her lips a tight pale line in her ruddy face. 'The de'il is in you and no mistake. Have you been mixing with those tinkers again?'

'Ay, Mam,' Ruth whispered, her own face flaming to crimson.

'I thought as much! Well, I tell you now, my girl, it will be the last time. It's that Rachel! Leading you astray. It won't happen again – oh no – you've defied me once too often.' Her blazing eyes fell upon Rachel, who had come further along the shore. She stood, straight and tall against the backdrop of the sea, arms folded behind her back, her dark, turbulent eyes boldly staring at Morag.

'Ay, she's a queer one all right,' Morag said, her voice strangely breathless. 'She gives me the creeps just to look at her. She is wild that one – like – like as if she had sprung from the very well o' tinker blood. Knowing that Annie I wouldny be surprised . . .' Her voice tailed off and she seemed to jerk herself back to reality, if such a state existed in her narrow, religion-bound mind. 'You will never play with her again, Ruth, do you hear?'

Ruth slowly raised her golden head to look up into her mother's strange glittering eyes. The coldness in them made her draw in her breath, and she was unable to answer. Morag shook her. 'Do you hear me, girl?'

Rebellion, strong, deep, overpowering, flooded Ruth's gentle soul. To give up Rachel was more than a punishment, it was a shattering of the only happy companionship in her life other than her father's. Her mother's punishments seldom took physical form, always they were designed to test heart and soul to the limit of endurance. Ruth bit her lip. She couldn't promise to relinquish the warm, stimulating friendship of fearless, exciting, untamed Rachel.

'Defiance, eh?' Morag's face was pale now, her voice low and flat yet charged with seething rage.

'No, Mam,' Ruth cried. 'It wasn't Rachel, it was me. I wanted to come down to the harbour! I asked Rachel to come!'

'A fine story, lies above all else!'

'Ask Mrs McKinnon then!' Ruth stormed tearfully. 'I made Rachel go into the house and ask her mother.'

'So, the minute my back is turned you go dancing about after fun. I won't let the de'il take you, my lassie! 'Tis all the more reason you must promise me you won't see Rachel again. If you don't I will be forced to take your jotters and pencils away from you. You idle too much time away with your father, writing down all these foolish notions that are in your head. There will be no more walks with him unless you . . .'

'No, Mam!' It was the protest of a tortured soul. The little girl threw her head back in appeal, her eyes drowning in tears of pain. 'I promise, I promise.'

'As well for everyone's sake, I'm thinkin'.' Morag

felt no triumph, only a flooding of shame at the sight of her daughter's face twisted in agony, but she couldn't relent, to do so was a sign of weakness, the first crack in the shell she had built round herself against softening influences that could so easily penetrate the unwary heart, make a body do things they lived to regret for ever . . . She held Ruth's hand firmly and led her up the path to the house. 'Your grannie has had a bad turn,' she told the child unemotionally. 'It was lucky that auld Biddy was passing, for I could not leave the house and, of course – you never at hand to run and fetch the doctor. Your father was expecting me back for teatime, but I will have to stay here tonight. Folks have a duty to their parents, so they have. Erchy is going over to Portvoynachan with the mail and I want you to go with him. You must make your father's meals like a good lassie. As a penance you will go without your dinner and mustny eat a bite till teatime – also you will go to your room when you have washed the teatime dishes and learn the Commandments till they are burned into your head . . . away you go now – you mustny keep your elders waiting.'

Erchy was leaning against his red post van, avidly devouring the headlines on each bundle of news-papers he had dotted over the bonnet for convenience. He was never in a hurry but Morag gave Ruth an impatient little push. The child hesi-tated, looking through the door of her grandparents' cottage.

'Is – Grannie going to be all right?' she asked fearfully, wanting to run inside and put her arms round old Isabel, whom she adored.

Biddy appeared, her dim eyes kind behind her specs. 'Ay, my wee lamb, she'll be right enough. It's just her heart gave her a fright. Don't you worry your wee head about her.' Biddy knew it was more than likely that a morning of Morag's spicy tongue had caused Isabel to have the shakes, but she held her counsel though the sight of Ruth's white strained face made her fume inwardly at Morag.

'Here,' she said, and fumbled in her pocket. Withdrawing a crumpled paper bag, she offered it to Ruth. 'You take some Imperial mints, they will keep your jaws busy till you get home.'

Ruth felt the waves of disapproval tautening her mother's body. 'No, thank you, Biddy, I'm – I'm not very hungry.'

'Here, what's all this?' Jim Jim appeared beside Biddy and put his hands out to his little granddaughter. 'Come in my wee one and have your dinner before you go home. Your father will keep for a whily and I will not have you going away from *this* house with an empty belly.'

Morag quelled him with a stony stare, but Ruth settled the matter by limping hurriedly to the post van and climbing into the passenger seat.

'My, my, some folks are aye in a hurry,' Erchy said, gathering the bundles of papers and throwing them into the back of the van, covering two hares he had retrieved from his snares earlier. On the journey over the high cliff road he whistled, talked, and offered the little girl chocolate but she refused and didn't respond to any of his banter. He had often told his cronies, 'She's a sad, sad wee lassie that Ruth Donaldson,' but now he glanced at her pale, set, plain little face and sensed something more than sadness. They were hurtling over the firm emerald-green of the links – cunning Erchy avoided the bumpy road whenever he could and knew every diversive route – but soon they were climbing a sandy sheep track and were back on the road again, in time to see Jon Jodl turning up the grass-rutted road to Croft na Ard, The High Croft. Ruth sat up in her seat and gave a shy wave, which made Erchy's eyes gleam with interest. 'Are you knowing the mannie, then?' he asked nonchalantly, the words jolting in his throat as the wheels hit a rock.

'No,' Ruth answered guardedly. 'We met him on the road earlier and Lewis told him the way to Croft na Ard.'

'Oh ay, young Büttger's place, eh? Does the hiker laddie know him then? A fine lad is Anton – for a Jerry – he will likely know lots of folks from way back.'

Ruth was caught off her guard and for the first time a spark of enthusiasm flickered in her eyes. 'You're right enough, Erchy, he is a friend of Mr Büttger's – Jon something or other – a strange name. They fought in the war together and crashed their plane on Rhanna the year I was born.'

'Get away now!' Erchy received the news with

such enthusiasm he almost ran over a group of cud-chewing sheep reclining on the verge. 'Jon – let me think now – a clever-looking wee lad wi' specs? Ay, ay, it's coming back – he was at the Manse ceilidh – oh hell!' Erchy slapped his knee in delight. 'What a night that was, me playin' the pipes and old Andrew the fiddle. This chappie – Jon Yodel – something like that – by God! Was he no' a marvel on the fiddle! Even old Andrew had to admit he was good.'

'He *is* a fiddler! Rachel and him and all the other fiddlers are going to be playing together while he's here.' Ruth's misery was swamped by eagerness. 'He's going to teach Rachel the dumb language.'

'Bugger me!' Erchy slapped his knee again and slid Ruth a sidelong glance. 'Another Jerry, eh? Are you no' feart you'll catch a dose o' the German measles from him?'

Ruth giggled despite herself. 'I don't care! I don't care, Erchy!' she cried, and Erchy, as pleased by her smiles as he was excited by the news, fairly hurtled towards Portvoynachan, hardly able to wait to tell everyone about Jon's arrival.

Jon trudged along, gazing over the lush green pastures to the ocean beyond. The white sands in the bay shelved into the water, turning it to shades of kingfisher-blues and greens, and further out from the shallows purple merged to deepest ultramarine. Several small groups of crofters were down by the shore, filling their carts with banner-like tangles of seaweed brought in by the spring tides. The carts were in the water, the ponies waiting patiently in the splashing waves, while all around them, against the pale gleam of sky and sea, was a bustle of activity as the men and women gathered the harvest of the sea to fertilise the land. A tractor purred busily in a nearby field and Jon wondered if it was Anton who was at the wheel. He was near the farmhouse itself now, a sturdy whitewashed building surrounded by numerous outhouses. Round a corner came a tall, fair, bronzed young man, stripped to the waist, his muscles gleaming with the sweat of his morning's labour. At sight of Jon he stopped abruptly, his keen blue eyes enquiring.

Jon smiled in delight at sight of his former commander but said politely, 'Excuse me – I wonder if I am on the right track. I am looking for a fellow by the name of Anton Büttger. Perhaps you know him or can tell me where I can find him.'

'I am he,' Anton said carefully and with slight suspicion. After more than four years on the island he was as wary of tourists as the islanders themselves. He plunged his arms into the water barrel and threw glistening flurries over his shoulders and face, keeping one eye on the visitor. Jon could contain himself no longer.

'Anton,' he breathed, suppressing his jubilation with difficulty, 'don't you know me? Have I changed so much? Don't you remember poor nervous little Jon Jodl – spewing into a tin while we were up there flying in the clouds?'

'Jon!' Anton came forward a few paces to look in

disbelief at Jon's shining face. 'Good God, Jon!' he cried with a little yelp of laughter. He strode forward and embraced the young man to him and for several moments they laughed and slapped each other and stood back to gaze and smile, and say each other's names over and over.

'Come inside and explain all,' said Anton after a while. 'You can have dinner with us, Babbie will be in shortly.' He led Jon to a side door and they went into a large airy kitchen with a flagged floor scattered with rag rugs, on top of which sat smugly comfortable-looking chintz easy chairs. The deep window recesses gave splendid views over the Sound of Rhanna; on the ledges sat posies of wild primroses; the rich smell of newly turned earth filtered in through the windows, mingling with the delicious fragrance of home-made lentil broth; snowy muslin curtains billowed gently in the breezes; the strains of a Gaelic air wafted up from the bay. A dark-haired young girl was busy at the table but she paused and looked up as the men came in.

'This is Jean,' Anton said. 'She comes up from Portcull every day and keeps the house spic and span for us.'

Jean darted Jon a shy smile but went smartly about her business as the men sat down and became engrossed in newscatching.

'So, you are in Oban now, Jon,' said Anton at last. 'That is wonderful. You can spend all your holidays here – but perhaps I presume too much – perhaps you go back to Germany whenever you can.'

But Jon shook his head. 'Not so often as I used to. You see, my gentle little Papa is dead now and –' he spread his long fingers expressively, 'Mamma gives me no peace: Why did I go away? Why do I stay away? It may be wrong of me, but I cannot stand to be in her shadow. She destroys the character, ruins the personality. She was one of the reasons I left home – the other, well that is easy, since the day I left Rhanna I wanted to come back and make my home in Scotland.'

'You are not married?'

Jon shook his head ruefully and gave a funny laugh. 'No, I think Mamma put me off all that. I've had enough of pushing and bullying to last me a life-time. Of course, not all women are like Mamma,' he hastened to add. 'You were lucky, Anton, you found the girl you love when you dropped in on Rhanna on a flying visit . . .' He laughed. 'But I make silly jokes – tell me about Babbie; it sounds like a fairy story with a very happy ending.'

Anton's blue eyes flashed. 'No endings, only lovely beginnings that are like chapters in a book. We are still getting to know one another though we have been married more than four years now. Ah, Jon, it was a long wait, Babbie here, me in the prison camp – but she waited. The war ended, I came back; all the lust for flying out of me and all the things my father taught me about farming unlocked from my head.'

'Did you marry here?' Jon asked eagerly.

'Where else? I went back to Germany after my

release but I felt only sadness. Babbie and I have no family; all her friends were here, and so now are mine. The Reverend John Gray married us in the church at Portcull – it was a wonderful wedding. Babbie's friend Shona was the matron of honour and McKenzie of the Glen gave Babbie away to me –' he said, his teeth flashing, 'the nicest gift I have ever had. The ceilidh went on for days afterwards, though the first one was at Laigmhor. At first we lived with dear old Biddy in Glen Fallan, but McKenzie of the Glen was all the time putting in good words for me in the ears of the Laird. Old Madam Balfour took a stroke soon after her son came back from the war and now cannot speak a word, or no doubt she would have put her spokes in the wheels. Burnbreddie himself is a good man and did not rebel too much at the idea of a German tenanting one of his farms.' He gazed round fondly at the white-painted walls. 'It was pretty run down when we took over. The two sons were killed in the war, and the old folk had not the heart to go on – we are still building it up, making the fields work again.'

'Burnbreddie is a man who does not hold grudges?' Jon said quietly.

Anton shook his head. 'No, he has the big heart and the hearts of all our friends are even bigger – after all, those boys, and many more, were sons of this island and we . . .'

'No – don't say it.' A flash of the old tension flitted over Jon's face. 'In my dreams I still remember and often I wake up shaking.'

Anton put a brown hand over Jon's. 'You are right, my friend – no sense in raking it up . . . Good God! I still cannot believe you are here! We have so much to talk about – but first you must eat!'

'Are there any little ones yet?' Jon asked with a smile, looking round in a way that suggested he might have missed something.

Anton laughed. 'No, you won't find any lurking in the corners, Jon. We don't have any yet and I am selfish enough to want to keep Babbie to myself for as long as I can. She is dedicated to her job, anyway, and I think she just might grow into another Biddy all over again . . .'

Wheels scrunched outside and Anton's eyes flooded with light. The next minute Babbie came flying in, her freckled skin glowing, her hat slightly awry.

'Liebling,' Anton greeted her, putting an arm round her waist and kissing her with unashamed love. It was then that Jon noticed his friend's right hand, three of the fingers missing, a reminder of the trauma he had endured after his nightmare landing on Rhanna. Jon swallowed but had no time for further thoughts. Anton was drawing Babbie forward. 'Look, liebling, see who we have here – my comrade, Jon Jodl. You remember one another, don't you?'

Jon had encountered Babbie only briefly on the night of the Manse ceilidh, but he had not forgotten the girl with the red curls and the odd, dreaming green eyes. Then he had sensed sadness in her, but there was no trace of that now in the radiant young woman standing before him.

'Jon,' she said, and held out her hand. 'Of course I remember you. You were pale and ill then, but behind that distinguished little beard you glow now with health.' She glanced at the rucksack lying on the floor. 'Where are you camping?'

'Nowhere yet,' laughed Jon. 'I have only just arrived.'

'Then you must stay here of course –' She held up her hand to ward off his protests. 'I insist – besides,' she said, her eyes sparkling mischievously, 'there are ulterior motives. Spring is Anton's busiest time – you will be called upon to work for your keep, young man, and while you're doing it you and Anton can catch up with all the lost years.'

Jon flushed with pleasure and Anton laughed deeply. 'You see, my friend, your papa was not the only one to marry a bossy woman – only one difference – I spank mine when she gets out of hand.'

Jean was hovering, waiting to serve the meal and Babbie pushed the men towards the sink. 'Wash!' she commanded. 'You smell of dung, Anton, and Jon looks nearly as bad as old Dodie.'

Jon paused with the soap in his hands. 'I met him today – in Glen Fallan – I also met some children, two of Mr McKenzie's sons and two little girls, one who was dumb and the other who limped badly.' He frowned. 'I was getting on well with them till they heard I was a German then they just took to their heels and ran, saying something about German measles.'

Babbie and Anton exchanged glances, the former remembering when Lachlan had found out that rubella, or German measles, could cause terrible defects in unborn children. There had been a mild epidemic of measles some weeks after the Germans' departure from Rhanna in the spring of 1941. Kirsteen, Annie, and Morag Ruadh had all succumbed to the rash in the early stages of their pregnancies and with the exception of Lewis, their babies had all been born with congenital defects. The illness had been discovered in Australia in 1940 and had gone under the microscope till eventually news of its effects on the unborn had filtered through to the medical world and Lachlan had had the answer to the thing that had puzzled him for so long. The islanders had soon heard about it, too, and the cry had gone up: 'German measles! The Jerries must have brought it thon time they were here!'

The belief had persisted for quite some time, during which an exasperated Lachlan had tried to reassure everyone that the illness was not specifically carried about by Germans. Gradually the indignation had died down till the whole thing became just a joke. On Anton's return he had been the butt for much teasing and leg-pulling and the islanders had taken an absolute delight in scuffling away to clear a path every time he appeared.

'But the children believe it still,' Jon said after hearing Babbie's explanation. 'They looked positively terrified.'

Babbie smiled. 'Children love to exaggerate, also

672

they love to scare themselves to death. They heard all the gossip in the beginning and are even more reluctant than the old folks to let it rest.' Her eyes fell on Jon's violin case and her smile widened. 'Mark my words, Jon, when next you see them you'll only have to start playing your fiddle to have them dancing behind you as if you were the Pied Piper himself.'

Jon lathered soap over his arms. The sound of the sea, the wind, wafted in through doors and windows. Jean was setting bowls of steaming broth on the table, the sunbeams pranced over the white walls and spilled blood-red over the ruddy flags on the floor. He smiled with quiet joy at the vision Babbie's words presented in his mind. How good, how very good to be back on Rhanna with people he had never forgotten.

Chapter Six

After the twins had made their departure on Conker, Fergus sank down into a chair in the kitchen and closed his eyes with a weary sigh. Janet Taylor, who lived at Croft na Beinn, but who came faithfully every day to Laigmhor as her mother had done before her, was hanging out teatowels in the washing green at the back of the house. She was an efficient worker though rather slow and dreamy and was often side-tracked in the midst of her chores. Now she left the washing to play with a kitten and in the interlude Kirsteen paused by Fergus's chair and stood looking down at him. The collar of his thin shirt lay open, showing where the mahogany brown of his neck merged with the pale smoothness of his shoulders. His firm mouth was relaxed and she longed as always to kiss it and to place her pinky into the deep cleft on his chin. His body was lean and lithe, the muscles in it so hard, not even repose relaxed them. There were more white hairs among the jet black of his curly thatch, but otherwise there was nothing to tell her that more than twenty years had passed since her first meeting with him in the woods by Loch Tenee. Her life with him had been turbulent, beauti-ful; full of problems and of joys; of soaring heights of ecstasy, of plunging depths of despair; but through it all, her love for him had grown and blossomed into a greatness beyond compare. He was often difficult to live with, quick-tongued and dour, but he tempered these things with the magnitude of his deep and abiding love for her. Often he goaded her to fury, but just as often he induced in her laughter, joy, pain, dear and tender adoration. He was the man he had been and always would be and she wouldn't have had him any other way.

Occasionally she invoked stark terror in herself by imagining what her life would be like without him, the kind of nameless fear she had experienced when he had been lost in the sea by the Sgor Creags, but quickly she pushed such thoughts aside and snuggled into the warm nearness of him in bed beside her.

She put out a finger and gently stroked the little white hairs above his ears. 'You're tired, darling, you should learn to ease up a bit.'

A smile curved his mouth but he didn't open his eyes. 'Havers, woman, are you hinting that I'm getting past it?'

She fell on her knees beside him, entwined her arms round his middle and put her head on his lap. 'Past it! After last night? No wonder you're weary, you passionate brute.'

Lazily he drew her up on his knee and cupping her face in his hand he drew her to him and nuzzled her lips with his. 'Mmm, you shouldn't have reminded me – couldn't you send Janet down the road on some pretext? We could always go upstairs and lie down for a wee while – seeing you think I need resting.'

She giggled and lay against him. 'I wouldn't put it past you – but seriously, you do work too hard. Never mind, though; in a few years' time you'll have the twins out in the fields with you. They can hardly wait to grow up and be farmers like their father.'

'Lewis perhaps,' he murmured into her hair, 'though he'll have to sow a few wild oats before he's ready to settle down. He's keen on the land, ay, but he's a restless lad. He canny seem to settle his backside for two minutes at a time.'

'Lorn will keep him steady, see he sows his oats in the right places. They'll both be a credit to you . . .'

'You set too much store on Lorn,' he said rather sharply. 'Don't do it, Kirsteen, you'll only end up getting hurt!'

'And you don't set enough store by him!' she said, equally sharply, pulling away from his enfolding arm to glare at him. 'Don't you know he worships you? Only wants to be like you . . . ?'

'Dammit! These are hardly the qualities that will make a farmer out of a lad like him! Kirsteen, don't let's go over it again! Time will tell but I warn you now, he hasn't the stamina for the land. The guts, ay, but the strength, no.'

Kirsteen's cheeks burned red. It was an argument they had had quite often in the past, but now that Lorn was getting older, more eager to follow the plough, the rows were growing more heated. '*That's* because you coddle him, Fergus. That was all right in the beginning, but not now. Oh, can't you see? He wants to grow, to expand, to have you show him how to do things the way you show Lewis.'

His eyes blazed like coals and he pushed her away. 'Are you asking me to kill my son? Are you, Kirsteen? Because in his condition it wouldny be hard . . .'

'Condition! Condition! You make him sound like a feeble baby! Oh, I know he's not strong, but he tries so hard and you never encourage him . . .'

'Kirsteen,' Fergus said, his voice softer now, 'I don't want to raise false hopes in him. Can't you see? It's because I love him I can't let him get hurt!'

'But he is being hurt,' she said bleakly. 'You hurt him almost every day of his life by refusing to let him do the simplest tasks around the farm – and I don't mean feeding the hens or – or patting butter into rounds . . .'

'You can be very stubborn when you want to be, Kirsteen,' he told her coldly. 'You are splitting hairs, talking about hurt feelings – I am talking about physical hurt. I'm afraid for him. Dammit all! Are you too stupid to see that!'

Her breath caught in her throat and her head went up proudly. '*I* can be stubborn! Well – if that isn't McKenzie cheek, I don't know what is. You're the most stubborn, pig-headed boor of a man anyone could possibly meet! How I've put up with your tempers and your sulks all these years I'll never know – and to think that only a few minutes ago I thought you were the most wonderful man on

earth –' She laughed mirthlessly. 'The most thoughtless would be more apt.'

'And what about you!' he lashed back, his jaw
working furiously. 'The girl of my dreams – my nightmares more like! You never give me a minute's rest;
you demand all the time – even in bed! Nag, nag,
nag. You're getting to be like that auld yowe Elspeth
Morrison and that's no mean feat.'

They stood glaring at each other, white-faced,
nostrils aflare, in the heat of the moment having to
exercise all their self-control not to lash out at each
other physically. He had never raised a hand to her,
but now she couldn't stop herself any more from
striking out, dealing him such a crack the force of it
spun his face to the side.

'So, I give you no peace in bed?' she gritted. 'And
all these years I thought you were enjoying it. Well,
if you're worried that I might keep you awake in
future, you needn't fear. I'll move your things into
Grant's room; I'm sure you can rake up some excuse.
Why not tell him that at fifty you're past it!' She was
horrified at the poison pouring from her lips, but she
had lost control and raced on. 'Alick and Mary will
be here in a few days – Alick always liked me, didn't
he? Why don't we swop? You have Mary for a few
nights and I'll have Alick – see what it was he was
going to give me all these years ago.'

She had gone too far, and she knew it. The time
when Alick had tried to seduce her – with all its
terrible consequences – was almost too much to
even think about and now she had brought it to the

surface where it reared between them like an ugly monster, spewing its venom over them.

Fergus had turned so white she thought he was going to collapse. His eyes were livid black pools, full of disbelief, hurt, shock – and something that was almost hate. Roughly he gripped her wrist and jerked her towards him till her face was inches from his. With clenched teeth he ground out, 'Never, never mention that again to me or you'll be sorry you ever met me . . .'

'What makes you think I'm not sorry now?' Her throat was tight, she hated herself, but the words were out before she could stop them.

Something deep in his eyes made her reel with pain, a hurt so raw he couldn't stop it showing. She felt weak. She was immediately sorry for all the harsh things she had said, but it was hardly the time to utter a feeble apology, and nothing she had said could ever be taken back.

His grip on her wrist slackened and she saw all the fire go out of him. He turned his head from her and the rays of the sun caught and gleamed on the snow-white hairs among the jet black.

She pressed the back of her hand to her mouth and reached out to touch him, but he pulled his shoulder out of her grasp.

'Fergus,' she rasped, the unshed tears making her voice harsh. 'I'm . . .'

Janet came rather warily into the kitchen. She had heard the tail end of the row but was unusually excited about something and pointed out of the window. 'Would you look at who's coming up the road.'

Fergus remained immobile, but Kirsteen went to stand by Janet. Up the winding glen came quite a procession led by Lorn and Lewis astride Conker. 'It's Shona and Niall!' Kirsteen cried, hastily patting her crisp curls and wondering how she could act normally after what had gone before. Peeling off her apron she threw it on the draining board. 'The wittrocks that they are – they're several days too early – there won't be enough dinner to go round.'

Fergus had joined the two women by the sink, his hammering heart lightening a little at sight of his daughter, slim and lovely, her auburn hair shining in the sun. She was leading the way through the gate and Fergus couldn't help saying, 'Shona – we'll have smiles about the place again.'

Kirsteen reddened and hissed at him furiously, 'Maybe I should go away for a while – it might be worth the welcome home.'

His eyes snapped and he turned away. The kitchen was filling with Fiona and Grant, Shona and Niall, with clamouring children, with hens boldly strutting, together with two sheepdog pups eagerly sniffing for scraps. For several minutes chaos reigned. Lorn and Lewis were talking excitedly, describing the meeting with Jon, the events at the harbour.

'Rachel made faces at the camera,' Lewis chuckled gleefully.

'Och, that Rachel,' Janet said in exasperated admiration for the little cousin who laughed at all the

681

conventions Janet herself hated but was too fearful to contravene.

Helen was wobbling on chubby legs, chasing the hens round the table before dropping on all fours to join the pups in their quest for crumbs. Grant watched her antics and his deep laugh boomed. 'Just as mad as her mother,' he quipped, giving Shona a brotherly squeeze that left her gasping. Kirsteen put her hands over her ears and shrieked, 'We didn't expect you two for some days yet! How on earth will I feed you all?'

Bob appeared and proceeded to remove his mud-caked wellingtons, which he clumped heartily against the outside wall. His dog, Meg, was immediately pounced on by her pups who proceeded to feed there and then, eyes blissfully closed as they clung to her teats, squeezing her belly with their fat puppy paws. Bob stopped his beating to gaze into the crowded kitchen with surprise. 'My, my, the gathering o' the clans right enough. I'm thinkin' I'll just get along home and have a sup o' milk and a bite o' bread and cheese.'

'No, no, Bob, wait!' Kirsteen cried rather dazedly, automatically picking Helen up from the floor to cuddle her. 'I'm sure we can sort something out.'

'Don't worry, Kirsteen,' Fiona said. 'Shona and Niall can come home with me.' She threw a meaningful glance in Grant's direction. 'You have your hands full here – all these helpless men to see to.'

'Away you go then, Shona. If you're lucky you

might get frog's legs for dinner,' flashed Grant, glaring at Fiona.

'Agree bairns, agree; for I hate to see peace,' smiled Fergus dourly, not deigning to notice the resentful look thrown at him by Kirsteen.

Shona hugged him. 'We only dropped in to say hello; we'll get away with Fiona. I'll be along later this afternoon while Helen's having a nap – come on, you wee devil,' she said, and scooped her daughter out of the big wickerwork dog basket and made for the door.

'Enjoy yourselves,' grinned Niall and went rather thankfully to join Shona and Fiona by the gate. The glen was peaceful with the hills drowsing in the heat and great shaggy Highland cows browsing among the lush grasses by the river. In the blue sky above an eagle planed lazily on the air currents.

'Phew,' Niall took a deep breath as he took his little daughter into the crook of his arm. 'To think Laigmhor used to be so quiet!'

Shona laughed. 'Och, it still is, we just disrupted everything, that's all.' She glanced around her with delight, her blue eyes brilliant with joy. 'It's so good to be back, to be home – oh, Kintyre is bonny but this,' she said, spreading her arms and skipping along, 'this is *me* somehow! Wild, peaceful, restless, dreamy – I feel like a daft wee lassie again when I'm back on Rhanna.'

'You *behave* like one!' giggled Fiona, taking the older girl's arm and skipping with her.

*

Phebie was in a chair by the table, napping in the rays of the sun pouring through the window of Slochmhor. She opened her eyes to see Niall standing grinning at her from the doorway and immediately she scrambled to her feet. 'What on earth – what may I ask are you doing here? You should have phoned – are you forgetting we have the phone in now?'

'Indeed no. I know you like surprises and we're about the nicest you could get. Fang let me away early; we came with Grant on the *Magpie*.' He advanced and Phebie made a clumsy scramble away from him. 'Don't you dare, my lad – I'm too auld for your capers now.'

'Havers, you're just a spring chicken, a nice plump one ready for the catching.' Niall's brown eyes were gleaming with devilment and Shona and Fiona smiled from the door, knowing what was coming. Round the table Niall chased his mother, the way he always did when he came home. Phebie shrieked, laughed, panted, and begged for mercy while Helen clung to her mother's skirts and observed joyfully, 'Gwannie's daft! Gwannie's daft!'

A chair was knocked flying and Niall caught his mother to lift her high in his strong young arms. Phebie had grown plumper with the years, but that didn't stop her son from running with her a few yards before he set her down, for good measure giving her a smack on her well-rounded bottom. Her round face was flushed pink and though she was breathless with laughter, she grabbed the dishcloth from the sink and swiped him over the face with it.

'Enough, enough,' he gasped. 'You win, I'm beaten, I give up.'

Lachlan came clattering downstairs, his thin face alight with enquiry. 'What is all this?' he grinned. 'I thought it was an invasion.'

'It is,' Phebie said fervently, sinking into a chair to fan her hot face with a corner of her apron. Lachlan swept his little granddaughter into his arms and danced with her round the room. 'My bonny wee Ellie,' he sang and the child crooned with him and grabbed a fistful of his unruly hair.

Phebie stopped fanning herself to say thoughtfully, 'How strange, I just remembered; when Niall was a baby he used to call Shona's mother Ellie.'

'It's nice,' murmured Shona, tucking away a wilful strand of her long hair. 'Not as formal as Helen.' She stroked the baby's satin-smooth cheeks. 'How would you like to be called Ellie, you daft wee thing?'

'Ellie, Ellie,' the child repeated the name happily.

Fiona sniffed. 'The only thing is, Ellie could be short for Elspeth and who in their right mind would want to be called after . . .'

'I heard that, miss.' Elspeth appeared, cabbages clutched to her bosom, a streak of earth lying over her gaunt cheeks. She went over to the sink and laid the cabbages down, her shoulders sagging slightly.

Fiona saw that her one-time dragon was now just a very lonely and rapidly ageing old lady and she was immediately repentant. Going over, she put her arm round Elspeth's shoulders and gave her a hug. 'I'm sorry, Elspeth, I'm a wee bitch to you, but you have to admit you've been an old one to me. I think Elspeth is a lovely name and to prove it I'm going to call my new white mouse after you . . .' She darted away as Elspeth turned on her. 'No really, it's a compliment. My mice are very special to me. Please smile, you look really nice when you smile, which isn't often.'

'I think I've come to the wrong house,' Niall said, shaking his head. 'This is all very undignified for me, you know. After all, it's not every day the son of this house becomes a junior partner in a thriving veterinary practice with his name just newly on the brass nameplate by the door.'

'Niall!' Phebie's face was glowing with pride. 'When? You never told us!'

'I'm telling you now – and since I'm such an important personage – isn't it high time I had my dinner? I'm starving.'

He picked up a buttered scone and proceeded to eat it, earning himself a smart rap on the knuckles from his mother.

'Just like old times,' smiled Lachlan, sitting down at the table and scraping in his chair. He caught Niall's eye and a glow of pride filled his heart. The tears and the laughter of his children's growing years echoed in his mind, a distant yet an ever-present melody that reached into the present to bring him joy.

*

Ruth let herself into the house. All was silent in the rather dingy, low-beamed, green-painted room, which, because half the things were packed in readiness for the move to Portcull, was even more spartan than usual. The air reeked of disinfectant. Twice weekly, Morag washed down the walls and floors with strong carbolic. The floor was bare wood, scrubbed white with only a rug at the fire to relieve the starkness. The mahogany sideboard, the bureau, and hard wooden chairs smelled strongly of polish, yet there was no shine on them. The house looked unlived in, there were no homely touches to add atmosphere, no cat or dog to give a welcome, as Morag had forbidden them in the house. The only ornaments on the walls were Bible markers, which were liberally scattered throughout the house.

A quick check revealed that her father was not in, and Ruth reasoned that he had most likely gone to share Totie's midday meal rather than have a solitary repast in that bare room. Ruth decided that a walk over to Totie's cottage would be lovely on such a day, and she stepped into the sunshine gladly. The cockerel was crowing loudly in the grassy run, as if proclaiming his relief at being released from his Sabbath prison, an upturned peat creel from which he could see the activities of the outside world without being able to join in. This practice of confining the cockerel on the Sabbath was by no means restricted to religious beings like Morag Ruadh. On crofts all over Rhanna, and indeed on islands throughout the Hebrides, it was considered immoral to have a cockerel roaming loose amongst the hens, so into creels, lobster pots, baskets, and fish boxes they went.

Despite everything, Ruth couldn't help feeling happy as she limped along to Totie's cottage perched high on the cliffs some distance from the village. The sun slanted over land and sea, making a bright mosaic of gold, green and blue; puffins, razorbills, and herring-gulls swooped, dived, and cried from the steep crags of the cliffs and rose up in thick clouds from the sea; the scents of wild flag and blue-bells mingled with the dank salt smell of the tangle left by the tide to dry in the sun. Ruth lifted her head and felt life bubbling into her until she shivered. It had been a wonderful morning; she was looking forward to going to live at Portcull – and she would still see Rachel despite her mother, because they would meet at school. She would have at least one friend there – perhaps the twins would speak to her as well. She liked them, especially Lewis; he didn't make her feel uncomfortable the way Lorn did. He was shy, like her; two shy people rarely invoked confidence in each other.

The skirt of Ruth's brown wool pinafore lifted in the wind. It was a hot, uncomfortable garment and the rough material made her knees itch. She wished she could wear a pretty cotton gingham dress like the one Rachel had been wearing that morning but she knew it was useless to ask her mother to make her anything that she considered to be flimsy and provocative. She hardly knew what that big word meant, but had an idea it was something to do with tempting boys – though she couldn't see how any girl of nine years old could do that. Still, Rachel had looked lovely in the simple pink frock; it showed off her suntanned limbs and black curls to perfection.

As Ruth hurried her calliper creaked slightly. She was to get a new one fitted soon, but even so she knew she would never be graceful or pretty enough to provoke boys.

The merriment of the morning came back to her; a smile lit her solemn little face, and she skipped as she approached Totie's cottage. As long as no one was watching she could skip quite well – and dance, too. Rachel had taught her how to do that in the shed behind her house and Ruth had forgotten her limp in the excitement of dancing with Rachel.

Totie's cottage, though windswept and bare of protective trees, was nevertheless well cared for and tidy, with its dazzling white walls and small patches of cultivated land. Totie was a capable woman who, despite all odds, grew all her own vegetables. The potato patch was in the process of being planted in a sandy soil sustained by great quantities of seaweed. A heap of seaweed and a barrowload of dung had been piled onto the earth, waiting to be dug in. Ruth walked over the unfenced springy turf to the door and was about to knock on it when her father's voice froze her action. His was a quiet voice but strong and deep and she heard plainly the words, 'Dear God, Totie, sometimes I don't think I can bear another day in that house with that woman. My times with you are the only things that keep me sane. If it wasn't for Ruth I swear I wouldn't stand another day of Morag.'

Ruth's heart hammered into her throat. That wasn't her father speaking, it couldn't be. But it was – his voice came again from a window at the side – from Totie's bedroom. 'I love that bairnie. The day she was born was the happiest in my life. She's the only joy in that godforsaken house. It's been hell for her since she was a babe and I'd give anything to see laughter in that sad wee face. If hitting Morag was a means of getting happiness for Ruth it would give me the greatest pleasure to do it – but she's stone that woman! A damned statue without a heart! How I rue the day I married her . . .' He gave a short bitter laugh. 'If only I'd known I didn't have to – from what I hear, Ruth could be any man's bairn – oh ay, the first and last time Morag let herself go she made a right proper job of it – and all those who have to live in her shadow have suffered for her sins ever since!'

'Ach, you should confront the pious bitch!' Totie said scornfully. 'Tell her you're not going to be punished for the things she did all these years ago.'

'I can't.' Dugald's voice was full of despair. 'Hell would be a nicer refuge afterwards – forbye, I must think of my wee Ruthie – I don't know why but I'm almost convinced she *is* mine. Yet, I'll never know for sure – that's the hell of it. Morag has damned us all.'

Ruth felt faint, so sick and giddy she leaned back against the doorpost and pressed the palms of her hands against the rough wall of the porch. She fought to control herself. It wasn't real – none of it was real – but she had to know more, had to find out if she was imagining it all – her father in Totie's bedroom, discussing things that made a mockery of her life. With her heart in her throat she crept over the springy grass till she was standing to the side of the bedroom window. There was silence now and she hardly dared to breathe. The green of the machair stretched before her staring eyes; far below, the blue sea eddied into bays of shimmering golden sands. It was such a beautiful world, such a beautiful sun-kissed day, but it was all crashing about her ears like a flimsy matchbox tower. She sucked in her breath and held it, hot unshed tears pricked her eyelids, her legs trembled till she thought she would fall. She leaned hard against the wall for support and threw back her head, her violet eyes staring up at the blue vault of the sky. Was God up there? Who was this God that her mother feared rather than revered? Where was He? If He existed how could He allow so much unhappiness? Her mother had turned Him into an invisible force that haunted them all.

Her grandparents spoke about God in a different way from her mother. Their simple faith had a beauty about it, and it was a joy listening to them reading from the Bible. Yet as soon as her mother intruded, God became different, a stranger without mercy for the smallest lapse from grace.

Standing alone on that sunlit day, Ruth's gentle soul became diffused with feelings of loathing – for her mother? For God? She didn't know. She only

691

knew that her being was so flooded with the powerful emotion she felt ill.

Her father's voice came again. 'Thank God for you, Totie. What I would have done without you all these years, I'll never know. It won't be easy seeing you when we move to Portcull, but I'll find a way – even if it means creeping out of the house in the middle of the night.' He was thanking the God who ruled his life – and he spoke of years with Totie . . .

With her heart in her mouth Ruth turned her head slightly and, raising herself on tip-toes, she glanced quickly in through the window. Her father lay in bed with Totie in his arms, his white head shining like a beacon in the shadows of the room. Ruth turned away and rammed her fist into her mouth to stop from crying out. She moved slightly and her calliper creaked quite loudly.

'What was that?' Dugald's voice sounded strange – faraway yet anxious.

Totie's voice came softly. 'Only the bedsprings – relax – we only have a wee while together.'

Ruth's heart fluttered and her face burned. Inch by inch she edged away from the window and at a safe distance from the cottage she began to run, a clumsy, halting gait that carried her back to the empty house and her own bleak thoughts. The one dear person she had thought was hers wasn't after all. She planted her small hands on the table and her breath rasped in her throat as the harsh sobs shook her body.

After a while the tears were followed by the dull ache of hurt, and then by anger, then rebellion. She wasn't hungry but she limped to the larder and cut a hunk of bread and a slice of cheese. Her mother had said she wasn't to eat a bite till teatime – who was her mother to tell her what to do? Tell her she mustn't play with Rachel, talk to boys? She was only nine years old but in her mother's mind she was already a Jezebel. Conflicting emotions raged through her. She stared at the bread and cheese lying on the plate and, picking it up, she crammed it into her mouth but the tightness in her throat wouldn't allow her to swallow. Coughing and choking she rushed outside and was violently sick. Going back to the kitchen she sat with her elbows on the table, her smarting eyes staring ahead of her without seeing anything.

She felt drained of all strength, all feeling. With her head in her arms she slept for a while and awakened with a start. Four o'clock and no sign of her father. He must have gone out in his van to deliver groceries from Totie's shop. She rose and automatically began to prepare a meal, and when her father's footsteps finally sounded on the path, the potatoes were boiling over the fire and the cold chicken left over from Sunday was neatly sliced on the plates.

Dugald came into the kitchen, his silvery hair slightly windblown. Ruth didn't look up but went on mashing turnips in a bowl with such vigour her arms ached.

'Where's your mother?' Dugald asked, putting his arms round the little girl and kissing her hot cheeks.

'Grannie took a bad turn so Mam had to stay – she won't be back till tomorrow. Erchy brought me home in his van.' Ruth was surprised at how normal she sounded.

'So it's just you and me tonight, my wee lamb?' His voice was light, relieved.

'Ay, Father. Wash your hands and sit down before the dinner gets cold.'

'Anything you say, madam.' He laughed, his steps light as he went into the scullery and poured water from a bucket into a bowl. 'You're a clever wee lassie getting the meal ready all by yourself,' he called over his shoulder. 'Have you been here all day, Ruthie?'

She hesitated only fractionally. 'Ay, Father. It was nice so I played outside for a while.'

By common, unspoken agreement they omitted to say Grace, a usual practice when Morag was in the house. During the meal Ruth was silent, toying with her food.

'Are you all right, Ruthie? Aren't you hungry?' Dugald asked.

She looked straight into his steady grey eyes. 'Not very, Father – I'm – I'm a wee bit worried about Grannie.'

'Ach, she'll be fine,' he reassured. 'She's getting on and gets flusters a bit. Your Grannie was never one to flap, but maybe she's getting a wee bit excited at the idea of us coming to live beside her.'

Ruth remembered the look on old Isabel's face when Morag had first told her the news. 'Ay, that will likely be it,' she said quietly and got up to clear the table and wash the dishes. Dugald grabbed a dish-towel and began to wipe the plates. Ruth moved away. 'I'll go to my room now,' she said and went to the door leading into the hall.

'But, it's only six o'clock, Ruthie – you don't have to go to bed yet. You and me could have a nice cosy evening together. I thought we might go for a walk by Aosdana Bay. We could watch the sunset from the top of the cliffs then come home and maybe write a poem about all the things we see. Over supper I had a mind to snuggle you on my knee and read you a wee story I wrote about the fairies that live over by Caonteach Cave.'

Ruth hung her head. How lovely to walk beside that tall dear man in the gloaming; to watch the fishing boats sailing in; to hear the sea lapping the shore, making the pebbles and shells sound as if they were chuckling; to perhaps gather some and bring them home to wash them in readiness to be laid into the little jewel box he was carving for her – but best of all – to sit on his lap by the fire and hear his voice weaving tales of the wee folk who, it was reputed, lived in the rock pools near the caves.

'I can't, Father,' she said, her voice low, 'I was bad today – I stopped at Portcull harbour to watch Todd's new car coming and Mam was so mad she said I was to go to my room after tea and learn the Commandments.'

His heart twisted. She was so vulnerable-looking, so sad and lost, so pathetic with her small body encased in the drab frock and her fair head bowed as if in shame of some momentous crime.

'Ruthie, my wee lassie.' He went to her and

stooped down to cuddle her to him. 'You have never done a bad thing in the whole of your little life. Bugger the Commandments! I'm sure you know enough of them to last you a lifetime. You get your jacket and come out with me.'

She raised her head in wonderment. 'But – what if Mam asks . . . ?'

'Let her,' he said firmly. 'I'll take the consequences. Now – put on your jacket and let's go.'

With her hand firmly in his they wandered silently over the white sands of Aosdana Bay, listening to the haunting song of the curlew, the whispering of the sea, the mating croon of the groups of scaup, drakes, with the purple-green gloss of their plumage making bright patterns in the translucent blue pools among the rocks. Then they climbed to the clifftop and sat side by side watching the sky turn from gold to pink and finally to a blaze of crimson that turned the Sound into a sea of blood stretching to the infinity of the horizon.

When they finally came home they shut the henhouses for the night, then went indoors where he made steaming mugs of milky cocoa, which they drank together by the fire's light. She went to rinse the mugs and came back to see him sitting on the old rocking chair by the range. In firelight and lamplight the bare room looked homely and welcoming, the feeling of oppression was gone and in its place was love – pure and real. He held out his arms. 'Come here, Ruthie,' he said softly and she climbed onto the lap she loved. He stroked her hair, curled a silken strand round his fingers. 'You have the bonniest hair of all the wee lassies on the island – it's like the hair on the heads of the fairy folk. I once saw a fairy who looked just like you – beautiful as a princess with hair as fine as gossamer, the shine to it brighter than fairy gold. But she wasn't a princess – oh no – she was a queen, the queen of all the fairies who live in the shiny rock pools by Caonteach Cave . . .'

Ruth lay back and listened, her heart touched with a joy that was almost pain. The arms of her beloved father were round her, holding her close to his heart and she knew that he *was* her father. Whatever her mother had done, whichever way she tried to atone for it, she could never, in all the days and years that stretched ahead, take away the beauty of this night, this now, this sweet ecstasy of a little girl's knowing that the arms that held her close were the arms of the father who loved her when perhaps no one else in the world did.

Lorn lay in bed thinking over the events of the day. So many people had been in it, but best of all were Shona and Niall. They were downstairs now with Phebie and Lachlan. Laughter drifted from the parlour. He wished Shona was staying at Laigmhor, but with Uncle Alick and Aunt Mary arriving soon, all the rooms were needed. The only room that was left was a tiny box room at the end of the passage and nobody ever used it except to store things. The scene at the harbour came to him and he smiled, then quite unbidden Ruth's face floated into his mind. She was a strange girl, gentle and shy, yet he sensed something great in her, something squashed so deep inside she probably wasn't aware that she had it. Someday it might get a chance to come out – someday . . . His child's mind grappled with the notion but couldn't quite make sense of it.

'Lewis – do you like Ruth Donaldson?' he asked suddenly.

Lewis's tousled head emerged from the blankets. 'Ach, she's all right – a bit soft, but, of course, she's a girl.'

'So's Rachel.'

'She's different, she's tough for a girl. She doesn't bother about being dumb the way Ruth cares about her funny leg.'

Lorn was silent for a few moments, then he observed slowly, 'Ay, but that Morag Ruadh is an awful mother to have – praying and scraping all the time – and I've heard her telling Ruth no' to drag her leg – as if she could help it. Rachel's mother is no' ashamed that Rachel's dumb – but she's queer in other ways. She lets Rachel run wild – as if she canny be bothered with her.'

'Och well, they're just girls,' Lewis said rather impatiently. Unlike his brother he rarely delved into the deeper issues of life.

'Still, I feel it's a shame for Ruth,' Lorn persisted, frowning in the darkness. 'Nobody bothers with her much.' He was silent again then said in a rush, 'I

wonder if Father's ashamed of me. Sometimes I think
he is.'

'Ach, you're daft then.' Lewis's tones were scornful.
'He's only feart you'll hurt yourself because of your
heart.'

'I suppose in a way I'm like Ruth and Rachel.'

Lewis punched his pillows in disgust. 'Stop
blethering and talk sense! I'm lying here thinking
about Todd's new car. I don't like cars as a rule, but
someday I'd like a car like Todd's – I'd like a fiddle
like old Mo's as well – it's no' just any old tink's
fiddle. I heard tell he got it from a man on Barra for
a few shillings. The missionary made the man feel so
ashamed for playin' on the Sabbath he sold it and
has wanted it back ever since, but old Mo wouldny
give it back for all the tea in China.'

'Maybe he would for all the whisky that's left over
from the *Politician*. Todd's brother-in-law from Uist
found a case a whily back when he was mending the
thatch on his hut roof and everyone left what they
were doing to have a big ceilidh.'

'Well, we'll be having a big ceilidh at Portcull next
week for Merry Mary's retiral. We'll get to play our
fiddles with old Andrew and Rachel and maybe that
Jerry hiker we met today.'

'I wonder if Merry Mary's wart might drop off in
the hall with all the dancing and hooching,' Lorn
pondered.

'I hope not,' Lewis returned fervently. 'Everyone
would see it happening and none of us would get

paid for it – and *I'm* going to be the one that will. When she retires she's going to try and grow a lot of vegetables to sell to the towrists and I've promised to help her to fetch seaweed and dung. That way I'll be able to keep an eye on her wart and if she knocks it off while she's digging I'll get to collect all the pennies from children all over the island who placed bets on it.'

'You would,' Lorn sniffed peevishly. 'You always get what you want.'

'I'll share the money with you,' promised Lewis sleepily.

'Would you?' enthused Lorn. 'In that case I'll come over to Merry Mary's with you and supervise – make sure you help her properly and don't knock her wart off with the shovel.'

Both boys collapsed in giggles at the absurdity and soon fell to discussing the fishing expedition their father had promised them during the Easter holidays.

Chapter Seven

While Lorn chatted happily with his brother, his parents were at that moment discussing his future with Lachlan, who had asked them to forsake the gathering in the parlour for a quiet talk in the kitchen. Kirsteen and Fergus had put a good face on things for the benefit of the company, but now, sitting together on the couch, they were both acutely aware of the barriers between them. Lachlan twisted his thumbs together for a few thoughtful seconds, then he looked from Fergus to Kirsteen and smiled wryly. 'I thought I was word-perfect in what I have to say to you, but now the time has come all the bonny rehearsals have gone out of my head. I'll have to be blunt – it's about Lorn – I've been keeping a close eye on him and have noticed how much he has improved this last year or two. When he was an infant he was too weak for me to even consider that something could be done for his heart – but now . . .'

Fergus had been sitting at the edge of the couch staring at his shoes but at those words his dark head jerked up and he stared at Lachlan enquiringly. A pink flush had spread over Kirsteen's face and she said tentatively, 'Now?'

701

Lachlan shifted, playing for time by filling his pipe and taking some time to light it.

'Och, c'mon, man, out with it!' Fergus said tensely.

'Well, I've been discussing your son's case with a colleague of mine, a chap I became acquainted with when I was away on one of my refresher courses. He's a heart specialist, a gifted man who's been doing some pretty wonderful things in his field. New techniques are being tried all the time in open heart surgery – and from what I've told Jack, he feels he would like to have a look at Lorn, see if surgery could possibly improve his condition.'

Hope and fear churned Kirsteen's stomach into a tight coil. 'What kind of surgery?' she asked.

'It's very difficult for me to assess without the proper tests, but I would imagine there might be some misplaced connections between the heart and the blood vessels – Jack would have to see Lorn to really know for sure what is wrong. On the one hand it might only mean one spell of surgery; on the other hand it could be a long, involved affair – perhaps several operations over a period of time, but in my opinion your son deserves this opportunity to improve the quality of his life. If all went well he could end up as sound as any other lad.'

'And if it didn't work, he could go through hell and end up the same – or worse than he is now,' Fergus stated flatly.

Lachlan spread his long fingers and shrugged. 'I can't promise miracles at this stage, nor at any stage for that matter. It's a chance I feel you ought to take, though – I cannot say more than that.' He leaned forward and tapped out his pipe on the grate then he swivelled round and looked them both straight in the eye. 'Don't feel you have to rush into any decisions now – talk it over between you; really thrash it out.' He put his hand over Kirsteen's and said gently, 'Believe me, I know how difficult this is. Take your time to discuss the matter thoroughly. However, I know you will both want to do the right thing for the wee lad's future – and surgery might provide an answer to what sort of future he'll have.'

Grant came into the room on a quest for food. 'Our visitors are starving,' he grinned cheekily, 'especially Phebie, who's fading away. I thought I saw scones being baked earlier and they smelled delicious.'

Phebie stood quietly in the background, knowing what the talk had been about. She caught Kirsteen's eye and her sweet face was full of sympathy. Later, when everyone was leaving and the kitchen was filled with chatter, she took Kirsteen aside and put a comforting arm round her shoulders. 'I know how you feel, Kirsteen,' she said quietly. 'Och, it's hard, so it is, so very very hard to try and think what's best for the bairnies we bring into the world. Sometimes it seems they bring us nothing but sorrow – but ach – what joy they give too – and they deserve to get the best deal possible.'

Kirsteen hugged her. 'Thank you, Phebie, you have been a wonderful friend and a comfort to me from the first day I set foot on Rhanna. Whoever gives you comfort, I wonder?'

703

'Lachlan and God,' said Phebie simply. 'If one fails me the other is aye to hand.'

Kirsteen gazed thoughtfully into Phebie's bonny face and thought, 'This woman is good, truly good. She has been through a lot herself, yet her belief in God has never wavered.' Kirsteen held her breath. When had she last communed with God in earnest? Not the automatic ritual of Sunday worship, but really and truly talked, asked, confided? She couldn't remember and as she bent to kiss Phebie's warm soft cheek she felt ashamed.

Everyone was moving out into a night of velvet sprinkled with stars. Fergus remained at the door, but Kirsteen went to the gate. The cool night air brushed her hot face, the dark moor stretched away, felt rather than seen; in the distance the sea was a subdued silver streak. Grant was walking the visitors up the road, but as the men moved away Shona paused at the gate and murmured into Kirsteen's ear, 'Next time I see the pair of you I hope you will have made it up.'

Kirsteen let out an audible gasp. 'How on earth –?'

'Ach, I'm not the daft wee lassie I once was; I've been married long enough to know the signs. Babbie taught me a thing or two a whily back when I could never see the obvious for looking – forbye,' she smiled in the darkness, 'Father always gives himself away. When you're not watching, he's watching you under his eyebrows and he's just a bit *too* nice to everyone, if you know what I mean.'

'Oh, but, Shona,' Kirsteen burst out, 'it's worse,

much worse than just a silly row!' She checked herself, wanting to pour her heart out, but knowing that to do so would be to betray others, to rake up things that were long buried. Also, she was hating herself for slapping Fergus, for hurling such cruel abuse at him. To have Shona hate her too was too terrible to contemplate. 'Thanks for the advice,' she said lightly then added, 'How very strange life is – to think I once taught you when you were just an infant, now you're teaching me.'

'I know.' Shona sounded rather sad. 'Life passes so quickly. 'When I was just a baby you were a young woman and there was no way we could bridge the gap – now we're both women and can speak to one another on the same level.'

'And you make me sound an absolute relic!' Kirsteen laughed. 'Get along now before I fold up and crumble away before your eyes.'

Shona giggled and sped away up the glen to catch up with the menfolk. Kirsteen felt exhausted, so drained she felt she would drop off the minute her head touched the pillow, but once in bed she didn't lie down. She hadn't carried out her threat of moving Fergus's things into Grant's room and she sat up, hugging her knees, waiting for Fergus to come up. The sound of his step on the stairs set her heart racing madly, but he didn't look at her when he came in. Instead, he went to the linen chest and took out a couple of blankets and a pillow.

'Fergus – we – we must talk – about Lorn.' Her voice sounded feeble, strange even to her own ears.

'Ay – we must,' he said shortly, the deep voice cold and distant. They might have been standing at either end of a long bridge – so far apart they seemed in those moments, as if all the years of their intimate loving had been wiped out like chalk marks on a blackboard. He said nothing more and walked with measured step out of the room and along the passage to the tiny box room at the end. It was a jumble of odds and ends, bits of unused furniture, discarded toys, the two wooden cradles that had rocked his baby daughter and his infant sons. The sight of them caught him unawares and he was whisked back to a long ago night of love, of laughter, of dancing with a baby in the crook of his arm, of Kirsteen standing with bowed head gazing tenderly at their smallest son. Now that infant was a boy – a boy whose future rested on an operating table under bright lights, surgeons' knives cutting . . . Fergus gave a little cry and threw an old rug over the cradles but he couldn't shut out the thoughts, the fears, the misery that engulfed him as he lay on the uncomfortable old horsehair sofa that had stood in the parlour in his father's day. His head ached slightly, but overriding all was the ache in his heart. Kirsteen had been cruel, so cruel – vicious almost. Why? Why? Why? The question banged around in his head. They had had rows before, some more heated than that of the morning, but never before had she said such venomous things – things he had thought buried. He had goaded her, of course, but hardly enough to make her rake up that thing about Alick, an incident that had cost him his arm, cost Hamish his life, caused him to lose Kirsteen for six long, heart-breaking years.

He tossed and turned. The sofa was full of lumps, draughts seeped in through the sparse coverings – he should have brought a quilt . . . Lorn, what about Lorn? The decision was too great, a burden of responsibility that crushed into him like a ton weight. Perhaps Kirsteen was right: maybe he had tried to shield the boy too much. He should have been harder with him, made him tougher – prepared him better for the harsher things in life and in that way he himself might have been better prepared for the enormity of what lay ahead. Help me, God, he prayed in despair. Help me – us – to do the right thing for our son.

Kirsteen remained sitting up long after Fergus had left the room. Her limbs felt so rigid they might have been locked. She heard Grant letting himself in and coming upstairs. There was a bump followed by a muffled curse. She smiled mechanically. Fiona infuriated him by putting all sorts of silly comparisons against his adolescent clumsiness: one day he was the boy with frog's feet, another his hands were likened to bunches of bananas.

A tremor passed through Kirsteen, and she shivered. Slowly she unwound from her cramped position and, throwing back the covers, she got up and padded to the wardrobe. Inside, hanging under layers of tissue paper, was the silver fox fur Fergus had given her after the twins were born. The joy and love of that night came back to her. She thought of how he had gathered clothing coupons together and had gone off to Oban on his Christmas shopping spree. He had brought back something for everyone, his eyes shining with the pleasure of giving – giving her red roses . . . She lifted the paper away from the jacket and buried her face in the soft fur. She hadn't worn it very often, at christenings, weddings – on a wonderful holiday with Shona and Niall on the Mull of Kintyre when they had all dined out and gone to several dances.

'Oh, my darling.' She bit her lip and threw back her head but she couldn't stop the tears spilling. It would be no use going to him in his present state of mind. It would only serve to make things worse. She went back to bed and in her despair she cried silently to God for help and drifted into a fitful sleep, waking before dawn to hear Fergus come quietly along the passage and downstairs. He had risen earlier than need be, so that none of the family would know that he and Kirsteen had quarrelled, that he had slept in a separate room.

Alick and Mary arrived a few days later, minus their fourteen-year-old twin sons who were now spreading their wings and had gone off with the Scouts to Easter camp. Mary immediately changed from her elegant town clothes into garments more suited for a farming holiday, while Alick and Fergus caught up with all the news. Alick was slim and distinguished-looking with his grey hair fashionably styled, his moustache and small beard neatly clipped: except for the dark eyes there was nothing in his appearance to connect him with tall, dark, hard-muscled Fergus.

The following day all the menfolk from Slochmhor and Laigmhor went off on a day's fishing expedition. The women had gathered at Slochmhor and Shona stood at the window, watching the men trudging away, wishing that she was going with them. Although Alick was wearing an old jersey and tweed trousers tucked into wellingtons he still managed to look sophisticated, but the illusion was shattered as, with his arms slung round the twins' shoulders, he let out a wild whoop of delight. It was a mild day with the hilltops shrouded in mist. It had rained in the morning but now a stiff breeze was breaking the clouds apart to reveal patches of blue.

'A grand day for a spot of fishing,' Alick observed. 'Even if we don't catch any it will be nice to sit at the lochside and eat all that lovely food we have in the baskets – and, just picture it – a whole day without a single woman's tongue flapping away in our eardrums.'

Lewis looked up at the sky. 'Look, it's a fluffy cloud day!' he yelled, pointing at the big clouds racing along. 'I can see a dragon's face in that one with a big pink tongue spitting out fire.'

Alick laughed. 'Shh! Maybe it's Elspeth sitting on a cloud watching us.'

Lorn held onto his father's hand and couldn't help giving a little skip of joy. He was with his father, he was one of the men, and it was a 'fluffy cloud day'. He loved his brother's fantasies about such days, often they spent ages watching the wind sculpting the clouds into fantastic shapes and human faces.

Shona, still watching from the windows as the men receded into the distance, said, sighing, 'Sometimes I wish I was a wee lassie again, running around doing things like guddling and fishing. It seems unfair, so it does. Men grow up, yet they never look out of place doing the things they did as boys. I feel like an old grannie left behind with my knitting.'

'Well, I'm glad Lachy's getting a break,' Phebie said. 'And that *I'm* getting one with him and Niall out from under my feet – besides,' she said, her eyes twinkling, 'they don't know it yet but they're taking us all for a picnic on Monday and we're all going to roll our Easter eggs.' She went into the pantry and came back with a basket piled high with big brown eggs. 'I boiled these last night – more than two dozen of them – enough for two each, and we are going to take chairs and sit outside to paint faces on them. I found a box of Fiona's paints at the back of a cupboard, and since tomorrow is Sunday they will all have to be painted today – so get your peenies on everybody.'

Shona chuckled with delight and immediately began carrying kitchen chairs outside to set them on the grass. Mary rushed to gather all the aprons she could find. 'What a marvellous idea, Phebie,' she approved as she went to the door with an armful of Elspeth's spotless linen aprons. 'I haven't rolled an

Easter egg in years.' She was a well groomed and elegantly coiffed woman, but after half an hour her hair had fallen down and streaks of paint covered her face and hands.

The sun was breaking through the clouds and Shona glanced appreciatively round, feeling it very good to sit there with the windbreak of green pines releasing a rain-fresh fragrance, the nearby sheep chopping away at the rich, sappy green turf, the hens strutting and clucking; shrieks of merriment from Fiona, who was having a wonderful time trying to make Grant's eggs' faces as disagreeable looking as possible. On one she had painted deep black frowns between eyes screwing up into a squiggle of black curls, on the other he was grinning foolishly above a ridiculously exaggerated dimple. On the back of each egg she had dared to write 'Dimples' in bold red letters.

'He'll throw them to the gulls,' Kirsteen predicted.

'Or he'll skite you round the lugs with them,' Shona said, giggling, deftly removing Helen's chubby fingers from the gooey paint box. 'Look,' she said, holding up an egg painted with big brown eyes and golden-red hair. 'Ellie's egg.'

'Ellie's eggle.' The little girl clapped with glee, lost her balance and landed on the grass with a soft thump.

On the face of it they were a jolly company, but Shona glanced at Kirsteen's face and knew that she hadn't yet made up with Fergus. She was laughing and talking as happily as the rest, but her blue eyes were weary and Shona guessed that she had been losing sleep over the matter.

A little black car came meandering along the glen road from Downie's Pass. It groaned to a halt at the gate and Babbie got out, her expression one of amusement as she observed the gathering outside Slochmhor. 'What on earth are you lot up to?' she asked, eyeing the heap of gaily painted eggs. 'Would I be right in thinking you are quite literally having a hen's party?'

'Ay, indeed you would,' Shona said, laughing. 'We're just getting a picnic prepared for Monday – why don't you and Anton come? You never seem to have time off these days – I've hardly seen you since I arrived. A break would do you both the world of good.'

'Sorry, I can't,' Babbie said and sighed ruefully, pushing a hand through her red curls. 'I have too much on my plate at the moment. Biddy helps all she can but even at that . . .' she smiled rather wearily, 'it's a bit like working on the Forth Bridge – when you get to the end you have to start all over again, and with me being off part of Saturday and all day Sunday, Monday is my busiest day really.'

Shona sprang to her feet and began to peel off her apron. 'Are you forgetting I'm a nurse – I'll come with you today and between us we'll get through your patients like a dose of salts.'

'Really – would you? But you're here for a holiday . . .'

'Am I? With Phebie making me work my fingers to

712

the bone painting eggs and forcing me to get up out of my bed in the morning in order to drag Fiona and Niall from theirs?'

'But . . .'

'Away you go, lass,' Phebie ordered kindly. 'I'll look to wee Helen though I can't promise you'll find me all in one piece when you get back. I thought Fiona was wild as an infant but this one beats all.'

'You see, no "buts",' Shona said, linking her arm through Babbie's and pulling her away. 'I'm quite looking forward to coming with you, it will be like old times, we can have a rare old blether and I'll get to see a lot of folk I haven't seen in ages.'

Mary had already endowed an egg with a squiggle of red loops and enormous green eyes and was starting to streak yellow locks over another.. Babbie turned back. 'I wonder – do you think you could do one with dark hair and specs and the name Jon, spelt J-O-N. I've a feeling Anton's friend would love to come on an island picnic.'

Fiona delved into the egg basket. 'Say no more,' she intoned authoritatively, and with fiendish delight swirled her brush into black paint and began drawing two black circles on Jon's egg.

Elspeth appeared with a brush in her hand. She had been upstairs tidying the bedrooms with such energy she had lost some pins from her severe grey bun, which Fiona had likened to a 'mouldering cow pat'. 'What's this, madam?' Elspeth asked tightly, eyeing Fiona's apron, which was patterned with livid splashes of red and blue. 'Is these my aprons? My beautiful aprons, just fresh from the wash line and newly starched?'

Phebie's lips twitched. 'We'll wash them, Elspeth,' she said soothingly. 'It will come out easily – it's only watercolour.'

'Only! Only!' Elspeth repeated menacingly.

Fiona's bright eyes glittered. 'Ach, you shouldny bother, Mother,' she advised mischievously. 'I think they look better with a bit colour in them, it makes them look artistic – like Elspeth herself – and . . .' she spluttered with mirth, 'she's got her brush all ready – only she looks more like a house painter than an artist.'

Elspeth screeched and, raising her brush, waved it threateningly at Fiona, who vacated her chair with agility to prance away over the turf, Elspeth on her heels, scattering sheep and hens in all directions, her hair falling in lanky grey loops down her back. Behind her wobbled little Helen, falling into sheep's sharn, picking herself up, waving her hands and screaming with joy, as she followed hot on Elspeth's heels. Mary clutched her stomach and shrieked so heartily her chair flew out from under her, and while Phebie and Kirsteen rushed to help her up, Shona took Babbie's hand and they flew to the car in fits of giggles.

Monday dawned in a haze of ethereal light that bathed the hilltops in gold and brushed the sea with bronze. By eleven o'clock, the world was awash with sunlight and on the journey over to Croy, with the company divided into three traps, each keeping pace with the other, everyone began to sing – all except Kirsteen and Fergus, who, making the excuse of being polite to their guests, sat on opposite seats, Fergus with Mary, Alick with Kirsteen. 'You can't say I'm not giving you the opportunity to get close to my brother,' Fergus had muttered to Kirsteen as they left Laigmhor. Kirsteen was still smarting with hurt at the remark, and now, to add insult to injury, Fergus was giving every appearance of enjoying himself, laughing readily at Mary's witticisms – and he had thrown his arm lightly round Mary's shoulders and was murmuring things the others couldn't hear but that were making her laugh. Kirsteen's cheeks burned and she felt panic rising in her. How long could this go on? The rift between her and Fergus was growing wider with each passing day. She had tried to talk to him, to tell him she was sorry, but always he had some excuse for walking away from her. Things weren't made easier by having to carry on normally in front of the visitors, but each night Fergus was careful to ensure that he was last to go upstairs and first to rise in the morning so that no one was aware that he was sleeping in the box room. Kirsteen wanted to stop the trap and run away – anywhere to hide her humiliation. Grant was driving the horses at a spanking pace as he happily bawled out a tune.

Alick glanced questioningly at Kirsteen. He was looking very handsome that day in a dark blazer and light grey flannels. 'Hey, what's wrong?' he enquired quizzically. 'Has the cat got your tongue? This is a picnic, not a funeral.' His voice was soft, well-modulated and rather pleasing to the ears. He grinned teasingly. 'What's the matter, Kirsteen, don't you like sitting beside me or is it just that you can't bear to let big brother away from your side for a single minute?'

Kirsteen gave herself a shake – she couldn't – she wouldn't – let Fergus see how much he was hurting her, and she forced herself to smile at Alick, her blue eyes very bright in her smooth-skinned face.

'*That's* better.' Alick looked at her appreciatively. She still had the figure of a girl – with breasts that were soft yet firm, skin that was smooth and golden, blonde hair a ruffle of curls in the breeze. Her white dress was simple, loose-topped, with a soft flowing skirt belted at the waist. It draped over the curves of her body, revealing without flaunting. A gust of wind at Downie's Pass made Mary yell and hold onto her hat, and without warning Kirsteen's skirt billowed in the air, briefly exposing her long shapely legs before she grabbed at the folds and tucked them firmly under her. Alick's eyes gleamed at the sight, and Fergus's mask of jollity fell away. A thundery shadow fell over his dark face and he glowered at his brother. A bemused Alick interpreted the message. 'This woman is mine,' it said more plainly than words. 'I know every plane of her body, the secrets of it are mine alone. I know how she looks in sleep, how she responds to me when she is awake.'

Alick sensed the tension and shifted uneasily. He realised for the first time since the start of the holiday that Fergus and Kirsteen were not on speaking terms.

'Big brother is watching us,' he mouthed in Kirsteen's ear. 'For God's sake, I don't want any trouble. Come on, sing – we're on a picnic and I, for one, am going to enjoy it.'

And sing Kirsteen did, in a rather shaky voice, and she kept on singing desperately till they arrived at Tràigh Mor Bay, Bay of the Great Sands. Here, on the cliffs above the bay, rising up from the machair, was a towering mass of soft rock, which rose up to a height of seven hundred feet, studded with hazel bushes and innumerable starlike primroses. Jagged cliffs of a harder rock divided Tràigh Mor Bay from An Coire Srùb Bay, Bay of the Spouting Kettle, where at high tide the sea thundered into vast underground caverns to gush spurting and foaming, fifty feet and more, from a spout-shaped vent above the splintered crags. The tide was in now and it was an awesome experience to hear the sea roaring into the vast subterranean caverns and to watch it spuming out of the blow hole, sending millions of glistening droplets high into the air.

'We'll have to wait till the tide goes out before we go down,' said Phebie, who was as jubilant as an excited child. It wasn't often that she and Lachlan had time to spend together, and they went off, arm in arm over the emerald-green clifftops, which were studded with numerous wildflowers. Grant was hoisting Lorn onto his shoulders and he held out a hand to Lewis. They ran laughing to watch the spout at close quarters, followed by Shona and Niall skipping like small children. Babbie and Anton followed more sedately, hands entwined, lost in a world of their own. 'Do you remember, liebling,' he whispered into her ear, 'that day we made love in the sands at Aosdana Bay?'

'As if I could ever forget,' she murmured dreamily.

His hand tightened over hers and he said tenderly, 'We had so little time to love then . . . now,' he said, gazing at the panorama of sea and sky, 'now we have it all – all the years of our lives to love.'

Babbie laid her curly red head against his fair one and they walked on, lovers even after four years of marriage.

Jon and Fiona were finding they had a good deal in common, for he, like she, was interested in flora and fauna, and they strolled away, pouncing every so often on unusual plant specimens.

Mary stood at the end of the cliffs in raptures. 'How perfectly wonderful!' she exclaimed in her high light voice. 'I've never been to this side of Rhanna before.'

The wind buffeted Kirsteen, tossing her curls, moulding her dress to her body, whipping up her skirt to once more reveal her long brown legs. She was unaware of the effect that the sight of her was having on Fergus. God, she was desirable, a creature that could tempt any man to – to – the muscle of his jaw tightened. If only they were alone in this place where passion had carried them heavenwards on effortless wings. Surrounded by such memories they could perhaps have made up – made love on the sands as they had done so often in the past . . .

Kirsteen staggered and stumbled on a rock. Alick

gallantly caught her arm, and without being able to help it, she found herself leaning against him. She felt awkward and unsure. Alick might go off with Mary, leaving her alone with Fergus and she didn't know how to handle him in his present frame of mind.

But then Fergus solved the problem for her. He was calling on Mary, his lilting voice snatched by the breeze: 'Mary! I'll show you round the place! I know it well. Come on.'

'What did you say?' Holding onto her hat, Mary bent into the wind towards him and he took her arm to pull her close, the wind giving him the excuse to shout louder than was necessary.

'I know how to get along Coire Srùb Bay without getting wet feet – even at high tide. I'll take you along by the reefs where you can see the Bodach Beag – when the tide recedes we'll go over.'

He was turning the knife in a wound already tender. Kirsteen swayed and closed her eyes. Coire Srùb Bay was *theirs*, where they had come in the wonderful days of their courtship; made love on the hot white sands – but most of all, Bodach Beag had belonged to them alone: they had laid claim to it on their first picnic in the bays of Croy. It was a tidal island, cut off from Rhanna at high water, a picturesque haven inhabited only by sheep who cropped the turf till it resembled a bowling green. The surrounding sea was broken by high craggy rocks and reefs bounded by pink shell sands. At the eastern end, abutting into the sea, was a round tower of rock shearing up to a tattered pinnacle fifty feet high. Its name, Bodach Beag, meant Little Old Man, and from certain angles it did indeed appear as a bent old man gazing broodingly into the frothing sea far below. Kirsteen and Fergus had gone to Bodach Beag on their first picnic together, they had been cut off by the tide but it hadn't mattered. They hadn't cared about time on that sunlit summer's day with the sea foaming at their feet and the great crags enfolding them as they made love on the sands with the water caressing them as tenderly as they caressed one another . . . Kirsteen gave a little sob and clamped her fist to her mouth.

Fergus and Mary had disappeared and Alick reached out to touch her. 'Hey, c'mon now,' he said soothingly. 'It can't be that bad.'

She passed a hand wearily over her eyes. 'Oh but it is, Alick, it is.'

'Everyone has rows in marriage,' he told her. 'Hell, I had enough of them myself at the start of mine.'

'This is more than just a row, Alick − it's − oh, I don't know what it is − I only know it's all my fault!' she cried despairingly.

'Nonsense, there's always two sides.' Alick glanced round. The clifftops were deserted, everyone having dispersed about their various pursuits. 'I tell you what,' he said, and taking her by the shoulders, he gently pushed her down on the grass and sat down beside her. 'We're going to sit here, in full view of everyone who isn't here, and you are going to use my shoulder − oh yes, I insist.' His dark eyes were

compassionate. 'You can·trust me now, really. I'm
not the silly young goat I once was – in fact I'd say
I've grown into a rather dignified and somewhat
respectable gentleman – in case you haven't noticed.'

Kirsteen gave him a watery smile. He had always
been able to make her laugh, to forget things – that
had been the root of the trouble all these years ago.

'But – you'll hate me when you hear – it's – it's
about you.' She clasped her knees and avoided his
eyes though she couldn't avoid hearing his startled
intake of breath.

'About me? I don't see . . .'

'Oh, it wasn't about you really, it was about Lorn
when it started. I wanted Fergus to stop shielding
him and let him do more about the farm. He got
angry – you know how afraid he is for Lorn – one
word borrowed another and – and it ended up with
me casting up the past – raking up that time when
you – when you . . .'

'Oh hell, no,' Alick protested, 'not that! No wonder
Fergus was looking daggers at me earlier. Oh, Lord!'
He drew up his knees and gazed broodingly at the
swirling sea below. There was silence between them
for some time before he burst out, 'But why,
Kirsteen? It's not like you to be so petty.'

Her face burned crimson and she shook her head.
'I don't really know. Well, perhaps I do – at least I
think I do – I felt as if history was repeating itself.
Lewis being made to feel he always had to play the
protector, fighting Lorn's battles – like – like . . .'

'Like Fergus and me,' Alick finished bitterly. 'Have

721

no fear of that, Kirsteen. The twins are entirely different from me and the big brother who did all my fighting for me. Lewis is the strong one physically, ay, but Lorn is the one with the backbone. Oh, don't get me wrong. Lewis is a grand little chap – a bit devil-may-care, but he'll settle down. He's too wise to ever let himself be leaned on by Lorn or by anyone else.'

'I'm sorry, Alick,' she murmured, 'I shouldn't have burdened you with this, and you on holiday.'

He smiled crookedly. 'Isn't that what brothers-in-law are for? To confide in now and then? I've always had the feeling that I owed you something, Kirsteen, and if a bit of advice from me helps you, then it is also salving my conscience to some extent. And I'll tell you something for nothing. Fergus is crazy about you – why else do you think he's gone off with my wife? Certainly not because he's ever been overly fond of her – I can assure you. He's behaving like a spoilt brat and the best thing you can do is ignore his behaviour. He'll be the first to come to his senses, believe me. He didn't search for you for six long years just because you happen to be a very lovely lady.'

'But I slapped him!' Kirsteen almost wailed.

'Really?' Alick grinned. 'Then no wonder he's sulking, I doubt anyone has ever hit him before. No doubt he deserved it, so stop worrying and let's go and enjoy ourselves. The tide's on the turn.'

They found the others on the beach, swimming or paddling, and without more ado Alick rolled up his immaculate trousers and went into the fray, leaving Kirsteen to go behind a rock and peel off her dress to emerge wearing a yellow swimsuit that made even Lachlan whistle in teasing admiration.

Fergus walked with Mary along Coire Srùb Bay. Now that he was out of Kirsteen's sight, his mask of jollity had fallen away, leaving his face dark and brooding.

In a way, Mary was glad to be free of his attentions, for while she had always enjoyed flirting with men, she had always instinctively known that Fergus wasn't the flirtatious type and she had felt somewhat uneasy when he had made such unusually friendly overtures towards her. She had never fully understood him, though she liked him a lot better than she had done in the beginning. 'Fergus, let's go back,' she suggested. 'I can see your Bodach Beag another time. I'm getting a bit peckish.' Hiding a smile at the alacrity with which he accepted her decision, she ran to keep up with him. She wasn't going to get her feet wet if she could help it, and she needed his help to negotiate the slippery reefs and rock pools.

Everyone was enjoying themselves at Tràigh Mor Bay. Fergus's eyes flashed at sight of Kirsteen in the yellow swimsuit, her limbs golden, her head thrown back in an agony of laughter as Niall and Shona splashed her with great handfuls of freezing sea. His absence hadn't affected her at all, and his frown deepened further when he spotted Lorn swimming happily, flanked by Lewis and Grant. A sharp protest rose to his lips but he quelled it.

Grant saw Fergus and unease clouded his young face in anticipation of the expected admonishment, but relief made him smile again as Fergus took off his shoes and socks and waded out to the shallows.

Lorn scrambled onto a rock, his breath coming fast but his blue eyes triumphant. 'I can swim quite well now, Father,' he said rather defiantly.

'So I see,' said Fergus dryly. 'You have obviously been practising.'

'I taught him, Father,' Grant said gruffly. 'I think everyone should learn how to swim. You never know when you might have to – do you?' There was a message in the words. Grant held his father's look boldly.

'Ay, you're right, lad,' Fergus conceded at last and understanding passed between father and son.

Rachel appeared over the cliffs. She had been to the tinkers' camp at Dunuaigh, which had been deserted except for old Mo lying in the sun in his pram. The old man and the little girl had spent a wonderful hour playing their fiddles, and Rachel was in a jubilant mood when she came to Tràigh Mor Bay and saw the frolics in the sea below. Without hesitation she raced with Squint down to the beach to stand for a moment curling her bare feet into the warm sand, savouring the feel of it trickling between her toes. She was wearing grubby blue shorts and one of her brothers' white cotton shirts and she looked like a beautiful boy with the wind tossing her short raven curls over her brow. Her eyes were turbulent, filled with a great restlessness,

an enquiring love of life that could find no expression in speech. Carefully she laid her beloved fiddle
on a rocky cradle, then ran straight into the sea to
splash joyfully over to Jon. Her fingers told him the
blithe message. 'The sun is shining and it is a beautiful day.'

'You remembered!' Jon cried in delight. 'You will
learn more of your special language, Rachel. I will
teach you many words before I have to go back to
Oban.'

Squint barked and threw his body into a curving
golden arch as he leapt like a dolphin over the
waves. He was a lovable clown of a dog, as much in
love with life as his small mistress, and the children
rolled him onto his back in which position he
remained quite contentedly, trusting implicitly the
human hands that held him as the sea cradled him
and swirled his floppy ears back and forth. His
tongue lolled from the side of his mouth and he
seemed to be grinning as one eye gazed thoughtfully
at the sky and the other kept guard on Rachel.
Later, when the eggs were being rolled over the
hillocks, he chased after them, pouncing on them,
tossing them into the air before fetching them back
uncracked to their owners. Everyone was in a state
of high spirits. For once Grant and Fiona were
agreeable to one another, and when he saw the eggs
she had painted for him, he let out a burst of
laughter.

Rachel stood with her arms folded behind her back
watching everyone rolling their eggs.

'What a pity we don't have one with her name on it,' Kirsteen murmured.

'Oh yes we do,' Grant said, and with a flourish presented Rachel with one of his eggs. She gazed at the loops of black hair, the grinning face and finally turned the egg round to see the word 'Dimples'. The ruse couldn't have been more successful. The dimples on her cheeks deepened, and brandishing the egg above her head she took to her heels, her brown legs a blur as she careered down the slope with Squint prancing beside her.

When the picnic was over everyone sat on the sands in replete contentment listening to Jon and Rachel, who sat side by side on the rocks playing their violins to the accompaniment of sea and wind. The melodies soared and blended with the sounds of nature, for nothing was more natural than to hear the music of instruments that were meant to be played in the open air. Terns, razorbills, and shear-waters cried from the cliffs and plummeted into the blue water as the strains of the fiddles filled the bay with sweet refrains. Jon's touch was sure, the bow silk against gossamer, the notes fine yet full of a liquid resonance that were one moment like the gentle waves lapping the shore, the next like the wild seas crashing, racing before the wind. Jon and Rachel were lost in the magic of music. The young man was enchanted by the untamed child, in his mind he likened her beauty to that of the wild hare-bells fluttering in the wind, fragile yet strong, a wildflower at one with the solitude and grandeur of nature.

Everyone had gathered into pairs. Lorn and Lewis sat side by side on the flat smooth stones over the rock pools, dangling their feet in the warm water; Shona's glowing auburn head was on Niall's shoulder, and little Helen was asleep in her arms; Babbie and Anton were perched at the entrance to a cave, his blond head close to her red one, her green eyes sparkling as he murmured things for her ears alone; Alick was with Mary; Fiona and Grant sat companionably side by side; Lachlan, his unruly hair blowing over his eyes, his thin face solemn as he listened to the music, had his arm protectively round Phebie's shoulders.

Only Fergus and Kirsteen remained apart from each other. Idly he played with the shells at his feet, picking them up, poking them back into the sand. He gave the impression of nonchalance, but every fibre in him longed to go over and crush Kirsteen to his heart, to feel her warm sweet nearness, to kiss her lips, caress her, tell her that he was sorry, for now that unreasoning anger had left him, he *was* sorry and longed to tell her so. He glanced at her from lowered brows. She was sitting against the shimmering blue-green backdrop of the sea, her hands clasped round her knees, the white dress blurring her curves to a softness that made her look not only gorgeous but strangely spiritual. Her fair head was thrown back, her chin proudly tilted; the symmetry of her profile was of the stuff that made poets pick up their pens; her skin was smooth and tanned, the tiny hairs on her arms bleached almost white after just a day in the sun. She was gazing straight ahead as if absorbed in the music. Fergus pulled in his breath – she was a million miles away from him, so aloof she appeared not to be aware of his existence. She had tried to speak to him, to tell him she was sorry – but he hadn't listened. Once more he had made the mistake of thinking he alone had the power to call the tune, but he had underestimated her own power, the strength of will that had once made her turn her back on all that she loved, to leave him knowing that she was carrying his child. The pain of his love for her ripped him apart. They had to talk – about Lorn – about everything, but she seemed now to be beyond his reach . . .

Jon was playing Rabbie Burns's *My Love is Like a Red Red Rose*. The beautiful evocative strains spilled into the air, liquid, haunting, accompanied by the pure, bubbling song of a nearby curlew. Kirsteen felt as if her heart was bursting with pent-up emotions. Red roses – Fergus – red rosebuds – the twins – laughing, crying – Fergus dancing on a night of love and laughter . . . Everything was a jumble in her mind. She felt Fergus's propinquity overwhelming her, sapping her of so much strength it took all her willpower to hold onto her mask of indifference. The exquisite notes flowed from Jon's violin and the words of the song beat into her, washing into her veins, swelling deep into her breast: 'And I will love thee still my dear till a' the seas gang dry.' She dug her nails into her knees in the agony of believing that the man she would love till the end of time seemed not to love her enough to forgive her for words spoken in the heat of anger.

Chapter Eight

The imminence of Merry Mary's retiral party was now uppermost in everyone's minds, and the day crept round at last, heralded by the arrival of slate-blue storm clouds building up on the horizon. An ominous calm lay over the glassy swell of the waves and old Joe rubbed his chin thoughtfully as he gazed out over the Sound of Rhanna.

'There will be a bugger o' a storm come nightfall,' he forecast with assurance, and one of the fisher-wives looked at him anxiously.

'The smacks were due in the day,' she said worriedly. 'And my man went out with them.'

'Ach, it will be all right,' Joe reassured. 'They'll maybe lie up at Mallaig for a while.'

'And maybe they won't,' the fisherwife said doubt-fully.

'Ach well, they know what they're doin',' old Joe soothed, though he looked again at the clouds and felt uneasy. If the men had indeed left the port of Mallaig they would be caught in the teeth of the storm long before they reached Rhanna . . .

Lewis squirmed as Kirsteen pulled the comb through his thick crop of curls but Kirsteen didn't prolong the agony and stood back to survey her twin sons with pride. Their faces were glowing from a brisk wash, auburn lights shone in their newly washed hair, and their blue eyes were big with excitement. Tonight they were playing with Rachel, old Andrew, old Mo, Jon, and one or two others who went to make up the 'Portcull Fiddlers'. They stood fidgeting in their white shirts and McKenzie kilts while Kirsteen gave them a thorough inspection. 'Right, you'll do,' she told them with a laugh. 'Take your jackets and go downstairs to wait for me.'

'I wish Grant was here,' Lorn said before he turned and followed Lewis downstairs. Kirsteen wished so too. Outside the rain slanted in horizontal sheets across the hills and battered against the window panes; the wind had keened over the moors and whined down the chimneys all day, sending so many blasts of smoke into the rooms that earlier Kirsteen had had to open doors and windows to allow the fresh air to swoop in and disperse the choking clouds. Out in the yard something clattered and Kirsteen prayed that it wasn't a part of the dairy roof, which had been mended during the winter gales. Fergus was out at the sheds now with Matthew, securing doors and windows against the fury of the gale. He had sent a message via Lewis that she was to go on ahead of him to the hall and he would be along later. She was dressed and ready but went along to her bedroom to pull back the curtains at the window. Rivers of rain gushed down the panes, interspersed with smatterings of hail and it was difficult to believe that only days before the weather had been so warm and springlike. She pressed the tips of her fingers to her lips and thought about Grant out with the smacks. His parting shot of four days ago came to her. 'Don't worry, Mother, I'll be back in time for Merry Mary's ceilidh – I wouldny miss it for the world. Press my navy suit and leave it ready on the bed – I must look my best for all those lassies waiting to pounce on me.' He had laughed, his dark eyes crinkling with mischief before he gave her a hurried kiss and went off.

'He'll be fine,' Alick had reassured her earlier. 'That lad could take on the Atlantic single-handed. He's got seafaring blood in him, with a few exceptions it runs in the family. I often wish I'd made a career out of the sea myself, though my view of it is maybe just a romantic one.'

Kirsteen could hear Alick talking with Mary in Shona's room as they prepared themselves for going out. Everyone was looking forward to the evening ahead. Part of Kirsteen didn't want to go: she wanted to stay behind and wait to see if Grant would come home; also – if she were here in the room when Fergus came in to get ready, they could perhaps at last make things up with no one but themselves in the house.

Absently she pulled a comb through her shining hair and almost without thinking went to open the door of the wardrobe to touch the wrappings on the fur jacket, wondering if she should wear it or if it was perhaps too grand for a village ceilidh . . . No – it wasn't just any ceilidh, this was a momentous night for little Merry Mary and it was only right that everyone should turn up looking their best. She took down the jacket and wrapped herself in its warm luxury. The fur collar nestled against her cheeks, she wished Fergus were with her to give her his approval, but they were still worlds apart, speaking without really communicating, and every night they went their separate ways to bed. It was such a strange situation. Kirsteen knew that it had to end, but at the same time she wondered just how long such a ridiculous state of affairs could go on. She buried her face into the collar of the jacket. Oh God! She missed him so: cuddled next to her in bed, talking over the events of each day, laughing over the little intimacies that only they shared . . .

The door burst open and Shona came in, her glorious mane of hair framing her sparkling face, the collar of her fur jacket pulled up cosily over her ears. 'Kirsteen, aren't you ready yet?' she chided. 'Lachlan's outside waiting with the car and Biddy's grumbling about the smell of it. She says she would rather have the smell of a horse's bum in front of her nose. You've to come with us though you'll be squeezed against Biddy. I'll have to sit on Niall's knee. The Johnstons are taking the twins and Mary and Alick –' She stopped in her outburst and her blue eyes shone. 'Oh, you're wearing your jacket, too! I brought mine hoping for a chance to wear it, but thinking it was a bit too showy for tonight. I'm looking forward to Merry Mary's ceilidh. Janet is looking after Ellie so I can stay out as long as I want. Isn't Father coming?'

'He'll be along later, he's securing things in the sheds.'

'You're still not talking, are you?' Shona sounded accusing.

'No-o.'

'I thought so.' Shona's face was serious as she faced Kirsteen. 'Now listen to me, Kirsteen. Niall and me only have a day or two left of our holiday, and before I go I want to see you and that stubborn father of mine on speaking terms. You're behaving like a couple of bairns, so you are! You both need a good skelping – and – and the cheek of you going all motherly on me and giving me advice about Niall a few years back. I haven't forgotten, in case you think it. You ought to be ashamed, the pair of you. Promise me you'll make it up tonight.'

Kirsteen's eyes sparkled suddenly. 'Yes, Grannie, I promise,' she said and giggled.

Little black specks were scurrying along the harbour, bending into a wind that was lashing the sea into white-veined rollers that churned round the reefs of Port Rum Point before throwing themselves violently against the Sgor Creags to roar and curl into the air in creamy plumes forty feet high. The fierce blasts of the sou'westerly shrieked low over the water, pushing the sea into the mouth of the harbour so that even in this normally sheltered anchorage, there was a violence in the waves lashing over the walls. The tops of the waves were being hurled onto the road, spattering over the hurrying figures making for the hall, but everyone was in a cheery mood and the stinging drops only made them shriek with surprise and scuttle along faster before another onslaught caught them out.

The village hall was no more than a converted barn, the term converted relating only to the addition of a new floor, some windows, and a mobile platform, a simple framework structure laid over with stout wooden planks. The hayloft still remained, much to the delight of courting couples who made full use of it when amorous feelings got the better of the desire to sing and dance.

Jon had spent a good part of the day helping the languid menfolk of the village to prepare the hall during the course of which there had been more discussion and banter than actual work, but with much tactful persuasion the young German had succeeded in accomplishing the task, and the hall looked splendid. It was hung with coloured lanterns and paper festoons, which, though made from newspaper strips coated with various hues of distemper, still looked very impressive – though here and there an odd item of news popped out.

Canty Tam, who revelled in gory details, leered at them and announced, 'I can see the headlines about thon murder where the mannie chopped his wife in wee pieces and fed her to the dog.' He leaned so far sideways in order to devour the exposed newsprint that he fell into a pile of chairs ably aided by Robbie, who clipped him on the ear for good measure.

Bundles of net floats hung round the platform together with bunches of balloons, and at the front was stretched a red banner on which Ranald had splashed in whitewash, A MERRY FAREWELL TO MERRY MARY. HASTE YE BACK.

'Here, what way are you putting that?' Tam asked with a derisive snort of mirth. 'The wifie is no' goin' anywhere; she's just givin' up the shop.'

But Ranald remained unruffled. 'Ach, it sounds fine, it's a poetic way o' sayin' things – though of course you wouldny know much about poetry. I read a lot and know fine there's more ways o' sayin' the obvious than just sayin' what is obvious.'

'Ay well, if that's what poetry does to the brain I'll stick to things that makes sense,' the grinning Tam returned.

But the crowd that poured into the hall that evening did not see the little flaws in the decor, and nods of appreciation followed the first swift appraisals. Merry Mary blushed with pleasure when she saw the efforts on her behalf and was amazed at the sight of the swelling ranks, but everyone who knew and loved the little Englishwoman with her limp ginger hair and big happy smile, was determined to give her a rousing send-off. She had served behind the counter of the village general store for more than fifty years, and as some of the older ones put it, 'was more native than the natives'. During her fifty years of service she had thoroughly enjoyed gathering and dispensing gossip, but had never done it in a malicious manner. For every bad word she had to say about anyone she had a dozen good ones to compensate, and everyone knew they would sorely miss the cheery smile they had grown so used to seeing whenever the bell tinkled above her door.

Merry Mary was radiant that evening despite a dress patterned with livid orange and purple flowers and, when Scott Balfour, resplendent in kilt and tweed jacket, came in accompanied by his attractive wife, Rena, a murmur went round the room. 'The Laird himself – Merry Mary is indeed honoured. He'll be here to make the presentations later.'

Elspeth, who herself had caused quite a stir appearing in a black dress with white ruffles at the throat and wrists, her grey hair attractively arranged round her gaunt face, her thin lips bearing a discreet smudge of lipstick, whispered to Merry Mary, 'It is a popular woman you are indeed, Merry Mary. I doubt there's naught but a handful here would turn up to see me off – no, not even for my own funeral.'

'Ach, I'll come anyway, Elspeth, never you fear,' the little Englishwoman said kindly. 'But it is talking of funerals you are and you lookin' so grand you might be goin' to your own wedding. Your hair is a treat, that it is.'

Elspeth blushed in confused appreciation of the compliment, but she said off-handedly, 'Ach, that rascal Fiona bullied me into letting her do it – she's a modern miss if ever there was one, though I'm glad to see she is no' wearin' the trowser tonight. I'm thinkin', though, that she's overdone things wi' my person, for I was never a one for fancy ways. But och, it's no' every day I get the chance to see one o' my friends off in style – mainly because there's precious few bodies I can call my friends,' she sniffed. 'I canny help but think o' Mirabelle betimes. She would aye listen to my troubles whether she felt like it or no.'

Merry Mary patted her scrawny arm. 'Well, you know you're always welcome at my cottage for a crack and a cuppy and you can bring me a bit o' gossip for I'll no' be gettin' so much of that now.'

Anton, looking exceedingly handsome with his fair hair brushed back and his blue eyes shining, approached and with a little click of his heels he first kissed Merry Mary's hand and then turned to Elspeth and made a similar gesture. 'Ladies, may I say how charming you look tonight and I am hoping that you will do me the honour of dancing with me later.' He looked Elspeth straight in the eye and she hastily composed her features into stern lines as he went on in his charming broken English: 'Frau Elspeth, I have never forgotten your kindness to me when I was ill and how you put the strength back in my "feets" with your home-made tablet. And though I don't see you often, I think of you and the times you came up to my room and fed me the Benger's Food – so tonight we will do the Highland Fling together, eh?'

'Ach, get away wi' you, your tongue is smoother than silk,' scolded Elspeth, acutely aware of Merry Mary's smile, though she was secretly thrilled at having been singled out by the young German for whom she had a soft spot (though never for one moment would she let the fact be known).

Anton turned away and Merry Mary nodded meaningfully and said, 'So, you were up in his room thon time he was laid up and near dyin' – and all the time you were puttin' it about you had no time at all for Jerries. Well, well, 'tis learnin' we are all the time, but –' she said, her eyes twinkling while Elspeth snorted, 'don't worry, Elspeth; I will no' be tellin' a soul about you and your wee secret sojourns in Mr Büttger's sickroom.'

'You are a silly woman, Merry Mary!' Elspeth blustered. 'That was years ago, and anyways, I have no intention of discussing it with you or anyone else.' She stomped away in high dudgeon.

Babbie watched her retreat and her green eyes positively danced. Grabbing her husband's arm, she smothered her giggles into his sleeve and hissed, 'You impudent young bugger, Mr Büttger! That was positively brazen. I've always known you had a certain charm, but that was bare-faced and calculated.'

Anton was unrepentant. 'Nonsense, liebling, I have made the night for a lonely old lady and I have also given Mistress Beag something to talk about – see how she scowls thunder at me.'

He was right. Behag had witnessed the exchanges and her jowls sagged over her neck as she told Kate, 'Hmph, did you see that? These two lettin' a German kiss them – ay, that Elspeth never did fool me. She is smoulderin' wi' passion under that sour face o' hers and of course, wi' her bein' a widow woman things will be worse for her – what I mean is, a pure body like myself has no knowledge of the lusts o' the flesh and has no need to hanker after them.'

'Ay, right enough,' Kate said, nodding in mock sympathy. 'Though wi' all that enchantment you hide so well 'tis a miracle you escaped intact.'

Behag affected not to notice the sarcasm and gazed round the crowded hall. 'A fine turnout I must say. I wonder will I get the same when I retire. I've missed hardly a day behind the counter o' the Post Office and I am a native of the island, after all – Merry Mary is just an incomer.'

'You'll maybe get a send-off you never bargained for,' Kate said, and dimpled. 'Right off that damty island if you don't learn to smile a bit more instead o' grumpin' your head off. Folks only get what they deserve in this life, and if you go on moanin' like an old hag you'll get no more than a box o' matches and a rocket when your time comes.'

'My, my, but you're a spiteful woman, Kate McKinnon,' Behag blustered and flounced away to seek out her brother Robbie on whom she continually vented her wrath.

Jon had been passing the time with the Rev. John Gray who had been delighted at the young German's return to the island and had given him a very cordial welcome. Everyone had been glad to see Jon and his popularity was proven when he had affectionately been bestowed with the nickname 'Jock'. The men didn't resent his intrusion into the life of the village – rather, they were glad to off-load the responsibility of organising Merry Mary's ceilidh onto his willing shoulders, and when he climbed onto the platform to arrange the children into their places, a cheer went up and cries of 'Good old Jock!' went round the room.

Jon had already taught Rachel much of the deaf and dumb language and the two now carried on an animated conversation with their hands. Annie felt a rush of pride as she beheld her raven-haired daughter on the platform. She wished Dokie Joe was here to see his beautiful, clever child. His weather-beaten face would have given little away, but Annie knew that while he was too slow to keep up with Rachel's mercurial brain, he was nevertheless so proud of her that often, when he'd had a bit too much to drink, he boasted about her to his mates. Annie sighed. She often wished that her husband didn't have to make his living from the sea. Forbye being a financially uncertain existence, it was a lonely one for her with him being away for days on end. He should have been due in with the smacks tonight but there was little hope of that with the storm blowing up.

Torquil Andrew, a tall strapping man with Norse colouring and looks that set female hearts fluttering, came up to Annie. 'I'll be keeping you company tonight, Annie,' he stated softly.

Her dark eyes glittered. 'Ay,' was all she said, and her thoughts turned away from the cold dark wastes of the sea and back to the pleasant realities contained within the big, softly lit barn.

Lewis saw Torquil's hand briefly touching Annie's

and he thought about the time he had chanced upon them standing very close together in an abandoned fuel shed – too close – the kind of nearness that made grown men tremble and caused women to make funny little sighing noises. The ruffled Annie had jumped away from Torquil like a scalded cat and had hissed at Lewis, 'Never you be tellin' a soul about this, Lewis McKenzie! Do you hear?' Until the tirade, Lewis in his youth and innocence had not realised there was anything for him to tell, but at Annie's words he had sensed there was an opportunity going to make a little money. 'Not if you give me sixpence every week till the day you die,' he had told Annie with a smile, and though she had raged at him, she had from that day paid him silence money.

Lewis smiled to himself and drew his bow over his fiddle with a gay little flip. He loved crowds. He enjoyed gaining their attention, and he liked to be liked; but if the occasion demanded otherwise, that was the way of life and he accepted the good with the bad, without fuss.

Lorn was nervous and sat quietly beside old Bob, who was helping him to tune his fiddle. His heart was beating rapidly and he tried to will himself into a state of tranquillity. From the side of his eye he saw Ruth sitting in a corner in the darkest recess on the other side of the platform. Although her mother had made her a new dress it had certainly been created by the hands of an inexpert seamstress. It was shapeless and ill-fitting and made Ruth look more ungainly than ever. She was sitting very still, her hands folded

743

serenely in her lap, but her violet eyes were huge with unease, and Lorn knew she was, like him, uncertain of herself, terrified of crowds. The sight of her made him feel more uncomfortable than ever, and he turned his head and looked up, catching his mother's eye. He smiled, a radiant smile that belied his racing pulse, and Kirsteen smiled back though she sensed his fears, and her heart twisted with the knowing that soon he could be facing hazards and pain that might prove too much for his sensitive spirit to bear. But the love of life was in his eyes: it leapt out like a living thing and she knew deep inside herself that he would bravely face anything the future might hold for him.

Old Mo was being lifted in his pram up onto the platform while his fellow tinkers were making good use of the opportunity to sell sprigs of dried white heather to the assembly. A smiling damsel, looking extremely pretty despite the fact that she was wearing dirty white sandshoes beneath a tartan dress, followed old Mo onto the platform and accosted Bob.

'Ach, get away wi' you, lass!' he told her irritably. 'We can get any amount o' that ourselves on the moors. It's the towrists you should be takin' in wi' your fancy talk, no' the folk who live wi' the damty stuff!'

'Ah, but you weren't thinkin' to be bringin' any with you,' returned the girl quick as a flash. 'Is it too mean you are to be buyin' a bit o' good luck for the old lass who has served you well all these long years?'

'You make her sound like a bloody cow,' grumbled Bob, but nevertheless he dug in his pocket for his coppers. Those standing nearby followed suit because the tinker girl was renowned for putting vicious curses on those unwise enough to reject her wares.

Up until then the majority of the gathering had consisted mainly of womenfolk but now the men, having fortified themselves in the Portcull Hotel, breezed in, merry and windblown, bringing with them the usual whisky fumes, though on this occasion the strong palpable smell of mothballs overpowered all else. Everyone wrinkled their noses though it was naturally assumed that the odour was just a stronger version of that which was experienced every Sabbath in kirk when Sunday best was brought out from wardrobes perpetually tainted by naphthalene. But there was another reason for the smell and it arrived when Dodie catapulted into the room, his aversion to social gatherings having been overcome by his desire to witness Merry Mary's official retirement. His entry caused all heads to turn and all murmurings to cease because, except for one other memorable ceilidh at Laigmhor, no one had ever seen the old eccentric so well turned out.

Although he still wore his greasy cloth cap, he was otherwise attired in a thin but well cut sports jacket with vented sides; his grey flannel trousers were immaculate, his white shirt spotless. He was obviously stunned with embarrassment at the sensation he was causing, and he stood red-faced, enveloped in mothball fumes, his lips stretched nervously in an attempted smile. The Laird, though startled, turned discreetly away, having noticed that Dodie's stout brogues were the very pair he had thrown into the dustbin some time ago and Rena whispered to him, 'Poor dear old Dodie, he wouldn't have taken them if I had offered them to him.'

'Mercy on us,' muttered a round-eyed Isabel. 'Would you look at that, Jim Jim. I'm thinkin' old Dodie has maybe come into some money.'

'Ay, ay, it's only towrists and gentry wear clothes like these,' said Jim Jim thoughtfully. 'But I'm thinkin' there's something gey queer goin' on, for he's reekin' o' mothballs like these other chiels that have just come in.'

Morag Ruadh tossed her red head and her lips tightened. Memories were stirring fires in her she had thought buried, invoked by the sound of Erchy and Todd tuning the pipes, a procedure that entailed much puffing and blowing in order to produce squeaks and groans and several other sounds that bordered on the unseemly. Morag felt a pang of excitement, which in turn made her feel uneasy. She had not had such feelings since that other night of the Manse ceilidh – a night she didn't want to remember. She had only put in an appearance tonight because Dugald was having the shop handed over and he had insisted that Morag be there. 'We are members of this community now, Morag,' he had told her quietly enough, though determination had edged his tones to sharpness. 'As my wife you will accompany me to this function and you will bring Ruthie. See she has a new dress, by the way. I will not have my daughter looking like a sack of potatoes in front of everyone, particularly the bairnies who will be her schoolmates after Easter is over.'

The fiddlers were practising now and the strains of a Strathspey filled the air. Morag's blood pulsed and she tried not to think of the minister's words to her recently. 'You must stop using the Lord as a vessel for guilt, Morag,' he had told her sternly. 'You can only be absolved if you treat God as a friend, not some sort of enemy who spits fire and vengeance. If you think like that, you are worshipping the Devil, and the Lord himself will have difficulty finding a door in your heart.' Morag glanced balefully at the Rev. John Gray standing at the foot of the platform talking animatedly to Jon Jodl; his hair was now silvery-white, his face full of a serenity that the last few years had brought him; contentment cloaked him like a mantle.

Anger swamped Morag. What gave him the right to be so smug and self-righteous? It had taken him long enough to come to terms with the islanders and in so doing coming to terms with God. His contentment had sprung from the night of the Manse ceilidh, while hers had been robbed from her – it was all Mr Gray's fault, really. She wasn't to blame, yet every waking day was a punishment for her.

'Here now, man, where are you gettin' things like these?' asked round-faced Robbie of the abashed Dodie. 'These is towrists' clothes.'

'Ay, and that shirt?' put in Tam, gazing round at a display of shirts the same as Dodie's, both in quality and naphthalene saturation.

'Did you get them from that mannie who's been goin' round the island sellin' things out o' suitcases?' enquired Torquil Andrew, whose deep chest strained against the fine material of his own shirt.

Dodie nodded eagerly and his carbuncle wobbled. 'Ay, that's right enough. He came by my door a day or two back.'

Ranald eyed Dodie's jacket and trousers. 'But these things cost a lot of money. Have you won the pools, Dodie?'

Dodie glowered at the money-conscious Ranald. 'Indeed no. I am not a one to gallop my money away on such things,' he said primly.

'But what you get in your towrist tin wouldny even pay for that bonny tie you're wearin',' Ranald persisted.

But Dodie wouldn't be drawn. He was not going to give away the secret he had kept since the *Politician* had been doomed on the rocks in Eriskay Sound. On one of his frequent beachcombing sojourns he had chanced upon a treasure trove of shirts floating in with the tide like disembodied ghosts. He had collected more than five dozen of them, and, stuffing them into his peat creel, he had hastened home to wash them in the purling burn near his cottage. With the sea water out of them, and the sun and wind endowing them with a dazzling whiteness, Dodie had felt rich indeed and had visualised the look on the faces of those who would receive the gifts. But news of the police and Customs searching the islands for contraband had reached his ears and in a panic he had stowed the garments away in an ancient bride's kist, together with a generous amount of mothballs. He had almost forgotten his treasure chest till the persistent rapping on his door had heralded a visit from a travelling salesman burdened down with cases which, despite Dodie's protests, he had opened to reveal garments the likes of which the old eccentric had only seen on the backs of the gentry. The salesman hadn't appeared to hear Dodie's refusals to buy nor had he seemed to believe that he was poorer than a kirk mouse just. Perhaps tales of country folk owning treasures they believed to be worthless had reached the salesman's ears, for he had craned his neck and gazed past Dodie to the dim interior of the house. 'Surely we can do a deal,' he had purred coaxingly. 'You look as though you could be doing with some new clothes. You must have some sort of valuables lying about gathering dust.'

'I tell you, I haveny anything, only my shells and stones fro the seashore,' Dodie had wailed and was about to shut the door when he remembered the shirts. 'Wait you here,' he had instructed, and closing the door in the man's face, he had plodded up the passage to the kist in the bedroom. The shirts were as perfect as the day he had packed them away and he had presented the naphthalene-smelling bundles to the salesman, who, holding his breath, had flipped through them quickly, almost immediately recognising

749

their quality, though he had said off-handedly, 'From the guff off them they must have been lying about for years. I'll give you three pounds for the lot.'

'Indeed you will no'. These is good shirts, and if you can't be doin' better than that I'll just be havin' them back.' But the man had quickly evaded Dodie's outstretched hands and for the next half hour the pair had bartered till in the end the exasperated salesman, realising that the old eccentric wasn't as simple as he had first imagined, had handed over a complete rig-out in exchange for the shirts. 'And I'll be keepin' one o' these to wear wi' my jacket,' Dodie had smirked, snatching a shirt back from the pile.

'No flies on you, old boy,' the man had said, grinning, and went off jauntily to make a good profit selling the shirts at croft and cottage, his smooth tongue gliding out explanations for the naphthalene odour.

Thus it was that the men, each believing they had secured a bargain, turned up at the ceilidh wearing identical shirts, and for once in his life Dodie felt like laughing himself into a fit as fishermen and farmers, crofters and shepherds, eyed one another in some discomfort.

Dodie galloped away from the scene to seek out Merry Mary to whom he presented a bottle of spray perfume. 'It's just a wee thing,' he told her with a gloomy smile. 'I know leddies need scent to make them smell nice.' From anyone else this would have been the ultimate insult, but from guileless Dodie it was a compliment, and Merry Mary accepted the gift with due appreciation, time dulling her memory to the fact that the spray bottle was identical to those given up by the *Politician* years before. Dodie had a tidy supply of the bottles which he kept for 'special leddies'.

Despite the fiercely competing aromas of whisky, naphthalene, and perfume, the evening was proving to be an unprecedented success. Outside the wind howled and the hail rattled against the windows but everyone inside gave themselves up to the gay tunes of pipes, accordions, and fiddles. Jon was in his element. He itched to play old Mo's violin, a beautiful creation of gold with deeper undertones of rich dark red. The old man obviously cherished the instrument, because it was in perfect condition. He looked rather worried by Jon's request to play a solo on it, but with a nod of consent he allowed the young German to pick it up. Jon was enthralled. He knew at once that this was no ordinary violin and as he guided the bow and touched the strings with his long intelligent fingers, evoking sounds hauntingly human yet that might have been the language of spirits, Jon knew that he held in his arms an instrument that could easily be 250 years old, probably a Cremonese, created by a great craftsman of northern Italy. Jon had seen a similar one owned by a well-known musician, but no two violins were alike; each had its own distinctive appearance and unique tone of voice. Jon closed his eyes and gave himself up to the ecstasy of being privileged enough to actually handle such a violin.

The minister was enthralled. Leaning his silvery thatch against the wall he closed his eyes, hugged one knee and breathed deeply. 'The boy is brilliant,' he murmured to his wife, Hannah. 'Ah, he makes me feel I am soaring on the wings of angels. What control, what sensitivity – and the tone of that violin – perfection.'

Rachel, too, was lost in enchanted admiration for the young man who had been so patient with her and taught her so much during the short time he had been on the island. Her eyes were dark with rapture as she watched his masterful fingers, listened to the notes spilling powerfully and evocatively, touching chords in her soul that pushed tears of pure joy from her eyes.

The last notes died away and the applause shook the rafters. Jon handed the violin back to old Mo. 'Thank you for letting me play it. It was a wonderful experience.'

The old man nodded and tucked his precious violin in at his side as if it were a baby. Jon realised he probably knew nothing of its value. An instrument like that could fetch a vast sum of money, but Jon wasn't going to tell old Mo that because he knew by doing so he would take away the only thing left to the old man, the deep contentment and joy he experienced every time he picked up his violin. He cherished it for that and to violate anyone's contentment would have been to Jon a sin. If the other tinkers found out its worth they would sell it, the money would be frittered away on useless modern trivia, and old Mo, already saturated in liquor, would just drink himself to death very speedily, his life joyless without his fiddle. At the moment he was quite happy; the violin brought him happiness as well as a fairly good profit and that, to Jon, was that, though as he parted with the instrument he felt that he was parting with a tiny part of his soul, for what musician would not yearn to own such a treasure as that owned by the old tinker.

The hall was now very warm and Phebie flopped beside Kirsteen on a bench to fan her face, laughing at the sight of Niall and Shona dancing a jig while everyone else did an eightsome reel. Fiona was a sparkling-eyed nymph in a pretty red dress, her long legs carrying her with ease over the floor. Captain Mac and his crew were present that night, having arrived into port before the full fury of the storm got under way, and Fiona wasn't short of partners.

'Thank the Lord she discarded her trousers in favour of a dress,' said Phebie. 'The besom wasn't going to, you know. She was all for coming in the trowser just to see the effect it would have on the cailleachs, but for once Lachy put his foot down and told her she could stay at home if she insisted on looking like a laddie.'

Biddy, who was comfortably ensconced nearby, sipping at a glass of rum, smiled sourly, showing her 'teeths', which she had remembered to wear for the occasion. 'Ach, you should leave the lass alone,' she scolded mildly. 'The bairnie has the right idea I'm tellin' you. Skirts are just a temptation to a man, but the trowser makes it easier for a lass to keep a finger on her halfpenny – and they must be cosy too. If I wasny such a cailleach, I'd wear them myself. They'd be fine for keeping out the wind when I'm on my bike.'

Phebie's eyes twinkled. 'Surely you aren't needing protection from men at your age, Biddy.'

'Ach, you daft lassie,' Biddy said, her old eyes crinkling. 'It's more like them needin' protection from the sight o' my auld legs. That bugger Todd told me the other day I looked like a bowly-legged hen wi' the gout – an' him wi' the most godforsaken knees I've ever clapped eyes on! Would you look at him up on that stage, wearin' the kilt and smilin' like he was proud o' knees like cow's knuckles.'

Todd was beyond caring about his knees or any other part of his anatomy. He and his cronies had made frequent trips outside where several bottles of whisky had been buried earlier. Bedraggled by rain and wind the men were now in stages ranging from merry to hilarious and turned deaf ears on nagging spouses. Old Mo, too, had quite a few bottles hidden in his pram and he, together with old Bob and Andrew, was decidedly under the influence. Even Jon was looking slightly flushed, and Anton murmured in Babbie's ear, 'I suspect our friend has had a drop of Tinker's Brew. His fingers are moving so fast, it's taking me all my time to keep up. I think we will go and sit by Frau Kirsteen – McKenzie is taking his time in turning up.'

Kirsteen was glad of their company. She had taken

part in one dance after another but still she felt lonely, waiting for the one person without whom her life seemed empty. The door opened and she couldn't keep the expectancy out of her eyes, but it wasn't Fergus and her face flamed.

Anton and Babbie both sensed her loneliness and the latter said with a laugh, 'Dance with Anton, will you, Kirsteen? He's got far too much energy for a tired old nurse like me.'

Anton was panting for breath but gallantly extended his arm. 'I would be honoured, Frau Kirsteen. You have grace, and I have a feeling you will not tread on my toes like my Babbie – her "feets" are growing more like Biddy's every day.'

Amidst skirls of laughter he whirled Kirsteen away and Babbie said to Shona, 'You know, if it was any of my business I'd give your father a good talking to, keeping Kirsteen waiting for him like this. He could easily have left the sheds to Matthew and Donald. It isn't often Kirsteen gets a night out. It will serve him right if, when he does arrive, she gives him the cold shoulder. He deserves it.'

Shona didn't say anything because Babbie had just voiced her own sentiments. Shona's deep blue eyes flashed. She thought of her own marriage with Niall. There had been a lot of rough patches but they were far outweighed by the smooth. Niall was an easy and wonderful person to live with, though often he had his hands full trying to deal with the frequent temper tantrums she threw. Shona sighed. Life would never be easy for someone living with a McKenzie, and she realised how lucky she was to have Niall and how fortunate her father was to have Kirsteen.

Alick shivered a little as he stood in the shelter of the porch where he had come to puff his pipe and get a breath of air – and to wait for Fergus. The wind tore in from the Sound, bringing blasts of salt-tainted rain in its freezing breath. Through the darkness Alick saw the sea, tossing and heaving, a white swirl of rollers that boomed and crashed into the harbour where they lost some power but were still vicious enough to heave themselves over the road and plosh against the sturdy walls of the cottages, some of the droplets showering Alick as he stood watching, awed and fascinated by the might of the elements. Voices floated and he stiffened – one of them belonged to Fergus. Matthew and his son, Donald, now a tall, fine-featured young man, went past Alick into the hall but Alick intercepted his brother with the accusing words, 'So, you've finally made it. What did you have to do? Re-build the dairy?'

Fergus was immediately on the defensive, his misery over his row with Kirsteen having resulted in a slow build-up of wrath against Alick. 'Just supposing I was! If I had to rely on you for help the damned place would be around my ears by now!'

'Oh, c'mon, big brother, Matthew and Donald would have managed fine between them,' Alick's voice was cool and controlled. 'Why don't you come right out and admit you were playing for time? Piling the punishment onto Kirsteen, making her suffer just a little bit more, nursing your grievances like a bloody baby! Well, sulking bairns don't make men big or turn them into all-conquering heroes . . .'

'You've a damned nerve!' exploded Fergus. 'Mind your own bloody business and get out of my way or you'll be sorry you interfered. I don't intend to get soaked to the skin while I stand here listening to you whining.'

'Me, whining? Well at least I say what's in my mind instead of putting the cork in and letting my grievances fester away like rotting sores! You'd better watch out, Fergus, don't push Kirsteen too far. If you think she's in there moping you've another think coming. She's a lovely and rather special lady, the men are queuing up to dance with her. One of these days you'll waken out of your petty little stupor and find she's not so willing to come running back at your high and mighty command – there's other fish in the sea you know.'

'Ay, and by God, wouldn't you like to be one of them!' cried Fergus harshly. 'We've already had a taste of you and your ill-controlled lust! It's strange how you invite trouble, from the day you walked, you lunged from one buggering mess into another. It's because of you we're in the damned state we're in now – but of course,' he said, laughing mirthlessly, 'you must know that already! It seems you and Kirsteen have been chatting cosily behind my back.'

'Too bloody true, but hardly cosily! That day of the picnic – when you were fawning over my wife

– your own was so flaming miserable I made her tell me what was wrong. By Christ! What she had to say made me feel uneasy all right. It all came back, all the things I tried to forget but never quite managed.'

A blast of wind hurled Fergus against Alick. The rain whirled and lashed about them, they were so close each could feel the other's heavy breath; in the darkness the brothers glared at each other, the pale blurring blobs of their faces only inches apart. Fergus felt dark bubbling rage overwhelming him. The truth of Alick's words had hit him like a sledgehammer, then, suddenly, Alick's fist shot out to land Fergus a blow on the face that sent him reeling backwards, away from the shelter of the porch, into the wind and the sleety rain that stung his eyes, blinding him for a minute. But Fergus's reactions were only momentarily suspended. Springing forward he caught Alick by the collars of his jacket and hauled him round the side of the building. The raging of a nearby burn was as nothing to the all-consuming rage that sped through his veins, charging him with a power that rendered the slightly-built Alick helpless. With a snarl Fergus pushed his brother into a rickety hayshed and threw him against the piled-up bales of hay. Then Fergus advanced, his black eyes throwing sparks in his deathly white face. 'You asked for this, little brother,' he gritted, and his knuckle of bunched steel smashed into flesh and bone.

Alick shook his head to clear it but he didn't cower

away as he might have done in days gone by. Fear ripped through him but instead of making him submissive it bolstered him into action. Dancing to the middle of the floor he faced the towering mass of bone and muscle that was his brother. 'Right,' he said quietly, 'all's fair in love and war, so the misguided saying goes. And with that in mind we'll do this fairly.' Tucking his left arm behind his back he went on tauntingly, 'I was the cause of you losing your arm, as you've just reminded me – and I wouldn't like to have an unfair advantage over a one-armed hero – so – come and get me.'

The soft light from the hall windows filtered in through the door of the shed allowing Fergus to see the dim figure of his brother standing watching him mockingly. In a blind fury Fergus lunged, but Alick intercepted the blow with an upward toss of his hand and before Fergus could regain his balance he was catapulted across the shed by an expertly-placed punch, which made his head spin. Surprise lowered Fergus's defences and he wasn't prepared for the next crack that sent him sprawling among the hay bales. Rage boiled in his blood, but as well as anger there was something else, something that reached down, plucking at the churning cauldron of his emotions: this was his brother fighting him, the one-time blubbering, apron-tied boy for whom he had fought endless battles, who was now fighting back – at last he was fighting back. Briefly, Fergus wondered when the change had come about. Certainly Alick had seemed different after the hellish nightmare all these years ago: the man in him had begun to creep out. But this – when had this happened? With little physique behind him, he was holding his own, winning by tactics that made Fergus look blundering and inexpert. Admiration flooded Fergus's being even as he went into the fray with his brother. They sparred, punched, hurt each other, while outside the wind howled, and the music spilled from the hall. Then, almost simultaneously they called a truce and collapsed onto the hay, panting, half-laughing, half-ashamed, wordlessly gathering breath from heaving lungs. Alick took out his hanky and dabbed a split lip tenderly before he said apologetically, 'We're even now for those years ago when you beat the hell out of me and I went scampering away with my cowardly tail between my legs.' He took a deep breath and in the darkness he smiled though it made him wince. 'God! I feel hellish – I'll ache for days – yet, I've never felt better in my life! We've never spoken about things – just locked it all away, now I feel I've crawled out of my hole to see daylight for the first time in years – and – it's a bloody marvellous experience, if you see what I mean?'

Fergus gulped a lungful of air. 'I know what you mean all right – what I don't see is how – how –'

'How I learned to use my fists? The Army taught me a few tricks, Fergus. I took up boxing for a giggle – well, I was always one for a giggle, as fine you know. But I became quite good at it – so much so I earned myself a bit of respect from the other lads. A

760

good feeling that – to be respected – to feel self-respect.'

'You kept it dark enough.'

'Saw no point in boasting – I did too much of that in my time and found I kept getting smaller instead of bigger . . . Anyway, tonight you dug up my well-kept secret.' He passed Fergus a cigarette and they sat on the hay bale puffing companionably for a few silent moments then Alick said deliberately, 'I just had to get a poke at you back there. You're so bloody stubborn, you'd never have listened to me otherwise. You feel pretty peeved because Kirsteen threw me in your face – right? Do you know why she said the things she did? It was a kind of chain reaction. She was terrified the twins were going to turn out like you and me – one being made to lean, the other to be leaned on – history repeating itself, if you like.'

'Hell no! I never saw it like that,' Fergus groaned.

'Neither did Mother, but sometimes love can be blind and very blinding.'

Fergus gripped his brother's arm roughly. 'Thanks – for helping me to see,' he said awkwardly.

Alick laughed. 'Think nothing of it, big brother. I owe you some favours – and now, it's time you and Kirsteen got down to brass tacks and decide what you're going to do about Lorn's future. Oh, don't start! I got it out of Kirsteen yesterday. She's beside herself with worry and had to tell someone.'

'Ay, no doubt.' Fergus stood up. 'I think – we'd better show our faces at the ceilidh,' he said sheepishly.

'Do you think they're worth showing?' chuckled Alick. 'I feel as if an elephant has pushed me into a door. Here – take my hanky and clean yourself up a bit.'

'I suppose we could always say we just bumped into each other.' Fergus's deep laugh boomed out, and with arms thrown around each other's shoulders, the brothers went to join the ceilidh in a jubilant mood and were able to slip into the softly lit hall virtually unnoticed. Everyone was intent on enjoying themselves. Bruised faces and cut lips weren't uncommon at the height of a good ceilidh. Tam and one or two of his cronies had already come to good-natured blows over the location and owner-ship of the hidden whisky, and they were now ensconced in a corner re-creating the scuffles with avid enjoyment.

Across the crowded room Kirsteen's blue eyes met Fergus's dark gaze. Although she was apart from him she saw the hungry yearning in the burning glance he threw at her. Her heart skipped a beat, her cheeks reddened. The notes from Jon's fiddle poured into her and made her tremble. It was as if she was hearing the music for the first time since the start of the ceilidh. Warmth flooded her being. It was going to be a perfect evening, nothing could go wrong now – now that she had interpreted the messages of love, desire – forgiveness – flowing out of the beautiful black eyes of the man she loved with such intensity it was an ache in her heart.

Chapter Nine

Out on the Sound of Rhanna lightning forked into the wind-crazed surface of the water. All day long the smacks had battled against the raging seas and the men were haggard with exhaustion. They had left Mallaig early, when the sky had given no hint of the brewing fury sweeping with insidious speed from the south-west. The sea had been calm, deceptively so, and it had remained like silk till the menacing banks of purple-black cloud had started rolling over the sky, blotting out the gold and the blue, spurring the waves to restlessness. By the time the men had realised a storm was in the offing, they were far out in the Atlantic and it was too late to turn back. Howling winds attacked the small boats, pushing them through endless successions of deep troughs. Smatterings of hail and snow whirled and eddied, blotting out the horizon, confining visibility to a few yards. The *Magpie* rolled and pitched and Grant staggered up from the fo'c'sle, feeling too sick to join the rest of the crew in the hearty meal of bacon, eggs and beans the cook had just prepared. He had managed to gulp down some hot black tea sweetened with condensed milk, but even that lay heavy in a belly delicate from a heavy bout of drinking the night before. He had matched dram for dram to keep up with the rest of the men, but now he told himself it was the last time – he wasn't a man yet and no amount of hard liquor would ever make him one.

The mate was at the wheel and he threw Grant an amused smile as the boy brushed past him and out of the wheelhouse. The wind caught and bullied him, spicules of ice froze his lips to numbness and he gasped for air. His belly heaved and he was catapulted across the sopping deck to be hurled against the rails with such force he felt as if he had been punched by a giant hand. He retched and his vomit was thrown back at him by the wind, making him shiver in disgust and recall vividly but too late Skipper Joe's warning, 'Never spew into the wind, she'll just throw it back at you like confetti.' Grant coughed and spluttered. He had thought he knew it all, but every fresh trip out at sea warned him he was a mere novice . . . A vision of his mother flashed into his swimming head. Thank God she couldn't see him now – grey, splattered with vomit – his father wouldn't much like the sight of him either. Fergus was a man who could hold a good dram. Vaguely Grant wondered if such a man had ever been foolish, had ever taken too much to drink – been sick with it . . .

A thirty-foot wall of water crashed over the stern, sucking it down into a trough as deep as a ravine. For a heart-stopping eternity Grant choked in a watery world, his knuckles white as his hands clamped round the rail like a vice. Gasping for air

Grant slithered down the slanting deck – straight into the arms of Dokie Joe, whose tight black curls and grey-flecked black beard made him look older than his thirty-five years.

Dokie's eyes were narrowed to slits in his sea-drenched face as he glared into Grant's salt-reddened eyes. 'What the hell do you think this is?' he yelled above the wind. 'A bloody joy ride? Get into the wheelhouse and give Dan a hand. I'll be back in a minute.'

'Ay, ay, Skipper!' shouted Grant and fought his way to the shelter of the wheelhouse.

Dokie Joe was soon back inside the wheelhouse as well, smiling now, his white teeth startling in a face whipped to mahogany-brown from years of fishing in all weathers. Through the whirling hail and snow – now turning to sleet – he had caught a glimpse of land. 'Port ahead, lads. Old Righ's light is shining like a bloody great star on top of a Christmas tree. I've never seen such a beautiful sight.' His mask of toughness fell. 'I tell you this – out there in that cruel bugger o' a sea I had my doubts, ay, I had my doubts – but,' he said, taking the wheel from Dan, 'the old girl got us home. She's all right, is old *Magpie*. I mind when I bought her and my mother saw the name on her: "Paint it out, Dokie", she told me, "call her something else. *Magpie* is unlucky, it will bring sorrow." Ay, but the superstitious cailleach was wrong, for I aye knew the old girl had a reason to her name – magpies pick up anything that's worth something, and on every trip my old girl gets to the herring shoals first.'

Dokie Joe was thinking about Annie even as he peered through the blizzard for a sign of the markers at the mouth of the harbour. Dokie thought of her warm curvaceous body pressed close to his in bed. Tonight he would lie with her after all, make love to her . . . Back there he had had his doubts about ever seeing his family again, but now he could almost feel the silk of Annie's breasts against his hard hairy chest . . . a pulse beat in his groin . . .

Dokie Joe's hand tightened on the wheel. The *Magpie* was bucking wildly in the tide race swirling into the harbour. He revved up the engine in an effort to pull the boat further back into the open sea so that he could make a wider turn into the harbour, but the *Magpie* didn't respond. Instead, she submitted to the pushing, bullying wind at her stern and pitched headlong towards the long dark finger of Port Rum Point. Dokie felt fear crawling over his skin, and despite the freezing cold deep in his very bones he felt sweat breaking over his body. His rough voice bawled out orders, which the crew scurried to obey. They trusted their skipper – he knew the sea, its moods, its wiles. In his fight with it he often behaved like a ferocious tiger; and in his admiration of its delusive beauty he became soft, resilient, relaxed as an alert cat; it was as if it transferred its moods to him like a lovely temperamental mistress might induce love, hate, respect, anger, admiration in a besotted lover. Dokie knew the sea all right, and that was why now his heart thudded up into his ears and his brusque comments were laced with oaths. His lips were pulled back in a snarl over his teeth as he held tightly to the wheel. The boat leapt and plunged like a mad dog and Dokie knew – he knew where the *Magpie* was taking him. The Sgor Creags! They were waiting for him and his men, always they were waiting, like grey, patient vultures waiting for prey. He stopped cursing and cried in a muffled voice, 'Oh God, help us!'

Quite suddenly Rachel's face bounced into his terrified mind. He felt her presence very strongly, as if she was standing beside him in the wheelhouse of the *Magpie* . . . He shivered and moaned slightly. Strange – she was a strange wee lass . . . he didn't understand her, but God! he was proud of her . . .

The *Magpie* bounced before a mountainous wave which caught her and smothered her in a wall of grey water. When it receded the men saw the Sgor Creags in front of them. Dokie Joe wrenched at the wheel but nothing happened. The boat was like a paper toy being sucked into the whirlpools that raged round the reefs. Dokie Joe's reddened eyes widened in horror. Those bloody rocks! They were reaching for the *Magpie*, pulling her towards them as if they were magnets and she were held in a vice-like grip from which there was no escape. The cruel grey pinnacles of rock reared up, gnarled, racked, twisted by time and wind into grotesque shapes; they towered like spectres over the frail little boat, while the churning fury of the dark rolling sea battered her hull.

Grant felt awe ripping through him. For the first

time in his young life he smelt and tasted real fear.

The crash as the *Magpie* hit the reefs threw the men to the floor. Grant heard the propellers racing uselessly, heard Skipper Joe's terrified curses as he realised the *Magpie* was caught amidships by two massive fragments of jagged rock. The deck tilted and swayed. Grant was thrown to his knees. Through the thudding of his heart he heard the sea snarling over the rocks; heard the groaning screams of the *Magpie* as the Sgor Creags began ripping her apart; felt the cold finger of death hovering over him, eager to reach out and carry him off in its pitiless clutches.

Todd was now holding the stage, his cheeks puffed into red pouches. The skirl of the pipes set everyone hooching and they whirled gaily round the floor, stirring up the chalky dust from the floorboards. The children climbed down off the platform and went to sit in the corner beside Ruth. The bench was immediately under the platform, hidden from the rest of the hall, and the children giggled as they received an unparalleled view of Todd's hairy legs under his swinging kilt. Ruth felt happier. Her mother couldn't see her from this angle and she was able to chatter to Rachel in peace of mind. Lorn was beside Ruth and all at once he grasped her arm and choked in a strangled whisper, 'Look, Ruth, Todd's drawers are coming down.'

Sure enough Todd's knees were being obliterated inch by inch by folds of wind-bleached cotton. The children clutched each other and gave themselves up to ecstasy.

Lewis leaned across to his brother and hissed, 'I bet you twopence they've got his initials on. Mollie puts initials on all her washing when the tinks are on the island.'

'I'm not betting,' Lorn stated with a grin. 'I *know* they've got his initials on – I saw them on the washing line yesterday!'

Old Mo spluttered into his whisky as he too espied the slow unfurling of Todd's underpants. 'Bejabers and bejasus, the bloody lyin' cheat,' he mumbled to Bob. 'Was he not after tellin' me just two minutes ago he never wears knickers under his kilt!' Todd was stomping his sturdy legs, keeping time to the music, obliviously abetting the descent of his drawers.

'Mercy on us, no!' stuttered a red-faced Mollie. 'He could never bring such shame to our good name. I told him, I told him this very mornin' he was needin' the elastic mended, but would he listen to me? No, oh no! I am just his wife! It's shamed I am just.'

A deadly hush had fallen over the floor as word spread like wildfire. The Laird had been discussing farming with Fergus and his was the last voice to die down, tailing off with a cultured if explosive, 'Poor old chap, I don't think he's aware of what's happening.'

Todd wasn't. In an inebriated haze he was blasting away merrily, stamping his feet, his eyes closed in his perspiring face.

'And there's a hole in them too!' Mollie almost

sobbed. 'Right where I patched them on the seam!'

With a triumphal flourish the underpants slid down to lie in dazzling folds at Todd's thick ankles.

'Ach God!' Kate clutched her stomach. 'He's unfurling his banners in style is our Todd! I wish I had a pair o' bellows. That would put the wind up him right enough!'

Todd was now aware of his imprisoned feet. With a drunken grin splitting his face he shouted, 'Ach, the hell wi' them!' and calmly stepping out of the cotton layers he stooped down and, picking them up, threw them with a flourish over his shoulder, intending in a burst of showmanship to catch them on the tasselled drones of his pipes. Instead they sailed over his head to land gracefully on the golden head of Squint, who was lying peacefully at Rachel's feet. The little dog looked with comical cross-eyed surprise through one of the wide legs before he shook the garment from his head and got to his feet to sniff blissfully, his inquisitive nose poking into the torn patch. For a moment the drawers hung suspended on the end of his muzzle then he went wild with delight. Although he had all the points of a good gun dog there was also something of the terrier in his nature. Holding the cloth firmly with his front paws he began pulling it up and down like strings of gum before gathering the lot in his soft jaws to go racing round the hall, throwing the drawers into the air, catching them, exposing to the hysterical gathering the initials T. McD. emblazoned red on white.

The hall went into an uproar with everyone clutching each other for support. Dodie's screeching wail of a laugh rang out; Biddy cackled so heartily her glasses slid to the end of her nose; the minister leaned helplessly against his dumpy little wife, who was wiping her streaming eyes with the first thing that came to hand – a corner of Merry Mary's new dress.

'Pour auld Todd,' Niall sobbed. 'He'll never live this down as long as he lives!'

In the corner the children were rendered speechless. Lewis had fallen against Rachel; and Lorn's earth-brown curls were touching Ruth's golden locks – in the sheer ecstasy of their mirth they had both forgotten their shyness and were now in harmony with each other, as was every other laughter-racked person in the room.

Alick was standing beside Kirsteen. 'Only on Rhanna could this happen,' he commented breathlessly. 'I always seem to get more laughs when I come home here.'

'You get other things as well – such as a bruised face and a split lip.' She looked him straight in the eye and he returned her gaze, his heart quickening slightly. 'Thank you, Alick,' she said quietly. 'I'm not going to ask what it was all about – I think I know. And I think you're a really special person – I just want you to know that. You're quite a man, Alick McKenzie.'

Alick flushed and turned away. Her words made him feel ten feet tall. Quite a man – at last – quite a man. He felt complete and proud to be a McKenzie.

Fergus looked over at his wife. They hadn't spoken a single word to each other yet; they were like shy children not quite knowing where or how to begin. Kirsteen felt excitement beating into her as she looked ahead to when they were alone, anticipated the first tentative kisses, the first gentle caresses . . .

Then Scott Balfour was climbing onto the platform followed by the minister, the doctor, their respective wives. The band re-assembled and Squint took up his position by Rachel's side, Merry Mary blushingly arranged herself between Phebie and Lachlan and the presentation speeches began. Plaudits were showered on the little Englishwoman from each of the menfolk in turn, and then the Laird made the presentations. The village had done Merry Mary right well: face afire with embarrassment, she received an elegant carriage clock to grace her mantelpiece; with trembling lips she stared in speechless gratitude at the silver tray complete with tea service, a personal gift from the Laird and his wife for 'keeping the Burnbreddie larder stocked through war and weather' – and when she was presented with a discreet plain envelope containing 'a wee thing from every man, woman, and child on the island', a sob caught at the back of her throat. Finally, when a tiny tot stumbled onto the platform bearing a huge bouquet, which she handed to Merry Mary with a big shy grin, the tears spilled over.

'Thank you, thank you everyone,' Merry Mary said and fumbled for her hanky. 'I meant to be very grand

and to say things that were light-hearted and funny – but now I find – I can say nothing except thank you to every one of my dear friends on Rhanna.' In confusion she melted into the background and resumed her seat. A rousing cheer went up then the Laird went on to the business of officially handing over the shop to Dugald, who, with his tall straight figure and mop of shining white hair, made a dignified figure on the platform.

Dugald wished Totie could have been there with him, but she had decided it might not be a wise thing. 'I'm jealous, Doug,' she had said bluntly, 'and I don't think I could bear to be in the same room with Morag and not show her my claws.' Dugald's eyes fell on Ruth sitting on the bench in the corner, and his heart twisted. Poor lonely wee lassie. She was gazing at him with pride in her huge violet eyes. For her sake he had to stick by Morag; a child as sensitive as Ruth might never get over the scandal of a divorce . . .

Morag listened while Dugald made a short but appropriate speech. Something tugged at her heart. She felt pride and something else, an affection that bordered on love – he was such a good man. They could have been happy together – if only – if only her soul wasn't so tortured by guilt . . . Morag shook herself angrily. He was a man like any other, men wanted things from a woman that made a mockery of so-called love. Always on the female scent they were – like – like dogs sniffing after bitches in heat. It wasn't clean – nor decent . . .

The Laird was holding up his hand, asking once

more for attention. To everyone's surprise Biddy was being invited up onto the platform.

Hearing her name Biddy grunted and stirred out of a rum-induced stupor but had no time to gather her senses. Babbie was beside her, helping her to her feet, escorting her up to the platform, placing her in a chair beside the minister.

'My damty specs, I canny *hear* without them!' hissed the old nurse, and with a smile Babbie retrieved the glasses and placed them on the end of Biddy's nose.

'It isn't my intention to steal Merry Mary's thunder,' the Laird began in his well-modulated, rather nasal voice, 'but I have a very special presentation to make, and while we are all gathered here tonight I can think of no better opportunity to carry out a duty that has fallen to me and that I am particularly honoured to fulfil.' He went on to explain that some time ago Lachlan had written to the Prime Minister recommending that Biddy, in view of her long and faithful service to Rhanna, be considered for an award.

The gathering in the hall gasped when the Laird read out the letter that Biddy had received from the Prime Minister's Principal Private Secretary, which ended by saying that His Majesty would be graciously pleased to approve that Biddy be appointed a Member of the Order of the British Empire.

The Laird cleared his throat. 'Biddy replied saying that she would be pleased to accept this mark of His

Majesty's favour, but she explained that she was too old and – hm – somewhat infirm to personally attend an investiture – and,' he said smiling, 'I have an idea that she thought that was that and promptly forgot all about the matter.'

Biddy glowered at Burnbreddie through the spikes of silver-white hair that escaped her hat. She was rigid with embarrassment. Had not the doctor coaxed her to write that damty letter of acceptance? It had all been just a lot of palaver that she didn't understand, and she had forgotten about it. She sucked in her lips with annoyance as a ripple of amazed comment bounced round the hall. She knew that for ever more she would be teased and tormented because she had omitted to tell anyone about the letter.

Her eye fell on Behag's sagging jowls and popping eyes. If it had been that cailleach, she would have told everyone: boasted, strutted, preened like a constipated peacock . . . Biddy sat up straighter and, puffing out her scrawny chest, peered haughtily down her nose. She was going to enjoy this after all, make the most of it, show old Behag she was some-body, an important personage of the island, a mother figure . . . After all, she had delivered three gener-ations of Rhanna children . . . Ay indeed, she smiled and nodded, was she not nurse, mother, grand-mother, to just about everyone present there that night? She folded her hands on her lap and settled herself back in her seat.

The Laird was continuing. 'Doctor McLachlan and

myself contrived between us to make sure that Biddy would receive her award, and I now have the honour, in place of the Lord Lieutenant of the county, who could not be here at this time, to carry out His Majesty's command . . .' He turned to Lachlan, who handed him a scroll and a small box, and then he went to stand by Biddy, his hand on her shoulder. 'It is with a feeling of great privilege and pleasure that I bestow upon Biddy the emblem and warrant of a Member of the Order of the British Empire as a token of His Majesty's awareness and gratitude for the many, many years of service our beloved nurse and friend has given to this island. She was just a slip of a lass when she took on her slim shoulders the great responsibility of nursing a community single-handed. She has through the years proven her worth, and has devoted her life to caring for others. Now she is an old lady –'

'Like a good whisky, the older the better,' Biddy interposed sourly, and a giggle went up.

'– she is now an old lady,' the Laird went on unperturbed, and with a smile, 'and as she says, like a good whisky she has improved with time. I know that all of you here share my hope that she has got many a good year left in her yet. She has assisted many here tonight into this world – she has watched us come – and – yes – she has known the heartache as deep as the mothers themselves of watching the sons of Rhanna go marching into two world wars – many of them never to return.'

Biddy's eyes were filling and Babbie squeezed her arm comfortingly.

The Laird turned, and with genuine affection, he said softly, 'Ay, indeed, she has watched us come and she has watched us go, she has burped us and she has blessed us and – as if all that wasn't enough – she has now brought great honour to our island community.' Leaning forward he pinned the insignia on the old nurse's jacket and, handing her the warrant, he took her rough old hand in his and shook it firmly.

Biddy stared down at the silver medal mounted by a crown attached to a red ribbon. A swelling pride surged in her breast. 'A damty fine brooch,' she said huskily and sniffed loudly while the Laird helped her to unroll the ornately inscribed warrant and then held it up for everyone to see. There were gasps of awe followed by thunderous applause. Babbie hugged the old nurse and whispered, 'I'm proud of you, you dear old cailleach – and – if I serve this place half as well as you have done, I will be well pleased.'

'Ach, wait you, I'm no' finished yet; I still have a few bairns to deliver before I go out.' Biddy tried to sound firm but her voice came out in a wobble, and as she was surrounded by people, hugging her, shaking her hand, patting her shoulders, the tears finally spilled over and she wept copiously into Babbie's hanky.

'Wonderful, wonderful,' beamed Mrs Gray. 'Now

I'm sure you could do justice to a nice cuppy.'

Biddy scrubbed her red eyes. 'Ay, indeed, a cuppy is just what I need, all this fuss just because I have done a job I have loved. The good Lord knows it hasny been easy, and betimes I could fine have seen it all far enough, but ach! It's my life, what I was put here to do, and there is no need to go giving me medallions for it.'

The minister was giving the vote of thanks, and Mrs Gray stepped discreetly from the platform. She had spent a good part of the morning baking delicious scones and pastries, which had been added to the batches prepared by the village womenfolk. These delicacies had been put to heat in the ovens of nearby houses and several of the women had already bustled away to fetch them, leaving Mrs Gray and her helpers to preside over the ancient but efficient tea urn. A lull followed during which everyone juggled with piping hot sausage rolls and mugs of strong steaming tea, discussing between mouthfuls the events of the evening. Quite a crowd was gathered round both Merry Mary and Biddy to admire the respective awards; old Mo was announcing in a loud voice that he had to pee or burst, and there was a scramble to get him down from the platform and outside; several children were gathered in the alcove by the platform, giggling as they dared one another to dart out and grab extra helpings from the trays; the courting couples had sneaked into the loft, and through the general buzz Rachel's keen ears heard the rafters creaking. She smiled and, nudging Ruth, she pointed above her head.

'I know, I saw them go up,' Ruth said, and laughed. 'Jean and that skinny-ma-link Harry the Bus – *and* I saw Colin McKinnon go up with Betty Alexander. He's only fourteen and she's just twelve, yet Mary told me that Betty lets Colin put his hands inside her –' Ruth lowered her voice to a shocked whisper – 'inside her blouse. Her bosoms began to grow when she was only eleven.' Ruth was thoroughly enjoying herself. She was a naturally outgoing little girl who had been unnaturally stifled, and normally she kept a tight rein on her tongue. Only with Rachel could she unwind and reveal in some measure her true self. Morag Ruadh had hovered around earlier but now she was helping dispense tea and Ruth felt unfettered.

Rachel listened to her friend with avid enjoyment. It had been a wonderful evening, one she would remember: Jon's playing, Merry Mary's tears of joy, the dancing and singing, Biddy's old eyes filling as she looked with pride at her brooch. Rachel loved the old nurse with her whimsical ways, her snowy hair, her grumbling good nature, her continual search for her specs and her teeths – Rachel stiffened – her father had burst into her thoughts, so real and near she could see his brown skin, his grey-flecked beard, his brown eyes wildly staring. The little girl felt a strange, cold premonition of danger touching her, pulling her down into a chasm of dread. She had

had these feelings before, things she didn't understand, but never before had she experienced such force in a vision, such powerful intensity of transferred thought it was as if her father was inside herself, hammering at her brain, clenched fists screaming at her to let him out – no – no – get him out – get help. She trembled and put her hand down quickly to Squint's soft head, reassured herself of reality by touching his cold nose, stroking his muzzle. He gave a little whimper, and she knew that she had conveyed her unease to him.

'Dad.' The word she had never been able to speak beat inside her head. She loved him, more than her mother, more than her brothers. He was tough, dour, silent, ignorant about many things, but often she sensed his love for her reaching out of his aggressive spirit to caress her, without words, without touch. When he was away at sea she ran wild; when he was home she became calmer, stayed nearer to home to cherish each minute he spent there. Sometimes he lifted her up in his swarthy arms and his beard scuffed the smooth bloom of her cheeks. Once, his dark, strangely gentle eyes had regarded her for a long time before he said in his gruff voice, 'My lassie – if only you could speak, tell me your thoughts. Those bonny eyes o' yours say things but I canny understand everything that's in them – I – you're my special bairnie.' She had laid her small hand on his arm and nodded, and from that day she had known what she meant to him. Now – now he was in danger – trying to reach her – to let her know . . .

She felt ice-cold: her dark eyes were wide and big as if she was watching some terrible disaster unfolding before her.

'Rachel, what's wrong? Are you all right? You – you look as though you'd seen a ghost.'

Ruth's voice came from a long way. Rachel shook herself and started to her feet just as the door burst open and Hugh McDonald, the young assistant lighthouse keeper, stood there, wind-tossed, rivers of rain and sea running from his mackintosh to lie in puddles on the floor. 'The smacks are in!' he shouted. 'All safe but for one – the *Magpie*'s on the rocks!'

In minutes the hall was empty but for old Mo lying in his pram, Biddy dozing in her chair, and Mrs Gray rushing to fill the urn in readiness for the men coming in from the smacks.

Chapter Ten

Grant thrashed in the freezing water, almost paralysed with cold and exhaustion, his brain so numb with shock he barely remembered being pitched from the *Magpie* into the black fury seething round the Sgor Creags. The spikes of rock had smashed a gaping hole in the *Magpie's* hull and she had keeled over to lie half-submerged. With her bow impaled on a shaft of rock, she looked like a dying whale raising her snout above the waves in a desperate bid to resist the relentless pull of the churning depths. Everything had happened so quickly there had been no time to make sense of the jumbled impressions of men shouting, the boat tilting, the fleeting glimpse of Skipper Joe in the wheelhouse, his face twisted in disbelief as he struggled up from the deck, blood oozing from a gash on his cheek. He had thrown his arms round the wheel as if it were a baby and had cried out in protest, 'Christ, no! Oh, dear Jesus, no!'

'Leave her, Skipper! She's breaking up.' The warning roar had come from Grant, in a voice that didn't seem to be his, so unreal was the screaming pitch of it. The timbers had groaned, squealing in the agony of dying, as the little boat had been torn apart by the pitiless sea smashing over the deck. Grant had staggered, slithered, screamed as the snarling water reached for him and pulled him down. His flaying hands had caught and clutched at the capping, and for a moment he had lain gasping before he was torn away, lifted by a giant wave, which hurled him relentlessly into the waiting sea. The roar of it filled his head, the embrace of its icy clutches seemed to reach right into his heart and squeeze it, so that it seemed to stop beating. Dan's white face bobbed near him. Grant reached out but was lifted and tossed towards the rocks. Adrenalin pumped through him, spurring him into frantic activity. Kicking frenziedly he swam for his life. Something black loomed. The *Magpie*. The water was swirling round her, fighting to claim what was left of her from the teeth of the rocks. Grant knew that he was trapped. Behind him reared the stark treachery of the Sgor Creags, in front of him was the *Magpie*, no longer a friend but an enemy blocking the way to safety, seducing the sea to rage as it sucked and roared, sucked and roared, into the yawning hole amidships. He stopped struggling and allowed himself to be pounded by the waves. His limbs were growing numb, he couldn't feel his legs . . . He closed his eyes, waiting for oblivion to release him from a watery hell.

Something rammed itself against Grant's rib cage and lifted him up. It was a piece of wreckage as big as a raft. His frozen fingers clawed at it and he heaved himself up to lie, gasping, on it. Deep in his consciousness, a jumbled prayer of thankfulness took form. From somewhere close at hand he heard something like a groan. He looked up and though his eyes were burning with pain he saw through a watery blur the black outline of what remained of the *Magpie*; the mast wavered for what seemed eternity then with a shuddering crack it crashed through the wheelhouse. A trembling scream rose above the snarl of the storm. The sound of it filled him with horror and he moaned softly and whispered, 'You shouldn't have stayed, Skipper; you should have let her go.'

The crowd that spilled from the hall surged onto the little strip of shore laid bare by the ebbing tide, some of the womenfolk running to meet the bedraggled fishermen coming from the smacks. Captain Mac and his crew made straight for the boathouse where the Rhanna lifeboat was kept. Righ nan Dul, Keeper of the Light, was an old man now, but tougher and wirier than many a man half his age. He welcomed the solid, cool presence of Captain Mac. They were old friends of many years' standing, and when it came to dealing with the sea, action rather than words was their keynote. Hurriedly they plotted a course of action, with Righ suggesting that they take the boat to the harbour mouth to see if they could pick up any of the *Magpie*'s crew.

Captain Mac nodded his bushy white head. 'Ay, the tide's on the turn, and I'd say the worst o' the storm is over – the bugger has blown itself out.'

There were many willing hands to man the lifeboat, which was no more than a long rowing boat.

The men piled in, the shed doors were opened, old Joe released the mechanism and the boat slid gracefully down the slip and into the water.

Kirsteen stood a little way back, watching, her heart in her throat, her icy fingers nervously winding together. The wind had abated a good deal, but it still moaned deep in its throat, a sound of menace that struck dread into her heart. The waves were silken, greeny-blue troughs of satin in the light from storm lanterns held aloft all along the shoreline. It was frightening to be standing so close to the pounding sea, seeing the litter of debris held in the clutch of the green swell thrashing against the land; seeing the foam spuming high into the air, carelessly tossing out seaweed and pebbles; hearing the thundering roar like a lion defiantly proclaiming its might, untamed, unconquered no matter how submissive it might sometimes appear. In the excitement everyone had left coats and jackets in the hall. Kirsteen shivered a little in the bite of the wind. Everything, everyone seemed to be in confusion. She felt panic rising in her. Her son was out in that godforsaken sea – out by the Sgor Creags – the rocks that had killed Hamish – been the means of Fergus losing his arm . . . Fergus – where was he? Where was everyone who meant everything in the world to her?

She turned blindly and fell into Shona's steadying arms. Niall, too, was there; calm, comforting Niall with his strong arms and his soft reassuring voice.

Shona held Kirsteen and murmured soothing words, but her thoughts were far away – in that relentless sea with the half-brother she cared for more than she would ever admit. Shona drew in her breath and closed her eyes. Niall led them to a spur of rock away from the wind – none of them saw the tall dark figure of Fergus running towards the base of Port Rum Point, scrambling over the slimy rocks to the tiny strip of land that lay exposed along the length of the rocky finger.

'Come back, Fergus!' Alick's voice bounced over the bay. 'You'll get swept away on that damt Point! The boat will pick the lads up.'

'For God's sake! It's my son out there!' Fergus threw back, and plunged on, slipping, falling, picking himself up, squeezing himself round barnacle-encrusted outcrops that dropped down into blackness. Time and again the sea reached out to him, drenching him, plucking at his feet with icy fingers. At one point the water roared into the dank black hole of an enormous cavern. He had to swim in order to bridge the gap and he felt himself spinning like a cork in the mêlée. Terror momentarily engulfed him, but concern for Grant imbued him with power and he lashed out with his legs. His hand brushed a rock and he hauled himself onto dry land once more. Soaked to the skin, his breath ragged, his throat raw and tight, he ran on. It seemed to him he had been running for ever with the wind tearing him and the sea lashing him. His eyes were so filled with salt he barely saw where he was going – only the thin irregular ribbon of silver sand kept him from plunging headlong into the water. The black holes of caves loomed like the wide mocking mouths of giants; his world was one of thunderous boomings; of dark towering crags; of searing, biting cold. The wind strengthened and he knew he had reached the tip of the Point. He was whipped and bullied by the elements, and he staggered as he strained his stinging eyes into the heaving blackness.

His eyes adjusted and new shapes emerged out of the wall of water facing him, causing him to tremble with a mixture of dread and hatred of those menacing splinters rising sheer out of the sea. The last time he had seen them at such close quarters was years ago – yet in those moments it might have been yesterday: the horrendous nightmare loomed like a spectre: Hamish's face floated beside him, his sightless eyes seeing nothing, the blood bubbling from the hole in his skull, the sea all around lathering to a pink froth . . . Fergus shuddered. Never had he thought to face these rocks again. He loathed them with a passion that terrified him.

He stared wildly and saw another shape – a great black snout rearing up to the sky looking for all the world like a giant whale rising for air . . . the bow of the *Magpie* . . .

'Grant!' His voice came out in a rasping bawl. Over and over he called his son's name, and over and over it was thrown back at him. Rage filled him. The sea would not get his son! Not if he could help it.

'Father.' He thought he imagined the sound but it came again faintly and without hesitation he plunged into the element he feared more than any other. A spike of rock bit into the flesh of his hip but his mind was so preoccupied he felt no pain. It seemed a miracle to him when, in that freezing hostile world, he came upon his son clinging to a great plank of wood that had wedged itself between two rocks.

'Hold onto me!' Fergus ordered.

Grant let go of the wood and Fergus felt himself sinking under the weight of him. Naked fear ripped through him and his limbs went rigid. A pinpoint of light pricked into the darkness then disappeared, but in that split second Fergus had seen a small familiar figure standing on the Point. Lorn or Lewis? He didn't know which . . . he felt himself spinning in a void as waves of faintness washed over him. The water swirled round his legs, sucking, pulling, Grant was a dead weight against him and they both went under . . . Fergus kicked and wildly flayed the water with his arm . . . water flooded his lungs . . . he and his son were caught in a whirling underwater current that wouldn't let go. Grant thrashed wildly and they both bobbed to the surface . . . and miraculously a lifejacket was there within their reach.

'It's all right – Father, I'm here – hold onto this.' It was the voice of a child, a breathless, weak voice.

Lorn! How could it be Lorn! That tiny boy with the weak heart and skinny body. 'Go back, for God's sake go back!' Fergus rasped. The child was gasping, struggling for air, but his thin little arms were reaching out, holding on, keeping his father's chin above water . . .

'Hold on!'

Alick's voice! Cool, calm Alick who had always been quite at home in the sea . . . Now other arms were there, too, carrying Grant and Lorn to safety, and now it was just Fergus and Alick, Alick uttering soothing words of encouragement, cradling his brother, taking him to the haven of dry land. Fergus was aware of figures moving, familiar voices tossing hither and thither. His chest heaved and he choked out the sea from his lungs.

'This – this is getting to be a habit – you pulling me out of the Sound,' Fergus joked feebly.

Alick laughed, but it was a trembling, weak attempt. With frantic fingers he loosened the collar at his throat. 'It – wasn't me this time – it – was Lorn who saved you – foolhardly – brave wee brat – I couldn't stop him.' The pain reached up to his neck and seared through his jaws. He had never known such agony, it was crushing the breath from his body, forcing him to lie down near his brother. All around him was blackness, blacker than the darkest night. Only the blob of Fergus's face above him was grey.

'Alick! Are you all right?' Fergus, barely recovered from his own hellish experience, looked at his brother lying gasping on the sands and felt he was caught up in a nightmare without end. He forgot himself, his chattering teeth and numb limbs. 'Alick!' he cried again harshly. 'What's wrong?'

'I – think – big brother – I've come to the end of my holiday. Us city gents are – too soft for midnight swims – can't breathe – I think – my heart.'

Fergus raised himself onto his knees. 'I'll get help

– hold on –' But Alick's trembling hand reached out to stay him. 'No – no – stay – stay with me. I've always been afraid – of the – dark. I need you – big brother.'

Fergus gathered his brother to his breast. The wet hair beneath his fingers was plastered with sand and gently he stroked it clean. Alick's breathing was more laboured, his head heavier than it had been a moment before . . . Fergus's thoughts flashed back to boyhood days, of Alick relying on him, leaning on him – worshipping him . . . and tonight, the two of them fighting, Alick proving that he was quite a man – had been for years without Fergus being aware of the fact. And now – Alick was dying – dear God! He was dying! The pain of love, for someone he had always taken for granted and who was now about to leave him, shot through him like a knife. He caught his brother's head to him and touched the wet hair with his lips. 'You don't need me – I need you,' he sobbed harshly.

'An unusual way to end – an unusual holiday – but then – I was always a one for anything – different . . .' gasped Alick painfully. The last of his strength went into the hand clasped round Fergus's arm. 'You know – even when I hated you – I loved you – I never quite grew up, you see – big – brother . . .' His hands relaxed and fell away, his head lolled to one side, and with a little sigh he died peacefully in his brother's embrace.

Fergus gathered him up and cradled him as if he was a baby. All around him the wind moaned, the black night closed in like a mourning blanket. A sob caught at his throat. He wanted to shout his hatred at the sea, which had robbed him of so much, to scream, to give vent to useless wrath. Instead, he sobbed quietly.

'We'll take him, lad.' Bob's voice came softly, gentle hands drew him up and led him away, and as he stumbled along he saw not where he was going for his tears.

Some distance away everyone waited anxiously for the life boat to come back. The lanterns picked it out, bucking towards the shore, the keel grounded, and an army of willing helpers plunged into the water to pull her up. Annie stood a little way back, her shawl clutched over her head, her limbs immobile and stiff.

'We got them all but one.' Captain Mac's voice was gruff as he jumped from the boat.

'Which one?' Old Joe's voice was tense. 'It – isn't young Grant?'

'No, he was rescued from the Point – it's Dokie Joe. He's trapped in the *Magpie*, a goner from all accounts.'

Righ shook his head. 'Ay, and there is no way we can reach him until the old girl breaks up – even then . . .' The remainder of his words went unsaid, but everyone knew what he meant. The Sgor Creags had been known to hold onto a body till it was no more than a skeleton picked clean by seabirds.

Torquil Andrew turned on his heel and trod heavily over the shingle to Annie. Without words he put his arms round her and drew her close.

'Oh no, oh dear God no,' she said, leaning against him and sobbing. 'It's a punishment – a punishment, I'm tellin' you, Torquil.'

'Weesht now, mo ghaoil, you mustny think like that. Dokie stayed wi' the boat – he could have got out but he stayed wi' her – it's the way o' things.'

Rachel stood alone in the cold dark embrace of night. She watched Torquil leading her mother away. In that moment she knew that her father was dead. Her great brown eyes stared wildly into space. Her big, dour, adored father had been taken by the sea. She felt her world crashing round her. He had been her security, the only person she had ever really trusted. She loved her mother, but she had always been aware of her mother's weaknesses, her inability to cope with loneliness. Her father hadn't been weak; he had been strong, strong, strong; he had been faithful – and he was gone from her. Her lips trembled and formed the word 'Dad'. She wanted to shout it aloud but her voice was locked inside for ever . . . Arms were enclosing her, Jon's strong young arms, holding her close, reaching out and soothing her in her moment of greatest need. He said nothing, just knelt beside her and held her. She laid her head on his shoulders and his long sensitive fingers stroked her hair. Then she felt herself being lifted up and carried away through the night, and as he strode with her he murmured, 'I'm here, jungfräulich, I will stay with you as long as you need me.'

Ruth watched and squirmed against her mother's painful hold on her shoulders, every fibre in her longing to run to her friend to give her comfort, but Morag Ruadh's hold grew stronger, her voice when she spoke was without emotion. 'No, Ruth, you will come home with me and pray to the Lord to give Rachel strength – her mother too.' Her lips twisted as she thought of gay, vivacious Annie with her lust for life and her discontent when her husband was away at sea. 'The Lord works in mysterious ways, mark my words. Sinners must be punished one way or another –'

'Rachel has done nothing wrong!' Ruth cried passionately. 'Why should she be punished! You're afraid of her – that's why you try to keep me away from her! She's strong and good and beautiful and she's my friend – and – and I won't keep away from her when she needs me most. I won't! I won't!'

Morag's face flamed red, her hand shot out to crack her daughter hard on the face. 'You learn to get your facts right my girl! I wasny meanin' Rachel, though she is just her mother all over again. Never – never speak like that to me again. You will obey me, you will obey the Lord's word. You are a daughter of God, do you hear me, child?'

'I am my father's daughter,' sobbed Ruth, but even as her mother yanked her away she wondered, as she had wondered so many times lately, just whose daughter she really was – it might be better to think of herself as God's daughter after all.

The men carrying Grant stepped out of the shadow

of Port Rum Point and Kirsteen ran forward, so full
of relief at seeing her son alive she couldn't speak.

'It's all right, Mother,' he said through chattering
teeth. 'I'm not planning to leave any of you for a
while yet – I never managed back for the ceilidh, but
at least I'm home.'

Kirsteen looked up and saw Lachlan running
towards the Point. Lewis, who had been watching
the unloading of the lifeboat with interest, was
running too, as if drawn by some sort of telepathy
towards the little group some distance away.

'It's Lorn,' Grant murmured, the impact of recent
events only now starting to come home to him.
'Would you credit it – the spunky wee bugger dived
into the sea and kept Father afloat . . .'

Kirsteen was gone, racing with pounding heart to
her youngest son. Grant looked up to see Fiona
staring down at him, the soft curves of her slender
body outlined against a watery light breaking
through the clouds. She felt strange, light-headed,
filled with something she could put no name to.
Before she could say anything he said, as teasingly
as his frozen lips would allow, 'Well, well, if it isn't
wee Robin – all dressed up in a frock like a *real* girl.
Are you disappointed to see I'm still alive and
kicking?'

Anger rose up in her. She tossed her head. 'I might
have known it would take more than a drop of the
sea to kill a McKenzie!' she spat vindictively.

'Ay, we're a tough lot,' he retaliated without spirit.
Without another word Fiona turned on her heel and

walked over to join Mary, who was enquiring of a group of fisherwives if they had seen anything of her husband . . .

It was almost three a.m. when Kirsteen eventually made her weary way upstairs. Lachlan, concerned for Fergus because of the weak lung he had had since his accident, had ordered him up to bed an hour before. He had gone with surprisingly little objection, his shoulders bent, his steps dragging. But he wasn't asleep. He lay very still, staring at the ceiling, his eyes hollow in his white face. Kirsteen went over to the dressing table, and, planting her hands on its smooth surface, she stood with her fair head bowed, every muscle in her body sagging with tiredness.

'How is everyone?'

She whirled round to look at him. 'Fergus – I – I thought you'd be asleep.'

'Sleep! How can I sleep after what's happened? I wonder if I'll ever sleep again.'

She clasped her hands and stared down at them. 'You mustn't worry about the boys – Grant is sound asleep, he's young and strong and is only very badly shaken up. Lorn – well – I can hardly believe he's all right after what happened, but he is – oh, naturally drained of course. Lachlan has told me to keep him in bed for a couple of days. Mary – she – Lachlan gave her a sedative. I don't think she's really taken in what's happened yet. She kept saying she didn't know how she was going to tell her sons.'

'Oh, dear God,' Fergus said, his voice full of disbelief, 'I've been lying here feeling I've imagined it all – I can't believe he's really dead.'

Kirsteen felt sorrow engulfing her and she put her hands to her face. 'I know. Oh poor dear Alick! He'd been so good to me this holiday – so patient and kind, I don't know what I would have done without him.'

'Don't rub it in,' Fergus said, his voice heavy with grief, 'I feel hellish enough as it is – as if everything is my fault. We had a fight earlier and he beat the hell out of me! My little brother turned the tables and fought back. He laughed about it – said how good he felt that everything we had buried for so long was at last out in the open.' He bunched his knuckle. 'And just when we might have made a go of things he died pulling me out of the sea. What does it mean, Kirsteen? It all seems so senseless – he was only forty-seven.'

Kirsteen said nothing. It seemed there was nothing she could say to ease her husband's torment of mind. He turned his head to look at her, noting her stillness, the feminine fragility that gave her such grace and beauty, the strength that emanated from her.

'Kirsteen,' he said, speaking her name softly, savouring the sound of it, 'Alick had a great respect for you – also I think he'd always been a little bit in love with you. Perhaps he was never really aware of it himself, but he loved you enough to face up to me tonight – to tell me things I was too damned stubborn to admit. My darling, darling Kirsteen, I'm so sorry for everything – I've missed you so – I need you –'

She raised her head and saw his dark eyes burning into her. The room was in lamplight, shadows danced and played, everything was soft and dim. His trembling hand reached out to her. 'I love you, oh God how I love you. I need you more than I've ever needed you in my life – you're part of me, Kirsteen.'

She had no recollection of crossing the room, she was only aware of his nearness, his lips kissing her hair, kissing away the tears from her eyes, caressing her ears, her neck, her breasts. The power of their love for each other reared up out of grief and misery. His body was hard against hers. Slowly she undressed and got into bed to lie down beside him. They spoke no words; there was no need for them. His arm came round to draw her in close to him, his lips touched her hair, her face, her mouth. They lay quite still in one another's embrace, savouring the close, warm comfort of being together again. They were enclosed in a sphere of their own, worlds removed from reality, each so aware of the other they were lost in the exquisite joy of their reunion. The grief and uncertainty of tomorrow would wait; tonight was theirs – fleeting, intangible, unforgettable. The dawn would bring renewed awareness of the world outside their love, but it could wait – it must wait . . .

Rachel stood very still, her hands immobile by her sides, her eyes seeing yet barely believing that the crumpled broken body thrown so carelessly by the tide onto the sands was really her father, her big, hard-bodied father who had strode so tall through life. The tide had carried him round Portcull Point to Mara Òran Bay, Bay of the Sea Song. She saw him as he had been, tough, sullen, his surprisingly gentle brown eyes lighting up at sight of her and her small brothers waiting for him at the harbour. She saw him striding homewards through Glen Fallan, mock severity in his glance at sight of her grubby knees and dirty face; then one huge hand would reach out to her while the other felt in his pocket, pretending not to find the sweets and toys till with a show of amazement he allowed the bulging pocket to give up its treasures. How could that man now be this poor pitiful sodden lump? The men had covered him quickly, but not quickly enough. She had seen his crushed chest; the congealed blood clogging his mouth, matting into his beard.

The morning was gentle and warm; the sea shimmered blue; the sky was wide and boundless; seabirds were making a noisy fuss as they poked for molluscs among the seaweed left by high tide. It was all as it had been, as if there never had been a storm – as if the world could never be anything else but serene and warm and bright – as if her father had never lived – or died. Rachel saw, she heard, her eyes remained dry, but silent screams thrust up inside her skull like shock waves inside a subterranean cave: booming, reverberating, pounding – yet unheard in the world outside. Everything that could be released by the human voice was locked away inside. She was a small cauldron of seething emotions that could find no outlet.

Her mother was standing by Dokie Joe's body, her hands over her face, her shoulders shaking. She looked small and young and vulnerable. Torquil Andrew appeared round Portcull Point and soon his arms were protectively round Annie. When he glanced up and saw Rachel, he held out a hand to her, but she stared past him into nothingness.

From the clifftops Ruth looked down and saw her friend standing alone and her heart brimmed over with pain for the little girl who had always run free but who now stood as if held by invisible fetters, a tiny statue, silent and unmoving. Ruth drew in her breath and began to limp towards the cliff track, but her mother emerged from the house and saw her. 'Ruth!' Her tone was imperative. 'Wait you there, your grannie needs you to run a message.'

Ruth lifted her head defiantly and kept on going down but her mother's hand on her shoulder stayed her abruptly, and she swung round. Her heart was beating very fast. She feared her mother's wrath more than anything else in the world because it was such unreasoning, unthinking anger.

For a few moments, Morag said nothing. Her green gaze travelled down to where Rachel stood on the beach. Morag shivered. The little girl always made her feel uneasy – she dreaded the open frankness of the big expressive eyes, she couldn't take the accusation in them. Rachel couldn't utter a single word yet those eyes of hers said it all. 'You must leave

Rachel alone, Ruth.' Morag's voice was strange and far away. 'She has something in her that's gey strange – she's no' a normal wee lass – she has – the power.'

Ruth's heart bumped, but she cried, 'Leave me be, Mam. Rachel has God in her, *really* in her – and she's just lost her father. Let me go to her, *please*, Mam . . .'

The blood had rushed to Morag's face and she began to shake her daughter till her golden head became a wobbling blur. 'You wee bitch! If I'm no' mistaken the de'il has got at you. What is it that's changed you, Ruth? You were aye such an obedient wee lassie before.'

Old Isabel came out of her cottage, anger in her kindly old face. 'Ach, will you leave the bairn alone, Morag?' she implored. 'What is ailing you now I'd like to know? Go on the way you're doing and I warn you – the bairn will grow up to hate the sight of you.'

Morag whirled round to face her mother, 'If it's any o' your business, Mother, I will no' be havin' my lassie mixin' wi' that wee – that wee witch down there! She's a wild one. She has a funny look to her, I've seen that look before – she has the de'il in her and no mistake.'

'And where have you seen it, Morag?' asked old Isabel ominously. 'In the mirror? If I didny know better I wouldny be wrong in thinkin' *you* have become the daughter of the de'il. I canny believe betimes that you are the same lassie I bore from my own body, for through the years you have changed, Morag, and that's a fact – ay, and fine your poor auld father and myself know it for you have led us a fine dance in hell for more years than I like to think.'

The grip on Ruth's shoulder had lessened and she hurried away, hating herself for leaving her beloved grannie to Morag's fury, yet unable to stop herself from doing so. She reached the beach and Rachel raised her eyes, for the first time recognising someone outside her private hell. The two little girls clung together. Ruth felt the tension in Rachel's body and her heart brimmed over with compassion. What if it had been her father lying crumpled and dead on the cold lonely sands? The idea was unbearable. He was her whole life. She couldn't imagine an existence without him.

Old Joe came over and pushed some things into Rachel's hands. 'These were in his pocket, lass,' he said kindly. 'They will have been meant for you and your wee brothers.' Rachel stared down at the toy cars and the flute. Before he had gone away, her father had promised to bring her back a flute 'so that you can play fairy music to me when I'm tired, lass'. Rachel felt that she was going to fall down and never get up again, so much did her legs shake beneath her.

People were crowding the beach, a few tourists but mainly villagers who stood in sad-eyed little groups discussing quietly the tragedies wreaked by the storm. Canty Tam's voice floated loudly and clearly. He was proclaiming to all and sundry, 'I was after knowin' last night that the Uisga Hags would have a Rhanna man; it was a night just perfect for all the witches of sea and land to get themselves up.' His eyes gleamed as he leered vacantly in Rachel's direction. 'Ay, and the evil caillichs were no' content wi' just one – oh no – they had to have another – a McKenzie, too.' He leaned further sideways. 'Of course, there are some who have the power to call the witches, ay indeed. Witches know their own all right – a fine job they made o' Dokie Joe –'

Ruth leapt at him like an enraged animal and he was thrown to the ground, terror in his pale blue eyes. 'Shut up! Shut up!' she sobbed passionately and began violently to tear at his hair. Dugald ran down the path with Jon at his heels, the former to pull his daughter away from Canty Tam, the latter to run to where Rachel stood immobile. Jon fell on his knees beside her and pulled her to him, his arms strong and comforting. 'Cry, cry, jungfräulich,' he implored her, his own eyes wet at the feel of her slender small body bending trustingly to him. 'Cry, my dear little maiden,' he whispered soothingly. 'It is the only thing that will help to wash away your pain.'

Rachel responded to his impassioned plea. She lay against him, her eyes wide and big and staring, and from them the tears rolled, spilling faster and faster, and all the while Jon soothed her with words of comfort and reassurance.

Among the rock pools some distance away, Lewis sat watching the scene in Mara Òran Bay. There was a strange look in his eyes. He knew that he ought to go and say something kind to Rachel, but he couldn't face any more grief and suffering. He had come here to get away from Laigmhor and all those shocked, dull-eyed people bowed down with the burden of grief. He couldn't bear to see the pain in his father's eyes, the numb shock on Aunt Mary's face, the sadness in his mother's glance. Laigmhor was filled with the presence of death and the strange sickly feeling of illness – Lorn's illness. His brother was in bed, weak and breathless, his flying pulse bringing a frown of concern to Doctor McLachlan's face. Lewis loved his brother but couldn't bear it when he was ill. He hated and feared illness and unhappiness, and when Lorn was ill he felt ill, too. Lewis shuddered. His thoughts strayed back to Lorn – Lorn who was soon to go away from Rhanna to the uncertainty of a big town hospital where he would lie on an operating table while doctors did things to his heart that might make him better – or might kill him. Shona had told Lewis that morning, and he had backed away from her shaking his head and saying, 'Don't tell me any more, I don't want to know.' She had looked at him strangely. She always gave him the impression that she knew what he was thinking. Those beautiful blue eyes of hers had regarded him with frightening perception on several occasions and this morning she had said, 'Och, come on now, Lewis, you have to be told. Father asked me to tell you. I only found out myself yesterday from – from Uncle Alick. Lorn will be going away soon and Father and Kirsteen will need our help. Lorn will need all the support we can give him.'

But Lewis was angry with Shona for telling him – there was enough unhappiness to cope with. He was angry at Lorn, too. Lorn's weakness had always made him uncomfortable. All along he'd had to appease him and reassure him about things, more for his own sake than Lorn's because in appeasing his brother Lewis was in some measure comforted himself. By rights they should have had wonderful times as twin brothers – they could have had a lot of fun – if only . . . Lorn's dark eyes floated into Lewis's mind, rebellion and impatience fighting up out of them. Lorn wouldn't be afraid of hospitals – he would go through anything to be as fit as any other boy . . . Lewis felt suddenly ashamed, yet his shame didn't lend him any strength.

He glowered over lowered brows to Mara Òran Bay: more death, more unhappiness. He threw a pebble in the air and, reaching up to catch it, he saw that it was a 'fluffy cloud day'. The cheerful face of a clown grinned over the sky. Lewis's heart lightened. Wait till he told Lorn about that – but the face of the clown was changing, the big lips were slowly turning down – even the clouds were in mourning.

Lewis felt unease shivering through him. He put his chin in his hands and gazed far away over the shimmering sea. One day he would be a farmer like his father, but first he was going to enjoy himself. The world was big and wide and wonderful . . . Rachel was looking towards him, and though she was some distance away he felt her wild turbulence reaching him, touching him. Rachel was dumb, but she was so full of vibrant life she didn't need words to convey how she felt. She was like him, thirsty for all life had to offer, taking happiness where and how she could get it – yet, there was something in her that wasn't in him, only he didn't know what it was. He looked up. The clown was smiling again. That was how a clown ought to look.

The clear notes of a flute were borne to him on the breeze. Jon was walking with Rachel and she was playing the flute – not a sad tune, either – one that was light and gay.

Lewis stood up, his earth-brown curls tossing in the breeze, his blue eyes brilliant. It was all right to go to Rachel now; she had turned her back on the pathetic bundle that had been her father and she was playing the flute.

Lewis ran, his sturdy tanned limbs carrying him swiftly to Rachel's side. She didn't look up at his approach, but kept on playing, her fingers moving nimbly. Her black curls were dancing in the breeze, he noticed, and there was a sheen of blue in them where they were touched by the sun. Her body seemed totally relaxed; the curve of her lashes swept the rounded bloom of her golden cheeks; she looked as she had always looked – a sun-kissed waif, a child of the sea, the sky, the sun. She was like him – death was something she turned her back on in her search for the sunshine. She raised her eyes to look at him, and the expression in the deep dark pools made him draw in his breath; they were pain-racked, filled with pathos, torture, despair. Her naked soul was in her eyes, and Lewis knew that carefree little Rachel would never be the same again, that part of her – her vitality, her childhood – had died the moment her father had taken his last shuddering breath out there in the sea that swirled ceaselessly round the stark pinnacles of the Sgor Creags.

Part Three

Summer 1956

Chapter Eleven

Lorn opened his eyes to see fingers of sunlight pouring through the window to make a golden pool on the mellow varnished wood of the floor. Lazily he stretched and drew a deep satisfying breath. How good to breathe like that, to feel life and strength surging through his veins. How good not to feel breathless or faint any more. He stared for a few moments at his upstretched arms and frowned a little – they were too skinny; he would have to get some muscles in them, to work and work till they were hard and strong. From where he lay he could see the rugged thrust of the peaks of Ben Machrie – he would work till he was as strong as a mountain – well, he grinned – as strong as dear old Conker anyway.

He swung his legs over the bed and put his feet on the soft rag rug that had been made by Mirabelle. As he dressed he looked at Lewis's side of the room: it was tidy now, but tomorrow it would resemble a midden because tonight Lewis would be home from school for the summer holidays. All the children of Lewis's age had gone away to complete their education at mainland schools – all except Lorn who had spent much of his teenage years in hospital.

Time had often hung heavy for him, especially during his earlier years when his stays in hospital stretched into months and his visits home were brief, worrying affairs for his parents. When he had become stronger Kirsteen had taught him at home. Often she had looked very tired, but determinedly she had set time aside each day to sit with him and a hard taskmaster she had been, too, never allowing him to fob her off with excuses. From Shona he had learned that his mother had been called a Tartar in the classroom.

'I could never understand that,' Shona had said, her blue eyes lit with amusement. 'Oh, she was strict all right and made us all sit up like pokers, but the bairns respected her for it and half the older boys were in love with her and used to sneak flowers to her when they thought no one was looking.'

Mr Murdoch, too, had given freely of his spare time, and Lorn had developed a real liking for the fussy little man with the worried frown and twinkling eyes. But best of all had been Ruth, though at first they had barely been able to communicate because of mutual shyness. His bed had been in the parlour then and Morag Ruadh had only allowed her daughter to visit him on the condition she read to him from the Bible. 'Only the passages that will benefit his soul most, poor wee cratur',' Morag had stipulated. 'Later, when he's stronger, you may read Kings to him, Solomon has a lot to say that might make young folks sit up and take notice – you mustny go near his bed, mind, it's no' decent for a wee lass to be in a boy's room, but seein' he's lyin' in the parlour, it will no' be so bad.'

'Ay, Mam,' Ruth had promised obediently, but on her first few visits to Laigmhor, struggling with her own self-consciousness, trying to break through Lorn's, she had barely been able to see a word, let alone read passages from the Bible. Long silences had passed between them during which he had fidgeted and wished she would go; and she had sat very still in the chair by the window with her hands folded in her lap, her great violet eyes gazing long-ingly at the long ribbon of the Glen Fallan road winding to the harbour. The first time she hadn't been able to bear it and she had risen and hobbled away, leaving behind her Bible, which had slid from her lap. But gradually each had glimpsed something of the other's true nature, and Kings was abandoned for stories from Ruth's jotters, for card games, Scrabble, mischievous chatter.

Every time Ruth returned from a visit to Laigmhor her mother never failed to ask, 'Well Ruth, have you and Lorn enjoyed reading the Lord's word?'

'Ay, that we have, Mam,' Ruth always answered soberly. Her visits to Lorn had eased her first months at Portcull school. In the beginning the children had christened her 'Saint Ruth', and she had held her golden head high and borne the gibes; but one day, riled beyond bearing, she had flown at her tormentor like an enraged wildcat. Some of the children had witnessed her attack on Canty Tam the day Dokie Joe's body had been washed up on the beach. Others had only heard about it, but now they were all made aware that gentle, shy Ruth was possessed of a courageous fighting spirit that had to be reckoned with. Rachel had watched till Ruth had reduced her tormentor to a snivelling bundle, and then she had pulled her friend away and with shining eyes had spelled out a message in the sign language: 'Good for you, Ruth, I knew one day you would fight back. They'll never call you names again.'

But primary school days were in the past now for Ruth, Rachel and Lewis, and Lorn no longer had their company except in the holidays. He wasn't strong enough for a secondary education that involved fatiguing trips from home. And there were also the spells in hospital to contend with, so he had to make do with tuition at home. But he was strong enough to be able to get up and about more. No longer were his days spent in the parlour waving to people passing up and down Glen Fallan. He was able to ride, fish and swim in moderation, and, best of all, he was able to help his father around the farm, though these were light tasks to begin with. Oh, what joy to work beside that tall giant of a man in the morning fields! In the gloaming at harvest time, when all the world smelled of earth and rain and warm ripe hay, his heart glowed with quiet appreciation as he worked with the other men. He would never forget the day he climbed to the top of Ben Machrie with his father, or the heady euphoria of sitting in the heather on that high, windblown place, drinking the sweet water of the hill. It was as if he had climbed to the roof of the world to look at a panorama of patchwork fields and amber moors, and all around the blue, blue sea stretched to infinite horizons, studded with the green and purple jewels that were the islands – Barra, Eriskay, the Uists – and far in the misted distance the craggy ethereal peaks of the inner Hebrides – Skye and Mull, Rum, Jura, Eigg. His father was a man of few words, especially when he was outdoors working, but Lorn was glad of that as he himself hated superfluity of speech. As the years passed he chattered less and less, expanded mentally, physically and emotionally, and in so doing grew to understand his father. Mentally they had become very close: they worked in harmony, attuned to each other, communicating by instinct rather than utterance.

But everything changed when Lewis came home. He brought excitement, laughter, nonsense – and had so much to catch up on he was never still for a moment and talked from morning to night. He had hated having to go away to school without Lorn, but had felt better when the Travers, retired now and living close to Oban harbour, had insisted that he stay with them rather than in a hostel. Lewis had suffered a good deal during the years of his brother's fight for survival. He had experienced phantom chest pains and knew exactly when Lorn was on the operating table. When the surgeons' knives had been at work, Lewis had felt genuinely ill and often had had to be excused from school. But now all that was over. Lorn had undergone his last operation some months ago, and in his uphill climb to good health, his brother climbed with him.

Lorn met him at the pier that evening. He was tall and broad-shouldered in his fifteenth year. With his white teeth flashing, his suntanned face and his blue eyes sparkling, he was dashingly handsome. His manner was confident and assured, his charm of manner and speech very arresting. When he spoke to females of any age, his lilting voice became soft and silken and was so obviously irresistible to the fair sex that one or two young tourists with whom he had become acquainted on the boat stood gazing at him with fluttering lashes before walking reluctantly away. Lorn felt dwarfed by him and was overwhelmingly conscious of his own pale face and skinny arms.

'Hey, hello there, little brother!' Lewis cried in delighted greeting.

Lorn flinched. 'Ach, I'm not so little,' he growled. 'It's just that you're so big –' He broke off as he saw over his brother's head Ruth and Rachel coming down the gangplank with Jon at their heels. Rachel had changed, that much was obvious from her newly sophisticated dress. She was tall, slender and windblown, her face was vibrant with life. Beside her Ruth looked small, dainty, and rather delicate. But there was a change in her too, Lorn noticed instantly: she was less ungainly, her once plain little face was sweeter, almost pretty in its youthful serenity. Her hair, which had grown even lighter, was a startling halo of pale gold next to Rachel's raven curls. Both of them had blossomed from flat-chested little girls into shapely young maidens, though there was still an uneasiness about the way Ruth carried herself, as if to stand too straight and show off too much was something to be ashamed of. Rachel, on the other hand, walked tall and straight, so that her firm young breasts were thrust out. There was also a sensuality in the way she moved: it was graceful yet provocative, and the directness of her gaze obviously tantalised men. One of the young deckhands was being very attentive to her.

Lewis grinned at the look on his brother's face. 'Ay, they've changed. Imagine, even you noticing that! I always had the feeling you saw girls as boys with frocks on . . .' He threw his arm round Lorn's shoulders and they walked along the harbour towards Glen Fallan. 'I'll tell you a secret, Lorn my boy, girls are made different from us . . .' His voice was bubbling with mischief and Lorn shook his head and laughed. 'Ach, wait till you hear the rest,' Lewis instructed. 'And don't interrupt. Before I left Rhanna, while I was still with old Murdoch and feeling a bit wild about having to go to Oban, I chased Mary Anderson through the fields and rolled her around in the grass for a wee bit of fun – but something happened – she had bosoms – she was more than two years older than me – and I touched them. She let me do it and after a while she let me make love to her.'

'You – you mean you kissed her.'

'Ay, that too and all the rest.'

'But – hell, Lewis! You must only have been twelve!' Lorn exploded in disbelief.

'I could have done it at eleven.' Lewis sounded very confident. 'Don't you tell me you never had funny things happening to you when you were eleven.'

'I was too busy being ill,' Lorn answered faintly.

Lewis laughed, a hearty booming laugh. He hugged his brother closer as they trudged up Glen Fallan. 'Well, you're not eleven or ill now and I'm telling you this, it was grand with Mary, but too quick and silly – it's much much better the more you practise, so start practising – it's what girls are here for.'

Laigmhor seemed to come alive that evening. Lewis's delight at being home was infectious and he carried everyone along on an exuberant tide so that his buoyancy filled every room in the house. Kirsteen skelped him on the ear for swearing, and in retaliation he got up and waltzed her round the kitchen. Fergus leaned back in his chair and roared with delight at the look of exaggerated outrage on her face, and Lorn watched his father and wondered why it was he never laughed like that with him – but Lorn knew – he was too reserved, too like his father, and opposites made the best companions – his father and Lewis were opposites. Kirsteen pushed Lewis away. Her curls were ruffled, her face flushed. 'Bed, young man,' she said firmly. 'You too, Lorn, you must be tired, you've been up since dawn.'

Lewis turned at the door. 'When will Grant be home?'

'Next week sometime.'

'Good, I'm dying to hear all his adventures. Sometimes I think I might join the Merchant Navy. He promised to bring me back a native girl – I hope he doesn't forget.'

'A what?'

'Ach, dinna fash, as Dodie would say – a carved one, for my bookcase – though a real one would be better,' he ended with a chuckle and dodged quickly upstairs.

Fergus looked at Kirsteen. 'Lorn is still a boy but Lewis is already a man of the world.'

A shadow passed over her blue eyes and she went to stand behind her husband to gently massage his shoulders. 'I know – were you at his age?' He pulled her hand towards his lips and kissed it. 'In some ways, ay, I would be lying if I said otherwise . . . In other ways I was still a lad till the day I wed.'

She bent and kissed the top of his silvered dark head. 'You always said he would sow some wild oats before he settled down – we can only hope he'll have the sense not to scatter them too liberally.'

'Ay,' Fergus said off-handedly, and she couldn't see the frown that darkened his brows.

Lewis was up first next morning, punching his brother into wakefulness with a pillow.

'Hey, get off!' Lorn emerged tousleheaded. 'What time is it?'

'Six-thirty. C'mon, get up, it's a grand morning, just right for a paddle in Brodie's Burn.'

In minutes they were dressed and running down to the kitchen where the rays of the sun patterned the brick-red floors. Lewis gulped creamy milk from the big jug on the table and stuffed his pockets with scones from the larder. He was like a small boy, eager to explore old familiar haunts. The gentle heat of the sun probed into field hollows, coaxing the steam to rise and billow out over the landscape. Wreaths of mist encircled the blue hill peaks; down by the harbour, peat smoke curled lazily from the chimneys. The warm smell of heather was sweet in the air; the pure haunting call of the curlew rose out of the moors where greens and ambers blended harmoniously together; the path to Brodie's Burn was a blue and lavender carpet of harebells and wild thyme. Long before they reached the burn the boys removed socks and shoes to walk barefoot through the scented wildflowers. Lewis threw out his arms. 'What a morning to welcome me back.' He grinned wickedly. 'Of course, the sun always shines on the good and pure – hey, little brother,' he said, and threw his arm round Lorn's shoulders, 'this is how it should have been from the start, you and me together doing all the things we're doing now. But we'll make up for it – only good times from now on. Promise me – only good times. I don't know what it is about twins, but it's true they share everything. It must be something to do with coming from the same egg, but I was pretty damned sick every time you went into hospital. I hated it.'

'I didn't like it too well myself.' Lorn's young face

was dark. 'And I didn't exactly have hysterics laughing when the doctors were cutting me up.'

Lewis was serious for a minute. He looked into his brother's deep, steadfast eyes and said slowly, 'I know I'm the selfish half of the egg. When it split up it didn't make an even job of it – all the goodness went to you.'

'Ach, get away! I'm no simpering goody-goody!' Lorn protested awkwardly. 'I want things, the same kind of things you want – only I'm too damned afraid to go after them.'

'Not afraid,' Lewis said softly. 'Canny's the word for you, my lad. You're like Father – canny, dour, and as stubborn as a mule's arse. You can wait for the things you want from life – I can't, that's the difference; I want it all and I want it now.'

Lorn glanced all around him. 'You've got it all now, you daft ass. Stop gabbling and let's get on.'

Ruth was sitting on a low shelf of the Seanachaidh's Stone, her feet in the bracing waters of Brodie's Burn. She had divested herself of shoes and stockings, her calliper lay by her side. She was absorbed, her golden head bowed over the notepad in her lap, the tip of her tongue protruding from the side of her mouth as her pencil flew over the pages. This was one of her favourite haunts, a place of solitude seldom visited by anyone. She often came here before breakfast, before her mother arose to begin another day of religious ritual. The sound of feet swishing through grass made her start up in fright: her violet eyes darkened with the awareness that she wasn't alone, and she had the look of a young deer ready to take flight. At sight of the twins her cheeks blazed and she hastily removed her feet from the water and tucked them under her dress.

Lewis plunked himself down on the bank and plunged his feet straight into the water, teasing her with his roguish grin, enjoying the blushes spreading over her fair skin. 'A fine mornin', Ruth, mo ghaoil.'

'Ay, it is that,' Ruth stuttered. She felt naked, so conscious of the calliper lying on the light grey stone she tried to cover it with the hem of her dress.

'Och, don't be so worried about that silly old calliper,' Lewis scolded, ducking his head to watch his toes wiggling in the peaty brown water. 'No use trying to hide it – you've got a bad leg, and that's that. Get your feet out from under your frock and put them back in the burn.'

Ruth felt better. She relaxed slightly. Lewis had always been able to ease her self-consciousness, make light of her disability – but Lorn couldn't – he was trying very very hard to simulate his brother's indifference, not looking at her, letting his fingers dabble in the umber trout pool some distance away, but she could sense his awareness of her feelings, and she felt miserable with embarrassment. She glanced at the top of his head. His earth-brown curls were tinged with chestnut lights, his shoulder blades stuck out through his jersey, the arm that hung downwards was thin and void of sunburn. She saw the reflection of his face in the pool, an ascetic sensitive face – like her father's. The thought startled her.

He said without looking up, 'You suit that stone, Ruthie, it might have been made for you – after all, it's the stone of the storyteller.'

Ruthie! Only her father called her that. She felt the heat go out of her face. 'I know the legend of this place,' she volunteered shyly.

'Tell it,' Lewis said absently. He had little time for things of the past – the present was far more exciting to him – but he felt that as Ruth was here, she might as well entertain him.

'It was told to old Andrew by Neil the Seanachaidh, and old Andrew told it to me before he died last year,' Ruth began, hesitantly. 'Brodie was a hill climber who got lost climbing the Rhanna hills one stormy night. He lay hurt and dying, crying for help, but no one came. He wept so many tears of anguish they flowed down the hillside, and a spring welled up at the spot where his body was found. There was a great landslide on the night of the storm: the boulders and rocks that rolled down crashed through heather and bracken and came to rest in the fields and moors far below – all but one – this one I'm sitting on now. It came to rest a few inches from Brodie's body.' Ruth's purpled gaze was faraway and very bright. 'Later, in the dark nights of winter, the seanachaidhs gathered round the peat fires to tell how Brodie's Burn came to be, and in the quiet gloamings of summer nights, at the end of the day's work, they came to sit on this stone to rest and to tell the tales of the old days to the young shepherd boys. That's how this stone got its name, and how the story of Brodie got handed down – and that is why to this day the folk of Rhanna come up here and bathe their feet in Brodie's Burn. The old folks say the water is his tears, and that it has healing properties – that is why I bathe my feet in it when no one in the world is looking.'

She uttered the last words without a hint of self-consciousness, so lost was she in the tale she told with such sincerity in her sweet voice. Both boys were completely entranced. Lewis's eyes were on her face, drinking in the almost ethereal quality of beauty the last few minutes had brought to it. Lorn looked down at his hands and murmured softly, 'You're a fine storyteller, Ruthie – just like your father. One day, I think, you might be famous.'

Ruth started out of her reverie and the crimson flooded her cheeks once more. In confusion she said, 'Oh, I must go, Mam will be waiting for me to help her with breakfast – I – I'm late as it is . . .'

Lorn saw her dilemma. She was in a panic at being late, yet if need be she would stay where she was for ever. Under no circumstances would she put on her calliper in front of them, and without it she couldn't walk. Lorn stood up and gave his brother a little push. 'Come on, big brother, Mother will have breakfast ready, and I for one am starving.'

'Me too!' Lewis was like an eager hungry young puppy. He began to run. 'We'll be seeing you, Ruth,' he called over his shoulder, 'goodbye for now.'

'Goodbye,' Ruth returned, and waited till they were just mere specks in the heather before she uncurled her legs stiffly from under her. For a moment she stared with dislike at her small wasted foot, then hastily she pulled on stockings and shoes and fitted the calliper in place. Lachlan had told her mother that exercises and physiotherapy might do a lot to improve the leg, but Morag Ruadh had scoffed at the idea and had told Lachlan it was the will of the Lord. When Ruth had told Rachel this, her eyes flashed and she had promised that during these summer holidays she was going to massage Ruth's leg for her and make her do all sorts of exercises. Ruth smiled as she recalled the glitter of determination in her friend's dark eyes, and, gathering up her notepad and pencils, she hobbled away over the fields to Portcull. She stood on the hilltop looking down at the village. A thin banner of smoke rose from the chimney of her cottage. Her mother was up and had most likely already scrubbed the kitchen floor with carbolic. She would be making the porridge about now, stirring, stirring, rhythmically banging the wooden spoon against the pan sides. Ruth was fascinated by the ritual. She often fancied that her mother was a red-haired witch standing tight-lipped over the fire, brewing some sort of evil potion, using the wooden spoon as an instrument to rid her of all the emotions she bottled up inside.

Sure enough, when Ruth opened the door her mother was at the fire pounding the sluggish porridge viciously. She barely turned at Ruth's entry yet the sideways sweep of her hooded green eyes

825

took in everything. 'You're late, Ruth, and you've got dirt on the hem of your dress.'

'Ay, Mam, I know, but it's awful hard to keep clean in a white dress.'

She stood waiting for the usual questions, a vision of summer in her pure white dress, the rays of the morning sun at her back making her look slightly insubstantial, a being not of this world with her violet dreaming eyes and the fluffy curling hair turned to threads of palest gold in the sun. For over a year now, except when she was away at school, her mother had insisted she wear nothing but white. The change from drab browns and greys had come about one rainy cold morning just after her thirteenth birthday. She would never forget the terror of that morning, or the lonely stark imaginings of a little girl who had been told nothing of the facts of life. She remembered the aching cramp deep in her belly, the misery of nursing her pain in silence, hoping it would go away. But it hadn't gone away, it had got worse and she had gone to her bed to lie down. Then had come the terror – of seeing blood seeping through her clothes – *her* blood – coming from some wound deep inside her body. In her ignorance that was what she had imagined, and, pale and shaking, her eyes huge with fear, she had limped through to her mother to cry out pathetically, 'Mam! Mam! I'm bleeding to death! Could you – would you help me, please.'

Morag Ruadh had turned round very slowly, her own face white and strained. It had been bad enough for her to watch Ruth's thin little body blossoming out – but this – this moment of truth was what Morag had dreaded more than any other. She had shut her mind to the inevitability of it, had refused to face the fact that one day it would happen. Her heart had gone queer within her and she had felt faint.

'Mam,' Ruth's voice had come again, appalled, shaken, fearful.

Morag had gazed at her child and the pathos and strain on the pale small face had twisted her heart. For the first time since the night of her baby's birth, all her motherly instincts were unleashed in one mighty upsurge of pure love. She had sat down in the rocking chair, had taken Ruth into her arms, and for the first time in many years had experienced the earthly joy of kissing and touching smooth skin and silken hair. 'My babby,' she had whispered huskily. 'You mustny be afraid, these things that are happening to you are natural – you've grown, Ruth, from a wee lassie into a wee woman. Weesht now, I will take you and bathe you and tell you what to do.'

Later, when Ruth was calm, her mother had held her at arm's length to gaze down on her and say, 'You mustny ever let boys come near you, Ruth, for they want nothing but to take away the purity of a young lass. From now on you will be dressed in virgin white, for nothing is cleaner that the white o' the driven snow. Heed what I say, my lassie, and remember – when the de'il tempts you, as indeed he will, you must remember my words and be mindful never to violate the purity o' the garments that clothe your body.'

Ruth never had forgotten that day or her mother's words, for each morning she was minded of them afresh when she arose to don white underwear and white outerwear. Boys whispered behind her back and christened her 'the white virgin', yet their glances were admiring, for with her fair skin and hair she was a vision of sweetness. The older folk had always pitied her in her drab frocks but now they called her 'the wee white angel' and their hearts warmed to her and grew colder to Morag Ruadh for stamping her daughter in ways that were enough to turn the lass to sin.

'And where did you go this mornin'?' Morag asked as Ruth busied herself laying the table.

'For a walk. It's a bonny morning.'

'And did you meet anybody at all?'

'Ay, the twins. Lorn is looking much better than he did,' Ruth answered carefully.

Morag glanced at her quickly and said meaningfully, 'Both lads are growing to be young men. You watch out, my girl, I don't take much to these ways you have o' goin' off first thing in the mornin' by yourself.' Ruth was saved further questioning by the arrival of her father. He gave her a quick wink and she winked back, enjoying the intimacy of one of several little habits that had sprung up between them over the years.

During Grace, Ruth sat with her eyes closed, thinking about many things, her mind drifting to

Rachel and the plans they had made for the long summer holidays. They would be aided and abetted in these by Ruth's grandparents, who, though now in their eighties, were still sound of wind and limb and had become adept at thwarting Morag's attempts to run their lives for them. They took a wicked delight in trying to outwit her, and Ruth dreaded the day when she would have them no more. She was far more at home in their cosy cottage than she ever was in the clinical confines of the place both she and her father referred to in private as 'the temple'. Here, all savoury smells were perpetually drowned in the ever-present fumes of carbolic and even the food itself seemed to be tainted by disinfectant.

'You're fidgeting, Ruth,' Morag inserted the reprimand into her own extended version of morning Grace.

Ruth folded her hands in her lap and prayed for patience. She was unusually restless that morning and in between polishing the furniture and black-leading the grate she kept going to the window to gaze with anxious eyes in the direction of the Post Office.

'Ach, what's wi' you, Ruth?' Morag demanded sharply. 'You're like a hen on a hot girdle.'

Ruth turned quickly back to her tasks but breathed a sigh of relief when Morag at last went into the scullery to fetch the meal basin and then took it out to the sunlit yard where she was at once surrounded by an eager army of hens. Ruth looked once more through the window and her heart leapt. Erchy was emerging from the Post Office and her grandparents' house was one of the first on his rounds. Throwing down her duster she limped to the side gate to burst shining-eyed upon Isabel and Jim Jim. She had only visited them briefly the evening before but it had been enough for them to slip her a letter that had arrived at their cottage more than a month ago. In wonder she had devoured the contents of it by the light of a torch in the privacy of the wee hoosie at the back of the temple. So exciting was the news contained in the letter that she had barely slept all night and had risen early to go and tell her grandparents her news before making her journey to Brodie's Burn. Her news had resulted in Isabel spending a feverish morning glued to the window. She had even supped her porridge there so that she would miss nothing of the comings and goings from the Post Office. Jim Jim had remained stolidly by the fire, smoking his pipe and spitting into the peats, but excitement had gained the upper hand in the end and the fire had been abandoned in favour of the window where he jostled with Isabel for the best viewpoint.

'Erchy's coming,' Ruth burst out breathlessly.

'Ay, ay, here he is now.' Jim Jim was at the door, grabbing eagerly at a package from the bemused Erchy's hands. He cocked a bright eye at Ruth who had grown pink. 'Love letters, is it? It's gey lucky havin' grandparents you can put things like these in care of.'

Ruth glanced nervously outside. Her mother had

fed the hens and had gone over a hillock to inspect her washing. Only her red head showed, and Ruth took the package from a disappointed-looking Jim Jim and said breathlessly, 'I'll have to be going now, but I'll come over at dinner time and show it to you. Quick, Mam's coming back, I don't want her finding out yet.'

Erchy scratched his balding sandy head and grinned after Ruth's disappearing back. 'Family secrets, eh? You haveny won a competition like our Todd did a whily back? My, I could fine picture a brand new motor car sitting at your door, Jim Jim.' He pulled up a chair and took the cup of tea proffered by Isabel. 'Were you after hearin' that a rich American lady has hired Todd's car for a fortnight?'

'Indeed no.' Isabel folded her ample arms on the table and comfortably settled down to listen to the latest gossip about Todd's car. He had never driven it since the day it arrived, and for years it had sat outside the Smiddy with a large 'For Hire' sign on the window. Tourists were amazed to come upon the incongruous sight of Todd and Mollie sitting outside on kitchen chairs beside the gleaming car, smiling benignly at the passing world, Mollie in her apron, Todd in shirt sleeves, hairy tweed trousers and cloth bonnet. So startling was the contrast between the sturdy whitewashed cottage, the homely old couple, and the sleek car, that the majority of visitors thought the whole thing was a joke and the 'For Hire' sign wasn't to be taken seriously. The car was popular for island weddings and funerals but was seldom used for anything else, therefore Erchy made much of the latest piece of news.

That day, Ruth spent so much time in the wee hoosie that Morag enquired sharply if her bowels were in good order. The minute Dugald came home he was accosted in the kitchen by his sparkling-eyed daughter. Morag had gone next door with a pot of broth for her parents, giving Ruth the opportunity to be alone with her father. She took him by the hands, propelled him to the rocking chair and made him sit down.

'What on earth's going on, Ruthie?' Dugald said, smiling, his eyes on his daughter's pink cheeks.

Ruth clasped her hands, and, putting the tips of her fingers to her lips, regarded him for a long silent moment. Then from the pocket of her apron she drew out her letter and handed it to him.

'Read it, Father,' she burst out in a strangely controlled voice. Slowly Dugald put on his glasses and glanced through the letter. It was from the editor of a well-known Scottish magazine informing Ruth that the short story she had submitted for consideration had been accepted for publication and would be appearing in the following month's issue. Ruth extracted the magazine from the breast fold of her apron, where it had been all day, and, spreading it open, she laid it on her father's knee. His eyes had grown misty and he had to remove his glasses to wipe the steam from them before he could commence reading. His voice was husky as he read out, '*Hebridean Dream* by Ruth Naomi Donaldson.'

He raised his head slowly and there was such a depth
of pride in his grey eyes that Ruth drew in her breath.

'Well, Father, are you pleased?' she asked somewhat shyly.

'Pleased?' His tones were tight, charged with so
many emotions he could hardly go on. 'My lassie,
you've done it – you've done it, Ruthie. In bringing
your own dreams to fruition you've made all my own
come true. I'll bask in your reflected glory and by
God! I'll bask in it till it dazzles me. I'm proud of you,
my lassie – so proud I – I think I'm going to cry.' The
mist in his eyes brimmed over, and, fumbling for his
hanky, he buried his face into it and could say
nothing further.

Ruth looked down at his thin shoulders, his bowed
silvery head. She remembered the days of childhood
rambles when all her world had revolved round him,
when his slow pleasant voice had woven one story,
one magical tale after another. She remembered
sitting on his knee by firelight, listening enchanted
as his fables lifted her and carried her up and out of
harsh reality into lands full of beauty and wonder.
He had been her guiding light, her teacher and
mentor. All his own dreams had been shattered by a
loveless marriage, but unselfishly he had encouraged
her, nurtured her talent, nourished her mind with his
vast store of knowledge, and in giving of himself, he
had given her treasures far greater than any worldly
goods. Love for him poured through every fibre of
her being, throbbed in each pulsebeat. She laid her
hand on his shoulder, and without looking up, he

took it and held it and shook his head, too full yet for words.

'You gave me my gift,' she said, her musical voice soft. 'I am your daughter – that's the truth, isn't it, Father?'

Slowly he lifted his head. His eyes were full of tears, the pupils of them black and wide with the pain and the pleasure of minutes he would treasure for the rest of his days. Her violet gaze was on him, calm, assured. Understanding passed between them and he knew what she meant. He nodded. 'Ay, Ruthie, you are indeed my daughter, and I thank God for bringing you into my life. You have been more than a blessing to me – you have been my salvation.' He reached up and touched her hair. 'The bonniest hair of all the lassies on the island. When I was a laddie my hair was the colour yours is now – ay, indeed, you are mine, Ruth Naomi Donaldson.'

She took something else from her pocket and held it up. 'This was in with the letter, a cheque for five pounds – it isn't much but it's a start . . .'

Morag came in, muttering about the cantankerous ways of her parents, but she stopped short in her tirade to look suspiciously from Ruth to Dugald. 'What's wi' the pair o' you – and why isn't the table set, Ruth? I turn my back for five minutes and –'

'Morag, will you be quiet for once in your life and listen to *us* for a change . . .'

Morag stared at her husband. His voice had been pleasant but firm, and in the same tones he went on to tell her the news. As she listened, Morag's expression grew strange; something that was indefinable crept into her green eyes.

'We should be very proud of our lassie,' Dugald finished softly. 'She is a daughter any parents would be glad to own.'

Morag turned away. Her shoulders sagged, and she put out her hands quickly to steady herself on the white scrubbed table. 'And why is it you had your mail addressed to your grandparents' house?' she said finally, not looking up but keeping her gaze glued on the table top.

'I was afraid you would open it, Mam,' Ruth said quietly.

Morag threw up her head as an angry retort sprang to her lips, but a glimpse of Ruth's steady frank gaze made her bite back the words. That look – had she not seen the same look in her husband's eyes every day of her life for the last fifteen years? No matter what she had done to him, no matter how much she had denied him, the steadfast honesty in his deep eyes had never faltered. The same look was there in Ruth, growing stronger with each passing year – and now, the thing that Morag had always scorned as 'fanciful nonsense' had taken root to become reality – the dreams, the fables had come out of the clouds and were there, spread out in black and white, on Dugald's knee. Ruth had been born with a gift – she was a gifted child . . . born of a gifted father. Morag's heart beat fast – was it possible? Oh God, that it were so . . .

Ruth was beside her, placing the cheque on the

table. 'This will maybe help with my keep, Mam. I know fine things are dear these days and with me growing so fast it canny make it any easier – get a wee thing for Grannie and Granda – some baccy and maybe a wee sweetie.'

There was no hint of condescension in Ruth's voice; it was tinged only with the pleasure of giving. Love for her child flooded Morag's heart. In a rush of impulse her long fingers clasped round Ruth's hand and she said awkwardly, 'You're a good, good lassie, Ruth – and the Lord knows I'm proud o' you this day.'

'I'll set the table, Mam,' Ruth said. Turning away she winked at her father as she passed his chair on the way to the big oak sideboard.

That night Dugald went early to bed and lay entranced as he read *Hebridean Dream*. It was an enchanting tale, written in such a simple, moving style, that long before he had finished it his eyes had grown misty. He leaned back on his pillows to gaze unseeingly through the window. Ruth had written this, his Ruthie had woven this tale of such enchantment it had been judged good enough to be actually published. Good enough! It was wonderful! Wonderful! Wonderful! And his daughter had done it, *his* daughter! His flesh and blood. She had known all along of the doubts surrounding her identity and she had never uttered a word of them to another soul. Dear God! She must have gone through hell in her mind-searchings, yet her love for him and her loyalty to Morag had never wavered.

'You gave me the gift, I am truly your daughter.' Her words rang in his ears and he turned his face to the pillow. He felt comforted and fulfilled beyond measure and for the first time in years the rigours of his existence faded into insignificance. He forgot the cold, sparse emptiness of his lonely bedroom and fell asleep with the glow of love and pride filling every corner of his heart.

Chapter Twelve

The news of Ruth's success spread round the island like wildfire. When it reached Rachel's ears she went racing down to the village, her long bare legs carrying her swiftly. Ruth was in the henhouses gathering eggs, but she got up quickly to see who could by flying down the stony road in such a hurry. At sight of Rachel she put down the egg basket. The two girls stood regarding each other with warm joy, then Rachel covered the short distance that bridged them and took her friend into a strong, congratulatory embrace. In those precious breathless moments of swift heartbeats, both girls felt that everything they had ever dreamed of was coming true. The world was at their feet, the fire and energy of youth pulsed rapidly in their veins.

Rachel herself was on the crest of a wave. After her father's death she had felt her place would be at home with her widowed mother, but just a year ago Annie had told her daughter that she and Torquil Andrew were to be married. Now, a tiny baby girl with blonde hair and brown eyes had arrived, and the couple were very happy. Rachel wasn't impressed by the new arrival. She had never been the sort of girl to fawn with wide-eyed adulation over babies, she had had enough of them with her young brothers – for whom she had been expected to fetch and carry. The thing that was important to her was that her mother now had someone to lean on, and Rachel had dared to hope that she could pursue a career of music. Jon, who had visited Rhanna as often as he could, had encouraged her all the way, and her ambition was to stay on at school to study hard and perhaps go on to the Atheneum in Glasgow. To her joy her mother had raised no objection – 'Ay, your father would have wanted that,' Annie had said without a great deal of interest – the girl's euphoria was threaded with the dark knowledge that her mother was too wrapped up in her new-found happiness to care very much about that of her daughter.

Torquil Andrew, though kind, was never quite at ease with Rachel. He sensed that she had always known about him and Annie. Although he was a sensible man, he was also a superstitious one, and somehow, in Rachel's company, he felt that the spirit of Dokie Joe was very much alive and would never be allowed to die. Rachel didn't need words to tell him that or the fact that, though he was now man of the house, in Rachel's eyes he would always be an intruder. Yet he knew that he had been the means of freeing her from her ingrained sense of duty to her family, and he knew that she was grateful to him for that.

Old Isabel came out of her cottage and saw her granddaughter with Rachel. Morag Ruadh had gone away up the Hillock to the Kirk to supervise the tuning of the ancient organ, and now a sense of freedom cloaked the temple and its policies.

'Go you away and enjoy yourselves,' Isabel instructed as she came through the gate. 'You don't get out enough, Ruth.'

'But I've still to peel the tatties and prepare the mackerel that old Joe handed in this morning . . .'

'Ach, get away wi' you; I'll do these in no time! Your mother might think Jim Jim and myself are hapless, but there she is far wrong, lassie.' She held up a plump hand. 'Don't argue – when your mother comes back (and the Lord knows when that will be, for she'll have thon poor wee mannie sweatin' over that damt music box for hours), I'll just tell her I sent you over to Nigg wi' a knitting pattern for auld Aggie. A trip like that should keep you away for a few hours, eh?' She beamed mischievously, and Ruth hugged her and peeled off her apron.

The girls went off arm in arm hugging each other with glee at the rather awed looks thrown at Ruth from people she had known all her life. Lorn and Lewis had been dispatched from Laigmhor to fetch some groceries from Portcull and they came along the glen road, Lewis swinging the empty shopping bag in the air. He immediately set about teasing Ruth. 'Is it permitted for a humble peasant like myself to speak to one so grand?' he grinned. 'You're a sensation – do you know that, Ruth Naomi Donaldson? Old Behag nearly had apoplexy when she saw your name in print. They have called out the fire brigade to put out her tongue.'

'And to think just yesterday I was gabbling on about you maybe being famous one day,' Lorn said, 'and all the time you already were.' He bent forward and dropped a kiss on her hot cheek. 'Congratulations, Ruthie.' His voice was soft and rather intimate in her ear. 'You deserve all the success you get, you'll make this island proud of you.'

Ruth was confused. The kiss had been brief, yet she had the oddest feeling that his warm lips were still there against her face. His blue eyes gazed into hers and something that neither of them could understand passed between them, a short sharp little shock of tingling awareness.

Lewis's hearty laugh carried them over the moment. 'Would you look at that, Rachel! At last! Little brother is finding out what girls are for. Go on, Lorn, she won't bite, will you, Ruth? She might be a writer but she's still flesh and blood.'

'It's strange,' Lorn said, his face red, but his voice thoughtful, 'one day a person that everyone takes for granted suddenly does something that changes them in the eyes of the world. They're still the same but everyone starts to see them in a new light. If they really get famous the world puts them on a pedestal. It becomes an honour to get close to famous people, to get their signature – to touch them.'

'I've only written one little story,' Ruth protested awkwardly, rather taken aback at Lorn's deep-thinking philosophies.

Rachel was nodding her agreement at the words, though she couldn't suppress a smile as Lewis gave

Ruth a ridiculous curtsey and said in a high voice,
'Please, may I touch the hem of your dress, my lady,
or will I dare to kiss your hand?'

Dodie came galloping down the hill path from
Nigg. Grinding to a halt he cried in tones more
mournful than usual, 'He breeah.'

The young people returned the greeting and Lewis
added, 'Fine the day may be, but you don't look too
pleased with yourself, Dodie. What ails you?'

'Ach, it's these damty towrists,' Dodie moaned. 'I'm
gettin' fair scunnered wi' them swarmin' up the hill
to look at the pattern on my wee hoosie.'

'Why don't you take the sign down?' Lorn
suggested. 'You'll get peace then.'

But Dodie's countenance became more sorrowful
than ever. 'Ach, it would be no use at all, they all
know about the pattern now. Like flies round a lump
o' dung they are, an' it's no' worth the coppers they
put in my tin – there was two foreign coins there this
mornin',' he ended with a sniff.

'Well, paint over it then,' Lorn said patiently.

Dodie's eyes filled. 'But I wouldny like to lose my
pattern – it's a fine pattern, so it is.'

'But you could still have it,' Lewis pointed out. 'On
the inside of the roof where only you can see it.'

Dodie brightened. 'Ay, that would be just the thing
– only I used the last o' my paint on the door o'
Ealasaid's byre – she'll be havin' her calf soon and I
wanted to make the place nice for it comin'.'

'We'll bring some over and do it for you,' Lorn
offered. 'Grant will be home in a few days and will

be looking for something to keep him busy.'

'Ach, it's kind you are just, just like your father.' He was about to take off, but stopped in his tracks to rub his grizzled chin and stare in rather stupefied awe at Ruth. He couldn't read a word of English and had scant idea of anything that went on in the outside world, but he had heard about Ruth's story appearing in print, and was greatly impressed by the fact. His gaze travelled slowly from Ruth's face to her feet then travelled back again as if he was trying to convince himself that she was real and not some kind of transient apparition.

Ruth shifted her feet in some embarrassment but managed to smile and say, 'I'm just the same as I ever was, Dodie, you don't have to look at me as if I was a ghost.'

'Ay, but you will never be the same as you ever was,' Dodie returned cryptically. 'Everybody will be readin' your story and seein' your name. You will no' just belong to the island any more, you will belong to other folks – folks like the towrists who come and gawp at my wee hoosie and at myself as if I was different. If folk like these found out you were a writer they would come and look at you for you are different – like my wee hoosie.'

For all his unworldly ways Dodie had an uncanny insight into more sophisticated minds, and it was perhaps this that made the islanders pause occasionally and say, 'Auld Dodie's no' as daft as folks make out. He has his head screwed on even though the Lord never fixed it into the right threads.'

Ruth felt uncomfortable and was glad when a diversion appeared in the shape of Todd's car slowly purring down the glen road. In the passenger seat was Biddy who, despite her aversion to cars, had been delighted at being offered a lift into Portcull. She beamed toothlessly at the little group by the roadside, and gave a coy little wave such as she had seen practised by members of the royal family. Behind the driving wheel sat the rich American lady, and she too raised a hand in salute.

Dodie, perhaps hoping for a lift in the car himself, galloped off after it, followed by the twins who had been given strict instructions to get to the shops before they closed. The girls went off to the moors to spend a pleasant afternoon, though Rachel kept her promise and made Ruth remove her calliper so that she could massage the twisted little leg. Ruth sat in the heather and watched her friend's long slim fingers patiently working away. Only with Rachel could she allow herself to be truly free, and she felt no embarrassment in exposing the limb that had caused her such distress all her life. Rather, she experienced a strange sense of relaxation as she felt the blood coursing under Rachel's sure touch, and when she finally put back the calliper, she was sure that it wasn't just imagination that made her feel a strength in her leg that hadn't been there before. She looked at Rachel's lovely face, noted the proud tilt of her head. If only Rachel could speak. Ruth was certain that her voice would have been as sweet as the music she made. It seemed such a sad thing that a beautiful girl like Rachel could never express all those deep thoughts and emotions that crowded into her eyes.

Rachel read her thoughts and with her hands she spelled out quickly, 'You mustn't feel sorry for me, Ruth. I don't for you.'

'I know, I know!' Ruth cried. 'I don't feel sorry, it's just – how I would have loved to hear the voice that might have been yours – just once, so that I could have a memory of it inside my head!'

Rachel's hands said slowly, 'And I would love to see you running like a deer – just once – but we are as we are. If we had been different we might never have been friends.'

Ruth nodded wonderingly. 'I never thought of that. You can't speak but you think out things that other folks wouldn't dream of. I'm too busy imagining things to sometimes see the truth, I think I'm what's known as a romantic, while you have your two feet firmly planted on the ground.' She giggled suddenly. 'I have an excuse – only one of mine is firmly planted. Isn't that a fine picture for you – one leg on the ground like a flamingo and my head lost in the clouds? No wonder Dodie was looking for me back there.'

Laughing they ran over the heather and parted at the bridge by Murdy's house. In the distance Rachel saw Stink the Tink and she ran to him. The tinkers had learned to understand her sign language and Stink watched as her expressive hands asked, 'Why haven't you got old Mo with you today?'

Stink leaned against his laden wheelbarrow and rubbing a tattered sleeve over his sweaty brow he said sorrowfully, 'The old man is not at all well, miss. His chest is rattlin' like a bundle o' dry hay. He has not been outside his tent since we came last week and we are afraid for him, miss. He has not eaten a bit for days and is only able to sup hot toddy – we are all thinkin' the good Lord has set His finger upon the old man.'

Rachel drew back in horror, her smooth brow furrowed. Her beloved old rogue of an Irishman couldn't be dying – her visits to the tinker encampment to see him were one of the highlights of her life. But old Mo was indeed very ill. That evening, when the sun was low in the western sky, Rachel ran over the heat-hazed moors to the hollow near Dunuaigh. The smoke from the tinkers' fires curled lazily into the gold-washed sky and in the little burn that purled through the heather the tinker children paddled their feet, while nearby the women washed clothes. The small round framework tents with their weathered coverings of grey canvas were dotted together in companionable closeness. It was a familiar scene to Rachel. She of all the people on Rhanna knew the tinkers as well as they knew each other, and as her long brown legs carried her swiftly through the tough moor grasses, the children glanced up and waved to her in greeting. She found old Mo lying on a tattered pile of bedding. His pram lay outside, abandoned and forgotten-looking – as if the old man who had occupied it for so long would never again ride upon its creaking chassis.

The sound of old Mo's rapid breathing filled the dark confined space. Rachel knelt beside him and put her hand on his damp brow. His mottled face was grey and gaunt, and he didn't stir at her touch. Beside him lay an almost full bottle of whisky, and to Rachel that in itself was a sign that the old man was not long for the world. In a panic she started up. She had to get help. He couldn't, he mustn't, be allowed to die. She ran outside and without preliminary, began hitching a cart to a fly-tormented pony who was searching the heather for clover.

'It is no use, miss,' Stink cried. 'There is no help for him. Leave the old man to die in peace.'

But Rachel paid no heed. She jumped on the cart and, grabbing the reins, coaxed the pony into a trot. One thought beat in Rachel's head: Help, she had to get help. The doctor was too far away; the nearest person with medical knowledge was Biddy – and it was to the sturdy grey stone house in Glen Fallan that Rachel guided the horse. Biddy was preparing for bed. The remains of her supper of oatcakes and creamy milk lay on the table. Halfway through eating it, she had fallen asleep and sat by the embers of the fire, her cat Woody ensconced on her knee, her white head nodding onto her breast. Rachel opened the door and went inside to shake the old woman gently by the shoulder. Biddy jumped and Woody clawed her knee in fright before leaping down to scamper under a chair.

'Ach, what on earth!' grumbled Biddy. 'Can't a

body have a snooze at the fireside without bein' shaken to bits?' She screwed up her eyes at the intruder, but without her glasses she was blind. 'Has the cat got your tongue?' she cried sharply. 'Get me my damty specs till I see who you are.'

She grabbed the proffered glasses and stuck them on the end of her nose. The vision of Rachel was a hazy one. 'Are you a spook or are you real?' Biddy demanded. 'What is it you're tryin' to tell me?'

But Rachel had no time to waste. She knew the old nurse could make little sense of her sign language and gently she began pulling Biddy to her feet. 'Please, oh, please,' the girl cried silently. 'Come with me. Make her come, God.'

Biddy sensed the girl's urgency. The dazzling child with her untamed quality and great expressive eyes had always been a particular favourite of hers. Stiffly she got to her feet. 'Go away ben the lobby and get me my cloak and my bag,' she ordered. 'I'm no' a mind reader but I'm thinkin' somebody must be ill.'

A few minutes later, they departed from the house and Rachel goaded the horse into a trot. The sun had set, diffusing the sky with fire. The cliffs of Croy were red in the glow, the sea a sheet of flame; the peace of night lay over the moors like an invisible cloak.

'It's as I thought,' Biddy said softly when the tink camp came into view. 'Yon auld Irish de'il I haveny a doubt.'

A tinker woman was bathing old Mo's brow; when she saw Biddy she shook her red head. 'It's no use me old woman, he's nearly a goner. Come mornin' he'll be wi' the fairies. You have had a wasted journey.' Biddy puffed out her scraggy chest. 'I'll be the judge o' that, my bonny woman. Bring me some clean cold water and dinna waste too much time about it.'

With difficulty she eased herself over to the old man and examined him quickly, screwing up her nose as odours of all kinds were released from his clothing. She shook her head and turned to Rachel. 'Pneumonia. Too far gone to help. The bodach is burning up. The only thing we can do for him is make him as comfortable as it's possible to make a dying body.'

Rachel recoiled as if she had been struck. Gently the old nurse took her hand. 'My bairnie, you are young and strong wi' life tumbling through your veins so fast it's like a burnie rushin' after rain – this is an auld man, the stream o' his life is dryin' up. Look at him, Rachel, he is very very tired. He wants to die; he needs to rest. When a body gets old and feeble, the dawn of each new day can sometimes be more a curse than a blessing.' She shook her head sadly and sighed. 'Fine I know it too, some mornin's I feel like closin' my eyes like old Mo here and givin' up the ghost.'

Rachel felt the sobs tearing at her throat. She looked at the old man's grey, sunken face. Biddy was right, he did look tired and very old; the stubble that sprouted from his sweat-lathered face looked like snow lying on grey earth.

As the hours wore on, Mo's breathing became

harsher. And when Biddy grew weary of bathing him, Rachel took over, gently washing the perspiration from his face and chest. The only sounds in the ghostly hours before dawn were Mo's laboured breaths and the resigned moans from a nearby tent where a young woman lay in childbirth. Sometime before dawn the old man stirred and opened his eyes. They were dazed, and he seemed to struggle out from a far distant place, but awareness came into them at sight of Rachel. He struggled to speak, but no sound came and Rachel bathed his cracked lips and lifted his head to allow him to drink some water. He spluttered and said in a strong voice. 'Water! Water bejasus! It's the water o' life I'm needin'! Where's me whisky?'

The mouthful of burning spirits revived him and Rachel spun round to Biddy with hope in her tempestuous eyes, a look that said, 'He's going to get well, I knew he couldn't die.'

The old man reached out to her, and his damp horny hand closed over her wrist. 'Mavourneen,' he whispered, and there were tears in his eyes. 'Did not we make good music with our fiddles? The finest ever heard in any tink camp.' He gripped her wrist tighter, his other hand scrabbled frantically under the blankets and he withdrew his treasured violin. 'Here she is, me beauty.' He pushed it at Rachel. 'She's yours now. Take her and look after her as I have done – and I tell you this, me lass, she played well for me, but she'll play even better for you. Give me a tune now – "Danny boy" – ay – no finer tune to play an old timer off the stage. Go on now, mavourneen.'

With tears flowing down her face Rachel took the beautiful instrument, and the strains of the haunting melody filled the tent. It was like some sort of signal to the other tinkers. In minutes a crowd had gathered outside to pay their respects to old Mo.

His eyes were closing. Rachel put down the violin and laid her cool hands on his brow. A smile touched the corners of his mouth, and the fear that had engulfed him some minutes before dissipated like mist. A strange peace stole over him. 'You have the touch of the angels in those hands, mavourneen. Indeed you have more gifts than you know of yourself – many of them at your fingertips.'

One of the women came in and whispered in Biddy's ear, and the old nurse rose stiffly. There was nothing now to be done for old Mo and she followed the woman to a nearby tent where a young girl, awash with the sweat of childbirth, was in the last stages of labour. Biddy hastened to wash her hands and deal with the delivery while just a few yards away old Mo was breathing his last. His hands were still at his sides but a twinkle lit the dullness of his gaze as he instructed Rachel, 'Be playin' me out in style now – only – the best is good enough for – an Irish leprechaun . . .'

Rachel took up the violin once more. The old man's respiration was shallow and irregular, and as he died peacefully to the strains of 'The Londonderry Air' the rising sun burst brilliantly over the sea, and the lusty cries of a newborn baby boy filled the air with life.

Stink moved into old Mo's tent and pulled the blankets over the craggy old face. There was about it a serenity that had rarely touched it during the course of his tough life. The struggle for survival was over.

Rachel stumbled outside blinded with tears. The morning was filled with the glories of summer; the scents of the moor were sweet and strong; the languorous sounds of land and sea broke through the silence like a melody.

'I'll be havin' that! It might fetch a few bob.' A rough-looking tinker was stretching out his big fist for the violin.

Rachel's nostrils flared and she held the violin to her breast, enfolding it protectively with both arms.

'C'mon now, me fine lass, let's be havin' it.' The Irishman made to grab at the girl to forcibly take the violin away from her, but Biddy intervened with a sharp, 'Leave the bairn alone! The fiddle belongs to her now. The bodach told her so wi' his very own dyin' breath and I was there to bear witness. Get away from her, Paddy McPhie, or it's the police I'll be havin' on you. A fine disgrace that would be to all of you, and you wouldny be welcome on this island again.' She stood at the door of the tent, her lined old face yellow in the morning light, her white hair straggling over her eyes, her toothless mouth pulled in so that her nose almost touched her chin. She looked very old and very tired, but such an authoritative air emanated from her that Paddy's meaty fists fell to his sides and he shuffled away in shame. 'And I'll be havin' a good strong cuppy and a chair by the fire,' Biddy told the other tinkers firmly.

'You'll be havin' more than that, me fine old lass,' beamed the young father of the new baby. 'You brought my firstborn into the world, and helped old Mo go out of it in dignity.' He escorted Biddy to the fire, then sent the children scurrying to fetch blankets and a torn but well-upholstered car seat. In minutes Biddy was comfortably ensconced, wrapped in a tartan blanket, drinking tea laced with whisky while she waited for breakfast to cook over the flames.

Rachel wasn't hungry. She wandered away from the camp and sat with her back to a rock to gaze out over the moors to the golden sea. For over two hours she sat lost in thought while Biddy ate, drank tea, and dozed by the fire. Then she got up and went back to the camp. Biddy looked at the girl's sad face, and, rising, she put her arms round Rachel's shoulders.

'Come on, my lassie, we'll go home now. Don't bother wi' the cart, I could be doing wi' a walk to ease my bones.' Her face glowed suddenly. ''Tis glad I am you came for me last night. It's no' often I feel needed these days – ay – it's a wonderful way the Lord has – an old life goes out and a new one comes in, and I was there to deliver the bairnie.'

It was well after nine when they arrived at Biddy's house. Woody was at the door, mewing a rather reproachful welcome. Biddy paused, her rheumaticky hand on the gate, her shoulders stooped. On an impulse Rachel took the old woman in her arms.

'Ay, ay, go away now and get some rest,' Biddy's voice was husky. 'You'll greet for the bodach in days to come, my lamb, but remember – he was ready to go, that he was.'

Rachel turned, and walking quickly away, crossed a bridge over the river Fallan so that she could walk home over the moors. Skirting a heather knoll she paused for a moment to run her fingers over the smooth red-gold wood of the violin. The screeching of brakes on the road far below made her whirl round in horror. There, just outside Biddy's house, Todd's car had ground to a halt, from it ran an agitated figure – and lying on the road, like a tiny broken doll, lay the figure of Biddy.

Rachel's flying feet hardly touched the ground. She heard her ragged breath deep in her throat, her heartbeat rushed in her ears. The American visitor was kneeling beside Biddy, her volatile cries of distress reeling through the air. She rose at Rachel's approach and ran forward, a haggard, nervous-looking woman of about forty-five with sad eyes and suspiciously black hair. Her clothes were beautifully cut, yet looked untidy on her. The immaculate slacks had brought forth the usual nods of disapproval from the island women though the younger ones were reserved in their judgement as many of them had a hankering after the trowser themselves.

Rachel paused briefly in her flight to stare at the scene in disbelief before she turned the full fury of her gaze on the American. 'Hey, don't look at me like that, kid!' cried the woman in near-hysteria. 'It wasn't my fault. The old lady just ran straight into my path – I wasn't even doing thirty – she went after her cat . . .'

Rachel pushed past her and fell on her knees by Biddy, whose eyes were closed, and who was a ghastly grey colour, but other than some cuts and bruises there was no outward physical damage. Rachel felt the hills closing in on her. Frustration boiled in her belly. She had pretended to Ruth that she accepted the fact that she couldn't speak but she had lied. She wanted to scream, to talk, to ask Biddy if she was all right. Gently she reached out to stroke the hair from the lined brow. Biddy's lips fluttered and her eyes opened. She didn't appear to be in any kind of pain, but her skin was cold and moist, her breathing shallow. The American woman came running with a coat, which she tucked round Biddy's prone figure.

'Rachel,' Biddy murmured. 'Lay your hands on my brow like you did wi' the bodach.' Rachel did as she was bid and a sigh came from Biddy's pale lips. 'The bodach was right – you have the gift in your hands to ease a body's fears. Hold my hand, lassie, and don't let go.'

There was another squealing of brakes as the island bus came to a halt at Downie's Pass. Erchy had driven the vehicle at a spanking pace over the narrow roads and now, despite the sudden halt, not a single word of enquiry came from the tourists. They sat rigid, the white blobs of their faces peering from the bus windows. Erchy ran from the bus, followed by Jon, who often rode with Erchy on his tours round the island. Close on their heels ran Kate, who had been spending the night with her daughter at Croft na Beinn. Erchy was removing his jacket as he ran, and in seconds he was tucking it under Biddy's head. Her lips moved again. 'Is that Kate McKinnon's voice I hear? Are you there, Kate?'

'The very one.' Kate knelt and took the old woman's frail hand in her big capable one. Kate was of an exuberant, earthy, boisterous nature, but she was also cool-headed, efficient, and calm in an emergency, and Biddy was grateful for her presence in those strange unreal minutes. She held Kate's hand and gazing up at the green hills she murmured, 'Oft, oft have I walked these purpled hills and watched the sun go down.'

The American woman wrung her hands. 'Gee, she's delirious, she's going on about all the things she loves . . .'

'Ach, it's you who's delirious,' Biddy said with a touch of her old asperity, 'I'm sick walkin' the damty hills and watchin' suns go down when all I wanted was my bed – I'm just tryin' to pass my time on this hard road while somebody goes to fetch Lachlan.'

But Erchy was already away, turning Todd's car at Biddy's gate and setting it on the road to Slochmhor.

'It will no' be Lachlan who will come,' Kate reminded her. 'He's away on holiday and won't be back for a few days yet – but thon nice young doctor who's doin' for him will soon see you right.'

'I don't want him – he has hands like putty – I want Lachlan . . .' She tried to raise her head. 'Where's my cat? The bugger ran out on me when I opened the gate . . .'

Jon came from the riverbank with the cat in his arms and placed him in his mistress's trembling arms.

Rachel turned away. The pallor on Biddy's face was the same as she had seen on old Mo as death had drawn near. She bit her lip and walked unsteadily to stand some distance from the scene of the accident. Suddenly Jon was beside her, taking her hands, making her sit down on the grassy bank. She looked at his honest brown eyes and the little beard flecked now with grey, like her father's. It seemed the young German was always there when she needed comfort. He had also been with her the day she found Squint dead in his basket. Gently Jon had lifted up the little dog, and the glint of tears had been in his eyes as he had taken Rachel's hand and said, 'Come, jungfräulich, we will bury him in a quiet place on the moors and I will make a cross to mark his resting place.'

She remembered her hand in his as they walked over the Muir of Rhanna to bury the dog who had been such a wise and faithful companion to a little dumb girl. Out there on the open moors, with the wind sighing and ruffling the bracken, Rachel saw again a small golden spaniel, his floppy ears flying in the breezes as he raced towards her over the heather, the expression of joy in his gloriously comical face making her laugh as he flopped by her feet to look up at her in cross-eyed adulation. Jon had given her strength then, and she often went to sit by the simple elm cross that he had carved.

Now, here was Jon again, his words of comfort, spoken in his charming broken English, reaching out to ease her sorrow. Todd's car appeared in a cloud of dust, and Rachel went back to Biddy's side as the young locum jumped out. In a short while Biddy was being carried into her house, hurling abuse in the doctor's ears and moaning for a cuppy. But her voice was weak and Kate's face was grim as she set about helping to get the old woman into bed. The doctor took Kate aside and told her, 'She is suffering badly from shock, which has affected her heart. I'm afraid it's rather serious, but I'll do what I can.'

Rachel crept away from the bedroom door and went slowly downstairs where Jon was waiting for her. He led her outside. 'Come, jungfräulich, I will walk home with you.' He glanced at the violin that she was hugging like a baby. 'Your old friend has gone?' he asked quietly.

She nodded and her head fell forward onto her chest. He felt her pain and misery and lifted a tentative finger as if to stroke the satin black of her hair, but then he thought better of it and his hand fell back to his side. 'I told you once before, Rachel, cry your pain away. Old Mo would not want you to be unhappy over him. He gave you his violin in gratitude for all the happy times he shared with you. This is a very special gift he left you – a Cremonese, made by a great craftsman of northern Italy, it is very old and very valuable. I noticed it on the evening of Merry Mary's ceilidh when the old man let me play it. It has the voice of the angels; under fingers such as yours it will make music such as is in heaven.'

Rachel knew that what Jon was telling her was of great importance, but just then she couldn't fully take it in. Old Mo was dead, he had given her his treasured violin, and that was all that really mattered – the thought, not the value. She handed it to Jon and signalled for him to play. Reverently he placed it under his chin, and drew the bow over the strings. The notes swelled and soared to join the summer song of the birds. Rachel's heart felt like bursting. She was sad, yet happy at the same time, and not even her mother's stern face at the window penetrated her emotions.

Annie's voice was sharp as she came to the door and cried, 'Well now, miss! What is the meaning o' this I'd like to know. Out all night, then comin' home over the moor playin' the fiddle wi' a Jerry as if . . .'

Jon laid a hand on Annie's arm. 'Rachel and Biddy have been sitting all night with old Mo. He died at dawn, and Biddy has just been knocked down by a car. Rachel stayed till the doctor came.'

Annie's hand flew to her mouth. 'Auld Biddy! Oh dear God, no!' She saw the anguish in her daughter's eyes and felt something of her frustration and grief. 'Rachel, 'tis sorry I am about old Mo. I was never happy about you spendin' so much time up by the tinks' camp, but I knew how much the auld de'il meant to you. I'm – sorry I shouted – I would have been angrier still at a lassie who had not the heart nor the courage to bide wi' an auld man in his last breath.' She held out her hand. 'Come you in and sup – you too, Mr Yodel, you have always been kind to my poor dumb lassie and 'tis grateful I am indeed.'

Jon flinched. 'Poor dumb lassie.' Was that how Annie saw her beautiful talented daughter? Rachel was holding her head proudly, and he couldn't tell if the words had made an impression or not. Her mother's expressions were probably commonplace to the girl, but as he sat in with the family and shared their breakfast, he sensed that Rachel was never quite at ease throughout the meal, that she tolerated rather than enjoyed her home life, that when she spread her wings into a wider world she would never be hindered by homesickness. In these respects she was like him. He enjoyed going back occasionally to Germany, but he dreaded going home to Mamma. Rachel adored Rhanna passionately, but had little attachment to a home where no one took any real interest in her life. Her father had done so up to a point, but he was dead now, and she had no one.

Jon glanced over the table at Rachel. The sun was streaming over her, turning her skin to gold, her hair to blue-black satin. Her eyes were shadowed pools, glinting amber where the sun danced into them. She had him! Always she would have him – as long as she needed him.

Chapter Thirteen

No titled lady in the land could have had more affection and attention than was lavished on Biddy over the next few days, but quite unlike the pampered rich, she had no need of wealth or position to further every whim that came into her head. The islanders came in a steady stream bearing delicacies to tempt her appetite and generally to make sure that her time spent in bed would not be weary. While gossip was exchanged in the upstairs bedroom, downstairs in the kitchen the kettle was never off the boil and tea was drunk in great quantities as everything from peat cutting to the price of sugar was discussed with energy. The menfolk sat on the crofter's bench under the window, smoking and adding the odd piece of sage argument to the current topic, but occasionally the voices grew hushed as everyone wondered quietly 'just how bad was auld Biddy'.

Kate came faithfully every day, but other than endless cuppies laced with brandy or whisky, Biddy ate very little. After a few days a dismayed Kate realised that all her culinary efforts were in vain.

'You canny live on whiskified tea!' Kate scolded when yet another meal was rejected, but Biddy put a frail hand on her arm and said, 'Mo ghaoil, my belly has been wi' me for a long time and knows what's best for it – besides,' she said, sinking back on her pillows and sighing deeply, 'there comes a time in a body's life when no amount of food will ever do any good – and my time's come.'

'Away! You've years in you yet, you silly cailleach,' Kate stated cheerfully, but when she turned away from the bed her eyes were sad and her steps heavy as she went downstairs to report the latest news.

If Kate hadn't put a stop to it, the children would have been swarming into the house in their droves to visit the old woman they loved. Instead, Kate allowed them upstairs in ones and twos, and then only for a few minutes at a time. But at Biddy's own request, a little impromptu concert was arranged and Jon, Rachel, Lorn and Lewis arrived to play their fiddles for her. One favourite tune after another filled the bedroom, and very soon her eyes were wet and she had to dab them furtively with a corner of the bedspread.

'Damty grand,' she said in husky appreciation.

Rachel threw back her head to stop her own tears spilling, and found Lewis's hand in hers under cover of the valance. She looked at him quickly, her heart beating very fast, the way it always did lately whenever she saw him or sat beside him. He smiled at her sympathetically and squeezed her hand tighter, and she knew that for the moment sympathy was all that he felt for her. Half the girls on the island were under his charming spell. He went from one to the other like a bee in search of the sweetest nectar, and she knew one day her turn would come.

Jon, sitting with his fiddle on his knee, saw the exchange and was minded afresh that Rachel was growing up. There would be boys – lots of them. And her need for him would grow less and less . . .

His musings were interrupted by Ruth's arrival into the room. Her mother had dispatched her to read the Bible 'for the salvation of Biddy's soul', but Ruth had slipped her notebooks into her pocket, and it was these she proceeded to read. Her face was pink and her voice shaky because she had never been good with an audience, but, as with Lorn and Lewis up by Brodie's Burn, she soon forgot herself, and her sweet voice grew steady.

Everyone in the room was enchanted by her stories and poems. Biddy lay back with a little smile lifting her lips, and closed her eyes in contentment; Lewis once more sought Rachel's hand; Jon looked from the window to the hills and tried to convince himself that Rachel's cheeks were burning because it was stuffy in the room; Lorn gazed at Ruth's bowed golden head and thought about a field full of ripe corn . . .

Ruth's face flushed again as she glanced up and caught him watching her. She closed her books. 'I think Biddy's asleep,' she said softly. 'We'd better go.'

'Asleep nothing.' Biddy's eyes popped open. 'My magazine's on that table; get it for me and read it, Ruth. Your voice is like a burnie purlin' through the heather and I want to hear you readin' your story from your very own lips. It's no' every day I get to hear a writer readin' to me.' So Ruth read *Hebridean Dream*, and half an hour later Biddy really was asleep, lulled by the girl's musical voice.

Everyone looked at each other; something other than the sadness of being by a beloved old lady's sickbed had touched them all, and they were each aware of it. The touching of hands had brought Lewis a step nearer Rachel; the arch of a slender neck and silken strands of hair had stirred something in Lorn's heart that had never been there before; Jon glanced at the four youthful faces surrounding him and felt old at thirty-seven. Life to him was a magical wonderful experience. It made him walk with a spring in his step and a lightness of heart. But the sight of the flush on Rachel's face made some of the magic go out of his life, with the result that his heart felt heavy inside him. Rachel glanced up and saw the sadness in his face, and she smiled, a vibrant radiant smile that told him of the new doors opening in her heart. He nodded and forced himself to smile back. She was so young. She had a right to every happiness that came her way – but he knew she would never find them in Lewis McKenzie, and he hoped she would discover that in time – before she fell too much under Lewis's spell.

When Dodie first heard of the accident he galloped into Biddy's house without any of his usual preliminary and went straight upstairs, his great wellingtons making sucking sounds in the hollows of the well-worn wooden stairs. For him to come straight into a house was unusual; for him to go into a 'leddy's bedroom' was unheard of, but to him the old nurse was not a lady. In his eyes, her standing went far higher than that of any other mortal female known to him, and no title on earth had yet been created for the grumbling, lovable old woman he had known all his life. Dodie had little recall of his own mother – who had died when he was only thirteen, leaving him to fend for himself – and Biddy was the nearest to what he imagined a mother to be. She scolded, nagged, occasionally cuffed him on the ear – but she also conveyed her affection in many ways. When she met him she always gave him a sweetie; when passing her house on his solitary wanderings, he had often been invited in for supper or breakfast. At Christmas she gave him baccy and made him plum pudding, but most wonderful of all, out of everybody in his world, she was the only one who remembered his birthday, and every year, without fail, she presented him with a small reminder of the day.

'I couldny forget the day you were born,' she unfailingly told him. 'Just like a wee squealing piglet you were, wi' ears on you like those on the wally joog in my bedroom.'

Dodie was never offended by these comparisons. In fact, they delighted him. They gave him a feeling of having some sort of roots, and he blushed and smiled, never tiring of hearing such things from the only person who could, like a real mother, give him anecdotes of his babyhood.

When he beheld Biddy in bed, white-faced and

hollow-eyed, her silvery hair brushed back and tied with a blue ribbon, he burst into tears. She appeared to have shrunk, and she looked very small in the big feather bed. But her voice when she scolded him was still as strong as ever. 'Ach, what's wrong wi' you, laddie?' she asked in disgust. 'It's me who's the one should be cryin' – lyin' here waitin' to see when will Lachlan arrive. Come over here this meenit and take this hanky to wipe your eyes.'

He shuffled over, and taking the proffered square of white cotton, proceeded to soak it in seconds. He stood over her bed, a figure of pathos in his threadbare coat, his stooped shoulders juddering with sobs.

'Ach, laddie,' she said, her voice soft, 'you are a good kind soul, and the Lord knows you were put on this earth for a purpose like the rest o' us. Dry your eyes now and take a sweetie. They're Imperials, your favourites.'

He took the sweet and sucked it loudly, his watery gaze fixed on her tired face. ''Tis sorry I am for greetin',' he sniffed dismally. 'It's just I was feart when I heard you had been knocked down by a motor car. They are dangerous smelly things, and I was aye thinkin' they would stay in the cities and never come to the islands . . . A horse would never knock a body down like that. Even when they are runnin' wild they will make a circle past anybody in their road.'

Biddy nodded in thoughtful agreement. 'Ay, you're right there, Dodie. But times are changin', and there will come a day when the likes o' Todd will no' be kept in business by just horses. Already he's havin' to take in bikes and make fancy gates to make ends meet – ach, these new-fangled ways will no' make for a better world. I'm glad I'll go out of it afore it changes too much.'

The tears sprouted from Dodie's eyes once more. He scrubbed them with his calloused knuckles, and hung his head to hide his shame.

Biddy was growing very tired. She was grateful to the islanders for sparing their time to fill her daytime hours, but she was thankful when night came and she could be alone. Babbie had only been one of many who had offered to stay with her at night, but she had declined all such offers with the reasonable excuse of 'being too weary come night to even hear a mouse fart'.

'Dodie.' She pulled herself up, almost knocking over her teeth in the glass by her elbow. 'Will you stop your blubberin' – or I'll get out this bed and cuff your lug, and you will no' be likin' the sight o' me in my goonie and woolly bedsocks. Now, dry your eyes and listen to me. I want you to do a wee thing for me.'

'Ay, anything at all, Biddy,' he whispered, keeping his head averted just in case she would keep her threat and get out of bed. He knew well that with Biddy anything was possible.

'You like nice things wi' patterns, don't you, laddie?'

'Ay, that I do,' he agreed dismally.

'Well, go over there to the kist and see me over the wee boxie right at the top.'

He did as she bade him, his pale dreaming eyes widening at sight of the wee boxie carved exquisitely in oak and inlaid with mother-of-pearl. The old lady fumbled for her glasses and her eyes grew misty as she touched the relief design of leaves and roses. In a husky far-away voice she murmured, 'My grandfather made this for my fourteenth birthday, the finest jewel box any young lass could wish for – ay, fine I mind him goin' to his wee shed and workin' all the hours God made. It was carved wi' love, for his auld hands were knotted like bits o' driftwood warped by the tide. He died just a fortnight after my birthday, and I have treasured this boxie all my life. But now I'm no' able to give it the care it needs. It has to be polished and kept in the manner it deserves, and you wi' your love o' treasures is just the one to do this for auld Biddy. Take it now and don't be tellin' a soul – you can use it to keep these bits and pieces o' shells and things you are aye gatherin' together.'

Dodie took the box and touched it with reverence, his rough fingers whispering gently over the mother-of-pearl inlay. 'My, my, it's beautiful just,' he said before he was overcome once more with emotion, his Adam's apple working desperately in a bid to keep back the tears. 'I'll be bringing her back to you when you're better able to look after her,' he promised in confusion.

'Ach, no, laddie!' The rebuke was sharp, but the fire had gone out of Biddy's voice. 'I'm giving it to you – as a present. I will never have need of it now.

It's for your birthday when it comes, a special thing to make up for all the years I won't be here to mind your birthday.

'Get away home now, I'm tired o' talkin'. Go you down and tell Mollie to send me up a cuppy.'

But Dodie was beyond speech of any kind. With the tears streaming down his face he laid something on the bed, and loped downstairs and out of the house.

Biddy reached out to the object Dodie had left lying on the counterpane, and as she held it against her bosom, the slow tears filled her eyes and affection for the old eccentric engulfed her. Wherever he went, whatever the occasion, he bestowed his unsophisticated gifts on people, and the uncanny aptness of them had touched many a sore heart. What had prompted him to bring her the thing she had pined for more than any other while lying in bed that hot summer's day, gazing from the window to the heathery hills lying so serenely against the azure sky?

'Oft, oft, have I walked these purpled hills and watched the sun go down.' She murmured the words again that she had tossed aside so scornfully when the American woman had suggested she was delirious. Ah, how often had she walked these dear green hills, sniffing the scents of wildflowers, watching the sun rising and setting, diffusing the sky and sea with breathtaking colours beyond all description. All her life, as a small barefoot girl, and as a black-stockinged old woman, she had freely roamed, revelling in her surroundings even while she grumbled at real or imagined hardships. Now, here she was, too tired even to get up and go to the window to breathe the clean air. She closed her eyes and lifting Dodie's gift to her nostrils she gulped in the scent of the moors. Dodie had made the sachet himself, a crudely sewn piece of muslin stuffed with wild thyme, bell heather, moss, meadowsweet, and an assortment of grasses. 'Ay, you have a fine sensitivity about you, Dodie,' she murmured. 'You might be a poor cratur' to some, but to me you are a child o' God.'

Light steps sounded on the stairs and Babbie came into the room. 'Talking to yourself you daft cailleach?' teased Babbie in greeting, though her bright green eyes noted that the old woman's condition had deteriorated. The young locum had confided in Babbie that he was amazed Biddy had lasted so long. Her pulse was weak and irregular, her respiration laboured, she hadn't eaten for days – yet she was lucid and bright, and Babbie knew that Kate was right when she said, 'She's waitin' to see Lachlan before she goes. I always said she would go when she was ready and no' before.'

'I am just sayin', Dodie and all cratur's like him could teach the rest o' us a lesson. They come into the world innocent and go out o' it the same.'

'He's been to see you then?' Babbie asked, though there was no need for she could detect the vestiges of the old eccentric's particular odour hanging in the air.

'Ay, that he has, he's left his smell but he also left this,' Biddy said, holding up the sachet. 'A wee bit o' the moors sewn into an old bitty curtain – money canny buy what I have here.'

Babbie sat down on the bed to look quizzically at Biddy's face. 'You're a blether – I wonder you have the breath for it. How are you today?'

'Near drawin' my last,' Biddy replied candidly. 'I will never get over the shock o' being knocked down at my very own gate – but it wasny the wifie's fault – it was this de'il here.' Affectionately she rubbed Woody's black head, then with sudden urgency she reached out and took Babbie's arm. 'My lassie, it's up to you now. It will no' be easy. There will be times you will feel like packin' your bags and fleein' away – but you have your man to help you and a fine loon he is too . . .' Her dim eyes twinkled. 'Betimes I forget he's a Jerry at all – he's that like ourselves now. Ay, you have your man to talk to and the best doctor on this God's earth to work alongside.' Her fingers dug into Babbie's arm. 'Is he home yet at all? I want to see him before I go.'

Babbie gathered the old woman into her arms and stroked her hair. Her eyes were wet but her voice steady when she said, 'He'll be home tomorrow and you'll be the first on his list.'

Biddy gave a contented sigh. 'The Lord be thanked, for I don't know how much longer I can hold on. The motor car didny hurt my body, but I'm thinkin' it knocked my auld heart for six. It feels gey shaky, I can tell you.'

873

Babbie didn't repudiate any of this. To do so would have seemed trite in the face of such courage. Biddy was not afraid of dying, but even so, Babbie could not suppress a sigh of sorrow.

Biddy pushed her away to look long and searchingly at a face that had grown contented over the past few years. The uncertainty of early youth had disappeared; the green, amber-flecked eyes were peaceful; the wide generous mouth bestowed its radiant smile readily. Babbie looked rather weary and sad just now, and Biddy patted her hand. 'You mustny fret for me, lassie, it's your wee shoulders that are going to get the brunt now, and wi' you bein' married, your responsibilities will be even more than mine.' She slid Babbie a sidelong glance. 'I was aye wonderin' – have you never wanted bairnies o' your own?'

Babbie's lips curved. 'You're a nosy cailleach if ever there was one.' Her expression became serious. 'It might sound selfish, but Anton and I always felt content with each other. I know the gossips talk and say it isn't natural, but it's what we want – besides,' she said, and laughed, 'how could I ever be another Biddy McMillan with a wheen of bairnies at my aprons? I'm too busy delivering them to have them. Now, where's your brush and I'll do your hair. You must look your best for all these men who keep sneaking up here to visit you.'

Biddy lay back and closed her eyes as the younger woman worked with her hair. A satisfied smile flitted over her face. 'At least, I got to bring another bairnie into the world before my number came up. A bonny wee thing wi' hair black as night. I hear his mother has given him McMillan as a middle name – ay – I'll be remembered all right.'

Fergus came with Lachlan the following evening. Biddy gazed up at tall Fergus and she said dreamily, 'You know what I'm lookin' forward to most of all? Meeting Mirabelle again. She was a bonny woman and the finest friend I ever had. My, how she doted on you and poor Alick – the cratur' – I'll get to see him, too. You and him were like her very own bairnies. Mind, the pair o' you were buggers betimes and sore tried that good woman's heart, but she saw the good in you and knew how best to bring it out. You miss your brother, laddie?' she asked gently.

Fergus nodded and said huskily, 'Ay, that I do. When he was here I took him for granted, and as you know we didn't always see eye to eye – but – on the night he died we had more or less called pax and then . . .'

His voice faltered and she took his big strong hand in her thin one. 'Weesht, I know fine how you feel, McKenzie o' the Glen – a grand title that, and it suits you, laddie. By God, the McKenzies – a stubborn bunch if ever there was one – wi' tempers like that bugger Satan himself. But you blow more goodness than you do fire – especially my wee Shona – aye was a lovable bairn for all her tantrums – I'd like fine to see her, so I would.'

Fergus felt his jaw tensing. The realisation that

Biddy was dying hit him like a sledgehammer. He had heard all the gossip about how ill she was but this was the moment of truth: the pallor of her skin, the blue veins showing under the skin of her temples, the purple hue of her lips and hands. She was a part of his life – everyone's lives – a part of Rhanna . . . 'You'll see Shona soon; she'll be home in a few days. She always makes a point of trying to be here when Grant's on leave.'

'She'll be home for my funeral then.' Biddy closed her eyes, and Fergus made to go out of the room, but she stopped him by saying softly, 'The twins, they're good laddies both of them – but Lewis – look to him, Fergus. He's no' strong like his brother. That sounds daft, I know, but there are different kinds o' strength. He'll need a lot o' guidance, but he'll shape up to a good man wi' your help.'

'Ay – I know that, Biddy,' he said, and went quickly downstairs, leaving Lachlan alone in the room.

Lachlan had barely been able to conceal his shock at the change in the old nurse, but he turned from the window and, smiling down at her, managed to say carelessly, 'Disgraceful! I turn my back for five minutes and you get into trouble. Come on, lift your goonie and I'll have a look at you . . .'

But she threw off the suggestion with an impatient grunt. 'Ach, leave me be, you and I know fine it's a waste o' time.' She perched her glasses on the end of her nose and scrutinised his face. It was obvious his much needed holiday had done him good. He was tanned and well-looking; the hollows of his face had filled, and the tired droop had gone from his shoulders. She giggled coyly. 'A peety I hadny been a younger woman – you and me could maybe had one o' they doctor-nurse romances you read about in wimmen's papers – eh?'

He sat down and took her hand, his brown eyes full of the compassion that had made his career as a doctor a unique success. 'You old flirt,' he said huskily. 'Don't you know I've always had a fancy for you? Who could help but love a lady who has given her life to tending others? When God made nurses he set one special mould aside for Biddy McMillan, and when you were created he threw away the design, for there will never be another one to match you. And if that isn't romantic nonsense I'll – I'll eat my stethoscope.' His voice broke and he turned his head quickly.

'Ach, dinna greet for me, laddie.' She tried to sound brusque, but her voice was weak and she fumbled for her hanky. 'See now what you've done?' she scolded shakily. 'I'm greetin' for myself like a daft auld fool. My time has come, Lachlan, and the Lord is waitin' for me – afore the de'il gets to me first!

'Will you do something for me? When I'm in my box at the Hillock, say a few words in the Gaelic in that nice voice o' yours. It was the only thing that kept me awake in Kirk, and, who knows, it might waken me from the dead just when everyone thinks they've got rid o' me. I have asked Mr Gray to do the ceremony. There was a time when I wouldny have gone to the wee hoosie to hear him, but he's changed over the years and is more like one of us now.'

The Rev. Gray had been touched when, on paying a visit to Biddy's bedside, she had said with dignity, 'After I am gone I will be feelin' my mind easier if you would be doing the service. Thon young minister is a fine laddie, but we are not knowing each other well enough yet for him to know the right things to say – and be seein' me out in the Gaelic. You haveny the voice for it, but at least folks will hear you – ay, even to the other side of the island, if you don't mind me sayin' so.'

The Rev. John Gray hadn't minded. In fact, he had been so overwhelmed by the old woman's request that he hadn't been able to say anything for a few moments. It had been one thing to have been accepted by the islanders, but to be singled out in this fashion by one of the most venerable inhabitants was the highest tribute anyone had ever paid him. He was retired now but he and his wife had decided to stay on in the island that had been their home for so long. ('We belong here, Hannah,' he had boomed, 'no sense in starting all over again in some strange place.') He had patted Biddy's hand and, swallowing hard had said, 'My dear Biddy, thank you. It's at times like these I know the work of my life has not been in vain. You are a brave woman to face up to death with such courage, and you can trust me to carry out your wishes.' His stern strong face had relaxed into a smile. 'If I don't do things to your satisfaction you have every right to come back and haunt me.'

Lachlan got up, and, going to the window, gazed

out at the shadowed night hills silhouetted against the midnight-blue sky. It was midsummer and on cloudless nights like this it would never grow truly dark.

'They're bonny, aren't they?' said Biddy softly.

'Ay, mo ghaoil, the hills of summer, so feathery and soft with new green you feel you could go and lay down your head on them.'

Her eyes closed and she quoted on a sigh, '"I to the hills will lift mine eyes . . ."'

Lachlan forced himself to become brisk. 'Phebie wants to come along and spend the night, if you'll let her.'

Biddy held up a blue-veined hand. 'Leave me, laddie. It's kind o' Phebie, but my house is no' my own all day and I'm glad o' night – for a bit peace . . .'

In a few moments Biddy looked to be asleep, and Lachlan went over and tucked her mohair shawl round her shoulders. He stayed for a long moment gazing down at her tired thin face, then with a shake of his head, he went quickly out of the room and tip-toed downstairs to join Fergus. Both men walked silently through Glen Fallan with heavy hearts.

Biddy stirred and shifted Woody from his favourite place in the warm crook of her knees. With trembling hands the old lady threw back the blankets and dragged herself from the bed. She couldn't rest, not yet; there were certain things that had to be done first. Holding onto the furniture, her legs shaking beneath her, she walked slowly to the window and stood looking out over the moors to the glimpse of silver-blue sea beyond. Her eyes took long to focus, and soon became blurred, but she could still see the dark bulk of the mighty hills rising up before her. She smiled, a wistful little half-smile and murmured, '"Soft as the wind blows over your brow there will my feets go freer than now."'

Weakness washed over her. Woody mewed from the bed. 'Ay, I'm comin' back, no mistake about that,' she murmured. Some minutes later she crawled between the sheets, retrieved her 'teeths' from the glass, inserted them, and lay back on the pillows feeling strangely content. Her hand strayed to Woody's head. It was warm and soft. 'Bide a wee, my lamb,' she whispered affectionately. 'It won't be long – not long now . . .'

Next morning, Kirsteen and Babbie found Biddy propped up on her pillows, her silvery hair carefully combed and tied with the blue ribbon. On the breast of her 'goonie' was pinned her silver M.B.E. medal. She had always referred to it as a damty fine brooch to the children who came and requested she take it from its box and pin it on them for a little while. Her hands were clasped over her bosom: grasped in one was the ornately inscribed warrant, in the other was Dodie's sachet of wildflowers. The last breath, the final memory, had been of the moors she had trod for almost eighty-seven years.

Kirsteen went over and gently touched a lock of her snowy hair. 'Goodbye, dear, beautiful old lady. You leave behind a great army of bairnies who will grieve sorely for you in the days and years to come.'

Babbie stood at the foot of the bed gazing at the face of the old nurse who had befriended her, guided her, given Anton and herself a home when first they married. In life Biddy had often looked grumpy and harassed, though a twinkle had never been far from her eyes. Latterly a sweet tranquillity had settled on her features though this was sometimes usurped by fatigue. Now she lay, a gracious, noble figure. Death had swathed her with peace, dignity, and an ethereal quality of grace that could only have sprung from a soul satisfied with a life well spent. Babbie knew she would mourn for Biddy, but gazing upon the calm dear face, she felt an odd peace stealing through her entire being. It was as if the old lady was reaching out beyond the grave and saying to her, 'Don't weep for me, lassie, I was weary and the Lord saw I needed to rest.'

'Look, Kirsteen,' Babbie said, indicating the empty glass at the bedside. 'She put in her teeths for the occasion. She used to say the one thing she dreaded was to die in her sleep without them.'

Kirsteen took out her hanky and blew her nose. 'She always did try to wear them for special occasions, and this was one time she didn't forget to remember.' Stooping she lifted the sleepy cat from Biddy's side. 'She asked the twins to look after Woody for her, and I'm thinking this is one cat who is going to lead the life of a very special lord – it's the least we can do for an old lady who always treated animals like humans – like her bairnies they meant everything in the world to her.'

Chapter Fourteen

If Biddy could have seen the masses of people who came from all over the island and beyond, she would have shook her head and said, 'Ach, it's just a lot o' damty palaver anyways.' But she would have folded her hands over her stomach and smiled rather proudly too, for she had often commented, 'Why can folks no' have their funerals while they're alive and able to see who will turn up? A fine lot o' good it does a dead body no' to be there to count how many friends come to see them off.' But it is doubtful if she could have counted the streams of men, women, and children who crowded into the Kirk and overflowed over the Hillock to listen to the burial ceremony. The flowers ranged from elaborate wreaths to bunches of wildflowers held in the hot grubby hands of the children, and it would have been these that Biddy would have treasured above all others.

Shona and Niall had come home for the funeral, and they stood close together as the coffin was carried from the Kirk to the graveside.

Lachlan began to say in Gaelic the words of the hymn, "'I to the hills will lift mine eyes.'" His clear resonant voice carried through the still air. When he was finished there was not a dry eye in the whole gathering.

Niall squeezed Shona's hand as he felt her shoulders trembling. 'I can't help it,' she gulped. 'She was so much a part of Rhanna; she gave so much. I'll never forget how kind and understanding she was to me when you were away at war and I was dreading telling Father I was expecting a baby. She never lectured or went all sour about morals – she just *helped*.'

'I know, my babby.' Niall put his arm round her shoulders and drew her close. 'Rhanna will never be the same without auld Biddy. She helped us all when often there was no one else to turn to. We would like the Biddys of this world to live for ever, but it canny be. Weesht now – and – and give me a loan of your hanky.'

Ruth and Rachel stood close together at the back of the crowd. Morag had been playing the organ for the service inside the Kirk, and it would be some time before she would emerge. Ruth put a comforting arm round Rachel's shoulders. Rachel had taken Biddy's death very badly, blaming herself for it happening. Coming on top of the death of old Mo, it was almost beyond bearing, and she leaned against Ruth gratefully. Through the gleam of tears in her eyes she saw Lewis McKenzie go forward to the graveside with his brother Lorn. Biddy had requested they play a wee tune on the fiddles at the graveside. Rachel had not been able to face it, and Jon had decided it would be more fitting for him to opt out too and leave it to the twins. Jon watched Rachel's face as the haunting notes of 'Amazing Grace' hushed the crowd. Her dark eyes were glazed with grief. As she listened to the beautiful music her face turned white, her eyes strayed beyond the branches of the elms to Lewis standing with his face resting on the gold wood of his violin, his earth-brown curls ruffling slightly as a breeze blew up from the sea. Rachel's eyes were dark with grief, hurt, and naked yearning. Jon turned away, and some of the feelings of inadequacy that had plagued him in his early youth returned with renewed force.

In her white dress Ruth stood out from the black-clad crowd like a lone snowdrop on bare winter earth. Not even for this occasion would Morag Ruadh unbend, and quite a few shocked glances had been cast at Ruth, though everyone reasoned, 'That besom, Morag Ruadh! Calls herself a Christian and doesny even allow her lassie to respect the dead.' But Ruth didn't feel as badly as she thought she might. Biddy had seen to that. 'Be wearin' one o' they bonny white dresses to see me off,' she instructed. 'I'll never know why folks deck themselves out in thon awful black. They a' look as though they were worshippin' the de'il! Ay, no doubt that rogue has a snigger up his black sleeve when folks turn up wearin' his colours for Christian burials.'

Through the tracery of green on the elm trees Ruth glimpsed Lorn as he played. Why did she keep remembering the way he had looked at her in Biddy's bedroom? A flushed, admiring, furtive look. Their eyes had met only briefly, but it had been enough for her heart to start fluttering too fast. The leaves swayed in the breeze, and he was lost to her momentarily – only to appear before her gaze with renewed force some seconds later. His hair was lighter than his brother's; a lovely coppery tinge gleamed through the rich earth-brown. Her violet gaze rested on him and stayed there, then quite suddenly he glanced up and seemed to look straight at her. Her heart bounded. He couldn't make her out from that distance of course. It was stupid! But he could, could! Her white dress, her pale hair. She stood out a mile away. A glow warmed her heart – then she saw a movement in front of the Kirk and an unmistakable red head. The glow in her heart vanished and she fingered the white ruffle at her neck nervously.

Grant stood beside Fergus and Kirsteen and looked to where Phebie watched the ceremony with Fiona, who had just arrived the day before. At twenty-two, she was a tall, attractive, assured young woman with lively eyes and an air about her that exuded something of the excitement and wonder of living. She had graduated with honours the year before, and had won a two-year travelling scholarship to study marine biology. Grant had heard Phebie confiding certain things to Kirsteen about her daughter: 'She will never settle down to normal life like other girls of her age.'

'Oh, she's enjoying herself.' Kirsteen had smiled. 'Plenty of time to settle down. At the moment she's playing the field.'

'I know, I know!' Phebie had cried. 'One affair after another, but she never wants to be tied to any of them. She always said she would never marry.'

Grant remembered that too. He couldn't help feeling amused as he recalled her passionate childhood sentiments. 'I'll *never* marry!' she had vehemently and often declared. 'Boys are smelly and noisy. Their minds are as dirty as their habits. All they ever seem to do is pick their noses behind their reading books and try to look up girls' skirts.'

A playful wind lifted Fiona's skirt slightly and moulded it to her hips, which were seductively rounded; her legs were long and very shapely. She turned her head and caught Grant watching her, and her nose went into the air. He reddened. Her opinions of him hadn't altered anyway.

The Rev. Gray began the service. He stood beside the coffin, and as he gazed round at the crowds filling every space he felt a lump rising in his throat. He straightened his shoulders, a fine figure of a man in his robes. Strength was in his face; his thick thatch of white hair was startling against his black cloth. It was a calm day with occasional meek puffs of wind. The sheep bleated from the mist-filled corries of the hills; a dog barked from some distant croft. Mr Gray cleared his throat, and as he began The Lord's Prayer in Gaelic, everyone joined in, murmuring the well-known words in whatever language was best known to them. Mr Gray then conducted a short but sincere service and all the old Gaels present thought how different were his sermons now to the dry theological affairs that had reverberated in the Kirk for so many years. Then, as the coffin was being lowered, Mr Gray began to sing a Gaelic lullaby that had been one of Biddy's favourites. It was so unusual to end a burial service in this manner, that at first the gathering was silent. Then, one by one, every man, woman, and child took up the song and it seemed, as the voices rose heavenwards, that there could have been no more fitting tribute to one who had all her life nursed children on her knee, and crooned lullabies to them in her lilting voice. The song was taken up by those who stood outside the mossy walls of the Kirkyard, and by others even further back, till it seemed the whole of Rhanna was singing in that final moving farewell to Auld Biddy. The tears flowed, for Biddy, for other loved ones gone before, for the uncertainty of life itself. Then the first scatterings of earth were being thrown over the coffin, and everyone was dispersing slowly, as if unwilling to relinquish the feeling of unity that the singing of a Gaelic lullaby had created.

When the graveyard was finally empty, a pathetic stooping figure crept rather than walked over to the fresh grave with its mounds of wreaths and flowers. Dodie had always believed in seeing the departed off in style. Funerals and ceilidhs were the one thing he made the effort to dress up for because he felt it was the least he could do for a departed friend. On this occasion though he was dirty and threadbare. The grey stubble on his face was days old; his eyes were sunk in his thin face and had a haunted look about them; the skin on his cheeks was rubbed raw from endless weepings and wipings. He loomed over the grave, a vexed lost soul, quite unable to take the harsh blow of Biddy's death. The tears poured afresh, a large drip gathered at the end of his nose. He shuffled his feet and then with an embarrassed movement reached up and removed his greasy cap to reveal a downy head of baby-fine white hair. Twisting the cap in his big workworn hands he bowed his head and sobbed, 'I'm – sorry I didny dress up for you, Biddy. I – I've no' been feelin' like myself since you went. I've looked after your bonny boxie, she's all polished and standin' at my bedside where I can be lookin' at her and be mindin' o' you. Ealasaid had a new bairnie last week, a real bonny wee calf – you would have liked her, that you would – I hope you dinna think it cheeky but I've called her Biddy after you. You're no' a cow, I know, but I felt I aye wanted to speak your name so dinna be girnin' about it.' He fumbled under his coat, and withdrawing an untidy wreath of meadowsweet, purple clover, and white heather, he laid it at the foot of the grave. 'It will bring you luck up yonder,' he said with childlike conviction and, turning, he stumbled blindly out of the Kirkyard.

A week later Lorn walked with Grant, Niall, and Shona over the hill road to Dodie's cottage. No one had seen the old eccentric since Biddy's death, and Lachlan, mindful of him since he had contracted a stomach ulcer after almost starving himself to death, had said to Niall that morning: 'I'm worried about Dodie. I've a mind he took Biddy's passing very badly. Maybe you and Shona could go along and see if he's all right.'

'I was thinking the same thing myself,' Niall admitted. 'Grant said something about painting the roof of his wee hoosie, so we'll call in at Laigmhor on the way.'

Shona immediately set about filling a basket with foodstuffs from the larder. Slochmhor had been her second home for years now. She was often ashamed of herself for thinking of the lovely rambling old house on the Mull of Kintyre as just 'the house'. She and Niall had lived in it for the past five years, yet she knew she would never think of it as home. Her roots lay on Rhanna, and she knew that one day she would come back to live on the island. She had talked the matter over with Niall and had discovered that he felt as she did. 'Give me a whily to build up some capital, mo ghaoil,' he had told her. 'Then we'll start seriously thinking about moving back to Rhanna. I fancy the idea of being an island vet. Island hopping is one way of making our dreams come true.'

Shona came out of the larder and bumped into Fiona, who eyed the full basket quizzically and enquired eagerly, 'Going for a picnic?'

'Just for a strupak over to Dodie's house.' Fiona's face fell till Shona added, 'We're going to paint the roof of his wee hoosie.'

Next to dabbling in pond life, Fiona enjoyed

dabbling in paint of all kinds, and she said, 'That's different! I could maybe paint some flowers on it instead of that German sign.'

'Come along then,' Shona said, and giggled. 'Might as well make a party of it. We're calling in at Laigmhor for Grant.'

Fiona's bright eyes snapped. 'Dimples McKenzie! No thanks! I'd rather spend my time looking at amoebae through my microscope.'

'Fiona, you're the limit. Why do you and Grant grab one another by the throat every time you meet?'

'Because he's rude, bad-mannered – and – and vulgar!' Fiona snapped then flounced away.

'He called her a cold fish the other day,' little Helen piped up. 'That's why she's mad at him.'

Shona laughed at the sight of her small daughter standing at the kitchen table enveloped in one of Elspeth's aprons, which was liberally sprinkled with flour. The old housekeeper had grown less spicy over the years, and though she could still wield a very able tongue, she had a lot of time and patience to spare for 'wee Ellie' as Helen was affectionately known. Shona looked at her angelic-looking little girl and a memory came of herself learning to make scones under Mirabelle's patient guidance. The child was very like herself at eight years old, though she had also inherited much of Niall's even temper. Shona would have liked more children, but time was passing, she was thirty-three now and still Ellie was an only child. 'We said we would fill the world with our children,' she had said rather sadly to Niall, but he had just answered quietly, 'We will, mo ghaoil, but just now Ellie fills our own little world, and if that's how it was meant for us then it canny be helped.'

'Are you coming with us, Ellie?' Shona asked, hiding a smile as the little girl energetically wielded a rolling pin.

'No, you and Father can go without me for a change.' She glanced up and her golden-brown eyes glinted with devilment. 'I'll let you have a rest from me and I'll torment Elspeth instead.'

'You'll do nothing of the sort, madam,' Elspeth said with asperity. 'Stop rubbing your nose with that floury hand this meenit! No one will want to eat scones covered in germs.'

'Och well. I don't mind. I'll get them all to myself then,' the child returned placidly.

Niall grabbed Shona's hand and they ran outside giggling. 'I'll say one thing for our wee Ellie,' he grinned. 'Unlike her mother she always "keeps the heid" as they say in Glasgow. She must have taken her good nature after me.'

'And her good looks from her mother!' Shona flashed. 'No one could ever accuse her of looking glaikit – not like a daft wee boy I once knew who called me names in the Post Office and was the cause of me getting a good skelping from Mirabelle.'

'Served you right – the best cure for that red-haired temper of yours!'

They arrived at Laigmhor in reminiscent good humour. Fergus came out of the byre, his black eyes lighting at sight of his daughter, who was a picture with her glowing face and her hair the colour of bracken on an autumn day.

'About time you two paid us a visit,' he greeted them. 'Kirsteen was saying only last night you've been neglecting us.'

'We're only here to collect the boys,' Shona explained. 'We thought we should pay Dodie a visit.'

Fergus looked thoughtful. 'Ay, he hasny been around for a time. He'll be taken up with the new calf, but it's as well to make sure he's fine. Grant and Lorn are in the barn, but you'll not get Lewis – he's supposed to be cutting the top field but a fine lot of work he'll get done with Eve at his elbow. Oh I know she's a dab hand around the farm, but lately she's taken to mooning about with her head in the clouds.'

Shona detected a note of annoyance in Fergus's tone, but she kept her counsel. Grant came out of the barn and hailed the visitors with delight. 'Nice of you to stop by once in a while to visit your ageing parents.' He ducked to avoid the swipe Fergus aimed at him and went to rummage in the shed for paint. Soon all four were swinging along the narrow road winding through the moors, waving to the groups of islanders who were up by the peat hags building the slices of turf into mounds to dry in the wind and sun. Except for a few sheep and some Highland cows cudding contentedly in the shade of the house, Dodie's place was deserted with not a single tourist to disturb the stillness.

Grant fetched a rickety chair from the porch, and

climbing onto it he saw that the roof of the wee hoosie was in a poor state of repair, the nails holding the metal tailpiece to the wooden slats rusted through in places. He called down, 'I'm surprised it hasny blown away years ago, there's only one or two good nails holding it down.'

'We'd best repair it before we paint it,' Niall suggested, and went off whistling to look for a hammer.

Lorn went with Grant to rummage through a tiny hut that held a jumble of driftwood and other things hoarded by the old eccentric, who could never bear to return from the shore empty-handed. Nails were obviously low on his list of useful items. A search in the barn and the byre, where Ealasaid was reclining with her new calf, also proved fruitless, and Grant ran a hand through his black curls in disgust. 'The old bugger collects everything *but* nails, as far as I can see. I'm away to look in the house, he's probably got box-loads hidden away in some corner.'

Lorn wasn't listening, he was too taken up with the new calf, and Grant stamped away. He had never been over the threshold of Dodie's house but boldly marched inside to gaze with interest at the dim interior. Ashes spilled from the grate, cobwebs hung from the rafters – more durable-looking than the ancient net curtains draped over the windows. The two car seats from Madam Balfour's abandoned car sat comfortably on either side of the grate. From the ceiling hung a bundle of onions, and Grant smiled, recalling Shona's tales of Mirabelle and her onions, and wondering if the old eccentric had somehow hit on the cure for 'a host o' germs'. Grant forgot about the nails and wandered up the short passageway to the bedroom. On the threshold he paused, mouth agape, hardly able to believe the sight that met his gaze. The room was literally papered with money, Jamaican ten-shilling notes – hundreds of them covering the dingy walls, dozens of them pinned jauntily round the muddy mirror of an aged dressing table. Grant stared in breathless wonder, his black eyes crinkled, and he hugged himself with pure delight. With a fingernail he scraped one of the notes away from the wall and it came off readily, having only been stuck on carelessly with a paste made from flour and water.

'The money from the *Politician*,' Grant breathed. 'God Almighty! The fly old bugger.' Racing outside he called to Lorn.

Shona and Niall had wandered away to look for Dodie but at the sound of Grant's excited voice, they turned quickly and ran over the turf. Soon all four were gazing dumbfounded at the treasure trove. Niall slapped his knee and exploded. 'Well, bugger me! It was always said that some old boy was sitting on a heap of Jamaican money!'

'And fancy it being old Dodie,' Lorn said, his thin face alight at the surprise of the discovery.

Shona's brilliant blue eyes were sparkling, as they had done on another occasion when she and Niall had come to the cottage and seen that Dodie had managed to collect his share of the 'spoils' from

Madam Balfour's car. 'He's the limit, so he is,' she said, giggling. 'But I'm glad he got it instead of the Crown Agents – it's just a pity he can never get to spend any of it.'

Grant's eyes gleamed. 'Oh yes he can –' he started to say but was interrupted by a wail of indignant outrage from Dodie, who had arrived home. All week he had been doing jobs to Burnbreddie in order to gather enough money together to contribute towards the purchase of a headstone for Biddy's grave.

'What are you doing in my house?' he babbled, terror rising in his pale eyes. 'I never stole it! I found it, years ago, comin' in on the tide. I knew it wasny real money so I dried it and stuck it up on my walls to make them look nice.' He sank down on the bed, and burying his face in his hands, began to cry in a storm of abject fear. 'Dinna tell the police! I don't want to go to jail! I would die in jail so I would. I couldny bear never to roam free again, and Ealasaid and my bonny wee Biddy would die too!' He rocked himself back and forth in an agony of stark misgiving. Grant went quickly to sit beside him and put an arm round the shaking shoulders. 'Weesht, weesht, Dodie, nobody's going to tell. We're all glad you found the money and you're wrong – it is real money, and you're going to get to spend it. Dry your eyes and listen to me a minute.'

Dodie drew a greasy sleeve over his face. Through tear-filled eyes he looked at Grant, who was one of his favourite McKenzies. Since the boy had joined the

Merchant Navy he had sent postcards to the old man from all over the world. Erchy's post van stopped regularly at Dodie's cottage, and together they gazed at pictures of 'furrin parts'. The cards were pinned proudly above the fireplace, and on long winter nights Dodie delighted in scrutinising them over and over again, smiling primly at pictures of 'exotic leddies wi' belly buttons', screeching at the haughty expressions on the faces of camels, puzzling as to why 'dark leddies' walked with pots attached to their heads.

'You know I visit places all over the world?' Grant started. 'Well, I could take some of your money away with me and change it for you. Only wee amounts at a time, mind you, but it means every time I come home I would have some money to give you. As long as the Jamaican notes remain legal tender I can go on changing them for you.'

Dodie understood very little of this beyond the fact that Grant could somehow change his bits o' fancy paper into real money. 'My, that would be grand,' he said enthusiastically. 'I could buy lots o' baccy and we could get Biddy a real fine headstone and,' he said, brightening further, 'maybe I could build Ealasaid a new byre.' His eyes roved round the walls and his face fell again. 'But – my bonny walls, they'll no' look the same without these.'

Shona smiled. 'You can buy real wallpaper, Dodie . . .'

'And I'll put it up for you,' Lorn promised rashly. With his interests lying mainly out of doors, he had

had little experience of home decorating but the smiles stretching Dodie's lips heightened his resolve.

Niall moved to the door. 'Come on, bairns, we'd better get the painting done before the rain comes.'

Dodie gave a great sigh of contented appreciation. 'I aye said that the doctor and McKenzie o' the Glen had good bairns,' he said, and nodded magnanimously.

Grant's laughing young face became suddenly stern. 'Not a word of this to a soul, Dodie, or we'll all be in jail.'

Outside Grant repeated his warning to the others, but Lorn knew the message was for him. He must not say anything to Lewis who, in his exuberance, often let things slip that had been told to him in confidence. It wasn't lack of loyalty that made him like this, just a love of the limelight, which loosened his tongue often much to his own regret.

'I won't say anything – to anybody.' Lorn's tones were sullen, Lewis was his twin, the bond between them was so strong that a strange telepathy existed between them. They confided everything to each other.

Shona saw his discomfiture and murmured softly, 'Some things are best left unsaid, Lorn – for the sake of other folks.'

Lorn stirred the paint energetically and said nothing. Dodie came galloping up, his arms filled with great sticks of juicy red rhubarb. 'These is for your kindness,' he told them joyfully. 'I washed it in the burnie and I have made wee polkies and filled

them wi' sugar. Come you inside and eat it now, a
fine treat it is – the best rhubarb on the island – ay,'
he said, 'the very best you could get.' He disappeared
into the house. The four young people looked at one
another; Niall and Shona held their breath, remembering a long ago day of sunlight, of argument and
laughter – of Dodie divulging to them the secret of
his flourishing rhubarb patch. Niall pulled Shona to
him and kissed her burnished hair. The laughter
bubbled up and out of them, echoed by Lorn and
Grant, who, with paint streaked over their faces,
had collapsed against one another in agonies of
smothered snorts of mirth.

Part Four

Christmas 1959

Chapter Fifteen

The awakening of Lorn's love for Ruth was like the slow opening of the tender buds of spring. But he wasn't sure if she returned his feelings. Whenever she saw him she seemed nervous, which gave her a remoteness that made him long for her all the more. Sometimes she smiled, a lovely, sweet, uncertain smile. The magic of her smile, the violet of her eyes turning to night, her exquisite stillness, sent pangs of aching hunger gnawing through every nerve in his body – but they seemed unable to find anything to say to each other. None of the things that meant anything. After the usual polite salutations she would walk past him and limp quickly away. Neither of them had matured yet: they hadn't passed beyond adolescent dreams, or the awkwardness of extreme youth and all the agonies of self-doubt that went with it. But she had blossomed over the years in other ways: the plainness of childhood had disappeared gradually, till now there was about her an almost unearthly quality of beauty: her pale silken hair framed an oval face, her slightly turned-up nose was lightly sprinkled with freckles, her skin was exquis-itely clear – and her mouth: it was beautifully shaped and oddly sensuous. She was small-boned, and rather too thin, though her breasts were full and firm, curving enticingly under the loose frocks her mother made for her. She had rebelled against having to be continually garbed in white and had had quite a scene over the affair, resisting fiercely the idea that she shouldn't be allowed to express her individuality. But Morag Ruadh had remained tight-lipped, adamant, and shocked at the idea of 'my very own daughter turning on me'. And after a few days of charged silences, of seeing her father and grandparents bearing the brunt of her mother's tongue, Ruth had given in. Nevertheless, she had managed to make it plain that she was a girl with a strong mind and a will of her own, and that it was for her father's sake that she had unbended and not because she went in fear of the Lord.

Ironically, Morag's intention to label her daughter as untouchable only served to heighten her desirability to the opposite sex. Despite her limp she walked with a grace of movement that was oddly rhythmic. To see her wandering along the hillsides on a mist-shrouded morning, clad in her white dress, her pale hair shining, added to the impression that she was a vision who was not quite real. It was also a temptation to the young males of the district to find out for themselves whether she was after all flesh and blood like other girls. But they kept their distance, partly because to do otherwise would be to incur the ungodly wrath of Morag Ruadh, partly because Ruth's shyness was in itself an almost insurmountable barrier, and partly because for any boy to be seen walking with the white virgin would have meant endless teasings and tormentings from young contemporaries.

But Lorn would have cared nothing for the teasing. He longed to walk with Ruth; to hear the sweet singing quality of her voice; to touch her; to find out if she would respond to him; to know if she felt even a little of what he felt for her. But he didn't know how to make the approaches and cursed his lack of self-confidence. Also there were other things to contend with. Only last year he had suffered a setback when he had collapsed while guiding the plough. He remembered the squeezing pains in his chest, the breath forcing itself from his lungs, the terror of not being able to get breath, the stifling panic of slipping gradually into unconsciousness. He had been taken by helicopter to Barra, and from there by plane to Glasgow where he had undergone emergency heart surgery. Dramatic though it had all been, the complication hadn't been a serious one. Lachlan had reassured Kirsteen and Fergus on that point, but Lorn had seen all the old doubts back in his father's eyes. He had forbidden the boy to use the hand plough. 'You'll just have to make do with the tractor,' he had said sternly. 'We'll keep the Clydesdale, though. She can live out her days in the fields, she deserves that much.'

So Lorn had bottled up his frustrations while Lewis strode with Fergus in the fields, shared his manly talk and laughter. More and more Lorn felt shut out and rejected. Everyone except him seemed to be getting on with their lives.

Ruth had become a successful writer, contributing regularly to Scottish magazines. The islanders eagerly devoured her tales and had grown so used to having an author in their midst they no longer went in awe of her, though they were quick to point her out proudly to visiting relatives. Ruth remained unaffected and unspoiled. 'I don't feel different or special,' she confided once to Lorn. 'Just silly when people look at me as if I had horns.' Then she had added with a mischievous smile, 'My ambition is to get a book published. If that happens I might look down my nose at everyone.'

Lewis had become an excellent farmer, though he never let work interfere with fun. Often he came home unsteady and giggling after a night of ceilidhing to recount his latest romantic venture to Lorn. He did everything with a dangerous abandon. When he went out riding he went bareback, galloping his horse at a reckless pace, his blue eyes snapping with exhilaration. When he went swimming he swam further out than anyone else dared. Even while working he had fun, yet no matter how much he tempted Providence he invariably emerged unscathed. Life to him was one great adventure to be enjoyed to the full. He said things that only he could get away with. Girls fell at his feet and made fools of themselves in their efforts to get him to notice them. His manner was charming, witty, outrageous, infectious – and though many an eyebrow was raised at his feckless ways, very few were able to resist his engaging grin.

'He loves people does Lewis McKenzie,' Kate had summed up. 'And there's no' many who canny take to him.'

'Ay, he was born wi' a silver spoon right enough,' Merry Mary had said and frowned slightly. In her opinion ulterior motives lay behind his bland talk and suave manners, her disapproval of him having arisen from the day she discovered that he had collected money from every child on the island after she had very painfully cracked her nose on the handle of her shovel, knocking off her wart in the process. Lewis had been helping her that day and had affected great surprise that the shovel had been left in a particularly slippery part of the vegetable patch. She had felt slightly uneasy as he had tried to hide a triumphant grin even while he fussed over her and marched her off to the doctor's to have the bleeding nose seen to. 'I prefer Lorn myself,' she had continued thoughtfully. 'Quiet he may be, but there's a strength there, ay, that there is. He's truly kind-hearted, too, for all he's suffered. I mind he came to help me in the garden after I hurt my nose thon time, and no' a penny piece would he take for it. His brother never came back – *he* got what he had been waiting for.'

Winter came early to Rhanna that year, with some weeks to go before Christmas. The winds swept in from the Atlantic bringing sheets of freezing rain that seemed to go on perpetually, blotting out the hills and bringing early darkness night after night.

'I hate when it's like this,' Kirsteen sighed one morning, glancing out of the window to the wind-tossed, rain-sodden landscape. 'I wish it would snow instead.'

Fergus got up from the table to stand behind her and nuzzle her ear. She leaned against him, enjoying the strength of his hard body, then with a little self-conscious start she moved out of his reach and ran her hands ruefully through her crisp hair. 'Don't,' she murmured, her fair skin flushing. 'You'll see my white hairs.'

He pulled her to him and kissed the tip of her nose. 'In this light?' he murmured teasingly. 'All I see is a beautiful woman who can still drive me crazy with her feminine wiles – besides, what can be lovelier? Silver threads among the gold.'

'Oh Fergus, don't,' she said uncomfortably, 'that makes me sound like a hundred – and fifty-three is bad enough.'

'Don't be daft,' he said tenderly. 'I still think of you as a girl and always will. Still, it's strange,' he continued thoughtfully. 'How quickly the years pass. I don't feel much older than I did at thirty, and it hits me hard when I realise I'm fifty-nine. Bob was right. I always mind him telling me that at sixty I would be thinking much the same things I did at forty – only then I didn't have a grown-up family, nor was I a grandfather.' He sighed. 'I often think I wasn't cut out to be a father, sometimes I feel I've failed in some way. I mind Murdy Travers telling me to treat my sons the same, but that hasny been easy the way things have turned out. I feel I have to protect Lorn and often wonder if Lewis feels left out.'

She stared at him. 'But – oh, my darling, I know it hasn't been easy. We went over all this some years ago and tortured each other with nasty words – but – you're wrong! I think Lorn is the one who feels shut out. I know you're shielding him because of what happened last year, but he's all right now, Fergus, and quite able to do as much as Lewis around the farm. Oh, don't look like that, darling! Sometimes when you're wrapped up in people you love it's very hard to see things in black and white – oh, look at the time, I must start breakfast.'

Slowly Fergus resumed his seat, his black eyes troubled. Surely – surely Kirsteen was wrong. Lorn couldn't think – mustn't think things like that . . . His thoughts were interrupted as the door opened and a cold blast of air catapulted Bob and the twins inside. Although Bob was in his eighties, he was hale and hearty, wirier and tougher than many a man half his age, though he now walked with a slight stoop and used his shepherd's crook more often to aid him over rough ground.

He now took most of his meals at Laigmhor. Kirsteen couldn't bear to think of him eating solitary makeshift meals in his lonely little cottage on the slopes of Ben Machrie. Folks said he was 'a crafty auld bugger', for it was known that he was quite capable of looking after himself, but Kirsteen shut her ears to the gossip and made the old shepherd welcome. The new arrivals crowded to the sink to have a hasty wash.

'I think old Rosie has a touch of milk fever,' Lewis called over the running water. 'She kicked the pail out of my hand when I touched her udder. It would be grand if Niall was here to see to things like that.'

'Ay,' Fergus responded absently. Lorn sat down opposite and Fergus glanced at his thin young face. 'You're good at things like that, Lorn,' he said, drawing his porridge towards him. 'You'll maybe look at her for me.'

Lorn didn't look up. 'Ay,' was all he said and lifted his spoon. Fergus frowned. Was Kirsteen right after all? Surely not! This boy was the one nearest his heart. They understood one another, had so much in common a telepathy seemed to exist between them. The joy of having such a son was an uncommonly rich and wonderful experience. Murdy's words came to him, 'Never show you have a favourite son'. He never had, by word or deed. Biddy's last words came to him: 'Look to Lewis; with your guidance he will turn out to be a good man.'

Had he in his anxiety to set Lewis's steps in the right direction unwittingly neglected Lorn? Lorn with the inner strength that glowed out of his eyes, who had been born physically frail but fiercely courageous. Had he in his eagerness to protect this fine son of his somehow only succeeded in making him feel cast out? The questions whirled round in confusion in his mind. What was right? God in Heaven, what was the right thing to do in his role as a father? He sucked in his breath and searched his mind for something to say that would be right. With a glance at the rain streaming down the panes he said more harshly than he meant, 'Maybe you'll come with me today, Lorn, and help me to take feed up to the yowes on the hill?'

Lorn, lost in his own deep thoughts, didn't answer, and Fergus, connecting his sullenness with the things Kirsteen had said, felt frustration boiling in him, tensing his jaw, darkening his eyes. Hell! Why did it all have to be so complicated? He was too busy a man to have the patience for all this – and patience had never been one of his strong points.

Lewis dug into his porridge and smiled. 'Don't fret over him, Father, he's just love-sick.' He nudged his brother, who scowled and drew away his arm. 'Never mind,' Lewis continued unruffled. 'The Laird's ceilidh should cheer us all up. A real grand do it will be from all accounts.'

'The Laird's ceilidh?' Kirsteen questioned, puzzled.

'Ay, Matthew was telling us about it in the dairy just now. Burnbreddie is throwing open his doors on Christmas Eve for all his tenants. There's to be a band, a bar, and a buffet table. In other words, a real grand affair, so you'd better think about getting Mother a new dress,' he finished cheekily.

'Things have indeed changed since her leddyship passed on,' Bob observed. 'I hear tell the old house has had its first coat of paint in years. The old lady wouldny allow a thing to be changed – said it all had to be as it was when old Balfour was alive.'

The atmosphere lightened as everyone fell to discussing the latest piece of news. Only Lorn remained silent and as soon as breakfast was over he went upstairs to throw himself on the bed and gaze at the ceiling. He should ask Ruth to the dance. She wouldn't go otherwise, as Dugald wasn't a tenant of the Laird. He had bought his house when he had taken over Merry Mary's shop. Lorn moved restlessly. The ache that had lain dull in his heart for months was growing worse. Was this what love was? A yearning that tore relentlessly at the senses, a burning emptiness that nothing could fill? Sleepless nights, a longing for more and more solitude in which to think – think of her? That shy lovely girl with her grace and sweetness and her uncertain awareness of her feminine power. For she did have power. For all her reserve, for all her shyness she was possessed of a power that overwhelmed him. He had to talk to her more, pluck up the courage to ask her to Burnbreddie's ceilidh – but would that witch of a mother of hers allow her to come?

Lewis bounded into the room but stopped short at sight of his brother. 'Thinking of *her* again? You're all flushed, Lorn my boy. No bloody wonder! Thinking's no use, doing's the thing.' He threw himself onto the edge of the bed. 'How the hell you've managed to wait so long for a girl beats me – no wonder I hear your bedsprings creaking in the night. You wake me up with your tossing and turning. Have you never done it with a girl?' he asked bluntly.

Lorn threw a hand over his eyes. 'Shut up! I'm trying to think.'

'From the look of you, you've succeeded. Why don't you ask Ruth to this dance? Burnbreddie's got some fine haylofts up yonder. I can recommend them.'

'Do you think I should?'

'What? Get Ruth into a hayloft?'

'No, daftie, ask her to the dance?'

'Of course you should. I'm worried about you. It's time you spread your wings a bit – after all, we'll be eighteen in a few days' time. If I get some birthday money, I'm saving it to buy Rachel a really fine birthday present.' He grew serious. 'I'm a bit like you at the moment. I can't get Rachel out of my mind. Funny she's been here all along, yet last time I saw her it was for the first time somehow. What a figure that girl's got! I've sweated over girls before, but Rachel – phew!'

Some days later Lorn and Ruth came face to face in the village. The wind was biting in from the sea and had whipped her skin to roses. 'Lorn, I was hoping to see you,' she greeted him breathlessly, a combination of swift heartbeats and fighting the wind. She rummaged in her pocket and with difficulty withdrew a bulky parcel, which she pushed at him. 'I've been carrying it around for days so it's a wee bit squashed. Happy birthday. I – I knitted it myself, so don't look at it too closely – I'm better with a pen than with knitting needles.'

Wordlessly he took the parcel. For a long tremulous

moment he gazed at her. The wind lifted and tossed her fine golden hair about her face. Her eyes were the colour of the purple-blue clouds racing over the sky, her lips were parted slightly showing her white teeth. For what seemed eternity he gazed at her mouth, then he dropped his eyes and said gruffly, 'Thanks for the present, Ruthie, I'll – I'll have to go now.'

'Ay, me too, I'll – I'll be seeing you.'

They started to walk away from each other though an invisible bond seemed to be tugging at them, slowing their unwilling steps. He stopped. 'Ruthie.'

She whirled round. 'Yes, Lorn.'

'Will you – do you – would you come to Burnbreddie's dance with me?'

Her colour deepened, the answer rushed to her lips though it came out slowly. 'Ay, Lorn, I'd like that.'

They stood apart, staring at one another, eyes bright with longing, then she turned and hurried away, blood pulsing, heart singing, even while she wondered what her mother would say when she asked her permission to attend the dance with Lorn McKenzie.

Lorn rushed home and went straight upstairs to tear open the parcel. It was a scarf, a blue knitted scarf, so long it took ages to pull it from the folds of tissue paper. Inside was a card, which simply said 'From Ruth to Lorn, with love'. With a little whoop of delight he wound the scarf round his neck and surveyed himself in the mirror. She had knitted this for him, especially for him. With her very own hands she had knitted and knitted and knitted – for him. He picked up the card to read it again. The word 'love' leapt out at him and he raised it to his lips to kiss it.

Lewis came in with a rush. He had just returned from Oban. 'It was grand in Oban, though too bad Rachel's in Glasgow now, or we could have met up. Murdy's getting a bit doddery. He keeps losing things and Maggie follows him around like a sheepdog finding all the things he's lost. I laugh all the time when I'm there.' He sat up and said eagerly, 'Wait till I show you what I got for Rachel.' Rummaging in his case he withdrew a flat box out of which he extracted an oyster satin nightdress.

Lorn stared. 'It's a nightdress – and so thin you can see through it.'

Lewis laughed deeply. 'Top marks! Can you picture her in it? I can, and I hope I'll get a chance for a private showing.' He paused. 'What's that you've got twined round your neck?'

'A scarf,' Lorn's tones were defensive. 'A birthday present from Ruthie.' Lewis scrambled up and hugged his brother. 'Well, things are moving at last! Get in there while the going's good – if not, some-body else might beat you to it. The way Ruth looks these days she won't be known as the white virgin for much longer. Too bad you didn't ask me to fetch her something from Oban. Girls love to get presents – and I don't mean things like woolly gloves or scarves that reach to your ankles!'

Lewis chattered on, but Lorn wasn't listening. He was furious with himself. Still, someone else was bound to be making a trip to the mainland before Christmas. He wondered what he could get her. He wouldn't have the nerve to give her a nightdress, only people like Lewis did things like that.

The Laird's invitation had given the villagers something to look forward to. Best clothes were hastily unearthed to be inspected, aired, and repaired. All over the island women sighed over the contents of their wardrobes and dropped broad hints to their menfolk about Christmas gifts. Kirsteen gazed at her collection of dresses in disgust. They were years old and out of date. Normally she never bothered to keep up with changing fashions, but now she longed for something new. With a sigh she got out her best old dress and set about altering it on the little treadle sewing machine Fergus had bought her after the twins were born.

Ruth was in the worst dilemma of all. She didn't want to go to the Burnbreddie dance dressed in the same boring white. She couldn't ask her mother for a new dress. In fact, she couldn't ask for anything till she first asked her mother if she could go to the dance with Lorn, which she kept putting off, knowing the showdown that would surely follow the request. She thought of doing it through her father, but he had been ill recently with flu, and she felt she couldn't burden him with anything else. She was in despair and resigning herself to the fact that she must tell Lorn she couldn't go with him, when Shona, who was home for Christmas, came to her rescue.

'I am hearing Lorn has asked you to the dance,' Shona greeted her. 'What are you wearing?'

'Nothing!' Ruth wailed, her violet eyes dark with unhappiness. 'I haven't asked Mam if I can go yet because she'll only say no.'

Shona's blue eyes snapped. 'Oh, is that so! We'll see about that! It's time you got to enjoy your life. I'm sure if your father knew he would move heaven and hell for you.'

'Och, I know that, Shona, but he's been ill recently and still very weak. He's not able to take trouble at the moment, and Grannie and Granda are over in Barra for a few days so I can't get them to help.'

Shona's nostrils flared. 'Well! You've got me then! Ask me back to your house for a strupak – now.'

Ruth looked at the lovely determined face, the fearless tilt of the auburn head, the fiery sparkle in the wonderful blue eyes – so like Lorn's. 'Will you come home and have a strupak with me, Shona?'

Shona proved a spirited and competent ally. Over tea and scones in the carbolic smelling kitchen she smiled warmly at Morag and said conversationally, 'I was delighted when Lorn told me had asked Ruth to the dance at Burnbreddie. She'll be the belle – no doubt about that. Nothing can be more exciting than a girl's first dance. I mind when Niall took me to mine – oh, it wasn't a grand affair, just a ceilidh in a barn but –'

917

Morag's cheeks had flamed, and her tones were ominous. 'What's that you say? Lorn taking Ruth to the Burnbreddie dance? It's the first I've heard o' it – of course, I'm the last to hear of her goings on these days. Well, you can tell your brother he needny bother, she won't be going. All thon dancin' and caperin' wi' boys is just a temptation to the de'il, and I made a vow that my lassie would never be tarnished by pleasures that are just excuses to dabble in the unseemly – a vow to the Lord it was and I will no' change my mind now.'

Ruth turned away to hide the tears of frustration and disappointment. 'The Laird has already included her in the guest list,' Shona lied sweetly. 'All the young girls will be going.'

'Well, my Ruth will no' be one o' them!' Morag returned in tight-lipped outrage.

'I'm thinkin' you're wrong there, Morag,' Dugald, white-faced and hollow-eyed, spoke from the rocking chair by the fire. 'I'm the man of this house, and it's time I damned well made you aware of that fact! Ruthie will go to the dance with young McKenzie, and that's final. It's time she started to enjoy her young life.'

The crimson flowed from Morag's face to stain her neck. Her tight lips parted as rage boiled in her, but before she could utter a word Dugald held up his hand and said firmly, 'Don't say it, Morag, you'll only be wasting your breath. Ruthie is going to this dance – and I tell you this – that will only be the start of it. If Lorn wants to take her out anywhere in future, he has my permission. She is, after all, my lassie as well as yours,' he finished softly.

The blood drained from Morag's face, leaving it deathly pale. He was warning her that he knew – knew that she wasn't entirely sure that he was Ruth's father.

'I'll buy the dress myself, Mam,' Ruth's voice came, anxious yet tinged with delight. 'I saved some money from –'

'*No!*' Morag's voice was taut with frustrated temper. 'There will be no new dresses. You can go to this dance, my girl, but you will go in one of your own white frocks!'

'But, Mam –' Ruth began tearfully, but Shona flashed her a triumphant smile.

'Your white dresses are lovely, Ruth, with a bit of alteration . . .'

'I will not alter one single stitch,' Morag stated. 'And that is that! I'm far too busy a woman for any o' that frivolous nonsense.'

'Och, don't worry yourself, Morag,' Shona said, her smile remaining fixed, though she could gladly have torn Morag's hair out by its red roots. 'Kirsteen is a dab hand with her wee sewing machine. Come on, Ruth, we will go and look at your dresses, choose the best one and take it back to Kirsteen – now.'

Dugald turned his face quickly to hide a smile as Shona, her head high, marched Ruth out of the room, leaving Morag standing speechless in the middle of it.

Kirsteen was at first dismayed at the challenge that

had been thrust upon her, but after hearing Shona's account of the scene with Morag she set her lips and went grimly to the task. Removing the long flowing skirt from one of her own evening gowns, she attached it to the bodice of Ruth's dress. To the neck and sleeves she added ruffles of pure white lace, and as a final touch she sewed a row of tiny pearl buttons down the front of the bodice. When Ruth arrived for a fitting she gasped in awe at sight of herself in Kirsteen's wardrobe mirror and whispered, 'How can I ever thank you, Kirsteen?'

'The look on Lorn's face will be thanks enough,' Kirsteen replied, her heart melting as the girl swirled round, sending the long skirt billowing, rejoicing in the fact that the ugly calliper would be hidden from view.

Kirsteen's wish for snow was granted. Three days before Christmas the wind abated and the stars glittered coldly in the night sky. Hoar frost rimed the heather on the hills, the icy grip of winter slowed the burns as icicles gathered. Gradually the fat grey snowclouds rolled over the sea, to be torn apart on the ragged hill peaks, sending snow cascading over the countryside. On Christmas Eve morning Fergus stamped the snow from his boots and, coming into the kitchen, said with a rather sarcastic smile, 'You got your wish, Kirsteen, now would you care to grab a shovel and come and help to dig the ewes out of the drifts? We need every pair of hands.'

At first it seemed fun, working beside Shona and

the men, the former sparkling as she pushed snow-
balls down Niall's neck and ran shrieking as he
chased her, but by mid-afternoon she was
exhausted, and after tea she dozed by the fire in the
parlour to wake with a start wondering what time it
was. As she dragged herself up to the bedroom she
sighed and wondered if all the romance had gone
out of her life. Fergus had been sharp with her that
morning, and at teatime he had hardly spoken a
word. He had murmured some things to Shona that
she hadn't been able to catch, and she had felt left
out and rather angry at the pair of them.

As she reached the door of her room she
wondered if she could possibly make some excuse
not to go to the dance. Every bone in her body ached
and she felt she could hardly walk, let alone dance.
She opened the door to see a warm fire leaping in
the grate. On the hearthrug sat the zinc tub piled
high with steamy soap bubbles; her fur jacket was
laid out on the bed – and beside it lay a gaily
wrapped parcel.

Shona put her bright head round the door, her blue
eyes full of mischief. 'Father's orders. We all helped
to fill it, including Niall, and – I hope you don't mind,
but Ellie poured nearly a full bottle of bubble bath
in. She says she's going to wait outside the door and
watch the bubbles oozing out under the crack!'
Shona said, and withdrew before Kirsteen could utter
a word.

Without further ado Kirsteen stripped and sank
blissfully into the perfumed water, chuckling as

bubbles popped under her nose, little drifts of them rising and floating in the draught from the fire. She soaked for fully fifteen minutes till all the tension left her and she emerged to wrap herself in a pink dressing gown, feeling relaxed yet tingling.

'Am I too late to dry your back?' Fergus's deep voice made her jump. The door shut with a little click and he came forward to press himself against her and kiss her. 'Mmm, you smell lovely, I had hoped to catch you in the tub. Too bad we have to go out.'

He smelled of soap and toothpaste. His fingers touched the tips of her breasts and she could easily have forgotten the Burnbreddie dance if he had stood beside her for one more minute. But he moved away, his face rather flushed. He went to the bed, picked up the parcel and handed it to her. 'Merry Christmas, darling, I hope you like it.'

'But we don't open presents till tomorrow.'

'You open this one tonight. I got Burnbreddie's wife to buy it in Oban. You and she are about the same size – anyway – see what you think.'

It was an evening gown of soft blue silk. He zipped her into it and stood behind her, his dark eyes full of love. 'You look beautiful.'

'Oh, Fergus, I feel it, it's just what I needed to boost my morale. If I had known I wouldn't have spent hours altering my old things.' She threw her arms round his neck and kissed him. 'Thank you – for this – and for being my husband.'

Some minutes later she knotted his tie for him. It wasn't often he had occasion to wear one, which was as well because with his one arm he found it a frustrating business to tie a neat knot. He was very handsome in his dark suit and a white shirt that emphasised the mahogany of his skin. Standing before the mirror he said rather jauntily, 'Amazing the difference clothes make. I look rather a distinguished gentleman, don't you think?'

Kirsteen turned from brushing her hair. 'How like Alick you sounded just now. He used to say that, in that light-hearted fashion, just as you did now. He was never like you to look at, but there were little things that marked you out as brothers.'

'Ay,' Fergus said, his tone thoughtful. 'Blood is thicker than water right enough. It's strange how much I miss him, yet look how we used to fight . . .'

From the room at the top of the corridor there came the sound of arguing and laughter. Kirsteen smiled. Lewis would be showing Lorn some last-minute dance steps. In all the excitement of the season Lorn had forgotten that he could barely dance a single step. A few nights ago he had suddenly leapt up from his chair and in a terrified voice had cried, 'I can't dance! I've asked Ruth to this big night out and I can't dance a single one! Bugger it! What the hell will I do?' Lewis had immediately got to his feet. With a deep bow he had intoned in a high voice, 'Please, my lady, will you do me the honour of dancing with me?' To which Lorn had acceded with a gust of laughter. Fergus had said to Kirsteen, 'Come to think of it, I ought to brush up too.' And he had swept her all round the kitchen. Then Niall and

Shona arrived, and they too had joined in the impromptu fun, and it hadn't mattered that the men wore working clothes and the women aprons.

Tonight, however, everything mattered very much to Lorn. He had been nervous all day and several times had been on the point of backing out. His courage embraced everything but social gatherings and on top of it all he had his feelings for Ruth to contend with.

'Those two will never fight like Alick and me,' Fergus said quietly. 'They are so alike in many ways, they share so much.'

'Let's just hope they never fall in love with the same girl – then the trouble will begin,' Kirsteen said. 'Oh, I know Lewis flits about from one to the other, but one day he will really fall in love – like Lorn at this very minute.' She sighed. 'He's so shy – so is Ruth. It won't be easy for them.'

'If they truly love one another it will turn out all right – it did for us.'

'That took years,' she pointed out.

He helped her into the fur jacket and she snuggled against him as he whispered into her ear, 'Ay, but it was worth it. The best things are worth waiting for.'

Chapter Sixteen

Ruth came slowly into the kitchen and stood sparkling-eyed in front of her parents. Dugald drew in his breath; pride brought a lump to his throat: tonight Ruth had grown from an uncertain child into a dazzling young woman. Dugald had given her a tiny pair of pearl earrings for her birthday. These, and a single pink rosebud pinned above her breast, were the only ornamentations she wore, the delicate colour of the rose matching that in her cheeks. She glowed with a radiance that seemed to spread out and touch the bare clinical room with light. He got up and took her hands.

'Ruthie, Shona was right – you will be the belle of the ball – no – more than that, a princess.' He took the mohair stole from her arms and wrapped it round her shoulders. She reached up to kiss his pale cheek then turned a radiant face to her mother and said rather hesitantly, 'Well, Mam?'

Morag cleared her throat and said gruffly, 'Ay, you'll do. You've grown into a bonny young woman – just you mind all the things I've told you and you'll be all right. You had better be going, see no' and keep the McKenzies waiting.'

Over his wife's head Dugald winked at his

daughter and she lowered her face quickly to hide a smile. At the door Morag rather furtively pushed a tiny Bible into her hands. 'Carry this – it will protect you.'

'Where will I keep it, Mam? I don't have a bag.'

Morag flushed and whispered, 'Tuck it into your drawers.' She glanced quickly round as if afraid that someone had overhead the ridiculous suggestion.

Ruth's lips twitched. 'I prefer the words of the Lord to be in my heart, Mam – not in my knickers next to my backside.'

Leaving her mother with her mouth agape, Ruth hurried out into the cold glittering night. A short distance away, parked outside the shop, she saw her father's van. Vehicles of every description were being used to transport people to Burnbreddie, all of them filled to capacity. The Laird had sent out his own cars to bring those whose only hope of getting to the dance would have been by shanks's pony. Everyone had worried that the weather might have prevented them getting over to Nigg, but while the snow had draped itself over hills and fields, the tangy air of the sea had kept the shore roads clear.

Dugald had been determined that for once his daughter would have some freedom, and he had left his van at the shop and given Lorn the keys. Before Ruth reached the vehicle Lorn was out, holding open the passenger door. His heart was beating a tattoo. Lewis had given him a short but uplifting pep talk in the bedroom as they were getting ready. 'Act very cool, even though you feel hot under the collar.

Open doors for her, lead the way, take her wrap, get drinks for her – in fact, behave like a perfect little gentleman. Girls love to feel special, and with a girl like Ruth you'll have to go all out in your efforts. She hasn't got any confidence in herself, you'll have to give her some even though you feel like fainting in the process.' His blue eyes had gleamed. 'It pays in the long run, my lad, believe me.'

Lorn stood by the door, erect and poised while beneath him his legs felt like jelly. On the journey he tried to act very coolly, and succeeded so well that Ruth felt a pang of dismay. This self-assured stranger with the clipped tones wasn't the Lorn she knew. She felt uncomfortable and uncertain, feelings that grew in magnitude as he became silent in his concentration of driving the van over the treacherous cliff road to Nigg. She stole a glance at him. All she could see in the darkness was an anonymous black silhouette sitting straight and rigid behind the wheel. The faint aroma of soap came to her, and her heart quickened further. For the first time in her life she was alone with a boy – and that boy was Lorn McKenzie, whom she loved so much her heart ached with the depth of her emotions. She gazed at the sea swirling and booming restlessly far below. That was how she had felt lately, unable to settle, forever seething inside, unable to find solace in anything, not even her writing. Car lights were behind and in front of them on the normally deserted road, and from the crofts and cottages at Nigg little black dots were scurrying, while a gay little melody drifted from Annack Gow's blackhouse. After a lapse of many years Tam had dared to get his still working again with the help of Graeme Gow and a few others.

The van swerved suddenly as it left the road and made a bumpy path over a lonely moor track. The engine stopped, silence and darkness shrouded them. Lorn's voice came breathlessly, all his composure crumbling away. 'Ruthie – I – before we go up I wanted to give you something – for your birthday and your Christmas combined. I wish I could give you a whole pile of things, but – och – here, take it and open it – it's – it's not much . . .'

The nervous monologue trailed off. He pushed the parcel at her. Briefly their hands touched, flesh burned into flesh, their pulses raced apace, then in confusion she moved away and immersed herself in opening the gift. The cold caress of marble lay heavy in her hands and he said, 'It's a paperweight with a pen sort of attached to it – like an old-fashioned quill, only it isn't. It's a fountain pen. The base is Skye marble, full of lovely colours – greys, greens, and a wee hint of purple, the same colour as your eyes when you're looking very serious.'

'Lorn.' Her voice was low, melodious. 'I can't see it – but it's beautiful.'

They laughed at the silly remark, then without conscious thought their hands entwined. He drew her towards him. The scent of roses filled his nostrils, her nearness made his senses whirl. Briefly he touched her soft hair with his lips. They both trembled, each feeling the tremors of the other. For an eternal moment they remained apart, lips close but not touching then with a soft little moan his mouth moulded to hers and all the longing and misery of endless days and nights melted into obscurity.

The kiss was fleeting, inexperienced, tender, but it was only the beginning of dreams, a warm sweet promise of greater things to come.

'I suppose we'd better go.' His lilting voice was shaky.

'Ay,' she said softly, unwilling to relinquish the intimate lovely experience of being alone with him. She had looked forward to the dance, now she knew she had only savoured the anticipation of being in his company. It would have been enough for her to spend the whole evening with him in her father's draughty van and her heart sank a little as they drove up to Burnbreddie House. Light flooded the silvered lawns, people laughed as they held each other upright on the slippery road.

The interior of the house had lost its gloomy look. The walls were bright with new paint, modern furniture had replaced the monstrous overstuffed sofas, in the hall a great log fire crackled up the chimney.

'Stay beside me, please,' Ruth whispered as they went inside to be swallowed up in an atmosphere of laughter and chinking glasses. In the background a band played soft music. Lorn's own composure was fast failing him but somehow he managed to carry out Lewis's advice. The Laird and his charming wife Rena were the perfect hosts, welcoming and smiling, making the guests feel relaxed and at home. The

Rhanna folk were used to homely ceilidhs but this was a much grander occasion, and an unnatural politeness prevailed. But nothing could dampen their spirits for long. Tam's eyes gleamed at sight of the bar set up in a corner of the room. Behind it presided his son, Angus. Tam rubbed his hands together and spoke to the Laird in his most polite tones, 'Is this no' terrible weather just? I will just go and have a wee dram to warm up my blood.' He winked confidingly. 'I am no' as young as I was and Kate would have me comin' out tonight without my combinations. Ay, ay – women,' he ended sadly.

Kate yanked him away. 'You liar, Tam McKinnon! It would take a hacksaw to cut you out these damt drawers o' yours. You sew yourself into them in September and never a chink o' air gets in till summer comes!'

Lorn squeezed Ruth's hand and they giggled. Rena spotted them and led them further inside, her warm smile lighting her face. 'How charming you look tonight, Ruth. Your dress is lovely. You're a very lucky young man, Lorn.'

Everyone else was also thinking how radiant Ruth looked that evening. 'A bonny, bonny lass,' Mollie murmured to Todd. 'I doubt it's the first time I've seen her alone at a gathering.'

Todd chuckled. 'Ay, thanks to our Shona. I hear tell she left Morag wi' no' a leg to stand on, and Morag's mouth dropped so wide you could have used it as a goal at a shinty match.'

The young men gaped openly at Ruth and some

of the happiness left her when she heard the whispers. 'Would you look at the white virgin,' and, 'In that dress she's more like the virgin bride. By God, I wouldny mind a first night wi' her.'

Lorn's fists bunched at his sides, and Ruth's face flamed. But she was with Lorn. As long as he stayed by her side she would be all right. He was so handsome that evening with his earth-brown curls shining under the lights. His face was filling out a little and he looked very tall in his dark suit. His hand was warm in hers. He was making her feel like a desirable young girl instead of plain little Ruth Donaldson whom young men avoided like the plague. There was a strength in him that made her feel safe – yet, he was like her – shy, afraid of crowds . . .

The first polite exchanges over with, the islanders became less constrained. Some of them were taking to the floor, awkwardly to begin with, but as the uisge-beatha warmed the blood, and the band struck up well-known Strathspeys and reels, the room became filled with swirling dresses and swinging kilts.

Lorn felt himself growing hot with unease. He couldn't possibly lead Ruth onto the floor; the few steps he had learned from Lewis sank to the pit of his mind and refused to re-surface.

He gave Ruth's arm a little squeeze. 'Go and sit down over yonder, Ruthie. I'll – I'll be with you in a wee minute.'

She glanced at him hesitantly but limped away to sit unobtrusively on a large antique settle with a high back. Lewis came over to Lorn, a frown darkening his brow. 'What the hell's wrong with you now? You've got the lass, now make the most of it. Get over there and dance with her.'

'I can't.'

Lewis deftly lifted a glass of whisky from a passing tray. 'Here, drink this, it will do you good. While you're at it, do I have your permission to ask Ruth to dance?'

'Ay, away you go, tell her I'll be with her in a whily.'

He fingered the glass of whisky. He seldom drank, only at weddings, funerals and Hogmanay, and then only in moderation. He watched his brother going up to Ruth, saw relief replacing the apprehension she had felt. With a decisive movement he raised the glass to his lips and downed the contents in one gulp. It gripped at his throat before it burned into his belly, but he felt himself steadying. Shona waved to him, his mother raised a sparkling face and smiled at him. She looked like a girl in the swirling blue dress. His father was straight and ruggedly handsome in his good suit. It didn't matter that it was slightly outdated. When folk looked at Fergus McKenzie they saw the man, not the wrappings. Lorn recalled his mother telling him that at one time Fergus had been so shy of crowds he had seldom gone to ceilidhs – but now his silvered dark head was proudly tilted as he swept Kirsteen round the room. Lorn straightened his shoulders. Maybe when he was older he would grow more confident but maturity was far away yet

for him – he had to find his courage now . . . Ruth
was dancing beautifully in Lewis's arms, forgetting
her limp, forgetting her nerves. Her hair was like
spun gold under the lights, she was no longer a
vision but a lovely desirable young girl . . . Lorn
heard snatches of a conversation some boys were
having: 'I wonder who will be the first to get the
white virgin.'

'Ach, it'll be Lewis, he has a way wi' the lassies.'

'Never mind the McKenzie lads. I might have a try
at her myself.'

Lorn swung round but the boys had moved over
to several giggling young maidens who had arrived
on the scene. Then Shona came marching over to
speak sternly to her young brother. 'What's this, Lorn
McKenzie? Lewis dancing with Ruth? I though she
was *your* partner.'

'Go on, man,' Niall urged. 'Once you're on the
floor it doesn't matter if you have three left feet. Look
at Tam and the others. They canny dance two right
steps but they're still enjoying themselves.'

They whirled away. The dancers were really
warming up with the Laird and his wife 'hooching'
as loud as anyone. The laughter began to get through
to Lorn, excitement surged in his veins – one more
drink and he would be ready for anything. Angus
McKinnon grinned at him. 'A dram or a beer, son?'

'A dram – a big one.'

'Coming up, I'll make it a treble seeing it's you.'

Lewis was strangely aware of Ruth's femininity as
he held her slender waist and felt the heat of her

body. Her head came only to his shoulder, the fragrance of roses filled his nostrils – but it wasn't Ruth he wanted. His eyes continually strayed over her head to the door.

Ruth sensed his inattentiveness and some of her confidence left her. She had forgotten her limp, forgotten the earlier remarks directed at her. Lewis was cool, assured, she felt herself floating in his arms like thistledown. He had paid her flattering compliments, whispered silly things in her ear that made her laugh – but now his restlessness came to her. She looked round for Lorn and an odd feeling of foreboding filled her heart when she spotted him over at the bar drinking, his dark head thrown back as he laughed with Angus. Misery engulfed her. Was he drinking to give himself courage to dance with a lame girl – a white virgin – a virgin bride? She stumbled as the dance came to an end. Lewis put a steadying hand under her arm and was leading her back to her seat when a buzz went round the room. Rachel was standing under one of the archways. She had just arrived and if she had meant to make an entrance she was certainly succeeding. She was sensational-looking in a long rich red evening gown with a low-cut front. A sheen of blue lay over the silken black of her hair, which was swept over one ear and pinned with a diamanté clasp. She moved across the room, a statuesque figure, her tilted head and slow measured step suggesting supreme self-confidence. The sensuous sway of her hips caused women as well as men to turn and stare.

'A Jezebel if ever there was one,' Elspeth said to Behag, who tightened her lips and shook her head in extreme disapproval.

Jon, who had been watching the door as anxiously as Lewis, started to walk towards Rachel, but Lewis was there first, taking her hand, leading her away. But Rachel had spotted Ruth, and with a seductive sidelong glance at Lewis, she broke away and went to greet her friend who received her with quiet pleasure. Physically they were completely opposite. Rachel was the picture of elegance in her red gown: her golden skin glowed, the dark eyes smouldered with life, her lovely body taunted every young red-blooded male in the room. Ruth, however, with her pale hair and milky skin, was a startling comparison. In her flowing white dress she looked fragile and vulnerable; her feminine appeal was subtle, faintly suppressed, yet there was about her small-boned body a faint sybaritic quality that was strangely, movingly sweet, ensnared as it was in a young woman who was still a child in so many ways. She and Rachel not only looked different, they lived in different worlds. Rachel had moved into a sphere of sophistication, her sights set firmly on a career as a solo violinist; Ruth was able to pursue her writing yet still remain on Rhanna. In every way she was a girl of the islands, yet the friendship, nurtured in the two from childhood, had never wavered. Though Rachel's chosen career had taken her away from Rhanna, she was at heart the same free spirit who had roamed barefoot over the moors and bays, and

935

she was always glad to be home. In a mixture of vocal and sign language the two exchanged news and gossip and commented eagerly on one another's dresses.

'Dance with me, Rachel.' Lewis's hand was on her arm, holding it in an urgent grip. With a provocative smile lifting her mouth, she allowed him to sweep her away. Her body was pliant in his arms, moulding to each of his movements. He said nothing, he couldn't, he was too conscious of her mouth, the exciting sway of her limbs, the enticing swell of her breasts.

The other girls watched and none of them liked Rachel McKinnon that evening. She had never been one of them; she had always been remote, untamed, cool, passionate – different from 'normal' girls. To some degree Ruth came into this category as well, but unlike Rachel she wasn't considered a threat, a competitor in the ring of eligible females. No one could imagine Ruth tempting Lewis into her arms; the looks that had been cast at her earlier had been merely amused. Lewis had taken pity on her, that was all – but it wasn't pity that flushed his face now, nor was the brilliance in his blue eyes the result of too much drinking. And so his entourage of female admirers and conquests past and present, glowered long and hard at the oblivious Rachel.

Lorn had witnessed the exchanges through a blur. His head was swimming and he felt sick. He knew he shouldn't have gulped down that last drink so quickly. He watched Ruth limping back to her corner, dejection slowing her steps. Perhaps if he went to sit by her, explained to her that he couldn't dance, had never danced, she would understand and be content just to sit and talk . . . The lights merged and swam; the room turned upside down. Teasing remarks came to him but barely penetrated the fuzz in his head. A group of boys sniggered as he swayed past, and some of the older men came forward to take his arm, but he shook them off and made his unsteady way up a long dim corridor to a side door, which he wrenched open.

The cold night air washed over him, the sweat dried on his body, making him shiver. Falling to his knees in the snow he was violently sick and in the midst of his misery, he hated himself: Ruth would never forgive him; she would think him a drunken coward. He felt degraded, cheated and ill, but above all he ached with humiliation and self-loathing.

Lewis danced Rachel to the side of the hall. She looked cool, but her heart was racing madly. How often she had dreamed of a night like this – music, dancing, laughter, the arms of Lewis Fraser McKenzie enfolding her, holding her close.

Without a word Lewis took her hand, and they slipped away. He had often been to Burnbreddie with his father and knew the lay-out well. He led her through the silent corridors to a room well away from the main hall. This was the Laird's study, an untidy, comfortable den with worn leather armchairs and a huge oak desk. A connecting door led to another room, full of cubbyholes, a filing cabinet, and a plush velvet sofa scattered with plump chenille cushions, and it was into this room that Lewis led Rachel and bolted the door after them. She didn't draw back, nor was she shocked at the boldness of the venture. Like him she was a daredevil; convention had never cluttered her life. He went forward to switch on a shaded wall light, then turned to her. Her lustrous eyes were dark with laughter – and something else: passion, smouldering, beckoning to him, taunting him. He came to stand by her. His eyes, a startling blue in his flushed handsome face, travelled over her face to her body, lingering on the curving swell of her breasts. The mellow light spread over her, deepening her dress to blood-red, her skin to golden-rose. He gazed at the arch of her throat, the graceful curve of her shoulders, then he focused again on her mouth: the red parted lips, the pearly teeth, the pink tip of her tongue showing between them. Slowly he bent and kissed the hollow of her throat, his lips laying a trail of fire up to her mouth. Over and over their mouths met in swift, breathless kisses that made them tremble.

'I got you a present, Rachel.' His voice was hoarse with desire, and with shaking hands he took the small parcel from his pocket and gave it to her.

She tormented him by slowly peeling off the wrapping paper. She smiled at sight of the nightdress and teased him by holding it against herself, moulding it to the curves of her body. With one hand she propped it against her shoulders, with the other she traced the shape of it – over her belly, her waist.

He could contain himself no longer; roughly he pulled her to him and claimed her lips, pushing them apart, his tongue probing, searching for hers.

She was in the arms of an expert lover, but she wasn't afraid; she had gained plenty of experience with men over the last year or two and knew how to handle them. She knew that playing the field was a dangerous game, and even at the height of desire one half of her always remained alert, aware of the price she might have to pay if she allowed herself to relax completely. She wanted Lewis – for a very long time she had wanted him, and she wouldn't rest till she had experienced the delights that she knew an affair with him would bring. She would take it all, and she would take it now, because later – later she had to give her all to her music and she would have no time to spare for the Lewis McKenzies of the world – except perhaps – occasionally . . .

His hands were on her thighs, pulling her in ever closer to him. With a little shiver of anticipation she heard the slow unzipping of her dress. Together they sank onto the couch. He was moving, lost, groaning with pleasure. She wanted him to go on, never to stop; she was burning, beating, pulsing with the need for him . . . With a supreme effort of willpower she tore herself free and began to pull her dress over her shoulders. She was trembling, panting, fumbling behind her back for her zip. It stuck. Darting to the door she threw open the bolt, wrenched the door open, went through, shut it, and with her back to it found the zip and began pulling it up. She heard him scrambling up, cursing her, and a triumphant smile lifted the corners of her lovely mouth. For years Lewis McKenzie had made her wait – now it was his turn. Just for a little while would she make him sweat it out – her legs trembled again – for a very little while. She began to run, through the corridors, tidying herself as she went. Lewis pulled open the door of the cubby room. Little bitch! Cruel, flaunting little bitch! He gritted his teeth, rage replacing passion. Snatching up the nightdress from the floor he was about to tear it apart but stopped. No! By God, no! Damned if he would ruin the thing. He had bought it for her and he meant to see it draped round that lovely body of hers if it was the last thing he did. His head was pounding as hard as his heart, and he passed a hand over his hot brow. Fresh air, he needed fresh air, had to cool down.

Stuffing the scrap of oyster satin into his pocket he went up a short passageway to a side door, opened it – and found Lorn sitting on the steps. His skin was clammy, he was shivering uncontrollably and he smelled of vomit. 'Lorn! God Almighty!' Lewis cried. 'What happened?'

'Nothing,' Lorn whispered miserably. 'I took a few drinks, came out here – and was sick.'

'How long ago?'

'I don't know – about an hour – I couldn't go back in.'

Lewis hoisted his brother to his feet and put a shoulder under his armpit. 'Hold on,' he ordered. 'I'll get you home. I'll take Lachlan's car. I'll explain when I bring it back; he won't mind.'

'What – about Ruthie?'

'Ach, I'll take her home later. Oh, don't worry, I'm no' going to steal her – I've had enough of lassies for one night – now hold on and shut up.'

Jon watched Rachel's departure also and his brown eyes were dull. He felt foolish and angry with himself. It wasn't right for him to feel this way about a young girl . . . Yes! Dammit! It was right! Love could never be wrong and he would go on loving, caring, protecting this beautiful child as long as there was breath in him. He was also concerned for her. He knew she'd had boys before, that was natural; but her time with Lewis McKenzie had come, and somehow he knew it was. what she had waited for. He knew that their affair would be a tempestuous one. Anton came over and touched his arm, his keen blue eyes full of understanding as he said, 'My friend, you love her very much, I watch you and I feel your pain. Am I not right?'

Jon flushed and nodded and Anton went on softly, 'She will come to you in the end, Jon. You and she were made for each other . . .' Jon opened his mouth to protest but Anton held up his hand. 'Ah yes, it is so. Age makes no difference with love to bridge the years. She is very young, and she is sowing the wild oats. Rachel is a very clever girl – she is sowing them quickly, because she knows that her kind of ambition will take all her concentration. There will be no time later for frivolous love affairs then – and that is when you must step in and be ready to take over.'

Babbie came over, lovely that evening in a green dress that matched her eyes. 'You haven't danced with me tonight, Jon Jodl. Why don't you ask me now?'

Jon shook his head, his thoughts were with Rachel and he couldn't bring himself to enter into the jollity of an evening where everyone in the gay whirling crowd seemed to have a partner. 'Thank you, Babbie, you are very kind, but I think I will go and keep company with the little maiden sitting over there in the corner. Like me she seems not to have a partner, and she looks as if she would like to curl up and die.'

Anton and Babbie watched him walking away. The latter took her husband's arm and murmured, 'Poor Jon, I hope he finds a happiness as great as ours. He's so nice and deserves only the best.'

'He will get it, liebling.' Anton gazed into her eyes and smiled. 'Take it from a great philosopher. Jon will have his wish; all he needs is patience and understanding.'

Ruth watched Jon approaching. She liked this kindly German who had integrated so well with the community. He had done a lot for it, but mostly he encouraged the island children to take an interest in music. He had succeeded so well that many had discovered hidden talents under his guidance. She knew he was in love with Rachel. From the beginning he had devoted himself to her unstintingly – he had encouraged her ambitions, had gone to endless trouble to help her fulfil her dreams – and now – like her, he was tortured by a love that seemed out of reach. She stood up, and when she spoke she sounded slightly breathless. 'Jon, are you enjoying yourself?'

He reddened again and smiled wistfully. 'Not very much, jungfräulich.'

'Then – will you take me home please? My father's van is outside – I – I don't feel very well.'

He put a steadying hand under her elbow, the trembling of her delicate young body came to him. 'I will be honoured to accompany you home, jungfräulich. Take my arm and we will walk to the archway there – no one will see us slipping away – they are all too busy enjoying themselves.'

It was later than usual when Ruth came into the kitchen next morning. Her parents were seated at the table and Morag raised her head to say somewhat sharply, 'You're late at table, Ruth. What happened last night to make you oversleep?'

'Nothing happened, Mam.' Ruth's voice was flat and lifeless. 'I'm still a virgin, if that's what you mean.' Ignoring her mother's shocked gasp she went on, her voice rising a little, 'There's not a lad in the whole of Rhanna who would dance with the white virgin for fear of being laughed at. That's what they call me behind my back, only last night it was worse – they called me the virgin bride instead. You've got what you always wanted, Mam, an untarnished daughter.

You've labelled me, you've made folks laugh behind my back and call me names, you always tried to make me believe that boys were dirty-minded and wicked – and now you've got a daughter who will one day be known as the virgin spinster.' At the door to the hall she turned, 'I've told a lie – someone did dance with me – Lewis McKenzie – because he felt sorry for me.' Her face was very pale as she went out of the kitchen, her limp more pronounced than it had been for years.

Dugald looked at his wife with contempt. When he spoke his voice was tightly controlled. 'Satisfied? You've used the innocence of that lovely young life to ease the burden of your own ungodly guilt. I saw bitterness in her just now, Morag, for the first time I saw bitterness and it was an ugly expression to see in my Ruthie's face.' He stood up, tall, over-thin, white with anger and sadness. 'I'm going up to her. You pray a lot to the Lord to save your soul, but you might remember that your family have souls too. I think the time has come for you to pray for us as well – if it isn't too late to mend the damage you have done.'

After a sleepless night, passing solitary hours thinking about Ruth, Lorn decided he must go to her and explain the reasons for his behaviour at the dance, and soon after breakfast he went over to Morag's cottage to ask to see Ruth. But Morag was outraged by his request.

'You leave my lassie be,' she told him through tight

lips. 'A fine mess we are all in because of you! What kind of laddie are you anyway? Asking a lass to a ceilidh, then creeping away to a corner to drink yourself stupid. Oh, ay, folks are talking right enough, news of that sort travels fast.'

'Ay, you're right enough there.' Lorn's voice was ominously quiet. 'Folks do talk. Has it ever occurred to you that folk might be talking about you? Or do you think you're so saintly there's nothing that anyone can find bad to say about you!'

Morag's face flamed red. 'How dare you speak to me like that you – you McKenzie upstart!'

'I dare because it's true – just as I've dared to come here this morning and ask to see Ruthie. I just want to explain something to her.'

Morag thought about Ruth upstairs in tears, and a fresh upsurge of guilt made her angrier still. 'Indeed you will not. You've done enough damage to be going on with. Fancy her coming home here and laying all the blame on me!'

'All the blame is with you!' Lorn couldn't help himself shouting. 'And I didn't get drunk last night because – oh – what's the use of trying to explain anything to you! You never hear anything for all the brimstone bunging up your lugs!'

Morag let out a yell of outrage and slammed the door. Turning, Lorn walked away, his shoulders stooped with dejection.

The next day he heard that Ruth's father had taken her for an indefinite period to Coll where he had relatives. Immediately Lorn went to get the address from Isabel, but she and Jim Jim were not yet home from their holiday in Barra. He thought about going to see Totie Little of Portvoynachan, whom he suspected was more than just a good friend of Dugald's, but Totie too had 'gone away for a whily', leaving the Post Office in charge of Jemima Sugden, a retired teacher of the area. Lorn was in a daze of despair. Just a few days ago he had been sublimely happy – now he didn't know where to turn. And there was no one he could find who would help him.

Part Five

1960

Chapter Seventeen

Rachel made an excuse to extend her Christmas holidays, and she and Lewis ran wild together, like children. They ran and played through the virgin tracts of snow on the moors, danced close together at the ceilidhs, walked hand in hand along the wide, windswept bays. They looked like beautiful children with the fresh bloom of youth on their cheeks, immaturity allowing them to indulge in the kind of things they might never do again with the onset of adult sobriety. But the passions that consumed them belonged to a man and a woman, and when childish things were done with they fell into each other's arms, eager for the pleasures of love. It seemed they could never tire of one another. He couldn't get enough of her silken body pressed against his – the sight of her long-legged, firm-breasted young body sent him crazy with desire – and they had to force themselves not to be seen touching in public places. Though Annie had always allowed her daughter to run free, though her own morals had often been dirty linen to be mulled over by the gossips, she had an inbuilt sense of propriety, which had been passed to Rachel. Oh, she was going with Lewis McKenzie all right, but she was careful to give the impression that, to her, he was just another boy. So while Behag, Elspeth, and others who came into the category of nosy cailleachs, tightened their lips and talked among themselves of sinful flaunting, the rest of the population looked and saw just a lass and a lad having a bit of a fling. But soon after the New Year Rachel went away, and Lewis seemed to retreat into himself. He had changed since his eighteenth birthday: he had laughed less, and had become moody and irritable. Everyone put it down to the affair over Rachel, but Lachlan, to whom Lewis went complaining of headaches, knew better. On questioning the boy Lachlan discovered he was suffering other symptoms as well.

'I get dizzy a lot,' Lewis told him off-handedly, 'and sometimes I can't get things into focus – and I'm getting as grumpy as old Behag,' he finished with a grin that didn't entirely hide his anxiety.

Lachlan bent over his desk, keeping his voice even as he said, 'Too much wine, women and song, you young rascal. Right, we'll arrange for you to have a thorough check-up. I'll give you some painkillers just now, and make the arrangements to get you over to Glasgow for some tests . . .'

'*Glasgow!* Och, c'mon now, Doctor!' burst out Lewis, his face going pale. 'It surely isn't serious enough for that!'

Lachlan's smile was warm, reassuring. 'Heads are funny parts of the anatomy, Lewis. It could be you're just needing glasses – it could be a thousand and one things – but I have to be sure, and I don't have the facilities here to carry out the necessary tests. I'll get a letter away to Glasgow and let your parents know . . .'

'*No!*' Lewis exploded violently. 'I couldn't bear Mother worrying over me and wondering about getting over to Glasgow to see me.'

'The tests will only take a day or two,' Lachlan said patiently.

Lewis looked him straight in the eye. 'On the other hand they might take ages.' He shook his head. 'No, Lachlan, I'm old enough now to do things for myself. I'll make up some excuse to be away from home for a while. If – if everything is all right I will have saved a lot of fuss, and unless I need specs, no one need be any the wiser.'

Kirsteen and Fergus had no inkling that Lewis was ill, they only knew that both their sons were becoming increasingly difficult to live with.

'Hell, Kirsteen, what are we going to do with them?' Fergus appealed one day in bewilderment. 'I thought it was bad enough when Shona was going through all this, but I didn't expect it with boys! They moon about like sick puppies and it's impossible to talk to either of them!'

Kirsteen sighed. 'Darling, darling, I know. We mustn't forget that we mooned about, too, when we were in a tangle over each other. I wonder if we were as difficult to live with. I want to help, but they just turn away as if they had been scalded. Lorn is impossible – and Lewis –' She frowned. 'Lewis is behaving very strangely – out of character. He's so bad-tempered and moody. It seemed to start before Christmas and has got worse and worse. Maybe it's the real thing with Rachel. Thank goodness Grant isn't here to bother us with the affairs of *his* heart – I couldn't take three of them moping about.'

Rachel was gone only two weeks when Lewis announced his intention of going to Glasgow to stay with Andrew McKinnon, a great friend of his, who had gone to the city to find work. 'It will only be for a week or so,' Lewis told his parents. 'I'll write.'

But the week stretched to a month, and Kate nodded her head sorrowfully. 'The laddie has got it bad this time. Fancy following Rachel to Glasgow – mind, who can blame him? Though she's my own granddaughter I have to admit she's a bonny bonny lassie – she has that tempting look about her men canny resist.' She pushed out her ample bosom. 'I had it myself in my day, but for all Tam noticed I might have been born wi' my head screwed back to front and my bosoms where my bum is!'

When Lewis returned, neither Fergus nor Kirsteen could get much out of him beyond the fact that Glasgow was busier but the same as ever it was.

'Did you see Rachel at all?' Kirsteen persisted, her blue eyes glinting with exasperation.

Lewis grunted and refused to expand on the subject.

Fergus glowered in puzzlement at the son who, from the start, had laughed at life. The boy had always eaten like a healthy young horse, now he toyed with his food, his face was thinner, he'd had his hair cropped in Glasgow and somehow the boy had left him, leaving in his place a stranger whom Fergus didn't know. 'Are you well enough?' he asked sharply.

Lewis's head jerked up, the blue eyes flashed. 'Of course I am – at least I was till I came home and you all started poking and prying into my affairs. Och – why can't you leave me be!' he said and angrily scrunched back his chair and stomped away out of the house to walk moodily through Glen Fallan.

Lorn pushed back his chair also, and moved to follow his brother, catching up with him by Murdy's house, where quite a little crowd were gathered. Then Andrew McKinnon stepped onto the road and hailed Lewis with delight. 'Lewis McKenzie, you young bugger! It seems years since I saw you. I heard you were in Glasgow and you never even came to see me. I could have shown you the town!'

Lewis's face reddened and he groaned, 'Oh, no.'

The crowd were staring at him. Murdy spat at the ground and murmured in an aside to his wife, 'Stayin' wi' Andrew indeed! The young stallion must have had a fine time to himself wi' that Rachel! Stayin' wi' her more like!'

Lewis clenched his fists. 'You can't get away with *anything* in a place like this. They all want to know your business, and by God! They make it their business to find out where you've been, what you've been doing! Christ Almighty!' he exploded. 'You can't even fart in this place but they all hear the bloody explosion!'

Despite himself, Lorn sniggered, and Lewis looked at him and laughed also, especially when a peacefully grazing cow lifted its head at his cries of protest and, as if on cue, lifted its tail and released a might ripple of wind.

'God! Did you hear that!' Murdy bellowed. 'It minded me of old Shelagh farting in kirk when the minister was bawling out thon awful sermons in our lugs!'

Lorn clapped his hand over his mouth and both boys erupted into laughter. 'I tell you what,' Lorn said, throwing an arm over his brother's shoulders, 'let's go back and get the horses out. A good ride over the sands might help us to get things into perspective. We're a miserable pair of buggers at the moment, and are making Father and Mother the same . . .'

They arrived back at Laigmhor with rosy cheeks and were in time to see Erchy whistling up the cobbled yard to the kitchen door. He popped his head round. 'Telegram. I'm thinkin' I will be waiting for an answer and watch your faces while I have a cuppy.'

Kirsteen had turned slightly pale. Telegrams weren't always the harbingers of good tidings. 'Is – is it happy news, Erchy?'

Erchy grinned and spooned generous amounts of sugar into his tea. 'Good, I'm thinkin'. Ay, damty good right enough.'

Kirsteen tore open the envelope. The words leapt out at her: 'Got married last week. Home in a few days. Grant.' She gasped and slowly read the news aloud.

'Where did it come from?' Fergus asked as the colour mounted in Kirsteen's face.

'Here, take it,' she said faintly and handed over the scrap of paper with shaking fingers.

'Country of origin, Kingston, Jamaica,' Fergus said. 'Well, bugger me! He's done it at last!'

Erchy slapped his knee and beamed widely. 'Ay, he was aye a one for surprises was young Grant.' His smile widened. 'It might be there's more to come – maybe he married one o' they native girls wi' the belly buttons he's always sendin' to auld Dodie.'

Lorn and Lewis came in to hear the tail end of this, and the latter picked up the telegram, his eyes crinkling, while Erchy indulged in further fancies. Everyone stared at him blankly for a few moments before they erupted into gales of laughter. Then Kirsteen went rushing over to Slochmhor with the news.

Phebie wiped floury hands on her apron and hugged Kirsteen delightedly.

'Does he say exactly when he'll be home?' Lachlan asked with a smile.

'No! That's just it!' wailed Kirsteen. 'It's obvious he's taking leave and flying back from Jamaica with his new wife. Och, I could kill him that I could! We must have a ceilidh and the house is a boorach! The only double bed in the house is in our room – we'll have to give them that. Fergus and me will just have to move another bed into Grant's old room because

Shona and Niall will want to come home for the reception – unless of course you put them up here. I hope she won't be one of those very sophisticated types . . . Erchy thinks she might be a West Indian girl, and knowing Grant I wouldn't put it past him! Oh, they're beautiful girls and I'm not in the least prejudiced, but can you imagine what the cailleachs will say! I've got absolutely nothing to wear either – nothing that's suitable that is. I wonder if it should be a formal gathering – oh, I wish I knew what she was like . . .' She paused.

Phebie had fallen into Lachlan's arms. The pair of them were helpless with laughter. 'You should hear yourself, mo ghaoil,' Lachlan gasped. 'You sound like an old gramophone record with the needle stuck!'

Phebie wiped her eyes. 'I tell you this – if that besom Fiona ever decides to get married I'll no' be working myself into a state over some laddie I've never met – ay – even supposing he was the future king of Britain and ate herring with a gold fork! Now, you calm yourself this minute. Am I not here to help you get the house in order? By the time we're finished it will be fit for a princess, and we might no' consider her good enough to set foot over the doorstep.'

Lachlan's mask of jollity fell as he watched Kirsteen going down the path. Only that morning he had received Lewis's reports from the hospital – to the effect that the boy had a deep-seated brain tumour, which was inoperable. He had sat, white-faced, staring at the words, unable to believe the evidence of his eyes. He was so shocked that Phebie, coming into the surgery, had glanced at the papers on his desk and gone quickly to get him some whisky. He had buried his face into her soft breasts and whispered helplessly, 'How am I going to tell him, Phebie? How? How?'

She had cradled him gently, her heart brimful of love for this dear husband of hers on whose shoulders so many burdens had been heaped over the years. 'I know how you must feel,' she had murmured. 'Dear God! I can't believe it myself! It might be better if he didn't know – if you just told Kirsteen and Fergus.'

'No, no.' He shook his head as if to clear it. 'He made me promise not to mention anything. As far as everyone knew he was away in Glasgow for a jaunt. He'll have to be told, Phebie, but he won't want a fuss. I've a feeling he'll make me promise not to tell another soul. He's funny about illness; even as a wee lad he hated to be near sickness. I mind once he turned and ran from the room when Lorn had a bad turn. No, he'll carry this alone; it will be easier for him than sharing it with those whose faces will remind him of it every waking day. I – I'll tell him in the morning.'

She put her hands on his shoulders. 'God be with you, Lachy; yours has been a difficult role but you've never shirked any of it.'

He took her in his arms and kissed her. 'Only because you have stood by my side all these years.

I wouldn't have got by without you – and now you're going to be called upon to be very strong indeed, mo ghaoil. If Lewis reacts the way I think he will, you will be called upon to put on the greatest act of your life for the benefit of the McKenzies.'

Next morning Lachlan walked over the fields of Laigmhor. The frosty air was fragrant with the scent of newly turned earth. Lewis was driving the tractor that pulled the plough. He was alone as Lachlan had guessed he might be.

At sight of the doctor walking along by the edge of the field Lewis's blue eyes darkened. Something was wrong. Lachlan wouldn't have come up here to talk to him if everything had been all right. Lewis shivered as the cold hand of fear clawed into his stomach. He jumped down from the tractor, and as he went to meet Lachlan he recalled his horrible time in hospital: the hellish apprehension; the bewilderment of never knowing what was going to happen next, bewilderment that turned to fear as days stretched into weeks and no one would tell him why he was being kept in, just the rather distant smiles and the stock phrases: 'Patience, young man, these things take time,' or: 'Won't be long now, lad, just another day or two.' Once Lewis had cried out, 'What things? What takes time? I want to know! It's *my* bloody head!'

Which outburst had sent ripples of shock through the hospital staff, who treated Lewis rather coldly for the remainder of his stay.

How different was Lachlan with his warmth, his

humanity – how different was a man who walked over the soil to personally talk to a boy who was so apprehensive his voice shook as he said, 'You've got the results of the tests, Lachlan, and if they had been good you would have had no call to come here and tell me.'

Lachlan's face was drawn, his brown eyes full of a terrible despair as he looked straight into the boy's eyes. 'Ay, you're right, Lewis, the news isn't good. I had a mind to tell your mother and father first – but I didn't think you'd want that.'

Lewis sank onto the bank. He shook his head and stared at his hands. 'No, whatever it is they mustny find out – tell me, Lachlan, and tell me quickly.'

When Lachlan's soft pleasant voice finally halted there was silence. Then Lewis burst into tears that rasped harshly in his throat, and shook his head from side to side in an agony of disbelief before he buried his face in his hands. Lachlan gathered him into his arms, saying nothing, letting the tears flow. When the boy was finally quiet Lachlan said firmly, 'We're going to fight this thing, Lewis. I'll arrange for you to have treatment . . .'

'No, no, Lachlan,' Lewis said, drawing away, his eyes full of a desperate pleading. 'I don't want to go through months of hell lying in some hospital only to die anyway. I hate hospital – being surrounded by sick people. Just leave things be. All I ask is that you won't say a word to anybody – promise – not one word – please.'

Lachlan drew in his breath. 'Ay, if that's what you want, Lewis.'

'It's what I want – by the way – I almost forgot to ask – how long?'

'Six months – a year perhaps – with treatment it could –'

'Lachlan – will you – could you go now? I want very much to be alone for a while.'

Lachlan got up and began to walk over the tracts of rich brown earth, his steps heavy.

'Lachlan.'

Lachlan spun round. 'Ay, son?'

'You won't let me suffer – will you?'

'No, I won't let you suffer, Lewis, I'll do everything in my power to help you.' He walked quickly away, aware of nothing but the pain of unshed tears and the sight of a young boy sitting alone in the fields knowing that soon he was going to die.

Lewis was thankful for the diversion that Grant's news had brought. He was able to be quiet without anyone noticing or asking questions. For the next few days Laigmhor was such a hive of activity that Fergus groaned at the disruption of normal routine, and old Bob grew so disgusted at being told continually to wipe his feet and watch where he put his pipe ash that he took a huff and stamped off to the peaceful disorder of his own little cottage. The news had soon spread and old Joe, who had just celebrated his 100th birthday, and who had received a telegram from the Queen to mark the occasion, shook his snowy head and chortled. To him Grant was still a boy, not long removed from golden childhood days when he had spent fascinating hours in the old sailor's company, listening to his tales of the sea. 'Fancy, that lad married,' he murmured, 'I wouldny be surprised if he brings back a beautiful mermaid . . .' His sea-green eyes were faraway. 'Did I ever tell you about the one I saw sitting on the rocks near Mingulay?' he said, and the small boy to whom he addressed the question shook his head and listened avidly to the unfolding of a tale that had been told to numerous children before him.

Some days later the McKenzies walked with the McLachlans down to the harbour to await the boat. The whole of Portcull had somehow contrived to be there too, and as the steamer pushed into the pier, everyday tasks were abandoned and all eyes were focused on the gangplank.

'She'll maybe be wearin' one o' they grass skirt things,' Tam said, 'though she'll no' be wearin' it long in this wind.'

His cronies chuckled with delight, but Ranald scratched his head with his paint brush and said in disgust, 'Ach, you're thinkin' o' the lassies from they South Sea Islands. The Jamaicans wear clothes the same as you and me.'

'Hairy jerseys and trousers?' Todd said. 'Ach no, young Grant was aye a one for legs. This lassie will no' be wearin' the trowser – mark my words.'

Shona and Niall came running down the gangplank with Ellie, now a tall leggy twelve-year-old, leading the way. She rushed at Fergus and he cuddled her to him and put out his arm to take Shona to him as well. 'It's nice to see familiar faces,' he said rather nervously. 'Go and buck Kirsteen up, will you? She's badly needing some female support.'

Shona's eyes twinkled. 'Och, Father, there's absolutely nothing to worry about, I can assure you . . .'

Kirsteen darted over, her fair skin stained with crimson. 'They're coming,' she gulped, 'I can see Grant . . . Oh, God. I hope she'll like her in-laws . . .' Her eyes widened. 'I'm a mother-in-law – I never thought of that . . .'

A black curly head bobbed among the crowd, next to it was a sleek brown one, and Fergus mouthed to Kirsteen, 'Hold on tight, darling, we're about to meet our new daughter-in-law.'

A gasp went up as Grant came into full view. Hanging on his arm was Fiona, tall and elegant in a smart, well-cut blue jacket, red polo neck jumper, and immaculate navy-blue trousers. Her glowing face was a deep golden brown and for a moment everyone wondered if she was a native lass dressed in the trowser, or that wittrock Fiona McLachlan flaunting the laws o' decency.

'Fiona.' Phebie was so surprised she could hardly say the name.

A smile curved Lachlan's mouth. 'It would just be like the thing if –' Fiona threw herself at him, smothering the rest of the sentence. Kirsteen was caught up in the embrace of her eldest son.

'Your wife,' she gasped. 'Where is she?'

Grant extricated Fiona from her father's arms and drew her forward.

'Right here. Meet Mrs McKenzie.'

'But – you two loathe the sight of each other!' Phebie cried, her round face both delighted and bewildered.

'Ach, we were just bairns then,' Fiona said, laughing. 'We had to travel halfway round the world before we discovered it was love. I was in the Caribbean studying its marine life when who should pop up but Dimples McKenzie.'

Grant hugged her to him and kissed her fringe of shining hair. 'The moment I saw my wee Robin again I realised why I'd never married any of the beautiful girls who had queued up for years . . .' He looked around at the rugged slopes of Sgurr nan Ruadh etched against the sky. 'One day we might build a love nest here and hatch out a whole clutch of wee robins with dimples. Now let's go, before Behag chokes on all those flies she's catching!'

Later that evening, when all the gossip was exhausted, Grant found himself alone with the twins and he ruffled Lorn's curls affectionately. 'To think I used to carry you on my shoulders,' he teased. 'If yours grow any wider you'll be carrying me.'

'Me too,' Lewis said, flopping rather wearily onto a chair. Grant looked at him, surprised anew at the change in this once dashing brother of his. 'You've grown thinner, Lewis my lad,' he observed with a frown. 'I've been hearing about this affair between you and Rachel. Don't let it get you down so badly. It might just be infatuation . . .'

Lewis jumped up, a dark flush spreading over his face. 'I might have known the gossips would be at it! I thought *you* at least would have had more sense not to believe all you hear.' He banged out of the room and Lorn spread his hands ruefully. 'You've touched on a sore spot. He's not long back from Glasgow but won't say what happened between him and Rachel. He's like a bear with a sore head.'

'Och well, he'll get over it, he's just growing up. Come on – upstairs, I've got presents for the pair of you. They might cheer you up.'

The next morning Dodie almost fell on his back when Erchy arrived at his door bearing an invitation to the reception that was to be held at Laigmhor that evening. 'My, my,' Dodie said, his voice husky as his big fingers caressed the silver-gilt edging on the card. 'I have never had the likes in my life.'

'Well see you have a bath and wear your best bib and tucker,' Erchy instructed severely.

'I will do no such thing,' Dodie intoned primly. 'I'll be wearin' a suit, my very best, bibs is only for babies.'

Dodie was thrilled. He loved and respected all the McKenzies, but none more so than Grant, who had been the means of bringing a few riches to his life. Many of his ambitions had been fulfilled. Ealasaid had had a roomy byre built for her; the interior of the cottage was gay with bright wallpaper and paint;

964

at the head of Biddy's grave sat a very unusual stone straight from the Rhanna shores, and inscribed on it in Gaelic were the words, 'Fàilte don Nèamh, Dodie', which, when translated, meant 'Welcome to Heaven'.

'What way are you puttin' that!' Tam had scoffed when first he saw it. 'It's the Lord will welcome her to heaven. You canny very well welcome her to yonder place from down here. You're daft, man!'

'Ach, it's you who's daft,' Dodie returned with asperity. 'Biddy knows fine what I mean, an' that's more than can be said for the likes o' you. I'm no' up there to welcome her so I can best do it from down here. Anyways, Biddy aye said heaven was all around us, so if she's as much down here as she is up there she will be havin' two heavens to keep her going.'

The reception relaxed the atmosphere at Laigmhor. The young couple radiated so much happiness everyone was touched by it, even the twins forgetting themselves in the festivities that went on for several nights. Because Grant had reached the status of Second Mate at this stage in his career, it meant that he could take his wife with him on his voyages, though Fiona had some very decided plans of her own for the future. But it was enough that at the moment they could be together, and they were both glowing with happiness as they stood at the rails of the boat waving farewell to the crowd on the pier. Lewis had taken his big brother aside at the last moment to apologise for his sullen behaviour.

'Ach, think nothing of it,' Grant had said. 'Girls do that to people; Fiona did it to me plenty.'

'When will you be back?'

'Hard to say, a few months anyway. Maybe longer.'

Lewis had taken his hand then and had squeezed it very hard. 'Goodbye then, I hope you'll both be very very happy.'

His voice had been very husky and Grant had looked at him keenly. 'Hey, c'mon now – things will come all right in the end, they always do.'

Lewis had nodded. 'Ay,' was all he had said before turning on his heel and walking quickly away.

Rachel came home briefly at Easter. Lewis arranged to meet her at the harbour, and together they walked along the rocky finger of Port Rum Point. She was different; he sensed it immediately. And she didn't look at him. She was barefooted, and as they walked she stopped every so often to curl her toes into the wet sands. He was reminded of the gypsy-like Rachel of childhood, running barefoot over moor and shore, her long brown legs carrying her swiftly to favourite haunts. Lewis found himself pining for those days again, all the carefree days of early youth when the whole world was his, when he had moulded life to suit his whims. Now he could command nothing – nothing. It was over between them, he knew even before she turned at the head of the Point to look at him. She gazed for a long time at this tall handsome young McKenzie, and her heart died a little inside her. She knew him so well – his strengths, his weaknesses. She would always love him, but there was no place in her life for passionate young men; she had to have stability and she would never find that in him.

He took her hands and murmured, 'Rachel, I've waited so long.'

His blue eyes were so miserable, she drew in her breath. This wasn't Lewis McKenzie, laughing, carefree Lewis who had chased girls since he was in short trousers . . .

'I've missed you so,' he went on huskily. 'You mean the world to me – no, don't move away from me, look at me . . .' She put a finger to his lips and stepped back, and he knew then what it was he had seen in Rachel a long long time ago: a strength of will that bordered on ruthlessness. She had always known where she was going, and would allow nobody to stand in the way of her ambitions – she could – and she would – turn her back on love, the kind of love that might hinder her chances of a brilliant career.

She turned her head to look back along the rocky shoreline. He followed her gaze and saw a figure sitting some distance away gazing thoughtfully into the water. 'Jon,' he said softly. 'It's him, isn't it? You're going to marry Jon?' She kept her face averted as she nodded her head. 'But he's old enough to be your father!' he cried so vehemently that Jon raised his head. Lewis paused and stared at her. 'That's what you want, isn't it? What you've always wanted since

Dokie Joe died on the *Magpie.*' Rachel turned her restless gaze towards the great glistening needles of the Sgor Creags. Her throat constricted and she nodded. He bunched his fists. 'What about me, Rachel? I need you, just now I need you very much.'

She looked at him steadily; his body was tight with hurt . . . Yet she saw no anger in him. Somewhere at the back of her mind she thought that rather odd. He was so easily moved to laughter, passion, anger – now there was none and she felt uneasy.

His shoulders sagged suddenly. 'Let me kiss you – one more time.'

His voice was soft, gentle, and she knew if she succumbed to his request she might never have the will to walk away from him. Briefly she touched his arm, and he made to take her hand, but she evaded him and began to run, back along the length of the Point – to Jon, who stood up at her approach and held out his arms.

Jon had seen that her eyes were too bright. She stopped a short distance from him and, leaning against a rock, closed her eyes so that he couldn't see what was in them. His thin arms enclosed her, protective and safe – so safe, she knew she would always find comfort in the gentle haven of his arms. She didn't want to look back at that strong young figure standing alone at the tip of Port Rum Point, but something made her want to look and look – for ever. To remember the wild, fiery passion of youthful love, the bittersweet ecstasy of living through a time she had always known could not last.

She would never know again such untamed joy, such burning, consuming desire – such laughter. Her memories of Lewis would be wonderful, yet always they would be tinged with poignancy. Somewhere, sometime, she would look back on her exquisite experiences with him – and she would cry. Love with Jon would be gentle and good; she would never betray him for other men – she had had her times of carefree love. Jon had understood that, and he had waited – so patiently and devotedly he had waited.

Rachel turned her back on Lewis and looked up at Jon, at his dear honest face; at the steady brown eyes; at the little beard flecked with grey. She had grown to love him dearly, he had taught her so much, and they shared so much. A sob caught in her throat. She took Jon's hand and made him run till they got to the harbour. She didn't look back again . . .

Anton and Babbie were thrilled at the news. With the exception of her mother, Rachel hadn't let Jon tell anybody else till she had first broken it to Lewis. Anton came in from the fields, his blue eyes glowing in his face at sight of Jon with his arm round Rachel's slender waist. 'I knew things would work out for you,' he laughed. 'My Babbie sometimes laughs at my philosophies, but I am quite often correct. We must celebrate . . .' He went to a cupboard and withdrew a bottle of whisky, which he held up to the light. 'You see, I now have the customs of the islands – we will drink a dram together.' He drew Babbie to him and kissed her red curls. 'If you find happiness like ours you will be rich indeed. Is that not so, liebling?'

'Ay, indeed, it is so,' Babbie agreed softly, her fingers curling over his hand. Whenever she saw him stripped to the waist like this, the mark of his scar standing out from the surrounding tanned skin, she was minded afresh of the day she had first seen him lying deathly pale on the scrubbed white table at Slochmhor, and, as always, her love for him flooded her heart and she wanted to take his fair head in her hands and kiss it where the sun had bleached it almost white.

She looked at the tall stunning girl by Jon's side, wondering if such a beauty would be faithful to a man so many years her senior. Rachel lacked speech, but with her kind of looks, that would never be such a great obstacle. Men would ogle her wherever she went: she exuded a magnetism that was definitely sexual; she was a very physical sort of girl – yet there was also about her an aura that was spiritual, a rare sensitive depth in her great burning eyes . . . Babbie went to fetch the glasses and she saw Rachel's hand go up to reverently touch Jon's little beard, her long fingers staying there for a moment before they moved up to trace the outline of his mouth. Babbie smiled to herself. It was going to be all right for Jon. Rachel would love him, and love him well – she would, in time, forget Lewis McKenzie.

As the toasts were being made, Jon drew Rachel's head towards his lips and kissed the raven curls. 'I feel I must be the luckiest man in the whole world.

I have here the perfect girl. With her there will be peace; I will hear only music – no nagging – no scolding. My poor little Papa was deafened by Mamma's voice booming in his ears telling him all the things he should and shouldn't do.'

Babbie smiled impishly. 'Rachel might not be able to nag you, but she could turn instead to hitting you – what will you do then, Jon Jodl?'

'I will have no option but to turn the tables and start nagging till she doesn't hit me any more.'

Everyone laughed, the glasses chinked. Rachel held onto Jon's hand and looked forward to the excitement of going to Germany to meet his mother. They were leaving on the morning boat. If she won the travelling scholarship she was working for, there would be a lot of excitement ahead. But all that was in the future, and at the moment she and Jon would take one step at a time . . . For a minute her mind strayed to Lewis, the rapture, the laughter – an indefinable sadness made her shiver . . . She gave herself a little shake and forced herself away from the past. She must look forward to a future filled with music, with the tender, undemanding love of Jon, the man who would never hinder her, but who would help her in all the years of their lives together.

Chapter Eighteen

Lewis walked slowly up to the headland of Burg. It was June, the mist of rain that swept over the cliffs was soft and warm. The clouds were breaking apart to reveal patches of cornflower-blue sky; a ray of sun spilled over a fat fluffy cloud and beat warmly on the green springy turf of the headland. He had recently returned from a two-week stay at the Travers'. Since Rachel's going he hadn't been able to settle to anything. Fergus had been patient but now it was beginning to wear thin. 'You'll earn your keep around here, my lad,' he had warned that morning. 'You can't go gallivanting off when it comes up your hump!'

Lewis dug his hands into his pockets and stared moodily down to the wide curve of Burg Bay, which lay north of the rock-strewn shores of Port Rum Point. He made his way down a rutted sheep track, kicking stones as he went, feeling a sensation of giddiness washing over him as he paused to gaze down at the rock pools far below. 'Lewis, you'll have to eat more.' His mother's familiar plea rang in his ears. 'If you keep on pining like this you'll make yourself ill. Do you think Rachel is pining for you? You must forget, Lewis, you must.'

He couldn't eat, he couldn't do any of the things that had once made his life so sweet. Even Lorn couldn't reach him these days – yet, they were so close, they always would be. On the evening of his return from the Travers' they had raced to the big barn to measure themselves on the growing posts. Lorn had only an inch to go now before he caught up . . . They had laughed; it had been like old times; yet he knew Lorn's jollity was forced, that his mind was on Ruth. He had changed: he had started going out more, to ceilidhs, with girls; his shell of shyness appeared at last to have cracked. It was as if they had reversed roles, and he was as Lorn had once been – intense, introverted, thoughtful. Lorn was doing all the things Lewis had once loved – yet Lewis felt it wasn't real somehow, that Lorn was forcing himself, rebelling against the image of his true self – trying to forget . . . Now Lorn, too, had gone away. He seldom left the island but just three days ago he had gone away on the steamer to spend a holiday with Shona and Niall on the Mull of Kintyre.

Lewis reached the beach and saw a movement on the rocks near the water, the glint of a golden head . . . Ruth sat hugging her knees, lost in thought. She heard nothing till Lewis was just a few yards away, then she started and lifted her head. At first she thought the tall boy with the thin haunted face was Lorn, and her heart began to race. She had seen this same boy last night. She had looked from her window and had spotted him walking along the harbour with Eve Patterson. They had been talking with their heads close together and she had drawn her head back behind the curtains, pain and hurt catching at her throat. He had forgotten her so easily – so very very easily. She had been gone for just over five months, yet for all he cared she might never have returned. She couldn't forget that evening on the moors, the sweet nearness of him, the innocent tenderness of that first beautiful kiss . . .

She started to her feet. 'Lorn.' The name was a mere breath on her lips – but then she saw it wasn't Lorn, it was Lewis – a vastly changed Lewis from the boy she remembered. His blue eyes were pain-racked; the hollows in his cheeks belonged to someone who was ill . . . Could love do that to a boy like Lewis? Break a heart that once had brimmed over with the love of life? . . . Yes! Yes! Love could do that to anyone – anyone. Her father had only come back from Coll because she had been so unhappy there; she had wanted to come back to Rhanna to be near Lorn.

Lewis came over and stood looking down at her for a long time before he said quietly, 'It's nice to see you back, Ruth. You look thin though, your holiday over on Coll doesn't seem to have done you much good.'

'No – I – I wanted to come back.'

'Lorn isn't here. He went away to Kintyre a few days back.'

'Oh!' she stammered out. So it hadn't been Lorn she had seen last night; it had been Lewis. She felt relief even as sadness drowned her. She had come back to see Lorn and he wasn't here. She couldn't bring herself to ask how long he would be gone, and there was silence. The sea bubbled to the shore, lapping the sands, swaying the fronds of seaweed back and forth.

Lewis sat down on a rock and picked up a shell, turning it over in his fingers. 'You shouldn't spend so much time alone, Ruth.'

'You were coming down here to be alone,' she pointed out.

'Ay, ay, you're right, I was.'

'Did you hear my father has bought a boat? He's giving up the shop and going to start lobster fishing. I'll be able to spend a lot of time with him in the evenings.'

'He did it for you, mo ghaoil.'

'And for health reasons too –' Her voice faltered and her eyes grew dark. 'Ach, you're right, he did it for me, but I think he'll be glad to get away from the shop. When the summer is over I might take over the shop myself – I like to keep busy.'

'To stop yourself thinking about Lorn?'

She flushed and bit her lip. 'Ay, that's right, Lewis.' She gazed at him steadily. 'You've changed, Lewis; you never used to take the time to analyse people – Lorn was the one who did that.'

He stared at the shell, a terrible dejection stooping his shoulders. 'Things change, Ruth,' he said at last, wearily. 'Folk change – circumstances, I suppose.' He got up and held out his hand. 'Will you walk with me, Ruth?'

She hesitated but only fractionally. She placed her hand in his. The strong brown fingers curled over hers. It felt rather strange to be walking over the beach with Lewis McKenzie, but it was oddly comforting to be with someone who understood how she was feeling.

After that day they met regularly. Often they walked to the wide sweeping sands of Aosdana Bay, the setting for so many of her father's tales. She recounted the days of her childhood to Lewis, telling him of the magical hours spent with her father. Quietly he listened to her musical voice talking about the legends of the Hebrides, and peace stole into his heart. Once he was at the bay before her. He was standing by the water's edge gazing far out to sea. He looked very lonely, and her heart went out to him. She went further up the shore to sit on the creels that lay piled against a sturdy stone boatshed. It belonged to an eccentric old man known as Hector the Boat. Every waking day of his life was spent either pottering with boats in the shed or fishing for lobsters out on the Sound. He was mending his pots and he peered at Ruth from lowered brows, smiling his one-toothed beguiling smile, his eyes crinkling in his rosy face. 'Will you be havin' a clappy doo wi' me, lassie?' he asked, indicating a driftwood fire on which sat a can filled to the brim with large mussels. Hector liked his mussels fresh from the shore, edging the shells apart with his tobacco knife and scooping out the contents, which he slithered down his throat with great enjoyment.

'No, thank you, Hector,' Ruth said and smiled. 'But – would you let Lewis and me have one of your boats for a whily? We'll collect some nice big clappy doos for you when the tide goes out.'

Hector acceded readily and Ruth ran to Lewis. Without a word she led him over to a small rowing boat tied up in a sheltered part of the bay. Together they pushed off and very soon they were bobbing peacefully in the translucent green water of Aosdana Bay. It was very calm and Lewis stopped rowing and let the boat drift gently on the wavelets.

'Talk to me.' Ruth's voice was low. 'Get it all out of your heart – it might help.'

She was surprised to see the glint of tears in the blue eyes of Lewis McKenzie. 'Could I, Ruth?' he asked huskily. 'Could I tell you everything? I have to tell someone or I think I might go mad.'

'I'll listen, Lewis, I'm a very good listener.'

Once he had opened up his heart it seemed as if he would never stop. There, out on the calm clear waters of Aosdana Bay he unburdened his mind and heart of things that had troubled it for a very long time. Ruth felt some of his pain washing into her. As the sea sighs over the sands and leaves behind that which it doesn't want, so Lewis left with her the unfettered debris of his mind. The lilting voice that was so like Lorn's flowed through her soul, and something of the terrible despair that was in him was left behind in her, and she knew it would never entirely leave her. When finally he stopped talking and there was only the sigh of the sea and the hush of the breeze, she buried her head in her arms and cried as if her heart would break. He stared at her bowed head. Her hair was like the sun, so bright it dazzled his eyes. Putting out a finger he gently stroked the silken strands and murmured, 'Sweet Ruth! And could you go with me? My helpmate in the woods to be . . .'

She raised her head to gaze at him wonderingly. 'But that's . . .'

He nodded. 'Wordsworth, the very mannie. It's Lorn's book but lately I've taken to reading a lot of things I never looked at before. That verse was meant for you, but the whole poem is more like Rachel – and myself really.'

'A slighted child, at her own will, went wandering over dale and hill, In thoughtless freedom bold,' Ruth quoted.

'Ay, that is very like Rachel. She always needed freedom, she would die without it.'

The boat rocked as he came closer. She gazed into his eyes – so blue, like Lorn's. Lorn and Lewis, they were so alike, they were of the same mould. She closed her eyes and felt the warm lips of Lewis McKenzie on hers. It was a fleeting kiss, very tender and gentle. 'You're a very sweet girl, Ruth, so very sweet.' The next kiss was longer, more demanding. She allowed herself to melt into his arms. A dew of tears lay on her lashes; she felt weak with love – for Lorn – weak with sadness – for Lewis. The two emotions mixed and merged and in the end she didn't know if she was crying for two boys who looked the same, who laughed and talked the same – or if she was crying for herself, for her own heartache.

The days of June slipped past. Every morning and evening Ruth went with her father to the lobster pots and almost every afternoon she met Lewis by Aosdana Bay. Morag Ruadh saw little of her daughter that summer of her nineteenth year, but she didn't worry unduly. Very often Dugald went out in the morning and stayed away all day, and Morag imagined that Ruth was with him. She didn't question him on the matter, and for the first time in her life Ruth knew unbounded freedom.

Fergus and Kirsteen didn't mind Lewis going off in the afternoons because he made up for it working hard around the farm morning and evening. He seemed to be happier; he had stopped snapping and going off in the huff, and Fergus said with a fervent sigh, 'Thank the Lord! We might get a bit of peace about the place now.'

'Ay, we might,' agreed Kirsteen, though inwardly she sighed. Rumours were beginning to circulate about Ruth and Lewis, and she dreaded to think what would happen when Lorn came home and found the gossip to be true.

On a hot day in midsummer Lewis met Ruth at Aosdana Bay. It was deserted. Hector the Boat was off fishing, and Ruth was very conscious of the solitude. With Hector around her meetings with Lewis seemed innocent and safe. He was wearing a blue shirt that day, a blue that matched his eyes, his earth-brown curls glinted chestnut in the sun – so like Lorn's. He was standing very close and she could see the pulse beating in his neck – the pulse of his life. Something tugged at her throat. He caught her and kissed her hair. It was warm and smelled of sunshine.

'Ruth, you're so sweet,' he whispered. 'I want to say so much to you. These last weeks I don't know how I would have lived without you – oh Ruth – mo ghaoil –' His lips came down on hers. He buried his face in her neck and nuzzled her ears. She felt the world turning upside down – if only this was Lorn . . . if only she didn't feel such sadness . : .

'Ruth,' his voice came again, slightly breathless in her ear. 'Let me love you, please please my darling little girl, I love you –' He put a finger over her lips. 'It's true, Ruth, I've never said that to any girl before – not even Rachel. I thought what I felt for her was love – now I know it was infatuation. I love you, Ruth, I really love you.'

'*No!*' She broke away from him and put her hands over her eyes to shut out the sight of his handsome young face – so young . . . She couldn't let pity for him engulf her . . . Even as she tortured herself, even as conflicting emotions whirled in her mind, she felt Lewis's arm around her waist leading her to Hector's boathouse. She stumbled, but Lewis held her tighter.

The shed was cool after the heat. It smelled of peat smoke and tar; cobwebs patterned the window panes; the sound of the sea ebbed and grew; ebbed and grew. Abruptly Lewis pulled her to him and kissed her throat, her eyes, her hot cheeks. She couldn't respond to him – she wouldn't. It wasn't right! It wasn't, it wasn't . . . His lips were warm, firm yet gentle, but she sensed his mounting passion. She didn't know how to kiss back – she didn't want to . . . His tongue met hers and something rose up inside her, commanding her tongue to meet and merge, meet and merge with his . . .

In a panic she pulled herself out of his arms. 'Please, I'll have to go,' she whispered. 'Don't – you mustn't make me feel I have to do this! It isn't fair, Lewis! You know it isn't fair!'

He was removing his shirt, pressing his naked body to hers. 'Weesht, weesht,' he soothed. 'Relax my dear little Ruth, relax . . .'

Her breasts tingled suddenly. He was touching her, doing things to her body that made her draw in her breath . . . Why, why was she caught up like this – caught between Lorn and Lewis? 'Lorn.' She murmured the name but Lewis was beyond hearing anything. He was fumbling with the buttons of her white dress, moving it down over her shoulders, pulling the sleeves down over her arms. Her throat grew tight. She tried to pull away from him but he was all at once strong yet gentle. With one hand he kept a tight grip of her arm; with the other he held up the dress to look at it almost reverently. It dazzled white in the sun streaming through the grubby windows.

'Pure, so pure,' he murmured beneath his breath before he tossed the garment onto a chair where it lay in crumpled folds. He turned his blue gaze on her; it was dazed, faraway. She was afraid now, her fear clawing inside her belly like a living thing, and with a sob she struggled in his embrace but his hands were grasping her shoulders, forcing her back – back . . .

'Ruth.' Her name on his lips was beautiful. 'You must give me this. I have no one now but you – only you.'

Her mind went numb. She had no recollection of him pushing her down onto the narrow bunk . . . She thought of her calliper – how ugly – how ugly – he mustn't be allowed to see . . .

Her breasts were in his hands, the skin of them milky white, the nipples like small pink rosebuds – so pure – so young. He bent his head to kiss them; a dew of sweat gleamed on his brow . . .

Briefly she saw sun, slanting, spilling its rays over his bronzed naked shoulders – and then there was no light, only his lips on hers, his body moving, his shoulders rippling beneath her fingers, his long lean legs pushing hers apart . . .

Pain ripped through her. She cried out once, then forgot the pain. He was murmuring her name over and over, stroking her hair, gently, so gently carrying her into oblivion. As the song of the sea swells and surges so she was swept along on waves of wanting – needing . . .

She forgot where she was, who she was with. This was Lorn loving her, wanting her – taking her . . . The sea rang in her ears, her heart pounded; once more she said the name: 'Lorn.'

She opened her eyes and saw not Lorn but Lewis, awash with passion, taking her – taking away her virginity . . . She clenched her fist against her mouth to stop from screaming out – his body was so tense the muscles were standing out. He quivered and cried out, then he fell against her, still saying her name, stroking her hair, kissing her lips . . . and she felt nothing – nothing except shame, and guilt so deep and raw it was like a knife turning inside her. Her hands fell away from his shoulders, her eyes were the colour of night, black with hatred of herself and what she had done. Crimson flooded her cheeks, her fingers clutched the blankets. Turning her golden head away from him she felt the tears falling slowly over her cheeks.

'I don't love you,' she sobbed. 'I hate myself. How can I ever face Lorn again? Everything is finished . . . finished – Now there is nothing . . .'

'No, don't say that, Ruth!' he cried then in a voice so low she barely heard it. 'Please, please don't say that. I couldn't bear it if you left me now.'

But she wasn't listening, all she could say over and over was, 'I hate myself, I hate myself, and Lorn will hate me too.'

He lay down beside her and took her in his arms. She didn't resist but lay passively against him while he soothed her as if she was a little girl. Eventually, when she had stopped crying and just lay staring unseeingly towards the window he said urgently, 'Promise you'll see me again, Ruth. You're the only one in the whole wide world who can help me. Don't let me face my future alone. Promise me; promise, Ruth.'

'I promise,' she said dully. Suddenly he was angry and he shook her slightly, as if trying to force her out of the torpor into which she had sunk. 'Ruth, look at me! Don't hate me! I couldn't bear it if I thought you hated me!'

She brought her eyes from the window and gazed into his tormented face. Her hand came up and she stroked the damp brown hair from his brow. 'I don't hate you, Lewis, I've never hated you. I like you – very, very much – and – I won't leave you.'

Lorn returned with Shona, Niall and Ellie at the end of July. Shona was so highly excited about something she could hardly wait till she got inside the doors of Laigmhor before she burst out, 'We're coming home, Father. Next spring! We've got enough capital saved to take a gamble. We'll buy a motor launch and Niall can go hopping about the islands. Ellie will be at school in Oban by then, so I'll have plenty of spare time on my hands. I thought maybe I could help Babbie out. She could be doing with it, so she could. While we're here this summer we'll start looking for a house . . .'

'You don't have to look very far!' Fergus's deep voice was full of joy. 'Biddy's cottage is still free. It will do you till you find something more suitable. Shona, mo ghaoil –' His voice had grown husky. 'To think it's nineteen years since you left Rhanna! And now you're coming back. I canny believe it – you'll have to give me some time to take it in. My mind is a bit fuddled these days – old age creeping in.'

Everyone laughed and began talking at once. Lorn grabbed Lewis's arm, and together they walked across the cobbled yard to the big barn. Lorn was tall and broad, his face had filled out considerably, and there was hardly any need for them to go to the growing posts to find out that the difference between them was barely half an inch.

'Hell!' Lorn was delighted. 'I'm six feet one and a half inches! Me! Skinny wee Lorn McKenzie!' He threw himself down on a bundle of hay and looked up at the cobwebby roof. 'It's grand to be back! I didn't want to stay away so long, but Niall was so busy I began going with him on his rounds and was able to help him quite a bit – especially with the cows and horses. When he and Shona come back here to stay I might get to go with Niall now and again. Father won't miss me, he'll have you; he always trusted you more than me to do all the heavy stuff . . .' He sat up, his blue eyes brilliant. 'I did a lot of thinking when I was away, and I've decided – no more of this moping around to see if things are going to work out between Ruthie and me! I'm going to make them work! I'm going to see her – tonight! I heard tell she was down at Mara Òran Bay . . .' He stopped suddenly and peered into his brother's face. 'What the hell's ailing you? You've hardly said a word since we got back. You're not still mooning around after Rachel, are you? I should have thought you would have got somebody else by now.'

Lewis was very pale. He was unable to meet his brother's eyes as he said, 'Ach, I'm fine! I just thought you and me could have spent this evening together. Ruth won't be back from the lobsters till late.'

'To hell with time!' laughed Lorn carelessly. 'I've let enough of it pass in misery. I'm going to see Ruthie, and I'm going tonight.'

Lewis turned away. He couldn't bear to see the eager shining hope in his brother's eyes, and he couldn't bring himself to take away that hope by voicing the things that had happened between him and Ruth.

The Sound of Rhanna was a sheet of purpled silver when Lorn finally came whistling down through Glen Fallan and walked along the cliffs above Mara Òran Bay. One or two fishermen were hauling their boats up onto the sand and Lorn went to give a helping hand.

'Is Ruthie back yet at all?' he asked of Fingal McLeod, who had sat down on a rock to unscrew his peg leg and swig at the hip flask contained therein. Fingal shook his head, 'Na, na, lad, but she'll no' be long. Look there she and her father are now,' he said, holding out the flask. 'Will you have a swallock? Warms the blood after the sun goes down.'

Lorn was about to refuse, remembering that it was the devil's brew that had caused the misunderstanding between him and Ruth in the first place, but his earlier confidence was seeping away a little and he thanked Fingal and took a swallow from the flask.

Fingal then got up and went away over the sands, his wooden leg leaving a thin winding trail behind him. The beach was deserted now and Lorn waited, his heart in his mouth as he watched the black little blob that was Dugald's boat coming closer. The sound of it scrunching on the shingle was like thunder in Lorn's ears. Ruth's back was to him as she helped her father drag the boat up above the tide line. Some distance away Lorn remained immobile, savouring yet dreading the confrontation. Ruth turned suddenly and saw him. Her heartbeat rushed in her ears and she almost fainted. Although Lorn was several yards away she could see his eyes quite clearly; they were a keen blue in his bronzed face. She felt he could see into her very soul, read her very mind. She felt soiled in his sight, degraded beyond all measure. She had waited for this moment, longed for it; now it was here and it was too late . . . too late . . .

'Ruthie, can I speak to you?' His voice was soft, breathless with hope and longing, his hands outstretched in appeal. 'We've both been very silly but – well – will you let me explain?'

'No, Lorn, go away, I don't want to see you.' It was her voice but it seemed to come from another self, a being filled with self-loathing. Anger was the only way she could bear to turn her back on him, and her voice was harsh with it.

Disbelief filled his eyes, that and a hurt so deep she knew if she went on looking at him she would cry aloud in her anguish. 'I'm sorry, Ruthie.' His voice was flat, dead. 'I was foolish enough to think you might feel a little of what I feel for you – I can see now I was wrong.' He stumbled up the beach, hardly able to see where he was going for the mist of tears that blinded him.

Dugald turned a troubled face to his daughter. 'What was that all about, Ruthie?' he asked with a frown. 'I thought you were more than fond of young Lorn. If I'm no' mistaking he was the reason we left Coll to come back here.'

She watched the tall, beloved figure of Lorn McKenzie walking away from her, out of her life – perhaps for ever. He would never lower himself to speak to her again. The McKenzie pride was in him. She could never face him and feel clean in his presence again – now now. The beautiful thing that had been between them was over almost before the buds of their love had ripened. They would remain like that, eternally unfurled, never to blossom forth into glorious flower.

She closed her eyes and swayed. Her father's voice came again from a very long distance: 'Ruthie! Are you all right?' She forced herself to answer normally. 'Ay, Father, I'm right enough. Come you home now, Mam will be waiting with the supper and if we're late she'll punish us by saying Grace after Grace before we can get a bite to eat.'

It was strange, on a small island like Rhanna, where gossip and talk abounded, that more than three weeks were to elapse before Lorn found out the reasons for Ruth's rejection of him. Lewis had taken to meeting her in the evenings, and Lorn assumed that his brother had got over Rachel and was starting to lead again a normal life. Lorn himself had rarely gone out since that fateful meeting with Ruth, but after tea one evening Fergus asked him to go over to Rumhor with a message. He was driving the trap back over the cliff road, and paused for a moment to look down on the wide sweeping curve of Aosdana Bay. Two people were walking hand in hand over the sands, a boy and a girl. Every so often they stopped and the boy bent his dark head to kiss the girl, whose hair shone golden in the light. Lorn's heart pounded and he felt light-headed. Lewis and Ruth! He didn't want to believe the evidence of his eyes, and for quite some minutes he stared in disbelief at the couple far below. Hurt filled his heart till it felt like bursting. So, that was why Ruth hadn't wanted to talk to him or have anything more to do with him! Lewis had found someone else all right! In his restless seeking after pleasure Lewis had turned to the very girl whom Lorn felt was his alone, who in time, Lorn knew, would come to him, and with whom the lovely thing that had been growing would blossom anew. With a strangled little sob he urged the pony forward and drove it back to Laigmhor at a reckless pace. Anger had replaced hurt, a fury so intense it blinded him. He would have it out with Lewis! By God! He would kill him for this! How could he? How could he do this to his own twin brother?

He made some excuse to remain out of doors and waited in the shadow of the barn for his brother's return. He had to wait for a long time, long enough for his anger to simmer steadily till it was at boiling point by the time he saw Lewis turn in at the field gate and come slowly along.

Lewis was looking neither to the right nor left of him. His eyes were on the rutted road, his steps were slow and seemed to drag. When Lorn jumped out into his path he started, but his eyes were strange, out of focus, as if he wasn't seeing properly.

Lorn's fists bunched. 'So! The wanderer has returned!' he ground out menacingly. 'You and Ruth must have had a lot to talk about – or did you have other things on your mind! The kind of things that have filled it since you had your first lusty roll in the grass with Mary Anderson!'

Lewis had gone very pale. He backed away from the dark-faced tower of revengeful wrath who blocked his way. He looked confused and passed a hand over his eyes as he muttered, 'Lorn, calm down, for God's sake, calm down. I'm sorry you had to find out this way about Ruth and me. Keep her out of it though. It wasn't her doing, it was mine. Just something that happened . . .'

'Too bloody true!' Lorn exploded. 'The way things always just happen for you. The minute I turn my back you're off with the one girl who means anything to me! You could have had your pick, but that isn't good enough for hot pants McKenzie! Oh no! The grass on the other side – eh, Lewis? Is that it! Finish with one and go after even tastier fruits! Oh, you had to have the first sampling, didn't you? Quite a challenge! To be the first! The first with everything!' he laughed bitterly. 'Well, there's a first time for everything; even I can see that though I was too blind and stupid to see what was going on under my very nose! We've never fought before, but the time has come for that too. I'm going to beat the living bloody daylights out of you. Get them up!' His fists were up in front of his face, his blue eyes were wild, his nostrils aflare in his chalky white face.

'Och, c'mon, little brother,' Lewis's voice was uneasy. 'Try to see reason. All you ever did was gawp at Ruth – at least I make her feel like the lovely girl she is . . .'

Lorn went berserk then. With a roar he rushed at his brother and punched him to the ground. Lorn hopped around him as he staggered to his feet then landed him another blow that sent him flying onto the grass verge.

The cows chomped peacefully nearby; the grinding of their teeth and Lorn's rasping breaths the only sounds in the world. Lewis lay in the grass, stunned and bruised, shaking his head, drawing a hand across the blood welling from a split lip. Grabbing at tufts of grass he got up once more but staggered and fell, sprawling his full length on the rut of grass growing in the middle of the track. Lorn fumed. He clenched and unclenched his fists.

'Playing possum!' he sneered. 'Get up! Get up, you coward, and fight back!'

Lewis did get up, so quickly that Lorn was taken aback as he watched his brother half-running, half-falling towards the stables. Lorn began to run to the stables also, but was almost sent flying as his brother raced past on his horse, riding it without saddle or bridle, urging it on over the fields in the direction of Portvoynachan. Lorn raced into the stables and, leaping onto Dusk's broad back, he kicked in his heels and the horse took off at a gallop. Away in front was Lewis, a fleeing dot on the horizon. Lorn goaded his horse faster and faster till he was within shouting distance of his brother. 'Come back! Come back, you coward!' he roared. Lewis was making for the cliff road to Portvoynachan. The ground flew by beneath his horse's thudding hooves, the drumming of them mingling with those of Dusk, the air reeling with the abuse Lorn was hurling. The air rang with his accusations, the ringing of hooves. Lumps of turf flew; the fields and moors became a brown and green blur. Lewis's horse bucked as he was guided towards the crumbling cliff paths, its eyes rolled in bloodshot fear as sods of grass and sand disintegrated under his hooves. But now they were on the beach. All was smooth and wide and clear. The sea frothed over the shell sands, rattling the tiny pebbles. Both horses thundered over the bay – Aosdana Bay – where the sea was pink and turquoise and great rocks rose like sentinels out of the water. Lewis's horse was running smoothly and faltered only slightly as his rider suddenly pitched from his back onto the rocks fringing the bay. There was a sickening thud as the dark head struck a spear of basalt.

Fifty yards away, Lorn couldn't believe the sight

that he had just witnessed. He pulled on his horse's mane and, jumping down, ran as he had never run in his life before to drop on his knees by his brother's side. The rock had torn a gaping gash in Lewis's head; the blood was flowing swiftly, matting Lewis's hair into red-brown tufts; his eyes were brilliant in his white face.

The sounds of Lewis's world came to him clearly. The bleating of the sheep rose up from the machair that lay between the north slopes and the shoreless sea to the north, ascending as the smoke of peat fires to the rosy vault of the heavens. It was a fluffy cloud evening, soft cirrus clouds floated over the emerald-green of the clifftops far above. Over the wide white sands the sea glistened, capturing in its vast reaches the blues, greens, and purples of an opal. The great mountains beyond the bay cast their purple-blue shadows on the still waters of inlets and bays that stretched as far as the eye could see. The fishing boats were coming home, their sails red in the fiery eye of the sinking sun. The tangible sense of life was all around, exquisite, timeless as time itself yet so swift in its passing it was almost a mockery. Lewis saw it all, a beauty that was partly physical, partly spiritual. Here he had walked, here he had talked – here he had loved – with Ruth. His lips were very white and trembled slightly. A little smile hovered and he whispered, 'Look, Lorn, a fluffy cloud night . . .' His hand came up and his finger pointed. 'See – up yonder – a face – with a little beard . . . I think – it must be the face – of God.'

Lorn's senses reeled; he felt as if he was gazing down a long long tunnel and at the end of it was the face of the brother he loved with his very soul. It was the face of Lewis – yet it was *his* face. He felt the tunnel whirling, spinning, round and round till Lewis's face was his and his face was Lewis's. Was this what it was like being born? A long tunnel, a vortex; pain; choking. Birth, death, birth, death. Lewis had come first into the world and he would be the first to go out of it – or would he? Lorn felt himself spinning through endless space, of time and tears yet to come, of grief blacker than space, of – emptiness . . . Lewis couldn't go – they were part of each other.

'Why did you fall? Why did you fall!' he heard himself crying. 'There was no reason, no reason . . .' His voice reverberated against the cliffs and then there was silence.

'Lorn,' Lewis's ghost of a whisper came from a long way off. Lorn spun back through the vortex, back to his own life, back to the white face of his dying brother whose head was cradled on his knee. The blood was seeping through his trousers – Lewis's blood? Or his? It was warm – warm and red . . . He whimpered and bit his lip. Strong, he had to be strong.

'Ay, what is it, Lewis?' His voice spoke the words automatically.

'I'm frightened, take me and hold me – the way I used to hold you in the sea.'

Lorn lay down on the sands and entwined his brother in his arms. Lewis smiled. 'Babies – we're both just big babies . . . Lorn, listen. Ruth – she loves you – I meant nothing to her – it was always you . . .'

'Shut up! Don't talk,' Lorn said fiercely.

'Why not – not much time left – for blethering –' His eyes grew big and wide. For eternal moments everything that was life was there in the blue brilliance of Lewis's eyes before they grew dull and heavy, like blinds shutting out the light of day. 'Is – is it dark?' he whispered in panic.

Lorn gazed at the vast red ball in the heavens shedding blinding sheets of flame over the sea. 'Ay, Lewis, it's dark,' he murmured.

'Then – I'm still – alive . . .' The words came out in a sigh, his eyes closed, and he grew still and heavy in his brother's arms.

Lorn never knew how long he sat there with his dead brother cradled to his breast, but the sun had long gone and the sea was dark when he finally came out of the deep trance into which he had sunk. The horses had wandered to the patches of machair among the dunes and were contentedly nibbling the sweet clovers. Lewis's arms were still where he had placed them in his dying moments, round Lorn's waist. Lorn never wanted to tear himself away from that last brotherly embrace, but the loneliness and grief were engulfing him; gently he eased himself away and stood for a few seconds gazing down at Lewis's body lying beside a rock pool in which was reflected the last remnants of gold from the evening sky; then he turned and ran. He had no memory of jumping onto his horse and riding over the cliffs to Laigmhor, of bursting into the kitchen to cry out in deepest anguish, 'I've killed Lewis, I've killed him, I've killed him!' The world went black then and spun mercifully away from him and he didn't hear his mother's agonised cries of protest, nor was he aware of Niall and his father carrying him upstairs between them.

Many miles away Rachel sat staring before her as one witnessing a dark and terrible dream unfolding before her strangely faraway eyes. More than half an hour ago she had experienced a cold eerie sensation washing over her as a vision of Lewis erupted into her mind. It wasn't the same Lewis who had loved her with such passion, but a hollow-eyed boy, pale as death, white lips moving, eyes dark with a terrible fear of being forced to travel to some unknown place far far away from the life he had so loved – it was the same feeling she had had when her father died, and Rachel shuddered and knew that Lewis McKenzie, the boy who was with her wherever she went, whatever she did, was no more of the earth.

Ruth wandered alone in the gloaming, not aware of distance or of time, and as she walked through the cool green valleys of the hills her troubled soul became calm, and she knew what she had to do. Lewis's funeral was now two days in the past. Only snatches of it remained fixed in Ruth's mind: the pale stunned faces of Lewis's family; Lorn, a shadow without control of himself, relying implicitly on others to guide his steps, his dry dull eyes telling of grief locked away, unable to relieve his agony in the healing balm of tears. Rachel had been there too. No one had told her of the tragedy, but she had been there just the same. She and Ruth had stood by one of the big elm trees at the top of the Hillock, watching the ceremony, neither of them speaking till it was all over. Then Ruth had turned to her friend and had said, "Tis glad I am you came, Rachel, but you're a bit late to give Lewis the help he needed. He turned to me for that and somehow everything went wrong. I'm sure you will be happy though – you will go far with Jon at your side.' Her voice had been very quiet, and Rachel had flushed and turned her face away. For the first time there had been reproach in Ruth's voice and Rachel could hardly bear that. How could she explain? How could she tell Ruth that she could never have forsaken her music for the love of a mercurial boy like Lewis? She turned her dark expressive gaze on Ruth, begging for understanding, asking for a return of the simple un-questioning faith they had shared for so long. She took Ruth's hand and held it very tightly, and for a long, long time they gazed at one another, both of them knowing that the lovely innocent years of child-hood were finally done with. They had been so close as children; theirs had been a rare friendship, one filled with simple trust. Now an even greater under-standing had to grow between them, and it had its first stirrings then, with the holding of hands, the dark deep pleas for forgiveness that were there in Rachel's eyes. Ruth felt self-reproach searing through her. It was wrong of her to blame Rachel; she hadn't known that Lewis was dying. Even if she had stayed with him she couldn't have saved him – nothing – no one could have done that. For a moment she was tempted to tell the other girl about Lewis, but the idea left her as quickly as it had come. She had sworn to Lewis that she would tell no one of his illness – that she wouldn't utter a single word about it till all the pain and grief of his death had departed from the lives of those who had loved him most. His death had been put down to an accident, and Ruth believed this to be the case also. She wanted to believe it. He had told her that he wasn't going to wait till his condition had deteriorated to the stage where he would be lying in bed with those he loved best watching him dying. He had meant to take his own life but Ruth knew he would never have deliberately done such a thing in front of his twin brother. She guessed he had taken one of his giddy spells and simply fallen off his horse. Some of his most profound words came back to her, so clearly she heard the lilt of his voice, the note of pleading. 'After I'm dead, Ruth, I want you to wait a whily before you tell my family I had a brain tumour. Mother would go mad thinking of all the things she should have done for me. Seven or eight months should see them over the shock of losing me. I want them to know why I was such a grumpy bugger all this time, but not right away. I am going to ask Lachlan to wait also, to hold his tongue till a few months after I am dead and gone – though of course I won't tell him how I plan to go. It's a lot to ask of you, Ruth, but do this for me – a dying wish if you like.'

There in the graveyard, Ruth had had no inkling of the quarrel that had taken place between Lewis and his brother or she would most certainly have run to Lorn and spilled out her heart to him. Instead, she had put her arms round Rachel and held her close. Raven curls had touched those of palest gold, and each of them had felt a great sadness for days gone, never to return.

Ruth's heart had felt numb. One day Rachel would go away, far away to foreign places, while she – she hadn't known then what she was going to do. She had stepped out of her friend's arms. 'I won't see you for a whily, Rachel, I'm going away, I don't know where yet – but I'm going away . . .'

Ruth stood amidst the heather and closed her eyes. She wished she was more like Rachel, able to turn her back on the kind of love that seemed to bring more heartache than joy – but she wasn't like Rachel. When she married it would be for love . . . Would she ever marry for that? She remembered running up to Lorn after the ceremony, taking his arm and saying quickly, 'I'm sorry – dearest Lorn – I'm sorry I've hurt you so – if only you knew . . . I hope one day you will understand . . .' He had stared at her dazedly as if he was seeing her from a very far distance. His earth-brown curls had been chestnut in a glint of watery sun breaking through the clouds, his eyes, for all their sadness, so intensely blue she could hardly tear her eyes away from them as for a brief moment they focused on her face. His lips had moved and he had whispered, 'Ruthie, it's you – it's you, Ruthie.'

'Ay, Lorn, it's me,' she had said, nodding, her voice so choked by tears she could hardly get the words out. His hand had come up to take hers, but she had stumbled away from him, away out of the Kirkyard to walk unseeingly past the schoolhouse and along the shore to the clinical confines of home.

Now as she stood on the brow of the hill, watching the sun go down behind the corries, she knew that she had to get away, away from Rhanna and all it meant. Yesterday she had met Shona, her auburn hair tossing in the wind, her blue eyes full of compassion as she said, 'If you want somewhere to be at peace for a whily, you are welcome to stay with Niall and me in Kintyre. Sometimes it helps to get away, Ruth. It helped me once when my heart was as troubled as yours is now.'

The words rang in Ruth's ears as she walked homewards through the darkening night. Her father was in the kitchen and she went to him, and putting her arms round him, said quietly, 'I'm going away, Father, just for a whily. Shona has asked me to go and stay with her and Niall. They're going away on the morning boat and I'm going with them. Don't tell anyone where I am, not even Mam; I must be free of everything till I get myself sorted out. Och, I hate leaving you, I love you, Father – I'll – I'll write. I'll send my letters to the shop and you can maybe answer them when you have the time.'

He seemed to expect the news because he held her at arm's length and his grey steady eyes were full of understanding as he said huskily, 'I'll miss you, my babby, but I think you're very wise. Don't give up your writing – whatever else you do don't give up your writing.'

She didn't answer. Going to her bedroom she hastily packed a small case and the first thing she put into it was the marble paperweight given to her by Lorn on a far off night when the world had been full of laughter, life, and the first tender stirrings of love.

Very early next morning Ruth came downstairs dressed in a neat navy-blue suit and a violet blouse that matched her eyes. She had bought the clothes from a mail-order catalogue whilst she was on Coll, and had smuggled them away, never knowing when she would get the chance to wear them. Now her chance had come.

Her mother was at the fire, pounding vigorously at the porridge, but at the opening of the door she turned her red head and the sight that met her eyes made the blood drain from her face. 'Where are you going, my girl?' she said in a flat monotone. 'And why are you dressed like that? Where is your white frock?'

'I left it upstairs, Mam.' Ruth's voice was calm, though her heart was beating so fast she felt she would faint. This confrontation with her mother was what she had dreaded more than any other. The thought of it had kept her awake all night, yet now she felt a great sense of relief coming on top of her apprehension, and her dark purple gaze never wavered from her mother's face.

Morag's hand tightened on the wooden spoon till

her knuckles were white. 'So, you've sinned in the eyes o' the Lord,' she gritted. 'Everything I told you, all the things I warned you against – you never heeded a word – no' a single word . . .' Her voice began to rise: 'You wanton, brazen wee hussy that you are! You're no better than that Jezebel, Rachel McKinnon! I warned you, I warned you about her, but did you listen? No, oh no! She contaminated you wi' her flirting and caperin' around wi' boys of all kinds. Tell me, tell me, girl, was it that Lorn McKenzie? Was it?'

'No, Mam, it wasn't Lorn.' Ruth wasn't frightened any more, her heart was as steady as her voice.

'Then who was it, girl? *Who was it!*'

Ruth's eyes were big and bright and beautiful as she answered, almost triumphantly, 'It was Lewis McKenzie, Mam, and he's dead so there is no' a thing in the whole world you can do about it.'

Turning round she kissed the white head of Dugald who had been standing close behind her all the time she was speaking, then, lifting her case, she walked across the carbolic-smelling floor, slipped unhurriedly out into the clean air of morning, and walked with her head high towards the steamer tied up in Portcull harbour.

Part Six

Autumn 1960

Chapter Nineteen

Kirsteen walked slowly upstairs and into her bedroom. Going to the dresser she pulled it open and took out the big family Bible that lay there. The pages fell open at the book of Job. Here lay the papery-brown fragments of the two rosebuds Fergus had plucked on the night their twin sons were born. How long ago it seemed – yet how near – the joy, the pain, the laughter – the uncertainty of those early days when Lorn's life had hung in the balance – the later uncertainty when he had undergone one operation, one crisis after another. Now he was big and well and strong – physically. Mentally he was ill. Since the death of his brother he had retreated into a world where nothing, no one could reach.

Everything that had meant anything in his life had gone out of it – first Lewis, then Ruth . . . Kirsteen lowered her head and a tear fell onto the withered roses pressed between the pages. The sounds of the late September evening came through the open window – the barking of the sheepdogs, the lowing of the cattle from the byre. A calf had been born that morning, new life, just as it had been at Laigmhor the night her twin sons were born . . .

Fergus came up behind her and pressed his lips

against her hair. He knew how her heart ached, the same deep pain lay heavy in his own heart – yet – he knew they had to go on – that life had to go on. Shona would be coming back to Rhanna the following spring, back to stay after more than nineteen years' absence. He couldn't help looking forward to her coming home, was unable to stop the little surge of joy that lifted his spirits every time he thought about it. He couldn't help but feel a small stab of hope on this sweet evening in autumn when the air was filled with the scent of peat smoke, and the golden leaves that littered the cobbled yard were frisking in the breeze. Yet, he couldn't shut out the sadness either nor help but feel something of Kirsteen's pain. He put his strong right arm around her waist and whispered in her ear, 'You must try not to feel so sad, my darling, it's not easy I know but you'll have to try.'

She shook her head. 'I know, but I can't help it. I'm sad for Lewis, for life – the beauty of it, the passing of it. Perhaps I cry for it all, all the remembrances – Mirabelle – Biddy – Alick – so many people who lived and loved and died. I might be crying because I am growing a bit nearer death myself. Oh – not yet! But it's nearer today than it was yesterday. Ay, I think I cry for that – and . . .' she turned and buried her face into the warm flesh of his neck, 'I cry for you too, my dearest, dearest love – just because I love you so much and don't know what I would ever do if anything happened to you.'

He drew her in close to him, conveying some of

his strength to her as he soothed her tenderly. 'Weesht, weesht now, my darling, you mustny think such things. We have many years together yet – we'll live till we're a hundred – if the Lord spares us, of course.'

She smiled and gave a watery sniff. 'Of course we will, how could I ever think we might only live to be ninety-nine?' She leaned against him. 'Oh, if only Lorn could find some happiness, I think then I might begin to live a wee bit myself.'

'Anybody at home?' Lachlan's deep voice came from below. He was sitting in the inglenook in the kitchen when they came down, his fine, sensitive face full of something that neither Fergus nor Kirsteen could define, a muted excitement mingled with a slight apprehension. Although he was past sixty he had never lost his boyish look. His hair, though slightly threaded with grey, was in the main still dark and thick. 'Sit you both down,' he instructed in his quiet pleasant voice. 'But before you do I think it might be a good idea if you fetched us a dram, Fergus. What I have to tell you might hurt and upset you – on the other hand it might take some of the weight from your hearts and help you to understand better the last few months of Lewis's life.' He smiled ruefully. 'It will lift a burden from my own mind, too. Ay, and poor Phebie's as well . . .' He hesitated. 'Actually the things I am about to tell you were meant to keep a whily longer, but I got a letter from Ruth this morning that changed my mind.'

'From Ruth?'

'Ay, as you know she's staying with Shona and Niall, and seemingly they got a letter from you to the effect that Lorn was eating out his heart, not only with grief but with guilt. I had no idea he blamed himself for Lewis's accident.'

'Neither did we until last week!' Kirsteen cried. 'On the night Lewis – died – Lorn came racing home here shouting that he had killed Lewis. We knew it was just shock, of course, and he never said any more on the subject. Then last week it all came spilling out. He and Lewis had had a dreadful fight. Lorn chased him over the shore and – Lewis fell off his horse. Lorn thinks that somehow he is to blame!'

'Ay, they did fight – about Ruth – as you've probably guessed,' Lachlan said gently. 'Ruth had no idea of this. Like everyone else she assumed the boys were joyriding on the beach when the accident happened. Shona confided certain things in your letter to Ruth, who immediately contacted me . . . You see, with the exception of Phebie and myself, Ruth was the only other person who knew the truth about Lewis.'

'What truth?' Fergus asked harshly.

'I'll explain – where is Lorn by the way?'

'Out in the stables with the horses,' Kirsteen said rather wonderingly. 'He spends a lot of time in there nowadays.'

'Ay, well best to leave him where he is just now. I want to talk to you both first.'

And talk he did. The hands of the clock crept round, but not one of them noticed the passage of time. It was almost midnight when Lachlan finally sat back, his brown eyes full of compassion as he looked at the two people sitting close together on the settle. Kirsteen was staring at her hands lying on her lap, Fergus's arm was round her, holding her very tightly. Finally she looked up, her blue eyes misted with tears as she whispered, 'Our laddie was a wild, wild devil in his day. Times were he was so fickle I could fine have skelped some sense into him but – oh God! He died a man, Lachlan, a fine young man with a brave brave heart.'

'Ay, he did that, Kirsteen,' Lachlan agreed softly. Reaching inside the breast pocket of his jacket he withdrew a bulky package. 'This is for Lorn – would one of you give it to him? The sooner the better.'

Fergus stood up. His eyes were very misty as he said huskily, 'I'll take it to him now – and –' he held out his hand to grip Lachlan's firmly, 'thank you, Lachlan, for everything. You and Phebie are more than friends of this family – you're part of us.'

He went quickly outside to the stables. They were warm and steamy and smelled of hay. Lorn was sitting in a corner, close by the big Clydesdale Myrtle, whom he loved fiercely. He was polishing her harness, talking to her quietly. He spent many of his free hours in the stables, grooming the horses, cleaning the stalls, tiring himself out so that by the time he crept up to bed, often in the small hours of morning, he was too tired to think – to remember. He didn't look up as Fergus came in, but went on rubbing at the harness, which was already shining from previous care lavished upon it. Fergus's shadow danced in the light from the lantern hanging from a beam. He held out the package, his eyes black with love and compassion for this haunted son of his who had blamed himself for his brother's death and who had lived neither in the land of the living nor of the dead for five long, weary weeks. 'This is for you,' he said softly, 'from Lewis.'

Lorn did look up then, his blue eyes wary, his voice harsh as he cried out, 'What do you mean – from Lewis?'

'Just what I say. Read it and read it well, son. I'll leave you in peace, for peace is what you need now, and I hope the things that Lewis has to tell you will bring you peace of mind in full measure,' Fergus said and went out, closing the door softly behind him.

For fully five tremulous minutes Lorn stared at the brown paper package on top of the golden bale of hay, then with a little cry he snatched it up and withdrew the contents, a large diary bound in red leather and a letter. He laid the letter to one side and ran trembling fingers over the gold-edged pages of the book. He had given it to Lewis last Christmas – the Christmas of 1959 – the day after that terrible evening of the Burnbreddie dance. His heart was beating very fast as he opened the diary. The first few pages were blank but just after the end of February 1960 the writings began, Lewis's large untidy scrawl filling the pages, and as Lorn read he heard the echo of his brother's voice inside his head so that even as he was reading the words it was as if Lewis was reading them out, keeping him company there in the stables with Myrtle and Dusk and the ponies peacefully lying in their stalls. Lorn settled himself back among the hay, and as he read the message, written to him alone, it was as if he and Lewis were the only two people alive in the whole of the quiet night world.

3rd March 1960

Lorn, by the time you get this I will be up in the great blue yonder. I don't think I will go to hell. I haven't been an angel but I haven't committed any great crimes, either. I have a brain tumour. Lachlan told me it was perhaps there when I was born but only started to become active recently. So I didn't escape after all. At first it was just bad headaches, which got worse. And then I went to Lachlan. I am not afraid – I am terrified! From the time I knew what death was all about it scared the breeks off me. Maybe some inbuilt instinct warned me that my time on earth was to be short. I don't know. All I know is I've been in hell since I found out, and I've put those I love most in hell with me. I wouldn't let Lachlan tell any of you. Mother and Father will suffer enough when it is over and done with, so why make them suffer now. I have been to Glasgow and had tests done and the doctors told Lachlan the tumour was inoperable. That is why I went away. Not to see Rachel, but to go to hospital. It was gey lonely there, I can tell you, and the longest month I ever spent. I'm going to enjoy the time left to me. I'll have a bonny time and to hell with tomorrow. I'm tired now, my head hurts a lot and I see things double. I'll speak to you again later.

April 1960

The spring is coming in and I've never been so aware of life as I am now. Lachlan wanted me to go to Glasgow for treatment, but I wasn't having it. I don't want to prolong the agony. Lachlan gives me painkillers. He and Phebie are wonderful. Have you ever noticed Lachlan's eyes when he knows you're feeling pretty damned sick and there's nothing much he can do to help? Of course you have, little brother, you've know illness since you were born. I'm not good at describing things, but Lachlan has God in his eyes.

These last few weeks I've been running wild. There's so much I want to do. If I sit still I begin to think and I get scared so I get up and go. I wander up to Brodie's Burn a lot and I remember the day we met Ruth up there. It helps just to sit and think about her tales of the past. I used to hate dwelling in the past, now it's all I ever want – I don't want to think of the future. As well as being sick in the head (don't laugh) I'm pretty sick at heart just now. I've got Rachel on the brain! She grows in there and, like the tumour she won't go away. Funny how girls can do that to men. I've had a lot of girls in my time. They meant nothing, I never felt for them the way I feel for Rachel. She's different, like a wild rose blowing in the wind, so beautiful I shiver whenever I think of her smooth golden skin and those big dark eyes of hers. Thàt doesn't sound like me, eh? For the first time I feel there's more to all this love business than just a quick roll in the hay.

Rachel has told me she's going to marry Jon. I can't believe it! Yet – I can. He can be trusted; he's like her father. I think that's what she needs, a father figure. Rachel has got a strength in her that's a wee bit eerie at times. She knows where she's going, what she wants from life; and she'll get it, too. I looked into her eyes today and an odd shiver went through me. The old ones are right. Rachel has the power. Whatever it is, she's got it.

May 1960
I watched you today, Lorn, and saw myself. You've grown, little brother. I won't be able to call you that much longer. You're getting stronger and I'm getting weaker. You deserve it, you skinny wee rabbit! (You can't hit me where I'm going.)

I watch Father and Mother too. I've taken to watching people. Mother is beautiful, more from inside now she's getting older. Yet, in some ways, she always seems young. Father is getting older too, it shows in his hair and the crinkles round his eyes – but that's all. His back is straight, he's hard and strong as an ox. In a way I'm glad I won't see them growing really old, they'll always be as they are now. I can't imagine Mother a wee old woman or Father a grey auld bodach. I'm smiling writing this, so you smile too – go on – smile, you bugger! The time for weeping is over. I'm thinking now of how I love our parents. Mother is a very easy person to love but my love for our father isn't so easy to explain. I've respected him all my life and there have been times when I have felt really close to him but never like you and him. He understands you because you're two of a kind, but I think I always worried him a wee bit. He's a hard man to live up to – not because he's ever been a Holy Wullie, God forbid! He's got a lot of ideals, though, and I think I was born without a single one. He's a dour, stubborn bugger – like you – but I love you both. Shona's a lot like the pair of you – stubborn as a mule's arse but there's a wonderful sunny side to her nature. She must have taken that after her own mother. She's always known I was a coward about death and sickness but she always had a lot of understanding for me. Many's the time I've blessed having a big sister like her. Grant's the happy-go-lucky one of the family – a bit like me but with more sense of responsibility. Maybe I should have gone round the world like him, but then I would have missed everything that's here on Rhanna. I've loved every minute of my life here and I thank God for letting me be born on a Hebridean island – here I can breathe and be as free as the wind – I'm talking about God now, thinking about Him in a way I never did before. Ruth has helped me there. Somehow, through all the hellfire and thunder dinned into her ears since she was born, she's managed to extract the truth from her Bible and to see God. She told me there was a time when she hated God, but the years have opened up her eyes to the truth and beauty behind it all – and now I'm going to sleep. Tomorrow I will write more – tonight my head hurts and I'm seeing everything double – even you lying in your bed snoring. I'm writing this by the light of a torch and it's strange to be writing to you when you're here beside me in the room.

It's June now. You're away staying with Shona and Niall and I miss you, little brother, always I miss you when we're apart. I walked over to Burg and met Ruth. She thought I was you at first. I saw the hope in those lovely eyes of hers then it faded when she realised it was me. She came back from Coll because she couldn't stand to be away from you only to find you had gone. You're a daft pair of buggers! All this beating about the bush because of a stupid mis-understanding. I told her the reason you got drunk at the Burnbreddie dance and she got quite angry about it. She says all you had to do was tell her you couldn't dance. She doesn't much like dancing either, and would have been quite happy just talking to you all night.

I've been meeting Ruth a lot over at Aosdana Bay. Today we got out one of Hector's boats and I poured out my soul to her. She cried for me and I kissed her. Ruth is like sunshine. Her hair smells of it. When she talks about you her eyes grow dreamy and go really purple, the colour of the heather hills in autumn. Her voice is like music. I could listen to her all day. The sound of her voice is like a burn tinkling over the stones on the moor. She called me Lorn when I kissed her the second time. Fancy the blow to my ego! Girls have always fallen at my feet now this wee lassie with the big dreamy eyes feels me kissing her and imagines I'm you!

Weeks have passed. I know now why you love Ruth. She's truly good. I've grown to love the innocence of this sweet shy girl with her lovely face. I love all her moods, her sadness, her joys. I feel a strange sort of rapture just being in her company. She's so different from Rachel. Rachel always gave out a sense of great power; Ruth is fragile and vulnerable. I feel I want to protect her, to keep her safe, yet she has an inner strength that is like yours. She's stronger than me. She's been my crutch these last weeks. When she knows I'm in pain she takes my head in her hands and soothes me. I knew Rachel wouldn't feel pity, that's why I never told her about myself, and to have her feel sorry for me would have been more than I could stand. Yet, even if she had known she would still have turned from me. She started off life with a show of toughness, time and events hardened her till her toughness became genuine. Ruth has no shell, she is laid bare to all the hurt the world can give her. Her only defence is shyness – yet, when she has to defend people she loves she's like a tigress. Mind what she did to Canty Tam when he sneered at Rachel? Well she did the same thing to me one day when I said you were soft. I was being jealous of all the talking she did about you and she turned on me like a wild cat and sent me off licking my wounds.

It's midsummer now and Hector has gone off for his annual holiday to Mull. Today I made love to Ruth. I know you will curl up inside reading this but don't hate me or feel anger against Ruth. She thought I was you, she called me Lorn and she cried and hated herself. I thought she wasn't going to see me again. She's all I've got now, the only person in the whole world who can help me in my last days here on earth. Whatever you do, don't blame Ruth for what happened. She's torn between her love for you and her sorrow for me – because that's all she really feels for me. I love her in a way I've never loved any girl before. I've never felt tenderness for any other girl, but that is what I feel for Ruth, tenderness. It's a good job I'm not going to be around for very much longer because I would have fought you tooth and nail for Ruth even though it would have been useless. She loves you and no one else. I only have her for a little while; you will have her for the rest of your life. Ruth has made me live even while I'm dying, so don't waste time holding grudges, just remember that in my last days Ruth comforted me, gave me light when there was darkness. Little brother of mine, I love you. You may ask yourself how can I say such a thing when guilt is tearing me in two and I know I can't go on seeing Ruth much longer for fear you will find out. But I can't say I don't love you just because we both love the same girl. That would be daft. You're my brother, my twin, you're me really and I'm you and all this is getting so complicated I'm laying down my pen. You're coming home tomorrow and I don't know how I'm going to face you, so I'm taking the coward's way out. I'll start seeing Ruth in the evenings so as not to arouse too many suspicions. I can't let go of Ruth – not yet.

12th August 1960
I'm feeling really bad today. I get dizzy a lot. When I'm supposed to be working I just sit up in the fields, seeing two of everything. I can't enjoy any of the things I love. I can't see to read now and it's getting more difficult to keep on writing in this diary. When I'm out riding I feel like falling off, everything just goes round in circles. I think that's how I'll go out. I'll take one of the horses and just pitch over the cliffs. I tell you this, I'm not waiting for this thing to kill me, I'm going to kill it first! After all, I'm a McKenzie and we're a family who don't like anything to get the better of us!

24th August 1960
How beautiful is this small island world of ours. I am aware of every blade of grass, every whisper of life in the forests and moors. The sky is so wide, I feel a great sense of freedom and space – as if I could spread my wings and fly like the birds. Just lately I have felt a strange peace coming over me, an accept-

ance of that which is to come. It might sound daft coming from me, but I'm not afraid of death any more. The folk of our island are beautiful, especially the old ones. They have got wisdom and contentment in their eyes. With a few exceptions the people of Rhanna are a serene lot.

I am going over to see Lachlan later this morning and I am taking this diary with me. I will ask him to give it to you eight months after I am gone and at the same time to explain to Mother and Father why I was such a dour, moody bugger to live with this year. I am going to see Ruth tonight and will make her promise not to say a word till the time is up. Why eight months? Well, I'm a bit in the dark when it comes to people's feelings on grief. I never wanted to know any of those things and always used to turn away from them. When I was in hospital there was a chap there who had not long lost his wife. I asked him how long it took to get over it. He said he never had, that you never do get over losing someone you love and that eight months passed before he could think of her without crying. Around that time he also felt that he wanted to start living again, to go forward, not dwell in the past. I mind too when Rachel lost her father it was April and for months after I used to shiver when I looked at her. She wore the same clothes as usual, yet I felt as if a thick black blanket was covering her. Round about Christmas that year I felt as if the blanket was growing thinner, letting Rachel shine out again. I'm a daft bugger but these are the only incidents I have to go on, so eight months it is. It won't be easy for Lachlan and Ruth but I have to make them see I'm doing it for my family – you will have gotten over losing me by then and better able to take all this. I know you'll miss me, of all the charmers who ever lived I think I must be about the nicest! With one exception, my wee brother, Lorn Lachlan McKenzie – my better half! Thanks for being my brother, I couldn't have had a better one. Don't think you're getting rid of me though. I'll be keeping my beady eye on you – sort of watching over you like a guardian angel. (I like the idea of that! I'll have wings like the birds and be able to fly.)

Have a grand life. On fluffy cloud days look up and remember me – who knows – you might see my face up there watching you, so be careful when you go rolling in the heather with Ruth. (On the other hand don't be too fussy, I might pick up a few hints.) By the time you get this you and Ruth might be married. If so, be happy and good in a naughty kind of way. (I always found being too good the most boring thing on earth.) Mo Beannachd leat, daonnan.

Lorn closed the book with a soft little snap. Lewis had died on the evening of August 24th 1960. For a moment it all came back, the horror, the grief, the heartrending pain. These last words, from Lewis to him, were the final thoughts, the final goodbyes. Then the ending of the diary came to him: Mo Beannachd leat, daonnan, the Gaelic for 'My blessings be with you always'.

The words rang in his head like a benediction, a prayer. Lewis had spoken, not from the grave but from life, all the eager thrusting force that had been in him, even to the end of his short young life. The experiences of his last months had been crammed into a few pages, yet they were so beautiful; wistful, yet so filled with every kind of emotion he had been like an atom, spreading outwards in the universe to embrace it and hold it to himself as if to savour all the wonder of creation. Lorn shivered and felt a thread of some of that wonder weaving its way into him till he felt like laughing and crying at the same time. A tear rolled slowly down his face to be followed by another. Faster and faster they fell, the first tears he had cried since his brother's going. His strong young body shook with a storm of weeping, and when it was finally over, when the great shuddering sobs had finally ceased, he felt as if a balm had been poured over his soul. Myrtle turned and nuzzled his neck with her velvety nose, and getting up he buried his face into her mane and said aloud, 'Thank you, thank you, big brother, you have set me free, I'm free now because I know the truth – and I don't hurt any more . . .'

His eyes fell on the letter lying on the bale of hay. The one word written on the envelope leapt out at him. That hand, he knew it, so well he knew it. 'Lorn' was all it said but it was enough for him to know who had written it, for had he not, over and over, looked at that very name inscribed into a birthday card given to him by Ruth to mark his eighteenth year? With trembling fingers he slit open the envelope and sank down against Myrtle to devour the letter with hungry eyes.

26th September
1960

Dearest Lorn,

I am sending this to Lachlan to ask him to give it to you along with Lewis's diary. You shouldn't have found out any of this for some months yet, but when I found out you blamed yourself for Lewis's accident I couldn't bear it and wrote to Lachlan. As it is, it has been a long and weary few weeks, and I'm glad the waiting is over and you at last know the truth. There is so much I want to say to you, so much you have to understand before you can even begin to forgive me. I don't know if you ever can. I have done things, so many things that have been hurtful and wrong but that were the only things I could do to give Lewis comfort when he needed it most. Often I remember and I hate myself. Lying in bed at night I cry thinking of you, your pain and your hurt. I want you in my arms, to have and to hold, and my body aches with loneliness. I miss so many people, my darling father, my friends on Rhanna – but most of all I miss you, my darling Lorn, and long to see you again.

Shona and Niall have been so kind to me, I will never forget how they helped me when I needed help most. They are like a pair of excited bairns at the moment and talk constantly about going home. They can't wait to get back to Rhanna.

I don't have many plans for my future. I tried to start writing a book, but it was no use. I kept seeing your face on every blank page so I have put my pen aside for a while and have taken instead to daydreaming. I might go back to my aunt in Coll, but wherever I go, remember this – every minute, every hour, every day of my life, I think of you.

Ruthie.

Lorn crushed the letter to his breast and sank down against Myrtle's soft flanks. The stable was peaceful and he had so very much to think about. He didn't go back to the house that night.

Fergus and Kirsteen slept fitfully. Like Lorn they had a lot of new thoughts that jumbled around in their heads before they began to settle into some sort of order. But just before dawn Kirsteen finally fell into an exhausted sleep. Fergus looked at her, the hands thrown over the pillow, the lock of crisp hair falling over her brow. She looked like a child in her repose, and, leaning over, he kissed her silvered hair gently then got up out of bed to get quickly dressed. It was a glorious autumn morning; the peat smoke was rising from the chimneys of Portcull; the fishing boats were sailing out of the harbour; the subdued clatter of milk churns came from the dairy. By the side of the road some distance away Dodie was sitting on a tiny stool by Ealasaid's flank, his big fingers gently extracting the milk for his breakfast. Fergus breathed deeply. It was the start of another day, a beautiful new day filled with all the promise of new life, new beginnings, new hope. He walked towards the fragrant fields; the rich smell of newly turned earth was strong in the air and he looked up. There on the golden horizon was silhouetted the figure of Lorn lifting the kale, in front of him plodded the noble sturdy form of Myrtle, the magnificent Clydesdale. Fergus swallowed the tears in his throat. 'This is my son,' he thought proudly. 'Against all the odds he has become a farmer and a true son of the soil.'

He heard himself calling, 'Lorn! Lorn!'

Lorn looked up, his blue eyes fixed on the beloved man who was his father. A great swelling joy exploded inside him. He began to run towards the lower fields, stumbling, falling in his haste, but someone seemed to be at his elbow, urging him on, helping him up. Lewis! Of course it was Lewis! Death could never rob him of the brother who had shared his life from the moment of conception. They were of the same flesh, the same heart beating – the same spirit. Lewis would go on living in him. As the years passed people would look at him and know what Lewis would have looked like that day – that tomorrow – that forever. They had both loved the same people – the same girl – perhaps one day Ruthie would come back to Rhanna – back to a love that could never forget her. If she didn't he would go to her – by God he would!

'I'm coming, Father!' he cried, the tears pouring unheeded out of his eyes. His heart was beating, pulsing, bounding with a joy he felt could never be exceeded – but it could – it could! One day it would – with Ruthie!

Fergus watched his son running swift and sure over the dew-wet fields. He saw him trip and almost fall, but in seconds he was steady again, his feet flying swiftly.

'Lorn,' whispered Fergus, the lump in his throat fading as tears dissolved it away. The boy reached him and pulled up short, shy for a moment, then he was in his father's strong embrace, the deep sure thudding of the beloved heart filled his ears. Fergus looked up and Lorn followed his gaze. Ruth was coming over the fields from Brodie's Burn, her slim body dressed in palest green, which blended harmoniously with the grasses.

'She must have come home on last night's steamer,' Fergus said softly.

Joy and hope accelerated Lorn's heartbeats; his eyes were filled with so much love they were luminous in their expression. Ruth spotted him, and her steps faltered, slowed. Lorn left his father's side and began to run, conscious of every ray of light, every sparkle in the diamond-like dew drops misting the fields. The dazzle in them found reflection on the teardrops poised on his lower lashes. Ruth had begun to run also, her hair a golden halo, now against the green of the grass, now against the deep blue sky. She was a vision of sweet and lovely girlhood with hardly a trace of a limp to hamper her graceful movements.

Kirsteen came out of the house and walked towards Fergus, hesitantly at first. Then she saw his powerful, dark face lifted up, transformed with the light of inner joy. She ran to him and he held out his strong right arm to take her in his embrace. Her gaze followed his and a little sob caught in her throat as she stood there with the man she loved, watching the two young people meeting and embracing on the brow of the silvered fields. The sun burst over the lower shoulder of Ben Machrie, morning broke in all its golden glory bathing the moors, brushing amber over the ethereal purpled peaks of the hills of Rhanna.

Rhanna at War

To Ray, Cathie, and Ethel, friends as well as sisters

AUTHOR'S NOTE

While I have tried to make the raids over Clydebank on 13th March 1941 as authentic as possible, there may be some discrepancies. According to statistics from German sources there was no bomber squadron I.K.G. 3 over Clydebank on 13th March 1941.

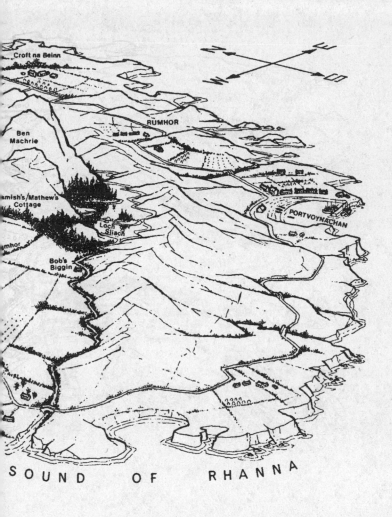

Croft na Beinn

RUMHOR

Ben
Machrie

PORT VOYNACHAN

amish's/Mathew's
Cottage

Loch
Sliach

mhor

Bob's
Biggin

SOUND OF RHANNA

Part One

Rhanna
March 11th 1941

Chapter One

Shona McKenzie stood with her arms folded on the rails of the steamer and watched with quiet elation as the tiny island of Eriskay in the Outer Hebrides appeared on the horizon in an ethereal haze of mist. The landmark of Eriskay meant that in less than half an hour the boat would reach Rhanna and Shona's pulse quickened at the thought. Soon – soon she would be back on Rhanna, amongst all the dear people whom she had known all her life and who were as much a part of her as the very soil of the island itself.

She lifted her face to the sky, shut her eyes and breathed deeply, letting the salt-laden air wash into her lungs. Aberdeenshire had been lovely with its rivers, glens and majestic mountains, but she had missed the sea, hardly realising how much till this moment of sharp air, wheeling gulls and warm winds gently rippling the surface of the blue water. It was an extremely mild day for March. At other times in the same season the sea could be a boiling fury with gales throwing waves forty feet and more into grey lowering skies. But no matter the weather, she loved her native land and had never thought she could ever leave it for more than a week or two at a time. But that had been before the war, before her childhood sweetheart, Niall McLachlan, had been badly wounded in the massacre of Dunkirk . . . and before her father had married Kirsteen Fraser, who had once been her teacher in the little school at Portcull.

For many years it had just been Shona and her father living at Laigmhor, the big rambling farmhouse in which she had been born. Just herself and her father had meant a lot of loneliness, but it had also meant a lot of shared confidences and a warm feeling that the happiness of one depended on the happiness of the other. Now there was another woman sharing her father's life, and Shona wasn't quite sure of her own feelings on the matter. She loved and respected Kirsteen, had done ever since the day the two of them had met in the little village school, Kirsteen as a young teacher just starting in her new post, and Shona, a small motherless mite of five years feeling desolate and lost in a strange new world. From the beginning she had wanted Kirsteen Fraser to take the place of the mother she had never known and it certainly had looked that all her dreams were about to become reality when she was eleven and her father had announced his intentions of marrying Kirsteen. But tragedy had befallen Laigmhor round about that time. Mirabelle, the dear motherly housekeeper who had reared Shona from birth, had died suddenly, then her father had lost an arm in a terrible accident when out searching for his brother, Alick, in the treacherous waters that swirled round the Sgorr Creags. And Kirsteen, believing that he would no longer want to marry her because of his pride, had sailed away from Rhanna carrying his child.

But all that was in the past. In the autumn of 1940, after a lapse of almost six years, her father had been reconciled with Kirsteen and she had come back to Rhanna with his son. The boy, Grant Fergus, with his black curls and dimpled chin, was unmistakably Fergus McKenzie all over again. Laigmhor had become a real family home where life and laughter abounded and where love embraced them all in a glowing little circle. Yet, despite all, Shona had felt an intruder. She had been still in the turbulent grip of some very recent crises of her own and had known she wasn't yet ready to adjust to a newly acquired little brother and another woman doing all the things at Laigmhor that had once been her ritual alone.

The idea of leaving home for a time had come slowly and conflicted greatly for a period with other instincts that would not let her relinquish, even for a little while, her beloved island. But she had felt strongly the urge to do something useful in wartime and notions of patriotism and feelings of superfluity continued to grow till eventually she had sailed away from Rhanna, a slender girl, not quite eighteen, wearing her uniform pinned with the Cross of St Andrew.

Now she had been ordered to take some leave: she had thrown herself into the job with such dedication she was physically exhausted. The leave had come unexpectedly, giving her just enough time to dash off a letter to Niall, who was at a college in Glasgow training to be a vet. At thought of Niall and of the letter she gave a little start of dismay. She had written the letter in great haste but had she remembered to post it? A rummage through her handbag revealed almost instantly that she hadn't and guilt raged through her. She loved him very dearly and her joy at returning to Rhanna was tinged with sadness that he wasn't here to share the holiday with her. What would he think of her for writing letters that she didn't post on time? At this very moment he would be thinking she was still working away in Aberdeenshire when all the time she was sailing over the sea to Rhanna. It had been a pact of theirs always to let the other know exactly where they would be so that each could think of the other in that particular setting.

Shona's friend, Babbie Cameron, came swaying over the deck towards her. Babbie was not a good sailor and despite the calm crossing had suffered from seasickness for most of the journey. As a result her normally glowing face was a sickly white colour, though nothing could take away the dazzling bright sheen of the sunlight on her red hair. Nor could it completely quench the sparks of mischief in those green, amber-flecked eyes that had the translucent look of a clear sea freckled with seaweed. They were odd eyes, dreamily masking a million secrets, yet they sparkled with soft lights of laughter and kindness. Babbie was five years older than Shona and though they had known each other only a short time, they were already firm friends. It was unusual for Shona, who had never been one for girlfriends. Most of her childhood had been spent playing with boys, especially Niall, and as a result she had always been something of a tomboy. She got on well with men; with them there were no petty little jealousies or frivolous gossip such as she had sometimes encountered with girls. But Babbie was different. She was sensible, honest and great fun to be with.

When Shona had first started her nurse's training with the St Andrew's Ambulance Corps, Babbie had taken her under her wing, always ready with helpful advice yet never too superior about it. Yet despite her open honesty and frank remarks, there was something very mysterious about Babbie. She was reticent about her private life, both past and present, yet this very enigmatic side to her only made Shona like her more. She felt that there was always something that was going to be new about Babbie, no matter how long she might know her.

'Haven't you found your sea legs yet?' Shona chuckled. 'If Canty Tam saw you now he would say you were a Uisga Hag – that means a sea witch. I thought I'd better warn you about such things now, for you'll hear plenty about them on Rhanna.'

Babbie smiled ruefully. 'A sick witch might be more apt. I can always tell people that instead of sailing to the Hebrides I spewed my way across.' She looked at the letter fluttering in her friend's hand. 'Is this you throwing guilty secrets into the sea?'

'Och, Babbie, I'm a silly bitch right enough! This is the letter I wrote to Niall and just remembered I'd forgotten to post. What will he think of me posting letters from Rhanna that ought to have been posted from Aberdeen? It's not as if things were all that good between us just now, certainly not good enough to allow mistakes like this.'

Babbie eyed her friend thoughtfully. Shona was a stunningly beautiful girl, delicate and slender with huge blue eyes and a thick mass of naturally waving auburn hair. Sometimes she looked like a small girl who had lost her way in a dark wood and didn't quite know how to get out of it again. She was looking like that now, tremulous and forlorn, yet the proud tilt of her head was defying pity or well-meant advice.

A few minutes of silence passed while the gulls wheeled and screamed above the ship's funnels and a crate of chickens covered by a tarpaulin clucked morosely in a corner. Nearby was a jumble of mail bags, paraffin drums and a mountain of coal which would keep the Rhanna folk supplied for two months or more.

'This Niall of yours,' Babbie said carefully, breaking the stillness, 'you've told me often enough how much you love him, yet . . . you also hint that things are not as they should be between you. It's none of my business I know but—'

'Ay, you are quite right, Babbie,' Shona interrupted angrily, 'it is none of your business. I'll have enough of the Rhanna folk prying into my affairs without you starting as well!'

'I'm sorry, really,' Babbie said turning away. 'I was always too outspoken. My sister was forever giving me rows for it. Forget I mentioned Niall and . . . everything.'

Shona was immediately sorry for her outburst and she gripped Babbie's hand tightly. 'Och, I'm the one who needs forgiveness . . . by a lot of people I love most. My temper always lets me down. Father says it's a family failing, and how right he is. All my life I've had to fight it and just when I think I've won, it comes right back at me and hits me between the eyes. I do want to talk about Niall . . . and before we get to Rhanna there's something I have got to tell you or nosy old Behag or one of her cronies will tell you for me. I've kept putting it off because I didn't know what you'd think of me . . . innocent little Shona McKenzie with a past as black . . . as black as that coal there! Oh God! If only it was possible to wind the clock right back!'

Babbie looked slightly uncomfortable. 'Shona, you don't have to tell me anything, we all have our secrets and the right to keep them as such. I won't listen to Behag or anyone else for that matter. You can trust me.'

The anger in Shona's blue eyes changed to a look of tenderness. 'I know that, Babbie. That's one of the things I like most about you. But I want to tell you . . .' She looked out to the sea and her knuckles turned white as she gripped the rail. 'I have to talk to someone and I hope – when you've heard all the gory details you'll still want to be my friend.' She took a deep breath and gazed unseeingly over the glistening blue reaches of the Sound of Rhanna which they were just approaching.

'Last summer, just about the time of the Dunkirk

evacuations . . . I . . . gave birth to a baby . . . a little boy, Niall's son. Niall was in France at the time and I thought he was dead. We got word from the War Office that he had gone missing, presumed to be killed . . . and I ran and ran over the Muir of Rhanna to a cave, our cave, Niall's and mine. No one could find me, they searched all day and all night. During the search my little dog, Tot, died trying to find me. That may seem a trivial thing to you but oh God how I loved that dear little spaniel with her wee pot belly and her white muzzle! I got her as a present for my fifth birthday and we grew up together. She died and my little boy died . . . was born dead . . . and all because of my stupidity. If I hadn't run away he might be alive now, but I thought Niall was dead, you see, and I couldn't bear to think about that, didn't believe it really, but of course I was living in a child's world, trying to pretend that things weren't true when they were going on all around me. I did it when Mirabelle died and when Father lost his arm and I did it again when I was giving birth to a tiny baby boy with Niall's fair hair and Niall's life inside him . . . And the guilt inside me is all the worse for knowing that I made Niall make love to me before he went away to France. I thought he might never come back and I wanted something that was his to hold on to! I made a mess of everything and I feel so guilty all the time. The lovely things I had with Niall, the innocence, the freedom of the carefree love we had between us – all has been ruined because of me. We were children together, before . . . before I turned it all upside down and now I can't look at Niall without feeling soiled, without feeling that our love has been ruined. I still love him, there never has been nor ever will be anyone else yet . . . oh, I can't understand it myself . . . but I don't want to let him kiss me or touch me or even *look* at me too closely because I think he's looking at me with accusation in his eyes. Och, he's not of course but I just *feel* he is and until I get rid of that from my mind then . . . things can never be the same between us.'

The tears were pouring unheeded down her face now and her breath came out in shuddering sobs. In a great rush of compassion Babbie took her into her arms and stroked her burnished hair. 'There, there now, have a good greet, it's the first step to healing that proud little heart of yours. I'm glad that you told me, if only to unburden yourself a bit . . . and I'm honoured to be your friend. Things will come right between you and Niall. I know they will, it will just take time, that's all. Here, take my hanky and give your nose a right good blow. It's my best linen one so don't blow *too* hard!'

Shona obediently blew and even managed a smile at Babbie's typically nonsensical words. 'Och, Babbie, it's me that's honoured to have *you* for a friend,' she said with a watery sniff. 'It's a good job we're the only ones at this side of the rails or I would have given more than just you a free show. I'm sorry for being such a crybaby but I feel a lot better, better than I did a whily back anyway. Here's your hanky back and don't worry, I'll wash it with my very own fair hands when we get home to Laigmhor.' She looked quizzically at Babbie and said hesitantly, 'I've talked a lot about myself and you've listened even though you look greener than a green Uisga Caillich. What about you, Babbie? I get this funny wee feeling that you hold yourself back all the time. You laugh a lot and talk a lot of daft nonsense but I think . . . the real you is hiding about somewhere under all the surface things.'

Babbie waved an airy hand. 'Ach, you and your funny wee feelings. I've already told you I was brought up in an orphanage in Argyll and that's all there is to it! Nothing exciting about my background at all.'

Shona's gaze held Babbie's for a long time before Babbie looked away with feigned interest at a seagull strutting over the deck. 'Maybe it was at the orphanage that you learned to hold yourself back,' Shona said softly. 'For you do it all the time, Babbie Cameron. I am not the only one to be sewing myself up and throwing away the scissors, as Mirabelle used to say.'

They both laughed and Babbie said gladly, 'Well, thank goodness, a Mirabelle saying from you means we're going to get away from all this serious talk. You invited me back to Rhanna with you for a rest, remember? And a rest I mean to have with a few of these ceilidhs you talk so much about and a crack or two with all those marvellous characters you've talked yourself blue in the face about ever since I met you.'

She pointed suddenly over the water. 'Look, isn't that Rhanna? It certainly looks like your description of it.'

A blurred mass of blue mountains had appeared on the horizon and Shona laughed aloud with pure joy. 'Yes, that's Rhanna! That's Rhanna! I told you it was beautiful, didn't I?' She had spread her arms wide as if to embrace the distant island to her breast and in her moments of surging happiness her face was a glowing cameo, full of childish delight and un-restrained love. It was the part of Shona that was best known to those who knew her best, an untamed wild spirit that had roamed free through the solitary wide spaces of her childhood. It was the part of Shona least known to Babbie, but now Babbie knew that she was witnessing the emergence of the real Shona. She felt the mood washing into her and despite the fact that a crowd of passengers had come round to watch the island looming nearer she too spread her arms to the heavens and shouted, 'Yes, yes, Rhanna *is* beautiful! The loveliest Hebridean island in the world!'

'Ach, you are a daft pair o' lassies right enough!' grinned one of the crewmen who was fiddling nearby with the ropes. 'It is a well-known fact that Barra has the rest of them beat. You can ask anyone that.'

'And is it not yourself who spends more time on Rhanna than anywhere else, Malcolm McKinnon?' Shona dimpled mischievously.

'Well now, and that is only because most of my brothers were daft enough to go and get themselves married to Rhanna lassies. A man has to go where his relatives are, indeed just.'

At the harbour of Portcull there was the usual air of restrained excitement whenever a boat came in. Men shouted instructions to each other, small boys darted to catch the ropes, chickens clucked, sheep bleated, engines churned the water till the waves foamed and slopped against the pier.

Shona's eyes raked through the throng on the jetty and almost immediately she spotted her father's jet-black head among the rest. 'Father!' she cried ecstatically though she knew he couldn't possibly hear her above the general din. But as soon as the gangplank was lowered she flew downwards like a young deer, almost colliding with Erchy the Post on his way up to collect the mail. 'Erchy, the very man! Would you put this letter into the outgoing mailbags for me? I forgot to post it on the mainland.'

'Indeed I will just,' Erchy grinned, glancing at the address with the usual curiosity displayed by the islanders. 'To young Niall, eh? 'Tis surprised I am you weren't after delivering it to him in person. It will be a whily now before he gets it.'

'Yes – I do know that, Erchy, and feeling bad enough about it as it is so don't you go rubbing salt into the wound.'

Erchy scratched his sandy head with a stubby finger and gave an apologetic grin. 'Ach well, I'll put it into the bag right away but don't ever say a word to old Behag or we'll never hear the end of it for she would have you goin' through all the palaver of postin' it proper in the pillar box an' then have me pickin' it up . . . mind you . . .' he rubbed his square chin thoughtfully, 'I'd say she has been so taken up wi' the contraption this whily back that she has no' been up to her usual sniffin' about like a starving bloodhound.'

'The contraption?' Shona exclaimed, puzzled.

'Ay, a radio thing wi' tubes sproutin' everywhere an' enough bits o' wire to make a fence round my vegetable garden . . . But look now, I have no time for idle bletherin'. You'll hear all about the contraption in good time. It's nice to see you home again, lass . . . and . . .' he gave a shy, sidelong glance at Babbie.

'My friend, Babbie Cameron,' Shona said quickly.

'Pleased to meet you indeed, Miss Cameron.'

'Just call me Babbie. Better to be informal from the start.'

Erchy looked at Babbie's exceedingly comely figure and his eyes gleamed. 'Ay well, right enough now, I'm no' a body for all this polite way o' doin' things myself. I'll be seein' you around then . . . Babbie.'

Shona was already at the foot of the gangplank struggling her way through people and a collection of horses and carts that had assembled at the pier to collect the coal and other items from the boat. Soon she spotted her father's black head bobbing and beside it the fair one of Kirsteen.

'Father!' Shona threw herself at Fergus and he laughed through the smother of auburn hair against his face.

'Hey, steady on. I'm just about choking to death and there's a whole lot of people gawping at us.'

'Ach, to hell with people!' Shona cried gleefully. She turned from her father to hug Kirsteen to her then she stood back to survey them both. They were a handsome pair with Kirsteen's corn-coloured hair a startling contrast to Fergus's jet-black locks. His side-burns were almost white but this only added to his powerful attractiveness. Kirsteen looked small and very feminine beside him, her fine-featured face alive with pleasure at seeing Shona. She had such a look of deep contentment in her blue eyes that Shona felt a sudden rush of gladness in the knowledge that the look sprang from the fulfilment that Kirsteen had with her father.

Fergus surveyed his daughter's pinched little face and said gruffly, 'It's just as well you're home for a time. You could do with a bit of fattening up.'

Babbie came struggling towards them, laden down with luggage. 'You left me to carry all this,' she accused Shona. 'You ought to know I'm far too lazy to enjoy such punishment forbye the fact I'm supposed to be here for a well-earned rest.'

'Oh, I'm sorry, Babbie,' Shona said with an apologetic grin. 'I was in such a hurry to get down to these two. This is my fa—'

Babbie held up her hand. 'I know who they are. God, girl, you've described them to me so often I see black-haired men and golden-haired maidens dancing in my dreams.' She stretched out a friendly hand. '*I'm* Babbie Cameron and I can only hope to heaven you got Shona's letter telling you you were about to have an unexpected guest. She has a habit of forgetting to post minor little things like letters!'

Kirsteen laughed. 'Short notice but enough to allow me to air the spare room and beg a pheasant from Robbie Beag.'

Fergus extended a cautious hand. He was always very aware of his missing left arm when first introduced to strangers, but he needn't have worried about Babbie. She took his hand, and shaking it warmly said, 'Now if we had both been left-handed this might have been a bit awkward, but we're not so it isn't and I'm very pleased to meet you, Mr McKenzie.'

The ludicrous statement put Fergus immediately at ease. Babbie had brought his disability straight into the open and looking at her steady green gaze and generous smiling mouth he knew that here was one girl who would never be accused of beating about the bush.

A small figure detached itself from a snowy-haired gnome sitting on the harbour wall and Grant Fergus came racing to throw himself at Shona though he was careful to check the immediate vicinity to make sure that no young male companions were there to witness such a 'cissy' demonstration. His sturdy little arms wound tightly round Shona's neck but for a moment he couldn't say anything. He adored his recently acquired big sister and her leaving Rhanna had caused him a good deal of anguish, though not by one word had he conveyed his feelings to anyone.

Shona felt a swift rush of love flooding into her heart. 'Shouldn't you be in school, you wee wittrock?' she asked breathlessly.

'Old Murdoch let me out for ten minutes seeing you were coming home,' he imparted off-handedly. 'Old Joe was telling me stories till the boat came in and I got so interested I forgot all about you.'

'Well, thanks a lot,' Shona giggled.

He looked up at her with dark solemn eyes, the mirror-image of his father's. 'I have to get back now . . . sums. I hate them! I wish I was going out fishing with Ranald . . .' His grubby little hand curled into Shona's and squeezed it tight. 'I'll see you later if I'm not too busy . . .' He threw a laughing glance at Babbie and darted off through the village towards the school.

The others began to move away from the harbour towards Glen Fallan. Shona gazed rapturously at the peaks of Sgurr nan Ruadh and asked, 'Anything new happening on Rhanna? Erchy mentioned something about Behag having some sort of contraption.'

Fergus threw back his head and roared with laughter. 'Ay, you could call it that right enough. Our postmistress is very full of her own importance these days. She is in charge of a wireless transmitter and we all have the feeling that she is just waiting to report some momentous event in order to cover herself in glory.'

Everyone smiled at Fergus's words and Babbie said, 'It might be that this contraption thing will keep her back from all the idle gossip I hear she's so good at.'

'*Nothing* will keep Behag from that,' Shona said
fervently.

'And nothing will keep me from the dinner that
Kirsteen has spent the last two days preparing in your
honour,' Fergus said. 'C'mon, get a move on you two.'

They were a happy throng walking up the winding
Glen Fallan road to Laigmhor, which lay amongst the
shaggy winter fields where there was nothing but a
few early cross-breed lambs to suggest that spring
was just waiting to creep slowly out from its long days
of slumber. Shona talked and laughed with the others,
but all the time her eyes were on the chimneys of
Slochmhor in the distance. This was where Niall had
lived and she looked towards the house longingly
with pain in her eyes.

Part Two

Clydebank
March 13th 1941

Chapter Two

Young Niall McLachlan slumped over the books which were spread out before him on the table in his cramped little lodging room on the fringes of Clydebank. He had embarked rather adventurously into reading a long chapter on bovine milk fever. With his chin cupped in his hands he plodded on doggedly, occasionally shuddering out an involuntary yawn. His cheery little Glaswegian landlady had just relentlessly filled him with a hearty meal of thick broth followed by an enormous helping of mashed potatoes, fluffy dumplings and mince. 'Ma Brodie', as she was known to young and old alike, was a thrifty soul who could conjure magical meals from apparently very little, the limitations of ration books no obstacle to her culinary prowess.

'How do you do it, mo ghaiol?' Niall had asked once, and she had put a finger to her lips and winked a knowing eye.

'There are wee ways, son, wee ways a body has,' she had said mysteriously and hastened away without enlarging on the subject.

Niall, well aware of the existence of the 'Black Market' but less aware of how it worked, had wondered if this endearing woman could be involved in such a thing. But in the end he had decided it was none of his business because she enriched the lives of those around her with endless kindly gestures. She always seemed to be hastening across the landing with a pot of steaming broth for gentle snowy-haired Miss Rennie whose bony frame suggested a spartan existence. And Mr Maxwell, the cantankerous widower one flight below, also found his life the richer by thick slices of dumpling and other tasty tit-bits. 'I'll be *her* tit-bits *he'll* be after,' Iain Brodie had winked to Niall and roared with laughter at his own ludicrous suggestion.

The Brodies had taken the young, handsome Gael to their hearts, delighting in his soft lilting tongue, his inherent politeness and his talk of the Hebridean island of Rhanna that was his birthplace. Their only son lay in a distant grave in France, killed in the very battle in which Niall had been wounded, and his heart wept for them and their unspoken suffering. He felt honoured to sleep in Tim's room and to use the things that Tim had used in life.

Undoubtedly Niall was happy living and working in Glasgow and seldom wasted time pining for dear familiar people and places, but occasionally his thoughts would drift, carrying him far over the western seas to Rhanna. It was a place where time itself seemed to stand still and the dour but fun-loving inhabitants retained a child-like innocence in their approach to life. Yet they were a powerful people, full of character and a strength of endurance born through the never-ending battle to reap a living from the harvests of land and sea. In amongst the dust and fumes of city life, Niall often found it difficult to remember the clean, wind-fresh air of Rhanna but sometimes it came to him in the diluted form of memories till he could almost smell the wild sweetness of tossed-heather moors, the nectar of summer fields, the piquant perfume of peat smoke, and, above all, the tang of salty sea. And of course there were the sounds of the Hebrides, the hill sheep bleating from mossy slopes, the ever-present sigh of the Atlantic Ocean, the gentle autumn winds rattling the seed pods of the gorse, heather bees buzzing . . .

Niall's elbows slipped and he sprawled into his heap of books. He'd been at it again, day-dreaming about Rhanna. Lately he seemed to be thinking about it more and more. He dearly longed to see his mother's bonny face, his father's brown eyes lit with a smile, the lively dark-haired nymph who was his little sister, Fiona, already using her feminine wiles to wheedle people round her little finger. But he wasn't sure when next he would be home because as well as being a student at the vet. college he was also a part-time member of Britain's Civil Defence, and with the Germans forever trying to get a foothold on British soil the country was alert and wary. It had been stipulated that anyone in a war-connected service should remain in their own locality.

Although Niall felt that the training he had received in the Regular Army was being put to some use, there were times when he felt a great sense of frustration and an anger against the enemy for rendering him unfit to take an active part in battle. By nature he was a pacifist and didn't believe in marching blindly into a foray for the sake of dying for King and Country. But in the exuberance of youth he felt he was of the stuff that went into one battle after another, always, in the height of his dreams, emerging unscathed and ready to start again. But he had fallen almost before he had begun his posting to Northern France in the autumn of 1939. After that it was only a matter of time before the Allied armies made the withdrawal from Dunkirk.

The horror of Dunkirk often tore his dreams apart till they became nightmares, but his daytime thoughts were even more vivid and real. He remembered now and lived again in the smell of unwashed flesh, the blood and guts pouring from the wounded. No one really knew what was happening, and some were too sickened and dazed to care. Like weary flocks of sheep they had been organized on to various embarkation beaches to await in a terrifying cacophony of noise the boats that were to take them home. Smoke, dust and acrid fumes filled everyone's lungs till it seemed it would be impossible ever to breathe clean air again. Thousands of men had been taken from the beaches but thousands more still had to wait. Moreover the place swarmed with French and Belgian troops and, adding to the congestion, hordes of empty-eyed and hopeless refugees. Niall now watched it all again with a feeling of utter despair. He felt that nothing was being achieved, that the fighting and killing was all in vain. He felt vulnerable and hopelessly inadequate and, seething with passion, knew that he would gladly tear apart a German soldier with his bare hands.

The voice of his mother came to his mind like the rippling little wind of a storm warning: 'How will it feel killing a man, Niall? You that never hurt a living thing in your life?'

He had shuddered then, hating a war that turned ordinary men into savage beasts. And while the hate churned inside him, an explosion rocked the ground nearby. When the smoke and dust cleared he looked round to see one of his comrades dying, blood spewing from a gaping wound in his neck. He was but a boy of eighteen with a light sprinkling of fuzz on his chin and it had worried him that his downy beard wouldn't grow into the wiry stubble of manhood. Lying together in the cold, dark trenches, he and Niall had laughed together as they dreamed up all sorts of ridiculous beard-growing potions. Looking at the round boyish face, Niall knew that the dawn would never break again for a life so young.

The youngster, nicknamed Billy Boy by the older men, shivered as the finger of Death loomed over him. His filthy uniform had been shredded to tatters by the blast, and Niall tore off his own battle-jacket, and pushed Billy Boy's arms into the sleeves in a rough frenzy of fear. 'This will keep you warm, Billy,' he choked harshly, the sob at the back of his throat making his whispers of reassurance sound rough. 'I'll get help, you'll be fine in no time.'

But Billy Boy reached out a smoke-grimed hand to grip Niall's arm. 'Don't – leave me to – die alone. You know there's no help for me now.' A weary smile touched his white lips and he looked up into the smoke-blackened heavens. 'I'll finish off growing my beard up there . . . though . . . I think it won't matter . . . any more.'

The feeble little joke was lost in the wisp of a sigh, and the long curling lashes of a young boy who had fought like a man and was dying like one, closed over eyes from which sight had already departed. In seconds he was gone, his head a dead weight on Niall's arm, the blood of his life still rushing from the hole in his neck. Niall rocked on his heels in an agony of grief but one of the older men came and tore him away. They stumbled along the beach together while above them the air attacks continued, the planes of the German Luftwaffe zooming in and out of the pallid smoke-clouds, dropping bombs with a fiendish certainty that they were bound to hit some target, be it human or otherwise.

Suddenly Niall felt the ground ripping apart and the sound of an explosion coincided with a searing pain in his head. He heard the older man screaming in agony and saw the blood seeping through the fingers held to his eyes. The world was a spinning blur of red, and the agony inside his head made him want to vomit. Before he sank into a thick blanket of nothingness he felt a rush of gladness that it was over and he could forget a world where power-hungry fanatics took away the freedom of peace-loving people.

But, Niall thought, coming back to his present state, it hadn't been over for him. He had lain unconscious in a military hospital in England and no one had known who he was because his identity disc had been blown from his neck and the rest of his personal belongings had been in the jacket he had given Billy. When he had finally come back to the living world he learned that his parents had believed him to be dead and that Shona, his childhood sweetheart, had given birth to a little stillborn son. In the agony of thinking him dead she had stumbled over the Rhanna moors to the place that had been their secret hide-out since early childhood. There, near the old Abbey ruins, was *their* cave, set into a heather-clad hillock called Dunuaigh. In it they had placed precious bits and pieces, there they had aired their childish dreams, had argued and laughed the years away till finally, in the passion of their youth, they had loved in a world-spinning union of body and soul. He had taken away her virginity and with it her childhood. She had been just sixteen then, he eighteen, and after the warm sweet days of their intimate loving he had gone away to war leaving his seed in her, a seed that had grown into a tiny son never to know the sweetness of life.

On his return to Rhanna they had both been over-whelmed with the joy of their reunion yet there had been a subtle change in their relationship. They had both suffered in their different ways. His war wound had left him almost totally deaf in one ear, but he could live with that. It was the memories of war he couldn't take. They had changed his peaceful soul into a restless spirit that yearned for revenge, both for himself and Shona whose experiences had robbed her of a lot of her gaiety and spontaneous affection. But it was too late now for regrets, too late to change what had happened . . .

The words on the pages blurred and his head sank on to his chest, the light from the gas mantle turning his hair into threads of gold. Under the fair strands at his neck stretched the tightly-drawn tissue of an ugly scar which split the curve at the base of his skull and distorted the delicate lobe of his left ear. Slowly he lifted his head and looked at the picture of Shona on the dresser. It had been taken during the Indian summer days of their breathless loving when she had still been a child. The picture was in black-and-white but he could see it in vivid colour; her slim, graceful body draped over a sun-warmed stone amidst the heather, the blue of her dress against the blue October sky, her long auburn hair vying with the bronze of the bracken . . . and her eyes, those incredible blue eyes of hers, filled with the love of life. He got up to snatch the photo to his breast, his thoughts carrying him away again, back to the cave on the Muir of Rhanna where first she had given her lovely body to him. He could see it now, the whiteness of it against the creamy wool of the sheepskin rug, her hair spread out in fiery strands, her eyes full of childlike innocence . . . until he had taken it away from her . . .

Since then she had once made a brief visit to Glasgow but she had been uneasy and out of place in the bustling city. Her discomfort had made him feel awkward and unnaturally polite, while deep down inside he had felt love and sadness churning themselves together. His proud, spirited lass had looked like a timid rabbit caught out of its burrow and he had known that she couldn't wait to get back on the train which would carry her away from smoke and noise and return her to green fields and purple mountains. But at the station he had taken her in his arms to kiss her and she had melted against him, her tongue touching his, and for a brief moment they had been, in spirit, lying on a bed of heather on the Muir of Rhanna, the bees buzzing in a frantic gathering of nectar, the sheep bleating from the wild summer mountains.

But then a nearby train had released a hideous bellow of impatient steam and they had jumped apart, the precious moment lost, and a few minutes later, her face hovering forlornly at the window, she was gone from him in a busy huffing and puffing and clattering of pistons.

The memories engulfed him so entirely that he forgot his studies, turned down the gas mantle and went to the window to pull aside the thick blackout drapes. A pale moon rode brilliantly in the vast spaces of the universe. He could picture it hanging over the Sound of Rhanna, weaving a pathway of rippling light over the deep Atlantic waters. He wondered how it would look to Shona in the grandeur of Aberdeenshire. Was she perhaps at this very moment peeping from her window to see the silvered ribbon of the Dee winding down through the glens . . . perhaps thinking of him as he was of her even while she looked at the sloping shoulders of the Grampians outlined against the sky?

The only things outlined for him were monotonous rows of houses with stack upon stack of chimney pots rising in the sharp silhouette of urban starkness. The long reaches of the Clyde estuary were hidden from his view by streets of tenement buildings. The subdued murmur of town life reached up from the street below. A dog howled unharmoniously with a wailing baby in the flat above. Somewhere in the backcourts a dustbin lid clattered and feline yowls of outrage followed as a well-aimed tackity boot found its mark. From the kitchen came the indistinct murmur from the wireless. Ma Brodie made a point of listening to the 9 o'clock news every night on the BBC Home Service. He knew she would be ensconced cosily by the range, her stockings rolled to her ankles, nursing one of the many cats which frequently adopted the house. Every so often she would murmur 'ay' by way of sympathy for the things that people were having to suffer in wartime.

Niall's reverie was broken by the thin wail of the air-raid sirens which suddenly pervaded the house. Ma Brodie raised her voice to shout, 'Would you listen to that! These poor souls in London are getting it bad. The sound of the siren is even coming through on the news!' Out of the blue, the Brodies' large ginger tom, known in the neighbourhood as Ginger Moggy, appeared in Niall's doorway, his fur on end and his green eyes narrowed to slits. He glared at Niall, his nostrils aflare with fright, and then shot under the bed to crouch there, howling and spitting. The sight of the terrified animal triggered Niall into action, for he realised that the sirens were not coming through the radio but were sounding in the immediate vicinity. Quickly he donned his coat and tin helmet and snatched up the case containing his gas mask. Outside on the landing there was a low murmur of voices and the sound of one or two doors banging on the landings above, but Niall knew that many of the residents of his building would not go down to the shelter. The experience of previous alerts had taught him that many of the residents would simply huddle under anything they considered might keep them safe, unwilling to leave the deceptive security of their homes.

Ma Brodie was in the lobby clutching a huge suitcase in which she kept her most personal documents. Her best coat and Iain's Sunday suit were still on their hangers, draped over her arm. She was always thus prepared for an air raid. 'C'mon, son,' she said stoically. 'I have everything that means anything to Iain and myself. If anything happens . . .' she paused for a moment, her thoughts on her husband out on fire-fighting duty. 'Ach, but it won't, it will likely just be another false alarm. I'd best get over to Miss Rennie and see if the auld scunner is hiding under her bed again.'

Niall went back to his room, grabbed Shona's picture and stuffed it into his gas mask case. As a last thought he reached under the bed for howling Ginger Moggy and bundled him inside his roomy coat. Ma

Brodie was on the landing helping tottering old Miss Rennie downstairs. But the old lady was loath to go.

'Joey, I must take Joey with me,' she protested. Joey was Miss Rennie's talkative budgie and the wailing sirens had excited him greatly. Boisterous cries of 'Mammy's pretty boy!' echoed from Miss Rennie's flat, and Ginger Moggy stirred in the depths of Niall's coat. Viciously, he clawed at Niall's chest till he was free, and bounded with a triumphant flick of his bushy tail through Miss Rennie's door.

'Joey!' the old lady cried and broke away from Ma Brodie to totter unsteadily back into the flat.

Niall was feeling uneasy. It was his duty as an Air Raid Warden to make sure that everyone was in safe cover, and something told him that tonight's alert signalled the real thing. Ma Brodie was seeing to Miss Rennie once more, so Niall bounded upstairs to check on the others before going off to his post. The top flats were empty but for one. Inside, sprawled in a shabby armchair, was Blackie O'Riordan, renowned for his drinking bouts and subsequent brushes with the law. He was drunk now, an almost-depleted bottle of cheap wine hanging precariously on the end of his fingers. At sight of Niall the slits of his eyes widened in glazed recognition.

'Young Niall! All dressed up like a soldier! Will you be havin' a drink with me?' Without replying, Niall yanked him to his feet.

'Will you stop pullin' at me!' Blackie yelled.

'C'mon now,' Niall said persuasively. 'The sirens are howling like blazes.'

'Up the sirens! I don't give a damn. Let the bloody Nazis fly about all night for all I care. I hate the bastards! They shot me out the stinking war but it'll take more than the crap Luftwaffe to chase me out my own house!'

Niall pushed his shoulder under Blackie's oxter but the brawny Irishman was built like a plough horse and tore himself free. His huge hands flew out and Niall found himself being propelled to the door and all but thrown out on to the landing, after which the lock shot home accompanied by a shower of abuse.

Finding himself alone on the landing, the blackout shutters on the windows muffling the sounds of the outside world; the stairs, lit only by the feeble flicker of a gas mantle, eerily deserted; and the high walls seeming to lean ever closer in claustrophobic conspiracy, Niall took the stairs two at a time, anxious to leave behind the ghostly confines. He followed the sound of friendly voices and soon found that everyone had crowded into the stuffy kitchen of the bottom flat because no one particularly favoured the damp brick shelters in the backcourts. Familiar faces wore cheery masks of composure. Gentle little Miss Rennie had the patiently resigned look of her generation, in the midst yet apart from the rest, her frail old arms clasped protectively round Joey's cage on her knee. Niall quickly realized that the stern dissatisfied countenance of Mr Maxwell was missing.

'He's maybe went to visit his sister in Dumbarton,'

someone suggested, but Niall ran out and back up the steep dark stairs. Bursting into the widower's house he found him comfortably ensconced under the kitchen table, a pillow at his head and a blanket tucked round his bony frame. A little Thermos flask stood conveniently at his elbow together with a large, tea-stained Queen Victoria Coronation mug.

'I'm stayin',' he told Niall bluntly. 'I'm no' goin' down to that house with everybody reekin' o' sweat and smokin' like lums.' At that moment the softly insidious drone of the first wave of German night-raiders wafted into the room. Niall cocked his good ear upwards and Mr Maxwell put a horny hand to one of his large lugs, moulding it into a wrinkled trumpet. 'They're comin',' he said incredulously. 'It's for real right enough.'

'Ma Brodie has dumpling and pancakes down-stairs,' Niall said in a persuasive rush.

'Ach, all right, anything for a bit peace . . . but mind now, if that auld Jennie Rennie and her damt budgie are down there I'm for comin' back up.' He crawled stiffly from under the table and allowed Niall to assist him downstairs and into the crowded kitchen.

Despite everything, the inconvenience, the appre-hension, it was a jolly company. The teapot was already to the fore and Ma Brodie was cutting thick slices of juicy dumpling. She slipped a generous portion into a bag and pushed it at Niall. 'Eat this when you have a meenit, son,' she ordered sternly. Then her face relaxed into a warm smile and she gripped his hand tightly. 'Take care, my laddie, the tea will be on the stove when you get back. You're like my own son . . . remember that.'

He stooped to hug her briefly, sensing her unspoken fears. 'Don't worry about me . . . or Iain. He can take care of himself.' At the utterance of the words a strange fear gripped his heart. He looked at Ma Brodie's smiling, kindly little face and on an impulse he stooped to kiss her cheek. 'Take care, Ma,' he said softly and then turned to abandon the warmth of the kitchen for the cold black streets. There, anonymous shadows flitted, felt rather than seen. The dark shape of a baffle wall loomed and he stopped for a moment to lean against it and to look up into a sky torn apart by the furring vapour-trails of the German bombers. The ragged silhouette of the town was already sharpened by the orange glow of fires. High explosives were falling in the lower parts of town, and fountains of smoke and flames licked into the sky. He watched the planes tearing past, small dots thousands of feet above, divorced from the earth by the power of engines, yet so easily able to tear it apart by the force of explosives. Panic closed in on him. It was here! It was real! No need now to go to war, it had come to him and to thousands like him. Incendiaries were raining down. One landed at the close entrance and he dashed forward to kick it away then he began to race towards his post. His thoughts were bitter, and the nerve-shattering experience of Dunkirk came to mind again in vivid snatches. Smoke and acrid fumes made his eyes smart with tears but they were also tears of anger at the destruction and grief that he knew the German Luftwaffe would leave in its wake. 'Nazi swine,' he murmured softly, the words, spoken in his lilting tongue, full of an uncharacteristic hatred in a boy who had never hated anyone in his life.

Chapter Three

The shower of incendiaries that came spitting out from the planes of the Luftwaffe, Third Air Fleet, were profuse enough for some to find their way into inflammable areas of industrial sites. The black spaces of the surrounding open fields pushed the orange flames into a giant torch which greedily began to devour the little town and spread thin curls of oil-laden smoke eddying through the streets. Another wave of bombers was arriving from the east, bearing down like evil birds of prey against the cold, pale sky. Within seconds they were dropping altitude and more bombs were falling, together with parachute mines, allowing no time for people in the target-area to sort out one thought, one fear, from the other. Enormous craters split the tarmac, blowing water mains and gas mains to smithereens. Because three Auxiliary Fire Service Stations had been put out of action earlier in the evening, the problem of dealing with the Clydebank inferno was overwhelming. Many of the hydrants were dry and the firefighters were driven to use the muddy water filling the craters.

Niall, working with a rescue party clearing the debris of a crushed tenement that had received a direct hit from a 500-kilo bomb, had lost his gas mask. He breathed in choking dust and hot smoke till his lungs were raw. Someone pushed a dirty hanky at him. 'Here, tie this over your face or we'll end up rescuing you!' Quite unexpectedly they had come upon a pile of battered corpses that were so twisted and bloody it was difficult to believe they were people. From out of the heap of dead flesh a terrified voice cried for help and they extricated a young woman, pulling at her arms as gently as they could, trying to ease her free from the ensnaring bodies that held on to her legs like the sucking mud of a bog. 'She's the only one in this lot,' said one of the men. 'Dear Jesus! There's dozens of them gone!'

A squad of rescue workers raced up, filthy spectres with reddened eyes and pale lips showing through the grime. 'The next street!' panted one. 'We need some hands!'

Niall ran, and somehow he knew, even before he turned the corner, that the place he called 'home' in Glasgow was no more. All of the façades of the buildings on his street had been sheared off as if someone had taken a giant axe and split bricks and mortar down through the centre. The portions of the front walls which had been blown away ludicrously exposed all the little domesticities of family life. In one kitchen an elderly couple were seated at the table as if about to eat supper. They had been killed by a bomb-blast which had left them whole but sucked all the air from their lungs.

Two houses along to the right, underneath the great mound of smouldering debris, were buried all the people whom Niall had helped to 'safety' just a few hours before. Old Mr Maxwell's table stood sturdy and intact amidst its humble surroundings. In the kitchen above, Miss Rennie's rocking chair sat by the jagged ruins of the range. On the mantelshelf china plates remained unbroken, on the smashed hearth a plaster dog lay on its side, its painted eyes staring out from the ruins. The Brodies' bedroom lay fully exposed to the elements. All the furniture was intact but the bed mat had flipped upwards to drape over the wardrobe and a lamp shade hung from a brass bed knob on the bed end. Eerie sights, made spine-chillingly macabre by the curious whims of blast.

Blackie O'Riordan stood at the edge of his kitchen on the top flat, waiting to be rescued. A torrent of abuse, directed at the bombers in the vaults of the heavens, drowned out the instructions of the rescue squad.

Some of the dead had been blown into the air and had landed so far from where they'd first been struck it seemed they might have been dropped from the sky. They littered the road like broken dolls, arms and legs twisted beneath them. But had they been dead when they were blown into the air? That was the question that drummed into Niall's brain as he stared around him in disbelief. He looked at a crumpled ball of orange fur lying on the cracked pavement and realized it was Ginger Moggy stretched in a pool of his own blood, his lips drawn back over his fangs in a grimace. He had suffered a painful death. Above him, alive by some freakish escape, Joey perched on a crazily-leaning lamppost, feebly muttering

'Good-night Mammy! Mammy's pretty boy.'

Miss Rennie's broken body was being lifted from the rubble, the jagged spars of Joey's cage embedded in her chest. Light pink bubbles of lung-blood oozed out of the little holes.

Half-sobbing, Niall ran to the heap of masonry and began to tear at it with the strength and blindly unthinking rage of a bull. Voices roared at him to be careful and several pairs of hands tried to pull him away but he shook them off and went on with his demented searching. There was no whimper of life from the piled rubble, nothing to tell him that a soul still breathed. He found Ma Brodie quite suddenly. Her eyes were open, gazing up at him out of the debris.

'Help me get her out!' he shouted desperately, but the other men were already pushing aside lumps of jagged stone, carefully freeing what was left of Nellie Brodie's diminutive frame. The teapot was still clutched in her hand, and fragments of a teacup were embedded into the flesh of her arm like crazed paving. Her rib cage had been smashed, and splinters of bone stuck through the gay, flowery apron Niall had given her at Christmas. It was soaked in blood which had congealed quickly in the powdered dust and crushed brick that had caved in on top of her.

'Ma Brodie – mo ghaoil,' Niall whispered brokenly and gently closed her eyes. He knelt beside her, too shocked to move. Deep within the crazily strewn heap of glass and masonry there came an almost imperceptible little sob. Holding his breath he cocked his good ear and it came again – the stifled ghost of a human voice. 'Someone's alive in here!' he called to the long line of men who were expertly shifting rubble in the fashion of a human conveyor belt. They scrambled towards him and carefully began the arduous task of rescue. An hour later they came upon a small boy, so petrified he was unable to move or speak, his life saved by a massive beam that had jammed above him to form a wedge-shaped tunnel. Niall was slim and agile yet neither he, nor any of the other men there, were able to wriggle in through the narrow gap.

'Haud on, I'll get in there.' Johnny Favour, named so because he was always willing to lend a helping hand, appeared at Niall's elbow.

'Johnny! I thought you were having a night with Shirley Temple!' Niall grinned, feeling a great sense of unaccountable relief at seeing Johnny's familiar, friendly face. He had changed his creased tweeds for a rather shiny navy-blue three-piece suit with a watch chain hanging from the pocket of his waistcoat. But he still wore his battered cap as proudly as a king might wear a crown.

'I left the wife at the La Scala,' he explained cheerfully. 'She'll be safe there and I'll be better use here.' He squirmed out of his jacket and handed it to Niall. 'Guard it wi' your life, son, it's my best. I'll get in beside the bairn and try to hand him out.' He disappeared in through the small opening, and a moment later his voice floated out. 'I'll need help, the lad canny move. I'll start making the hole bigger from this side. We'll shore it up with some bits of wood.'

Fifteen minutes later Niall was able to crawl in beside Johnny. The child lay in a bed of suffocating dust. He was a ghostly little figure with his face and hair coated in white plaster but Johnny was saying things that made him laugh and one side of his face bulged with toffee from Johnny Favour's trouser pocket. His legs were pinned under a lump of concrete but he showed no pain and Johnny whispered to Niall, 'At a guess I'd say the poor wee bugger's legs are crushed. I'd be a lot happier if he was greetin'. Then we'd know he was feeling something. C'mon, let's get to work.'

The job of freeing the child was painfully slow but eventually his torn and bleeding limbs were exposed. Both men knew the child would never walk again.

'Sod it!' Johnny drew a grimy hand across his face. 'Sod the bloody lot of them!'

A First Aid party had arrived. One peered through the opening. 'Can you get him out to us? We've got an ambulance waiting.'

'Pass us a blanket,' Johnny said tonelessly. 'He's shivering a bit.' They wrapped the child carefully and then, at Johnny's insistence, tucked the shiny navy-blue jacket round the small shoulders. 'You're a wee man now, son,' Johnny grinned down at the boy's pale face. 'And just to prove it . . .' he whipped off his battered cap and placed it on the child's head. 'There you are. It's maybe no' much to look at but it'll keep your brains warm.'

The little boy peeped out from the peak that came over his eyebrows. 'Ta, Johnny. I'll wear it when I'm playin' football – well, when I'm doing my goalie. Goalies always wear a cap.'

'You do that, lad,' Johnny said. 'Get going now. You get out first, Niall. Take his shoulders.'

In a short time Niall was placing the boy into the arms of the First Aid party who bore him quickly away. Niall felt dizzy with relief. At least one small life had survived the holocaust, but what of the others? The boy's parents? Old Mr Maxwell and his little Thermos flask and his assurances that he would be safe under the kitchen table. He would still be alive if he had stayed there! And Ma Brodie! The dear, big-hearted warmth of such a wee body – dead – and for what? He remembered the teapot still clutched in her hand, a symbol of a life that had cared unstintingly for everyone she met. What of Iain Brodie? Coming back exhausted from the fires. Back to what? His wife, his memories, all gone forever in a senseless waste of everything that made life tick sweetly for the average home-loving man.

The ground trembled suddenly and the tunnel from which Johnny was just emerging caved in. He made no sound as he was first smothered in dust and then crushed under the tons of rubble that came down on top of him. When it finally settled there was no whisper of life and the men knew that Johnny had performed his last favour.

Niall's mind was going numb with shock. He stared at the dull gleam of Johnny's watch chain caught among the bricks, and everything swam in a watery mist. The rescue squad were telling him to get out of the danger area but he barely heard. He was thinking of the senseless waste of good lives. Just a short time ago some faceless nonentity had pressed a button and a bomb had dropped. The mind that guided the hand would forget quickly each press of the button, giving no concrete thought to the agony and grief invoked by just the flick of a finger.

If Niall's own thoughts had been more rational, if he hadn't been so emotionally exhausted, he would doubtless have exercised more care in his movements. But his tiring feet were clumsy and he slipped on loose masonry. The beam that had saved the child dislodged from its precarious hold and came toppling down towards him. He tried to struggle upright but couldn't and in a mesmerised trance he saw the whole thing in slow motion and lay helplessly, waiting for the blackness to engulf him. Hefty arms grabbed at him, dragging him away from the deadly hail of bricks and glass, but they weren't quick enough, and the beam pinned his right arm into a bed of plaster, close to the spot where only minutes before a small boy had lain, too frozen with terror to do more than whimper like a lost puppy.

Chapter Four

Carl Zeitler, the pilot of one of twelve Heinkel bombers of Bomber Squadron IKG3, rocked gleefully in his seat. He squinted down through the Plexiglass panels of the gun cupola to the pink glow where the incendiaries and the rapid flashes of the H.E. bombs had split enormous craters in the ground and turned the little burgh of Clydebank into a raging inferno.

The rest of the group were heading back to base; but Zeitler, in a gluttony of excitement, was taking the risk of making one more bombing run over the burning town. With skilled airmanship he steeply turned the lumbering bomber for a triumphant sweep above the murky clouds of smoke. The feeling of power was strong within him, and the rhythmic throb of the Junker's Jumo 211 twin engines seemed to beat right into his heart, giving him a confident sense of security. He was an excellent pilot and, though he was barely twenty-five, already had an exemplary career behind him. He had brought his plane safely over Scapa Flow, Narvik and Dunkirk, with little more than some superficial damage to show for it. True, on one occasion his navigator had been peppered with flak and he had flown back to base with the dying man's cries of agony filling the plane. Another time he had lost his rear gunner. No one had known he was dead till the ground crew had slid open the rear door and were bathed in the blood that gushed from the holes in the gunner's face. Dunkirk! The remembrance of it always made Zeitler smile. All those stupid bastards strung out on the beaches like flies on a wall! Just asking to be picked off! He must have wiped out dozens of them. The French had been beaten and the Allied British had taken to their heels with their tails well tucked between their legs.

Even as he turned to make the final sweep over Clydebank Zeitler felt echoes of the thrill Dunkirk had given him. His very bones shivered with delight and he threw back his wedge-shaped head in an arrogant smile. But anger mingled with his pleasure, anger at the British for still managing to remain on their toes despite the concentrated blitz. Europe had gone under like a drowning dog! All except the bulldog British. Despite the hammering they had taken those proud, clever bastards were still keeping their heads above water. For someone like Zeitler, tuned in to Hitler's wavelengths like a well-programmed robot, the pill was a bitter one to swallow. Deep in his heart he admired the cool-headed British for their fighting spirit and their admirable allegiance to the British Premier, Winston Churchill. There was a leader for you! A good soldier too, experienced in the fields of both war and politics. But Churchill was the enemy and Zeitler's hot-headed fanatical devotion to his own leader, Adolf Hitler, soon blotted out his rare moment of level-headed thinking.

He stared through the Plexiglass. The moon was

beautiful, a cold bluish disc hanging in the sky. But Zeitler didn't see it as an object to be admired. It was there in the sky to aid the success of these night attacks. This raid was strange, they had come quite some distance to reach this industrial complex in Scotland. The targets were the docks, shipyards and oil depots. Difficult. The target area was small over this point. The landscape showed a lot of dark patches that were fields. Spasmodic streaks of flak spattered up from the fringes of the town. It was all quite different from the big raids over London and Coventry. These night raids on England had caused terrible havoc, yet still she remained unconquered. The damned place had nearly been blown off the face of the earth but still Britain popped up smiling, each time with a new trick, a new defence, up her voluminous sleeve.

The pilot's thoughts made his pale blue eyes bulge with chagrin. Dark rings under his eyes made him look older than his twenty-five years, and normally the illusion was completed by premature balding, but with his head enveloped in his leather flying helmet the effect was lessened considerably. He removed a large, gloved hand from the control column to adjust his face mask. 'Die Späten answers well, eh, Anton?' Zeitler yelled through the intercom.

Anton Büttger, bomb-aimer and commander of the aircraft, lay belly-down on a foam rubber pad in the nose of the gun cupola. The muscles in his jaw tightened and his keen blue eyes snapped like firecrackers. He guessed that the reason Zeitler was making the unnecessary fly-over was so that he could gloat. The destruction caused by the raid was pleasing him, exciting his cold, calculating emotions. Whenever bombs smashed into concrete, Zeitler showed his immense pleasure by sucking his breath and rocking his pelvis in a strangely sensual way. Though Anton couldn't see Zeitler from his position, he now heard the familiar sucking sound. During a sortie Zeitler's favoured expression was, 'Don't shit! Hit!', a phrase Anton had heard through the intercom so many times in the last twenty minutes that the young commander couldn't keep back his seething feelings of dislike for the pilot. Zeitler was so completely cast in the mould of so many hot-headed Nazis that he seemed to have no individuality, no character of his own. His personality was about as pleasing as a chunk of cold metal.

'Go now, Zeitler,' Anton ordered. 'Make a mess of this one and your days in the air are numbered.'

Zeitler hunched his shoulders, sucked his breath, and straightened the rudder. Soon the Heinkel was ripping through the cold night sky.

Anton relaxed slightly. He tried not to think of the scene below but couldn't keep the pictures out of his brain: the spilled blood, the cries of terror . . . the moments of death for the women and children. The hearts of the living would be filled with anger, frustration, compassion. He shuddered. It was easy to press the bomb-release button. Too easy. There was no challenge, no feeling that you had achieved something the way you did during air combat. He had joined the Luftwaffe because he loved flying. He had never imagined his career would one day turn sour on him. Up here in the vulnerable position of the gun cupola he always felt a certain measure of unease, often long after a raid was over. The bomb-aimer, and the gunners, perhaps, always had more on their conscience than the pilot. But it might be that not everyone felt as he did. He would rather be at the controls, but Zeitler was the better pilot and was arrogantly aware of the fact, using any opportunity to display his prowess and undermine Anton's authority. In an odd kind of way Anton understood: he was younger than Zeitler, and had only recently taken over command of the plane. Zeitler had made umpteen bombing raids with the usual commander, Willi Schmitt, who had been grounded because of illness. Anton knew you had to fly with someone a long time to get in tune with him.

'We have managed to make a pretty little bonfire!' It was Zeitler again, his lips stretched in a gloating leer which the other couldn't see but could feel. 'Look! Down there, the flames leap high. An oil depot perhaps! Drop the rest of the high Es, Anton. Might as well put them to good use instead of wasting them in the sea!'

Anton didn't answer. His fingers touched the bomb button but he didn't press it immediately. He knew he should. If he didn't lighten the load now he might have to later . . . perhaps in a field, or an open stretch of water . . . or on a little country farm with all the people in bed, unsuspecting, unprepared . . .

He felt very tired. The kind of dull, heavy tiredness that fills the veins with lead instead of blood. When this kind of exhaustion swept over him he remembered things he had thought forgotten: far-off days filled with happiness; small-boy days when his world was of green fields and golden corn; ambitions to be like his farmer father; the dreams of childhood. The grown-up Anton loved aeroplanes. When his father had spoken about cows or horses he had thought about aeroplanes, not so much about their operational functions as of their performance, engine power and attainable height. He thought about diving and banking, the sensation of zipping through lacy cloudbanks to the blue roof of the sky, and then looking down at the clouds drifting lazily over the world. His visions of flying hadn't included war and the personal tragedies it brought, the raids over Berlin in the late summer of 1940.

Late summer . . . his father out in the fields, working on after last light . . . his mother in the kitchen baking the bread for morning, the fragrant smell of it filling the room . . . his two little sisters, asleep upstairs. At least they'd had no time to know the terror his mother had known, buried in the rubble of the kitchen. She had lived for a short while after rescue, his father a few weeks, all because of one bomb, one stray British bomb that had missed the town and fallen on a little country farm . . .

A sob caught in his throat and for a moment he didn't care about the hail of flak that crackled in the air like sparks in the blackened chimney of a cosy farmhouse kitchen . . . 'Take her up, Zeitler!' he said in a slightly breathless voice. 'The searchlights are on us!'

'Did you drop the bombs?'

'Damn the bombs! Get her up!'

The searchlights were criss-crossing into the skies, violating the blue-black reaches. Zeitler throttled forward and the Heinkel responded by gaining height steadily. But still the beams were on them, clinging like leeches to a leg. Something inside the pilot's head, a built-in instinct of impending danger, warned him that this time his conceit had tempted Providence too far. His knuckles tightened on the throttles and he knew an unaccustomed rush of apprehension.

In his place in the gun turret, Ernst Foch, the wireless operator, watched the flak and the searchlights through the Plexiglass fairing. Their time over the target-area was up, and now they would be heading back to base. Every sense in him was alert but thoughts of his family back home in Germany strayed briefly into his head. It had been an eternity since he had last set eyes on his pretty wife, Helga, and his small sturdy son, Franz. He wondered why it was sometimes difficult to remember their faces. Little scraps of dear, familiar things came to mind but the memories did nothing to soothe him. He wondered how long the war would last. Like Zeitler he was devoted to his country. From the age of fourteen he had been a member of Hitler's youth movement, proud to wear his brown uniform and to carry a dagger like a man. His young mind had been very receptive to the Nazi regime, and he had felt part of a glorious system. But the softening influences of a wife and child had dulled his enthusiasm for mass regimentation. He didn't want his son to grow into a puppet with a master-mind controlling his life. It took more than a uniform and a dagger to make a man. There had to come a time when common sense and the need for individuality came to the fore. He wondered about Zeitler up front in the pilot's seat. The man was a brilliant pilot but a mindless fool otherwise. If the Führer ordered every Nazi to burn piss holes in the snow in the sign of the swastika then Zeitler would be the first to open his fly.

Far below, the gun crews on a Polish destroyer, docked in John Brown's for repairs, stood by their ack-ack guns and sent an almost constant barrage of shells tracing upwards to the aircraft caught in the beams of the probing searchlights. The smoke from the fires made visibility difficult though John Brown's shipyard was comparatively free of serious blaze.

Jon Jodl, the lower-rear gunner, lay on his belly near the ventral sliding door, in front of the machine-gun housing. 'Why is Zeitler hanging about?' he thought. 'Get out of it!' He watched the flak shells exploding about him. Down here it was cold but he felt a trickle of sweat running between his shoulder blades. One of those shells was going to pierce the Perspex door or the stressed skin and plating shell at any moment. A tremor passed through his body and somewhere inside his thin frame a tightly coiled knot of nerves made him feel sick.

At 1000 metres, Zeitler sought cover in a massive cumulus cloud, maintaining climb on his blind-flying instrument panel, and the searchlights and the tracers disappeared from view. Jon reached out to the tin can that was jammed between two metal plates and retched miserably into it. He was neither a coward nor a hero and he didn't give a damn about the Führer and his greedy dream to conquer the world. All his life Jon had been plagued by feelings of inadequacy even though he had shown great proficiency in his academic studies. His very appearance was stamped with a studious sagacity, from his thin clever face to his long, tapering musician's fingers. But he had never been 'one of the crowd' and he had always walked alone, though sometimes this introvert nature of his made him deeply unhappy. He had seen the German Luftwaffe as an escape to freedom, a chance to prove to the world he was as much of a man as the next. His big domineering mother had not approved. 'You were not made for such things, my Jon,' she had told him firmly. 'You must continue with your music, it is what you were born for.' But at the first opportunity Jon had taken himself off to an air crew training school. With his natural intellect and manual dexterity he had eventually passed out as an air gunner. The mathematics of airborne shooting had come easily to him, as had the required mastery of gun-assembly and fault-finding and an understanding of the intricate equipment inside an aircraft. All the other boys had wanted to be top pilots but not Jon. What he had chosen to do took courage enough. However, with the coming of war he quickly realized he didn't have the 'guts' to cope with the rigours it brought. His tightly strung nervous system simply couldn't take the strain. After all, his world was in Hamburg with his gentle little henpecked papa and his large, over-powering mamma who was like an indestructible mountain. All his life she had pampered him and he knew now that he wasn't strong enough to break away from her shadow. 'You were not made for such things, my Jon!' Her words echoed emptily inside his head. But it was too late now, there was no turning back. Jon was at breaking-point but tension was such a familiar thing in his life he wasn't aware that his crawling nerves were stretching tighter with every turn of the airscrews.

They flew out of the cloud and back into a criss-cross probe of searchlights. The flak was falling short. The crew breathed sighs of relief and Jon Jodl felt the sweat drying under his helmet. 'Thank you, my God in Heaven,' he prayed childishly and shut his eyes in gratitude. Another raid, another test of nerves was over for a while.

Then suddenly the flak from an ack-ack gun on the fringe of the town caught them unexpectedly and a hail of lead peppered the fuselage.

'I couldn't get her up high enough!' Zeitler roared in disbelief. 'You should have dropped those bombs, Anton!' The burst of incredulity momentarily suspended his reactions and the aircraft staggered along for a few seconds then terrifyingly dropped thirty metres. Zeitler felt his backside rammed down into his seat. The others hit the floor like stones. Shuddering gently, the Heinkel was suspended for a split second in the sky, and Zeitler, using his innate airmanship and the visibility that was left, levelled out and stabilized flight without recourse to instruments. 'Get up here, Anton, and check the damage!' Zeitler yelled through the intercom.

Anton lurched into the cockpit, head down to scan the instrument panels. The lights were gone, several of the needles were dead, others swinging senselessly.

Jon, detached from the intercom, saw Anton yelling at him and pulled aside his helmet to hear Anton shouting, 'Watch fuel and oil, take this torch.'

Zeitler waved a gloved hand at the blind-flying group of instruments in front of him and then squinted out through the windscreen. High above, cirrus blanketed off the moon, and below a bank of mist and low stratus obscured the earth.

Anton was rapidly checking the instruments and saw that the altimeter, airspeed indicator, artificial horizon and gyro compass were either destroyed or useless. 'Zeitler, set course 155 degrees!' he commanded sharply.

At that moment Zeitler sighted a cloud bank looming ahead and told Jon to shine his torch on the grid-ring of the magnetic compass beside his knee. Silently Jon did as told and squinting down, Zeitler set 155 on it.

Anton realized he would have to read off height and airspeed to Zeitler from the bomb-aimer's panel and began to crawl back up towards the cupola, but at that moment Zeitler was blinded by a searchlight's glare reflecting off the instrument panel. The aircraft entered cloud and Zeitler fiercely hauled the plane into a steep port turn, his eyes glued to the bank-indicator and engine revolution gauges, his sole remaining assurances against complete disorientation and a fatal fall.

They were still in cloud when the crump of a shell shook the Heinkel violently. Zeitler glanced down-wards and saw that the compass light was now gone and that only the needle and grid were faintly visible. Panic gripped him just as they flew out of cloud and into clearer skies and he kicked viciously at the rudder bar. The rear part of the fuselage was being tugged from side to side in a crazy motion and though they all knew that the air was streaming over a damaged rudder, Zeitler continued to drum the useless pedal with his foot. For a long moment nothing happened but Zeitler persevered grimly and eventually managed to get the rudder under control with Anton assisting him to stabilize course and level by use of trim and servo. They flew on through the clouding night sky. Everyone was very quiet, even Zeitler, who could sense the others' resentment at his putting them all at risk for a few moments of greedy triumph.

'Go back to the bombsight, Jon,' Anton said quietly. 'Keep reading height and airspeed to Zeitler through the intercom.'

They were now down to 950 metres and Anton suspected that they were leaking fuel. 'Throttle back,

Zeitler,' he ordered. 'Maintain cruising speed of 250 kilometres an hour.'

Zeitler didn't answer. He felt drained, so exhausted that he felt if he shut his eyes just then he would die.

'Ernst,' Anton said through the intercom, 'how are things up there with you? Radio intact?'

'Kaput!' Ernst answered shortly. 'The aerial! Tell Zeitler he's a bloody maniac, not fit even to ride a bicycle in a cemetery!'

But Anton, alarmed by the low readings on the still-intact gauges, made no comment. He checked his map and rapidly wrote up his log sheet. Wind speed and direction he could only estimate, and now one hour from target-area, he marked a reckoned position . . . well into the north of England. Through the intercom, at regular intervals, he heard Jon read to Zeitler. Both exchanged comments on the heavy cloud layer beneath them and simultaneously they spotted a breakaway. Visibility was clear below and the moon slanted its pale beam across the sea. Apprehension flooded Anton's brain and he checked his map again. He realized that they had crossed the English coast and were now over the North Sea. Alarm made him feel weak. Navigational conjectures flashed through his mind. A westerly gale? Zeitler's compass course? Compass deviation induced by airframe damage?

'Coastline ahead!' Jon called through the intercom.

All of them peered towards it. They were flying at less than 1000 metres and could see plainly the moon-flecked waves breaking surf on land. Anton saw that it curved away to port and starboard . . . An island? But where? There were no such places in the North Sea! He examined the compass closely, shading his torch beam with his bare hand, for the luminous paint in the dial was old and long overdue for renewal.

That was it! Anton gave a muttered curse and cried, 'Red on blue, Zeitler! We are heading for the Atlantic . . . been flying reciprocal last hour! No hope of reaching base now . . . Circuit this island, everybody on recce lookout!' Anton had been briefed and mapped only for the operation over the Clyde and had little idea as to where they were. Zeitler had committed the cardinal error of setting the reciprocal course on his compass which meant he was 180 degrees wrong, and had headed north-westerly instead of south-easterly, but Anton bitterly blamed himself. He should have checked sooner. But there was no time now for self-recrimination.

The starboard wing was dropping. Anton had released the remaining bombs into the black depths of the sea but even so the Heinkel was losing altitude. The engine could burst into flames at any moment though there couldn't be much fuel left in either tank because the fuel change-over had been made some time ago.

'Get ready to jump!' he ordered his crew imperatively.

'On that postage stamp?' Zeitler squawked.

'All right, we go in the sea then!'

'I prefer to swim in kinder waters,' Zeitler returned sarcastically.

Jon swallowed his rising gorge, the thought of the inevitable jump bringing him out in a cold sweat. Anton shoved a tin at him and said kindly, 'Don't keep it back, Jon. Airsickness is nothing to be ashamed of. What about Kommodore Vati Mölders? Look at the position he is in despite airsickness.'

'Unlike Mölders I have no ambition to be a pilot, ace or otherwise . . . but, thank you for understanding, Anton.'

Anton crouched by Zeitler. 'Take her round once more. The island is split by a range of high mountains but there is a good stretch of open ground just beyond. We must all try and land there.'

'I will stay with her,' Zeitler said.

'You will bail out, and that is an order!' Anton snapped. 'It would be madness to attempt a night landing. Look at those mountains . . .'

The aircraft gave a sudden downward lurch. When she steadied rather shakily, the starboard wing was dropping dramatically and the exhaust manifold was spitting a rush of bright red flame.

'Try to maintain height, Zeitler,' Anton said. 'Ready now! Jon, you go first, get it over with.'

He accompanied Jon to the hatch. The smell of the red-hot manifold made them splutter. Jon swayed dizzily, looking down to the sickening curve of the watery world below.

'Now, Jon!' Anton ordered and Jon jumped. The airstream grabbed him and hauled him away from the aircraft. Before he pulled his ripcord the speed of the drop churned his belly. He choked on his vomit and barely had time to get his wind before the pull of his released chute brought him up with a jerk. Now he was floating like a piece of thistledown to the dark little patch of moor. Ernst had followed close on his heels and was just above but behind him.

'Now you, Zeitler,' Anton said firmly. 'I will fly her now.' He was taking no chances with the dogmatic Nazi whose arrogance had led him to believe he was the master of any situation. Zeitler's eyes flashed but he unbuckled his straps and went without a word, leaving Anton at the controls.

Part Three

Rhanna
March 13th 1941

Chapter Five

Angus McKinnon hurried along the shore path that skirted the harbour. The moon had ridden out from its curtain of cloud to shed a pale brilliant light over the now calm Sound of Rhanna. The horizon seemed a timeless distance away and the great stretches of the Atlantic Ocean lay placid and hauntingly beautiful. The River Fallan rushed down from the mountain corries in mercurial wanderings and the sound of it thundered in Angus's ears as he crossed the bridge. For a moment he stopped to lean on the rough stone parapet, bowing his head to watch the frothing flurry of river tumbling into the sea.

'Uisge-beatha,' he murmured softly and smiled benignly at the 'water of life'. The smell of it was like nectar to his senses. On its journeying it had gathered the crystal-clear air of high mountain places; on its flight across the moorlands it had claimed the tang and tinge of peaty heather roots, which gave it a clear, amber glow and made it an altogether soft, fragrant concoction. A light came into Angus's eyes and his smile was one of triumph. 'Lovely Uisge-beatha,' he addressed the river with approval. 'Tonight you will be proving you are more than just a pretty sight. I'm goin' now to be havin' a taste of you.'

He lumbered on over the bridge but a sound, other

than that of the whispering sea, made him stop again and peer upwards into the sky. Was it his imagination or was that a plane he was hearing? It seemed to him he was always hearing planes these days, and without quite knowing why he felt uneasy. He hated the sound of aeroplanes. They sounded peaceful but he knew that was only an illusion. The war had changed everything. No matter how hard he tried he was haunted by an ever-present sense of guilt, which was made worse by the knowledge that two of his brothers had joined the navy. His supposedly bad back gave him no more than an occasional twinge; the heart murmur discovered during his medical examination did not detract from his easy, peaceful life, yet it and the backache had exempted him from active service. But the general opinion was that he was just lazy.

'The Uisga Hags will get you if the Germans don't,' Canty Tam had warned, grinning his aimless grin and staring out to sea as if willing all the water witches of myth and folklore to come leaping out to grab Angus in their evil clutches and carry him off to sea.

'It's a useless idiot like yourself they're more likely to be after,' Angus had answered with confidence. Nevertheless he hastened to pray to St Michael, the guardian of those on land or sea, and he was careful to wear his Celtic cross even if he was only mucking out the byre.

A little wind ruffled the sea and to one cursed with guilt it was easy to imagine that the sigh of Hag voices rode in on the breeze. Angus shivered, pulled his coat collar closer round his ears, and went quickly on his way. He was making for his father's wash-house, a place that had been grandly christened 'the Head-quarters'. Here a number of men met once-weekly, widely broadcasting the fact that they were, for all intents and purposes, patriotically keeping fresh all the instruction they had received during the Home Guard training courses.

He knocked hurriedly on the stout door of the wash-house, and there was the sound of scuffling and loud whispering before the door creaked open. 'You're late,' came Tam McKinnon's muffled reproach. 'We have started long ago.'

'Ach, I'm sorry, Father. Wee Colin fell out o' bed and I had to go for Nurse Biddy. Then she was fetched to go over to Todd's. Was he here when he was taken bad?'

'Ay, and a terrible job we had carrying him outside, for he was drunk as a lord. In the end we just put him in the wheelbarrow and took him home while Ranald went up for the doctor. How is things with him now?'

'The doctor had him opened up when last I saw him.' Angus gulped at the memory. 'He says he just caught the appendix in time.'

'Ach, poor Todd, a shame just,' Tam said sympathetically. 'But come away in now, son. It is even better than we thought. Like nectar it is, so easy it goes down.'

Angus had forgotten Todd. He stood in the doorway of the wash-hoosie like a child on the threshold of Wonderland. A suffocating heat rushed out to meet him coupled with the palpable, over-powering fumes of whisky. 'I could get drunk just standin' here,' he said happily, staring into the little room where flames from a peat oven gleamed warmly on a pot that was set into a corner of the room. A concoction of pipes and tubes sprouted from it in a glorified jumble that would have baffled the casual observer. But the sweating, glassy-eyed assembly in the wash-house had had plenty of time to acquaint themselves with the still and its intricate workings.

Tam McKinnon had acquired the antiquated machinery in a most unexpected manner. He had been fixing the thatch of a blackhouse at Nigg which was used by blind Annack Gow to keep peat and other fuel, though it wasn't unknown for her to live in the house during the winter months because she claimed it was cosier than the 'modern hoosie'. A rummage in the byre for a hammer had revealed the pot still, sitting like a nugget of gold amidst an assortment of farm implements and a pile of cow manure. Excitement choking him, Tam had hastened to Annack with an offer to clear out the accumulated junk in the byre.

'How much will you be wantin'?' she had barked, peering at him through her thickly-lensed specs. 'An old body like myself has no money to spare with my man gone and only myself to work the croft.'

'Not a farthing, Annack,' Tam had choked. 'Just the odd bit of junk you will never be using. Being a handyman I can make use of some of it.'

'Ay, well, don't be stealing my dung while you're about it,' she had returned suspiciously. 'I need all I can get for my vegetables . . . and a creel or two of seaweed wouldn't go wrong either,' she had ended cunningly.

Tam's face had fallen at the thought of gathering seaweed and humping it over the hill to Nigg, but the temptation of the still had been too much and the deal had been made. In the process of clearing the byre he had found all the bits and pieces relating to the still and happily had trundled the lot home on his cart.

Tam had been already adept at making beer and had enjoyed long years of solitary tippling, but the delicate art of making malt whisky needed several pairs of hands, and he had taken into his confidence those of his cronies whom he considered tight-lipped enough not to give his illicit little game away. With much patient devotion the men had carried out the various stages of the whisky-making process, working willingly, the sting of the task taken away by visions of ever-flowing golden whisky. The most critical stage of the business was fermentation and distillation and the men had taken it in shifts to make sure the temperature of the still was kept constant. Bewildered wives, wondering at their menfolk sneaking off in the middle of the night, had been fobbed off with a variety of excuses and long before Tam's still was ever to prove its worth many a Rhanna wife had harboured suspicions about the faithfulness of her espoused.

But that was all in the distant past. The first batch

of malt, lying in cool wooden casks carefully prepared by Wullie the Carpenter, was ready to be sampled; perhaps a little too soon for proper maturation, but the men could wait no longer to reap the rewards of their labour. In defiance against superstition they had chosen the thirteenth night of the third month for the tasting ceremony. For weeks they had waited for 'the night of the Uisge-beatha'. Now it was here. Tam had gone into the cool little closet extension of the wash-hoosie and, with the delicacy normally reserved for the handling of the newborn, had brought forth the first cask of matured malt. Quite unconsciously, every man in the gathering had removed an assortment of headcoverings in a moment of homage to the Uisge-beatha, and now they lay about the floor, each in a different stage of inebriation.

In their midst, propped shoulder to shoulder, sat Kate McKinnon and Annack Gow, a long history of temperamental differences drowned in the happy delirium induced by the Uisge-beatha. Annack's arrival had caused quite a stir, for she had come on the arm of Tammy Brown, one of the confraternity. It had soon transpired that Annack was neither as senile nor as blind as her demeanour suggested.

'You silly bugger!' she had scolded Tam McKinnon. 'Did you really think I was not knowing it was my Jack's still you were after? Clean out my byre indeed! You that canny even keep your own grass cut! It's the sheeps that do it for you!' Here she and Kate had exchanged hostile glances. 'No, it's not daft I am, Tam

McKinnon,' she had continued with asperity. 'My Jack was brewing the malt while you were still cutting milk teeths!' A dreamy look had come into her short-sighted eyes. 'My, the times we had in the blackhoosie . . . up there in the wee secret room . . . ay, they knew how to build hoosies in those days. My grandfather was the one to start the still and the secret of it was passed down to my Jack . . . ay, and much as I've missed him it's a wee taste o' his whisky I'm missing too. Yours will never match his but since you're a beginner to the art I will give you fair judgement.'

'But how did you know it was tonight, Annack?' Tam asked humbly.

'Hmph! Anybody with half a nostril could tell, so don't think I'm the only one to be knowing. Every time I am passing your house my nose is telling me the malt gets riper. I have been keeping a sharp guard on Tammy here . . . all that snooping about at all hours. I knew there was something brewing all this time so I threatened Tammy with the Customs mannie and he couldn't get me along here fast enough.'

But Tammy and his ready treachery had been soon forgotten in the spree that followed. The whisky, its attraction doubly enhanced by its rich amber colouring, had soon transported everyone into an idyllic world where no enmity existed.

And so it was when Angus came into this gathering and the door of 'the Headquarters' was securely bolted. The uninhibited sounds of hilarity in the wash-hoosie very effectively shut away the sounds of the outside world and no one heard the drone of an aircraft circling low over the island.

Shona had gone up to bed early and lay looking at the moonbeams spread over the floor of her room. It was a habit of hers to keep the curtains open so that she could lie and look at the night sky before falling asleep, and also to see what sort of day it was as soon as she wakened. Even if it was a grey, wind-tossed day the bright yellow cloth always gave the room a sunshiny feel. She always insisted on yellow curtains because somehow they were a part of her childhood and gave her an odd feeling of security, something that didn't change when everything else did.

Just before New Year, Kirsteen had wanted to put new curtains into her room but she had refused the suggestion vehemently enough for Kirsteen to look hurt and slightly bewildered. Shona was sorry she occasionally showed her temper to Kirsteen, but it was something she couldn't help, that and the feeling of being on the defensive at a lot of the little changes that Kirsteen naturally enough wanted to make to Laigmhor. But the last two days had been wonderfully happy for her. It was so good to be back on Rhanna. Her separation from it had made her appreciate it all the more. Her outlook on life had broadened a good deal in the last few months, and coming home had let her see just how lucky she was to have Kirsteen and her father to come home to, and though she had been away from them she was somehow now closer to them than ever. Her father was so different from the proud, aloof creature who had mourned in his heart for many years, first for her mother, then for Kirsteen during their long period of separation. Finally, his deep, dark eyes had lost their look of sadness and now glowed with the joy of living. Then there was Grant Fergus, a manly, dimpled little boy with the looks of a cherub and the gruff façade of a child with a heart so soft he had to try hard to hide it all the time. He tried with Shona but never quite succeeded, and into her own heart crept a real tenderness for the small stranger who was her half-brother.

But if only Niall was home and they could get together again, be the way they were before the war, young and carefree with no heavy burdens of the heart to weigh it down and make it ache all the time. Shona felt about under her pillow and her fingers curled round the locket Niall had given her as an engagement present before he had gone away to France. His picture was in it, beside hers, and the only time she took it off was when she went to bed. She trembled suddenly and put up a slender finger to trace the outline of the little damp patch above her bed which was shaped like the head of Jesus. 'Oh my dear sweet Jesus,' she whispered, 'you are the only one who can help me now for I feel I can't help myself any more. You know what I did with Niall was wrong but somehow I know you've forgiven me for that. But it's myself that can't forgive myself, if that doesn't sound too daft, so please help me, dearest Lord, to overcome myself. Let Niall know in his heart that I love him more than anyone else in the world. He's so nice and dear and it worries me sometimes that someone else just might come along and take the feet from under him and I couldn't bear that. If Mirabelle is there beside you at this very moment let her know that I love her and still miss her so. I can still see her nice rosy face and her white hair shining out from under her mutch cap. Good night for now, Lord.'

Her prayers to God were always very simple, child-like affairs but were so satisfying for her that they never failed to bring her a certain measure of comfort. She stared through the window up into the velvet blue-black night where millions of stars glittered brightly. It was so beautiful she pulled herself up in bed to get a better view of the night world. The moon was peeping sullenly from behind a big silver-lined cloud, its pale halo making the heavens vast and coldly infinite. The ragged peaks of Sgurr nan Ruadh reared up to embrace the great emptiness of space with intimate approval, shutting out the tiny speck of Man from the secrets shared by the heavens and the highest places of Earth.

A light tap came on the door and Babbie whispered, 'Can I come in?'

'Yes, I'm not asleep.'

The door opened and Babbie flitted over to sit on the bed. 'Of course you're not asleep, you daft thing. If you had been you wouldn't have answered me, would you?'

'I might, I sometimes talk in my sleep,' Shona giggled. 'Will I light the lamp?'

'No, the moonlight's lovely. Just let me snuggle my feet under a bit of your blanket. Then we can have a cosy talk before bed.'

'Have you just come up?'

'Yes, I was helping Kirsteen fill the zinc tub. She's having a bath in front of the fire.'

'But, wasn't Father there to do that? He usually makes it his business to do such things for Kirsteen, for myself too for that matter.'

'He went up to bed early-ish so I stayed behind to have a chat with Kirsteen. She's a dear. Interesting and a lot of fun. She has a great sense of humour. Funny little things pop out when you least expect them. I knew you wouldn't be asleep, that's why I looked in. You were thinking of Niall, weren't you?'

'Ay, as a matter of fact I was.' Shona's tone was wary. 'Isn't it natural to think of someone you love? Bed I always find is the best place for such thoughts because during the day everyone about you prattles on about nothing that matters and you can't get a thought in edgeways. Don't *you* ever think about your most secret things when you're in bed?'

'Of course I do,' Babbie laughed lightly. 'That's why I always try to go to bed as late as possible so that I don't have the strength left to think.'

Shona put out her hand and clasped Babbie's firmly. 'You daft thing,' she said affectionately. 'Would you like me to get up and make you a nice big mug of hot cocoa? I know we've already had some but a second cup won't do any harm . . .' She smothered a laugh. 'Just as long as you know where to find your chanty in the middle of the night.'

'How could I miss it?' choked Babbie. 'These country chamber pots are so enormous you could have a bath in them! I think we'll forget the cocoa though . . . After all, Kirsteen is having her bath in the kitchen.'

'*She* won't mind. I often wash her back for her.'

'Maybe you'd best leave that to your father this time.'

'But he's in bed and likely asleep by now!'

'I wouldn't be too sure.'

Babbie sounded so mysterious that Shona burst out, 'Ach, you talk in riddles, Babbie Cameron!'

'And you're so naïve at times I feel like giving you a good spanking. You're often too old for your years but sometimes you're like a little girl who can't see what's under her nose. Your father and Kirsteen haven't been speaking to each other since we came.'

'But . . . they've been talking their heads off! You're a witch right enough, Babbie.'

'Oh, they've talked all right, but only for our benefit. When she isn't looking he's making sheep's eyes at her and when he isn't looking she looks as if she might eat him at any moment. What better way to make up than over a bath tub?'

'Oh.' Shona wasn't too sure she liked the idea of that and easily betrayed her thoughts by her tone of voice.

'Listen,' Babbie laughed, 'if you were Kirsteen and Niall was your father wouldn't *you* take advantage of a midnight bath in the kitchen?'

'I don't know,' Shona said doubtfully.

'Ach, of course you would! Me too for that matter. We're *all* human, Shona McKenzie, and like it or no, your father and Kirsteen are so much in love at the moment they're like a couple of bairns playing at houses. You and me are going to have a nice long talk even if it's only a lot of rubbish. Stop grabbing at the blankets and give me a nice big bit to wrap round my legs. Hand me one of those rag dolls of yours to cuddle then we can both be comfy. Fancy, rag dolls at your age! You're worse than me with my teddy bears!'

Babbie was right about Fergus and Kirsteen. For two days Kirsteen had been cool with him because of a tiff over a matter so trivial that both knew they were being foolish but neither would give in. Earlier that evening she had kept her fair head averted all through supper. He had watched the fine beauty of her slender body and had wanted to crush her to him because she was even more desirable when she was aloof. Covertly she had observed his strong rugged features with his stubborn set of chin and, as always, the sight of him, his sweet nearness, had turned her heart to jelly. Looking at the little white hairs in his raven sideburns always brought a strange choking feeling to her throat, and just to see the muscular hardness of his body thrilled her with its maleness, yet she had eluded his burning black eyes. It was childish of her, she knew, but somehow the little times of disagreement between them made the making-up doubly exciting. He had gone to bed early but she hadn't followed and he had tossed and turned, unable to sleep without her at his side. Now it was late, but he finally got up and went quietly down to the warm kitchen. She had just stepped out of the zinc tub and her glistening body was tawny in the glow of the firelight, her crisp hair a deep golden halo of ruffled wet curls. For a moment neither of them spoke then she said coolly, 'It seems I am afforded no privacy of my own, no matter how late the hour.'

He felt the laughter rising in his throat. 'My darling!' His lilting voice was deep with joy. 'Am I to spend the rest of my life finding you in dark corners wearing nothing but your birthday suit?' He was thinking of their first meeting in the fragrant woods above Loch Tenee when he had come upon her drying herself after a swim. It had been the start of a long and turbulent affair that had finally culminated in a promise of marriage. But that had been before he had lost his arm in the accident, before she had sailed away. Now she was his wife of nearly six months and he felt that all the years of unhappiness were just a bad dream. Everything in his life was now doubly precious, and Fergus strode tall and proud, paying no heed to the gossip that had begun in the first weeks of Kirsteen's return.

'His lordship will no longer be standing on his pedestal,' Behag Beag had sniffed to her cronies. 'First his brother Alick gets a girl in trouble and has to be sent away in disgrace. After that we are seeing the terrible shame of his daughter with child and the little hussy holding up that McKenzie head of hers like she was royalty. As if that wasn't bad enough our ex-schoolmistress comes back to Rhanna complete with McKenzie's son born out of wedlock. 'Tis a bad name they will be giving this good place and I hope the Lord will forgive them indeed.'

At that point Erchy the Post had sent everyone scuttling about their business by opening the door and saying in a loud voice, 'And it is yourself, Mr McKenzie! Just in time for a nice cosy gossip!'

But now, with the worst of the talk behind them, Kirsteen and Fergus lived a relaxed and happy life. Occasionally there was a clash of personalities because the dominant Fergus liked to get his own way. But Kirsteen had acquired a strong willpower of her own during her years of independence and he was quickly learning that his moody tempers held no threat for her. Also, there was the problem of getting to know the little stranger who was his son. On the whole Grant Fergus was a good-natured child, but he was possessed of a temperament that could change like quicksilver from one mood to another. Fergus didn't want to introduce the heavy hand too soon but he was a disciplinarian and unable to repress the urge to control the boy. This had brought a spell of resentment, but it was short-lived because the little boy's irrepressible sense of fun wouldn't allow him to stay sullen for long. His respect for Fergus was growing stronger with each passing day, as did his sturdy admiration for the big man who had so recently materialized into the father for whom he had always longed.

Overriding all was the warm, wonderful sense of Laigmhor, once more a family home. For too many years it had been a place with an atmosphere of waiting for an infusion of the life that Fergus's first wife, Helen, seemed to have taken with her on the night she had died giving birth to Shona. But all that was over now. Fergus was fulfilled and happy. The days were busy with the work of the farm, the evenings filled with the warmth of family togetherness. And the nights belonged to two people making up for their years apart.

At Fergus's reference to their first meeting at Loch Tenee Kirsteen's lips curved and she peeped at him from lowered lashes. Despite the power of his body he looked like a small boy eager to make up for being bad. Her breath caught in her throat and she felt the tears of her love for him pricking her eyelids. She was unable to retain her dignity any longer and a soft chuckle escaped her.

'Fergus.' She whispered his name enticingly and in moments he was crushing her against him, fierce in his passion, his lips hard on hers.

His heart was beating rapidly. The smell of her was like the sweet, fresh air on the top of a summer mountain; natural, unmasked by perfumes and cosmetics. She was that kind of woman: clean as a mountain burn and uncluttered by feminine trappings yet so utterly desirable in her own right that his senses reeled with her nearness. For a moment he remembered the first night of their marriage with the bed cool and remote-looking, spread with sheets of pure white linen. Unaccountably he had felt awkward and shy, like a young boy entering an unknown phase in his life. She had entered the room looking like a mythical goddess dressed in a white silken nightdress, her hair shining like the pale gold of a summer cornfield. They had been like young lovers, awkward and unsure, lost for words in those first breathless moments. The new white sheets had rustled in the quiet room, adding to their embarrassment; then their feet had touched an assortment of brushes and other bristly accoutrements, placed there by Shona in a moment of mischief. The incident had broken the ice and they had shrieked with stifled merriment, finally falling into each other's arms in a passion of untamed desire. The memory made him catch his breath with tenderness even while his mouth crushed her lips and his tongue played with hers. Her skin was like silk, parts of it still damp from the bath, the intimate parts that made him forget all else but his need for her.

Suddenly she pushed him away, her eyes going to the windows, which, though heavily curtained, were a distraction to her senses. 'Not here, Fergus,' she whispered. 'Let's go up to bed.'

'No, here, Kirsteen . . . by the fire . . . like the night at the schoolhouse.'

'But – we were alone then, my darling. Shona and Babbie are upstairs, they could come down . . . Grant might come into the bedroom looking for me – you know he does that sometimes and . . .'

'No, I'm not having that!' he laughed. 'All those excuses. The house is asleep . . . and I can't wait . . .' He kissed her again and her resolution left her, it always did when he was beside her, doing things to her body that made her forget all else. The hard strength of him excited her; the heat from the fire seemed to burn right into her, till every life force within cried out for release.

Anton Büttger had noticed little white dots of habitation below and he wanted to get the crippled plane away from them. The only uninhabited area appeared to be the dark stretch of land where the others had jumped. He was over it now and would have to try and come back. He looked at the starboard wing. The fire had fizzled out. It meant the fuel was almost gone. A series of shuddering spurts of speed brought him round the western curve of the island once more. At a dangerously low altitude he flew past humping black mountains and his heart pumped into his throat. He had to get the plane higher in order to jump safely. Relentless slopes rushed to meet him, and even while his pulses raced he thought, 'There are no houses on top of a mountain. It might be better if she crashed now . . .'

He tugged at the controls but there was no response. His face was awash with sweat. This was it! Miraculously the Heinkel then responded to his wild handling and lumbered upwards into the sky . . .

high enough for him to make the jump. He wondered if he ought to try to climb out of the sliding hatch above the pilot's seat . . . . No, there wasn't enough time to manipulate himself through the small opening. He ran aft and jumped out of the rear-gunner's door. The freezing night air whipped him cruelly, and the jagged edges of a massive peak reared up to greet the frail speck of life. Frantically he guided his chute away only to see the cold face of a tiny basin of water sparkling in the moonlight.

At Laigmhor, the kitchen drowsed on warmly: Snap and Ginger slept peacefully atop the oven; the clock tick-tocked on the mantelshelf; somewhere behind the skirting-boards a mouse scurried among the plaster. But the things Fergus was doing to Kirsteen were drowning out all her usual senses. All she heard was his harsh, quick breathing, his lilting endearments. She stroked his thick dark hair, her love for him meeting and whirling with her passions. He had pulled the zinc tub away from the fire and the rug was soft and warm. For a moment she saw the shadows leaping about the ceiling then he pulled her down and in towards him; and her eyes closed, driving another of her senses inwards. In his rough search for fulfilment he brought her both pleasure and pain, so deep inside that she could hardly distinguish one from the other. Somewhere, in the world outside, a plane pulsated, robbing the night of silence; then it was gone; and the island dreamt on undisturbed.

Kirsteen felt the mist of tears in her eyes and she held his head against her breasts. 'My Fergus,' she whispered, 'tonight we have made a child. At this very minute our baby is being conceived.'

He looked at her for a long moment, cupping her chin in his hand, his black eyes alight with his love for her. 'I had thought that Shona was the only one in the household with a fancy to her imagination. I can see all that folklore you are hearing at the ceilidhs is getting at you too.'

But her smile was full of conviction. 'You wait and see . . . I'll give you the second of those five sons I promised . . .' She giggled. 'In fact – just to spite you I might have twins – if Alick and Mary can do it, then so can I.'

Somewhere in the distance the German bomber crashed, sending shock waves through the glen. The soft breath of the wind carried mere ghostly echoes of the sound, but they were unusual enough for Fergus to say uneasily, 'What the hell was that . . . ? I wonder . . . did you hear a plane a whily back?'

'Yes, but . . .'

A sudden high eerie wailing just outside the door made them both scramble quickly to their feet. Kirsteen wrapped herself into her woollen dressing-gown while Fergus, angry at the interruption, whatever it was, quickly made himself decent. He composed himself for a few moments, then wrenched open the door to find Dodie, the island eccentric, standing out-side. Dodie lived a lonely spartan existence in his tiny isolated cottage on the slopes of Sgurr nan Ruadh and it wasn't unusual to see him on any part of the island, day or night. He was a simple soft-hearted creature, as much a part of Rhanna as the very soil itself. Childlike in his innocence he was unable to understand the complicated natures of those around him and was very easily hurt. He was so introverted that he would come to a house only if invited, and something momentous indeed must have happened to make him stand and wail for help outside Laigmhor's door. He was a sorry sight to see, weeping into his big calloused hands, his stooped shoulders shuddering with long drawn-out sobs. He was a bedraggled, unhappy spectacle, and Fergus, who had a soft spot for Dodie and who also admired the way he worked so hard to provide the simple necessities for himself, said kindly, 'Och, c'mon, now, man, what ails you?'

Dodie looked pathetically forlorn and so afraid it was a long moment before he said in a whisper of embarrassment, 'Ach, Mr McKenzie, it's feart I am! I was just out lookin' for Ealasaid when one o' them airy-plane things swooped low over the moor like a damt great eagle and near took my head off. I started to run but it ran after me and . . . just as I was coming over the glen it came right round the hill so low I could hear the whistle of it in my eardrums. I'm not knowing a thing about airy-planes or the war and nobody is ever telling me anything . . . and . . . and Ealasaid's out there and I'm too feart to go and look for her. It's ashamed I am just!'

'Ealasaid can take care of herself,' Fergus soothed, knowing how much Dodie loved his wanderlust cow.

'Come you in now and Kirsteen will make you a bite to eat.'

Just then Shona and Babbie came piling down to the kitchen.

'I thought I heard thunder,' Babbie said breathlessly, 'but there's hardly a cloud in the sky. Is it always as quiet as this on Rhanna?' She was quietly pleased that Fergus was standing with his arm protectively around Kirsteen's slender shoulders. It was obvious the pair had made up their differences.

'I may be wrong but I'm sure I heard the roar of a plane just minutes ago,' Shona said, her blue eyes big in her pale face.

'I think we heard it too,' Kirsteen faltered, her face reddening.

They all jumped at the sudden appearance of Bob in the kitchen. His gnarled fingers were bunched on the bone handle of his shepherd's crook and he wasted no time with pretty words of apology. He had witnessed the spectacle of the bomber heading for almost certain destruction on Ben Machrie. 'Are you deaf, man?' he asked Fergus sarcastically. 'The damt thing must have come right over Laigmhor! It came down so low it rattled the dishes on my dresser!'

Before Fergus could answer, the sound of the kirk bell could be heard pealing over the countryside. It was pulled by Righ nan Dul who, from his elevated position on the windswept cliffs of Port Rum Point, had seen the bomber juddering round the village of Portcull.

For a long incredulous moment he had watched it

embracing the slopes of the mountains, heading for a crash on the quietly menacing slopes of Ben Machrie. 'Jesus – God – St Michael! Help us all!' he had muttered aloud to all those unseen guardians of life, and then taken off, limping hurriedly down the spiral stairs to emerge atop the smooth, cropped turf of the Point. To the left of it lay the needles of the Sgor Creags – grey, jostling pinnacles of treachery, the swish of the sea deceptively peaceful in its picturesque frothing round the slimy, barnacle-encrusted rocks. To the right of it lay the natural little harbour of Portcull, protected from the worst weather by the long finger of Port Rum Point. Righ had scuttled along the path to the kirk, which sat starkly aloof at the top of the peninsula. With its creaking elms and black, huddled headstones casting long moon-scattered shadows, it was an eerie place, but Righ had no time to let himself be haunted by monuments to the dead. His thoughts had been for the living and he had given the gate a mighty push that had set it creaking on its rusty hinges. The kirk was never locked. On Rhanna people seldom locked anything and to the Bible-thumping Reverend John Gray an ever-open kirk door meant an ever-available sanctum to repentant sinners wanting to unburden themselves to the Lord.

For several minutes Righ kept doggedly at the ropes, until finally, with aching arms, he withdrew from the kirk and hobbled away through the other old gate set into the wall atop the Hillock. He emerged to find little black blobs were scurrying from all quarters, hastily pulling outdoor clothes over night

1121

attire. The tall figure of John Gray came rushing from the Manse, followed closely by his small dumpy wife who was inserting her false teeth as she ran. No catastrophe on earth was worth the price of her dignity, to which she clung fiercely on an island where many of the older generation wore false teeth only on Sundays or at funerals.

Even while Righ was delivering his message to the community straggled out on the slopes of the Hillock, the bell he had recently rung was finding its echo all over the island. It was a pre-arranged signal to everyone that something connected with war had come to Rhanna.

At Portvoynachan, four miles to the east, Mrs Jemima Sugden, the elderly schoolmistress of the tiny school in that area, was vigorously ringing a huge handbell though she had no earthly idea what was happening. Elsewhere on the island general confusion followed, but after a few bewildering minutes a certain order began to emerge as the Home Guard assembled at their various posts to await orders. The efficiency of the Home Guard was hampered somewhat by those members who had come staggering out of the Headquarters in a merry drunken heap, but in the excitement of the moment, no one minded too much. Left behind was Annack Gow who sat with her arms lovingly entwined round the cask of malt, her head resting on the barrel in a manner that allowed her generous nose to inhale unhindered the strong sweet fumes of the Uisge-beatha.

Chapter Six

Tom and Mamie Johnston of Croynachan, who had been wakened rudely by the dreadful tearing of metal ripping through earth, were hardly able to believe their eyes when they rushed out to see bits of a German bomber strewn over their field.

'Don't panic, mo ghaoil,' Tom soothed his wife. 'It's only bits of an old aeroplane.'

'A *German* plane,' Mamie said faintly, quickly following her husband who had rushed into the kitchen to fetch his shotgun.

'You stay with the bairns,' he told Mamie. 'Lock all the doors and open them only to the neighbours or myself when I get back.'

Tom saddled his horse and galloped to Croft na Beinn, then on to the tiny clachan of Croy, quickly and efficiently gathering together every able-bodied man.

But the people of Nigg had no need of warning bells to let them know that something unusual had happened. Old Madam Balfour of Burnbreddie was standing on top of the high tower of her gloomy old house, lustily banging a dinner gong and shouting at the top of her high-pitched, hysterical voice. Her bedroom lay at the top of the big square tower and the German bomber on its third sweep round the island had flown at such a low altitude she had fully imagined it was coming in on top of her. With her only son, Scott, the young laird of Burnbreddie, fighting with the British Army somewhere in Greece, she felt vulnerable and abandoned despite the fact that she had the companionship of Rena, her very able daughter-in-law. Having screamed to Rena that the house was under air-attack she had made a very agile flight to the roof to bang her gong and shriek. Rena's two children, hearing their grandmother conducting herself in a manner that would have frightened the Uisga Hags themselves, began to scream also and Rena had her hands full trying to soothe everyone.

But Righ had dispatched several members of the bicycle brigade to places that were bereft of menfolk, and before long, frightened women and children were receiving welcome comfort. Meanwhile, other squads of bicycles and horses, gathering on their way the various little bands of men assembled at their posts, were moving up to the eastern end of the island, from where the sound of the crash was thought to have come.

The sight of the twisted wreckage of the plane near Croynachan brought gasps of incredulity from all who gazed upon it. The starboard wing lay in the Johnstons' field, and the stench of red-hot metal oozed from the exhaust manifold, mingling with the sharp air washing over the moors. Ragged ailerons, trim tabs, the tail wheel and tail gun littered the ground. The fin had snapped from the fuselage in a ragged fracture, and the rudder hung by mere scraps of material. The bold, sharp symbol of the swastika gaped mockingly, looking terrifyingly out of place in the wild, peaceful stretches of the Muir of Rhanna. There was no denying it: the Germans were actually on Rhanna and the evidence was there for all to see.

As the islanders bore down on the plane like a horde of ants, excitement made them revert to their native Gaelic, yet caution hushed their voices when the men spread out over the moors, their steps taking them warily through the snagging clumps of gorse. Out here in the open a keen little wind moaned in from the sea and wailed softly around the cloisters of the old Abbey ruins situated near Dunuaigh, the Hill of the Tomb. It was a lost, lonely place and in normal circumstances the islanders gave it a wide berth, even in daytime. Now, in the hushed shadows of night, it brought chilling fears to the more superstitious, magnified a thousandfold by the thought that Nazi Germans might be lurking among the time-worn stones.

A few minutes later Fergus and Bob arrived with Dodie, who had been so anxious about his cow that Fergus had allowed him to come. As Fergus and Bob wandered off to join the men, Dodie stared at the wrecked plane with joy, his tall ungainly figure a looming spectre at the feast. His fear of the Germans forgotten, he looked lovingly and longingly at the tail piece with its swastika plainly visible in the light of the moon peeping round the shoulders of Ben Madoch. ''Tis nice colours on it,' he whispered childishly. 'A nice pattern so it is.' But no one heard him, concentrating as they were on the search that was taking place somewhere in the darkness below.

It was Fergus who found Jon Jodl, sitting on the ground, huddled against a mossy boulder, staring dreamily out over the wild, dark moors.

'Up you get now, man,' Fergus said quietly. 'You will not be hurt if you do just as you are told.'

Jon didn't understand a word, but he knew what was expected of him and slowly unwound himself from his parachute and got to his feet.

In the pale glimmering of the moon's light Fergus saw the strained white face of the youth and the German flying suit stained with vomit. 'You are just a laddie and ill by the look of you,' Fergus said, compassion making his voice soft. He hadn't been able to imagine what his feelings would be coming face to face with a German. He had expected to feel some sort of resentment, or anger, and had good reason to feel both because of the indirect sufferings that war had brought to his own family. But the slim boyish figure of Jon Jodl, stamped with the vulnerability of the young, brought only feelings of pity. Yet . . . this was the Enemy. God alone knew what lay in the mind behind the face of the boy!

Fergus's thoughts were interrupted by the others, arriving on the scene in a clamour of excited Gaelic. Jon swayed on his feet and Doctor Lachlan McLachlan strode over. 'Get away from him!' he ordered sharply. 'Can't you see the laddie is in a state of shock? He needs all the air he can get! Let me examine him!'

Some distance away the keen air of morning was

bringing Tam quickly to his senses but he wasn't able to join the search for the Uisge-beatha that had filled his bladder, and, handing his shotgun to Jock the Ploughman, he stepped behind a bush – and tripped over Ernst Foch lying in the heather. A guttural roar of surprise split the morning asunder as Ernst sprang to his feet and a highly indignant Nazi and a white-faced terrified Gael faced each other.

'It's sorry I am indeed, just!' Tam gabbled, forgetting for a moment that he was addressing the Enemy. He stood transfixed, unable even to make the effort of doing up his fly.

A stream of islanders soon descended and Ernst was then bundled into a trap beside Jon Jodl. 'Jon!' Ernst cried, glad to see one of his own kind. 'You came down safely? I am glad.' His eyes raked the moors. He wondered where Zeitler and Anton had landed, there seemed to be no sign of them.

Everyone else was wondering the same thing. But as the various search parties drifted back to the scene of the crash, in the midst of one group was the bull-headed Zeitler, dragging his feet and scowling when he was shoved unceremoniously into the trap beside his companions.

The islanders stood around talking in subdued tones while they observed the captives with dismay. They had been so intent on the search that no one had given a thought about a place suitable enough in which to keep German prisoners.

'It would be fine if we could just chain them up in the Abbey ruins till help arrives from the mainland,'

Ranald suggested hopefully, his ideas influenced by the adventure stories he read so avidly. 'I was reading a war book about prisoners put in shackles in a cellar and fed on only bread and water.'

Tom Johnston snorted and said sarcastically, 'Ay, and that was maybe taking place away back in the Dark Ages. They are human beings though they are Jerries and must be treated with respect.'

Doctor Lachlan McLachlan stamped impatiently, his compassionate brown eyes fixed on the wearily crumpled figure of Jon Jodl. 'I want to see to that lad and I don't care if I have to take him back to my house to do it! I have a spare room . . . Phebie always has it ready,' he added quietly, and Fergus looked at him admiringly.

'Hold on! I'm coming! I will take them into *my* house!' the Reverend John Gray yelled as he burst on to the scene. He was dishevelled and dirty and a little stubble of beard made his face look haggard, even in moonlight. Rhanna, used to a neatly-turned-out minister with never a hair out of place, stared as one man. 'I was helping with the search,' he explained with dignity. 'And I got rather off the beaten track. I am not used to the moors, but the Lord guided me.' He looked at his flock sternly. 'We should *all* have faith in him. He is our comfort and stay.'

The men muttered and one or two bowed their heads but old Bob said something in Gaelic and the minister glared at him. He had never troubled to learn the native tongue and was continually frustrated by the dour Gaels who took every opportunity to make him feel an interloper, though he had been preaching on the island for many years.

'These men will be safe in my house,' he continued. 'God will guide us all to His way. Their stay will be brief but I would not be doing my duty if I didn't try to nourish their thoughts with the love of God . . . take their minds off war . . . I can speak a little German, we will understand each other.'

A gleam came into the eyes of the gathering. What could be better for the enemy than a day or two of bible-thumping under the minister's roof? He would be in his glory trying to save the Germans' souls, and they would be only too anxious to save their sanity by getting off the island the minute they could.

'Ach, it's a good man you are just,' Angus said solicitously.

Bob's weathered face broke into a mocking smile. 'Ay, good to be learning the German but never a word o' the Gaelic.'

The full implication of his words hit home. Everyone looked at each other quizzically and Fergus rapped out impatiently, 'Why don't you put your knowledge to good use, Mr Gray, and ask these men a few questions? There's a lot we would like to be knowing.'

'Hmm, yes, you're quite right of course,' the Reverend Gray muttered immediately, 'but I don't think we will find out very much. Nevertheless, I'll lend my hand to it, with God's guidance, of course.'

Ernst gave surly replies to 'the interrogation', repeating his name, rank and serial number so many times that even the minister's patience began to wane.

'It's as I told you,' he said to Fergus finally. 'He will tell me nothing of his mission but I gather he is concerned about his Commander.'

Fergus nodded. 'One more to be found, but I think we should leave him to the Military. If Mistress Beag got her message through, help should be arriving quite soon. If not, we will continue the search in daylight.' Wearily the men agreed and everyone began to move away from the scene of the crash.

Little Grant Fergus was marching up and down the drying green of Laigmhor with a meal basin on his head and a stout tree branch hoisted against his shoulder. He was practising 'being a soldier' and Kirsteen, watching him from the window, was angry at the influence of war reaching out to her son.

'Ach, don't worry yourself, Kirsteen,' Shona assured her. 'All wee boys play at soldiers – girls too – I did it myself when Niall and me were bairns.'

She folded the dish towel and turned to pick up a basket from the table. 'I'm away over to Tina's with a bite of dinner, and I'll do some wee odd jobs while I'm there. Matthew says she can hobble about the house but can't get out much to see to the beasts.'

Kirsteen looked at Shona's white face and felt a great surge of affection as, unbidden, a memory came of a slender little girl starting her first day at school; a child with glorious auburn hair tied back with a blue ribbon and skinny legs clad in black woollen stockings. Little had Kirsteen thought in those far-off days that one day she would marry Shona's father and become the mistress of Laigmhor . . . She had always got on well with Shona but her time of separation from Fergus had also separated her from his daughter, the only female in the household after the death of dear old Mirabelle. She could sense Shona's well-hidden resentment of the situation but understood her feelings on the matter. Impulsively she reached out to grasp Shona's hand and looked into her incredibly deep blue eyes.

'Shona,' she sighed, 'you're so sad inside – I can feel it even though you try so hard to hide it. I know what it's like – to love someone and be apart from them. What's wrong between you and Niall?'

For a moment a veil of hostility hooded Shona's eyes. She was growing more like Fergus every day, jealously guarding her most private feelings. But then she saw the genuine concern on Kirsteen's face. 'It's not Niall . . . it's me, Kirsteen. I need time to sort out my feelings. I love Niall, I think I've loved him since we were children. It was like a fairy story . . . the way we grew up together then discovered how much we cared . . . but . . .' she hesitated then went on in a rush, 'it never ended like a fairy story – that's the trouble with real life. I blame myself for that, everything that happened to make it all go wrong. It's like a dream now . . . the cave . . . me bringing that little life into the world . . .' She stared at Kirsteen with huge eyes then went on in a whisper, 'I didn't give him life – I gave him death. The only time he lived was when he was . . . in here.' She touched the flatness of her belly with trembling hands. 'When I knew Niall was coming back from France I thought I had forgotten that time in the cave with that poor little dead baby but I hadn't. It seems to get worse and worse all the time. I go over it and over it in my mind . . . it's like a nightmare without an end!'

Kirsteen put her arms round the girl's slender shoulders and said tenderly, 'Shona, we're all guilty of something. Your father and I could spend the rest of our lives feeling guilt, but our time is too precious to waste on useless self-reproach. A lot of our years were wasted because we were both foolish. Don't make our mistake, Shona.'

Shona forced a smile. 'You're right, of course, but it's easy to be wise after the event – I don't mean that to sound cheeky, it's just the truth. Och, it's lovely to be back on Rhanna, yet it won't be the same till Niall is here too.' She paused to look out the window to the misty blue of the mountains. 'This is where we both belong – no matter where I go my heart is always on Rhanna.'

'If you really love Niall, you would follow him to the moon. He won't be studying forever, you know.'

Shona went towards the door where the hens were cocking beady eyes into the kitchen. 'I'll have to go now,' she smiled. 'Thanks for listening to all my worries.'

'Be careful out there,' Kirsteen warned. 'Your father was making quite a fuss about that missing German. He doesn't think it safe for us defenceless females to be wandering about unescorted. Shouldn't Babbie go with you?'

'Ach, the lazy wittrock is sleeping late after the excitement of last night. I took her up a cup of tea but she just turned over and went back to sleep.'

At that moment a yell came from the garden where Grant had missed his soldierly footing and fallen into the thorns of the rose bed. Kirsteen rushed to the rescue while Shona grabbed a broom and chased the hens from the kitchen.

A crestfallen Grant came over the cobbled yard. 'Can I come with you, Shona?' he called. 'Mother's out of temper and there is still a while to go before school.' Mr Murdoch, the balding, fussy master of Portcull school, had gone to assist the Home Guard in their search for the Commander of the German bomber, giving all the children an unexpected morning off.

'Aren't you wanting to go down to the harbour?' Shona asked. 'If old Joe's there he might tell you a story.' The little boy loved the harbour with its collection of boats and old men always ready to recount an adventure of the sea. Already he knew a lot about fishing, jumping at any chance to dabble about in a boat. Whenever he could he went to help with the lobster creels and accompanied some of the older boys when they clubbed together to hire one of Ranald's boats for a day of sea fishing.

Grant hesitated at Shona's words, but seeing her basket of food, decided that a cosy strupak would better pass what remained of the morning. 'Old Joe has a bad head,' he told Shona in his precocious manner, his cultured English already showing traces of the lilting island tongue. 'I think, too, he is weary from chasing Germans all night and he told me earlier he was going to sleep off the effects of some meeting to do with the war.'

'The war was it?' Shona smiled. She had already heard about the 'disgraceful drunken behaviour' of the Home Guard. 'On you go and ask your mother then,' she conceded, 'but mind, you mustny bother Tina with your blethers.'

He ran to tell Kirsteen that he was going with his big sister to 'protect her' and a few moments later his grubby little hand was curled trustingly in hers. The misted fields were frosted with white which scrunched crisply underfoot as they walked, and the child's normally pink cheeks were soon like red apples in the stinging air. He was a picture with his black curls, snapping black eyes and dimpled chin. Tunelessly he began singing a sea shanty taught to him by the fishermen and after a minute Shona joined in, feeling something of his exuberance and youthful buoyancy.

Soon they were in the field that sloped upwards to a tiny cottage huddled under the brown heather slopes of Ben Machrie. Here Matthew, grieve of Laigmhor, lived with Tina, his ample, easy-going young wife and his two children, Donald and Eve.

Little Donald, a big-eyed dreaming child, was quietly pleased to see Grant and took him off to view a golden plover's nest he had chanced upon.

'Don't be going far,' Shona warned. 'Remember what Father told you this morning.'

Grant gave her a cherubic smile. 'I'm minding, Shona, don't worry . . . anyway . . .' he pulled a roughly-fashioned wooden dirk from his pocket, 'I'll kill any Germans with this! I'll not let them touch Donald or myself.'

Tina came limping from the byre, clutching a bucketful of manure mixed liberally with hen's feathers which drifted like snowflakes from the brimming container. At sight of Shona she put up a languid hand to tuck away strands of fine hair into two kirbys that were meant to be supporting a lop-sided bun. The grips were totally inadequate for the purpose and loops of hair descended in fly-away abandon.

'Ach, bugger it,' she swore mildly, her good-natured face showing not a trace of dismay. The boys scampered off and she told Shona consolingly, 'Don't you be worrying your head about wee Grant. Donald might be looking like his head was up on the moon but he is all there and knows every inch of the moor. I was hearing anyways it was only one airy-plane that came down though there were rumours of there bein' three. It's all a bitty mixed up. Matthew says he caught two of the Huns last night an' the soldiers will find the other later.'

Shona had to hide a quick smile. Tina's simple, devoted faith in her husband was such that she believed everything he told her. Her vision of an all-conquering hero was limited entirely to her spouse.

It was perhaps her acceptance of his manly boasting that made the marriage one of rare, uncomplicated happiness.

'Ay, you'll likely be right, Tina,' Shona said. 'Though I hear tell that some of the men have gone out to guard the plane. Father was a bit worried about Grant and myself coming out of the house at all this morning.'

'Ach, you'll be fine wi' me. If there is one smell o' a Jerry I'll set my dogs on the buggers!'

They had wandered into the house by now and Shona, looking at the jumbled assortment of canine and feline bodies that were heaped contentedly on hearth and sofa, wondered if even a whisker would have twitched if a dozen Germans had come marching into the room.

Little Eve, who had been having her morning nap in the commodious bottom drawer of the dresser, tottered through from the bedroom, rubbing the sleep from her huge bright eyes. The drawer had been her bed from babyhood and she simply popped into it when the mood took her. She was a rosy, intelligent child, delivered by Shona the Christmas Eve before last. The very timing of her birth seemed to have bestowed on her everything that was reminiscent of Christmas: roly-poly legs supporting a plump little body; stars shining in velvet eyes; a halo of flaxen hair that was a startlingly beautiful feature in a child otherwise so dark. At sight of Shona she giggled with glee then, turning very solemn, lifted her dress and stretched the top of her knickers till it seemed the elastic must surely snap. Peering over her pot belly she pointed between her legs. 'Wet!' she announced and collapsed on the rug in an ecstasy of baby chuckles.

'I've been training her to sit on the po,' Tina explained, 'but I'm no' able to bend much just now.' She collapsed into the depths of a huge armchair, pinning the tail of a skinny white cat against the springs. With a terrified squeal it struggled with the ensnaring layers of flesh till Tina was forced to ease herself up an inch and in doing so upset the brimming pail she had carried in from the byre. Dung and feathers littered floor, furniture and animals.

'Fevver!' Eve squealed, crawling amongst the mess to stick fluffy bits of down into her hair.

'Ach, my,' Tina clucked in slight anxiety. 'This damt ankle is keeping me back right enough. Matthew will be in for his dinner an' me that's so quick with everything will never have it ready, just.'

Shona's spirits were rising rapidly. Tina, with her effortless air of unruffled peace and uproarious overstatements, was a breath of spring sunshine. 'Don't upset yourself, Tina,' she instructed laughingly. 'I didn't just come over to blether, you know. I've brought some nice things for a strupak, then I'll get Matthew's dinner going.' She eyed the dangling pail in Tina's hand. 'Where were you going with that when I came along?'

'Just over to the midden. I'm saving it for the vegetable patch but I'm not wanting Matthew to know. I'd like fine to surprise him with a fine crop this year. Last year the tatties were like bools and the turnip so dry no' even the sheeps would eat it. Matthew hasny the time for it, the soul works that hard. I was having a mind to gather seaweed as well but this damt ankle has slowed me down with everything.'

In a few minutes Shona had swept the floor clean and the kettle was puffing gaily among the peats. Then she settled Tina and Eve with tea and scones and went to get the hens' pot from the jumbled array of cooking containers in the little stone-flagged outhouse Tina grandly called a kitchen.

The hens were gobbling greedily when Grant and Donald burst out from the windbreak of firs that sheltered the house from the windswept moors. They were arguing the way children do when greatly excited. It soon transpired that they had wandered up to the shores of Loch Sliach to look for rabbit burrows but had been frightened away when they saw a 'monster' floating on the loch.

'It was all spread out with humps on it!' said a round-eyed Grant. 'And it was moving about and making noises!'

'Ach no!' Donald's protest was faintly scornful of an incomer's inability to relate a properly embroidered tale. 'It was a Ullabheist right enough but it was dead because it was all white and limp. It was not making one sound but a water kelpie on the wee island was greetin' an' moanin'. Maybe it was crying for the Ullabheist though I don't know why 'cos they are feart o' them as a rule and should be glad it was dead!'

'We ran away,' Grant put in rather feebly, his pale face showing he had suffered quite a scare.

Shona was about to dismiss the childish ravings as of little import but her quick mind suddenly recalled Righ's saying that he thought the German bomber was surely bound to crash on the slopes of Ben Machrie and that instead it had careered round the mountains to come down on the open moor. Everyone had assumed the pilot would have bailed out on to open ground . . . but supposing there hadn't been time? Donald's Ullabheist sounded very much like a parachute.

Making a quick decision she bundled the protesting children into the cottage just as Matthew arrived for his dinner. Taking him into the kitchen on some pretext she hastily imparted the news to him. 'Get away now!' exclaimed the youthful grieve of Laigmhor, good-natured and easy-going like his wife, but, unlike her, possessed of an energetic taste for adventure.

'Can you get some men together?' Shona whispered.

'Ach, it would take too long. The last I am hearing they are all up at the airy-plane. Anyways . . .' he puffed out his well-developed rib cage. 'I'm here! I'll get my gun and I'll be goin' . . . you will maybe stay here and send some help after me.'

But Shona was not a McKenzie for nothing. 'Havers! I'm coming with you. I'm a nurse, remember, and the pilot of that plane might be badly injured. It's not a silly wee girl you are talking to, Matthew.'

'But Tina has that bad leg and will no' be able to send for reinforcements. I'm no' mindin' going to look for this Jerry so long as I know the lads will be up at my back. The island is crawling wi' strange men. Totie Little of Portvoynachan saw them early this mornin' rowing away from a big boat out on the Sound. They came over in rubber dinghies and hid them in the caves at Aosdana Bay. It's surprised I am you havny heard!'

But Shona's brilliant blue eyes were smiling. 'Ach, that's just a lot of rumour. Father thinks Behag sent a wrong message and it is soldiers – *our* soldiers who have come to Rhanna. There will be ructions and no mistake.'

Matthew's eyes were bulging and he hissed, 'I am hearing it was Robbie took the message to Behag!'

Shona nodded sympathetically. 'Poor old Robbie. Behag will never forgive him, his life will be worse than ever. But c'mon now, it's time Grant went down the road to school. I'll get him to stop off at Laigmhor and ask Father to come with Bob and the others.'

Grant was given instructions and, fairly bristling with importance, scampered off with Donald at his heels, leaving Tina to mourn gently about 'poor Matthew's empty belly'.

The path through the woods was a thick carpet of russet pine needles which muffled their hurrying foot-steps. There, in the cathedral of tall trees, it was dim and mysterious, a world apart from the surrounding open spaces. Matthew's steps were a little less jaunty now and he took frequent peeps over his shoulder.

'Did the bairns say something about a Ullabheist?' he asked nervously, the threat of the ethereal appearing to worry him far more than the possible presence of Germans.

'Ach, don't be daft, Matthew!' Shona scolded. 'The boys were exaggerating and fine you know it! Look, we'll go over the burn here and come out of the woods quicker.'

They wobbled their way over slippery stepping stones and, skirting a rise, saw Loch Sliach below. It was a dark, umber pool with the steep crags of the mountains on one side and the amber stretches of the moor on the other. A tiny tree-clad island rose in the centre, separated from dry land by a wide area of water. Billowing out from the island was a long length of translucent white material, humped into odd shapes where pockets of air lay locked in the folds. And plainly, on the cool breath of the calm, frosted air, there came an unintelligible thread of sound . . . human, yet, there in the shadow of the sleeping Ben, with the ever-present sigh of moor and sea, frighteningly uncanny and unreal.

'It's a spook or a Uisga Hag wandered inland,' Matthew gulped. 'I think we'd better be wise and wait for the lads, Shona.'

'Nonsense! You have a boat tied up here, Matthew, for I know you go fishing on the loch with Robbie. Where is it?'

Unwillingly he pulled aside clumps of bracken to reveal the boat in a hollow of sand, and with a distinct lack of enthusiasm helped Shona drag it into the water. As she sat in it, gently bobbing in a scurry of wavelets, she looked at him with quizzical eyes, and a few moments elapsed while he stood on the shore, embarrassed but unmoving. She grabbed the oars and began to pull away.

'Wait! I was just coming!' he said peevishly. 'I will not be having a lassie doing a man's work.'

They reached the islet in minutes. Matthew made a great fuss about tying the boat but Shona climbed quickly ashore and in a very short time found the delirious figure of Anton Büttger lying on a bed of frantically gathered heather and bracken. His eyes were closed but his head was moving from side to side in the madness of his inward nightmares. His uniform was a cold, sodden mess. Of the trousers only tatters remained, and blood seeped from a jagged gash in his leg. But it wasn't that which made Shona's hand fly to her mouth. She was staring at his stomach where a cruel finger of rock had ripped it open, allowing part of his intestines to escape in a red congealing mass. The skin of his legs was blue with exposure, but worse, the fingers of both hands were waxen white with frostbite – the ragged fragments of his flying gloves having afforded him little protection from the elements. The pathetic vulnerability of him lying there, his partially covered genitals giving him the innocence of a small boy, made the tears of pity well into Shona's eyes, and she forgot that this was the Enemy, a young man trained to take life. She forgot that long months of worry over Niall and the subsequent loss of her tiny son had been brought about by the Nazis and their greedy war. She saw only a critically injured human being, lying as Niall had lain, in a foreign land without consciousness to aid the instincts of self-preservation.

'My God, what way did he survive?' a wildly staring Matthew muttered before he rushed behind a bush to vomit.

Chapter Seven

Babbie, rising soon after Shona's departure, had taken herself off on a walk to Portcull to fetch some groceries for Kirsteen, and when she entered Merry Mary's shop the atmosphere was charged with excitement.

Little Merry Mary was an Englishwoman who had for many years been labelled as an 'old incomer' which she regarded as an honour. But now, after more than forty years she was regarded as a native, and with her quaint tongue and equally whimsical ways she might indeed have sprung from Hebridean soil. Limp ginger hair hung over a bright, inquisitive face from which protruded a square nose, dubiously decorated with a large brown wart. Unknown to its host it had been an object of great interest to the island children over the years: the first child to notice its demise being promised a monetary reward from every other youngster on the island. Like everywhere else Rhanna suffered from inflation and likewise did the value of Merry Mary's wart. Happily she was as unaware of her wart as she was to the mischievous attentions paid to it, and in her delightfully jumbled shop that morning her tongue was wagging busily, entirely oblivious to all but the latest events on the island.

The tiny shop was crowded, tongues clicked, heads

nodded, and curious looks were directed frequently towards the Post Office. The news about the ludicrous situation that had arisen on the island because of Behag's misleading message had reached every corner of Rhanna and it was a near-certainty that the subject was being analysed with thorough enjoyment over dinner-tables everywhere.

Soon Erchy the Post came strolling out of the Post Office, a nonchalant whistle on his lips. He walked very casually over to Merry Mary's but his composure failed him at the last moment and he almost fell in the door.

'Well! And what is she saying for herself?' came the inevitable cry of unconcealed curiosity. Under normal circumstances the islanders gave the impression of being uninterested in gossip even while they listened avidly. If a stranger was in their midst a gently malicious tale would cease and the interest would quietly be transferred to something mundane. But as events that morning were of a great magnitude and kettles had been singing over peat fires all night, no one paid the slightest attention to Babbie, who was gazing at the array of glass sweet jars with what seemed to be undivided curiosity. During her childhood in the Argyllshire orphanage Babbie had picked up a fair Gaelic vocabulary from an ancient gardener and, although it was a vastly different Gaelic to that of the Hebrides, she nevertheless got the gist of the conversation. Furthermore, one or two of the younger islanders lapsed frequently from Gaelic to English, which was a great advantage.

Erchy ran a hand through his sparse sandy hair and looked faintly bemused. 'She is not saying a word! Not a single word. It is like the shock has taken her tongue. Poor auld Robbie is begging her to speak but the bitch is just standin' at the counter with her lips tighter than the backside of a day-old chick. 'Tis lucky she is human enough to have calls o' nature like the rest of us, giving Robbie a chance to tell me the news . . .' He paused importantly while sounds of encouragement echoed round him then went on. 'Well, Robbie was thinkin' there were three German airy-planes over the island last night. Righ said it was a Heinkel three and Robbie thought he said three Heinkels and told Behag so. Well, you see, she reported that parachutes were droppin' everywhere and help was to be sent urgently. It was Totie Little saw men landing over at Aosdana Bay before dawn this morning and she told that writer, Dugie Donaldson, who told the Home Guard. For a whily everyone was running round in circles dodgin' the lads from the boat till they found out they were Commandos come to rescue the island. A lot o' them have gone away again but a few have stayed to help wi' the Jerries. Just as well, too, I'm thinkin', for Robbie was after tellin' me that one o' the Jerries has escaped from the Manse . . . that big bull-headed one wi' the bulging eyes. He ate a slap-up breakfast given him by Mrs Gray then just buggered off. He knows he won't get off the island but being the type he is just wants to make things more difficult for the soldiers. Time is precious to these lads and there's

1147

goin' to be a fine stramash over the whole affair.'

There was a gasp of surprise over this last piece of news and everyone looked at each other rather fearfully.

'They will take the contraption away from Behag!' said someone in awe.

'Totie will be gettin' it in her Post Office,' put in Morag Ruadh, the nimble-fingered spinner who also played the ancient church organ which Totie had itched to play for years. 'Totie always has her eye on other people's occupations,' she finished with a toss of her red hair.

'Ach well, she is having a clever head on her shoulders,' hazarded Mairi McKinnon, Morag's cousin.

Morag's eyes blazed. 'And what are you insinuating, Mairi? There is *some* brains in the family!' Morag had a spiteful tongue, more pronounced since her dithering, simple younger cousin had, by means more innocent than calculating, got herself pregnant which in turn had got her swiftly to the altar, a fact not easily borne by Morag, who was at a loss to understand why she had never arrived at that revered spot herself.

Tears sprang to Mairi's guileless brown eyes. Her happy life had been shattered since her adored William had gone marching away to join the navy and she was more easily hurt than she had ever been. Kate McKinnon, fresh-faced and full of her usual energy despite her nocturnal activities, rushed to defend her daughter-in-law to whom she had grown close after an initial spell of resentment. 'Ach, leave her be!' she scolded Morag Ruadh. 'Can the cratur no' make a simple remark without you jumpin' down her throat?'

'Simple right enough,' Morag muttered, but Kate's boisterous voice drowned out all else as she addressed Mairi earnestly.

'And how is your poor father, mo ghaoil? It was a bad state he was in when I was last seein' him.'

'Ay, well, he's right enough now,' Mairi faltered, recalling to mind the picture of Todd being trundled past her window in a wheelbarrow before midnight. She had merely thought he was being delivered home by his crapulous friends and no one had told her otherwise till the operation was over because she was useless in an emergency. 'The doctor made a fine job of him but we were thinkin' that someone would be over to see was he better this morning but neither the doctor or Biddy has come.'

At that moment, Elspeth Morrison, the gaunt, sharp-tongued housekeeper of Slochmhor, pushed into the shop. Her life had been embittered by her childless marriage to a fisherman who had met his end through drink. Her saving grace was her dour devotion to the doctor and his family and she jealously guarded her position in the household.

'The poor doctor is exhausted being up all night,' she imparted haughtily. 'He is in no fit state to be gallivanting after people who bring illness upon themselves! A fine thing indeed to be operating on a man pickled in drink and the stuff so scarce it is a mystery how he managed to get so much of it inside himself!' Here she looked meaningfully at Kate who was looking at bobbins of thread with great interest.

'Biddy is the one should be seeing to Todd,' Elspeth went on. 'Knowing her she will have had her fill o' sleep. The doctor was sayin' she must have decided to bide the night at Todd's because she was feart to go back over the glen with the Germans about, but she should have checked in at Slochmhor to see was she needed this morning . . .' She snorted disdainfully. 'The doctor wanted her to call in at the Manse to see how was the Germans. I wouldny blame Biddy if that was maybe why she is makin' herself scarce!'

Mairi, looking uncertain of her facts, murmured, 'Ay well, she was not near the place this early morning and Father worrying a bit about his stitches too tight.'

Elspeth put her sharp nose in the air. 'And tight they would have to be to keep all that liquid from oozing out . . . he will be uncomfortable for quite a whily,' she ended unsympathetically.

The subject of Todd's health having been exhausted the shop then turned eagerly to fresh speculation over the fate of Behag Beag and the two Germans who were still wandering loose on the island.

Babbie, having made her purchases, hurried back to Laigmhor, and mischievously imparted all the gossip she had heard. To Fergus, who had been at dinner with Bob when Grant burst into the kitchen with the garbled message, it only confirmed what he already suspected, for by the time he had heard his son's tales of 'monsters and ghosts' on Sliach he was in no mood to believe in further ridiculous rumours. Nevertheless there was still the question of the two missing

Germans and, though they would soon be found by the efficient Commandos, he felt he couldn't take any risks till the whole affair was sorted out.

As Fergus pushed away his half-eaten food and began to struggle into his jacket, Bob wiped his mouth with a horny hand and said gruffly, 'The bairns are havering, man! We have no time to be chasing fairy tales!' Old Bob was annoyed at the disruption the German bomber had wreaked in his normal working routine. At sixty-eight he was gnarled and tough from a lifetime of working in every kind of weather the winds brought to Rhanna. He revelled in the hard work his job as shepherd brought him, but it was a time-consuming task which left little room for interruption.

Fergus looked at his black-eyed son and solemn-faced Donald standing with his hands folded behind his back, but before Fergus could speak Kirsteen intervened.

'I know when Grant is lying,' she said quietly. 'And I don't think Shona would have sent him to tell a fairy tale.'

Grant looked up at his father. 'Shona said the monster was a parachute . . .'

'And the kelpie on the wee island was likely a German,' Donald added breathlessly.

It was enough for Fergus. 'You get on with your work, Bob, I'll go over to Sliach and see what all the fuss is about!'

But Bob suddenly felt ashamed. He knew Fergus wouldn't ask help of any man unwilling to give it and if it wasn't for Kirsteen's kindness his midday meal would be nothing more than bread and cheese washed down with milk. He scraped his chair back and strode to the door to push his feet into muddy wellingtons. 'I'll get along with him, lass,' he told Kirsteen. 'Thankin' you for my dinner.'

She gripped his knotted brown hand briefly. 'Thank you, Bob,' she said simply, but he knew what she meant. He made to follow Fergus but she stopped him by calling in rather awed tones, 'Shouldn't you take a gun? It – might be dangerous.'

'Ach, no, Matthew will have his! If the German has come down on Sliach it's more likely prayers he'll be needin'.'

'Can I come with you, Bob?' Grant asked anxiously, the idea of chasing Germans far more appealing to him than an afternoon with school books. 'I have a fine gun I made myself.'

Seeing Kirsteen's rather harassed look Babbie put down the dish cloth and began to peel off her apron. 'I'll take you to school . . . the pair of you,' she said firmly. 'But we'll go to the harbour for a wee while first and chase the seagulls.'

Grant snorted, feeling himself far too manly for the pastimes he had revelled in only recently, but Bob was already hurrying away, calling on Dot, his sheepdog, who had rounded up a dismayed squadron of hens.

When Bob saw the young German airman he knew it was well that he had come because Fergus with his one arm and a visibly shaken Matthew would never have managed Anton into the boat.

But at first Fergus had no intention of doing such a thing. His dark eyes had snapped and the muscle of his jaw had tightened. It was one thing for the men of the island to deal with the Enemy, but it was entirely another to see his daughter tenderly ministering to one of them. And as he watched her frantically tearing strips from the hem of her white petticoat to make them into bandages, he was consumed with rage. A German lay on Rhanna soil and his daughter was behaving as if his life was a precious thing that had to be preserved.

His hand flashed out to grip her roughly by the shoulders and haul her to her feet. 'Get away from him!' he ordered harshly. 'Bob and myself will see to him!'

Tears of anger glinted in her eyes. 'Will you, Father – will you see – to this?' She pulled back the blood-saturated cloak to reveal the terrible wounds.

'Dear God, help him!' Bob muttered, swallowing hard.

'God – and Lachlan!' she cried passionately. 'He needs attention quickly or he'll die . . . if he doesn't anyway,' she added so sadly that Fergus put his arm round her and whispered huskily, 'I'm – sorry, mo ghaoil – it was just – things that bother me sometimes.'

He raised his voice. 'Matthew, row like the devil then get along over for Lachlan! Tell him to bring his trap as far as your house!'

Matthew, glad of something to do, almost fell into the boat and splashed away hurriedly.

Fergus looked down at Anton. 'Is . . . there anything you can do for him, Shona?'

Wordlessly she laid a broad strip of petticoat over the gaping viscera. Bob and Fergus gently lifted Anton's body till a thick wad of material was fixed in place. It was immediately soaked in blood and Shona stepped out of what remained of her petticoat and bound it over the bloodstained pad.

'My, but you're a bright lass,' Bob said admiringly. 'There's more in your head than was put there by a spoon.'

'But I can't do any more.' Her voice was filled with frustration. Her experience of nursing was of a limited nature though her few months' training had equipped her with an efficiency that was at times even a surprise to herself. Her legs were shaking and she felt sick with reaction. Silently she sent up a prayer that the doctor hadn't been called to another part of the island. She looked at Anton's face. It was drained of colour and the congealed blood on his forehead leapt out from the whiteness in a vicious riot of purple and red.

It was very quiet. The cold green water lapped the little island. A lone Red-throated Diver paddled hurriedly by, uttering its melancholy mewing wail, annoyed that its chosen nesting territory had been violated by humans. Over the crags of Ben Machrie a great bird soared majestically.

Bob's hand rasped over the stubble on his chin, his eyes raking the misted azure of the sky. 'Damt eagle,' he muttered uneasily. 'It's roamin' up there like it's

waitin' for the lambs comin'.' But his unease wasn't
incurred by the sight of the eagle whose home lay in
the remote mountain ledges. His eyes kept straying to
Anton lying like one already dead and his grip tightened on the bone handle of his shepherd's crook.

Fergus leaned against the bole of a tree and lit his
pipe with a show of calm but his mind was racing.
He tried to keep from looking at Anton but couldn't,
the anger in his heart now replaced by a pathos he
could barely understand. It wasn't right to feel like
this about a German. He struggled with his thoughts.
What was right? To hate because it was the proper
thing to do in war? The night before he had looked
at Jon Jodl and had felt only pity. They were all the
victims of circumstance. This dying youngster was
just another victim in a world created by the greed of
his so-called leaders; another pawn in the deadly,
intricate game of war. There was something else, too,
that leapt into Fergus's mind, that reared up from the
depths of the past: his terrible battle with the deadly
waters round the Sgor Creags. The frail speck of his
life had struggled with a sea that had wanted to crush
his body to pulp and that had mangled his left arm
beyond repair. Lachlan had amputated it while he lay
in a world of hellish delirium; when he'd been
without his senses he'd had to depend on the help of
the people who loved him most. And now the
wounded German was unconscious and dependent.
But if he wakened at that moment who would be
familiar and beloved enough for *him* to ask, 'Will you
help me?'

Fergus blew a mouthful of smoke into the hazy blue air. For a moment it hung suspended, and when it gradually dispersed all the prejudices that had swathed his thinking went with it. Shona twisted round in a gesture of impatience and caught the look of tenderness in his black eyes. 'You're a fine nurse,' he told her quietly. 'You did a grand job. I'm sure he'll be grateful to you.'

'I don't want his thanks, Father, just a chance of life for him, that's all. I wish Lachlan would hurry.'

Dot was barking impatiently from the shore. She had followed Matthew through the woods but realizing that her master wasn't coming behind she had come back to look for him. The sound of her yelps echoed into the corries of the Ben, then rebounded back over the loch to be lost over the shaggy moors.

'I'll kill that damt dog!' Bob cursed as the eerie ghost bark bounced again and again off the face of the mountain. In normal circumstances he would have roared at Dot to be quiet but hard and tough as he was he felt himself to be in the very presence of Death and his watery eyes gazed broodingly at the unrestrained antics of the lively dog.

Time is an eternity when filled with urgency, but barely thirty minutes had passed when the tall, slim figure of Lachlan finally burst through the thicket of pines on the opposite shore and jumped quickly into the waiting boat. As he pushed it off and came gliding through the calm green water, the men let out sighs of relief and Shona gave a welcoming cry, for the sight of his black bag and the air of reassurance that seemed to enshroud him brought both peace and hope to everyone there. As everyone on Rhanna knew just to look at Lachlan McLachlan was to know love: his tanned face was finely drawn, his mouth firm and sensitive. But it was in his eyes that anxious souls found peace, where they beheld the compassion of his heart. It was the last thing that many of his patients saw before letting go of life.

When Lachlan reached the island he looked at the neat bandage Shona had made and patted her arm. 'You've done well, mo ghaoil,' he approved quietly before starting on a swift examination of Anton's broken body.

Fergus stood against the tree and watched Lachlan's long, sensitive fingers. The doctor had removed his coat to cover Anton and his shoulder blades showed through his pullover. He was thin and still boyish with his dark curling hair that always strayed over his forehead when he bent over. So Fergus remembered the doctor Lachlan who had tended him so devotedly, and for a moment Fergus held his breath. How he loved the man who was both doctor and companion to him. But it hadn't always been so. Fergus's first wife, Helen, had died giving birth to Shona and in his grief Fergus had blamed Lachlan, and it was only many years later, at the time of Fergus's accident, that the two men had healed the rift between them. Something caught in Fergus's throat. How bitterly he regretted those lost years. He had wasted so much precious time that could have been richly spent with the man who healed with skill and unstinting devotion.

As Lachlan began slowly to remove Anton's helmet Fergus knocked his pipe out against the tree and went to kneel by the doctor. 'Does he have a chance, Lachlan?' he asked softly.

'It's difficult to say till I get him back to the house. I've sent Matthew over to fetch Biddy, and Phebie is getting the surgery ready. He ought to be in hospital,' he continued. 'With complete asepsis and every modern surgical technique . . . but I'll do my best.' He passed a hand over his brow. He was always doubtful about his abilities as a surgeon. Working on an island with limited facilities, he'd had to deal with many emergencies over the years – and the patients who had come healthily through surgery carried out in crude, makeshift conditions were a testimonial to his capabilities. But he was completely without ego and it was perhaps the lack of it which endeared him to so many.

He paused as he lifted the helmet off the wounded man's head. The young man had already reminded him of Niall with his youthful features and firm chin, but now, the crop of fair curling hair completed the illusion. He gently ran his fingers through the thick blond thatch. 'He's got concussion, but the helmet saved him from more serious damage. It's the shock I'm worried about . . . he's lost so much blood.' He looked at the little boat rocking peacefully. 'In my haste I brought only my bag – could you – all of you – take off any clothing you don't need and pad out those planks a bit?'

Wiry old Bob was coatless but he pulled off a

tattered cardigan and stood in his shirt sleeves without the hint of a shiver. Fergus removed his jacket and felt the goose pimples rising, but he moved to the boat and began to lay the pitifully inadequate coverings on the bottom. Bob came at his back armed with a bundle of dead bracken which he pushed under the clothing.

'You have a head on you, Bob,' Fergus commented and he too began to gather moss and bracken. In minutes a soft bed was made and the arduous task began of getting Anton into the boat, which was no easy job, for, though slim, he was tall and muscular. Bob and Lachlan grasped his shoulders, Shona supported his middle in an effort to keep the wound from opening further, and Fergus took his ankles in the strong grasp of his right arm. Fergus got into the boat first and his stomach lurched as the frail little craft tilted alarmingly. For a moment he hesitated and looked down. There was no gradual shoreline from the tiny, rocky islet – the land dropped down immediately into deep black depths – and the sight of it made him shudder. Water had frightened him from boyhood. The land was his backbone, water something to be admired so long as his two feet were firmly on the ground. He stumbled against a thwart and the little boat responded by bucking alarmingly.

'Steady, man,' Lachlan said quietly, and the moment was over. Soon Anton was lying on his bed of mossy bracken but taking up most of the confined space.

'Only two of us will get in wi' him,' Bob muttered,

blowing his nose into a grimy hanky with a non-chalant air. 'It's how we'll be managing on the other side that worries me.'

No one looked at Fergus, for never by a word or glance had any man suggested that the loss of his arm was an inconvenience to him. But he was always quick to sense unspoken thoughts and he said roughly, 'Get along over, I'll wait here.'

Shona slid a thin arm round his waist. 'I'll wait with you, we can keep each other warm.'

He looked at her anxiously. She had divested herself of most of her warm clothing to cover Anton, and Fergus felt a rush of protectiveness. He pulled her close and she felt the warmth of his body burning into her, the very nearness of it dispelling the chilly tremors that were bringing her out in goose pimples.

Bob pulled swiftly at the oars. In his days of tending sheep and cows he had seen many a sickening sight, but they were of things within his experience. The sight he had just witnessed was without those bounds, and his tough old stomach churned, making him row the harder. Dot saw him coming and her barks grew in volume, but her sense of devotion was lost on her disgruntled master. He lunged at her with his boot the minute he jumped ashore, whereupon she tucked her tail well between her haunches and slunk into the bushes.

'Come back till I toe your arse, you bugger!' Bob cried in frustration, and then turned his attention to helping Lachlan. Both men were grimly aware of Anton's open wound and were able to ease him over the planks only a few inches at a time, a task made no easier by the swaying of the boat. Bob stopped to wipe watery mucus from his nose. 'It's no damt use, Doctor!' he spat. 'We'll never manage the lad between us! I'd best go back for McKenzie! We need another pair o' hands!' Which last remark was proof of Bob's invincible faith in Fergus. But before they could move, Dot began making a nuisance of herself again, whimpering in the bushes and making excited half-yelps. The distraction was too much for Bob and he roared, 'Shut up, you brute, or I'll skin your hide—'

He wasn't able to finish the threat. The dog suddenly shot out of the undergrowth, followed by the muzzle of a murderous-looking Tommy gun held by a man attired in khaki battledress and a tin helmet from which sprouted sprays of fir branches.

'Your dog was causing a bit of a nuisance,' he pleasantly told a surprised-looking Bob. The soldier then turned to Lachlan. 'You look like you could be doing with a bit of help?' but before Lachlan could answer he called into the trees, 'Out of it, lads. We need some muscle here.' Magically there appeared from bush and tree half a dozen young men all sporting a variety of natural camouflage. Without a word they went straight to the boat and lifted Anton out as if he were thistledown. Bob immediately climbed back into the boat to row to the island for Fergus and Shona, leaving Lachlan to introduce himself.

'Pleased to meet you, Doctor,' said the thick-set, heavy-jawed young man whose gun had sent Dot yelping. 'I'm Dunn, the officer in charge of this charade.' His teeth showed in a flash of amusement before his eyes travelled to Anton. 'I see you have found another of the bomber crew?'

Lachlan nodded slowly. 'Yes, he's very badly wounded and needs immediate attention. My house is a fair distance from here but I've brought my trap to the clearing at the edge of the wood. We'll have to carry him to it . . .' He spread his fine hands in a gesture of despair. 'I'm worried about the bumping he'll get on the way down. The track is a rough one.'

Dunn grinned reassuringly. 'Don't worry, Doctor, we'll get him back to your house.' He turned to the others and there was a swift exchange. Before Bob was half-way over the loch the men had removed their battle-jackets, fashioning them into a strong, pliable stretcher into which they placed Anton. There was no regimental dividing line between officer and men. They worked together as an efficient team and Lachlan looked on admiringly. Soon they were all making their way through the dark, silent wood with a subdued Dot slinking at Bob's heels. Fergus had wrapped his jacket around Shona who was carrying her bloodstained cloak over her arm.

Dunn looked at it and his professional mask fell for a moment. 'He's lost a lot of blood. Do you know how he came to injure himself?'

'Probably on the mountain – coming down,' she said quietly. 'There's a lot of jagged rocks on this side of the mountain.'

'And you've just found him?'

'Ay, the children heard moans from the island.'

'So he's spent most of the night in the open?'

'And most of the morning. He's suffering badly from exposure.'

'A real tough-skinned Jerry!' Dunn's words were harsh but Shona knew they were only a cover.

When they reached the clearing Dunn nodded towards the trap. 'You get in, Doctor, and lead the way. It's better that we should carry him, lessen the risk of rattling him around.'

Fergus fell into step with Dunn who was at the head of the stretcher party. 'It's been a wild-goose chase for you,' Fergus said in his deep melodious voice. It wasn't a question, but a blunt statement of fact.

The officer appreciated it, and laughed. 'Wild geese would be a bloody sight easier to catch than the ghosts we've been chasing. We were told the island was invaded by German paratroops and were sent over to investigate – can't be too careful – never know what the bastards will be up to . . .' He checked himself and went on pleasantly, 'We've got on to Naval Patrol to let them know it's a bit of a false alarm . . . some of us are staying though . . . there's still the pig-headed one of the crew to locate and it seems your Home Guard are having a bit of trouble running him to ground. We met some of them over on the north side of the island but they didn't seem too keen to hang around there.'

Fergus smiled at this but Bob's weatherbeaten countenance creased into a frown. 'No one in their right senses will be staying round that damt place for long!' It was a cryptic remark, one typical of the superstitious older generation, and Bob, being one of the best Seanachaidhs (story tellers), was renowned for his ability to arouse curiosity in the least imaginative beings, but the officer merely smiled politely and said nothing.

Bob's gnarled fingers curled tighter round his crook. 'The De'il deals wi' his own,' he snarled, defensive yet assertive about his beliefs. 'It is a consecrated place yonder at Dunuaigh. The monks will no' be likin' the intrusion that is goin' on wi' folks of all nationalities trampin' over their restin' places!'

Shona smiled impishly. 'But Bob, there is only one German likely to be wandering – and no doubt wishing he hadn't been so hasty in escaping from the Manse this morning.'

''Tis enough! 'Tis enough!' Bob barked and he stamped away to begin his belated work, calling impatiently on Dot who went scampering after him gladly enough.

Tina was standing at the door of her cottage. She raised a languid arm in the manner of one acknowledging a carnival procession, her only betrayal of surprise manifested by the slightly breathless utterance, 'You have caught the German laddie then?' Which singular observation rendered the sturdy presence of the Commandos as of little import. 'If any o' you are seeing Matthew, send him home for his dinner,' she added in slightly accusing tones, then turned to scoop Eve from the water barrel into which she was gleefully climbing.

Shona ran ahead and climbed into the trap beside Lachlan who immediately tucked a rug round her legs. 'You take care, mo ghaoil,' he told her. 'We must have a nice rosy lass waiting for Niall when he gets home.'

She laughed, tucking her arm through his. 'Don't worry, Kirsteen has stuffed so much food into me since I came home Niall will think I'm a prize turkey when he sees me. A good excuse for him to thraw my neck!'

Their laughter drifted back to Fergus who had just heard from the officer about the raids over Clydebank the previous night. First-hand news could be had from the accumulator-powered wireless sets owned by those interested and affluent enough to possess one. Fergus had one in his parlour but the morning had been too rushed for anyone in the household to think about switching on. The officer went on to say that it was believed the bomber that had crashed on Rhanna was one of a group which had taken part in the raids, and then, having been hit, had lost all sense of direction.

'Oh God, no!' Fergus breathed. 'The doctor's son stays in Clydebank. He and my daughter are sweethearts! Good God! Is there no end to it?' It was a cry from the heart and Dunn looked at him in sympathetic enquiry. 'Niall was injured at Dunkirk,' Fergus explained. 'Lachlan, his wife, Shona – all were wild with grief because they believed him to be dead – but he came back with a wound that meant no more fighting for him . . .' He smiled wryly. 'It would seem the war has caught up with him anyway. How am I to tell his parents that?'

Dunn cleared his throat. 'Would – you like me to do it?'

Fergus hesitated as he watched the stretcher party marching carefully down the grass-rutted track. It was very peaceful there among the fields, with the crushed grasses releasing an almost forgotten scent of summer. The dairy cows, released from winter byres, let out soft little half-bellows which they blew into each other's ears. The frost of the morning had disappeared and there was a gentle heat in the haze of the sun, a delicate promise of the green, Hebridean spring to come. Banners of blue smoke curled from croft and farm, rising to hang in tattered shrouds against the misted purple of the mountains.

Down below Lachlan and Shona turned, curious as to why Fergus and the officer had stopped.

Fergus wondered wildly what to do. How would Shona feel having an echo of the past brought back? Phebie would react typically, with a quiet display of normality hiding her deepest fears . . . And Lachlan, the doctor in him rising up out of his despair to try and save the life of a German . . . But how would Lachlan the man feel afterwards? How would they all feel till news of Niall filtered out of the confusion of an air raid? Shona . . . Again Fergus hesitated. She had come back to Rhanna for a holiday, to rest that tightly-strung little body which Fergus was still inclined to think of as belonging to a child. But even though she had been home such a short time he was seeing a change in her. She had gained a lot of poise, her emotions were under a tighter rein. Once, Rhanna and all it meant had been her only horizon, but now there were others which seemed to have broadened her whole outlook on life . . .

Fergus straightened his shoulders. 'I'll tell them,' he said abruptly to Dunn and ran down the rutted track to catch up with the trap.

Lachlan heard him out in silence, a faint flush high on his cheekbones the only sign of his inner fears. Shona, her deep blue eyes wide, stared at her father as his firm lips formed halting words into some kind of meaning. She wanted to put her hands over her ears, to scream at her father to be quiet, to shut her mind to the facts. It had been easier in childhood when little fantasies had helped her over the many hurdles of her young life. But she wasn't a child any more, there were no little illusions to help her now. In a dream she heard herself saying, 'No one will be knowing the facts yet. It – will be some time before we hear any news?'

'I'm afraid so,' Dunn murmured, coming up behind Fergus. 'Everyone is too shattered and harassed to make much sense of anything. I believe it all started last night and the all-clear didn't come till just before dawn this morning. Everything will be in a turmoil but I'll get some enquiries through if I can . . .' He smiled kindly and went on, 'Mr McKenzie tells me the young man has had experience of battle and is at present with Civil Defence so I'm sure he knows how to look after himself.' What he didn't add was that there was a strong likelihood the German bombers would return to Glasgow and Clydebank that night but he felt he had already said enough on the subject.

The stretcher party had halted some distance ahead, and Lachlan turned to Shona. 'Go home, mo ghaoil. I'll understand.'

She put her small hand over his and shook her head vehemently, tears welling up in her eyes. 'No! You'll need all the help you can get! If I sit at home I'll just dwell on all the things that might never happen. It would be useless to try and contact Niall, all the usual communications will be down but . . .' she turned appealingly to Dunn, 'if you hear anything further or can get any sort of enquiries through would you let me know immediately?'

'Count on it,' Dunn nodded.

Fergus took her other hand and crushed it tightly. 'You take care, Ni-Cridhe,' he told her softly.

Shona caught her breath. 'Ni-Cridhe' was the Gaelic endearment for 'my dear lassie'. It wasn't often he expressed himself so freely in public and she knew that he was feeling something of her pain. It was his way of telling her how much he cared. 'I'll take care, Father,' she whispered.

'We'll expect you in for tea,' he said, and then turned abruptly on his heel and strode away.

Chapter Eight

A curious crowd had gathered outside Lachlan's, ample proof that Matthew's tongue had been busy. When the stretcher party hove into view everyone began to talk among themselves as if by doing so they were proving that their presence in that remote spot of Glen Fallan had no bearing whatsoever on the latest events. So absorbed did they appear that it seemed an impossibility their interest could lie in anything that was happening outside their own little circle. As Lachlan came by in the trap, heads lifted one by one in a great display of surprise.

'It is yourself, Doctor,' acknowledged Kate McKinnon innocently. 'We were just thinkin' over the things o' last night and wondering where the other two German lads wcrc hidin' but I see you have another one there.' With one accord they all turned to look upon the deathly pale face of Anton being marched past their vision.

Lachlan got down from the trap and said with a deceptively charming smile, 'And you have all left Portcull to have a little chin-wag in the middle of Glen Fallan?'

Old Joe's sea-green eyes betrayed nothing. 'Ach no, not at all, Doctor,' he rebuked gently. 'We are waiting for the lads to come over the glen to see will they have news for us.'

'Ay,' put in Erchy the Post who, with his satchel slung over his shoulder and one foot on the pedal of his bike, had the air of someone who had been rudely interrupted in the middle of a busy day. 'That is a fact, Doctor. Also Matthew was asking us to wait and tell you that Biddy is not at home.'

'But I know that!' Lachlan cried. 'She spent the night at the Smiddy!'

Fingal McLeod, a tall lanky young crofter who had lost his leg to a fox snare, nodded wisely. 'Well, well now, that is likely why she is no' at home.'

'But I told Matthew she would be at Todd's,' Lachlan said.

'Ach well, that's where she'll be right enough,' Erchy murmured.

Lachlan was growing exasperated. The islanders could be trying and unhelpful when they had a mind, and it was obvious they were in no mood to be helpful now.

Shona felt her temper rising. It was a trait over which she had to exercise control but just then it erupted in a mixture of anxiety and grief. 'Well!' she cried hotly, 'one of you get along over to Todd's and fetch Biddy!'

'Matthew will be over there now,' Fingal said soothingly.

Shona tossed her auburn head and her eyes sparkled with rage. 'You are just like a bunch of old women! The laddie you are gaping at so eagerly may die! Lachlan can't do everything himself and I'm not fully trained to help properly! For God's sake! He's a German, I know, but he's also a human being!'

Lachlan had disappeared into the house leaving Elspeth listening at the door. Her strangely immobile face was gaunt with outrage at the very idea of a German, wounded or otherwise, being allowed to cross the doctor's threshold. In Elspeth's mind, Slochmhor and everyone therein owed all to her efficiency as a housekeeper and she felt it was her right to exercise her opinion as to what went on there. When Phebie had asked her to help prepare the surgery for an emergency case she had agreed willingly enough, scrubbing and cleaning till the air reeked of antiseptic. But not until the Commandos crossed the doorstep with Anton did she realize that for the past hour she had been preparing the way for a German airman, and she was speechless with indignation. Now, though, at Shona's words she found her tongue quickly. 'Wait you there, Erchy McKay!' she said to Erchy, who, shamefaced, was straddling his bike ready to push off. 'It is the King's business you should be about! You have no right to be gallivanting off when you are on duty!'

Elspeth was coming down the path into the crowd and Erchy stopped in mid-flight, his kindly face bewildered and angry. He was about to tell her that the 'King's business' was only a part-time job on an island that received mail only three times a week, but before he could speak another figure came flying past on a bike, pedalling swiftly along the bumpy glen

1171

road. It soon proved to be Babbie Cameron, her wind-tossed hair a fiery beacon, her pale, freckled skin whipped to a delicate rose. The bike had been left in the ditch by Murdy the night before and Babbie had simply borrowed it. It was a rusted heap with a wobbling front wheel and Babbie now discovered it had no brakes. Babbie's feet rasped along the stony road in an effort to stop the machine, but she catapulted into the crowd, sending everyone scattering. Gallantly the menfolk rushed to her aid, having to make no excuses for hands that grabbed at forbidden fruits in order to avert a catastrophe.

Babbie was an attractive sight standing against the backcloth of the mountains. Her red hair, which breathed of sunshine and all the bright fire of autumn, made the slopes of Sgurr nan Ruadh look dull in comparison. The pallor of her skin was startling in its glowing frame yet oddly in keeping; her mouth was too generous for her to be beautiful, but her smile was so radiant that to observe it was to know enchantment. She was slim to the point of being skinny but though her sweater was in itself shapeless it couldn't entirely hide the curving swell of her breasts. Rhanna men liked their women 'well padded', and no matter how beautiful the face or figure of a slim woman she rarely merited a second glance after the first swift appraisal. But it was a different matter if the slimness was enhanced by properly placed padding, and Babbie fitted this category. While she panted for breath the men fussed and Elspeth glowered.

'Sorry everyone . . . and thanks,' Babbie smiled, adroitly removing Fingal's hand from her left thigh. She turned to look at Shona. 'Your father popped in to tell us about – things . . . I thought I might be needed.'

Shona felt like hugging her there and then in the middle of the glen. Instead she put out her hand. 'You're just in time, Babbie – the doctor will be waiting.' And with her head held high she marched with Babbie up the path to Slochmhor, an outraged Elspeth forced to make way for them at the gate.

'I'll be telling Biddy to look in on her way home,' called a rather subdued Kate. 'She will not be liking it if she feels left out.'

'As you like,' Shona said from the door. 'Though 'tis a pity you were not thinking about it sooner.'

The villagers ambled back to Portcull in a somewhat embarrassed silence, Fingal and Erchy breaking away from the others at the hill track leading to Nigg. Erchy's satchel already contained two rabbits which he had collected from his snares half an hour earlier. He pushed his bike into a clump of bushes and grinned at Fingal. 'Let us go about the King's business then,' he said in a hideous falsetto. Both men roared with laughter, made all the merrier at the prospect of an afternoon poaching Burnbreddie.

'We might find the other Jerry waiting to ravish her ladyship,' Fingal snorted ecstatically. He halted for a moment to sit down on a mossy stone. 'Wait you, Erchy, I will have a wee look to see have I got everything we need.' Carefully, he unscrewed the bottom half of his peg leg, peered inside, and then, satisfied as to its contents, fixed it back in place. 'Old Peggy is fully equipped,' he grinned. 'I have an extra flask of Tam's whisky in there too. We will no' go thirsty.'

In the surgery at Slochmhor, Lachlan, too, was finding every reason to be grateful to Tam. Earlier in the day he had pressed a generous bottle of whisky into Lachlan's hands, and nodding and winking he had warned, 'Don't be telling a soul, Doctor. 'Tis for your nerves when you have to be doing these awful things like Todd's appendix.' Lachlan had put the bottle to the back of the cupboard thinking it unlikely that it would be needed in the near future, and now he smiled wryly at the small glass in his hand. Todd's appendix was nothing to what waited for his immediate attention. Anton lay scrubbed and ready . . . Ready for what? Life or death? The responsibility lay with Lachlan and the thought made his hands shake.

'Ready, Doctor?' One of the Commandos, a sturdy young man with a strong stomach, who had volunteered to stay behind and help, popped his head round the door.

Lachlan gulped down the whisky and spluttered, 'Yes, I'm ready.' He smiled. 'I don't make a habit of this, Private Anderson.' Anderson looked at the whisky bottle with interest. 'Would you like a drop?' Lachlan asked, amused despite himself.

'I don't mind, sir, I really don't mind.' He gulped down a generous mouthful, straightened his shoulders and followed Lachlan briskly into the surgery.

Phebie was just coming out. Inside, her stomach

was churning with misery, and all she could think about was Niall, her son, her beloved eldest child, once again bringing anxiety and deepest despair to all those who loved him most. Her bonny plump face was strained and pale but she managed to smile at Lachlan and whisper 'Good luck, Lachy. Shout if you need me.'

He gripped her shoulders tightly and bent to kiss her cheek. 'It's you I should be with just now,' he said huskily. 'You're always such a tower of strength, yet I know . . . even the strongest of towers needs a bit of propping up now and then. Our son will be all right, my darling. The young rascal has come through worse. I'll be in there operating on a mortally wounded German laddie but my prayers will be with Niall.'

'Mine too,' she said shakily and stood back to let him pass, hardly able to see for the tears drowning her eyes.

Babbie, masked and gowned, stood looking down at Anton. He was wrapped in wind-bleached folds of gleaming white linen which seemed to match the deathly pallor of his face. His forehead was patterned with bruises whose livid colour leapt out from the white skin. He looked very young and completely helpless and Babbie thought, 'So, this is a German. If you had been ugly . . . perhaps just a little bit evil-looking, Anton Büttger, I might have hated you . . . but you're not, you're not! If you had been then I might not feel so obliged to help try and save your life. Damn you, Anton Büttger,' her heart cried.

'Damn you for looking so young and innocent. I hate you for making me feel that I must do all the right things to give you a chance of life!' Her thoughts made her feel sick and her hands trembled.

Shona saw the hesitation and though her own legs were shaking, she said reassuringly, 'You're doing fine, Babbie. The beginning's always the difficult part.'

'Are you all right, Babbie?' Lachlan asked a trifle sharply, all the old doubts about his own abilities piling into his head at sight of the young German's ghastly wounds.

'Yes . . . I just skipped eating most of my dinner with all the upsets,' Babbie said faintly, her green eyes full of an odd apprehension. 'It's just hunger pains.'

'Would you like me to get you something?' Anderson asked. He had not batted one eyelid at the sight of Anton's stomach piling out from the surrounding flesh.

'No – no, I'm fine now.'

Lachlan gave her a worried look. 'You have had experience of surgery, Babbie?'

'Oh yes, yes of course . . . it's just . . . never with a German.'

'You must put that out of your head,' Lachlan said gently. 'Just think of him as a patient who deserves all our skill to pull him through.' Then Lachlan turned to begin the operation, and as he worked he forgot all about his doubts and concentrated solely on the task at hand. His long, sensitive fingers worked with a faultless skill that made everyone in the room glow with admiration. His aura of confidence seemed to reach out and embrace them all and after the first few minutes they were working together as an efficient team.

Biddy grumbled long and loudly as she struggled awake. With a dry mouth and an aching head spinning alarmingly, she hastily closed her eyes again. She felt sick and for a moment couldn't sort out one thought from another. Then the smells of the Smiddy came to her: horse manure, leather, fragrant hay and rusting bits of iron. For a few seconds she lay unable to believe it was daylight and that she must have spent the night in Todd the Shod's barn. Bits of hay had worked their way into her clothing and were making her very uncomfortable. Carefully she moved an arm in an experimental gesture. Well, one limb was still intact anyway. Slowly she shifted the position of her cold, cramped body and immediately a searing pain shot through her ankle. 'Damt bugger!' she swore through gritted teeth, the pain bringing her sharply to her senses. Wincing, she raised herself on an elbow to grope for her glasses, but they eluded her searching fingers. Screwing up her eyes she peered round the big shed but there was no sign of life. The visiting horses had probably been collected earlier by their owners, and as she was ensconced in a pile of hay which was almost smothered by a jumbled heap of ironmongery, she must have escaped notice.

Biddy's first feelings of surprise soon turned to

extreme indignation. What kind of place was it where people went about everyday affairs without a thought to the nurse who had tended them so devotedly for years? The cold of the night had played havoc with her circulation. Her extremities were like lumps of lead, especially her feet which were nearest the side door. 'Damt Germans!' Biddy muttered under her breath. 'I'll kill the buggers if I catch them!' Then she raised her voice, uttering appeals for help which flowed with such lusty frequency that the pigeons in the loft fluttered up in a cloud of dust and made a hasty exit. Then Mollie McDonald came running in, a red-faced bustle of amazement.

As Mollie stood in the doorway, taking in the sight of the old nurse, toothless and without spectacles, lying among the junk and hay, her mouth fell open. It was well known that Biddy was fond of 'a wee tipple'. She carried a hip flask wherever she went and fortified herself whenever she felt the need. It was purely for 'medicinal purposes only' she told anyone who questioned her, but few did. Hers was a job that called her out at all times and in all weathers and so devoted was she that no one blamed her for 'having a wee snifter to warm her auld blood'. Indeed, the islanders saw to it that her flask was never dry and frequently topped up her 'firkin for the fireplace'. But Mollie was in a mood that morning to blame the 'Uisge-beatha' for a great many things. Her good nature allowed her to overlook many of her husband's little misdemeanours, but the manner of his arrival home the night before had caused her some embarrassment. And now Biddy was lying in their barn hideously glassy-eyed and stupefied, her wiry grey hair hanging in limp strands over her lined, yellow face. She was obviously suffering from a massive hangover. Mollie folded her arms and moved forward into the shed.

'Well now, Biddy McMillan!' she said, her voice taut with disapproval. 'A fine thing this is indeed, and you with your reputation to uphold. It's a reputation for an alcoholic cailleach you'll be earning and no mistake. I knew last night there was something funny goin' on wi' Todd and his cronies but never – never– did I imagine that yourself of all people would be in on a thing like that. You're worse than auld Annack Gow and that's sayin' something for she was never sober when Jock was alive if I'm mindin' right!'

Biddy was speechless. She had found her specs and had hastened to put them on in order that she might hear better the words of sympathy that would surely follow her discovery, for it was a belief of hers that glasses aided not only the sight but also the hearing. Small inarticulate grunts escaped her toothless mouth.

Mollie snorted and continued softly. 'Ach, but it is terrible just. The world is goin' to ruin! Germans and soldiers all over the island an' our very own nurse lyin' drunk in my Todd's place o' business. 'Tis no wonder you were not over seeing to him this morning,' she clucked reproachfully. 'Biddy, mo ghaoil, if you had to sleep it off could you not just have stayed in the house to be decent-like?'

Biddy removed her specs because she could hardly believe her ears. Her ankle was throbbing, she was frozen to the marrow, and instead of sympathy she was receiving abuse. 'Is it blind you are, Mollie McDonald?' she gasped through tears of exhaustion and self-pity. 'It is the doctor I am needin' this very meenit! I feel like I am dyin' wi' exposure and my ankle is broken! Get help quickly, you silly woman – and put the kettle on for a cuppy.'

But before Mollie could hasten away Kate McKinnon appeared, and she too stared at Biddy. 'What way are you lyin' there for, you daft cail-leach?' she twinkled. 'It's no wonder Matthew couldny find you! They are needin' you over at Slochmhor.'

Biddy's howl of derisive indignation split the air asunder. 'Needin' me! God! It's the doctor I am needin' and quick! Go and get Matthew and get me in that house before I die!'

Matthew came running at Kate's boisterous call, and between them they carried Biddy into the house amid a shower of abuse, instructions and complaints.

'Go you and fetch the doctor, Matthew,' Kate ordered. 'And don't be longer than two minutes.'

An astonished Todd, wallowing in self-pity over his post-operative discomforts, found his martyrdom seriously undermined by the advent of Biddy who was placed near him on an adjoining sofa. Mollie hastened to swing the kettle over the fire while Kate went upstairs to look for spare blankets.

*

The operation was well underway when Matthew's voice, loud and excited, drifted through from the hall, mingling with Phebie's soft and pleasant tones. Moments later she tapped on the surgery door and put her head round. 'Biddy had an accident last night,' she explained in some harassment. 'She was asleep in Todd's kitchen when she thought she heard noises in the Smiddy. She went out to look, thinking it might be Germans and she tripped on some junk and knocked herself unconscious. Mollie found her just a short time ago and it seems as well as everything else she has hurt her ankle rather badly.'

'Damn!' Lachlan cried, exasperated. 'I can't possibly leave this.'

'I'll go,' Shona said rather gladly, her first experience of surgery rendering her so nauseated she had been wondering how long she could go on without fainting. 'It sounds like something I can deal with.'

'Biddy says she wants the doctor!' Matthew's voice echoed from the hall.

'Well, she'll just have to make do with me!' Shona said firmly. 'I'm better at the Jack-and-Jill stuff anyway . . .' She took a last look at Anton on the table. 'A lot better than anything I can be doing for him. Is it all right, Lachlan?'

'Run along, lass,' Lachlan said kindly. 'You've done a grand job here. If Biddy starts grumbling at you just you tell her I'll be along later to sort her out.'

On the sofa Biddy groaned loudly with pain in between gulps of hot tea laced with brandy. 'It's broken, I know the bugger has broken itself!' she proclaimed loudly, addressing her swollen ankle.

Kate helped herself to tea from the huge pot, then sat down on the edge of Todd's sofa to eye Biddy thoughtfully. 'It's an assistant you should be having, Biddy,' she began sternly, pausing to let the inevitable barrage of protest subside before going on. 'I was just thinkin' the thing last night when I heard you had to sprachle out your warm bed to see to Todd here. It's too much to ask o' an auld chookie and now you are having this accident and maybe endin' up wi' piles and piddle trouble wi' the cold gettin' up your passages all night.'

Biddy wrapped a patchwork quilt round her knees and glowered into her tea. She knew Kate was right but she wasn't going to admit it because to do so, even to herself, was a signal that she really was getting beyond nursing the island single-handed. There had been an assistant several years before but she hadn't stuck the post for more than a month, and this fact she sourly pointed out to Kate, who made a gesture of impatience with her big, capable hands.

'Ach, c'mon now, mo ghaoil! Is it any wonder the poor soul skedaddled like a fart in front of a turd? You never gave her a chance! Criticized everything she did . . . in front o' her patients too. I mind her saying to me, "I am not able even to give an enema but that old bitch is peering over my shoulder to see am I putting the tube in the right passage". Near to tears she was telling me that, and myself knowing she was good at it, too, for she gave me one thon time I was laid up wi' my back.'

Todd had been mending the handle of a goffering iron with what appeared to be single-minded intent but when he looked up, the smile on his craggy face showed otherwise. 'It will not be a man causing a mistake like that,' he observed with an avidness that was out of keeping with his supposedly delicate condition. The profundity of the statement seemed to surprise even himself and thoughtfully he spat on the peats from the conveniently placed sofa, and then watched the results with every sign of enjoyment.

For a few moments the sizzling of roasting saliva filled the kitchen until Biddy said with slow deliberation, 'It is well you are not yet knowing what we had to sew up last night, Todd McDonald. Ay me, the Lord giveth and the nurse taketh away . . .'

Kate spluttered into her tea, Todd's guileless blue eyes glazed over and Mollie, coming back with a bowl of cold water from the rain barrel for Biddy's ankle, stood in the doorway, her loosely-hinged jaw once more falling to its lowest extent.

'Ay, ay,' Biddy continued wisely. 'It can happen! These scalpels is sharp things and your belly that round a wee slip's no' an easy thing to avoid – but, ach – don't worry, Todd, at your age it won't be mattering too much and it will never be noticed! Lachlan is a great hand wi' the embroidery and I am having a fine wee keepsake o' yourself to be remembering you by. It's fine for an old body like myself that never was having a man to occupy me, as you have told me yourself on more than one occasion.' She sighed regretfully. 'I can be lookin' at it and thinkin' "Ay, poor auld Todd, he was aye generous wi' himself right enough".' She fixed him with a fond gaze. 'Just think, you will go down in posterior like that other chiel . . . Napoleon I think it was. There was always a rumour they preserved his in a wee boxie.' She stirred her third cup of tea with a great show of calculated sorrow. Todd's face had grown bright red and he was glaring at Biddy with malevolence.

'It is no' an assistant you are needin', Biddy McMillan! It is a replacement! I am going to write to the Medical Board and ask for one to be sent right away!'

Kate threw herself back on the sofa in a fit of laughter and Todd yelled in pain as her weight pinned his legs. 'Ach, but you should see your face, Todd,' she screeched. 'It is yourself will be needin' the replacement and maybe Mollie another husband, for who would be wantin' a man that's nothing more than a castrated ram!'

Mollie's mouth quivered but she managed to scold sternly, 'It's your tongue should be cut out, Kate McKinnon! Todd is all the man I need. Poor soul, he is no' able to take any more shocks, he had enough last night to last him for a whily.' She turned to Biddy. 'Now then, Biddy, Kate and myself will see to that ankle o' yours.'

'It's broke I tell you,' Biddy protested, but Mollie quelled her with a stern eye and Biddy allowed her shoe and one of her black woollen stockings to be removed.

Mollie's lifetime of administering to a slightly hypochondriac husband had hardened her sympathies and she was inclined to think that everyone exaggerated their ills. 'Ay, you've only twisted it,' she asserted with a nod.

'I tell you it's broke,' Biddy said faintly although she knew by experience that her ankle was only badly strained.

Todd's post-operative pallor took on a distinctly rosy glow during the removal of Biddy's stocking. It was one thing for a Gael to make jokes about the female form but quite another to have a feminine leg exposed to his vision, even though the limb in question resembled a badly warped spurtle. 'Here,' he protested, 'this is no place for a woman to be doing such things.'

Kate got to her feet with a mischievous grin. 'Ach, the poor bodach is right enough! Him bein' a virgin mannie now won't be having the thrill of a woman's leg any more. He'll be celebrite like thon monks in the monkeries!'

'Damt women!' Todd exploded, while Kate, with a great show of solemnity, fixed a blanket between the sofas so that it formed a screen.

Into this unexpectedly merry gathering came Shona who looked at the scene with some surprise. 'I was told to expect a house full of invalids and here you all are looking as though you are having some sort of concert party.'

'Ach, it was poor auld Todd,' Kate said placidly. 'He was feart the sight of Biddy's ankle would set his passions leapin' so I fixed up the blanket to keep him from doin' himself a mischief!'

'Well, I've been sent over to see to the pair of them. Lachlan is busy operating on the bomber commander but he will be over to see to you both later,' Shona imparted, hiding a smile at sight of Biddy's outraged expression.

'Hmph!' Biddy snorted. 'No doubt I'll keep yet for a whily. I've survived this long after lyin' half-dead all night while the doctor attends to Germans,' she ended with an air of blatant martyrdom.

'Ach, c'mon you silly cailleach, let me see your ankle,' Shona said affectionately. The swelling had subsided slightly, thanks to Mollie's administrations and Shona praised the act.

'Just as well she did something,' Biddy grunted, 'for when her and that Kate found me they just stood looking at me like a couple of spare farts! It's a wonder I didn't die before they got me in the damt house!'

Shona began to strap up the ankle and Biddy noticed the dark circles under the girl's eyes and the dispirited droop of her shoulders. 'My bonny wee lassie,' she murmured tenderly. 'Here is me rampin' on like a bull wi' the skitters and your poor hert breakin'. I can tell something is ailing you.'

'Niall is ailing me that's what, Biddy. The Germans bombed Clydebank last night – and – and I have no way of knowing if he's dead or alive.'

'Ach, my bairnie,' the old midwife drew Shona's head down to her scraggy old bosom. 'Greet now my wee one, it will help the pain.' And cry Shona did, softly and helplessly, while Biddy stroked her hair and crooned loving words. Behind the curtain Todd gave a small forlorn sigh.

'What ails you now, Todd? Is it a hangover you are having?' Kate dimpled mischievously.

'Indeed I am not!' he protested with dignity. 'It's my stitches too tight and myself wishing the doctor could be here to see am I all right.'

'They'll be tight for a whily,' Biddy told him, 'but no tighter than you were yourself last night so it serves you right if you are uncomfortable. The disgrace of it! But never mind, Shona won't mind taking a wee look at them I'm sure.'

Todd was aghast at the idea of a young girl 'looking at his condition'. 'Indeed she will not!' he asserted quickly. 'I will not have a bairn like Shona looking at my belly and if I have to die waiting for the doctor to do it . . . then die I will.'

In spite of herself Shona smiled. 'Ach, away, Todd. My friend, Babbie, is a trained nurse. I'm sure she won't mind helping Lachlan for a wee while.'

'Oh, but it will have to be done through the authorities,' Biddy imparted dourly. 'They'll have to send a spare nurse . . . just till I'm back on my feets,' she added hastily.

'We'll see.' Shona wiped her tears away impatiently and went back to her ministrations on Biddy's ankle.

Chapter Nine

In the little guest room at Slochmhor, Anton Büttger lay like one who had already passed through the Valley of the Shadow. It was now evening and the soft lamplight shone on his fair curls crisping out from the layer of bandages encasing his head; his thick eyelashes lay on high cheekbones; and a fine little stubble of hair shadowed the hollows of his cheeks, making his face look thinner than it was. A faint dew of sweat gleamed on his upper lip and Babbie stooped to wipe it gently away. Despite his fever his hands were still clammily cold and again she put them under the blankets, stopping for a moment to check the bandages that swathed his middle. Shona plumped the pillows on the shake-down bed set in a corner of the room, and tried to dispel the numbness that surrounded her thoughts like a cloying shroud. She had listened to the tea-time news about the raids over Clydebank and Glasgow. It was a depressing account of devastation, of a chaos from which no order could yet emerge. A lot of people had died, a lot more had been injured, and there was simply no way of knowing if Niall was among the living or the dead. More raids were expected that night – tonight . . .

Shona shuddered and looked from the window to the moon breaking through the mist. It was 10.30. At that very moment the German bombers might be sweeping over Glasgow, crushing out the lives of innocent people, wrecking the lives of those that were left. She imagined Niall then: tall and handsome with his sun-tanned limbs and boyish smile, his corn-coloured curls glinting in the sun, his firm lips close to her own . . . She could feel them brushing her face . . .

She started and pulled away the net curtain that had blown softly against her cheek. The keen air from the moor whispered in through the slightly opened sash, laden with the sharp clean smell of the frost-rimed bracken on the hill. She turned and looked back at the room – at the bed occupied by the young German airman – and her memory took her back over the years to when, as a little girl, she had lain in the same bed. It was during the time that Mirabelle had died, and Hamish, too, the big laughing Highlander who had been grieve at Laigmhor, and whom she had loved. He had given her Tot, her dear little spaniel. The pup had been a present for her fifth birthday. Hamish had died on the treacherous rocks of the Sgor Creags in the same sea that had crushed her father's arm to pulp. It had all happened at once and she had spent her nights at Slochmhor, a frightened little girl unable to sleep. Niall had come to her then, an awkward boy of twelve, his thin arms enclosing her with his boyish comfort. 'I'm just through the wall from you – we can tap out messages to each other.' His words tossed back at her over the years and a sob caught in her throat.

Babbie looked up quickly. 'Are you all right, Shona?'

'Yes, I'm fine.' She composed herself quickly and added, 'How is he? Will he pull through, do you think?'

Babbie shook her bright head. 'Only time will tell that. He's young – strong – the doctor did a wonderful job. You're lucky to have such a man on the island.'

'Yes, I know, he puts up with a lot but seldom complains.'

'Some would say he was wasted here.'

'Wasted! He probably does more healing in this wee island than many doctors do with all the modern aids of the big hospitals.' She looked at Babbie quizzically. 'Can you really see Lachlan swallowed up in a big city practice? Here he is somebody, he stands out . . . do you think that's as daft as it sounds?'

'I know what you mean,' Babbie said softly. 'He's special. I watched him today, Phebie too, working like Trojans to save a German even though they are worried to death about their son.'

'You worked pretty well yourself – though – I got the strangest feeling it went against your grain – working to try and save the life of a German.'

Babbie glanced at Anton but her face betrayed nothing. She gave a small shrug. 'It's as Lachlan says; he is a patient like the hundreds of other patients I've had to see to in my time.'

'Ay, but this one is a German and the idea of it affected you, Babbie, deny it how you will. You helped to undress him, you saw the Iron Cross. Young he may be, but he has killed, Babbie, and somehow you can't forgive him for it . . . Och, I hate this war! It does things to nice people, makes them all bitter – and – and horribly irrational in their thinking!'

Babbie left the bed and went over to Shona, her eyes dark with sympathy. 'You have a soft heart, Shona McKenzie. Despite all your tempers you're softer than butter. I wish I was a bit like you – you get it all out of your system and things heal up quicker inside you. I keep it all inside and it's as well folks can't see what's in my heart at times, times like today when I looked at Anton Büttger and for quite a few sick moments I wanted him to die! But you! You worked like a wee fury though you had just heard that Germans . . . like him . . .' she inclined her head towards the bed, 'had just killed and injured a lot of people and your Niall was right in the thick of it all. I admire you, Shona . . . but I don't understand you!'

Shona took a deep breath. 'I didn't want to think. I've discovered that's the worst punishment of all. It's the not knowing that's worst. It's like being in a dark tunnel, never knowing whether you're crawling towards the light – or going back into the darkness.'

'Yes, I know, it's the most terrifying feeling on earth . . . yet – somehow – in some strange way, one gets used to the dark.' Babbie spoke almost to herself. She sounded so strange that Shona looked at her sharply.

'What a queer thing to say, Babbie.' She forced a laugh. 'If the old islanders could hear you they'd be getting the shivers and saying you were a spook wandered from the tombs at Dunuaigh.'

'Sorry, I have a habit of saying silly things. The nurses at the home told me I gave them the creeps and now I'm doing it to you.' She was herself again, apologizing in characteristic fashion, the radiance of her smile lighting her weary face.

'It's bed you need,' Shona said firmly. 'I hope you manage to get some sleep, you look exhausted.'

'Don't we all? It's been a long day. Don't worry about me, you know what I'm like once I get into bed.'

Shona laughed. 'I'll be sorry for the man you marry, you'll never get up on time to see him off in the morning.'

A shadow flitted over Babbie's face but she forced a rueful smile. 'Ach well, I'd better stay the way I am, I'm heading for the shelf now – twenty-three and no man to warm the sheets of my bed.'

'A real grannie,' Shona giggled, feeling oddly cheered by the older girl's careless good humour, too careless in that moment for it to be really genuine, but Shona sensed the barriers were up once more and didn't pursue the conversation.

Babbie turned to her small suitcase and began to look out nightwear. She had been adamant about moving over to Slochmhor to be immediately at hand. Lachlan had protested even while he had desperately wanted to accept help. He had been exhausted after a night with little sleep and a day spent battling to keep the Angel of Death from taking the young German. With Biddy laid up, things were even more complicated, so after a lot of persuasion on Babbie's part he had given in and Shona had helped her move her things from Laigmhor.

'You don't know what you're letting yourself in for,' Lachlan had warned. 'Even though the lad can barely lift a finger the island will have you labelled as a lassie with loose morals. Ay, and a hundred times looser because the lad is a German.'

Babbie had laughed gaily. 'But Biddy would have done the same thing surely?'

'Ay, but there's a queer difference between you and Biddy! At her age she's not likely to do much damage, now is she?' They had both laughed, Babbie indifferently because in her compassion for the sick she cared little for the wagging tongues of the healthy.

Lifting a green nightdress from her case she looked at it in disgust. 'I suppose I'll have to wear it under the circumstances. I like to sleep in the raw but I can hardly do that here. The gossips would set their tongues afire if they heard about it.'

Footsteps crunched on the path under the window, plainly heard because the rest of the household slept and everything was very quiet. Shona looked from the window and saw a dark figure coming through the gate. 'It's one of the Commandos,' she reported. 'The one who helped in surgery today.'

'Yes, he was good, wasn't he? I suppose he feels personally involved. Go down, Shona, before he wakens the house. I can't be bothered with anyone just now. Tell him the usual things . . . Mr Büttger is holding his own, etcetera.'

Shona was back in a few minutes. 'He wanted to

come up and see Anton but I told him you were getting ready for bed. They were hoping to be off tomorrow but it seems they haven't found the escaped German yet and I have the oddest feeling that Anderson at any rate isn't too worried. I gather he just happened to pass Tam's house on the way over here and I think our young surgeon is a little bit merry. He put his arm round me and tried to kiss me . . . the cheeky bugger! He's waiting now to escort me up the glen just in case I come face to face with the wandering German!' With a weary little laugh she turned again to the door. 'I'd better away now or Father will be out looking for me. It's daft, I suppose, but he still thinks I'm a wee girl yet.'

'At eighteen – you are,' Babbie murmured.

Shona's blue eyes widened in surprise. 'How *old* you sound, Babbie, and how can I still be a bairn after all the things I told you about myself?'

'Because at eighteen you haven't really grown up. You think you've had all the experiences but there's so much more for you, Shona. You still have a bit of growing up to do.'

'You sound as if you've known me all my days.' Shona tried to sound light-hearted but the look in Babbie's eyes made her shiver, a look in which she glimpsed the wisdom that lurked in the faraway eyes of the very old.

'You're a witch,' she said lightly. 'Niall would call you Caillich Ruadh which means red witch. It's what he calls me to get me angry. Maybe there's a bit of the witch in us all. With Father I often know what he's

1195

thinking, and he seems always to know what I'm feeling. We're tuned in I suppose. Maybe that's why he likes to keep me in sight, though often he hardly says a word when I'm with him. I can just *feel* him caring.'

'You're lucky.' Babbie sounded wistful. 'It must be a good warm feeling to have a father – or a mother – or both. You have one, I have none, yet most people have both and never appreciate the fact.'

'Och, c'mon, Babbie.' Shona's voice was gentle. 'You must have someone . . . surely everyone has someone.'

'No, not everyone. I was lucky, I had an older sister – we were in the orphanage together. She left before me and though she married we always kept in touch. We were always fighting in the orphanage – you know what sisters are – oh, but of course, you don't – so sorry.' She paused for a moment then continued slowly. 'They say that sisters who fight a lot as kids are really very close even while they're pulling lumps from each other. Well, it's true, the closeness I mean. We had wonderful times when we grew up, even after Jan got married – then – she died, three years ago now – she was twenty-six. I still miss her so.'

Shona caught her breath. 'Oh, dear God, how sad you must be, to have someone you love die so young. How can you bear not having anyone in the world you can call your own?'

A little smile hovered round Babbie's lips, and her eyes were very faraway. 'But I'm not alone, Shona. I have friends. I have you here, I have others scattered everywhere and . . .' She laughed suddenly: 'Underneath all my heathen ways I'm really very close to my Maker. I'll see Jan one day, I know that for sure. It's quite exciting when you stop to think about it.'

A little groan from the bed made them both jump. 'Our young hero is still in the land of the living anyway,' Babbie said. In seconds she was a cool, efficient little nurse again, whose devotion to her patient seemed to divorce her from everything that went on in the world outside the sickroom, and Shona slipped quietly out of the house to meet Anderson and walk with him up the lonely moon-washed glen to Laigmhor and the people she loved.

Anton's brain was swimming. He felt as if he was in a vortex which was spinning him round and round, carrying him in a sickening whirl of motion towards the face of the mountain. He struggled to get away from it, to rise upwards and outwards from the gyrating force that held him, but he hadn't the strength to struggle, or even to cry out. All he could do was pray silently, 'Please my God, do not let me die now. I am sorry, I am sorry – for everything.'

A river was rushing down the face of the mountain. He could see it glinting in a strange heavenly light, some of it was splashing on to his cheeks, but it wasn't cold like he thought it would be. It was warm, warm and salty . . .

Salt water did not run down the face of a mountain. He put out his tongue slowly and licked the water . . . only it wasn't water – it was tears, his tears!

Commander Anton Büttger was crying like a baby. 'Don't let me die a coward. Oh God! Please don't let me die a coward!' he sobbed in a demented torture of mind and body. His head was throbbing and something deep in his belly was burning like the fires of hell. Was that it? Was he dead and already in hell? Was this his punishment for killing all those people he had killed when he was alive? A bubble of sheer terror rose in his throat. 'Please God not this!' The thoughts clamoured into his aching head. 'Let me live a little while longer to let me prove I am worth somewhere better than hell.'

'*Please, God!*' he cried aloud, opening his eyes suddenly. But everything was in a mist. The mists of hell! Smoke from the fires? The fires of hell or the fires of burning towns? The haze was lifting a little, his eyes were beginning to focus and he saw that he was in a little room with rose-sprinkled wallpaper, canted ceilings, and a tiny deep window looking out to bronzed hills basking dreamily in the sun. He was back home, in Berlin, in his own bedroom; his mother was downstairs cooking breakfast. The fragrant smell of sizzling bacon drifted up to his nostrils. The door opened and someone came in. He struggled to sit up. 'Mother! Mother, is that you?' But it wasn't his mother, it was a young woman with eyes the colour of emeralds and a halo of hair which made him think of the setting sun. She put out a cool little hand and touched his forehead.

'Are you – an angel?' he said in some bemusement. 'Am I in heaven?'

Babbie smiled and said dryly, 'An angel? With hair this colour? More a devil I'd say, Mr Büttger?'

'I was never lucky with women,' he said with a little smile, his eyes still drowsily half-shut. 'But I can tell . . . you are Scottisch. A Scottisch devil might not be so bad. My mother, she spent a holiday in Scotland once and she tells me, when I am a little boy, the Scottisch, they are kind. Are you kind – Fräulein?'

'You speak English well, Mr Büttger.' Babbie was struggling to remain aloof. She was looking at the tears glistening through his lashes, at the pale handsome face lying on the pillow. It was a fine face, sharply chiselled, boyish, very delicate in the morning light with faint purple shadows under his eyes. He had come through a night of hell. She had bathed him, talked to him soothingly in the delirium of his nightmares, touched him and all the time she had had to keep reminding herself he was a German, a young man who flew planes and committed himself to killing other young men, young men with boyhood still stamped on their features . . .

'You do not like Germans, Fräulein.'

The statement caught her unawares. 'Nonsense,' she said brusquely. 'Come now, enough chatter. I want to examine you . . . Oh, it's all right, Mr Büttger, I am a fully-trained nurse. To me you are just another patient.'

At that moment he opened his eyes wide and the blue brilliance of them in his white tear-stained face made her catch her breath. They were luminous eyes, and even though he was ill, keen and sharp and clear. She felt as though he could see right into her very soul. Already the sight of his frost-blackened fingers had brought a lump to her throat, and now – those eyes, looking at her with unwavering perceptiveness . . .

'How are you feeling, Mr Büttger?' she said briskly, trying to hide her confusion.

'A short time ago I thought I was dead – dead in hell . . . When I saw you coming through the door I thought I must be mistaken . . . and I was instead . . . in heaven.'

'I'll get the doctor to come up and have a look at you,' she said, tucking his hands back under the blankets.

'Can you tell me first – what happened, where am I . . . and what day it is, Fräulein?' His voice was cultured, his broken English utterly charming, like little notes of sweet music occasionally touching the wrong chord.

'You hurt yourself when you baled out of your plane and Doctor McLachlan operated on you yesterday. You are in Scotland, on an island in the Hebrides – and today is March the 15th . . . two days after the first attack by German bombers in Clydebank and Glasgow.'

Babbie was immediately sorry for her last words. Anton had turned his head away from her and was looking unseeingly at the rugged slopes of Sgurr nan Ruadh. One hand came out of the blankets to grip the white counterpane but only two fingers moved, the rest lying immobile, rendered useless by the ravages of frostbite.

She bit her lip. 'Are you hungry, Mr Büttger? If you managed to eat something it would do you good.'

'I was, Fräulein,' he whispered through white lips. 'When I smelt breakfast frying I felt very hungry. I thought, you see, that I was home in Berlin and my mother was up already preparing the morning meal . . . But I was dreaming – my mother is dead, and so too are the rest of my family. No, Fräulein, I don't think that I am very hungry any more.'

'I'll – I'll see if I can bring you something to tempt your appetite . . .' She faltered and ran downstairs and into the kitchen where Phebie was at the stove and the rest of the family seated at the table.

'Mr Büttger is awake,' Babbie reported tonelessly. 'I think he might eat something if coaxed enough – but his fingers are in a bad way. I fear he may have to lose them after all.'

'I'll go up and have a look,' Lachlan said, rising at once and going to the door where Elspeth was hovering, having arrived just in time to hear Babbie's words.

'Hmph! A fine thing indeed,' she snorted, outraged, 'when a German comes into this good home and uses up the rations that are scarce enough as it is!'

'He can have my rations,' eight-year-old Fiona piped up, her bright eyes flashing in her rosy face. 'I like Mr Büttger, he's a very interesting-looking German with all those bandages all over him and eyelashes like butterflies' wings.'

'And who asked your opinion, Madam?' Elspeth flashed. Behind her back Fiona made a hideous face. The unlovable old lady was as attached to her as she was to the other McLachlans, but Fiona, being the youngest member of the family, received most of the brunt of her razor-sharp tongue and was forever trying to get her own back. From time to time she played terrible tricks, sometimes contenting herself by just casting spells over Elspeth from the safety of her bedroom, but none of them had ever worked, and in the end the little girl had decided that a toad was a far nicer creature to look at than Elspeth and didn't deserve the fate of inhabiting Elspeth's bony frame for the rest of its life.

'I'm saving my butter ration for Mr Büttger,' Fiona persisted, 'and for Niall, too, when he gets home. I wish he'd hurry up. I want to show him my frog spawn.'

At her words Phebie's eyes filled with tears and the pan of frying bacon wavered before her eyes. Babbie went to her and put an arm round her shoulders. 'Please, don't – don't worry yourself so. It will be all right. He wasn't spared the war for nothing. There's a better plan for your son's life.'

'But – there's been no news – nothing, and I don't know how long I can go on,' Phebie said brokenly, dabbing her eyes with the corner of her apron. A sob of despair broke from her and she rushed out of the kitchen and into the parlour. The picture of the boy Niall was there, on top of the dresser, smiling his beautiful, cherubic smile while the sparkles of mischief exploded from his eyes and brought smiles to the lips of all who looked into them. Phebie ran a tender finger over the glass, tracing the handsome young features she knew so well.

'So that's Niall,' Babbie said softly, coming up behind her.

Phebie nodded, her plump sweet face pink with pride and grief. 'Ay, my laddie, at fourteen. He's bigger now but he still does daft things, like pinching buttered scones behind my back and chasing me round the kitchen table . . . and sweeping me up in his arms when he comes home . . . and . . . and . . .' Her voice faltered and she couldn't go on.

Babbie took her into her arms and let her cry against her shoulder. She looked at the picture of fourteen-year-old Niall. Something about the boyish face tugged at her memory but the abrupt arrival of Lachlan in the room startled her back to reality.

'No breakfast for Anton, I'm afraid. Those fingers will have to come off. Today, this morning.' He strode over and took Phebie from Babbie and into his arms. He stroked her hair tenderly, and over her head his eyes met Babbie's. 'You've had an exhausting night, Babbie, and could be doing with a good whily to yourself. I canny ask you for any more help. I'll manage the operation myself . . .'

Babbie was aghast. 'And do you think I would stand back twiddling my thumbs and let you carry on, on your own? Oh, no, Lachlan, you're not getting away with that . . . !' She paused and gave a little laugh. 'Just promise me one thing – when this is all over – will you call me Florence Nightingale?'

His brown eyes flashed for a moment and he put out his free arm. 'Come into the bosom of the family – Miss Nightingale.'

Her green eyes smiled, hiding the turmoil of doubts, fears and apprehensions that slid through her mind in a crazily jumbled procession.

Part Four

Rhanna
March 16th 1941

Chapter Ten

As Niall watched Portcull coming nearer, specks in the bay resolved into the warm-hearted, familiar folk who had filled his thoughts constantly in the last few days. It was very early on Sunday morning and the scene was even more peaceful than usual because, as Niall knew, most folk were indoors donning Sunday best as they prepared for kirk.

No ferries travelled to Rhanna on Sundays but he had been lucky to arrive at Oban to find one of the Rhanna fishing trawlers ready to leave with the tide. He had managed to get some sleep in a cramped little cabin below decks but still felt heavy and weary. He hadn't been able to get word through to his folks that he was on his way home, and his thoughts were full of anxiety as to how they must be feeling. The picture of the Clydebank holocaust was keen on his mind. He couldn't forget the first night of the raids when his duties as an Air Raid Warden had taken him from horror to horror, and finally into hell on seeing that the place he called 'home' in Glasgow was no more. Despite a broken right arm and multiple bruises he had stayed on in the devastated areas of Clydebank to assist the rescue parties and help with the evacuation of the homeless thousands.

He stood on the deck of the boat and with hungry

eyes devoured the serenity of the Hebridean island of his birth. After the chaos of Clydebank it was strange to look at a place where people ambled rather than walked, and never ran if they could possibly avoid it. The morning sparkled in a palette of breathtaking colours: the purple of the mountains thrusting stark peaks into the soft blue sky; on the hill slopes a faint fuzz of light green showing through the tawny patches of winter bracken, contrasting with the darker spires of the tall pines. Skirting the harbour, the cottages stood out like dazzling white sugar lumps, each one sending out fluffy banners of variegated smoke, and below it, a tranquil blue sea lapped the silvered white sands. Niall watched it all come closer, and he sniffed the well-remembered scent of peat fires. Closing his eyes he let the babble of the gulls and the slop of the waves wash over his senses till his heart surged with joy. And in the ecstasy of the moment he imagined Shona would be there to meet him as in days gone by . . . But that was all in the past. He wondered if she was thinking of him now in Aberdeen, wondered if she had heard about the raids and the destruction of his 'home' . . . .

As the trawler puffed into the bay, pushing and slapping against the pier, a row of pipe-smoking old men sat on the harbour wall, watching the proceedings with languid interest. Old Joe, perched on a lobster pot, and looking like a snowy-haired gnome with his pipe sending busy little blue-grey clouds into the face of a sea-stained crony, suddenly let out a cry. 'St Michael be blessed!' He had spotted Niall coming down the gangplank. 'It's young McLachlan back from the bombs!' he yelled, rushing forward. At old Joe's signal, Ranald, who divided his time between tarring his boats and reassembling a collection of ancient black bicycles with the intention of hiring them out to unwary summer tourists, threw his tar-clogged brush into a sticky tin and rose quickly to run to the pier. Others followed in a hurry, and soon Niall was surrounded by the men, who greeted him eagerly, eyeing his plaster-encased arm with sympathetic interest.

'My, my, you've been in the wars right enough, lad,' old Andrew observed gently.

A smile lit Niall's weary face. 'Ay, but I'm home now for a while. My studies will have to wait for a bit.'

'True enough, son, you wouldny get much on paper wi' that arm,' Jim nodded wisely. 'No' unless you are amphibious. Some folks are – it means you can do things with both hands the same.'

Niall laughed and looked round the harbour with hungry eyes. 'It's as peaceful as ever. And wonderful to be back. I don't suppose much has been happening on Rhanna.'

A clamour of protest followed. At that moment the crew of the trawler, who had been away from Rhanna for several days, joined the gathering and everyone vied with each other to regale the audience with greatly embroidered tales about the crashed German bomber. Canty Tam, always to be had wherever there was a crowd, gazed vacantly but smiled with satisfaction at the goriest details. Old Andrew prodded his pipe into the sky, making exaggerated circles to demonstrate to a young fisherman how the bomber had thundered over the village before its final wild flight to the mountains. There were a few moments of pipe-sucking, thoughtful silence with all eyes fixed on the upper corries of Ben Machrie where trailing wisps of vapour drifted in and out of high secret places.

'It must have been quite a sight,' was the eventual general verdict.

Tam McKinnon nodded seriously. 'Terrible just,' he stated lugubriously. His cronies then nodded in sad agreement though, with the exception of Righ, not one of them had witnessed the event. But Righ was fast asleep in the lighthouse cottage and Tam was able to embroider his tale, helped by the bobbing heads and sympathetic 'Ays' of the others.

Canty Tam smiled secretively at the sky, addressing it with a grimace of conviction. 'And was my mother not after telling me you was all drunk that night?' he accused the lacy cloudbanks pleasantly. 'She said to me only that morning while I was supping my porridge, "You keep out o' Tam McKinnon's house, my lad, for he is after doin' things that will bring the Peat Hags on him."' He brought his gaze from the sky to grin at a vexed Tam. 'She told me lots more but there was no need for when the bells were ringin' I saw you all comin' out o' your Headquarters an' you was drunk! That German airy-plane was already on the island then!'

There was a howl of derision from the fishermen

that brought blushes to the faces of the Home Guard.

'Och, c'mon now, lads,' Tam soothed earnestly. 'Surely you are no' believing that foolish cratur. We might have had one or two wee drinks but needin' them indeed for we were out all night lookin' for the Huns!'

But young Graeme Donald, a grand-nephew of old Annack, smiled with quiet radiance into the salt-washed faces of the other fishermen. 'Are you hearing that now, lads? Everywhere else whisky is scarcer than virgins and here is our Tam bathing in the stuff. Great-aunt Annack might be a cailleach but, by God! she has some nose on her face for sniffing out the hard stuff! She told me the time was near ripe for Tam's whisky an' it's here, lads! We just arrived in time!' His words were met with a great whoop of approval that sent the gulls screaming from the harbour walls.

'I was goin' to tell you, lads,' Tam assured them plausibly. 'What way would I be wantin' all that whisky to myself? There's more than enough and I was just thinkin' comin' over the track that a shilling a pint wouldny be too much to ask—'

'Sixpence!' cried a hard-bitten old sailor. Tam looked sad but he was already leading the way to his house followed by an eager, thirsty mob.

'The minister will be down on your heads!' Ranald called piously.

'Ach, him, is he no' after sayin' he is holdin' a ceilidh tonight for the Germans . . . and on the Sabbath too!' Tam returned placidly.

'A ceilidh . . . for Germans?' Niall asked incredulously.

'Ay, to give them a taste o' Scottish hospitality afore they leave,' Ranald imparted, scratching his head absentmindedly with his tar-stained fingers. 'The Commandos have still to find one big Jerry who got away from the Manse on Friday morning but they have narrowed the search down enough to think they'll get him today. The German officer o' the plane was torn to ribbons on the mountain comin' down an' damt near dead when we found him. Your father had to sew his stomach back in but some o' his fingers were rotting away wi' frostbite an' had to be cut off. The lads are guardin' him day an' night for you never know wi' Jerries . . . stayin' at your house he is.'

'My house?'

'Ay, he couldny be moved for fear he would die,' Ranald nodded eagerly, poking his fingers further into his thatch of brown hair.

'The airy-plane came over from blitzed places near Glasgow,' Canty Tam beamed. 'Everyone was sayin' they likely killed a lot o' people before endin' up here!'

'Be quiet, you glaikit bugger!' Erchy warned, coming from the boat with a creel of enormous crabs.

Niall had turned white at the news. The memory of his landlady with the teapot clutched in her hands and her dead eyes staring was extremely vivid. And Iain Brodie, smoke-grimed and red-eyed after endless hours battling with endless fires, his face empty and hopeless on learning the news. Niall felt the bitterness surging through him again, taking away some of the joy he'd felt at coming home. It seemed after all that the scourge of war had touched Rhanna. The thought of a German under the roof of Slochmhor made him feel sick with anger. How could his father calmly have taken the enemy into his home? Hot tears of rage pricked his eyes and he turned quickly away, his blurred gaze coming to rest at the Smiddy where a much-recovered Todd the Shod was sitting outside enjoying the spring sunshine. Beside him Biddy reclined on a wooden bench padded with cushions. They were both waving at him frantically and he raised his arm to wave back.

'Dear old Biddy,' he breathed thankfully. 'It will be good to have her moaning and fussing around me.'

Erchy shook his sandy head ruefully. 'Ach, not yet for a whily. The cailleach hurt her ankle and is stayin' at the McDonalds' till she is better. Todd had his appendix out and the pair o' them are driving each other daft.' A gleam of mischief came into his eyes. 'We had a fine young nurse lookin' after us for a whily. A right nice bum and bosoms she has too. We were all thinkin' up ways to see will she come and cure us . . . My ulcer has been bad this last day or two,' he finished, suddenly rubbing at his middle.

'But it's better you are now.' Jim Jim removed his pipe and spat malevolently on to the cobbled pier. 'They are after sendin' over a spare nurse . . . came on the boat yesterday afternoon . . . like a gallopin' hairpin she is wi' a face like a forgotten prune! There she is now, goin' up to the Smiddy. Todd has not

1213

moved since his operation, though Mollie has been givin' him enough liquorice powder to shift a horse. He will be gettin' soapy water through a tube now – I forget what they calls it but I am hearing it does queer things to the bowels – makes them squeal like the bagpipes tunin' up.'

Todd watched the lanky figure of the 'spare' nurse coming towards his house and he squirmed with apprehension. Biddy watched also and her lips folded into a thin line of disapproval. Babbie had been to see her twice, and like everyone else she had fallen under the girl's infectious charm, but now she wished she hadn't been so persistent about a spare nurse . . .

'My God!' Todd gulped, his round face crimson. 'She is comin' this way!'

'Ach, never mind,' Biddy consoled. 'If it's an enema she's come to give I'll see she does it right. She has hands like frogs' feets and will not be gentle wi' the tubes like myself.'

'Hell no!' Todd couldn't stop the protest. 'Not *two* of you! I canny take any more o' this! That wee Nurse Babbie would have done fine for a whily!'

The nurse came through the gate, burying her long nose in the depths of a large hanky. 'I have had nothing but sneezes since I came yesterday,' she complained. 'How are you today, Nurse McMillan?'

'Fine – oh ay – much better, thankin' you! It won't be long till I am up on my feets!'

'Good, then we will all be happy! How are you today, Mr McDonald?'

'Never better, indeed no! I will be back at the Smiddy much sooner than I thought!' Todd gabbled in agitated confusion.

Biddy straightened her specs. 'Where is the young nurse? She said she would be over to see how was I keeping.'

The nurse sniffed disdainfully. 'Too busy with that young German! Said something about changing his dressings. Well, she's welcome. I wouldn't touch him with a ten-foot pole. The child from the big farm was there too, the one with the long hair and inno-cent eyes.' She sniffed again. 'Looks like that are so deceiving. She and the nurse are fawning over him like sick kittens. Now . . .' she became suddenly brisk, 'will you come inside, Nurse McMillan – I'll do your enema first.' She smiled sourly. 'Ladies before gentlemen.'

'*Me!*' Biddy's yell of indignation sent a clutter of crows into the sky where they flapped angrily.

'Yes, indeed, Nurse McMillan. I met Mrs McDonald last night and she told me that for days you haven't been near the – er – toilet. She said you had only been passing water into the – hm – chamber pot.'

'That Mollie!' Biddy roared while Todd shook with delighted glee. 'I'll – I'll never bandage her varicose veins again!'

Niall managed a smile as Biddy's indignant yells filled the harbour. 'Well, *she* hasn't changed anyway! Still the same grumbling Biddy!' He began to move away and called back, 'I'll see you later, lads.'

'Ay, come to the ceilidh tonight at the Manse. The

minister said it was a praise meeting for teetotallers only but he'll no' find many of these around here!' Ranald grinned. 'You will likely get a try of Tam's Uisge-beatha. Like nectar it is.'

Niall nodded appreciatively, and walked towards Glen Fallan, lifting his face to breathe the wild, sweet scent of sun-warmed heather. In the high fields above Laigmhor, Fergus and Bob strode among the flocks of sheep; a few tiny early lambs wobbled unsteadily near their mothers, and the sheepdogs ran purposefully about their business, answering to the different whistles with an eager obedience that reflected Bob's training. Fergus rarely went to kirk and shocked the minister and many of his neighbours by doing work on a Sunday, which normally was taboo. Bob was a regular kirkgoer but his work came first with him, especially at lambing time, so today he wore his best suit under baggy plus-fours and a roomy tweed jacket, ready to take off as soon as the kirk bell tolled over the island. Niall looked with delight at the familiar scene and he raised his arm. The men were engrossed in their work but a moment later they waved in response and Fergus's voice drifted faintly but joyfully, 'Hello there, Niall! We'll see you later!'

When Niall reached Slochmhor he found it quiet and deserted. For a moment he thought there was no one at home. He knew that Fiona would be outdoors, making the most of her time before getting ready for kirk, and that his father would be out on a call somewhere but, though he wasn't expected, he had anticipated his mother's welcome and felt unreasonably cheated. He had pictured her face on seeing him, the surprise, then the gladness bringing the roses to her cheeks. If it hadn't been for his arm he would have swept her up high and she would have giggled and spilled a tear or two, but as he couldn't do that he had planned to chase her round the kitchen table till she clouted him with the dish-cloth . . . Niall looked round the kitchen which was warm and homely with two cats sprawled by the fire, one of them using Lachlan's slippers as a pillow. On the window ledge a vase of pussy willows managed to look graceful alongside a jar of frog spawn floating in obnoxious green water. Niall chuckled. Fiona was still pursuing her keen interest in all forms of insect and amphibious life. It was her favourite hobby. She was a child who kept pet spiders in jars and studied minute creatures with the aid of one of Lachlan's old microscopes. After eight years of struggling to keep her tom-boy daughter's room as feminine as possible, Phebie had gradually given up the fight and had ceased to be disgusted by the odd assortment of creepy pets she encountered while cleaning.

- A little laugh came from upstairs and Niall stiffened. The laugh was so familiar to him yet the unexpected sound of it made his heart race madly. 'Shona . . . what the hell –' he whispered and bounded upstairs. Even while he burst into the little guest room Niall realized this was where the wounded German lay, but on entering Niall got the impression that he had intruded into an intimate little world. Anton, pale but handsome, was laughing up at Shona whose hand was clasped in his, her blue eyes alight in her animated face.

'Shona!' Niall shouted her name in surprise.

'Niall!' She turned from the bed, to stare at him in joyous disbelief. 'Oh, thank God!' she said, rising to meet him. 'I prayed and prayed you would come back to me soon! We could get no news of you! I didn't know when you would be coming or I would have met you! You're hurt, my darling, what have you done to your arm?' She put out a hand to touch him but he pulled away.

'I didn't know you were back on Rhanna.' His voice held a note of suspicion.

'But – I wrote to you when I left Aberdeen! I told you I was coming to see you in Glasgow the minute I could. I'm home for a rest – I haven't been too well.'

He saw then her pale little face and her incredible eyes, smudged with a delicate blue-black under the lower lashes. He had forgotten how blue her eyes were, how beautifully shaped her small sensitive mouth. Her auburn hair was swept up from her face but gave it no maturity, instead it emphasized her cameo features and pointed chin. She looked like a little girl trying to appear grown up and the nearness of her overwhelmed him for a moment. He longed to crush her to him, to pour words of love into her ears but the picture of her with Anton had roused a stab of jealousy in his breast.

'I didn't get your letter,' he said briefly and bitterly. 'Mrs Brodie no longer has a letter box – it may still be attached to the door buried beneath the rubble of what was her home! Not that Mrs Brodie will worry about that now . . . she's out of it all . . .' He glanced at Anton accusingly. 'Mrs Brodie doesn't need her home now, but Iain Brodie needs it – and thousands more like him who lost everything in the raids last week!' His voice rose menacingly. 'Ask your German friend how he would go about helping the people he helped to kill . . . you might not find so much to laugh at then – *Fräulein!*'

'Niall!' She stared at him, shocked. 'Stop that! You're raving like a madman!'

'Maybe I am mad – mad enough for a bit of revenge! I keep seeing corpses, they're in my head and I can't get rid of them! I go to bed at night and see my land-lady – a tiny wee body who never harmed a soul – lying among the bloody tons of rubble that buried her alive!'

'Niall.' Her voice was gentle because she saw the terrible tension in him. 'You'll have to try and forget. The raids were horrible, we all know that . . .'

'Do you! Were you there? Pray God you'll be spared anything like it . . .' He nodded towards Anton. 'He'll know, he was over the place! He must have seen the hell of it all. After all, he must have dropped some of the incendiaries that lit up Clydebank like a Christmas tree. Maybe his was one of the bombers that strafed the streets, splattering bullets about just for the fun of it! Ask him if he knows what it's like to be holed up like a terrified rabbit waiting for a bomb to drop!'

'Ask him yourself.' Shona's voice was barely

audible. 'He can speak English quite well.'

'The intellectual type!' Niall answered scathingly.

Anton had struggled up in bed, his eyes meeting Niall's angry gaze. 'Niall.' He spoke the name with respect. 'Fräulein Shona tells me about you all day. We laugh just now about your times together as children.'

To Niall the words were flippant, designed to get him off the subject of the raids. 'So you know my name,' he said sarcastically. 'And you laugh. I wonder if we'll laugh when we know the names of all the people killed in Clydebank and Glasgow – and all the other cities bombed by the Luftwaffe!'

'Anton's mother, father and sisters were killed by the British in an air raid over Berlin.' Shona said the words quietly, her mouth frozen with dismay.

Anton had fallen back on the pillows, his eyes gazing unseeingly at the wall and he raised his bandaged right hand to pass it over his brow in a defeated, strangely touching little gesture. 'I hate the war as much as you do,' he said wearily. He reached to the dresser and picked up an Iron Cross which he dangled idly in his fingers. 'This little decoration is meant to signify bravery – all it means is I have killed a lot of people. I am not really proud of it – but I wear it – in the same way the British wear their medals.' He laughed without humour. 'I am very relieved that I do not have to pin it to my pyjamas – I can forget it for a while.'

Niall suddenly felt deflated and uneasy. He hadn't expected to come face to face with an entirely whole

German, and on the other hand he hadn't been prepared for one so obviously badly injured. Restricted though Anton's recent efforts at mobility had been, they had left him sweating and exhausted, and his rapid breathing filled the room.

A shower of sparks exploded from the coals in the grate and the clear, fluted call of a curlew came sweetly from the glen. Shona felt her heart beating swiftly. She could feel the tension spewing from Niall. It showed in his white young face, the clenching of his fist. He looked so forlorn, so unlike the loving, carefree Niall of her memories, that for a moment she was afraid. He'd come through the horrific experiences of Dunkirk, scarred but still buoyant of spirit. The war had wounded him yet again but she knew it wasn't that which had so crushed him: the first time he had gone to war expecting to meet death and destruction, but the second time war had come to him and she realized he hadn't been prepared for it.

'Niall . . .' she began huskily just as footsteps clattered and Babbie arrived breathlessly into the room.

'Oh – sorry.' She drew back at the sight of Niall. He turned and her hand flew to her mouth. *'Niall!'* The cry was one of disbelief.

He stared at her. *'Babbie!* What on earth – how did *you* get here?' They gaped at each other till Babbie finally stuttered, 'Shona brought me – at least she asked me to come back with her to Rhanna for a holiday . . . I'm in Aberdeenshire now . . . you know me, always jumping around! Pastures new all the time. Your name has been mentioned here constantly but I never dreamt – I never connected . . . I saw the picture of you downstairs and I thought the resemblance to you was uncanny though of course you've changed since then – amazing the difference a few years and a little moustache can make to a boy. It's such a coincidence . . .' She was unable to go on.

Shona looked from one to the other. 'It would be silly to ask if you know one another.' She laughed as lightly as she could. 'It seems you certainly do!'

Niall pulled himself together with an effort. 'Only vaguely,' he said briefly. 'Isn't that right, Babbie?'

'Oh yes, hardly at all. I didn't even know your surname – till now.'

From the collar of her dress, Shona pulled out the little locket that Niall had given to her as an engagement present. She snapped it open and said to Babbie, 'I should have shown you this sooner, Babbie, then you might not have been surprised to see Niall here on Rhanna.'

Babbie looked in some confusion at the little heart-shaped photos of Niall and Shona fitted into the locket and forced a smile. 'I wish you had, Shona. It would certainly have put me in the picture, as it were.'

Despite the careless words, Shona sensed unspoken questions bouncing between the two. They were trying too hard to be casual, Babbie fussing with Anton's bedclothes, Niall paying a great deal of attention to a loose thread on his sling. He looked up and caught Babbie's eye. She seemed flustered, with a pink tinge staining her pale face and her green eyes unnaturally bright.

'Your walk has given the roses to your cheeks,' Anton commented carefully, sensing that a situation had arisen which needed some delicate handling. 'It gives the sparkle to your eyes.'

'Yes, I went over by the cliffs at Aosdana Bay – the Bay of the Poet,' Babbie said. 'It was lovely there – peaceful – a good place to think. I didn't mean to go so far but I forgot time. I am finding that this island does that to one – time begins to mean nothing.'

She was chattering too much, too nervously. Shona held her breath but no matter how hard she tried she couldn't stop the suspicions crowding into her mind. Niall and Babbie! There was something between them, something they were trying very hard to hide. Her heart beat swiftly in her throat. She felt weak with emotion but she forced her head high. 'I'll have to go now. Father will be in soon from the fields and I promised Kirsteen to lay the table before kirk. I'll see you – Niall.'

'Wait!' Niall stayed her hasty flight. 'When will I see you – Ni-Cridhe?'

He said the endearment softly and a sob rose in her throat. 'Ni-Cridhe!' My dear lassie. How long she had waited to hear the caress of his dear, lilting voice but her reply was non-committal. 'Whenever you want – though not this afternoon. I'm going over to help Tina – she has a bad ankle.'

'I could come with you. I'd like fine to see Tina and the bairns.'

'Och, but I'm just going to wash and set her hair. You would feel in the way.'

A flush of anger stained his fair skin. 'I'm having a taste of that already! Tonight then? There's a ceilidh at the Manse – for the Germans, would you believe! But we don't have to speak to them. As far as I can gather the islanders are going to make a bonny night of it with Tam's Uisge-beatha.'

'You and Babbie go. She hasn't been to an island ceilidh yet. I'll sit with Anton.'

'Please, Fräulein Shona, do not deny yourself for me!' Anton cried anxiously. 'My little friend, Fiona, will tell me some of her fairy stories and show me some of her pets,' he laughed. 'She reminds me of my small sister with her caterpillars and her frogs.'

'Count your blessings then!' Niall gritted so harshly that even Babbie glanced at him in some dismay.

'Well, are you coming tonight or not?' he demanded of Shona.

Her head went up again at his tone. 'I'll sit with Anton,' she persisted.

'Oh, grand! Just grand! I'm sure you and he will have a lot to talk about! You can always tell him about the baby you lost because you thought I was dead in Dunkirk! Away you go then! A lot of folk are waiting on you it would seem!'

Shona flew downstairs and hardly saw where she was going for tears, and later, at Laigmhor, she flounced about, clattering things on the table.

'I see Niall's home,' Fergus said carefully as he and Kirsteen exchanged looks.

'Ay, that he is! With a broken arm too! Niall always

seems to be in the wars.' She kept her tone on a conversational level.

'And now you and he are at war with each other,' Kirsteen said deliberately.

Shona looked up quickly. 'If it's anybody's business, then you are right enough, Kirsteen!' she cried hotly. 'Niall would fight in an empty house . . . his temper is even worse than mine now!'

Fergus smiled faintly though a muscle was working in his cheek. 'That would take a bit of doing, mo ghaoil. I won't stand for it in this house – and I'll thank you not to talk to Kirsteen in such a disrespectful manner.'

Shona dumped a pile of plates on to the table with such a clatter that Ginger, a big placid tom, shot out of the door in fright. 'And who have I to thank for *my* temper?' she demanded wildly and stamped out of the kitchen in high dudgeon.

Chapter Eleven

The Rev. John Gray had never in all his years on Rhanna felt quite so fulfilled or so important as he had done since the captured Germans were delivered into his care. He had always felt uncomfortably out of his depth when carrying out his pastoral duties among a people who sensed his lack of confidence and also his slightly superior attitude towards them. He had always given them the impression that he regarded them as heathens whose only salvation lay in a conscientious kirk attendance coupled with a selfless devotion to 'The Book' and its teachings. But his methods of trying to bring God to the people were hopelessly out of keeping with the simple faith of the Hebridean people. His theological sermons were away above the heads of the majority of parishioners and matters weren't helped by his stern refusal to learn the Gaelic which was the only language that many of the older inhabitants understood. He had of course picked up the odd Gaelic word, and an intelligent man such as he could easily have learned it all. But he felt to do so would be to encourage the easygoing islanders to take a step back in time. What he had failed to see was a proud little community of Gaels struggling to hold on to a culture that was their inheritance. In the name of progress too much had already been taken away but no one could rob them of their individuality. They had met the so-called civilized world half-way, but had no intention of stepping over the border to be swallowed into anonymity for ever more. And so the Rev. Gray laboured on under his delusions and the barriers between him and the people of Rhanna remained firmly erect.

Hannah Gray was a much less overpowering personality than her overbearing husband. Her years with him had taught her that silence was the best form of defence against his forceful outlook on life.

When her husband had first suggested a ceilidh for the Germans the idea at first dumbfounded her, but the more she thought about it the more excited she became. She had often longed to throw a ceilidh in keeping with tradition, but her husband wouldn't hear of it, telling her sternly that such events were only excuses for uninhibited drinking bouts and an invitation to the Devil to wreak havoc in drink-weakened minds. Over the years Mrs Gray made do with giving strupaks; but her visitors were stiffly formal and always looked poised ready for flight. By contrast, whenever she dropped into a neighbour's croft, a strupak was a gaily informal affair. She had never ceilidhed in the long, dark nights of winter, and when passing a cottage gay with laughter and song, she had often longed to join the merrymakers but knew that her presence would only embarrass them. But now she would have a ceilidh of her very own! The very thought sped her steps to the kitchen which was soon fragrant with the smell of baking. Normally such activities in the kitchen were banned on the Sabbath but in this instance such restrictions were dropped.

'It must be referred to as more of a praise meeting,' the minister had warned righteously, but when Torquil Andrew, a strapping figure of a man whose Norse colouring and piercing blue eyes, which made him a great favourite with the women, had appeared at the kitchen door with the sack of potatoes she had asked to buy from him, she gaily told him the news.

'A ceilidh, Torquil,' she had beamed happily. 'Here in the Manse tonight. Tell your friends about it . . . but . . .' she had put a warning finger to her lips and screwed her face into a conspiratorial grimace, 'you know Mr Gray doesn't like the drink . . . so only those who don't.'

Torquil's handsome face had broken into a wide grin at the idea of a whiskyless ceilidh. Laughing aloud he had pulled the small dumpy Mrs Gray into his bronzed arms and waltzed her round the kitchen. 'A ceilidh, Mrs Gray! Just what we could be doing with. Mind though – some might no' like the idea o' drinkin' tea, wi' the Jerries. But I'll be gettin' a few folks together, never you fear, mo ghaoil,' he had said, and went off to spread the news.

Mrs Gray peered with pleasure into the oven where a batch of scones were rising in fluffy puffs. 'It will be a fine ceilidh,' she whispered into the depths of the oven. 'And even though John will make everyone sing hymns I'm sure it will be a success just the same.'

But not even Mrs Gray was quite prepared for the unprecedented triumph of her first ceilidh. It started quietly with only a handful of islanders shuffling through the door to look in uncomfortable silence at Jon and Ernst sitting meekly together on a huge wooden settle.

'My, it's a terrible night, just!'

'Cia mar a Tha!' (How are you?)

The first arrivals muttered embarrassed exchanges in a mixture of English and Gaelic, then arranged themselves in silence around the big cosy room.

'A dreich night,' Merry Mary observed sadly, unwilling to relinquish the safe topic of the weather conditions.

'Ay, ay, right enough,' came the sage agreements, but after one or two similar observations the company grew unnaturally quiet and the focal point for all eyes became the crackling coal fire which everyone stared at with undivided attention.

Mrs Gray looked round in dismay. But for the two Germans, old Andrew and Mr McDonald, better known as Jim Jim, the company was made up entirely of elderly women, and Mrs Gray knew that a good ceilidh needed a fair number of each sex to liven proceedings. She looked at old Andrew who sat with his fiddle cuddled on his knee. He appeared faintly out of his depth among such an odd company, fidgeting first with his bow, then with a pipe-cleaner which he poked into the depths of an ancient briar, extracting a great amount of an obnoxious tarry substance, and then depositing it carefully on the bars of the fire. Jim Jim was sitting about three feet from the hearth, a distance that was no deterrent to the well-aimed flow of spit which he shot across the intervening space at regular intervals. The sound of it roasting on the coals filled the room and the gathering stared at the popping bubbles with what appeared to be an avid interest.

Mrs Gray leaned over to Isabel McDonald and said in an anxious whisper, 'I wonder what has happened to Torquil and the other men. He seemed delighted when I told him about my ceilidh. What if no one else comes?'

Isabel McDonald looked at her in wonderment. 'Ach, mo ghaoil! It's the way o' things. The younger ones will ceilidh at each other's houses first! They always do. When they gather up enough o' a crowd they will be comin' round here sure enough – or maybe staggering more like!'

Mrs Gray looked at her in horror. 'Oh, but John will never . . .' At that moment the Rev. Gray came running downstairs and into the room. 'What . . . nobody singing yet?' he bellowed lustily. 'Where is Morag Ruadh? She should be at the piano by now!'

Isabel McDonald knew that her red-haired, quick-tempered daughter was passing the time at the door with two Commando guards. For long, Morag had been a source of worry to her elderly parents because though past forty she had, as yet, failed to find herself a suitable marriage partner. Morag, with her red hair and nimble body was not an unattractive woman but she laboured under the delusion that she alone

1231

was responsible for the welfare of her ageing parents. This had embittered her outlook on life to some extent and her scathing tongue quickly scared off any would-be suitors. Contrary to Morag's beliefs, her parents were longing to be free of her spicy tongue and they were quick to encourage the attentions of any men who chanced their daughter's way.

'Morag has been kept back tonight, she will be along later, Mr Gray,' Isabel said glibly.

The minister's voice thundered out imperatively. 'Where is everybody? We must have more men for the singing. Bring in the guards! There's no need for them to be out there now!'

'There I must disagree wi' you,' Jim Jim said in tones of slight reproof. 'You mustny be forgettin' there is still another Hun to be caught. You wouldn't like a big German charging in here to us defenceless people and shootin' us all down like dogs. Would you now?'

'Pray God, of course not, but –'

'Then leave the sojers be the now. You can be bringin' them in when the other lads bring in the Hun, we'll be needin' guards then wi' three Jerries in the place.'

'Well, all right . . . yes, surely, you're right, Mr McDonald.'

Jim Jim sat back amid nods of righteous approval from the gathering while outside Morag Ruadh was carrying on in an unusually abandoned mood.

Earlier in the evening she had complained to Kate McKinnon of feeling 'a cold coming down' and Kate had made her drink a generous amount of the

Uisge-beatha. After the first mouthful and the first indignant spate of outrage at what she told Kate was 'an evil trick, just', she had thirsted after more of the water of life, whereupon a liberal Kate had sold her a pint for just ninepence. Arriving home Morag had informed her parents she was going into the scullery to 'steam her head'. With a great show of preparation she had put Friar's Balsam into a bowl of hot water and then repaired to the privacy of the scullery where she spent a solitary hour alternately 'steaming her head' and tippling from the cough bottle that she had carefully filled with whisky.

Now she was ready to throw caution to the winds. She was neither drunk nor sober but had arrived at that happy state where no obstacles loomed in the horizons of life and all things were possible, even for a forty-two-year-old spinster. Her gay mood showed in a softening of her ruddy features. She looked almost pretty with her green homespun shawl reflecting the green of her eyes and showing to advantage the bright gleam of her fiery hair. It mattered not to her that the Commandos were years younger than herself. They were men, exciting men at that, so different from the withdrawn, easy-going males of the island. She giggled and gave the guards sips of whisky from the innocent-looking brown cough bottle. The men were glad of the diversion. The superb-tasting whisky was a welcome change from the endless cups of tea provided by the kindly Mrs Gray and the surprising heat of the home-brewed malt quickly melted any doubts they might otherwise have felt at being obviously seduced by a middle-aged spinster.

Morag looked at the black tracery of the elm branches lurking in the chilly mist. With an exaggerated shudder she drew the folds of her shawl closer round her neck. 'Look you, it's a bitty cold out here,' she said softly, her legs beginning to tremble in a mixture of anticipation and surprise at her audacity. She lowered her voice to a hoarse whisper. 'It's – it's warm in the fuel shed over yonder. A nice bundle of hay there too . . . just to be resting in for a whily.'

She drifted away into the mist and the older of the two men handed his gun to his companion. 'Me first, Thomson,' he said with a chuckle. 'She's asking for it and I've got it. By God, I'll put a smile on her face that will stay there for the rest of her days.'

While Morag was arranging herself enticingly in the hay, the minister was loudly bemoaning her delay in arriving. 'We must have Morag Ruadh for the piano!' he cried, running an impatient hand through his thick mop of grey hair. 'I asked her to come early! What can have happened to her? Morag has never let me down yet.' He swung round to Isabel who was gazing sleepily into the fire. 'Can something have happened to her?' he demanded.

'All things are possible,' the old lady murmured, hastening to add loudly, 'Do not be worrying yourself, Mr Gray. Morag was feeling a cold coming and you know she is always feart of gettin' stiff hands and feets, her a spinner needin' all her fingers – and there is the organ, too, of course. Morag would never forgive herself if she was never fit for the organ on the Sabbath. She has already steamed her head, now she will likely be rubbing herself with liniment to keep supple. She'll be along right enough in her own time.'

'Well, we'll have to do without the piano!' The minister frowned round at the motley company. He felt very disappointed. His big idea of showing the Germans a real display of Scottish hospitality wasn't getting off to a good start. He had visualized a devoted Morag Ruadh stolidly accompanying an enthusiastic crowd singing rousing songs of praise all evening. Instead there was only a handful of dejected-looking islanders who were being un-naturally polite to each other. They were also inclined to murmur to one another in Gaelic, which made the minister even more frustrated.

Suddenly Jon Jodl startled everyone by getting swiftly to his feet. His thin, boyish face was alight as he addressed the minister in excited German. The exchange brought a smile of delight to the Rev. Gray's face.

'The boy's a musician!' he boomed joyfully. 'And he has offered to play for us. Be upstanding everyone and give thanks to the Lord. Then we will start with the 23rd Psalm – and I want to hear every voice raised to the Almighty . . . in English.'

'Balls,' old Jim muttered but his wife nudged him and hissed a warning 'Weesht, weesht!' but he paid no heed, standing up to sing, defiantly, the 23rd Psalm in Gaelic. The well-known strains drifted out into the frosty night where the solitary Commando guard began to hum under his breath while he strained his eyes into the ghostly darkness surrounding the Manse and awaited his turn with Morag.

Shona didn't see Niall till well after tea when he came walking down Glen Fallan with Babbie. She was securing the hen-houses and heard their laughter long before they reached the gate in the dyke.

'We're away over to the Manse!' Niall called. 'Are you coming along, mo ghaoil? Mother is going to keep your German friend amused so he doesn't need you to hold his hand!'

The sarcasm of his words and the sight of them together brought fresh anger and a swift rush of jealousy to her heart. She felt hurt and cheated. When she spoke her voice was high with a mixture of rage and tears. 'No, you two get along! I'm – I'm busy and I'm in no mood to go ceilidhing.'

'Shona, *please* come,' Babbie pleaded. 'I – can't bear to see the two of you like this . . . after all the waiting.'

'Ach, go away, go away and leave me alone!'

Niall said nothing. He just stood looking at her for a long moment and then linked his arm in Babbie's and pulled her swiftly away. Shona stood looking after them, unable to believe the turn of events. She couldn't believe that Niall and Babbie were nothing more than casual acquaintances. Was it possible that Babbie, whom she loved like the sister she'd never had, could have engineered her stay on Rhanna in the hope that she would be near Niall? Their surprise on seeing each other had seemed genuine enough . . . yet they certainly appeared to know one another quite well, there was no denying that – or the looks they had exchanged in Anton's room. She felt sick with misery and shivered uneasily.

She looked back at the big farmhouse with its soft lights glowing from the windows. It was warm and inviting but in her present mood she felt it wasn't inviting her. Kirsteen's light laugh rang out followed by Fergus's deep happy voice. For a moment she wished it was just herself and her father again. She could have talked to him in the intimate way they had adopted through the years. Sometimes just a word from him made her world seem right again; he had a knack of making her worries seem trivial . . . Then she remembered the years of his loneliness and she hated herself for grudging him one moment with Kirsteen. If it was difficult for her adjusting to the new way of things, then how much more difficult it was for them, starting off together in married life and her throwing tantrums like a baby . . .

When she went back inside Fergus turned from the table. He was enveloped in a large pink apron that was liberally coated with flour. 'This daft woman is showing me how to bake bread!' he said, his black eyes snapping with delight. 'Me who knows better how to plant grain! But I'll show her the McKenzies aren't to be so easily beaten, eh, mo ghaoil?' There was a message in the laughing words and their eyes met in a moment of understanding.

'Hey, I thought I was now a member of this mad clan,' Kirsteen said, rubbing her nose with a floury hand.

Shona giggled. 'You both look members of a ghost clan . . . and I'm sorry to the pair of you for this afternoon . . . Now . . .' she rolled up her sleeves to wash her hands then went merrily into the fray.

'I thought you were getting ready for this mad Manse ceilidh that's the talk of the place,' Fergus objected. 'You and Niall . . .'

'He's taking Babbie. She hasn't been to an island ceilidh yet. They know each other, you know – Niall and Babbie – met in Glasgow. I'm going over later to sit with Anton.'

'But . . .' Kirsteen began, but Shona held up a floury hand. 'No more talk about me. I'm sure you're both heartily sick of me and my bothers.'

Fergus was about to reply when Shona interrupted with a shriek.

'I can smell burning! I think your bread is on fire, Father!'

'Bugger it!' He rushed to the oven. Kirsteen glanced at Shona and they both collapsed into helpless laughter as Fergus glowered at his burnt loaves and the three of them spent a light-hearted hour together before Shona went upstairs to tidy herself.

When she arrived at Slochmhor, Phebie was hauling a protesting Fiona from Anton's room. 'The little devil simply won't leave poor Anton alone!' Phebie panted. 'A grass snake this time – that after a frog, a newt and—'

'But he wanted to see them!' Fiona wailed petulantly.

'Well, it's bed for you now, Madam, and no nonsense or I'll give you a skelpit leathering!' She looked at Shona enquiringly. 'I thought you would be at this praise meeting-cum-ceilidh. I told Niall I would stay with Anton, though I fancy he would prefer you to an auld wife like me.' She put her hand on Shona's arm. 'Isn't it grand our Niall's come home to us, mo ghaoil? I feel ten years younger already!' She looked ten years younger with her bonny round face flushed and her eyes shining.

'Ay, it's wonderful, Phebie,' Shona agreed while her heart turned over. 'I told him to take Babbie out tonight. She's worked so hard here and she – the two of them – deserve a break. I don't mind keeping Anton company for a while.'

'You're a good lassie,' Phebie said while inwardly she wondered what had gone wrong between her son and his sweetheart. 'I'll go down and make Lachy some supper to come home to. He went away over to see Todd and Biddy – evidently she is not very happy with this unfortunate *spare* nurse the authorities have sent.'

Fiona popped her head out of her door. 'I think tomorrow I'll put a lump of frog spawn into Elspeth's sago pudding. We always have sago on a Monday and . . .'

'Bed!!' Phebe cried and made a lunge at Fiona who evaded her and went running round her room shrieking with glee.

Anton smiled at the sounds of merriment. 'That little Fiona, she is heaven and hell all rolled into one. I see frogs till I am green! But, what are you doing here, Fräulein Shona? You should be enjoying yourself. I don't need anyone to hold my hand – and I have no wish to make things worse between you and Niall.'

Shona sat down by the bed. 'Ach, don't worry about us. I came over to cheer you up. I thought you would be pleased to see my bonny face.'

'Bonny?'

'A saying – it means – well – nice-looking, though not in that way exactly.'

'No, I would say more like – beautiful? Niall is a very lucky fellow – and also a very angry young man.'

She flushed. 'Ay, he is that, but not at you really, you just happened to be handy, that's all.'

'Because I'm a German. It's all right, I understand.'

'But – you shouldn't understand! How can you understand! To be hated because you are a German!'

He took her hand gently. 'It is natural, Fräulein Shona. When first I knew my family had been killed by the British I hated them. Before that they were just people to fight because fighting them was the right thing to do in war. But when the killing involves you personally it becomes a private war. Niall saw people he loved killed just a few days ago. The hate is strong within him – also he hates because he doesn't understand what has gone wrong between you and him, neither of you can. It is the baby he says you lost while he was in France. You cannot yet bring yourselves to speak about it – really bring it into the open

1240

and talk it out of your hearts. It will go on poisoning you both till you do, the mixing up of your feelings will just go on and on . . .' His blue eyes flashed and he smiled. 'And I will go on talking too much. My mother, she used to say to me, "Anton, you are like an old gramophone, wind you up and you never stop".'

Shona saw the quickening of the pulse in his neck at the mentioning of his mother and a sadness stole into her heart. 'You are a very nice person, Anton Büttger, and even yet you cry inside for the family you have lost – and – and I think you are also very brave because not once have you bemoaned the fact that some of your fingers had to come off yesterday.'

He held up his bandaged hand and looked at it. Lachlan had removed two of the fingers, hoping that the third, which hadn't been too badly frostbitten, might heal with time. 'I am not brave, Fräulein, I have lain in this bed and felt very sorry for myself indeed, but I could have been worse off. You tell me your father lost an arm in an accident . . .' he said smiling ruefully. 'I am lucky I still have an arm with at least some of my fingers attached.'

There were a few moments of silence between them. Shona got up and went to look from the window. The mist had rolled in from the sea and the moors shimmered in a thick blanket that seemed to stretch to eternity. It was an odd feeling. Rhanna was just a tiny island, isolated far out in the Atlantic, yet certain weather conditions made the great undulating shaggy blanket of the Muir of Rhanna reach out to drape over the world. During the long sparkling days of the Hebridean summers the illusion was heightened even further. The deep blue of the ocean, glimpsed between distant outcrops of perpendicular cliffs, was the cradle on which the heather-covered mattress lay, with the heads of the mountains rearing up into shrouds of gossamer mist. Then the land and the sea became as one with nothing between them and eternity.

As Shona watched a meek little puff of wind occasionally blew the mist into swirling wisps, revealing the blurred face of the moon peering in sullen anonymity through the hazy curtain.

'You look at the moon and you think of Niall and Babbie at this ceil – ceil . . .'

'Ceilidh,' Shona supplied. 'It means a sing-song and perhaps a dance and a story. I hope you will experience one before you leave Rhanna. Ay, you are right, Anton, I was thinking, but I've had a lot of experience of that.'

'Has Babbie been your friend long?' he asked tactfully.

She shook her head and Anton could not help thinking how beautiful she looked standing against the moonlit window. 'No, not long at all. In fact I know very little about her, but enough – well, I thought it was enough – to feel as though I'd want to have her for a friend for the rest of my life.'

'She is another one who does not like Germans.' Anton said the words in a matter-of-fact way but with such assurance that Shona choked back the protest that had risen to her lips. She was remembering Babbie in the surgery, trembling, looking at the unconscious Anton with a strange, indefinable look.

'It is true, Fräulein Shona,' he continued rather wearily. 'I feel the things that people feel. I look at Fräulein Babbie's sweet and honest face and sense the battles that go on inside her head all the time. She appears calm but inside she fights many emotions. It is against her nature to dislike anyone but she dislikes Germans – and I am a German. Oh, she attends every one of my needs with devotion, but it is training – not trust or fondness – that makes her do so.'

His was such a frank assessment that Shona could find nothing to say to contradict him because she knew he would know she was putting on an act. He was watching her face with those perspicacious blue eyes of his and she found herself reddening.

'Babbie is a very mysterious sort of girl,' she said finally. 'As I say, I know very little about her so I can't tell you much about her feelings on certain matters.'

'You are kind, Fräulein Shona,' he smiled. 'You do not wish to hurt me, and while we are on the subject of people and the things they do, I believe it is you I have to thank for saving my life.'

Embarrassment made her suddenly brisk. 'Och, that is just a lot of blethers from a lot of old women. Donald and my wee brother, Grant, found you. They thought you were a monster, or a ghost,' she laughed. 'And looking at your white face now I'm beginning to think they were right. It's high time I went and let you get some sleep.'

He had sunk into his pillows, hollow-cheeked and strained with exhaustion and as she tucked in his blankets Lachlan popped his head round the door and in a whisper beckoned her out into the hall.

'Shona, mo ghaoil,' Lachlan said as he put his hand on her arm, 'Niall hasn't said anything but I know all is not what it should be between you.' His deep compassionate brown eyes seemed to look right into her troubled heart. 'You must stop torturing one another, mo ghaoil, or one day you will waken up and find it is too late for either of you. You are like my own lassie and my dearest wish is to see the pair of you settled. Take heed of what I say. It's you who should be up at the Manse with him this very minute and fine the two of you know it. Sometimes I wish you were bairns again then I would have an excuse to take you over my knee and give you a good leathering!'

'Ach, you were aye too soft-hearted even to beat a doormat,' she said and they both laughed.

When Shona reached Laigmhor it was warm and quiet. Although Fergus and Kirsteen were still up in the kitchen, Shona managed to avoid them and crept wearily into bed. But she couldn't sleep. She was thinking of Niall and Babbie at the ceilidh. It would be a merry affair. The Rev. John Gray might start off with psalms and hymns but the islanders would see to it that it turned into a proper ceilidh. Niall and Babbie would dance together . . . he would hold her close . . . and then they would go back to Slochmhor together because Babbie was still staying there, though she had moved out of Anton's room. She was in the little box room – which was on the other side of Niall's room!

'Oh God,' she whispered, 'please help me to be less suspicious – and – jealous. I can't help it, I love Niall so much yet every time we meet we seem to fight all the time . . .' She snuggled into her pillows and wept. Her arms ached to hold something. Tot, her faithful old spaniel, had shared her bed for years, but Tot was dead now and she felt terribly alone.

Mirabelle's rag dolls sat in a floppy row on the shelves. Whenever she looked at them she thought of the plump, homely old housekeeper who had been mother to her during the vulnerable years of her childhood. The old lady had lovingly stitched every one of the dolls and now they were all somewhat dusty and bedraggled, but on the whole they had stood the test of time. On top of the dresser was the splendid 'town' doll given to her by Fergus's brother, Alick, on one of his summer visits to the island. The extravagant beauty of the doll had taken her breath away and for a time Mirabelle's rag dolls had been cast aside. But the 'town' doll was cold and hard with none of the cuddly qualities of the others. She had never taken it to bed. Eventually it had become an ornament, a pleasant reminder of the uncle whose affection she had always appreciated though she knew he had caused so much trouble in the past. She hadn't seen Alick since last autumn. He had joined the army, surprising a lot of people except those who knew him best. He was still trying to prove himself, making up for the years of self-indulgence of his early manhood.

Shona looked at the 'town' doll with its prettily painted face. 'Poor Uncle Alick,' she said softly and, getting up, she retrieved it from the dresser, picked out her most favoured rag doll, and then padding back to bed she cuddled the toys to her like a lost child.

Chapter Twelve

When the Commandos had come to the island, expecting to round up a whole flock of German invaders, and had discovered that the whole thing was a false alarm, Dunn had quickly dispatched a message back to base to the effect that the mission would be accomplished much sooner than expected. He had used Behag's 'contraption' to send out the reports and at first she had received him into her Report Centre with utmost tight-lipped suspicion. But he was a young man possessed of fine tact, and in a few words he had dispelled Behag's guilt and made her feel an important ally in the war game.

'I need your help, Mistress Beag,' he had told her courteously. 'To be truthful, I am not acquainted enough with the machine to get the best from it. It is not exactly the most up-to-date transmitter but I am sure that is no deterrent to a woman like you . . . you are in a very important position you know, Mistress Beag . . . you and the Coastguard are probably the two best assets on the island.'

Behag had blossomed then like a wilted plant revived by water. Her jowls, which lay in several wizened layers on her neck, had unfolded one by one into taut furrows as she slowly tilted her head heavenwards and in a silent flurry of gratitude had thanked the Lord for allowing her to keep her dignity despite all the gossip she had endured since the arrival of the bomber. Later, when she could justifiably lift up her head again, the population of Rhanna was destined to hear repeatedly the story of the gallant Dunn, 'an officer and a gentleman, just', who, when her very own kith and kin had forsaken her, gave her the strength to carry on.

At first the Commandos had been disconcerted by their plight, but after a few days in the peaceful environment of Rhanna their initial irritation at the situation had evaporated quickly. Without being able to help themselves, each man had felt a reprieve from the serious and dangerous duties of the war. Despite a lack of military skill the islanders had somehow managed to net three Germans. Only one remained to be taken, and on a small island like Rhanna that seemed an easy enough task. But they soon discovered how wrong they were.

Earlier in the day Dunn had told the Commandos on guard duty at the Manse that the capture of the fourth German would almost certainly be accomplished before nightfall, but night had fallen hours ago and there was still no sign of the other Commandos and the members of the Home Guard who formed the search party. In the hours of daylight the interest of the Home Guard had been sharp enough, with each man feeling a throat-catching excitement at the idea of being the first to capture the elusive German. But the twilight had brought strange looming shapes to play on the whispering amber grasses. And when night fell, and the mist draped itself over the island like a shroud, cloud patterns danced on the aloof ruddy face of the winter moon and shadows loomed over the moor. At such time, the imaginative mind, fed from the breast on myths and folklore, saw the flapping cloaks of spooks and peat hags gliding over lost lonely places, and heard the thin voice of the sea, riding in on the wind, breathing the life of the past into the eerie shadows. These were the nights of the witching moon when fancy ran free and the crofters left the comfort of their homes only to see to their beasts or to walk a short distance to ceilidh in another warm house.

The Commandos had had a long and tiring day, but that they were able to take in their stride. The usual hazards of wide open spaces had presented no problems: they knew about peat hags and peat bogs; they were familiar with the ebb and flow of the tides and, with the added advice gladly given by Righ, had already explored many of the deep dank caverns that yawned into the cliffs surrounding the greater part of the coastline. But what they weren't so prepared for was a people so incurably addicted to the mythical legends of the moors that certain parts of it were taboo unless absolutely essential. The search for the German had been considered necessary and, on the whole, had been undertaken with curiosity. But the nearer the search got to the Abbey ruins the more the Home Guard's enthusiasm began to wane. Lusty cries of merry banter became more subdued till eventually everyone spoke in whispers and took frequent peeps over their shoulders. Much of it was exaggerated but the effect was such that even the Commandos had now lowered their voices to eerie whispers.

'Is it the German you're afraid of?' Anderson mouthed to Torquil.

Torquil didn't answer for a moment. He drew a big strong hand over his shaggy thatch and his blue eyes contemplated the craggy grey stones of the Abbey hunched together like old men sharing secrets. 'Na, na . . . tis no' the German,' he said finally without a hint of discomfort. 'Thon's the place o' the ghosts and they don't like being disturbed.'

'But it's only an old ruin,' Anderson persisted.

Torquil looked at him with pity and said heavily, 'And all you know, eh? Thon's the place o' the tomb, man. Underneath these hillocks is caves full of coffins. Walk on the turf above and waken the dead beneath!'

'And you all know where the openings of these caves . . . or tombs – are?'

'Some, ay, some no,' was the general agreement.

'But they're all grown over and mustny be disturbed,' old Andrew, who was one of the best Seanachaidhs on the island, and who was possessed of an imagination that turned the most mundane event into a thing of magic, whispered. He looked hastily over his shoulder and added, 'The mist is gathering. Look now! It's creeping in from the sea and the Uisga Hags will be hidin' on the rocks near the shore. Sometimes they come right ashore in a mist

and before you know where you are they are lurin'
you out to sea where you will be after drownin'.'

'The – Uisga Hags?' came the Commandos' query.

'Ay, ay, the green water witches,' old Andrew
explained patiently. Thoughtfully, he gathered a gob
of spit into his cheeks which he inflated several times
before spitting to the ground with an expertise that
left no traces on his lips. Staring at the frothy strings
dangling on a grassy tussock he went on in deliberately dramatic tones. 'They're the spirits o' witches
cast out o' the island hundreds of years afore, an' they
have just hung aboot haunting us ever since.
Beautiful mermaids they be one minute but if you are
out at your lobster pots an' dare to take your thoughts
away from your work, one look into the wicked
green eyes o' a mermaid witch an' you're done for.
There she changes into a wizened crone wi' whiskers
an' warts an' she carries you off to the bottom of the
sea to show you off to the other hags.' His rheumy
blue eyes twinkled mischievously. 'Hard up for men
they are down there on the bed o' the ocean, an' the
first thing they do is take your trousers off. It's the
surest sign a man has been taken by the hags when
his trousers float all limp and empty to the surface o'
the sea!'

It was the cue everyone needed to let out a
subdued bellow of laughter, for there, on the open
moor, with the wraiths of haar curling into the
hollows, the tale and the tone of old Andrew's voice
sent shivers up the spine. But the Commandos were
in no laughing mood when not long afterwards most

of the islanders drifted away in twos and threes as silently as their stoutly-booted feet would allow. And so, left without the willing guides they needed, the soldiers abandoned the caves and the moors, and now narrowed the search to Nigg and the Burn-breddie estate.

On the hill track to Nigg they came upon Dodie leading Ealasaid home to her byre. The old eccentric had by now learnt to tell the difference between Germans and Commandos and at sight of them he began to gesticulate wildly and babble in Gaelic. He was in a pitiful state with his grey-green eyes sunk into his face like currants in a wizened treacle dumpling and the grey-black stubble on his chin heightening the illusion of a fungus-covered reject. Fortunately some staunch, if not daring, members of the Home Guard had remained and it soon transpired that Dodie had spent a harrowing, sleepless night.

'The big Hun was here,' Robbie translated for the Commandos. 'Poor auld Dodie says the man burst into his house like a raving bull, took all Dodie's food, and then slept most of the night and part of today in a chair by the fire. He went away only a wee whily ago and Dodie just galloped off to look for his cow . . . he loves the beast more than anything else in the world.'

'Ask him if he knows which way the German went.'

Dodie was now weeping into his big calloused hands, his stooped shoulders shuddering with long-drawn-out sobs, the tears running in dirty rivulets through his fingers. For the first time in his life Robbie thought seriously about Dodie and his lonely simple world. It was bad enough to know about things that went on in the war but to a simple soul like Dodie, his mind groping at half-formed notions and solitary imaginings, it might be utterly terrifying. Not one of them had ever spared the time to explain to him what went on in war and Robbie realised that the arrival of the big German into Dodie's innocent world must have been a frightening ordeal. Robbie felt a great lump of self-reproach in his throat and he threw a firm arm round Dodie's bent shoulders.

'Look now, Dodie, I'm here, dinna greet any more. Just tell me which direction the big Jerry took.'

Dodie waved his arms in the direction of Burnbreddie. 'I saw him goin' in there when I was looking for Ealasaid, by the wee rustic gate in the bushes!'

Dunn looked at Robbie. 'Will you stay with him for a while? He looks like he could be doing with some comfort.'

Robbie was torn. He had looked forward to the Manse ceilidh, seeing it as a reprieve from Behag who was still giving him the 'silent treatment'. 'All day I am hearin' nothing but silence,' he had told his cronies dejectedly. 'I used to think it would be heaven to hear her mouth shut; now I am thinkin' she's even more hell wi' her lips closed.'

'Ach, all right,' he said finally, 'I'll bide a whily. Look you now, Dodie, I'm comin' in to ceilidh wi' you whether you like it or no'. I have some o' Tam's whisky here and we'll have a fine old time.'

Dodie raised a tear-stained face. It was grey and utterly woebegone in the pale glimmer of moonlight filtering through the haar, but a small ghost of a smile lit his weary face. 'Will you really stay wi' me, Robbie? My, it would be right nice, so it would . . . for a wee whily just. I'm – I'm feart o' being alone till the big German is caught but at least . . .' he blinked away the last of the tears, 'I found my Ealasaid and will get some milk to drink, for that big mannie took all I had in the house.'

It was an easy enough matter after that to trace Zeitler to one of the big haysheds inside Burnbreddie. His face was haggard and he succumbed quite meekly to the Commandos, though his look of arrogant disdain said quite plainly that he was proud of the trouble he had caused everyone in the last few days.

Thomson was back in his place outside the Manse door, shakily lighting a cigarette, when old Angus drove the trap containing Zeitler and the Commandos up the steep brae. Madam Balfour of Burnbreddie had kindly and willingly loaned both her groom and the trap to the Commandos.

'We must all do what we can in these troubled times,' she had imparted graciously, looking with disdain down her nose at Zeitler. She had fussed greatly over the Commandos since their arrival, inviting them to meals and at one point lending them her precious car that they might get about the island quicker. But the car had been of little use on the stony island roads and had got stuck in a bog on the Muir of Rhanna two nights previously where it still remained because no one had had the time to get it out.

'You have been very kind,' Dunn had said, taking the old lady's hand. 'First your car, now your trap. Thank you for all your hospitality.'

'A pleasure, I'm sure,' the old lady had fluttered, her veneer falling away for a moment to show a lonely old woman, but just as quickly she had been herself again saying, 'I'll get Angus my groom to drive you over to the Manse. He detests work you know but then, these people have no ambition, none at all! There's talk that they're brewing their own whisky, you know! Oh, I wouldn't put it past them, drink all day if they could . . .'

Old Angus had chortled wickedly as he guided the horses up to the Manse. 'The old bugger has done me a favour sendin' me out for I'll be gettin' to this ceilidh after all. I was rackin' my brains all night for an excuse to come.' He now glanced at Zeitler huddled in the back seat. 'We'll be showin' the Jerries a bit o' life right enough but I'm hopin' this one will be changing his clothes and scrubbin' himself. He smells terrible just!'

When the crowd piled into the Manse Jon Jodl was playing a gay little melody which brought forth smiles of appreciation from the new arrivals. In the hubbub Carl Zeitler was whisked away to the wash tub in the scullery. There, watched over by two soldiers, his urgent need for hygiene was speedily undertaken. Mrs Gray, glad to get away from the hymn singing for a while, presided over gallons of water heating on the range in the kitchen while in the scullery the men divested Zeitler of his repulsive-smelling layers of outerwear. Sounds of merriment came from the drawing-room and Mrs Gray smiled to herself. It was going to be a good ceilidh after all.

'I will just heat this – er – gentleman some food,' she said politely, glancing at Zeitler's brooding face. She looked up at the two Manse guards, Thomson and Cranwell, whose faces were rather haggard in the light of the lamp. 'Poor lads,' she murmured sympathetically. 'You look done in . . . but never mind, there's enough hot water for you all to have a nice wash. I've made lots of lovely food so nobody will starve.'

Torquil Andrew came into the kitchen, a pretty dark-haired girl hanging on one arm and a basket of food on the other. 'Some bannocks and scones,' he explained with a flash of his white teeth. 'I told Mother I was coming over to the Manse to sing hymns and she was that pleased to think I've changed my ways she started baking right away.'

'Oh, Torquil, you shouldn't,' Mrs Gray beamed in delight while in the scullery Zeitler was making strangulated sounds of protest because someone had left the door open and he sat in his zinc tub for everyone to see.

After Torquil there came a stream of people all bearing a little offering of some sort. Mairi handed over a pot of crowdie cheese. 'It will be nice on the bannocks – the way Wullie likes it,' she explained sadly before her brown, rather vacant, gaze came to rest on Zeitler. 'My, my,' she said with mild astonishment. 'You would never think he was a German without his clothes – I suppose it's just you expect that funny wee Hun sign to be everywhere on them – even their bodies!'

The earlier arrivals breathed sighs of relief when the familiar faces of the more rumbustious islanders appeared through the door. In the excitement everyone forgot inward promises of abstinence in all things the minister might consider improper. Despite the restrictions caused by rationing, the generous islanders passed round packets of cigarettes while the older men lit smelly pipes. Old Andrew, who, in the first part of the evening had done everything with his pipe except smoke it, thankfully accepted a good fill of 'baccy' from old Joe then reached for his fiddle to tune it. The Germans accepted cigarettes and, after introductions, smiled in some bemusement at the various nicknames bestowed on them. A shining Zeitler was brought in to join the company, one or two children sneaked in by the side door, and the once silent and empty room was soon filled to capacity.

A rousing welcome greeted Niall's entrance, ample proof of his popularity with everyone, while Babbie received a reserved introduction together with a swift appraisal from the womenfolk and sly glances of appreciation from the men.

'Good! Good! We're all here now!' the Rev. Gray boomed, looking round the gathering with some dismay because he hadn't expected such an enthusiastic turnout for a praise meeting. 'Now we shall really raise the roof with our singing!'

The door opened once more to admit a serenely contented Morag Ruadh who came on the arm of Dugald Donaldson. Dugald, determined to follow up the activities of the German invaders, had cycled over the rough moor road from Portvoynachan, his pockets bulging with notepads and pencils. Morag, having allowed herself some time in the fuel shed to 'gather herself up', had emerged to meet Dugald at the Manse door and had surprised him thoroughly by hanging on to his arm and chattering with unusual animation.

'Ach, that is good, now!' Tam McKinnon approved at the minister's words. 'Erchy has brought his bagpipes and we'll have Andrew playin' the fiddle. 'Tis a pity poor auld Todd is laid up for it's handy to have two pipers at a ceilidh. When one gets out o' breath you can just hand over the pipes to the other while the bag is still full of air.'

The minister looked at Tam with disapproval. He had told Mrs Gray to ask only teetotallers to the ceilidh and here was Tam McKinnon who, it was rumoured, was actually brewing his own whisky. In fact, on looking over the new arrivals, the minister saw only those who were notoriously fond of 'the devil's brew'.

'You cannot sing hymns to the bagpipes, Tam!' he said sternly.

Erchy grinned mischievously. 'No, but she'll play

them. Wait you and you'll hear what I mean.' He patted his pipes affectionately. 'Just right she is for a good blow. I've given her some treacle to keep her supple and a droppy whisky to give her a bit of life.'

It was Erchy's habit to fondly give his bagpipes a female gender but while everyone else smiled appreciatively the minister's frown deepened. 'I have no idea what you are talking about, Erchy, but there will be no whisky-drinking women in my house. Now . . .' He turned to Morag Ruadh and smiled ingratiatingly. 'Morag is here at last and only too ready, I'm sure, to relieve this young man at the piano – isn't that right, Morag?'

Before leaving the fuel shed Morag had consumed the remainder of her whisky and she was now seeing the world through a rosy glow. She smiled charmingly at the minister, and confounded him by replying, 'Indeed, I will not! I'm for the skirl o' the pipes and a good bit story from Andrew and Joe. 'Tis a night o' fun I'm after.'

The minister's jaw fell and everyone looked at each other in astonishment.

'It's no natural, no' natural at all! Morag Ruadh is no' herself,' was the general verdict.

Jim Jim and his wife looked at each other. 'Here,' Isabel said, 'was you thinkin' earlier that Morag was actin' a bit funny?'

Jim Jim nodded. 'Ay, indeed. I had a mind I was smellin' the drink off her, but knowing Morag I thought it couldny be. My God, would you look at the smile on her face. She's been havin' a bit fun out

there and well she looks on it too. I never thought o'
Morag as bein' bonny before but tonight she has the
look o' a new woman.'

The blast of the bagpipes filled the room and with
a mad 'hooch' Morag was the first to get to her feet,
turning to pull Dugald after her.

Isabel nudged her husband. 'Look at that now. She
and Dugald Ban are right friendly all of a sudden.'

Jim Jim removed his pipe from his mouth to make
a faultlessly aimed spit at the coals, despite the
swirling skirts that flounced wildly to the tunes of the
pipes. 'Well now, there's a thing,' he said thoughtfully. 'A fine thing, just. Dugald Ban would be just
right for Morag and him wi' his ambitions will maybe
become one o' they famous people wi' plenty money.'

Jon Jodl and Ernst Foch had risen to their feet and
were clapping their hands and stamping their feet in
time to the pipes. Only Zeitler remained staring
broodingly into the fire but even he could not resist
the music and one foot tapped almost automatically
on the hearth.

Niall gripped Babbie's arm. 'Well, what do you
think of the praise meeting?'

Her green eyes were sparkling. 'It's – it's magic, I
shouldn't be feeling like this, all happy and bubbly
inside, but I can't help myself. Oh, I wish Shona had
come. People will be wondering. Already we're
getting some queer looks.'

'You, you mean, the men can't keep their eyes off
you. Shona could have come if she had wanted. She's
behaving like a spoilt baby!'

'Och, c'mon, Niall, you know that's not true! You were horrible to her today and fine you know it.'

Niall's brown eyes were full of misery. 'I know, God, don't rub it in! But it was seeing her with that – that German. If he hadn't been in bed so badly broken up I swear I would have punched him. Don't tell me either that you particularly like the idea of mending a German or have you changed your mind about that sort of thing?'

She put her fingers to her forehead and shook her head angrily. 'Of course I haven't. When I saw him in Lachlan's surgery I thought for a moment that I wanted him to die!' She looked up suddenly and continued in a shocked voice, 'Isn't that a dreadful thing for a nurse to admit! I hated myself at the time and I hate myself now for ever having thought it! For three days now I've looked after him and now I don't know what to think. I look at him and I see only a wounded young man who has lost all his family in the war. I have to force myself to be cool to him and all the time he's so quiet and grateful for everything I do.'

Niall's nostrils flared. 'The best killers have the nicest smiles. He's a German and that's all there is to it!'

'Well, there's Germans here, aren't there? Why did you come tonight? After all, Niall, this ceilidh is in honour of them!'

Niall looked contemptuously at Jon and Ernst who were now jigging round the room with the utmost enjoyment. Commandos, islanders, Germans, all

1261

mixed together, 'hooching' and skirling, caught up in the irresistible wild rhythm of the pipes and the fiddles. 'I shouldn't have come.' Niall sounded defeated, with all the fight suddenly gone out of him. 'I shouldn't have done a lot of things today, but I did, and because of it Shona's not speaking to me and I'm damned if I'm going crawling to her to say I'm sorry! *I* wasn't the one fawning over a German!'

'You're jealous, Niall, so jealous you can't even think straight! I think it might be a good thing if I leave Rhanna by the next boat! Heaven knows what Shona must be thinking about you and me, first finding that we know one another then coming here tonight together and leaving her out in the cold. I'm too fond of her to hurt her!'

'And by God, no wonder. Both red-haired witches with tempers like devils! It would be fine of you to leave the island now with Biddy laid up, a spare nurse that's got one foot in the grave, and my father with so much to do he looks ill on it! Granted I could hit him for taking that German under our roof but he is my father and he needs all the help he can get!'

They were both shouting at one another but above the noise of the pipes no one heard except for those sitting close by. Old Isabel leaned forward confidentially. 'Where is our Shona tonight, laddie? I had thought that we would all be comin' to your weddin' soon and here you are, at a ceilidh wi' another lass. It's no' right, no' right at all.'

In Niall's present mood it was fortunate for Isabel

that the pipes stopped playing just then and everyone flopped exhausted into chairs. Jon Jodl came over to where Babbie was sitting and addressed her quietly in German.

'He is asking how his Commander is keeping, Miss Cameron,' the minister said.

Babbie reddened as all eyes turned towards her. 'Oh, tell him he is improving. He was very badly wounded but the doctor brought him back . . . from the dead. He has lost some of his fingers from frostbite but – otherwise he is perfectly whole.'

'Ach, the soul,' Kate sympathised solicitously. 'We are hearing that he brought his plane over the village and took an awful risk jumping out over the mountains so that he wouldny harm anyone.'

'Ay, he's no' bad for a Jerry,' Tam said enthusiastically.

'Speakin' the English too,' put in Erchy somewhat breathlessly. 'But we are after teachin' him some o' the Gaelic. Already he can say a few words.'

Tam looked at Ernst and Jon. 'These lads are no' like the real Nazis – except for the big Hun in the corner.'

Ernst looked over at Tam and said carefully, 'Uisgebeatha?'

Tam's mouth fell open and Torquil said, 'I think he's asking for some o' your whisky, Tam.'

Tam grinned delightedly. 'Well, damn me – and using the Gaelic name for it! These Jerries are clever right enough . . . here, Bullhead.' He held out his hip flask. 'Take a real good swig – you ugly big bugger,' he added in rapid Gaelic and everyone roared with laughter.

Ernst took the flask, but passed it to Jon. 'You first, Jon.' Jon took the flask and raised it high. 'Slainte!' he cried and the islanders took up the cry.

Mrs Gray was coming into the drawing-room with a tray of tea. Behind her tripped a merry procession bearing plates of food. The room was in a happy uproar. An exhausted Andrew had handed his fiddle to Jon whose long, delicate fingers extricated tunes that were unknown on the island but were so irresistibly gay they invited hands to clap and feet to tap. The Commandos and the Germans had all partaken freely from the brown cough bottles such as might be found in any medicine cupboard on the island, and an air of comradeship existed between everyone. Only the Rev. John Gray remained soberly reserved and his mood wasn't improved by his first sip of tea which Torquil had laced with whisky while it lay steaming on the kitchen table.

'Hannah, this tea tastes terrible,' he said tightly, but Hannah was beyond caring.

'Well, John, if you don't like it . . . away through and make some more,' she told him flippantly, but he was of the breed who believed the kitchen was only a woman's domain and he had no intention of domesticating himself now. Several minutes later he held out his drained cup and requested a refill.

'Ach, you enjoyed that,' Kate grinned, going off to fetch the teapot into which Tam had poured a good measure of whisky. 'There now,' she said, handing the minister the replenished cup. 'It is tastin' a wee bit funny but the water is that peaty the now it canny be helped.'

Babbie's face twitched and she let out a smothered laugh. Niall too could not contain himself and he let out a great guffaw of mirth that seemed to release all his pent-up emotions. 'Will you dance with me, Babbie?' he twinkled. 'We might as well enjoy ourselves now that we're here and if I don't grab you Erchy or one of the others will do it for me.'

They whirled merrily into the crowd while the minister, his face somewhat flushed after consuming three cups of tea, leaned towards Kate and gave her a conspiratorial wink. 'Good tea, my dear, very good! I must say there's something to be said for peaty water! By jove, it has really warmed me up and I am hoping you can squeeze another cup from the pot.'

Kate obligingly 'squeezed' the pot and put her lips close to his ear. 'There now, it's as dry as a fart in a corpse!' she imparted in a bubble of merriment.

'Mrs McKinnon!' the minister exploded, but the ghost of a smile hovered at the corners of his mouth. 'You know, for the first time since I came to Rhanna I feel really close to you all. I am very glad I held this ceilidh tonight, very glad . . . Would you care to dance with me, my dear?' he added as Jon broke into the wildly stirring *Czardos*.

A hotch-potch of an Irish jig made the floorboards jump beneath the rugs; everyone had reached the stage when anything with a rhythm made their feet itch to dance. Nearly all of the men present saw to it that they danced with Babbie. She was wearing a dress of softest green wool which complemented her amber-flecked eyes and luxuriant red curls. She had a knack of making every man she danced with feel as if he were the only man in the room, and when Niall finally managed to get to her he said with a teasing little laugh, 'You're a flirt, Caillich Ruadh. You've got all the men making sheep's eyes at you and all the women throwing daggers! I can see clearer than ever that it would be a very easy thing for any man to fall in love with you.'

'I'm in no position for anything like that ever to happen,' she answered, a little frown creeping into her radiant smile.

'You like Anton, don't you?' he said curtly and unexpectedly.

'Niall, for heaven's sake, what's got into you?' she said in hurt bewilderment. 'It's perhaps just as well we didn't know each other too well in Glasgow because I don't like the Niall I'm getting to know better now. Don't complicate matters any more for me! You keep on and on about Anton. I don't like him and I don't hate him! Does that satisfy you?'

He shook his head as if to clear it and looked at her with the shadow of fear darkening his eyes to black pools of misery. 'I'm sorry, mo ghaoil. I'm not myself, that's for sure. I'm saying things I don't mean to say. They just come out and I canny seem to stop them. Forgive me, mo ghaoil.'

Babbie said nothing but squeezed his hand reassuringly. He smiled and put his lips close to her ear.

'Would you look at our minister. That rascal, Tam, has been putting whisky in his tea!'

The Rev. John Gray was snoring on a hard wooden chair, his hands clasped over his chest, his legs stretched like pokers; he was in danger of sliding off his perch. 'The Lord is my – Psalm twenty-six – I have trusted also in the Lord; therefore I shall not slide – tea terrible . . .' he muttered insensibly.

'To hell wi' Psalms,' Robbie chuckled. He had arrived late at the ceilidh and was determined to enjoy the rest of it. 'Away you go over to the Headquarters, Tam, and be bringin' up some more of your cough mixture. It's early yet and I'm no' goin' home to have Behag sniffin' at me like a ferret and shoutin' at me wi' her eyes.'

'Ay, I will that,' Tam responded willingly, whereupon Kate set about collecting the bottles. Tam stuck out his large square palm and cocked his eye at the company. 'Cross my hand wi' silver and I'll be bringin' back full bottles.'

'Ach, you're worse than my Aberdeen cousin!' old Angus exclaimed. 'He looks for change out o' a farthing.'

'Well, it's more than a farthing I'm after,' Tam smirked, and though everyone grumbled they handed over their money willingly enough. Tam closed his hand and winked at Mrs Gray. 'You won't be saying a word in the wrong ears, mo ghaoil?'

'Tam McKinnon!' she said sternly. 'If people want to buy your cough mixture it is nothing to do with me.' She put her hand in her pocket and then slyly put some coins into his hand. 'And I'll be having a drop too. I think Morag must have passed her cold on to me. I'll never get the chance of medicine like yours again.'

Tam looked at her with reverence. 'Mrs Gray, this will not be your last ceilidh on this island,' he intoned in a respectful whisper. He stretched out his hand and dropped her coppers back into her pocket. 'Be putting them in the kirk plate for me next Sabbath,' he said benevolently, then turned to follow the sound of Kate's clanking bottles outside.

Chapter Thirteen

Niall turned restlessly in bed and wakened abruptly at the sound of stealthy footsteps climbing the stairs. Then he heard a faint exchange in German and realised that the Commandos had taken Jon to Anton's room to say goodbye. The three healthy captives were due to leave that morning, and Niall found himself fuming, unable to get back to sleep though he was still tired. Dawn was filtering over the night sky but his room still lay in darkness. He lay on his back, staring up at the ceiling, thinking about the German lying on the other side of the wall from him, comfortably lying under the roof of Slochmhor with his German companions coming to bid farewell to him. But hardly comfortable! Mixed up as Niall's thoughts were he couldn't deny even to himself that Anton most certainly must be suffering a good deal, though there was hardly ever a cheep of complaint out of him. 'But why should there be?' he argued with himself. 'His set-up couldn't be more perfect: a doctor at first hand to mend him with absolute skill and then to be right on the spot should anything go wrong; an attractive young nurse to tend him hand and foot, wipe his nose for him if need be; bed, board, all laid on with hardly even the snap of a finger to fetch him attention. The snap of a finger!

The poor bastard had hardly any fingers left to snap!'

The door opened softly and Fiona crept in, a ghostly little wraith in her long flannelette nightdress. 'Niall, are you awake?'

'Ay, and you should still be asleep, you wee wittrock! What ails you at this hour of the morning?' The next moment he felt the slight weight of her on his bed.

'Ach, don't grump at me, Niall. Mother and Father are still in bed and Father being so put upon this whily back I didn't want to waken him in case he would grump at me too. In a way you're the next in line as head of the house so I thought I would ask you if it would be all right for me to get up and go over to Aosdana Bay to see the Jerries off. I'd be back in lots of time for school and if I ran and ran I could catch up with the traps taking the Jerries from the Manse and get a lift. All my friends are going over—'

'*No!*' Niall bawled out the refusal even as his un-injured left arm shot out to grab his little sister by the shoulders and shake her till her teeth rattled. 'Don't you *dare* ask such a thing of me, you wee bitch!' he gritted furiously. 'Do you think it's a picnic? Haven't you had enough of Germans on the island without wanting to go and wave them goodbye? Wave them good riddance more like. Don't you know what they've done! Do you never listen to *anything*? No wonder old Murdoch feels like belting you round the lugs sometimes! It's likely you never take in a word of anything he tries to teach you!'

Shock froze the child's reaction for several stunned

moments, but then she opened her mouth and gave her lungs full throttle. Fiona was a little girl who could throw tantrums at the drop of a hat. They were so devilish and noisy that Niall always dreaded them and was never quite sure how to handle them. He was usually the quiet one of the family, the complete opposite of self-willed little Fiona. Occasionally he smacked her bottom, mostly he simply left her to shout herself out of a temper. But this time it was neither temper nor stubbornness that made her cry. It was pure hurt at him for flying out at her for no reason that she could really understand. Her yells brought him swiftly to his senses and in a mixture of anxiety and shame he pulled her into the cradle of his strong good arm and crushed her soft little mouth against his face. She smelt faintly of lavender soap from her bath of the night before. 'There, there, my babby,' he soothed. 'Weesht, weesht now. I'm sorry, I'm sorry I shouted at you. It's just – some unpleasant things happened a few days ago in Glasgow and I can't seem to forget them. I'm being an irritable old tom cat to everybody.'

'Please don't ever get like Elspeth,' Fiona sobbed against his neck. 'I know she's lonely and that makes her peckle her nose into everybody's business like an old woodpecker and snap at me because I'm the littlest in the house. I can stand it because I have Mother and Father and you when you come home. I look forward like anything to you coming back here because you smile a lot and like all my pets but you're not smiling this time and I hate it!'

He nuzzled her soft fragrant hair and cuddled her closer. 'I promise I won't get like Elspeth,' he chuckled. 'It would be too difficult anyway since she's a woman.'

She giggled. 'Is she? I mean, you would never think it because she's hardly got any bosoms or anything, has she, *and* she's got whiskers growing, they stick out of her face like little stiff pins on a pin cushion. Still . . .' she sniffed, 'she's better than that other old witch that's come in Biddy's place. She and Elspeth are becoming friends. Can you think what life will be like for me then? Old Elspeth biting my head off and Prune Face waiting around like an old Peat Hag for me to take an illness so's she can jag me on the bum! She loves jagging people. Old Malky of Rumhor got bitten on the leg by one of his pigs and Prune Face has already jagged him twice . . . and always on the backside. He says it's no' decent, an auld wife like that looking at men's private parts though I don't know what he means by that 'cos with him being the father of six children his parts couldn't have been all *that* private!'

Niall choked with laughter into her hair. 'You know too much, you wee devil. Look, hush now and coorie in beside me till it's time to get up for school. You can bring me up a cup of tea when you go down.'

As Niall and Fiona rested quietly and watched the day slowly dawn, a bleary-eyed and very subdued Rev. John Gray rudely awakened old Angus, sound asleep under the sofa in the drawing-room, to take charge of Burnbreddie's trap. They were to take the prisoners and soldiers over to Portvoynachan when the Commandos returned with Jon. 'Ach, but her leddy will be wonderin' where I am lost,' Angus grumbled, but the minister would have no excuses and Angus went stiffly to get the horses ready.

When Angus was out of the house, the minister shuffled into the kitchen and sat down at the table, his voice full of self-recrimination and dismay as he divulged to his wife that certain parts of the ceilidh were a complete blank in his mind.

'We all have our weaknesses, John,' Mrs Gray intoned prudishly while her heart surged with delight. 'You are only human after all.' In a neat, grey wool dress, her hair in a prim bun, she was Mrs John Gray, the minister's wife once more, instructions ringing in her ears about the church flowers and other such sober affairs. But nothing could keep the twinkle from her eyes. The ceilidh had opened doors that hitherto she had been too wary to enter, and now she knew that the cloak of convention would never again stifle her individuality.

'But I drank only tea!' His voice was almost a wail. '*You* know that, Hannah!'

'Of course, dear, of course,' she said soothingly but in such a way as to leave doubts in his mind which would never be dispelled.

'Whisky was in that tea, Hannah,' he said accusingly.

She patted his arm kindly. 'Then knowing that you shouldn't have touched it, John. Take your breakfast now before it gets cold.'

Soon after the Rev. had sullenly gulped down his

meal, old Angus rapped on the door to say that the Burnbreddie trap and the minister's own were ready to go. The Commandos and Jon appeared then and the minister insisted on squeezing the prisoners and all of the soldiers into the two vehicles for the trip across the island. Mrs Gray had prepared an early but abundant meal for the departing group, and she watched rather wistfully as the Commandos with their stomachs full and the Germans with theirs empty, for they had not felt like eating much on this uncertain morning, rumbled out into the hazy morning light. She had grown quite fond of her charges and would miss their presence – and the attention they had brought her.

Early though it was, half the population of Rhanna had contrived to be at Portvoynachan on some pretext or other. Because school hadn't yet opened, many of the children, too, were at large, and the normally deserted stretches round Aosdana Bay were reminiscent of a Sunday-school outing.

'My, my, would you look at what's coming now?' old Joe commented, looking up from mending a fishing net draped over a large boulder near the edge of the cliffs.

Jim Jim looked up, his netting needle poised in his hand. 'Ay, ay, the Jerries must be goin' away,' he commented with a bewitching show of innocence.

Canty Tam looked out to sea where, in the soft mist of morning, the grey ghost shape of a naval patrol vessel lurked. 'I wouldny like to be goin' out there in one o' they rubber balloon things,' he intoned, leering at the pearly turquoise of the early sky. 'The Uisga Hags have long claws for tearing things up. Yon rubber is no' safe, no' like a real clinker, the Caillichs will just rip the bottom out on them.'

'Ach, be quiet, man,' spat Jim Jim. 'Or it's your bottom will be ripped. Get hold o' one o' they nettin' needles and make yourself useful for a change.' As the traps came nearer Jim Jim suddenly abandoned his task to move closer to Morag Ruadh. 'You were a long time outside wi' these soldiers last night,' he said conversationally.

Morag examined her long fingers with great interest. 'Ay, you're right there, Father.'

'They wereny doin' you a mischief, mo ghaoil?'

'Indeed, hold your tongue, Father! You mind your own business!'

Jim Jim looked crestfallen but pursued the matter grimly. 'Now, now, Morag, as my daughter you *are* my business. I am hoping you are remembering the identity o' the men you were wi' last night – just in case,' he finished in a daring rush.

Morag tossed her red head haughtily. 'Your mind is blacker than the peats you damp all day. I will not be listening to another word!' She flounced away down the stony track to the bay.

Old Joe watched her and gave Jim Jim a conspiratorial wink. 'She'll have her man yet, Jim Jim. Look now, there she goes, straight to Dugald Ban. These two were more than a mite friendly last night.'

Jim Jim looked at his daughter talking animatedly to Dugald and a smile creased his brown face. 'By

God, you're right, Joe,' he said happily, and leaving his nets once more, went down to join the crowds on the white sands below. When he arrived, the Commandos were retrieving the dinghies from the deep, dry caves that pitted the cliffs. Soon Dunn emerged, a frown creasing his brow.

'One of the dinghies appears to be missing,' he informed the crowd in general.

'Ach, is that not strange now?' Ranald shook his head sympathetically.

'Are you sure you have looked right? It is easy to miss things in these caves.'

'Hardly something so obvious,' Dunn said dryly.

'Maybe it was taken away by a water witch,' Brown said with a smothered laugh. But he hadn't reckoned with the islanders who immediately met the suggestion with an eager barrage of superstitious comment.

'All right! All right!' Dunn cried. 'We'll make do with what we have. C'mon now, lads, get cracking!'

There was a general bustle to the water's edge and the dinghies were lowered into the speckled green shallows. Dunn looked at Tam McKinnon whose undoubted popularity singled him out as the unofficial leader of the island's Home Guard. 'You will keep an eye open at the doctor's house,' Dunn instructed. 'I am relying on you, Mr McKinnon. I know McKenzie of the Glen is the Chief Warden, but his farming duties take up a lot of his day. In a few days' time the military medics will be back to see how the German officer is progressing.'

Tam's face was red with importance. 'We will do a

good job, you can be sure of that, sir. We will make damt sure Mr Bugger will no' run away.'

'And we will make sure that Behag is getting her signals right in future,' Robbie put in, his round face completely cherubic.

'You will *all* get your signals correct in future!' Dunn said sternly. 'No more crossed wires . . . do you hear?' His face relaxed suddenly into a wide grin. 'Thanks, lads, for a great time . . . we'll maybe come back one day for a drop more of the water of life.'

'You'll no' be tellin' a soul – over there,' Tam said anxiously, nodding towards the horizon as if he were referring to another planet.

'Not a soul – scout's honour,' Dunn said solemnly.

Jon Jodl was sitting quietly beside Ernst in one of the dinghies. He looked at the green water lapping the edge of the sand. It was a peaceful morning filled with the tang of peat smoke and salt. Even the seabirds were in a placid mood. A curlew poked for small crabs in the shallow pools; a colony of gulls flopped lazily on the gentle swell of the waves. Above the cliffs the sheep cropped the turf with unhurried intent and two Highland cows watched the scene in the bay with silent interest. Jon looked at it all and swallowed a lump in his throat. For a little while he had found peace on the island. He felt lulled in mind and body. No matter what his future held now, he knew he would never cease to bless the reprieve that the landing on Rhanna had given him. The warmth of tears pricked his eyelids and he swallowed again. 'Farewell Paradise,' he thought sadly. The memory of

Anton strayed into his mind. Dunn and Anderson had escorted him over to Slochmhor before dawn. For a brief moment Anton had opened his eyes as Jon stood over the bed. 'You take care, Jon,' he had whispered. 'I'll see you – sometime.'

'Soon – soon, sir,' Jon had said and left quickly with the Commandos to meet the traps coming down from the Manse. In a way, Jon envied Anton his prolonged stay on the island but he was immediately ashamed of himself for thinking in such a way. Anton was still very ill. The doctor had made a fine job, but Anton had lost some of his fingers. That was not a thing to envy. It could have been him lying there, his fingers gone . . . a musician needed all his fingers to play the piano, the fiddle . . . 'God forgive me,' Jon thought. 'And let Anton get better so that he can enjoy this place the way I have enjoyed it.'

Suddenly he got to his feet, making the dinghy tilt alarmingly. 'Slainte!' he cried wildly. 'To Anton!' His blurring gaze swept over the homely faces of the people who had been so kind to him, and a sob caught in his throat. 'Slainte!' he cried again and Ernst was beside him, echoing the words, quietly at first, then in a great surge of sound.

'Heil Hitler,' Zeitler muttered, but no one heard him because Jon's cry was echoing out joyfully from the gathering on the shore. 'Slainte, Jon! Slainte, Mr Foch!'

Dunn was politely thanking the minister for his hospitality but the great swelling of the Gaelic 'Health!' bouncing from the pillars of the cliffs and reverberating through the caves, drowned his voice.

Dunn turned and stepped into the nearest dinghy and he too took up the cry. Then the crowd rushed to the water's edge to wave and shout and the Rev. John Gray stood alone.

'Slainte!' He heard Jon's voice above the rest, and a hot flush of shame darkened his face. He had been on Rhanna for more than twenty years and never in all that time had he uttered one word of the Gaelic. Jon's stay had been a matter of days and he was proudly shouting the Gaelic to the skies. The dinghies were now little dark blobs on the sun-flecked sea, yet still the cry of 'Slainte' tossed back at the crowd surging round Aosdana Bay.

'Slainte,' the Rev. John Gray whispered and turned abruptly on his heel to hide the red face of humiliation from the world.

Having forgotten now about the goings-on at Portvoynachan, Fiona snuggled against Niall contentedly and thought about Anton alone in the adjoining room. She opened her mouth to tell him how much she liked the young German but her better senses warned her against it and she said instead, 'I like Babbie being here, she's nice and she says funny things. I let her see some of my spiders and she didn't scream like some of these silly big girls do. That stupid Agnes Anderson screams all the time, especially if there's boys around. I love Shona for that too. I'm glad she's home. It means she'll be here a lot because you're here too. I'll hate it when you're married though and likely leave Rhanna. It's a pity people have to get married all the time. I don't think I ever will, you have to do awful things like wash your husband's socks and drawers and some of them have terrible smelly feet. Johnny Taylor is only nine and his feet are . . .'

'Weesht, you wee chatterbox,' he scolded gently. 'You'll wake Mother then *I'll* get skelped lugs for encouraging you.' The child's mention of Shona had brought back all his doubts and self-recriminations. He knew he was the one in the wrong. That it was he who ought to make the first move and go over to Laigmhor to tell her he was sorry. But then he would have to explain about Babbie and at that moment in time he felt he wasn't prepared for more emotional questions, upsets – perhaps even tears. He was too tired mentally and physically to sort out other people's feelings, let alone his own . . .

Half an hour later the house was up and bustling. Elspeth always came at eight o'clock sharp to help Phebie prepare breakfast. With the household's vastly increased numbers there was more work than ever to be done. Elspeth grumbled a good deal over this but her efficiency couldn't be denied and Phebie shut her lips and let the housekeeper ramble on.

A sparkling-eyed Fiona danced up to Niall's room with tea and toast. 'Mother is walking with me to school because she wants some things at Portcull. Elspeth's moaning about the rationing again so Mother's going to try and wheedle some stuff from Merry Mary. Babbie's going over to Tina's to see to her ankle. I think really she's getting out the house quick before Prune Face turns up. When she does you've to tell her to go over to see Todd and Biddy. Mother says it will serve you right for lying in bed!'

'Won't Father be here to tell her?'

'No, he's been called out to Old Malky at Rumhor who sent word that he thinks his leg is going to drop off at any minute with pain . . . so you'll be in the house with Prune Face and Elspeth.' She snorted with ecstatic laughter at the look on his face and didn't hear him mutter, 'Not forgetting Jerry next door.'

Babbie looked in a few moments later to bid him a hurried goodbye and then went to Anton's room, staying there for quite some time before her footsteps clattered away downstairs.

With everyone gone the house seemed very quiet. It was a dewy morning with banks of mist lying in the hollows of the moors and clinging to the mountain tops like big lumps of fluffy cotton wool. Niall felt very peaceful lying there in his own familiar bedroom at Slochmhor. It was what he needed, to be alone, to have time to sort out his thoughts and feelings . . . but it would have been more peaceful still if Anton hadn't been in the next room. Returning from the ceilidh the night before Niall had been tired and drunk yet unable to sleep. Shona, Babbie, Ma Brodie – Anton – they had all crowded into his mind till his head had whirled and he had felt sick, hate curling his stomach into a tight knot. He had never hated anyone before and the things it did to him had frightened him. Yet all through the feeling he had reasoned that he didn't know Anton enough to hate him, it was what the young German stood for that he hated: Britain was at war with the Germans; the Enemy were to be despised for the things they did; Anton was the Enemy – he was to be despised . . .

A terrific thud from the room next door shattered his thoughts. He sat up in bed, his heart hammering into his throat. There was the sound of scrabbling now, and the unmistakable moans of someone in pain. Niall quickly got out of bed, rushed out to the landing, and threw open the door of the spare room. Anton was on the floor, on his knees, his hands clawing frantically at the bedclothes in an effort to get back into bed.

'Christ Almighty!' Niall exploded. 'What in heaven's name are you playing at, man?'

'Playing – no – and certainly not on my knees – praying!' Anton gasped. His face was a ghastly white colour. 'I reached – for a glass – of water – I fell.'

Niall was across the room in seconds, trying frantically to pull Anton upright. Once deposited back on his bed, Anton lay sprawling and panting, his mouth twisted in pain, his bandaged hand groping inadequately for something to hold on to to aid himself upright. Niall saw with alarm that blood was seeping through the wadding across his middle and he said harshly, 'You've hurt more than your pride, Jerry! You're bleeding!'

Anton closed his eyes as he struggled to regain his breath but a bitter little smile twisted his fine mouth. 'Do not concern yourself for me. No doubt it hurt you very much to have to lower yourself to help a Jerry, as you call me, but you do not have to go beyond the call of human decency to do any more for me. Leave me alone now.'

'Too bloody right I will!' Niall said, but with uncertainty rather than anger. In a flash he saw not a German but a fair-haired, blue-eyed youth, very badly injured and undoubtedly in great pain. Then he saw the Iron Cross on the bedside table and his hatred returned anew. 'At least you're lucky you're alive and bleeding! Dead people don't bleed! It congeals too damned quickly once the heart stops beating! You've spilled plenty of blood in your time, now it's your turn! It's called poetic justice!'

As Anton struggled for breath, he allowed Niall to go raving on and heard the words being lashed out at him but did not really take in their meaning. His head felt light, there was a queer sensation in his belly, a feeling of nausea, of burning, of tearing apart. At first his mind was filled only with the sufferings of his body, but at Niall's last words the sufferings of his emotions took precedence. He could take no more: no more hate, accusations, rejections. He felt himself trembling but could do nothing to control it. He shook his head from side to side on the pillow in a demented silent torture of body and soul and gritted his teeth to stop from crying out, but it was useless.

'Will you stop it!' He screamed the words at the ceiling. 'You talk about justice! What the hell do you know about justice? Was it justice that killed my mother, my father? Two little girls who were too young and innocent to think they would ever be killed by a bomb? I loved my family, I still love them! Only they are no more! I will never see their faces again! I will never hear my mother singing or watch my father working in the fields – ever, as long as I live. Heidi – my youngest sister – she was like yours – playing with spiders and frogs and loving her life! I go to bed at night and I see her face, her smiling face! I hear Olga talking about her ambition to be a nurse, to help people who are suffering! I see, I hear – and I cry . . . do you hear me? I cry!' The tears were running unchecked down his face, drenching his neck. He struggled to sit up and even though his eyes were swimming the blue hurt and pain in them seared Niall's soul. 'You are a very angry young man, Niall McLachlan! But I too am an angry young man . . . angry and lonely and wishing at this Godforsaken moment that I had crashed to my death up there in the mountains! What is left for me? Tell me that! Tell me that if you can, damn you!'

Niall put his fist to his mouth and squeezed his eyes shut. 'Oh God! God!' he whimpered in utter despair. He fell to his knees by Anton's bed and buried his head into his plaster-encased arm. His sobs were harsh and dry at first, but then the tears came, flowing endlessly, while his shoulders shook and he rasped for breath. His heart was so full that it felt like bursting, but the tears were like a balm, and the more he cried the calmer his heart and mind became. They cried together for what seemed eternity but what in reality was but a few minutes, Niall on his knees by Anton's bed, Anton lying back on his pillows letting the pent-up tears of many months course freely till the pillows and the collar of his pyjamas were soaked in them.

Anton drew a shuddering breath and choked out, 'Our cup runneth over. We are indeed a lucky pair of fellows.'

The remark was both apt and silly. Niall choked on a mixture of laughter and tears. He lifted his head and looked at Anton's swollen eyes beginning to twinkle in his chalky white face. 'Not a word to anyone about this – do you hear?' Niall said. 'If the lads of the island heard about it I'd never live it down.'

'Do you take me for a fool?' Anton returned, drawing a hand over his eyes. 'Am I going to tell – Babbie for instance – or Doctor McLachlan that while they are out of the house I cry my eyes out . . . "Oh, don't worry about me, Doctor, I pass my time nicely while you are gone – I weep like a baby." He would think I am insane above all else.'

Niall got up from the floor and sat shakily on the edge of the bed. 'You know, old Mirabelle was right,' he said thoughtfully. 'She used to say, "A good greet cures a host of ails", and she's right, it does. I feel as if a lot of poison has just been washed out of my system.'

'A – good – greet?'

Niall laughed, his brown eyes, though swollen, shining for the first time since his return home. 'A Scottish way of saying a good cry cures a lot of troubles. You know, maybe that's how girls get things into better perspective than we do, they cry a lot and seem to see the world through a clearer pair of lenses.'

'Then – perhaps Fräulein Babbie would be the better for a good cry. She smiles her smiles of sunshine but inside – she bottles up.'

'You see a lot of people's feelings, Büttger.'

'I see in her what is inside myself – too much keeping in the thoughts that hurt – that is, until this morning when I had my good greet.' He smiled and his keen blue eyes looked straight at Niall. 'Please, do not call me "Büttger" or, worse, "Jerry". My name is Anton. I think friends should call each other by their Christian names.'

Niall took Anton's hand and squeezed it firmly. 'All right – Anton – later we'll talk some more, keep each other company while we're both convalescing, but right now I'd better get dressed and get downstairs to meet Prune Face and give her the morning's instructions.'

'Prune Face?'

'Nurse Millar,' Niall chuckled. 'Fiona christened her Prune Face which is appropriate, if unkind.'

'Ah, yes, I know the one. She came up to look at me yesterday and I really mean *look*. She just stood in the doorway with her hands folded very primly over her stomach and just *looked* at me. I felt like some sort of exhibit, tagged and laid out for inspection.'

Niall shuffled uncomfortably. 'Ay, well, Nurse Millar isn't the only one guilty of prejudgement – anyway, I'd better get washed and dressed or Mother will come back and clout me on the lugs for being lazy.'

But Babbie's arrival into the room delayed his departure. She looked at the sheepish, tear-stained faces of the two young men and knew immediately that they had made up their differences. She was surprised at the relief she felt, and it added to the sense of well-being she had come away with after her visit to Tina's cottage. The young woman had greeted her with easy-going pleasure and had admitted her into a cluttered small world of lazing animals, jumbled furniture and drowsing peace. But Babbie's professional composure had almost failed her when, over a strupak, Tina had observed casually, 'I am hearing that you are doing a grand job sleeping wi' the German laddie.'

'Not sleeping *with* him,' Babbie had spluttered into her tea, 'sleeping *beside* him, in the same room, to be near him the first night he was so ill.'

'Ach, well, is it no' much the same thing?' Tina stated placidly. 'And working so close to him, healing him and talking with him you will be seeing another side to him that maybe no' even his Jerry friends ever saw when they were all fightin' together. He is just a human being like the rest o' us and though some of them are real Nazis and never think about anything else except killing and winning, this one is quite a young gentleman from what Matthew was after telling me. He will likely be more an ordinary laddie than he is a Hun. It will make it easier for you to forget he is a Jerry, him bein' so nice – and good-lookin' too from all accounts . . .' Tina's eyes sparkled. 'You had better watch out or he will be after fallin' in love wi' you. Men always fall for good-looking young nurses.'

Babbie had said nothing but unworldly Tina had given her much food for thought. They were true, the things Tina had said. Babbie *was* beginning to forget that Anton was a German. In fact she was at the stage when she had to keep reminding herself of the fact in order to remain impersonal towards him. With the passing of the days she knew all too well that his charm was bewitching her, and doubly so because it was a natural rather than a calculated charm, a personal charisma that seemed to reach out and embrace her every time she entered his room. But she had to keep herself aloof, there was no room in her heart for sick young men, no matter how handsome or charming they might be.

Anton's face had lit up at her entrance and his blue eyes had become bluer and deeper as he gazed at her.

'I bumped into Nurse Millar downstairs,' Babbie said lightly. 'She was full of moans about the walk from Biddy's house and told me that she ought to be staying here to be right on hand and that I, if I had any common decency, should pack my bags and move back to Laigmhor. I didn't think poor Phebie or Lachlan would take too kindly to the idea of Nurse Millar under their roof, and just stood there, not knowing what to say, when old Elspeth came to the rescue. She said Nurse Millar was welcome to stay at her house, which isn't too far from here, and the old dear jumped at the offer. I think really she feels too isolated at Biddy's house and as she and Elspeth seem to have become friendly, the arrangement suits them both. They can moan at one another to their hearts' content. Now Nurse Millar is away over to see to Todd and Biddy with something on her face that could actually be described as a smile!'

'Fräu Morrison is a very soft-hearted old lady underneath her steel,' Anton observed, holding up his hand to ward off the barrage of disbelieving comments with which his words were met. 'It is true, she hides it well under a face which shows nothing, she complains about everything – yet – she finds time last night to come up to my room with a bowl of something she calls Benger's food. She frowns at me and tells me I look like death then sits on my bed to spoon the food into me as if I was a little boy.'

'*Never!!*' Babbie and Niall cried simultaneously.

'Oh, but yes. She is a very lonely old woman with a great capacity for love. It is squashed away inside her heart but occasionally – it shows.'

'You are quite the young philosopher,' Babbie said dryly.

'Nothing so grand, Fräulein. I just observe people, that is all, and lying here, with nothing to fill my time, I observe more than ever.' A spasm of pain crossed his face and Babbie was immediately alert.

'Observing you I would guess something is wrong,' she said briskly. 'Where does it hurt?'

'It is nothing,' he said weakly.

'I found him crawling about the room and saw blood on the bandages round his middle,' Niall volunteered somewhat sheepishly.

'And you sit around gossiping like a couple of old women knowing that!' Babbie scolded angrily. 'Och, men! What makes you all think it's brave to tear yourselves apart and then say nothing about it?' She threw back Anton's covers and saw at once the blood seeping through the bandages. His hand was over the wound, as if trying to staunch the blood which was profuse enough to seep steadily through his fingers. 'Oh, let me look!' Babbie cried furiously. 'A philosopher you may be but certainly not a wise one! You've probably gone and burst your stitches. Niall, go down quickly and ask Elspeth for a bowl of hot water . . . and bring some bandages from the surgery!' she yelled after his departing form.

'Fräulein . . . Babbie . . . don't be angry.' Anton laid his bandaged hand on her arm. 'There was something that had to be settled – something far more important to me than a few burst stitches. Do you understand?'

'Ay, well enough,' she replied shortly. 'Now lie back and be quiet, you've talked enough for one morning.'

With the bandages removed and the wound cleaned up Babbie soon saw that the damage wasn't as bad as she had imagined. Only two of the stitches had torn apart but even so, Babbie was in an awkward position. She knew she couldn't get Anton down to the surgery to administer to him properly, but he read her thoughts.

'Do it here,' he told her, 'and please, without ether, it makes me sick and stupid and I've already had enough of it.'

'Oh, but . . .'

'Please – Babbie. I am just beginning to enjoy food again . . . and . . .' he looked at Niall. 'I have some company around me that is just getting interesting.'

'Father has some of Tam's whisky in his cupboard,' Niall said. 'I'll go down and get it.'

Niall fed Anton the whisky while Babbie repaired the damage. He watched Babbie's sure, steady fingers gently but firmly closing up the raw, gaping aperture in Anton's belly and was filled with admiration for her coolness. Anton said nothing. He spluttered on the whisky, gritted his teeth and held on to Niall's arm with such force that the mark of his fingers lay on Niall's flesh in a vivid white pattern. Only when Babbie was finished did she show some reaction, and to steady the trembling of her legs she raised the whisky bottle to her lips and took a good draught.

'God bless Tam McKinnon,' she choked, and Niall followed her example.

'Slainte!' he cried.

'Slainte,' Anton muttered feebly though he had no earthly idea what it meant.

They all looked at one another and smiled.

'Well done, Nurse Babbie,' Niall said softly.

'And Niall McLachlan,' Anton muttered with a little laugh.

Babbie gazed for a moment into Anton's eyes which, though dazed with pain, still shone in his face in all their startling acuity. 'Well done, Anton Büttger,' she said huskily. 'You deserve a medal.'

1291

A flush stained his pale face. 'No more medals, please. Just a good strong "cuppa" as you say, with plenty of sugar . . . that is . . . if it can be spared, of course.'

Later that day Niall went up to Anton's room armed with a pack of cards and an account of an exploit that had happened over lunch and which had almost sent Elspeth away from Slochmhor for ever. It transpired that Fiona had danced home from school simply because sago pudding was on the menu that day and it was her favourite. Phebie had entirely forgotten her daughter's threat of the previous evening about doctoring Elspeth's pudding with frog spawn, and had not been even suspicious when the little girl had volunteered to go into the kitchen to fetch the pudding. But when Fiona had returned, proudly bearing the dish, and had placed it in front of Elspeth, the old woman had stared for a long moment at the lump of white jelly dotted with little black spots wobbling on top of her sago, and then let out a wail that made everyone jump. Without being able to help themselves the entire company had erupted into spasms of agonized mirth, all except Nurse Millar who had glowered at everyone and commiserated with Elspeth in a nasal, monotonous flow of useless adjectives. Phebie had bulldozed Fiona out of the room and into the hall with the intention of spanking her soundly, but on looking at the child's unrepentant grin she had instead collapsed on to the stairs where both mother and daughter had clutched each other in an ecstasy of pure, unadulterated, silent mirth.

The unfolding of the tale made Niall bellow with renewed laughter while Anton clutched his stomach. 'Please, no more, I want to keep my stitches for a while yet. Ah, she is truly a devil, your little Fiona. But, why did she do it?'

'A build-up of many things, but mainly for you.'

'Me?'

'Ay, she was mad at Elspeth for going on about rationing and you being here eating all the food that we don't have and which you were too ill to eat if we did have. But, Fiona's like that. She always protects those who can't speak up for themselves.'

'She is a little girl who goes for the underdog, eh?'

'She is also very fond of you.'

'Then, she is an angel. Heidi – Fiona – little devils with haloes, in Heidi's case perhaps even more appropriate now. But, poor Frau Morrison, she talks only for the sake of listening to her own voice. It is perhaps the only thing she has sometimes to keep her company.'

'Ach well, never mind that now, how about a game?'

'Fine, but you should be with your Shona at this moment.'

'Should I?' Niall said sharply.

'You know it or you would not shout.'

'You know too much, or you think you do!'

'Don't you love her? If she was my girl I wouldn't lose sight of her for a moment. She is very beautiful.'

'Perhaps I – love her too much.'

'No one can ever be loved too much. Listen, Niall,

I don't give a damn whether you take your feelings out on me or not, but don't take them out on that lovely child you call your sweetheart. Because – she *is* a child, Niall,' he went on earnestly. 'You have only to look at her to know that. Eighteen, it is very young, she hasn't yet learned to say "sorry", but you, you are a man, a boy in many ways but the war makes people grow up quickly, with too much of a jolt perhaps, but it does the job a lot quicker than nature intended. So, stop behaving like a spoilt little boy and go and get off your chest whatever it is that makes you moon about by a German airman's bedside instead of facing up to reality.'

'You cheeky Jerry bastard!' Niall grinned.

'I know,' Anton said simply.

'Girls,' Niall said ruefully.

'What would we do without them? So, today, games; tomorrow, Shona. All right?'

'You win,' Niall laughed. 'But I hope not at cards. Hell!' he glanced at his plastered right arm then at Anton's bound fist, 'look at us, like a couple of Egyptian mummies! Bugger it! How are we supposed to deal with these useless things?'

But Fiona, popping her head round the door at that moment, solved the problem. 'Cards! Can I play?'

'You can deal,' Niall said promptly, and he and Anton squealed with joy which was lost on the adroit Fiona who proceeded to deal, called on all the games which she knew best to play, then completely foiled her partners by winning time after time till, exhausted, the men declared themselves well and truly beaten.

'We really ought to play for money,' dimpled the little girl as she whirled out of the room with a triumphant whoop.

Chapter Fourteen

Early next morning Niall met Fergus at the gate of Laigmhor. Fergus looked at Niall's plaster-encased arm and his dark rugged face broke into a smile. 'We have one thing in common – for a time at least.'

Niall leaned against the dyke and looked towards the sea gleaming in the sun-bathed morning. 'There's a lot we have in common, Fergus, though at one time no one would have thought it. For one thing we both love the same girl – with one difference – you know how to get the best out of her. There was a time I thought I could do that too, but growing up has brought changes to us both . . .' He shook his fair head, at a loss how to explain further.

Fergus lit his pipe and stood puffing it for a moment, his thoughts on the last two difficult days during which both he and Kirsteen had talked to Shona about the foolishness of wasting time on petty quarrels and how she had only to cast her mind back to the precious years he and Kirsteen had wasted to realize how time could slip by too easily through pride and misunderstanding. Shona had listened, quietly and respectfully, without any fight or argument whatsoever, which very fact had puzzled and worried both Kirsteen and Fergus because it was so unlike spirited Shona. In the end Fergus had lost his temper and told her she was behaving like a spoilt child and if she ever wanted any happiness out of life then she would first have to learn to grow up and do a bit of giving as well as taking. Losing his temper had been a mistake, of course, because then Shona lost hers also and more or less told him to mind his own affairs. He had been able to sense the misery engulfing her and had wanted to take her to him and hold her close but the barriers had been too firmly up for that and it was with a sense of relief that he now handed the problem over to Niall.

'Take a bit of advice, lad . . .' he said, 'I haven't had a lot of experience with women – God knows I mucked up my own affairs pretty thoroughly – but I've learned that it's no use hanging around waiting for time to sort things out for you, you've got to do it yourself. Time has a knack of changing things, sometimes not to very good advantage. I know my daughter. She's a stubborn wee bitch at times . . .' He smiled. 'What else can you expect from a girl with a father like me? You'll have to show her who's boss, be a little domineering! She's in there now, mooning around, waiting for you – get in there and be firm with her! She can't go running off into tantrums for the rest of her life!'

It was a big speech for someone usually so thrifty with words, and Niall sensed the caring that had prompted it. He gripped Fergus by the shoulder. 'Thanks,' he said briefly then went through the gate and up the path.

Shona was putting away the breakfast dishes. She

had seen him at the gate and kept her back to him as he came through the door. She knew it was a foolish gesture. She had waited for this moment for what seemed eternity. Now it was here and she didn't know quite how to handle it.

'Right now, we'll have no more of your sulks!' Niall said firmly. 'It's a lovely day, just right for a brisk walk over the moors!'

She turned a crimson face, opened her mouth to speak, but he gave her no chance. 'Be quick now, get your peenie off. You'd better wear your wellies, for the dew is still heavy on the grass.' With that, she flew upstairs, her heart singing, and was back in minutes with a blue cardigan over her shoulders.

'Put your coat on too,' Niall told her sternly. 'There's a bite in the wind despite the sun.'

'You sound like Mirabelle,' she laughed happily and they went out into the sunny morning. He put his arm round her shoulders and they walked in silence to the hill track that wound over the high moors. The wind blew against the tough sedge grass, rippling it into tawny waves; green fern curls prodded through the tangle of dead bracken and nebulous webs glistened on the rich carpet of moss at the edge of the track.

On the ridge of a hillock a small group of islanders were already skinning fresh peat hags. Laughter and banter went hand in hand with such work because it involved both sexes. Peat skinning meant a lot of hard work yet a casual observer might have been forgiven for thinking the fun-loving islanders were literally having a picnic. Yet, despite the banter, the hags were worked with a skill that could only be carried out by a people imbued with generations of self-sufficiency. While the men cut deeply into the banks with the broad-bladed rutter the women expertly skimmed off the top layer of turf with flaughter spades. At regular intervals the workers fortified themselves from the milk luggie into which they simply plunged a ladle to fill with thick creamy milk.

'It's early for the skimming,' Niall commented.

'The weather has been so fine here,' Shona said almost apologetically. 'There's a good skin on the hags.'

'Ay, it has been warm for the time of year,' Niall said absently. 'Though I canny say I noticed too much blue skies. Smoke hangs about a long time after the fires have died down.'

Torquil Andrew's voice came floating down and they looked up to see him waving his spade. 'Were you enjoyin' the ceilidh last Sunday, Niall?'

Niall waved and answered in the affirmative.

Shona's head went up. 'So, you had a fine time the other evening, Niall McLachlan!' she said.

'Indeed I did so,' he said defensively.

'And Babbie too, no doubt?'

'I think so. She went home earlier than the rest.'

'And you went with her?'

'No, I did not. Nancy and Archie saw her along. She was tired with one thing and another!' He stopped and faced her squarely, the wind tossing his fair hair into his eyes and whipping at the old kilt he always wore when he came back to Rhanna. 'If you must know, you wee spitfire, I got well and truly drunk at the ceilidh. To put it rudely, I got pissed! And all because of you! Good God, you little bitch! I've longed to see you for months – when I do I find you hanging over a German airman as if you never knew Niall McLachlan was born!'

She stared. 'You're jealous, Niall McLachlan!'

'All right, I'm jealous, dammit! I have a right to be jealous. If I could look at you without trembling I might not be jealous! But I am, and I do, and if that sounds like a lot of seagull shit you can throw it back in my face if it makes you feel better . . . go on then, start throwing!' he finished passionately.

'It was your attitude to Anton,' she said gently. 'I know he's a German – the Enemy – but he's first and foremost a human being and you spoke to him as if he were a bit of cow dung!'

'I know.' His voice was subdued with shame. 'I apologized to him yesterday. After I got home from the ceilidh, I was in my room, drunk as a lord, hating the thought of a German through the wall from me! I spent a good long while feeling sick and hating Anton. I wanted to go through and spew on him! Then the next morning I heard a thud and went in to find the poor bugger had fallen out of bed trying to reach a glass of water. He burst some of his stitches and Babbie had to sew him back up again – all without ether. Later we talked for ages . . . about the war, what it does to people. He's all right is Anton.'

Shona reached up and pushed a lock of hair from

his eyes. 'When I saw him, lying so hurt and helpless, it was you I saw on a bloody beach in France. His face was your face. I had to help in every way I could because, in a way, it was you I was helping. I suppose that sounds silly.'

He laughed then, his brown eyes crinkling with joy. 'The daftest thing in the world, but I love you for it!' He drew her to him and kissed her harshly, his lips forcing hers apart till the warmth of his tongue briefly touched hers.

'Oh God.' Niall breathed into her silken hair. 'I've dreamt of this moment for so long. I want to kiss you forever! Do you think people are allowed to kiss each other in heaven? If not then I'm never going to die!'

Shona laughed gaily. 'I think people kiss all the time in heaven. How else would they know they were there?' She lay against him for a moment then murmured casually, 'And what about Babbie?'

The question took him unawares as indeed she had meant it to do. He blushed and drew away from her, not meeting her eyes. 'Babbie, ay, we must have that out. It's what I brought you out to talk about really.' He sat down on a mossy boulder and idly pulled at the dried heads of dead heather. 'We weren't lying when we said we knew one another only briefly in Glasgow . . . on the other hand we weren't being exactly truthful either. We met on a blind date and before we really knew what was happening had poured out all our troubles to each other. I think we both had wanted just a shoulder – you know the sort of thing. I found out she was married . . .'

'Married! But she doesn't wear a wedding ring!'

'It's on a chain round her neck. Babbie is a very private person. When I met her she had just had word that her husband had been reported missing, believed killed. They had been married only six months when he went to war. At this very moment she is in the most private hell of all . . . not knowing if he is alive or dead. That's why she doesn't wear her ring for all the world to see, she can't bear all the questioning.'

'Oh dear God! Poor Babbie!' Shona cried in anguish. 'I know only too well what she's going through, the terrible suspense, the hoping when you've almost given up hope. It's cruel, so cruel you wish that half the time you were dead yourself yet you have to keep hanging on . . . in case . . . just in case there might be a chance . . .'

'Oh, my darling,' he murmured huskily, 'you understand it all so well. In a way I wish you didn't because it makes the next part so difficult to tell.'

He turned his head suddenly and the rays of the searching sun vividly betrayed the deep purple scar beneath the golden fuzz of hair on his neck. A sob caught in her throat and she had to press her fists to her mouth to stop from crying out that she loved him no matter what he had done. But first she had to know! To hear it from his own lips.

Niall went on talking, his voice barely audible. 'On that date, Babbie and I got a bit drunk. We went back to her flat . . . and went to bed. I wanted to make love to her, I tried to make love to her . . . but I couldn't – my body wouldn't let me betray you. I kept

1303

seeing your face and hearing your voice . . . and – anyway – we both sobered up and felt horribly ashamed but glad that neither of us had betrayed the people we really loved – Oh God,' he lowered his head and hid his face in his hand, his voice breaking on a sob. 'That sounds such a poor way of wriggling out of the fact that we tried to make love!'

Shona didn't look at him or speak and eventually he burst out, 'Aren't you going to slap me . . . or – or shout or *say* something!'

'No.' Her voice was taut with unshed tears. 'I'm going to cry. I try never to cry! It's so silly to cry! Girls cry far too much and I always vowed that I would never be silly – and – and – cry . . . but now I can't help myself.'

And cry she did, the tears pouring down her face, the sobs breaking in all their harsh misery. She cried and sobbed and trembled and he rushed to hold her to him and cradle her head under his neck. 'Weep, my babby, let it all go. Remember what Mirabelle said. Cry, my lovely darling for – I am crying with you,' he soothed brokenly while his own tears washed down unchecked over his face.

Shona gave a watery sniff. 'Don't, please don't love me too much at this moment because I have something to tell you too. When I was in Aberdeen I went out with a couple of boys – one of them I liked very much – so much in fact I began to doubt my love for you. I thought perhaps that we had made a mistake, that when we thought we were in love it was only really a physical thing we had discovered when we grew up. We were so young then, without any experience of any kind. After our little baby died I really began to feel that I would never want you to make love to me again so I started to wonder if I really did love you. I enjoyed the company of this other boy and we went out a good deal. Then one night he tried to make love to me and I was so shocked and horrified that I had let it get to that stage that I bawled at him like a fiend and went into one of my worst tempers. He got such a fright I never saw him again, but I knew after that it was you I loved and always would . . . but I did kiss him and let him pet me a bit – and that's all.'

'So, the odds are even, then.'

Niall's tone was so strange that she looked up at him and giggled.

'So, it's all right for you but not for me. You can be jealous of me but I can't be jealous of you!'

He chuckled. 'Ach, you win, mainly because what you say is true. Will – will any of this make any difference between you and Babbie? She thinks the world of you and was so upset by meeting me on Rhanna that she was all for leaving that night at the ceilidh though I persuaded her against it.'

'If it hadn't been Babbie it would have been someone else,' she said wisely. 'You were ready for the comfort of someone else's arms – we all were. Naturally I will look at her and think of the pair of you together but I'll get over that. In a way I love her more than ever after what you've told me. Of course I won't let on I know about her husband, but at least

I can understand better when she goes into one of these queer green-eyed moods of hers.'

'Ay, I've noticed them, too, and the habit she has of going off to Aosdana Bay. It's one of her favourite places.'

'The Bay of the Poet,' Shona said slowly. 'Yes, one or two people have seen her walking there – alone – always alone. Some of the old folks say she is drawn there by the spirit of the young man who died there long ago.'

'She goes there to have a good think more like. You see, I have an idea she is falling in love with Anton. She doesn't really know it herself yet or is only half-conscious of it and is having to fight with herself to stop it happening. I watched her with him yesterday, all very cool and nurse-like, but when she thinks he isn't watching she watches him with the eyes of a girl who is in love.'

Shona leaned back against a heather-mound in despair. '*That* makes everything a hundred times worse. Her loyalties are with her husband who might be dead and her heart is with Anton who is alive but who will eventually have to leave Rhanna and go off to a prison camp somewhere. Oh, sometimes I wish I was a wee lassie again because being grown up is so complicated and makes everyone else around you complicated too!'

'I know, and we still have one very complicated matter to sort out. Right now I want you to come somewhere with me.'

'Och, Niall,' she scolded happily. 'You know I'd go anywhere with you.'

'Even to the – cave at Dunuaigh?'

Shona immediately recoiled from him. 'No, no, Niall! Don't ask that of me!'

'Please, Shona,' he begged earnestly. 'I have my reasons.'

'Very well,' she faltered unhappily. 'But there are nicer places on a beautiful day like this.'

In days gone by they had sped to the cave on swift, carefree feet but now she was pale and apprehensive as Niall put his arm round her firmly and led her towards the long heat-hazed stretches of the Muir of Rhanna. The sun beat down warmly, the dry heather rasped under their feet. Niall was very quiet. Shona looked at his boyish profile and wondered why he was taking her to a place that had no meaning for her now. They were skirting the edge of Burnbreddie Estate. Very soon they topped a rise and stood looking down at Dunuaigh with the Abbey ruins nestling in a hollow. It was very peaceful. The shaggy sheep of the hill cropped the new, sweet grasses; contented cud-chewing cows sat in the cool shadows of rock outcrops; and in the distance the deep blue of the Atlantic sparkled to the boundless horizon. Shona drank in the scene avidly.

'It's so beautiful here,' she said wonderingly. 'I'd almost forgotten the enchantment of it.'

'Come on,' he said softly and they ran then to the sun-drenched hollow where the silence of forgotten places descended on them in a thistle-down blanket of peace.

'Oh!' Shona was staring at the little birch tree that Niall had planted to mark the entrance to the cave. It was less than a year since her last tortured flight to this place of memories. How eagerly she had looked then for the little birch tree and how near to panic when her desperate gaze had nearly missed the twisted little sapling that had weathered the terrible winds that howled over the moors. She couldn't miss the tree now. Though warped cruelly by the weather it had grown bigger and sturdier, its silver bark shining in the sun, its slender bare branches throwing shadows among the gorse.

Niall glanced at her. 'It's weathered the storms all right. Can we say the same, mo ghaoil?'

But Shona didn't answer. She was running to the cave, pulling back bramble and bracken, snagging her clothes, pricking her fingers, pulling and tearing while the tears choked up into her throat. 'Hey, steady on!' Niall said as he rushed up to her, but she wasn't aware of him. She sat on her heels gazing into the cool, dry cave, going over every little detail that was etched in her memory. Mirabelle's dolls flopped on the shelves, jostling with cups. The cruisie, containing the remains of the candle that had given her light during the agonizing hours of her labour, still hung from its chain; the wickerwork chairs, carried over the moors on a far-off morning of childhood, still sat, one on either side of the rough stone fireplace. And in the corner, the roughly-hewn bed of stone, piled with cushions and a sheepskin rug now grey with dirt. Everything was covered in cobwebs. It was neglected and forgotten, but she looked and remembered: the happy echo of childish laughter; the whispered hopes and dreams; the discovery of carefree young love. She tried to push her mind on further but couldn't. The agony of her lonely childbirth was a blank in her mind and the lifeless body of her tiny son a dim blur almost beyond recall.

Niall slid his arm round her waist. 'Well, my darling little girl, what now are your strongest memories of this place? Sadness or happiness?'

'Happiness . . . oh, so much happiness I can hear the laughter now!' She buried her face into his neck. 'I can look down the years and it's all so real – you and me and dear old Tot . . .' She pulled away to look at him and continued slowly, 'The only thing that isn't real to me is – the – the last time! Oh God! I feel so guilty! It's my last experience of this place, yet it's the dimmest. In my mind I can see Tot with her golden ears covering her white muzzle – yet – I can't see the face of our little baby! Why, oh why can't I?'

'There now,' he soothed. 'I had an idea this place would get things into perspective, that's why I brought you. You can see the old spaniel because she lived before she died . . . our little boy didn't,' he finished gently.

They were quiet for a long moment, and then he asked, 'Well, am I going to be a bitter bachelor all my days or an old married man?'

Shona reached out and touched the scar on his

neck. 'An old married man, so long as you're married to me. You didn't have to bring me here to make up my mind. We've already wasted too much time looking back to things that can't be undone, and we're not going to waste any more. I did a lot of practical thinking while I was waiting for you to come out of the raids and praying you would be safe. Rhanna will give me back my health . . . When I'm ready to go back to nursing – I want to take my full training – and what better place than Glasgow? Being married means terrible things like bills. We'll need money for all that – so don't tell me I can't do it.'

Niall smiled wryly. 'Who ever tried to stop a McKenzie? But I won't have a wife of mine being the sole breadwinner. Glaikit wee Niall will find himself a weekend job . . .'

'And we have Mirabelle's legacy to tide us over at the beginning . . .' Shona caught her breath. 'I wish she was here now, I owe her so much. Oh God! It's wonderful not to feel guilty about the baby any more!'

'He'll come back to us.' Niall took her hands and looked at her with quiet joy. 'We'll have other sons – and daughters – lots of them – we'll fill the world with our children!'

As their shouts of laughter echoed through the cave, he embraced her and they sank to the heather as one, their mouths meeting over and over. His tongue touched hers and she responded wildly.

'My dearest, dearest love,' he murmured unsteadily. 'I feel so lucky to have you back again.' He caught her again and she tilted her head for his kiss, delighting in the firm strength of his young body. Her face was cupped in his hand and she could feel a small pulse beating in his thumb, the rhythm of his life throbbing steadily. She heard a sob catching in his throat and saw that his eyes were clouded with tears, those beautiful brown eyes of his that mirrored so many of his emotions. Now the look was one of tenderest love, his love for her, and she felt herself drowning in his tears, in his love. She had thought she would be afraid to give her body to him again, but love, tears, joy, washed away fear and carried her swiftly on a tide of pure ecstasy. The days of the fumbling, inexpert Niall were far in the past. His body was hard and demanding against hers and his lips moved over her face to her neck and then to the soft flesh above the swell of her breasts. He was no longer an unsure boy. His touch was masterful and certain. He was warm, flushed and powerful in the silence of his searching passion.

His plastered right arm made him momentarily clumsy as he unbuttoned her dress, and they both laughed, but softly, burning with the fires that consumed them. She helped him to undress her and for a moment he drank in the loveliness of her creamy-white body, marred only by the little stretch marks of pregnancy on the soft curve of her belly. With reverence he kissed them, and the feel of his lips on those parts of her made her cry out and close her eyes in an anguish of longing. She wanted to reach out to heaven and take all the pleasures of the universe swiftly and without measure of time. But he

1311

had yet to rouse her to a pitch that would make his own the doubly satisfying. The first time he had entered her body roughly, with thoughts only of himself and his needs. But now, though parts of him were hard, his limbs were tensile and he made her relax too and wait for the exquisite moments to come.

The sun wandered in through the opening of the cave, warm and fragrant with the scents of the moor captured in its rays; an early bee buzzed restlessly in a search for nectar. Far out on the open moor, a curlew bubbled out a song of pure joy, which reached deep into their souls where it was magnified a thousand times till it became a rhapsody to love. And then he went into her, pushing and seeking, while his mouth played with the delicate shells of her ears and he pledged his love for her over and over. They moved together, in the sweet delirium of their joining, washing away all the doubts and hurt of the last few months in soundless tears, and little cries of untamed excitement. The song of the curlew grew in intensity till it reached notes of highest perfection which carried them with it, up, up, to the top of the world, till together they touched the stars, and their cries ringing out, the echoes mingling, and in her greatest moment of agony he kissed the little dew of sweat on her brow and stroked the silken strands of her burnished hair. When it was over they lay together, trembling with reaction till they grew calm and slept, still as one flesh, to one another as a foetus is in its mother's womb.

Later, when Shona opened her brilliant blue eyes,

Niall was watching her, studying the composure of her relaxed little face.

'Why are you staring at me?'

'Not staring, admiring. And congratulating myself for having the good taste that I have. Beautiful children with bodies like goddesses are not thick on the ground, my darling . . . at least, I haven't found it to be so. Now, tell me. You say – or rather you said – you thought you might be afraid to love me again. What are your feelings now on the matter?'

'I think – that we've given in to ourselves again and it's just as well we're going to be married because this sort of thing can't go on . . . but, it was wonderful . . . and . . .' she laughed sleepily, 'you're a young stallion. I couldn't wait – yet I wanted it to last forever.'

His eyes held hers intently. 'It will, my darling, when we're married I'll show you that today was just the beginning – but – no more till then. It's enough at the moment that your fears have been taken away. We'll keep the rest of the treats till there's a ring on your finger. But I warn you now, after our honeymoon you'll be wishing you could have a holiday away from me!'

She shrieked with laughter and smothered his face with a cushion. Then they both got dressed and walked hand in hand into the sunshine.

'Will folks *know*?' she wondered aloud. 'I mean, do we *look* different?'

'Yes, daftie, we do,' he said tenderly. 'We look happy.'

Dodie was coming along the moor track from

1313

Croynachan, carrying a laden creel. He gave a start when he saw them and looked somewhat guilty. 'It's too early yet to be gathering in the peats,' Niall joked.

'Ach, I know that, laddie,' the old eccentric rebuked gently, 'it is hardly even time for cuttin' them. Are you forgettin' these things living in the big city? I am hearin' the fumes o' they motor cars can poison folk's brains and make them forget easy.'

'I was only pulling your leg,' Niall grinned. He paused and looked at Dodie's lumpy face with concern. 'You're looking a bit thin, Dodie. Are you all right?'

Dodie seemed embarrassed by the question and for a long moment looked with sorrowful reproach at the tawny slopes of Sgurr nan Gabhar before stuttering quickly. 'Ay, ay, right enough.'

'Father was saying he hadn't seen you for a while,' Shona said kindly. 'The wee lambs are beginning to come and you always help him at lambing time.'

'Ay well, I've been busy,' he answered evasively, his dreamy eyes raking the far reaches of the moor with unusual impatience.

'I'll help you to carry your creel,' Niall offered, reaching out a hand, but Dodie backed away.

'Ach, no, it is kind you are but I'll be managing fine by myself. I'm after lookin' for Ealasaid too and she might no' come to me if there's a crowd to hand.' Then he galloped away and was soon just a black shape flapping in the distance.

'If it's possible, I'd say old Dodie is acting queerer than usual,' Niall commented thoughtfully, but Shona laughed and linked her arm through his once more.

'He lives in his own wee world and has his secrets like the rest of us. We'd better hurry too for it must be near lunch time . . . and wipe that smile off your face before we get home or folks *will* know we've been up to something!'

Almost a week later Fergus leaned against the dyke and looked beyond the bridge to the hill-track leading to Dodie's house. 'I thought Dodie would have been down to help out,' he said to Kirsteen, Shona and Niall rather irritably. 'We're getting busier here and could be doing with an extra pair of hands. Bob and myself have other things to see to forbye the ewes.' Kirsteen stood beside him, nursing an orphan lamb, giggling as it slobbered greedily into a feeding bottle.

'You're holding it like a *real* baby,' Shona said, smiling as she reached out to stroke the lamb's curly fleece.

'It *is* a real baby,' Kirsteen laughed. 'It's how you must have sooked your bottle, and how Grant did too. He was so greedy he used to have most of the milk finished before I knew he had hardly started.'

'Shona and myself might take a walk over to Dodie's house,' Niall volunteered. 'I'm beginning to wonder about him myself and folks in the village are saying they haveny clapped eyes on him for some time.'

'You usually sit with Anton about now,' Shona pointed out.

'He's getting up today and Babbie is supervising so I thought I'd best keep out of the way.' He crooked his arm to Shona in a dashing manner. 'Will you do me the honour, my leddy?'

They went off giggling and Kirsteen smiled at Fergus. 'They have made up beautifully wouldn't you say, Fergus?'

He kissed a lock of her golden hair. 'Almost as well as we did on a certain night not too long since. I only hope . . .'

'Fergus,' she reproved quietly, 'everything is all right. They are very young and very much in love. You haven't forgotten what that is like, have you?'

'Ay, I'm beginning to . . . let me see, it must be nearly two nights now and *that* seems an age away. You wouldn't fancy a quick scrub in the tub before dinner, would you? I could always do your back . . .' They hugged each other with delight, and then he grew serious, his eyes dark with his love for her. 'Every day I watch you and I thank God for my happy life. Each morning I love you more than the one before which means all our tomorrows will be better than our yesterdays . . . and Good God! Here is me a farmer, turning into a poet. Get on your way, woman, and take the bairnie with you before it bursts with all that milk you're feeding it!'

Shona and Niall walked over the hill hand in hand, occasionally breaking into a run to chase each other like children, and by the time they reached Dodie's cottage they were hot and breathless.

'For goodness sake! What on earth is *that?*' Niall cried, pointing to a ramshackle creation of wood and metal huddled into the bushes near the cottage. The wind soughed through it, rattling metal against metal, eerily whining into cracks in the wood. They didn't need to look too closely to realize that Dodie had built himself a 'wee hoosie' using materials from the wrecked German bomber. The tail piece of the plane served as the roof with the bold symbol of the swastika breathtakingly displayed to the world. Niall and Shona gaped in astonishment, then sped over to examine the monstrosity at close quarters. The door scraped open on ill-fitting hinges. In the middle of the black cavern sat Dodie's large chamber pot, looking like the proverbial pea in a drum. On a small wooden shelf a large assortment of aircraft equipment jostled with a pile of neat newspaper squares. To the right of the chamber pot the control column was stuck into the ground at a crazy angle; propped in a corner was the broken barrel of a gun; under it, decoratively arranged, a band of ammunition.

Shona pointed at the control column and hissed, 'What is *that* for?'

'The mind boggles – but that's not all – look at this! Dodie is certainly going to be well amused when he's using his wee hoosie!' Affixed to the back of the door was an array of plane's instruments looking decidedly incongruous in such odd surroundings.

'Och, he's the limit!' Shona giggled. 'He's made his wee hoosie like the inside of a plane so that he can pretend to be flying when he's in here!'

Niall let out a bellow of mirth which coincided with a terrible bellowing that suddenly erupted from the cow shed. Ealasaid stood in her stall looking greatly distressed and Niall saw immediately that her udder was so distended the veins stood out like knotted rope. 'She hasn't been milked,' Niall said, frowning. 'Something's wrong with Dodie. He would never let Ealasaid suffer like this.'

They raced to the cottage and tiptoed in. They hadn't visited the place since they were children but it hadn't changed. Threadbare curtains covered the tiny windows, ashes spilled from the grate, treasures reaped from sea and land lay everywhere, lovingly gathered by the old eccentric who saw great beauty in the simple things of life. But one difference was immediately apparent. The old rickety chairs had been replaced by two well-upholstered car seats. They sat, one on either side of the fireplace, comfortably ridiculous-looking. Various other car accessories were scattered round the room and Shona held her breath in delight. Madam Balfour's car was one of two cars on the island; the other was owned by Lachlan.

He had been talked into buying it by a doctor acquaintance who was shocked to find his colleague still using outdated modes of transport. After much persuasion Lachlan had acceded to the suggestion of a car, but he felt embarrassed and out-of-place in a vehicle that made all eyes turn, and he began to find the car more trouble than it was worth. Machines of any sort were regarded with amused suspicion on Rhanna. Few of the men were mechanically minded, including Lachlan himself who found it easier to manipulate a horse or a bicycle than he did a contrary starter motor. Moreover, with the advent of war, fuel became difficult to obtain and the car had since lain in a shed, and was used only for the most urgent cases on the farthest corners of the island.

Like Lachlan, the young laird, a keen horseman, seldom used his car, which had been purchased at his mother's insistence that 'people of our standing ought to have a car'. But unlike Lachlan, Madam Balfour revelled in the attention paid her when her son drove her round the bumpy island roads. However, with his going she could find no one else willing to drive the vehicle. Angus, the aged groom, had been shown how to drive, 'Aying' his way through a course of instruction, but he had tucked the knowledge away in the farthest recesses of his mind in the hope he would never have to use it. Used to a lifetime of caring for horses, he resented the space the car took up in the stable buildings. Madam Balfour had been furious when he had refused to recover the car after the Commandos had left it near Croynachan, and by the time she had coaxed Lachlan into fetching it, it had been completely dismantled. Only the chassis and the body shell had been left to rot on the Muir of Rhanna.

It had been difficult to lay blame at any one door, and finally Madam Balfour had tried to enlist the services of Dugald Donaldson who was a retired policeman. But he had refused to get involved and eventually she had contacted the Stornoway police, from whom she was now awaiting an official visit. Rhanna was visited seldom by a policeman. The one who usually came was related to nearly everyone on

Rhanna and spent his time ceilidhing at relatives' houses. But it had been rumoured that 'Big Gregor' had been transferred to Mull, and when Madam Balfour's plans became known there had been a scuffle to cover up any little misdemeanours that might warrant investigation. Tam McKinnon had been particularly disturbed by the news and had made haste to transfer his 'still' back to Annack Gow's secret room inside the blackhouse. A delighted Annack had been only too willing to oblige, and once again her secret room was fully operational, as it had been in the days of her forebears.

Thinking back on all those events, Shona smiled to herself as she looked round the room. She knew that no official being would hazard a visit to Dodie's cottage and she hugged herself with glee at the idea of his getting away with a large share of the spoils.

'Are you about, Dodie?' Niall cried and was rewarded with a soulful 'He breeah' from a door leading out of the kitchen. They went up a short passageway, hung with driftwood cupboards, and came to the bedroom. Dodie's particular odour pervaded every cluttered corner. His old mackintosh hung from a hook on the door over a layer of tattered oilskins. Under the window stood his huge wellingtons and Shona rushed forward to throw open the sash, allowing the fresh, clean air from the moor to swoop in and absorb the smell.

'Ach, dinna open that window!' Dodie cried in alarm. 'I'm just about dead wi' cold as it is!' He was terribly embarrassed, cowering under the threadbare sheet like a frightened animal. He was a pathetic sight with his gaunt, grey face covered in stubbly little patches of hair. On a locker by his bedside a Delft cup held ancient dregs of tea, and on a saucer beside it two mouldy crusts adhered to a festering slice of cheese. Grimy tears coursed down the sunken indentations of his face, his mouth was twisted in pain and a band of perspiration glistened beneath the rim of his greasy cap.

'I have a terrible bellyache,' he wailed, scrubbing his tears with one hand and rubbing his middle with the other. 'It's been on me for a time now but it has just got worse this whily back. I'm near dyin' wi' the pain . . . and – Ealasaid, my poor beastie, is ill too. I havny been able to rise out my bed to milk her. She's roarin' in pain and breakin' my heart hearin' her.'

'I'll go and milk her now, I saw a bucket in the shed,' Shona said, thankfully escaping the room.

'And I'll go and fetch Father before he finishes in the surgery,' Niall added quickly. He eyed a heap of gay patchwork quilts lying on an antiquated bride's kist. 'Would you like some of these quilts on the bed, Dodie? You're shivering.'

Dodie looked terrified. 'No, no, I dinna want them! Just shut the window.'

Exasperated, Niall banged the window shut and turned out of the cottage. Leaving Shona to keep an eye on things he ran back over the hill track to Slochmhor. He found his father at once, and having managed together to get the neglected car started, they hurtled over the narrow track, the sound of the roaring engine making the crowd at the peat hags stop work as one.

'An emergency, just,' commented Erchy.

The others nodded in sad agreement. 'The doctor is having a busy time these days,' was the general verdict.

'Who will it be?' wondered Kate.

'Lachlan will see them along,' Jim Jim said with conviction.

'If the Lord spares them,' Isabel sighed sagely.

There was a move towards the milk luggie where creamy milk was amiably dispensed, together with much speculation about the 'emergency'.

When Lachlan arrived the hens were squawking dismally in the kitchen while Shona boiled a rather sparse 'hen's pot' over a fire made up hastily with cinders and kindling. She knew Dodie would be embarrassed by her presence and Lachlan went alone into the bedroom.

'You dinna have to look at me, Doctor,' the red-faced Dodie sobbed. 'I know fine what ails me.'

'Indeed, and what might that be, Dodie?'

Dodie looked with horror at the pile of patchwork quilts. 'It's *these*! I know it's these! I've been *smitted*, Doctor!'

'Smitted with what?' Lachlan saw how distressed the old eccentric was and his voice was gentle.

'With *Shelagh*! You mind, Doctor, she always said it was the winds she had, but I know fine what killed her.'

'But, Dodie, that was years ago,' Lachlan protested.

'I don't see what it has to do with your condition.'

'I have it, Doctor, the cancer! The same as Shelagh. Before she died she told me I was to have these lovely quilts made by her very own hands. After she passed on I took them . . . just to please her because she was always my good friend. My, but they were warm right enough but I havny used them since my bellyache started.'

Lachlan sat down on the bed which sagged alarmingly under the extra weight. Patiently he explained. 'You don't catch cancer, Dodie. It isn't a germ like a 'flu or cold. Please believe that. I'll examine you and tell you what I think you've got.' Despite vigorous protestations he proceeded with the examination, inwardly shocked when he saw how thin Dodie was. A few minutes later he looked up, a warm smile lighting his face. 'Stop worrying, Dodie, you don't have cancer but you do have an ulcer, probably a duodenal.'

Dodie looked terrified. 'Ach, Doctor, that sounds worse than the other!'

'It won't be with proper treatment and diet. What on earth have you been eating, man?'

'Nothing, Doctor.'

'*Nothing!* But you must be eating something!'

Dodie turned his face to the wall and his big calloused hands worked nervously on the sheet. Lachlan felt a great surge of remorse and compassion for the old man. His life had been one of misfortune from the start. Against all odds he had battled on, catering for his simple needs by the sheer hard work that had been his lot since he was old enough to hold a spade. Everyone on the island genuinely liked him, but his fierce independence made charitable acts difficult and he was more or less left to his own devices. It never occurred to anyone that the show of independence might be a form of pride born in a man deprived of the basic things in life that everyone else took for granted. His was a big heart with a great capacity for loving all the creatures, great and small, that God had put on the earth. In his simple world he had created for himself a life far happier than that of many who had all the obvious requisites. But it was a lonely existence and no one needed to be that lonely.

'Come on, Dodie,' Lachlan coaxed, taking one of his big hands and squeezing it reassuringly. 'You can tell me, I'll understand.'

'Och, Doctor, I'm starvin' so I am! I used my ration book to help light the fire one morning – I didny know what it meant for I canny read things in the foreign language. When I went to Merry Mary's for my messages, she asked me for it and I didny like to tell her I burnt it. She would think I was daft, and it bein' a Government thing I thought I would get into trouble so I just stopped goin' to the shop. My tattie crop was a bad one last year and all but ran out on me after the New Year. Then that big Jerry wi' the square head burst in on me and ate everything that was left . . . even the few neeps that I had. My poor hens have gone off the laying without the right food – it's terrible to see them starvin' to death.'

'You could have boiled one to yourself, Dodie.'

'Och, no, never! I wouldny kill the poor beasts!' Dodie was horrified at the suggestion.

'So, you had only Ealasaid's milk?' Lachlan said quietly.

'Ay, but never even that sometimes for she has never been the same since that big German chiel hurt her udder tryin' to get milk out o' it.' He put out a big hand. 'Doctor, it's my baccy I miss most. You wouldny have a wee bit – would you now?'

Lachlan extracted a tin from his pocket. 'You keep this, Dodie, but don't chew any till you've had a bite to eat. It's not the best thing for an ulcer but it will do wonders for your peace of mind. Now put your clothes on. I'll take you down in the car to Slochmhor.'

'But . . . what about Ealasaid?' came the inevitable wail.

'One of the lads will drive her down.' Lachlan's smile lit up his boyish face. 'How would you like to go and stay with Mairi for a wee while?'

Dodie's face glowed through the tears. 'Mairi,' he breathed happily.

'Ay, you know how she loves looking after people. With Wullie away she's at a loss . . . You and Mairi get on fine together, and she'll put Ealasaid in with Bluebell.' Lachlan was rewarded by Dodie's radiant eyes. He knew he wasn't taking a liberty, because Mairi had often confided to him her desire to give Dodie 'a good bit loving care and plenty food.'

Lachlan went out to explain matters to the young

people who were tidying the kitchen.

'Poor old Dodie,' Shona breathed.

'It's up to all of us to see this never happens again,' Lachlan said. 'He could have died up here and no one the wiser.'

Niall swallowed hard. 'Surely – Erchy must pop in sometimes with the mail?'

'What mail? I don't think Dodie has ever had a letter in his life. Just now I noticed a picture postcard above his bed. It was tattered almost out of recognition by continual handling . . . probably the only postcard he's ever had.'

They went outside and stood silently, each appalled and saddened by their thoughts. Niall looked at Dodie's pitiful attempt to build a 'wee hoosie' in order to be like the majority of the islanders, and he said huskily, 'Come the summer Dodie will have the finest wee hoosie on Rhanna. I asked Wullie the Carpenter last night if he could give me a job during my summer holidays. I should learn how to knock a few nails into wood. I'll get some of the lads to help me. We can scrounge some bits and pieces from Tam. He has a shed full of junk.'

'Good idea,' Lachlan approved.

Just then Dodie appeared, apologetic because he had taken some time to gather together his most treasured possessions into a large, spotted hanky.

'My hens, what about my hens?' he whispered, holding on to a gatepost for support.

'They'll be looked after too,' Lachlan said patiently and bundled Dodie into the car.

When they arrived at Slochmhor, Dodie underwent the rigours of a steaming carbolic bath, but the comforts that awaited him more than made up for such indignities. For the first time in his life he was made to feel cherished and important and was the first to admit he owed it all to a 'leddy'.

Part Five

Rhanna
Spring 1941

Chapter Fifteen

Shona walked quickly over Glen Fallan to Slochmhor. Anton was leaving the island next day and Niall had asked Shona to come over to the house early because he had planned some sort of outing. They were all sorry that the young German was going. Lachlan had kept the military medics at bay with various plausible excuses but there was no denying that Anton was now fit enough to go.

The April sun cascaded over the countryside, the heat of it abundant for the time of year. The air was fragrant with the scent of clover, crushed by the frolicking hooves of the lambs scattered in the fields, and Shona lifted her bright head and breathed deeply. She loved the spring, with each day bringing the promise of the long, golden summer ahead. The last few weeks with Niall had been full and happy. In a way, they both seemed to be getting to know each other all over again. Sometimes the past loomed very near, at others it was so far away it was like a dream, a mad jumble of hurried moments in which everything happened too quickly for there to be any lasting impressions.

Shona's thoughts drifted as she went up the path to the house. As she expected, it was very quiet. Phebie had worked so hard the day before, preparing for the surprise ceilidh they would hold that night, that Lachlan had decided to leave his patients to the tender mercies of Nurse Millar and take Phebie away for a day off. They had gone off with Fergus and Kirsteen to picnic in one of the sheltered coves near Croy. Elspeth, too, was away. She had passed Laigmhor earlier on her way to the shops at Portcull, and now Slochmhor looked rather deserted nestling against tall green pines.

When Shona reached the kitchen she saw Niall standing outside the kitchen door with Babbie in his arms, her head resting on his shoulder. He was stroking her fiery hair tenderly and she was leaning against him crying quietly. In her hand fluttered a buff envelope and Shona remembered that Erchy had gone whistling away ahead of her up the Glen. That envelope! Those tears! So unlike cool, self-possessed Babbie to cry. A pang of jealousy shot through Shona's heart at sight of her friend in Niall's arms but she knew she was being unreasonable, that something had happened to cause the scene.

Niall looked up suddenly, saw her standing there, and pushed Babbie, who hadn't seen Shona, gently into the house. Then he came dashing back to grab Shona's arm. 'Listen, something's happened. I can't tell you now because I want this morning to be special for everyone.'

Shona looked into his honest brown eyes and wanted to tell him that she knew, that he didn't have to pretend, but instead she said, 'All right, Niall, let's make it special. What do you want me to do?'

'Just behave normally, that's all . . . No, listen, Shona, we're all going away for the day . . . you, me, Babbie and Anton. We're all going over to Portvoynachan in Father's car. Babbie wants to go to Aosdana Bay.'

'The Bay of the Poet again. Yes, Niall, I understand, but who will drive the car? Anton isn't quite up to it with half his fingers gone.'

'I will – I learned in the army.'

'But – your arm . . .'

'Never mind my arm, I'll manage.' He looked at her pleadingly. 'You saw me with Babbie just now but I want you to trust me, darling – and – and no matter how you feel right now act as if you're having the time of your life! Laugh, sing – anything. I'll tell you why later!'

They collected the bulging picnic hamper Phebie had left on the kitchen table and then went to the shed where Lachlan kept the car.

'Does your father know you're taking it?' Shona asked quietly while a strange feeling of dread squeezed icy fingers round her heart.

'No, it only really occurred to me after he left and Babbie mentioned Aosdana Bay. I had intended getting one of Ranald's boats out for the day, but don't worry about Father, he'll understand – he always does.'

Babbie came out of the house with Anton leaning on her arm and she remembered suddenly the first day she had got him out of bed, surprised at how tall he was, how the trusting feel of his thin arm round

1333

her shoulder had made her quite suddenly want to cry. He had laughed a little and been embarrassed at having to rely so much on her help. His smile had reminded her of another young man, the fleeting, anxious smile of a very new and youthful husband leaving her behind at the station, the sight of his beloved face at a window, a million years of love in his eyes . . . mixed with fear and doubt as they both wondered if that farewell kiss might be their last . . . then the whistle blowing, his eyes gazing into hers wordlessly as the train pulled away . . . his hand raised – and soon the face that she loved just a dim little white blur framed in the carriage window of the train taking him out of her life. His body had been hard and strong – as Anton's was now, now that he was recovering his strength a little bit more every day . . .

'I will give you money for your thoughts.'

His voice brought her out of her reverie and she forced a laugh. 'Only a penny. They might be worth more, but only to me.'

They all piled into the car, Babbie and Anton in the back, Shona beside Niall at the front.

'I'll steer with my left hand,' Niall told Shona laughingly. 'And you can work the gears . . . Don't worry,' he stemmed her protests. 'Fiona could do it, it's so easy. I'll be working the clutch with my foot. It's a simple matter of coordination, mo ghaoil.'

She forced the laughter he had requested, but as they got going on the journey she found herself responding to him with a spontaneity that was entirely natural. Niall was in a wild, abandoned mood.

His head was thrown back, his brown eyes sparkling as the car hurtled over the rough moor road. Just outside Portcull, the road was no more than a horse track over high cliffs whose basalt columns dipped into the swirling sea far below. At times the way was so narrow it seemed a certainty that the offside wheels would career into thin air. Natural corrosion had eaten away the soft crumbling earth on the clifftops, which were now held together by only a tangle of roots. To the nearside was a deep soggy ditch flanked by stony turf, and on the narrow grass verges groups of cud-chewing sheep stared un-blinkingly into the distance. Rhanna sheep gave no precedence to anything on wheels. The island was theirs to roam as they liked and the noisy motor car was just another intrusive object to bleat at with disdain.

Niall weaved the car around potholes and seemed not to notice the horrific drop to the sea. For a time everyone was silent but soon the road began to wind over the moors and they all began to sing, the jolting of the car distorting their voices and choking the merriment in their throats. Anton and Babbie clutched each other, the former lapsing into German in his excitement. His pale, handsome face sparkled, and he chuckled as Babbie, thrown against him time after time, finally gave up the effort of trying to stay upright. She leaned against him and they both jolted in unison.

Niall began to sing a Gaelic song and immediately everyone else took up the tune despite the fact that they didn't know the words. It was a discordant mêlée but no one cared. They were all mad and young together, their voices careering out over the moors, tossed by the fresh spring breezes into a wild concoction of sound. Crofters stopped work to watch the passing 'contraption', and rosy-cheeked children stood by the wayside to wave at it solemnly.

'This day will last forever!' Anton cried, his arms embracing the world.

'Forever and ever!' Babbie echoed, while tears of sadness and joy clouded her mysterious green eyes.

Soon they reached Aosdana Bay, which was drowsing in the quiet of morning, its silver-white beaches inviting them towards the effervescent blue sea.

'C'mon, I dare you all to have a paddle!' Niall said sitting down on a rock to pull off his boots and stockings, and in minutes a variety of footwear dotted the sands and everyone was dancing to meet the foaming surf, shrieking in agonised ecstasy as the freezing water splashed their naked skin. They joined hands and ran to meet each wave, and though skirts were tucked into knickers and trousers rolled to knees, the hems were soon soaked.

For a time the world was theirs to command. Blue sky and sea reeled round as they danced. Aosdana Bay belonged to them. The beauty of youth reflected gloriously in each bright face in those carefree moments. Two fiery-haired girls, two fair young men, pranced together like children and though one of them was a German it mattered to none of them.

'Oh, I'll have to stop,' Babbie gasped eventually. 'Remember, you're just babies compared to me. I can't keep up.'

'I am twenty-four, Fräulein, older than you,' Anton pointed out soberly.

Babbie smiled carelessly. 'Men are slower to grow up. To me you're just a boy.'

'The day I joined the Luftwaffe I became a man,' he said with dignity but she merely smiled because he looked like a small boy in the huff. When Niall went with Anton to retrieve the hamper they had left in one of the cool caves, Shona said quietly to Babbie, 'You'll miss Anton when he's gone, won't you? You've been closer to him than anyone else these past weeks.'

'He has to go sometime,' Babbie said before turning away to spread a rug over the sand.

Niall and Anton returned shortly, and then they all feasted on chicken sandwiches and fluffy scones, and afterwards lay down on the warm beach. Shona turned her head to look at Niall and his hand came out to squeeze hers till it hurt, the strength of his love reaching out to her, but a moment later he jumped to his feet and pulled her up with him. 'C'mon, lazy,' he said lightly. 'You know we said we would pay Alasdair Robb a visit.' Shona began to protest but he led her away, saying casually over his shoulder, 'We'll see you two about an hour from now. Don't be running away, Anton. Remember you're in my charge.'

When they reached the top of the cliff Shona turned on him. 'Niall, if I didn't know you better I'd say you were going a bit daft! I thought we were out for a picnic.'

'And it seems I don't know you at all, Shona McKenzie. I credited you with a pretty keen sense of perception.'

'You mean – it's true about them then?'

'It's so obvious I thought the whole of Rhanna knew. Mother and Father saw it long ago. They're daft on each other though neither has yet admitted it to the other. She's mad on him – yet her heart is breaking because – of circumstances.'

'Oh God, I love you, Niall!' she breathed, drawing him into her arms and laying her warm cheek against his.

'We're lucky, my darling,' he said softly. 'We've had time to know what love is like. And how much better it will be with the passing of each day . . . They have only a little time left, which is why I wanted them to make the most of it. Can you imagine what it's like? To be in love and never to be alone together?'

'There is something else, though, isn't there? That letter in Babbie's hand earlier? It brought back a memory to me, one I want to forget . . . a letter in a buff envelope telling me you had been reported missing, believed to be killed. I was in Slochmhor alone, it was quiet and deserted, the way it was this morning when Babbie got her news . . . It was about her husband, wasn't it?'

'Ay, it was to tell her that he had been definitely classified as killed in action. The waiting for her is over but it doesn't stop her feeling as if she is breaking in two – one part of her crying for the young husband who is dead now – the other loving Anton but everything in her fighting against it because to admit it will make her feel a traitor. She's got a lot of loyalty in her has Babbie.'

Shona felt drained with sadness. 'And we thought we had troubles,' she whispered.

He kicked the ground fiercely. 'Life can be a damned cruel thing sometimes. She comes to a remote Hebridean island to nurse her hurt and anxiety over her husband and ends up falling in love with a German airman. Ironic, isn't it?' His brown eyes were dark pools of compassion and she drew him into her arms once again. They clung together in the warm, sweet heather and cried for two young people with so little time left to love.

Anton watched Shona and Niall disappearing over the line of the cliffs and then twisted round to take Babbie's cool little hand. 'You are shivering, Fräulein. Are you cold?' he asked in his attractive broken English.

She shook her head, her oddly mysterious eyes clouding with the sting of tears. 'Not cold – happy in a sad sort of way. It's been a wonderful day . . . thanks to Shona and Niall.' She looked down at his hand resting in hers. The three little stumps of his lost fingers had healed beautifully but the sight brought a sob to her throat. 'What will happen to you, Anton?'

He shrugged. 'I do not know. A camp, in Scotland or England. It doesn't matter. My home was in

Germany with my family. I don't pine for a place where they are no more.'

'Poor Anton,' she breathed softly.

Anger flashed out of his blue eyes. 'I hate pity! Please don't pity me!'

'I don't pity you, Anton, I was thinking how strange everything is. In a way we are both orphans. No family for either of us to go home to.'

'Babbie.' His voice was soft again. Very gently he touched her hair where the sun turned it to fire. 'Your hair, it is like summer. Whenever I think of you I will think of a summer sun blazing red at the end of the day. These weeks you have nursed me like an angel.' He smiled. 'You also make jokes like a little devil. I have laughed – and looked – and – loved . . . *Liebling.*' The endearment made her heart beat rapidly and she couldn't trust herself to look at him. '*Liebling*,' he said again, his voice barely audible. 'I love you and you know it. Niall gave us this time alone together – you know that, don't you?'

'It – it looks that way. He came to Rhanna like a young warrior – now he plays at Cupid,' she whispered, looking up then at the clear-cut structure of his handsome young face so that she would remember it for the rest of her life.

Slowly, he leaned towards her and she shut her eyes to feel his lips caressing her eyelids and when his mouth came down on hers she made no resistance. Instead she put up her hands to trace the curve of his ears, tenderly urging him to kiss her harder. They were timeless moments. The gulls mewed softly, the sun beat down warmly, the creamy foam of the incoming tide rattled the tiny shells of the smooth white sands.

He undid the top of her dress and played absently with the little gold ring attached to a chain round her neck. 'Did it belong to someone you loved?' he asked tenderly. 'My mother had a ring her grandmother gave her and she, too, wore it round her neck on a chain.'

'Yes, someone I loved,' she said tensely.

'*Liebling.*' His voice was taut with passion. He touched the softness of her breasts and she cried out, wanting him to love her but afraid that he would hurt himself. A soft dew of tears shone on his fair lashes. 'Please, Babbie, let me love you – tomorrow I go away – let today last forever.'

She was unable to resist his pleas. 'All right, Anton, but gently – for your sake.'

With trembling legs they walked to the great columns of rock beside the caves. There, in the shadow of the sentinel pillars, he made love to her with such tender devotion she had to press her knuckles between her teeth to stop from crying out in those exalted moments. When it was over they lay quietly, Anton in Babbie's arms, his head pillowed on her breasts. The peace of Aosdana Bay, that had, in years gone by, inspired love, hope and finally tragedy in a lovelorn young poet, washed into the souls of the two lovers with so little time left to love. They listened to the timeless wind and tide that had swept the Bay for aeons past and both of them knew these were the memories they would carry into eternity.

But their time together was coming to an end and Anton finally broke the spell of silence. 'Babbie, I want to ask you to be truthful to me. Our acquaintance has been very short yet my feelings for you are so deep it seems you have always been in my heart. If I am lucky enough to be sent to a Scottish camp then we wouldn't be so far apart. Could you – would you – wait for me?'

The welling of her tears drowned out the world for a moment and it was while she couldn't see the love shining in his eyes that she managed to say lightly, 'Och, c'mon, now, Anton, be realistic! You'll forget all about me in a little while. Young men always fall in love with their nurses. It's a part of convalescing.' Still she couldn't see him but she heard the deep hurt in his reply.

'Forget you, Babbie! How can I forget today – yesterday? You can't forget love! But perhaps – I just imagined that you loved me too.'

'You will forget, Anton, and some day you'll meet a really nice girl.'

'I don't want a nice girl – I want you!' he cried passionately.

She smiled through the mist of tears. 'That's not very complimentary, Anton.'

He was angry now, his blue eyes bewildered. 'You know very well what I mean! Good God, Babbie . . .' He spread his hands in appeal. 'Don't play games with me now. Tomorrow I must leave this island – I want to know what you feel for me!'

She turned away from him because the pleading in his eyes was taking away all the resolution in her breaking heart. 'I – my dear Anton – I feel a great affection for you, but . . .' Her voice broke on a sob. 'That's not enough for the thing you ask of me.'

He slowly got to his feet and stood looking down at her. 'Thank you, Babbie, at least you are truthful,' he said huskily. 'I will always remember today – even though you may forget.' He lifted his head proudly and she stared up at him outlined against the blue sky, tall, slim, fair threads of hair glinting in the sun, already a million miles away from her.

Niall and Shona appeared on the skyline then and Anton cried brightly, 'Hey there, you two, you are just in time! I was beginning to miss my escort. You have grown on me like a bad habit!'

It seemed that the whole of Portcull was crowded into the parlour at Slochmhor for the ceilidh. Most of the menfolk had donned kilts for the occasion, anxious to show Anton what a real island ceilidh looked like. Todd had recovered sufficiently from his appendix operation to be there complete with bagpipes though Lachlan warned him not to blow on them too hard or he would do himself an injury.

'Ay, and we're no' wantin' any more of the Ballachulish bagpipes for a whily,' put in Biddy who had hobbled along on sticks and was back to her usual grumbling good nature.

Todd looked uncomfortable. The 'Ballachulish Bagpipes' was Biddy's quaint way of referring to an enema, and the memory of Nurse Millar 'wi the tubes' was still keen on his mind.

It was a laughing, carefree gathering and Anton looked round at all the faces that had become so familiar and so dear to him and he felt a lump rising in his throat. This ceilidh tonight was in his honour and he felt like laughing and crying at the same time. The room was cosy with a peat fire leaping in the hearth and lamps burning softly, giving a glow to the colourful array of tartans. The womenfolk had changed out of rough homespuns and were wearing dresses of softest wool in a variety of rainbow hues. Some wore tartan shawls, caught at the neck with Cairngorm stones encased in silver. The skin of these island women was, in almost every case, soft and dewy, flushed into rosiness by generous amounts of good, clean Hebridean air which was about the only 'cosmetic' that any of them had ever known. Even the men had this fine complexion, a sparkling look about them that made their faces come alive and their eyes glow with the joy of their living. The freshness was not taken away by advancing years and indeed many of the old ones had only snowy locks and wisdom in their eyes to show for the years they had been on earth. Agility was another thing common to both old and young and it was no surprise to anyone that old men of ninety still worked a croft and old women of the same years ran a home with complete thoroughness and tended their animals into the bargain. If one of their kind was taken from their midst at the comparatively young age of sixty, heads would shake sadly and they would tell one another, 'And him in his prime, wi' all his life in front o' him.'

Anton had noted all these facts long ago and he sat in the midst of the Rhanna folk and wished that he could stay with them for the rest of his days, to discover the secrets that made for contented minds and to be rewarded with the elixir of youth that the simplicity of life on Rhanna seemed to bring.

Tam had brought along a good supply of 'the water of life' and glasses were filled with the amber liquid, chinked together solemnly in those first sober moments, while cries of 'Slainte' filled the room.

Babbie had not wanted to come down but had been persuaded to do so by Shona, and now she sat in a corner, hardly daring to look up for fear she would meet Anton's blue, questioning gaze.

The fiddles began to play and soon the room was filled with haunting melodies that spoke of the ocean and of young men who had died in treacherous seas while out with the fishing boats. After the fiddles came the rousing tunes of the pipes and soon everyone was up dancing, 'hooching' with wild abandon, a swirling mass of tartan kilts, fine hairy legs and flouncing skirts.

Fergus whirled Kirsteen round in a gay eightsome reel, his deep laugh booming out, so unlike the Fergus of yesteryear who had sat alone in corners during times like these, brooding over the girl he thought he would never see again. Now, here she was, one minute out of his reach, the next, warm and desirable in his grasp, her golden hair shining, her white teeth flashing.

'Don't whirl me so fast, Fergus,' she protested at one point. 'I'm dizzy enough as it is.'

'Do you think it's true then?' he murmured delightedly, 'the thing you told me on the thirteenth night of last month?'

'If it isn't then my name is not McKenzie!'

Everyone seemed to have a partner and the two who might have made the happiest partners of all sat miserably alone in their respective corners, pretending to be enjoying themselves, smiling without the smiles reaching their eyes – apart, yet so aware of each other's presence they might have been locked in the other's arms, whispering the words of love that so overflowed in their hearts.

'You'll be having another dram, Mr Bugger?'

Anton smiled up at Tam and accepted a fill of the Uisge-beatha. 'Thank you – Tam, and please, don't call me that – my name is Anton. You are Tam, I am Anton.'

'Ach, of course you are, son. Slainte, Anton, and get up off your backside and dance. There's a fine wee lass over there in the corner. Our very own Nurse Babbie.' Tam leaned forward confidentially. 'I would ask her myself but Kate would have me out of here by the skin of my lugs before you could blink.'

But just then everybody flopped down exhausted and it was time for the Seanachaidhs to tell their strange tales of myth and legend. Jim Jim had been watching his daughter with Dugald Donaldson and as soon as the red-faced Erchy stopped to gather breath, he spoke in a voice so mysterious that all eyes in the room turned towards him.

'I am thinking of a very odd story told me by Black Ewan that time I was over in Barra helping wi' the mackerel shoals.' At the very mention of Black Ewan the atmosphere in the room was charged with a subdued excitement. Black Ewan of Barra was well known throughout the Western Isles for his strange powers of second sight and his spine-chilling tales that went hand in hand with his 'seeing eye'.

'It was a gey queer tale but true – true according to Black Ewan,' Jim Jim went on, pausing to let his words take effect in the intervening hush. Erchy's heavy breathing and the sparkling of the peats in the grate were the only sounds that filled the silence for a few moments.

'Go on now, Jim Jim,' Bob encouraged, his curiosity getting the better of his resentment of Jim Jim's taking the limelight away from himself and Andrew, the two recognised Seanachaidhs in the room.

'Well, it was about the time o' the Great War,' Jim Jim continued slowly. 'And you mind Black Ewan was out at sea wi' the Naval Patrol vessels?'

'Ay, ay, that was the time he found the barrel o' rum floatin' in the sea,' Ranald supplemented with a beaming smile, 'and was so drunk on it his mates tied him to a chair in the wheelhouse because it was the safest place for him.'

'Look you, that has nothing to do wi' my story,' Jim Jim said scathingly. 'It is about one o' the lads on the boat who was always boastin' about the amount o' women he managed to have and never after marryin' one o' them. Black Ewan warned the chiel to stop his mischief and with his seeing eye he foretold the man was going to seduce the daughter o' a witch. If he wasny after marrying her he would have a fate that no mortal could foretell it would be so evil. Well, it happened right enough and worse than anyone imagined. Out at sea, with no land expected for miles, an island just appeared out of nowhere. On it was marooned a lovely young maiden, hair black as night and eyes like the black peats on the moor. All the men on the vessel were terrified but no' the seducer. He landed on the island an' promised himself to the maiden if she succumbed to him. Well, she did right enough, the bad bad lassie, but then he was all for leavin' her to go back to the ship. Just then a fearful hag rose out o' the sea, green wi' slime and black wi' warts. She screeched an evil curse on the seducer that was terrible to hear. He remembered his mother tellin' him "Never look into the eyes of a Green Uisga Caillich and their curses might no' work", but he was so taken aback he stared straight at the hag. There and then he was turned into a lump o' black rock, all twisted like he had died in agony. On the top was a black skull wi' two empty sockets where his eyes had been.'

Jim Jim paused for breath and a round-eyed Mairi said wonderingly, 'Och my, the poor mannie, it must have been sore on him.'

'Ay, but that's the kind o' things that happens to

men who go around seducing innocent women then leave them in the lurch,' Jim Jim nodded with a meaningful look at Dugald Ban, named so because of his mop of white hair.

Morag Ruadh threw back her head and gave a shout of laughter. 'Ach Father, you'd best stick to damping peats with your spit for you're no use at all as a story-teller . . . as Bob and Andrew will be after tellin' you from the look on their faces.'

'I did not understand it all but I think it is a very interesting story,' Anton said courteously.

'Will you tell us a story about the legends of Germany?' came eagerly from Ranald. 'I was reading a book about it and there's a lot o' strange things happen there . . . other of course than thon funny wee man, Hitler.'

Anton smiled. 'Not a story about Germany, Ranald, but something that I remember and always brings my home back into my thoughts.' He sat with his hands between his knees and slowly looked round the company. 'I am not one for too much talking and never could I tell a story like Jim Jim. These are memories I tell you now. When I was a little boy back home in my father's farm in Berlin, he used to say to me – round a fire like this, "Love each season for they are God-given. Love each day for each day is a gift. Love each moment, like moments in heaven . . . love, never hate for life is too swift." I have never forgotten these words and though I did not fully understand them at the time, I do now. I have not always found it easy – never to hate – but here, tonight on Rhanna, among people who have become my very dear friends, I understand fully the meaning of my father's words. Tomorrow I leave you all and never have I been so loath to leave a place as I am now.'

There was complete silence with all eyes on the young German whose boyish figure was outlined against the glow of the fire. He raised his head and smiled warmly at Lachlan and Phebie standing together. 'To you I raise my glass and say, "Slainte" – good health in return for mine. If all doctors were like Lachlan and all doctors' wives were like Phebie, then the world would be filled with health, and peace . . . and, most important of all, love. To Shona and Niall I give thanks for many things – friendship, companionship, for laughter when I didn't want to laugh . . . to my little Fiona I am deeply indebted for keeping me supplied with pets till my bed jumps with them and I almost undo all of Lachlan's good work leaping about after them. Frau Morrison I thank for her Benger's food and for keeping my bed so tidy I am almost afraid to lie in it – and . . .' he looked straight at Babbie, 'to Babbie, who nursed me like an angel, I give thanks for memories that will go with me for the rest of my life. To you all I give my gratitude for making the days of a German airman those that he will never forget. To all of you I say, "Slainte" and God bless you all!'

The silence in the room had deepened till it was something that could be felt. The islanders did not like sentiment openly displayed and were always careful to hide their deeper emotions in frivolous words and happy banter, but at that moment there was hardly a dry eye in the room. Elspeth rose hastily and rushed into the kitchen to stand with her hands planted firmly on the table in an effort to stop her gaunt frame from trembling with all her suppressed tears. Lachlan and Phebie held on to each other and smiled with eyes that were too bright. The rest of the gathering shuffled in embarrassment. And when Anton looked at Babbie's corner he saw that she had fled, taking his heart with her.

'Ach, you are a good laddie, right enough,' Biddy sniffed gruffly. 'The Lord will spare you wherever you go, I'm damt sure o' that.'

'Ay, indeed just,' was the general murmur round the room.

Niall jumped to his feet, raising his glass to the ceiling. 'Slainte to you, Anton! I never thought I'd ever say that a Jerry was – is – one of the best friends I ever had – but I'm saying it now – tonight! To Anton I say, haste ye back for auld lang syne!'

The room rose as one. 'To Anton, haste ye back!'

'And God bless you, Anton Büttger,' Phebie whispered shakily and buried her face in Lachlan's shoulder.

The island gave Anton a good send-off. Cries of good wishes for his future well-being filled the harbour at Portcull. He stood for a few moments, observing it all, the spring green on the mountains, the smoke that drifted as dreamily as the people of Rhanna, the bronzed slopes of Sgurr nan Ruadh that reminded him of a girl with hair the colour of a fiery sunset. He looked at the water remembering eyes that were like pools of amber-flecked sea, and he smiled and felt like weeping. In his pocket were several packages, one a bottle of Tam's Uisge-beatha, the other a small parcel which Elspeth had pushed brusquely at him when he left Slochmhor for the last time.

'Some tablet to put strength in your feets,' she had told him sourly. 'With the sugar on rationing it wasny easy but we must all share what we have – after all – we are all alike in the eyes o' God though sometimes I think He must be needin' specs.'

He had surprised her by taking her hand and saying quietly, 'Mein Frau – thank you – and it is not God who is needing the spectacles – it is ourselves. He will bless you for your thoughtfulness – Elspeth.'

His pronunciation of her name was beautiful and, with crimson staining her cheeks, she had hurried quickly into the house to dab at her eyes with the corner of her apron.

Fiona also had given him a present, a glass jar containing a large hairy spider. 'For luck,' she said briefly for it had cost her a lot to part with her most prized specimen. 'His name is Geallachas, which is the Gaelic for faithful, so mind you take care of him. Keep the jar open so's he can catch flies and get a parcel of midgies together. Mind give him a drop of water too for spiders get gey thirsty.'

Anton had laughed and stooped to look into the child's bright eyes. 'Thank you – *jungfrau* – that is the German for maiden. I know Geallachas will bring me luck – perhaps enough for me to come back to this island and marry a beautiful princess called Fiona McLachlan!'

'Ach, you'd be too old!' she told him, but her smile was coy and she threw her arms round his neck to kiss his forehead.

The military escort were impatient to be on their way but Anton's blue eyes were scanning the harbour hoping to catch a last glimpse of Babbie. She hadn't said goodbye to him, she had barely spoken a word to him since yesterday. There was no sign of her at the harbour and his heart lay like a pebble in his breast.

He extended his hands to Shona and Niall who had come down with him. 'Fräulein Shona,' he whispered, 'my beautiful maiden who rescued a monster in distress.'

'A monster who changed into a handsome young airman,' she said as lightly as she could, hardly able to bear looking at the pain of hurt in his eyes.

'Hey, enough you two,' Niall laughed, 'jealousy is rearing its ugly head again!'

Anton turned to him. 'Thank you, my friend, for yesterday. It is a day I will remember. Will you tell Fräulein Babbie I give to her my love. Thank her also – for healing my body – just say that, Niall.'

Niall gripped Anton's hand so hard he winced. 'I'll tell her, Anton.' Desperately he tried to think of something comforting to say but there was nothing. 'She couldn't come to see you off,' he said as the young German turned away. 'She said you would understand.'

A pink stain touched Anton's pale cheeks. 'Perfectly,' he said shortly and walked quickly to the waiting boat.

In the distance a figure came flying down Glen Fallan. Shona saw it first and hope fluttered in her breast. A few seconds later she saw the unmistakable gleam of red hair as Babbie ran past the War Memorial near Murdy's house.

'Anton . . . wait!' Shona's voice was a strangled little sob of sound.

Anton turned and in that split second the despair in his eyes was replaced by a jostling welter of emotions, with hope, that bright spark which buoys up the spirits in their most flagging state, struggling upwards from the depths of his being.

'Babbie.' He murmured the name huskily. 'Babbie.'

She came fleeing towards him without pause, straight into the water to wade towards the boat, without heed for anything or anyone.

'Anton!' His name soared towards the heavens. 'Anton! I love you!' she yelled in an ecstasy of joy. She fell into his arms and he caught her, laughing into her hair, burying his face into her breasts. Their tears mingled as they kissed and the military turned discreetly away.

'Anton, I couldn't let you go,' she sobbed almost incoherently. 'I thought about you all night long . . .'

He smothered her words with another kiss and she struggled to say breathlessly, 'I have so much to explain to you, Anton – all the reasons why I thought I couldn't love you – but I do – I do! You must send me your address and I'll tell you all in a letter . . . and I'll wait, I'll wait my darling . . . forever if need be!'

'I don't think the war will last that long!' he said, sparks of joy flashing from his blue eyes. 'And time will go quickly. I'll write you twice a day . . .'

'Once will be enough,' she laughed. The engine started up and they clung together. 'Oh, my darling, I don't want to let you go,' she cried. 'I want to hold you and love you and touch you.'

They drew apart, hands clinging, eyes saying a million things as yet unvoiced. Briefly he touched her hair, her face, then almost roughly he pushed her away from the boat. His eyes sought out Shona and Niall on the shore. 'Goodbye, my friends,' he breathed, while the man in him fought back the tears of such a bitter-sweet parting.

The boat's engines whirled the water into foam and pulled it steadily out of the harbour yet still Babbie stood up to her knees in the sea with tears coursing down her face. Anton's head was now a golden crown, a minute later just a bright gleam far out in the water. 'I love you, Anton, I love you,' she sobbed into her hands.

Niall waded out to fetch her back to shore. 'That's right,' he said gently. 'Greet your heart out. It will do you good, myself and Shona found that out a whily back. Take my hanky and give your nose a right good blow.'

She obeyed with such ardour that the sound of her blowing her nose was like a miniature foghorn and all three burst into subdued laughter.

Babbie gave a watery sniff. 'Fiona told me she gave Anton a spider for luck – and it worked – that and the pair of you going off yesterday and leaving me alone with him.' She twisted round to look at the boat which was now just a black speck in the water but Shona took her firmly by the hand and led her past a gaping throng of islanders towards Glen Fallan and the welcoming banner of smoke from Laigmhor's chimneys.

Part Six

Rhanna
Summer 1941

Chapter Sixteen

Rhanna droned lazily in the heat of high summer and Shona ran swiftly over the green fields of Laigmhor. Out on the Sound of Rhanna the ferry sounded its deep mournful horn and she stopped to watch it gliding into the harbour before she walked into the cool, silent woods that skirted the road. Pine needles rustled beneath her feet, the sunlight dappled the rich brown earth. She sat down on a mossy tree stump to hug her knees while she waited for Niall the way she had waited countless times before. She was wearing a dress of palest green which was a perfect foil for the deep gold of her suntanned limbs and the luxuriant auburn hair which she had swept upwards and pinned carefully into place.

She had taken overly long to get ready that morning, exasperating both Kirsteen and Fergus by running downstairs during breakfast, deciding to change from her white dress into a yellow one before the meal was over, deciding she liked neither and changing to the green. She had wondered whether to wear her long hair up or down and when Fergus said, 'I like it flowing down your back the way it was when you were a wee girl,' she had answered, 'I am *eighteen*, Father!' and had gone immediately upstairs to pin up the thick waving curls.

'You're too grown up for me to *talk* to now,' Grant told her disgustedly.

'And you're too much of a baby for me to care!' she had snapped at him. She was tense and irritable as so often happens when a keenly anticipated event is nearly reality.

Sitting among the cool trees she was ashamed of her outburst. The atmosphere at Laigmhor was usually one of happy contentment and it was wonderful to live in a house where laughter prevailed above all else. The weeks since Niall's going had been calm and uneventful except for an outbreak of measles which had affected a good part of the island's population. At Laigmhor, Grant had gone down with the rash first, followed by Kirsteen, who had laughed and felt ridiculous contracting measles at her age. Shona and Fergus had administered to the invalids but it was a mild form of measles and both Grant and Kirsteen were soon up and going about as normal. There was going to be another child in December. Kirsteen had confided the news to Shona and Grant a fortnight ago and they had celebrated by holding a gay ceilidh.

Grant's feelings were mixed on the matter. He dreaded the idea of a 'silly wee sister' and half-heartedly decided a brother might come in useful 'once it grows from a smelly baby into a real human'.

'Are you pleased, Father?' Shona had asked.

Fergus's black eyes had regarded her for a long moment. 'Ay, delighted,' he had said eventually. 'But no matter how many bairns may come along there will never be one to match you.'

'That could mean a lot of things,' she had answered with a smile.

'You know what I mean, mo ghaoil,' he had said with an intensity that made her put her arms round his neck and nuzzle his thick dark curls.

'I know, my dearest father,' she had said gently. 'It's easier for me, I have only one father to adore . . . you have more than one child – and you must love them all equally.'

Shona clasped her knees and thought about her father. The years they had spent together at Laigmhor had been stormy but beautiful years in her life and she knew she would always treasure the memory of them. But always there had been Niall. All through her tempestuous childhood he had been the other prop in her life and undeniably an even stronger one than her father whose pride had been the cause of unhappiness for a lot of people.

She watched a baby mole ambling blindly among the moss. A squirrel washed its whiskers on a branch above her head and she held her breath, loving the peace of the pine-scented wood, treasuring it even more because it was a part of Rhanna, the island she loved with every fibre of her being. Yet soon she must leave it if she wanted to remain with the man she loved. Niall had given her an ultimatum. 'When I come back to Rhanna in the summer I want your answer, Shona. You must decide when we are going to be wed.' Those had been his parting words when he left to go back to his studies at the vet. college.

A jaunty whistle came faintly on the breeze. Niall!

At last, Niall! The thought of him so near quickened her heart. That whistle! It suddenly came to her that she hadn't heard it for many months. It had always been part of Niall yet on his last visit to Rhanna she hadn't heard it once. The gay sound of it came closer and she got to her feet. Niall was back! The Niall of the carefree years before the war! The dear, sweet Niall of her early memories. She saw him through the trees, tall, sturdy, his hair gleaming like a field of summer corn. His hands were deep in his pockets, his stride firm and sure as he walked on past the woods and into Glen Fallan.

'*Niall!*' She burst from the trees in a breathless flurry and he turned, holding out his arms to embrace her. He held her away and looked at the graceful beauty of her golden limbs and slender body. The upswept hair enhanced the curves of her delicate neckline and showed to perfection the symmetry of her pointed little face.

'Hey!' he laughed joyously. 'You're all grown up! My God, you're beautiful. I won't tell you that too often though in case you get big-headed. And that tan – you make me feel like a ghost!' Tenderly he tucked away a small tendril of fine hair. 'You've got your hair up again, I see.'

'Yes, do you like it? I did it especially for you.'

'It makes you look – sophisticated – the way some of the town girls look. I always thought of my Shona as a tom-boy, hair flying all over the place.'

'You don't like it!'

'I never said that – Caillich Ruadh!'

'Don't call me a red witch again, Niall McLachlan! You know I hate it!'

'Temper! Temper!' he scolded, his eyes dancing. 'Now, if you were Fiona I'd take down your knickers and skelp your wee arse!'

'You're a barbarian, that's what you are – and a glaikit one at that! I don't know why I bother with you!' she cried, her cheeks red with rage.

'Because I'm irresistible, that's why.' He grinned delightedly. An ancient van trundled towards them on the dusty Glen road. Behind the windscreen two heads bobbed in unison, one a flaming red, the other a startling white. Morag Ruadh beamed at them, her ruddy face radiant, and Dugald Ban peered out, nodding in acknowledgement.

'*That* was Morag Ruadh!' Niall gasped. 'What is Dugald Ban doing riding around with that Caillich Ruadh?'

'It *was* Morag Ruadh,' Shona said politely. 'Now Mrs Dugald Donaldson, mistress of Dunbeag, Port-voynachan.'

'Never – never Morag Ruadh! How did she do it?'

Shona couldn't help laughing. 'In the same way as her cousin Mairi, only Morag Ruadh, the one-time saint of Portcull, was far more blatant than poor Mairi. Old Behag says she's never seen such sinful flaunting in anybody – but of course she says that about everyone who strays from the narrow path . . . I got it all, too . . . and from Morag as well, the besom.'

'But how did poor old Doug get caught? I thought he and Totie were pretty thick!'

'They were – up until that time the Commandos came and there was a ceilidh at the Manse. It seems Morag and Doug were very friendly that night. When Morag knew she was pregnant she blamed him, and Isabel and old Jim Jim gave him no peace till he took Morag to the altar. The baby's due in December. The cailleachs are saying that the Manse ceilidh was no more than an excuse for drunken lechery.'

'One up for Morag,' Niall grinned. 'Though I'll never know how poor old Dugald Ban got himself into that one.'

'Neither can anybody else. The gossips' tongues are red-hot, for some say that Doug wasn't the only one with a hand in the affair. When Jim Jim first asked Morag who was the father of the bairn she said calmly, "Will you take your pick, Father? I have been a loose woman." When Jim Jim heard that he nearly went up in a puff of peat smoke and said he hoped the father wasn't a Jerry. After that Morag pinpointed Doug. Morag was such a confirmed saint Doug just took her word for it so he must have been *one* of them.' She giggled. 'All these years, Morag without a man and suddenly we are to believe they are queuing up!'

'Totie must be furious! She kept Dugald dangling long enough.'

'She doesn't mind at all. Morag is kept so busy typing all Doug's notes and looking after the house she doesn't have time for the kirk organ so she signed it over to Totie. Doug got himself that old van and takes Totie's goods all over the island. She's delighted but Behag and Merry Mary are furious because it has taken business away from them.' They arrived at the gate of Laigmhor in a merry state.

'Let's go off on a picnic,' Shona suggested. 'I'll go in and get some stuff together while you go up and change into your Rhanna clothes.'

'Good idea, I'll see you in twenty minutes.'

They met at the dyke outside Laigmhor. He put his arm round her and led her towards the long heat-hazed stretches of the Muir of Rhanna. The sun beat down warmly. Needle-whin and broom nestled among tawny tussocks of sedge, and banks of butter-wort popped shy violet faces through the leaves of the more boisterous marsh trefoil whose dazzling white-flower spikes carpeted the moor bogs. A Hebridean rock-pipit winged overhead, muttering deep in its throat; bees, already laden with little sacs of pollen, prodded frenziedly into the bell heather; and delicate moths fluttered uncertainly over the wild flowers, restlessly roaming from one clump to the next.

Niall sniffed deeply. 'You know, I really love coming home to Rhanna. I used to think it was quite exciting going away to new places but I've got that out of my system now. This is where I really belong. I feel it more and more strongly each time I come back. We'll settle to live here one day.' He said the words with conviction but she looked at him with both doubt and hope in her eyes.

'But – how can we? You're going to be a vet. You would never find enough to keep you going here.'

'I've already thought about all that,' he said happily. 'I could divide my time up between Rhanna and some of the other nearby islands. A kind of travelling vet. I'd be here maybe four days out of seven – the rest of the time I'd be away . . . but it would be worth it – don't you think so, mo ghaoil?'

'Too wonderful to believe,' she breathed. 'It would be a dream that might never come true.'

'Dreams do come true if you work to make them real. It's a thought for the future anyway.'

'Oh, yes, yes, Niall,' she cried and threw herself into his arms to kiss him till they drew apart to look at each other longingly.

'Enough,' he said shakily. 'Two minutes of you and I'm shaking like a leaf.'

A sprite of mischief danced in her eyes. 'It's a good job you've got your kilt on, Niall McLachlan! Being the bull you are you wouldn't have room in your trousers.'

His brown eyes glinted. 'Remember old Burnbreddie? In the hayshed rutting at some old yowe? He wore nothing under his kilt then. How do you know I'm decently covered? Would you like a quick peep?'

She got to her feet in an outrage. '*Niall McLachlan!* You dirty bugger!' She ran and he chased her, in and out of the crumbling pillars of the Abbey.

He caught her and held her head between his hands. 'I love you! And I wish we were married right now because this waiting takes a bit of doing.' He studied her intently for a few moments. 'Something's missing! That beautiful hair, sliding through my fingers like silk! Let me unpin it so that it flies loose and wild like it used to. We'll be children again for a while! We'll dance and sing like idiots and we won't grow up till we're ready! We have the whole lovely summer ahead of us!'

For a brief moment their hands entwined, and a playful breeze lifted the loose strands of her hair, blowing it over her face, throwing it into a ruffled bronze mane behind her back.

'Race you!' he shouted. Their feet took wings and they were running, children again, their breath catching with laughter in the mad flight over the perfumed shaggy moors.

They were married when the soft, golden days of the Hebridean summer were growing shorter. The island waited with a subdued excitement for the event while Laigmhor and Slochmhor bustled with unhurried preparations.

The Rev. John Gray spent many hours rehearsing the wedding ceremony in Gaelic while his long-suffering wife sat with her knitting and made automatic sounds of approval. In her opinion his loud, booming voice was entirely unsuited for the soft pronunciation of the Gaelic language. Once she said mildly, 'You must speak softer, John, and you need some lilt. If you listen to the islanders you will hear the lilt.'

'I *am* lilting, Hannah!' he roared indignantly. 'Your trouble is you don't listen properly. Put those knitting needles away and you will *hear* my lilt!'

It seemed as if the whole of Rhanna was crowded into the Kirk on the Hillock to watch the ceremony. Mary, Alick's wife, was there with her twin sons. A letter had arrived from Alick. 'I can't be at the wedding of my favourite niece but my spirit is with you, mo ghaoil. I will picture you looking beautiful in front of the altar. For God's sake try to keep your temper for once and when the toasts are being made at the reception say one for me. God be with you both and may you be blessed with the thunder of many tiny feet.'

Babbie had arrived the day before, a new kind of radiance in her dancing green eyes. Anton had kept his word and letters had come for her every other day, tender love letters full of an impatience to be with her again but a certain contentment between the lines indicating to her his deep happiness that one day they would be together.

With Biddy's full approval Babbie had applied for the post of assistant nurse on Rhanna. The 'galloping hairpin' had long ago departed the island, glad to escape Biddy's criticism and the eccentricities of the older inhabitants.

'You're up on your feets I see, you auld cailleach,' had been Babbie's laughing greeting to Biddy. 'If things go right I should soon be having the pleasure of hearing you telling me how to give enemas properly.'

'I will never utter the words,' Biddy had growled while her old heart glowed. Babbie had become like a daughter to her and they were able to argue without

animosity and hug each other with laughter over all
the funny little happenings that could not be avoided
in work such as theirs.

Shona was radiant in a simple blue dress with white
marguerites braided into hair that tumbled down her
back in rich thick waves. At the altar Niall stood tall
and straight in a lovat tweed jacket and McLachlan
kilt, his fair skin flushed with a mixture of pride and
nerves. Strong, rugged Fergus wore the McKenzie kilt
with pride but he felt a moment of panic at the idea
of walking into kirk and all eyes staring as he gave
his daughter away. Then Shona was beside him and
he braced himself.

'Well, Father,' she whispered, 'another man will
have to put up with my tempers now.'

He nodded slowly. 'Ay, you're right there, lass. Not
only your tempers but those awful dumplings you
make and your cheek at the breakfast table . . .' His
black eyes were very bright. 'And your singing when
you're doing your chores and your wee voice bidding
me good night . . . these are all the things I'm giving
away to another man, together with a million other
things I love about my lass.' He gave a wry smile.
'You didn't know your old man could make speeches
like that, eh?'

'Not my old man,' she said with a little sobbing
intake of breath. 'My handsome big boy, remember?
I haven't called you that in years but I still think it.'

Behind them, Fiona and Grant fidgeted impatiently.
'I'll *never* marry,' hissed the former, pulling disgustedly at the frills on her dress.

'Nobody would want to marry *you*,' Grant returned. 'You're more like a boy than a girl.'

'I'm glad of that; even though boys are horrible they're better than silly girls. I'm going to be an explorer when I grow up and live in a tent in the jungle.'

'I'm going to be a fisherman like old Joe and sail all over the world. I'll never get married either 'cos it's stupid. Mother and Father fight one minute then make goggle eyes at each other the next – *and* they have babies all the time,' he finished in aggrieved tones.

Inside the kirk, Totie pedalled energetically in an effort to get the bellows of the ancient harmonium fully inflated before she began to play and in the red-faced fight with the instrument she wondered, not for the first time, why Morag Ruadh had put up such a struggle to remain the kirk organist all these years. Totie pedalled and puffed, the harmonium wheezed into life, spluttered for a few nerve-shattering moments, and then graciously the notes soared forth, sweetly and beautifully, and Totie knew once more the reasons for Morag's reluctance to let someone else play. The Wedding March soared majestically to the roof, the door opened and the ceremony began.

The Rev. John Gray had listened to his wife after all. His subdued tones lacked the 'lilt' but his Gaelic was perfect, and the old Gaels looked at each other with a mixture of surprise and delight.

'Ach, he's speaking the Gaelic in English,' Jim Jim muttered.

Isabel poked him in the ribs. 'The man is doing his best. He means well right enough. Just you leave him be, Jim McDonald.'

Despite the lack of the lilt, the ceremony was beautiful. The Gaelic words echoed round the old kirk and the ancient walls seemed to soak them in for a moment as if joyfully savouring a familiar tongue, then they were released again to go bouncing from wall to wall, one upon the other.

'Oh God,' Phebie gasped, dashing away a tear. 'I promised myself I wouldn't cry.'

Lachlan moved closer to her. 'Lend me your hanky,' he said with a watery sniff. 'Men aren't *supposed* to cry at weddings.' He gripped her hand. 'If they have a marriage like ours – then they couldn't ask God for more . . . my bonny plump rose.'

'Ay, you're right, Lachy – my darling,' she said huskily and blew her nose as quietly as she could.

Kirsteen felt a strong movement inside her womb and glanced towards Fergus, tall and dark, handsome in his kilt and tweed jacket. It seemed just yesterday that they had stood at the altar taking their vows, and now here she was, his flesh growing inside her, growing from the love and the happiness they had shared since their marriage. He caught her eye and smiled, an intimate secret smile, and she felt her heart glowing.

When it was over and they were all moving outside, Erchy and Todd stood one on either side of the door, and the bagpipes wheezed into life, the gay tunes filling the air. Laughing, the islanders linked arms and began to dance. The ceilidhing was already starting.

Shona and Niall were accosted from all sides, but Biddy, her ancient box camera at the ready, was the most persistent. 'Look you now, will you be standin' away from these gravestones,' she commanded. 'Todd, get out of the way! I'm no' wantin' your hairy legs in my picture.' Dodie galloped up, knocking her elbow just as the shutter clicked. Turning, she clouted him on the ear as if he was a small boy. 'You are just like a herd o' elephants!' she scolded. 'Now I have nothing but a fine picture o' the clouds!'

'Ach, I'm sorry, Biddy!' he wailed. Mairi had restored him to such a degree of good health that his cheeks popped out from his face like wizened brown apples and his bony frame had filled out considerably. But he was a creature who needed the freedom of wide places. After weeks of cosseting he was glad to escape to his lonely cottage in the hills though he showered Mairi with such a continual flow of simple little gifts it had been suggested to her by the opportunist Ranald that she should open up a craft shop for the summer tourists.

Dodie turned hastily from Biddy, knocking her hat off in the process and amid a stream of abuse he shouted to the newly-weds, 'Will you be waiting a minute. I have a wee wedding gift for you, that I have.' It was a dewy spray of harebells, bog myrtle and white heather, lovingly wrapped in a square of toilet tissue such as was used at Burnbreddie.

'It's a lovely present, Dodie,' Niall said gratefully.

'Ach well, it will be mindin' you of the moors when

you are being gassed by the smelly smoke in the city. The heather will bring you a lot o' luck. I had a job findin' it but I wanted to give you something after the fine job you made o' my wee hoosie.'

'Is it all right then, Dodie?'

'Ay, lovely just.' His grizzled face shone with pride then he looked ashamed. 'I am after putting back my own roof wi' the nice pattern.'

'But, Dodie,' laughed Niall. 'That's the sign of the swastika – the Nazi sign!'

Dodie's face showed no comprehension. 'Ay, ay, a lovely sign it is! I like it fine,' he enthused.

'Daft, daft, he is,' Canty Tam smirked. 'The British planes will be shootin' his wee hoosie down in flames else the Peat Hags will haunt him for takin' the pattern away from them.'

Shona had stolen away from the crowd to the part of the graveyard that held the remains of so many who had been her dear friends in life. Pausing at each grave she laid a single white rose on the grassy earth, each one plucked from her wedding bouquet. The only person she had never known was the one who had given her life and for a long moment she stood looking at her mother's headstone, then she stooped to lay her garland of marguerites on the mossy brown earth. 'Thank you for my life, Mother,' she said simply and turned to walk down to where her father was waiting quietly a few yards away.

'She would be proud if she was here today,' he said softly.

Shona looked straight into his dark eyes. 'I think

she is here today, they're all here, Mother, Mirabelle, Hamish, old Shelagh . . . everyone – and –' she smiled, 'just think, what a grandstand view they must get of everything.'

Babbie was standing on the fringe of the crowd. Off her guard for a moment she looked alone and vulnerable. Shona raised her arm and threw her bouquet – straight at Babbie.

'Oh – I caught it,' Babbie said with such surprise that Shona chuckled.

'I didn't mean it to fly to the moon, daftie.'

'If all goes according to plan I should be where he left me when the war is over.'

'What! Up to your knees in the middle of the sea?'

'Ach, you're even madder than usual,' Babbie giggled. 'All this excitement has gone to your head.'

The Rev. John Gray was standing at the kirk door and Shona went over to take him warmly by the hand. 'Thank you for such a lovely service. The older Gaels were able to understand every word. You will of course be coming to the ceilidh?'

'Well, I . . .' he began then stopped. 'I'll look forward to it my dear.'

Shona stood on her tiptoes and planted a kiss firmly on his cheek then did the same to a beaming Mrs Gray. 'The flowers were beautifully done, Mrs Gray. You have both given me a day to remember.'

A hard lump that had come suddenly to the Rev. Gray's throat made him cough and he stared after Shona's retreating back with eyes that were very bright.

'You know, John,' Mrs Gray said thoughtfully, 'I'd say that you have seen more than one kind of light in the last few months.'

He took her by the arm. 'Hannah, my dear, I do believe you're right. I have wasted a lot of years with my head in the clouds with the result that I couldn't see what was under my nose. These islanders are a fine people and for the first time I feel that I have taken a wee step closer to them . . . however, I warn you, Hannah, no more of that peaty tea tonight, I have to set a good example, you know.'

They chuckled and went off arm in arm to the Manse to get ready for the ceilidh.

That evening Tam's Uisge-beatha rocked the foundations of Laigmhor with its happy effects. At ten o'clock Niall and Shona stole away and sped hand in hand over the dark fields to the harbour where Ranald was waiting to take them out to a fishing boat. It was sailing with the tide to Stornoway where they were to spend their honeymoon.

Ranald's face beamed at them in the darkness. 'I kept a special boat for you,' he confided. 'I've been waitin' for a chance to use it and it bein' your weddin' night you must have everything done proper.' He led them to the dark blob of a rubber dinghy floating in the shallows. 'In you go now, mo ghaoil,' he said, courteously helping Shona aboard. 'If you feel like you've been walkin' all day on air then now you're goin' to be floatin' on it.'

'But, Ranald, this dinghy belongs to . . .' She stopped short and chuckled. 'Ranald McTavish,' she finished and the wily Ranald said a polite and utterly innocent, 'Right enough, now,' and began to row away from the shore.

Shona looked at Rhanna slipping away. The rugged peaks of Ben Machrie and Sgurr nan Ruadh were outlined in the remnants of a deep golden sunset that still hovered in the north-western sky. Sounds of merriment came faintly on the breeze; on the sands skirting Port Rum Point a family of gulls squabbled quietly; the dark shape of a lone heron glided on silent wings, uttering a sharp 'Cra-ack' as it passed over the dinghy. Shona's heart rose into her throat but Niall's arm came round her and his warm lips touched hers.

'Slainte – Mrs Niall McLachlan,' he murmured softly. 'You belong to me now.'

'We belong to each other,' she said firmly, dashing away the tears that had sprung to her eyes. 'Always you seemed to leave me behind on Rhanna . . . you can't do that any more – and I'm happy to be coming with you – my darling husband . . .' She pointed upwards to where the sliver of a young moon peeped out shyly from a fluffy cloudbank. 'Look, Niall, the new moon! Mirabelle always made a wish whenever it appeared. We must each spit on a piece of silver, hold it in our hand and wish.'

Solemnly they carried out the ancient ritual. 'I've made mine,' said Niall seriously. 'I hope it comes true.'

She nodded with assurance. 'It will – so long as you never tell anyone what it was. Some of my best wishes came true on the new moon.'

High in the fields above Laigmhor a tall figure looked out to the Sound of Rhanna, watching the dark little blob of the dinghy moving over a velvet sea faintly flecked with gold. It was a lovely autumn evening, filled with the sharp tang of peat smoke and fresh salt wind, the kind of weather Shona had always loved. Fergus breathed the scent of it deeply into his lungs, looking at the picture before him till it became a blur.

'Goodbye – Ni Cridhe,' he said, so quietly it might have been the sigh of the wind.

Kirsteen came up behind him and slid her arms round his waist. 'I knew you'd be up here,' she murmured, 'saying goodbye to her. Don't be sad, Fergus. She'll be back.'

'Only to visit us,' he said huskily.

'Perhaps – she has her own life to lead now but I think one day they'll both come back – to stay. I have some news for you that will most certainly take your mind off things. I didn't say anything till now because I didn't want to steal Shona's thunder. Lachlan examined me yesterday and heard *two* heartbeats. We're going to have twins, my darling.'

Fergus let out a roar of joy. 'Heaven help us! If they're girls Grant will have a fit! We'd better break the news to him gently or he'll be borrowing one of Ranald's boats to leave home in!'

She linked her arm through his. 'Talking of Grant, I'm sure that wee devil Fiona gave him a glass of sherry. He's doing a Highland fling with Biddy and her teeth and specs are rattling like mad! Come down now, darling, and help me to get him under control or the minister will never come to another island ceilidh again.'

Turning his back on the sea Fergus put his arm round her waist and they walked over the dew-wet fields to Laigmhor. As they walked the happy sound of laughter drifted to them on the playful breezes which eternally caressed the lonely high places of Rhanna.